BLADE OF FIRE

Stuart Hill

2 Palmer Street, Frome, Somerset BA11 1DS

Thanks are very much due to Mariam Ashraf-Shah for her invaluable advice.

I'd also like to mention Louise Walker, Barmy Beryl and the Bean, and Esther, Sarah and the Clan Cameron for conversation, cats, beer and curry. And Nigel for years of support.

I am also indebted to Immers for her supreme patience, and to all at The Chicken House.

And finally, Pauline McClelland; author, historian, raconteur, artist and complete Renaissance woman.

Text © Stuart Hill 2006
Cover illustration © Mark Edwards and Carol Lawson
Inside illustration © Carol Lawson

First published in Great Britain in 2006
First paperback edition 2007
The Chicken House
2 Palmer Street
Frome, Somerset BA11 1DS
United Kingdom
www.doublecluck.com

Cover design by Ian Butterworth
Designed and typeset by Dorchester Typesetting Group Ltd
Printed in the UK by CPI Bookmarque, Croydon, CR0 4TD

1 3 5 7 9 10 8 6 4 2

British Library Cataloguing in Publication data available.

ISBN 978 1 905294 29 9

Praise for THE CRY OF THE ICEMARK

From The Chicken House

I couldn't wait for Stuart Hill to welcome us back
to his wild world! Now he takes us on a journey
to the hot southern region, and introduces us to a
new generation of characters.

Scipio and his two cruel sons seek revenge, and
the children of Thirrin and Oskan must struggle
with witches, werewolves and vampires against
impossible odds!

Thrilling! Awesome! Epic!

Barry Cunningham
Publisher

To Clare for being there.
To Mam and Dad and to
Leicester's own Adams Family.
Also to the G and G, TM, TG and all the Ts.

CHAPTER 1

At the Hub of the World, Queen Thirrin was in the Leopard Hold watching the finishing touches being added to the coming victory feast. The alliance of human, Snow Leopard and Wolf-folk had defeated the fearsome Ice Trolls in a vicious battle, and the victors were assembling, ready to mark the event with mountains of food and rivers of beer.

Much had changed since the first time she and Oskan had come to the capital of the Snow Leopards almost twenty years before. For one thing, the Royal Court now held its gatherings in this massive ice cave deep within the everlasting snows of the Hub Mountains. Not only did this provide shelter for the human ambassadors and other dignitaries who visited the Kingdom of the Snow Leopards, but it also added greater majesty to the Royal Court.

The cave was packed with long tables around which sat leopards, humans and werewolves, all talking and laughing at once, filling the air with a tangle of voices and a frosting of breath that wafted like vaporous banners. In the centre of the cave a huge fire roared, its heat and light erupting into the freezing air before climbing higher and higher into the roof, which arched over the feasters in a single elegant leap of ice that no human architect could ever hope to equal. Here, the firelight ignited a thousand glittering reflections on the surfaces of the ice, while at floor level, the entire cave glinted and sparkled with braziers and torches that spiralled out from the central fire. The effect on the eye was that of a mesmeric, never-ending cascade of light.

Thirrin wondered why the flames didn't cause a localised thaw, but one glance at the misted breath of the leopards and humans in the hall made the answer all too obvious. It may have been warmer inside the cave, but the temperature was still barely above freezing. Even the large central fire could make little impression on ice that had been frozen for thousands of years.

In fact, Thirrin could hardly believe she'd ever be truly warm again. Wearing her sumptuous furs of State, she sat next to her own personal brazier, yet still her feet seemed as cold as the icy floor beneath them. Next to her sat Oskan, wearing his usual black robes and looking as relaxed and comfortable as if he was in the Great Hall at home in Frostmarris. Only Thirrin knew that under his tunic and cloak he wore about ten layers of furs, all fluffy side inwards, and more socks than she'd ever realised he owned. She reached over and took his hand, and was almost gratified to find that it felt like a glacier, even through both their gloves.

"Do you remember warmth?" she murmured so that none of the other guests would overhear.

"I've heard it exists somewhere," he murmured back. "But I think it's one of those silly legends, like dragons and leviathans." He caught her eye and grinned, reminding her sharply of the boy she'd married when they were both still so painfully young.

A sudden fanfare crackled on the frigid air. Thirrin and Oskan rose politely to their feet to welcome their hosts, along with the hundreds of other humans, leopards and werewolves who were guests at the feast.

Tharaman-Thar and his mate Krisafitsa-Tharina now processed into the Leopard Hold at a magnificently dignified pace, followed by the tumble and tangle of the Royal Cubs.

There were five altogether: the eldest, Talaman, was the Pro-Thar and carried himself with immense dignity, spoiled somewhat by the youngest cub, Kirimin, who had her eldest brother's tail gripped firmly in her teeth and was doing her best to drag him backwards. Being less than a quarter of his size she was failing miserably, but true to her character she fought gamely on. The other three, Tadadan, Krisilisa and Thuraman, gambolled and rolled about in front of a long line of human chamberlains who were carrying ornate platters and trenchers brimming with an array of different foods. The servants, with an air of long practice, gravely stepped over the cubs playing in front of them, and tried not to be jostled backwards into the barrels of beer, wine and mead that the werewolves were carrying in behind them.

Thirrin watched Tharaman, Krisafitsa and their cubs approach the raised dais where she and Oskan were waiting. The Tharina was as tall as her Royal mate, but her head and shoulders were far more delicate, and she walked with the grace of flowing water. She and Oskan shared the same slightly waspish sense of humour and often giggled together over the peculiarities of one or other of the courtiers, but her favourite human was Thirrin. The young Queen had attended the Snow Leopards' Royal Pair-bonding, and afterwards, at Tharaman's invitation, she had extended her official State visit. It was then that she and the Tharina had forged their friendship, spending the long dark of that winter discussing many things, including their mates. "Just like ordinary young wives with no worries of State or Government to bother them," Thirrin had said. They'd found the male animal was remarkably similar whether human or leopard, and had laughed affectionately over their funny ways.

Thirrin smiled at the memory as the Snow Leopards reached the platform. The great cats inclined their heads and Thirrin replied with a deep curtsey, while Oskan bowed. Then, formalities over, Tharaman threw back his head and laughed enormously.

"Let the feasting begin! Ethelbold, send round the beer and wine!"

A supremely neat human chamberlain raised his hand and immediately servants scurried amongst the trestle tables in the lower hall, pouring drinks into waiting cups, flagons and bowls.

Tharaman fussed over his Tharina, making sure she was comfortably seated next to Thirrin and Oskan. Then he ushered the Royal Cubs into the keeping of their nurse – an elderly Snow Leopard who would have been the fiercest sort of headmistress if she'd been human. And finally, he lowered his Royal rump on to his favourite fluffy cushion and looked out over the feast. He purred thunderously, then catching sight of Olememnon sitting next to the Basilea and her Consort further down the table he bellowed, "Fancy your chances in a drinking competition, Ollie?"

"Whenever My Lord is ready!" the veteran warrior

shouted in reply, and raised his flagon.

"Erm . . . before you get too involved in your competition, I'd like to clear up a few points about the Ice Trolls, if I may," Thirrin interrupted.

"Certainly, my dear," Tharaman said, turning to her politely. "My drinking bowl doesn't seem to have been filled yet anyway," he added pointedly, and raised a regal eyebrow at Ethelbold the chamberlain who hurriedly waved up a scullion with a wine jug.

Tharaman purred with satisfaction. "Now, what exactly do you wish to know, Thirrin?"

"Well, firstly, the Ice Trolls were carrying metal warhammers instead of their usual stone clubs and antler spears, and I suppose it's pretty obvious they've been armed by the Polypontian Empire. I think we have to accept that Bellorum is up to his old tricks again. But why did they get the trolls to attack in the depths of winter, when the passes into the Icemark are blocked by snow and no invading army could attack anyway? Surely it would have been better for the trolls to keep you busy during the summer so that no Snow Leopards could come to the aid of the Icemark when the passes are open and the Empire invades again?"

"That's quite simple, Thirrin dearest," the Tharina's beautiful singsong voice interrupted gently. "Ice Trolls hibernate in the summer; they can't abide daylight. It blisters their skin and blinds them, so during the six months of summer when the sun never sets they burrow down into the deepest levels of their caves and sleep until the dark and the cold return."

"Precisely!" Tharaman agreed. "They couldn't attack during the summer. No doubt old Scipio Bellorum hoped that arming the Ice Trolls, and encouraging them to send the biggest army they've ever mustered, would be enough to destroy us and leave us completely unable to send help to you during the campaigning season." The leopard paused to lap at his bowl of wine. "I don't suppose it occurred to him that our alliance is reciprocal and that you'd send human troops to help us in our war against the trolls. I'm sure he still thinks of me as some sort of giant palace cat that you keep as a useful pet."

Krisafitsa giggled. "And so you are, my dear. A big, soppy old pussycat that likes a comfortable place next to the fire."

Tharaman raised his head and gazed regally down from his enormous height. For a moment Thirrin thought he was offended, but the effect of Royal disdain was completely spoiled as pendulous droplets of wine slowly ran down his whiskers and a large tongue quested forth to lick them up. "A comfortable place next to the fire *and* a bedtime bowl of beer, if you don't mind," he said in his most refined and cultured voice.

"But of course!" Krisafitsa agreed. "How could I forget?"

The Thar suddenly called down the table, "Ollie! I've drunk one bowl. What's your tally?"

"Hah! I'm on my third already," Olememnon answered.

"Yes, well. You have me at a disadvantage; we've been discussing matters of State up this end of the table."

The evening continued with a seemingly unending supply of food and drink, and soon the warriors were singing the usual selection of offensive drinking songs, led in the main by Tharaman-Thar and Olememnon.

Thirrin and Oskan, like everyone else, ate enormous amounts in an attempt to keep out the ever-present cold, but there were limits to what anyone could eat and eventually they slumped back in their seats and held their hands protectively

12

over their distended bellies. They were relaxed and happy; the Ice Trolls had been defeated, and a winter of peace stretched before them. Even so, the dangerous problem of the Polypontian Empire was still very much on their minds. This was only a short enjoyable respite before they'd have to travel home across the Icesheets to begin preparations for warding off the growing threat.

In the years following Scipio Bellorum's defeat in the war with the Icemark, many nations under the control of the Empire had seized the chance to rebel against it. If a small country like the Icemark had been able to defeat the General and his enormous army, then so could they! It had taken the Polypontians almost fifteen years of constant fighting to crush the rebellions in every part of the Empire. But the last guerrilla army had finally been defeated, and in the ensuing five years Bellorum had reorganised his forces *and* added two new territories to the Imperial possessions. These last two campaigns had obviously been a warning to the known world that he was well and truly back and was looking for new lands to conquer.

Then, a little over a year ago, werewolf spies had picked up information from the birds and animals beyond the southern border of the Icemark: the Polypontian armies were once more starting to muster. Immediately, Thirrin had ordered the spies to seek more information, and the werewolves had slipped over the border like the shadows of thought. Travelling only in the dead of night, and following the most secret and wildest of ways, they had spoken to the watchful creatures of the land and discovered that Bellorum was preparing a war of revenge.

In response, Thirrin had moved her own forces to defend the border, and put them on a permanent state of alert. But so far, nothing had happened.

"Well, if Bellorum himself invaded tonight he'd have to wait until I'd slept off supper," said Oskan, patting his belly tenderly.

"Don't even joke about it!" Thirrin snapped. "It was only because the borders were frozen solid that I dared send our troops to help Tharaman."

"Don't worry. When the sea freezes as far south as the coast of the Polypontus, and pine trees explode because their sap has frozen, *no* army can march."

"*We* managed it, and fought a war," Thirrin pointed out sharply.

"Yes, but we had warriors with long experience of cold conditions, Snow Leopards to ride over the frozen wastes, and Ukpik werewolves to draw sledges loaded with supplies. Bellorum has none of these advantages. He'll have to wait for the thaw, and then we'll be ready for him."

Thirrin nodded grudgingly. But when it came to Bellorum, she was always wary of trusting to luck and the weather. The Polypontian General was completely unpredictable, and she'd only be really happy when she was back home, personally supervising preparations for the coming war.

"Iphigenia!" she suddenly called down the table to the Hypolitan Basilea. "How long before your soldiers are ready to march?"

The young Basilea had to lean a long way over the table to see round the massive bulk of Taradan the Snow Leopard, Second-in-Command. "Three days, Ma'am."

"That long? Make it two," Thirrin said gruffly.

"But there's equipment to clean and pack away, transport to be arranged for the wounded, and everyone needs a rest after that last battle."

"Two and a half days, then," came the reply. Then turning to look beyond Oskan, Thirrin said, "Urik. How long will the Wolf-folk need?"

"We're ready to march now," the werewolf Commander answered. "We have no equipment, and the wounded will have to manage."

Thirrin nodded. "Two and a half days it is, then."

"In the meantime, let's enjoy the feast. The ability to take fitting pleasure in a task well done is the sign of a truly refined mind," said Tharaman-Thar, his beautiful voice having a calming effect on the entire table.

"Hah! That's my tenth!" Olememnon suddenly boomed, and hiccuped as he smashed his tankard down.

Krisafitsa giggled, and Tharaman's eyes suddenly glowed with the light of battle as he nodded at the wine steward.

"Right," he said. "We'll see about that!"

CHAPTER 2

Charlemagne Athelstan Redrought Strong-in-the-Arm Lindenshield, youngest child of Queen Thirrin and Oskan Witchfather, was less than happy with his name. He was fourteen years old, small for his age, and always treated as the baby of the family.

But on this winter afternoon it was his name that was really annoying him. He hated the way he always had to tell strangers how to pronounce it. *"Sharl-a-mayn,"* he would say, patiently or sharply depending on his mood, whenever anyone new to the Court stumbled over it. Often, people shortened it to *Sharley*, then the other palace kids would call him *Shirley* and he'd end up fighting . . . and losing.

"Stupid, horrid name!" Charlemagne whispered to himself, so that he wouldn't wake Maggiore Totus who had fallen asleep at his desk again. If he kept quiet, he might get through the entire lesson without having to do a stroke of work. Maggie was always falling asleep, but nonetheless the Prince's mother insisted he continue his lessons with the ancient Royal Adviser. He had to admit that sometimes they were interesting, and even exciting, but there was something special about a lesson spent doing no work at all.

Once, Maggie had told him his name was that of a great king who'd ruled in the country of Gallia many centuries ago. King Charlemagne had been a brilliant statesman and a great warrior who had defeated the Desert People when the rest of the world seemed ready to fall beneath the hooves of their unstoppable cavalry. This information had cheered Sharley up for a while and he had almost learned to like his name, but then one of the palace youngsters would call him Shirley, and he'd be fighting – and losing – again.

Weak winter sunlight moved slowly across the room as he sat watching motes of chalk dust blaze silver-gold in its rays. Then, seeing the sun was shining full on Maggie's sleeping face and making his eyelids twitch, Charlemagne hopped out of his chair and closed the shutters that looked out over the ice-locked palace garden. Maggie snorted once, then settled back into a deep sleep.

The young Prince grinned happily and began to walk back to his desk, but he clumsily caught the edge of a stool, which fell over with a clatter like an avalanche of logs down a wooden mountain.

Maggie snorted enormously. "Open your book at page forty-three," he murmured, and sank back into sleep again. Charlemagne heaved a silent sigh of relief. He was always doing things like that: walking into furniture, falling down, or tripping over steps that had been there since long before he was born. It wasn't really surprising, he supposed; he *did* have one leg that was weaker than the other, and it sometimes refused to do what he wanted it to. Most of the time he tried to pretend there was nothing wrong with his leg at all, but there were always those occasions when it let him down, usually when everyone was watching.

He hadn't been born with a "gammy" leg, as he called it. Ten years ago, almost to the day, a plague had hit the Icemark. It had arrived at one of the southern ports just after Yule and swept through the country, striking down children and paralysing them. In some cases, even the muscles that worked their lungs were seized in its terrible grip, and they died of suffocation. At the time, Charlemagne had been five, and even though his father had ordered that the city be placed in quarantine, the plague had still found its way into Frostmarris.

Charlemagne remembered nothing of his illness, but Maggie had told him that his father, Oskan, had fought night and day to save him, calling on all his vast knowledge and experience as a healer to bring him back from the brink of death, again and again. And when Charlemagne's lungs became paralysed, Oskan had breathed for him. He blew air into his chest while directing Maggie to hurry to the artisans' quarters to fetch a bellows and something to make a mouth-piece, rigging them up so he could keep the boy breathing.

Charlemagne had survived, and Oskan, as Head of the Order of Witches, had called his people to Frostmarris and explained how to use the new breathing device. Thousands of children were saved. But thousands also died, and many of those who lived were left with arms or legs permanently with-ered by the illness.

"Polio Leg. Polly Leg," Charlemagne muttered to himself as he limped back to his desk, making a chant of the cruel nicknames some of the palace youngsters called him. Overall, names were a major problem for him. But nothing was as big a problem as his leg. Thanks to his limp he wasn't allowed to train with the Weapons Master, and the Horse Mistress would only let him ride a quiet mule, very like his father's old mount, Jenny. He was a Prince of the House of Lindenshield, yet he couldn't use a sword or axe, nor could he even lift a Royal Housecarle's shield. He might be of a slight build, but so was his eldest sister Cressida, and *she* was heir to the throne and could throw a full-sized axe and hit the target nine times out of ten.

But of all the Royal children, at least Charlemagne knew he was the favourite. Cressida might be the heir, Eodred a great horseman, Cerdic a brilliant swordsman, and Medea the inheritor of their father's Gift, but he, Charlemagne, was loved by his parents above them all. Oh, they'd never admit it – not even to themselves, and certainly not to anybody else – but they cared for their youngest child with all the depth of love they'd had to call upon when his life had been in such terrible danger from the polio. But he never used this knowledge against his brothers and sisters. They were all close – apart from Medea – and they protected their "little snotling" like a wolf pack whenever he needed it. There'd been several nasty punch-ups when the Royal children found the other palace kids teasing him, but there was always so much trouble afterwards that Charlemagne now preferred to fight his own battles. Even if he did always lose.

Maggiore Totus snorted again, and seemed to be waking up. His long grey beard swept a small clean patch in the chalk dust on his desk as his mouth opened in a cavernous yawn and he murmured something in the singsong native tongue of the Southern Continent. Immediately, Charlemagne opened his textbook and started to write notes. The ancient scholar coughed, sneezed, and then his finger found his ear and

19

wriggled furiously in its depths. Finally, a sleepy eye opened and was instantly joined by the other.

"Ah! Ah, yes! Where were we?"

"I was just taking notes on the palace rituals of the Wolf-folk," said Charlemagne innocently.

"Were you? I mean, yes you were!" said Maggie decisively. "Have you finished yet?"

"Not quite. Almost."

"When you've done that you may go," said the old scholar, and noticing that all the sand had trickled through the hourglass on his desk, he grinned. The deep wrinkles on his face gathered in an intricate pattern of amusement around his eyes and mouth so that he looked like one of the comedy masks worn by actors from the land of the Hellenes. "You've let me sleep through the lesson again, haven't you?"

"Well, it seemed a pity to disturb you. You looked so peaceful," Charlemagne replied, grinning in return.

"There are times when you remind me so much of your mother," said Maggie, his expression fading to a gently reminiscent smile. "Except that your mother would have crept out of the classroom, and I'd have found her practising battle tactics with the Weapons Master."

"That option's not open to me," said Charlemagne, his voice suddenly sharp. "And I didn't particularly fancy going for a five-mile-an-hour jog on my mule, so I thought I'd stay here and listen to you snoring."

Maggie nodded sympathetically. The blood of the Linden-shield clan ran true in Sharley's young veins; he was a warrior at heart, but his weakened body stopped him from fulfilling his true potential.

"Perhaps you should see your . . . problem as a test of

character," said the old scholar. "A sort of endurance test, like the forced marches the housecarles subject themselves to. Rise above it, beat it, show you are greater than the limitations imposed upon you."

Charlemagne thought for a moment, his face a sullen, bad-tempered mask. "Nice try, Maggie. It would be a good way of looking at things. But eventually even the toughest housecarle will collapse from exhaustion and have to drag himself off to rest. But I can't do that. I can't stop being a cripple when I get tired. It's with me for ever."

Maggiore Totus let the silence that followed stretch out into discomfort before he finally said, "Prince Charlemagne, you have a withered leg. Don't let your natural anger about that cause your personality to wither too. *You* are more than your limitations, you are more than your inability to fight with a sword, or ride a cavalry stallion. I sometimes see a boy full of laughter and fun; at other times I see consideration and kindness lurking under the surface of your frustration. Let them out. Let the rest of the world see who you truly are. Or you'll become known as 'Prince Sour Face', 'Prince Misery'."

Charlemagne felt his eyes fill with tears, and he blinked them away angrily. "Do people say that of me?"

Maggie ached with pity when he heard the small and vulnerable voice, but he hardened himself and replied simply, "Not yet."

The young Prince nodded, and retorted sharply, "But it's just a matter of time. Is that what you're saying?"

"Perhaps. But people still remember the bright-faced child who used to follow his brothers around so doggedly, and so hopefully. They've forgotten your disappointments – if they ever knew about them at all. They don't understand why

21

you're so sullen. They only see a young boy growing up in comfort and privilege, when throughout the land so many go hungry, and others with disabilities like yours are forced to beg on the streets."

Charlemagne listened, feeling a turmoil of emotions. He knew a lot of what Maggie said was true, but he wasn't being entirely fair.

The old scholar seemed almost to have read his mind, because he added, "Perhaps I am being a little unjust. You're carrying the burden of adolescence as well as your disabilities, something that many would find nigh on impossible. But if you can't be a soldier of the Icemark, then you should prove your strength, and true worth, by surmounting your difficulties."

Charlemagne was incensed. All of his problems had been dismissed as a simple case of teenage angst. He rose from his chair, and after bowing long and low to Maggiore, left the room. Once outside, he stormed along the corridor in a characteristic lope as he forced his withered leg to keep up with his furious pace. He had to get out of the palace, and get away from stupid people who would stop him and ask in their reedy, whiney, sympathetic voices if he was 'all right', and was there 'anything they could do to help?'

Almost without thinking he headed for the garden. On reaching the door that led into the small private enclosure, he burst through and slammed it behind him. There was nobody about as he stomped across the frozen snow to where the fountain stood, packed with straw and sacking to protect it from the vicious Icemark winter. The freezing air felt as if it was scorching his throat as he gulped down great lungfuls, but nothing seemed to calm his mood, and he continued to stomp around the small intricate pathways that radiated outwards from the fountain as though running a race. Just as he'd started his second circuit he slipped on a glaze of ice and crashed to the ground. For several long seconds he lay staring up at the brilliant blue of the frozen sky, then his eyes filled with tears and he wept like the child he desperately didn't want to be.

Gradually, the sobs slowed, subsiding into an occasional gulp or sniff, and he hauled himself to his feet using the stonework of the fountain as an impromptu crutch. Things, he knew, would have to change. There was nothing he could do about his leg. He would just have to rise above it all, as Maggie had said. It was bad enough being denied the normal rights of a Lindenshield Prince, but to also lose the respect and liking of his family and the populace of the Icemark would be too much to bear. A surge of determination thrilled through his frame and, climbing to his feet, he headed for the doorway.

At the classroom window, Maggiore heaved a sigh of relief as he watched the small figure limping along the pathway. He'd witnessed everything, and when Charlemagne had fallen he'd almost called for one of the housecarles to run and help. But the young Prince with the flame-red hair had eventually stirred and climbed to his feet. Even so, Charlemagne was young and vulnerable enough to need watching, and the ancient scholar seized his stick and banged it rapidly on the wooden floor. Within seconds two young housecarles appeared in the doorway.

"Ah! Canwulf and Aelthric. You'll find Prince Charlemagne coming in from the garden. Keep an eye on him, will you? I've been brutally honest with him, I'm afraid, so he'll need some friendly support."

The two soldiers saluted and hurried off. Maggiore raised

his head and listened intently to a faint howling that was spreading itself across the frozen sky beyond his window. A werewolf was relaying a message. It was probably only a routine report, but with the Queen away and Bellorum's troops moving beyond the border, any news could be important.

Out in the garden Charlemagne stopped in his tracks and listened. As the final drawn-out syllables became clear, he grinned. His parents would be home within a few hours. Giving a yelp of joy, he leaped into the air despite his leg, and hurried back into the palace.

Maggie rapped on the window with his stick, but Charlemagne didn't hear. The old scholar sighed. Now he'd have to wait until someone thought to come and tell him the news.

His thoughts were cut short by a loud thump on his door, and Charlemagne himself burst excitedly into the room. "Get your glad rags on, Maggie. Mum and Dad are coming home. They'll be here by tonight!"

The old scholar smiled, then asked eagerly, "Any news of the Ice Troll war?"

"Well. We already knew they'd won that days ago. What more do you need to know?"

"Numbers, dispositions, tactics, casualties . . ." Maggie listed.

"That sort of detail you'll have to get directly from Mum tonight. They're not going to risk information like that on a relay that can be heard by anyone."

Maggie shook his head in tired amusement. Youth always assumed the whole world had access to its skills. "Not everyone speaks the language of the Wolf-folk, Charlemagne."

"No? No, I suppose not. Well, whatever, there were no details in the report."

Just then, a member of the werewolf guard arrived, and saluted smartly. Maggie listened in fascination as he and the Prince spoke rapidly in the strange snarls and guttural grunts of the Wolf-folk tongue.

"Captain Blood-Lapper wants to know if a full guard of honour will be needed tonight," Charlemagne translated, after politely waiting to see if Maggiore had understood.

"Yes, I think so, Captain," the old scholar answered, in his capacity as Senior Royal Adviser. "After such a fabulous victory the Queen should be greeted with full ceremonial."

"Yes, My Lord," the werewolf replied in the language of the Icemark, his voice booming around the small room. Then, with a final salute, he withdrew to pass on the order to the human housecarles and his own warriors.

Maggie sighed in sudden contentment. Charlemagne's mood had changed for the better, and he also seemed to have forgiven his old tutor's earlier bluntness. "Well, there are enough of the Yule supplies left to make a scratch feast in honour of your parents' return. Though I wish they'd given us a little more warning. What's the point of setting up an efficient werewolf message system if they don't use it?"

"I suppose they were preoccupied and just forgot," Charlemagne said. "They have just fought a war, you know." Then, grinning, he added, "Mum was right. She warned me you can be a bit of an old woman when you get going."

"'Old woman'! What do you mean?"

"Always fussing and nagging."

Maggiore sniffed and drew his dignity about him like a large protective cloak. "I'll treat that remark with the contempt it deserves."

* * *

Charlemagne had been standing on the battlements of the citadel for almost an hour listening to the werewolf messages coming in. Despite several layers of furs and the blazing brazier beside him, he was freezing. Even so, there were compensations. Not only would he be among the first to see the Queen and her army come into view, but the sight of the near-full moon rising over the frozen land of the Icemark was achingly beautiful. Its subtle light reflected off the snow and diffused through the myriad ice crystals suspended in the frigid air, so the entire world seemed steeped in misted silver and smoky shadows.

"'A night for magic,'" Charlemagne murmured, remembering the times from his early childhood when his father would conjure little images from the 'muscle and texture of light itself' and set them skipping and dancing on his bedcovers just before he went to sleep.

His thoughts were interrupted by the lonely sound of another werewolf howling into the cold night air. It was nearer than the last couple of calls, which was hardly surprising – the Wolf-folk were reporting on the progress of the Royal Army, and each time they passed a lookout point another message was sent.

An acknowledging call was relayed back from one of the werewolves at the main gatehouse. And judging by the average marching pace of one of Thirrin's expeditions, Charlemagne quickly calculated it would be twenty minutes before the army came into sight. He beckoned a nearby housecarle.

"Tell the kitchens the army'll be here in less than an hour," he instructed. "Then tell Maggiore."

The soldier saluted and hurried away.

A noise on the spiral stairwell behind him told

Charlemagne that his brothers and Cressida were on their way up. All of them spoke some werewolf and would have understood the relay, though none were as fluent as Sharley.

Cressida was first to emerge through the narrow doorway of the turret. "Ah, there you are, Sharley," she said, smiling. "I knew you'd have heard the werewolves. How long before Mum and Dad get back?"

"Another hour or so. But they should start coming out of the forest in about twenty minutes."

His twin brothers, Cerdic and Eodred, struggled through the narrow doorway. At sixteen they were already larger than most housecarles, and Maggiore said they took after their granddad, King Redrought, except that they both had jet-black hair. Redrought's hair had been as flame-red as Thirrin's, and as that of Cressida and Charlemagne. But, as if to compensate for the difference in hair colour, both twins had inherited their granddad's inability to say anything quietly. They boomed and bellowed and laughed with the volume of a thunderstorm in the mountains, added to which they also had Redrought's slapstick sense of humour, and when they laid aside their axes and swords, they were as boisterous and fun-loving as kittens. Even now, as they stretched their huge frames after climbing up the confined spiral staircase, they were nudging and shoving each other, trying to make one another slip on the ice. Cerdic scooped up a double handful of snow from the battlements and stuffed it down Eodred's neck and the following squawking and giggling echoed over the silent citadel as if a pack of manic hens had been released into the night.

"Stop it, you two!" Cressida said with all the authority of her seventeen years and her position as heir to the throne. "We won't be able to hear the Wolf-folk messages if you keep mucking about."

The twins immediately settled down, despite the fact that they towered over their slightly-built elder sister. But they continued to poke and nudge each other slyly whenever she wasn't watching.

"Hiya, Sharley!" Eodred boomed, as if only just realising he was there. "When will Mum and Dad get back?"

"I've already asked that, thickhead!" said Cressida. "They'll be here in about an hour. Where's Medea?" she suddenly thought to ask.

Charlemagne shrugged. "Who knows? Doing whatever it is our sister does so much of the time. She'll turn up when she's ready, I suppose."

Cressida frowned. "She could at least make the effort for Mum and Dad."

"Do you think they'll bring us something back from the Icesheets?" Cerdic asked excitedly. "Perhaps a troll's war-hammer, or maybe a piece of those falling stars Tharaman told us about last time he visited?"

"That's Tharaman-*Thar*, to you," said Cressida sharply. "And don't you think you're getting a little old to expect presents every time Mum and Dad have been away?"

"No, *actually!*" Cerdic answered forcibly. "It's traditional for monarchs to present their friends and allies with gifts!"

"But not their small-minded offspring!" his sister answered in a dangerously quiet tone that made both twins subside immediately.

"I bet they *will* bring us prezzies, anyway," Cerdic muttered rebelliously, but quickly closed his mouth when Cressida shot him a warning look.

"You don't have to wait out here in the cold if you don't

want to, Sharley," Cressida said, sounding concerned. "We can send word as soon as the army comes into sight."

Charlemagne sighed quietly. Even his sensible elder sister treated him as though he was constantly on the point of collapse. "I'm fine," he snapped with a frown. "At least I'm wearing furs. You lot are likely to freeze if you don't get something warm on over your armour. I suppose you've been training in the lists."

"With the Weapons Master, yes," Cressida answered, deciding to overlook her youngest brother's tone. "We're perfecting some of the finer points of the shield wall technique. I think we've got the hang of it now."

Charlemagne nodded silently. He sometimes watched them training, but his need to join in had become almost too much to bear, so he'd reduced the time he spent spectating on the sidelines.

Cressida knew the root cause of Charlemagne's silence and put her arm around his shoulders. She was just taller than him by about two inches, and their bright red hair and green eyes would have proven to any stranger that they were brother and sister. "Come on, Sharley. We have to accept what we are."

"You sound like Maggiore Totus," he answered sullenly.

"Do I?"

"Yes. He said just that, this afternoon."

"Well, he's right. Look at old Carnwulf, the porter. He was a housecarle, and one of the best, until he lost his leg to the green rot after he was wounded. But you don't hear him moaning or going on about the unfairness of life."

"And I do, I suppose."

"That's not what I meant, Sharley, and you know it," Cressida answered sharply. "Not all warriors carry swords and shields."

Charlemagne felt his face redden in a confusion of embarrassment and anger, but before he could say anything a call rose up from the werewolves at the gatehouse. Immediately, all four children of Queen Thirrin Freer Strong-in-the-Arm Lindenshield, Wildcat of the North, stared out over the snows to the dark and glowering eaves of the distant forest. For a moment it seemed that the trees themselves had begun to march out over the plain, but then the sharp eyes of the Royal siblings slowly distinguished cavalry horses and the raised spears of marching infantry. The army had come home.

As they watched, the soft diffusion of moonlight seemed to gather about a tall figure riding a long-eared mule, until a brilliant shooting star of light illuminated the marching housecarles and the distinctive white forms of the Queen's bodyguard of Ukpik werewolves. This was Oskan Witchfather's signal to his children who, he knew, would be watching from the walls.

A call rang out from the Wolf-folk down at the main gatehouse, and after a few moments a faint reply came from the Ukpik bodyguard. All four siblings scrambled for the stairway, eager to be first to greet their parents.

In one of the highest towers of the citadel, Medea looked out over the snows beyond the city walls and watched as her parents marched home. A year older than Charlemagne, she was of the same slender build, but where he had the red hair and green eyes of his mother and Cressida, she had the same dark colouring as Oskan. Once, a Court poet had even compared her deathly pale complexion and black hair to snowfall in a shadowed forest, though Medea's cold silence in response had ensured that no other social-climbing artist had ever again tried to win her support with flattering verses or songs.

Medea's feelings were a tangled knot of contradictions. She was happy that Thirrin and Oskan had arrived home safely, but she was angry that they would greet everyone before her and she was overflowing with a fierce resentment.

Medea burned with the jealousy she felt for her elder sister and her brood of brothers, Charlemagne in particular. She had been six years old when polio had nearly killed him, but when he'd survived with a crippled leg Medea had realised that the attention and pampering her parents were lavishing on him would be his for life, now that he would never be strong enough to fulfil his role as a fighting Prince of the House of Lindenshield. Medea felt as if she'd been forever demoted in the pecking order of the family, and rising above them all was *Charlemagne*, untouchable because of his disability, and for ever steeped in his parents' love. It was then that she knew she would always hate her younger brother and she did her best to make his life a misery.

With a smile she remembered a time when, soon after he'd recovered, Charlemagne had broken his favourite toy horse. After weeping over it for a minute or two, he had set about repairing the damage. Of course he made a terrible botched job of it, all gobbets of glue and legs set at odd angles, but he seemed quite pleased.

"I could mend it properly for you so that you couldn't even see the joins," she'd said after watching him struggle with his toy for almost an hour.

He'd looked up then, his innocent face alive with hope. "Could you?"

"I could. Would you like me to show you?"

"Oh, yes please!" he'd squeaked, and had handed the horse to her. He'd then watched every move she'd made in rapt

31

fascination, trusting his sister to make the world right again.

For several minutes her Magical Eye had inspected the fabric of the toy until she'd finally understood how grain meshed with grain, how molecule combined with atom to make the wood of its form. She'd then drawn on the energy she needed, and had unbroken the splits and breaks, tying splinters back into a flawless surface, smoothing away all signs of damage and at last returning the toy to Sharley.

Medea had let him play with the little horse for a while until, satisfied he trusted her, she'd said: "Give it back to me a moment, I want to show you something." And she'd made him watch tearfully as she broke off the legs again, one by one.

The insane jealousy of the memory still boiled in her veins, but at least her Gift ensured that she still got some of her father's attention. As the only other member of the family with Ability, he was the one who put her through her magical paces and devised different training regimes for her. For several nights a week – until she'd Come of Magical Age at fourteen – he had gone to her tower, and together they'd created landscapes and cities from the ectoplasm of moonlight and shadow, or sent their Sight far out into the night, viewing the world or sometimes even spying on the housecarles in their mess hall. She'd been thrilled to find that her Far-Seeing abilities were stronger than her father's.

Now, on this night of her parents' return she extinguished all the lamps and candles in her tower room and, opening the shutters wide on the freezing night, secretly watched her sister and brothers waiting on the walls. She had no intention of joining them yet. Only when the sickening screeches and tears of greeting were over and done with would she go down, knowing that at least Oskan would be looking for her.

CHAPTER 3

Glad to be home, Oskan stretched his feet towards the fire and sighed contentedly. It was the first time he'd felt truly warm in nearly two months, and the addition of a very fat Primplepuss curled up in a purring heap of tabby fur on his lap somehow added to the sense of comfort. He stroked her gently, grateful for the medical skills that had kept the ancient cat alive for almost twenty years. When Oskan had first met Thirrin, Primplepuss had been a tiny kitten, a scrap of fur nestled in King Redrought's huge war-callused hand. But now the animal was a massively fat matriarch of a large dynasty of palace cats that stalked the corridors and halls in search of any rodent stupid enough to try and raid the pantries and store-houses.

Meanwhile, out in the Great Hall, the sounds of trestle tables being set up and of servants scurrying about told Oskan that supper would soon be ready. Recently, he and Thirrin and their five children had taken to eating as a family in the private apartments – with the permanent addition of Maggiore – but tonight would be different. This was their first meal since returning home from the Ice Troll wars, and although it wasn't exactly a banquet with important guests and dignitaries, Thirrin had thought it best to show themselves to the household.

Oskan stroked Primplepuss, making her purr ecstatically like a hive of happy bees, and waited in warm contentment for the return of 'the rabble', as he termed his family.

Medea was somewhere in the citadel. She'd put in an appearance almost an hour after the rest of the children, and welcomed them home, although, as usual, she'd been as reserved and mysterious as a locked box in a secret room. The rest of his brood were with Thirrin, who had been forced to go to the lists with the twins and Cressida to see their latest accomplishments in battle tactics, and of course Charlemagne had insisted on going with them. Why could that boy never sit quietly? He always had to torture himself by watching his siblings train in ways he never could. Perhaps one day he'd redirect his energies into something other than his burning ambition to be a warrior, but Oskan suspected Sharley would be old and grey before that happened.

All of a sudden he sat bolt upright, causing Primplepuss to look up in alarm. He'd felt the unmistakable touch of the Gift nudging him, whispering into his mind from its deep mystery, and sending tell-tale shivers down his spine and thrilling down to his fingers.

"What . . . what? The boy? . . . Charlemagne!"

But the moment had passed, the Mystery curling a protecting veil around information he wasn't yet meant to know. Oskan slumped back in his chair feeling the familiar sense of draining that even the gentlest touch of the Gift always inflicted on him. The details would come in time . . . perhaps. But whether they did or not, Oskan felt a sudden upsurge of pride for his youngest child. Perhaps little Charlemagne had a destiny that would overshadow even those of his sisters and brothers . . .

The familiar uproar of the twins began to echo faintly across the Great Hall. He smiled to himself. The twins certainly took after Thirrin's side of the family. He could never fathom where they got all their energy from, and neither could he understand why everything they did needed so much noise!

He listened now to Cerdic excitedly greeting one of the palace wolfhounds, and the playful barking and giggling as Eodred tried to get on the dog's back to ride it round the hall as he used to do when he was little. Thirrin's sharp voice soon stopped the horseplay, and Oskan smiled as a familiar rebellious muttering rose up from the twins, and was followed by another sharp rebuke. It was only then that he realised it wasn't Thirrin's voice, but Cressida's. How like her mother she was: strong, capable and, it had to be said, bossy and domineering.

"Just right for the heir to the throne," he murmured, bracing himself for the dramatic entrance.

The salute of the housecarle on guard duty was followed by the twins exploding into the room. "Hiya, Dad!" Eodred boomed. "Bit quiet in here isn't it?"

"Not now it isn't," Oskan answered.

"Yes it is!" Cerdic joined in. "I can hear spiders tap-dancing across the ceiling." This was considered so hilarious by the twins they began to giggle.

"Good evening, dearest. We're not disturbing you, are we?" asked Thirrin, a small ironic smirk on her lips.

"Not in the least. I love spending an evening in the quiet company of warriors."

"Sharley's not a warrior," said Cerdic, immediately going a

brilliant crimson as he realised what he had said. "I mean—
ow, that hurt!" he finished, frowning at Cressida and rubbing
his arm where she'd hit him.

"It was meant to, you oaf," his sister hissed angrily.

Diplomacy was never going to be either twin's strong point,
Oskan thought to himself.

"Well, come in and find yourselves chairs," he said.
"Supper's going to be served soon. While we're waiting, you
might as well tell me what you've been doing."

A sudden movement at the door caught his eye, and he
tried hard not to look surprised as Medea slipped into the
room, as quietly and as stealthily as a hunting cat. He smiled
at her and almost got a response, but hardly noticed it as he
tried to fathom why she was deigning to visit her family for
the second time in one evening. Perhaps she'd actually missed
her parents and wanted to make up some of the lost time. It
was a happy thought, but one Oskan didn't believe for a
moment. Medea was far too self-sufficient; there must be
another reason.

"We can all hold the shield wall now, even with the most
experienced housecarles trying to break us!" said Eodred
proudly.

"Good, good," said Oskan, trying to sound interested. He
would have to puzzle over the enigma that was Medea later.
"And what about horsemanship?"

"Oh, that's always good," said Cerdic.

"Especially mine!" Eodred put in. "I'm working out ways
to use the cavalry to break a shield wall."

"You're more likely to break your neck," said Cressida
sharply.

"And what about you, Charlemagne?" Oskan interrupted

36

hurriedly. "What have you been doing while we were away?"

His youngest son looked at him moodily and shrugged. "Nothing much. Lessons with Maggie, mule riding, vegetating."

"I'm sure you've done more than that, Charlemagne," said Thirrin gently. "I've been told you've missed none of your lessons."

"No, but I bet he let Maggie sleep through half of them," said Cerdic, and laughed.

"Shut up, bonehead," said Cressida. "Let Sharley answer for himself."

They all looked at Charlemagne, who stood next to his mother. Even Medea, who'd positioned herself in the shadows by the door, turned her blank eyes on him. He went crimson, and desperately tried to think of something interesting he'd done while his parents had been away on the Icesheets. But nothing came to mind. He'd spent the entire time in one long boring round of lessons, eating and sleeping. Eventually, he just shook his head, completely defeated."Well, I'm sure if you really put your mind— *Quiet!*" Thirrin interrupted herself as Oskan suddenly slumped forward in his seat, his jaw working and his eyes rolling back in his head. "Leave him! It's the Sight. Just wait."

All the children had seen their father go into a trance before, but not so often that it wasn't still terrifying to watch. Only Medea observed everything with calm fascination as Oskan's Gift worked to take control of his mind. She'd sensed something magical might happen that night, and she knew it would have something to do with a family member. The rest of them waited breathlessly as Oskan slowly sat upright, his white eyes staring out over their heads, and a low growling sound rumbling in his throat.

He drew breath, and a deep inhuman voice boomed into the room. "Charlemagne Athelstan Redrought Strong-in-the-Arm Lindenshield, your fate – your Weird – will take you to the south, over burning sands, to a people of one god. Their cavalry was once dreaded by all, and will be again; they wait to be woken by the shadow of the storm. There will be your fulfilment, Prince Charlemagne, and you will return to the north, a blade of fire in your hand, at the head of—"

Oskan suddenly choked and slumped forward again.

"Eodred, fetch wine. Cressida, keep the guard out," Thirrin ordered. "We don't need any rumours of this getting round the city."

Then, taking the beaker her son held out, she put an arm around Oskan's shoulders and trickled wine into his mouth. Thirrin had seen her husband's Gift grow since they were both in their teens, but there were still times when she felt she hardly knew the man who'd been her Consort for almost twenty years. When the moon was full his aura changed from that of a quietly amusing individual who was more than happy to play with his children, to that of a cold and distant *Practitioner of the Art*. He coughed again, and Thirrin poured more of the wine into his mouth. He swallowed greedily, then seized the beaker and drained it.

"More," he whispered, and when a second beaker was put into his hand he drained that too.

They all waited, stunned into a quiet intensity. But then Oskan smiled, and sat upright. "I wish they'd give me more of a warning," he said, as though talking about unexpected guests. "So, what did I say?"

All eyes now turned to Charlemagne, who stood open-mouthed in exactly the same position he'd been in when his father had first collapsed. Then, all of a sudden, his weak leg gave way and he fell to the floor with a crash.

Medea's normally white face blazed crimson. She glared at her brother with undisguised hatred. She'd hoped her father's prophecy might have related to her in some way, but she'd been overlooked again, and her youngest brother was once more the centre of everyone's attention. Angrily, she slipped away and sought the sanctuary of her tower and the sweet bitterness of solitude.

The Great Hall wasn't overly full, Charlemagne noted as he ate his supper. Just the family, the housecarles, and the werewolf guards who weren't on duty. It felt almost intimate compared to the crowds and noise of official banquets. Musicians were playing softly up in the minstrel's gallery, and housecarles were greeting each other in the traditional manner. There was a contented burbling of: "Eh up, hairy arse! How's things?" and "Great, fathead, just great," as they sat down at the long trestle tables. The central hearth roared mightily with what looked like half a forest of logs blazing and crackling in it, and sending great billows of smoke up into the rafters where only some of it escaped through the vents.

Charlemagne was relieved to be able to sit in the relative quiet without almost jumping out of his skin every time one of the werewolves roared with laughter, or a housecarle bellowed the punchline of a filthy joke to his mates. Besides, he wanted to think over what his father had said when he had fallen into his trance earlier.

His Weird, his fate, lay in the south over burning sands. What did that mean? He and his family had discussed it in the few minutes before supper began, but then his mother had told them to keep quiet amongst the soldiers in the Great Hall, so no proper conclusion had been reached. Charlemagne was both afraid and excited. He'd expected to spend his days like a poor relation, hanging around the palace, tolerated at best by whoever was in power. But his dad's Sight had shattered that notion. For the first time in his life, Charlemagne realised that although the future he'd expected might have been boring, it would at least have been comfortable . . . and safe. Where were the burning sands? Who were the people with only one god? He could hardly think straight; he continued to munch his supper without tasting a thing. And what was that about *the shadow of the storm* and *a burning blade*?

The silken rustle of his mother's second-best dress didn't disturb his troubled thoughts, but when she laid her hand on his he suddenly started and looked up at her. As always, he was struck by her beauty. At thirty-three her hair blazed in all its fiery glory and her green eyes sparkled with the mixture of a warrior's fighting ferocity and her determined spirit. No one could have doubted she was a queen, even if she wore rags.

"Having a quiet think?"

He nodded, then said, "Dad's never wrong, is he?"

"Never," she answered with simple conviction. "Even when his prophecies seem ridiculous, they always come about."

"Then I'll be leaving the north. I'll be leaving you and Dad and . . . and everyone?" His voice cracked, and he stared down at the supper slowly congealing on his platter.

Thirrin gazed at her youngest son, so slight and small for his age, and felt a sudden longing to gather him up in her arms and keep him safe from the world and all its horrors. But she determinedly thrust aside such thoughts and, carefully controlling her voice, said, "You are a Prince of the House of Lindenshield, and at fourteen you're ready for the responsibilities of manhood, whatever they may be for you. Are you prepared for this? Can you take up the burden?"

"No . . . yes . . . I don't know," he almost wailed. "How can I say? I don't even know where I'm going."

She nodded. "Exactly the right answer. None of us can ever know, but remember that Dad's prophecy said you'd come back – *how*, we don't know, nor when, but there certainly was no mention of anything lowly or dishonourable about it."

Charlemagne nodded vigorously, grasping at the truth of what she said. "That's right, it did say I'd come back, didn't it?"

Thirrin nodded. "And don't worry about being ready. Life has a habit of preparing you and giving you abilities you never knew you had. At fourteen I found myself the Queen of a country at war and I was sure that I'd fail, but with the help of your dad, and Maggie, and countless others, we survived."

Charlemagne nodded. He was well aware of his family's history, and just hoped he'd be able to live up to such an impressive past. Even if he had only the smallest role to play in future events, he wanted to carry out his duties as well as he could, and with as much dignity as his position as the limping runt in a family of warriors would allow.

He squeezed his mother's hand, and she smiled at him. He was shocked to see that her blazing green eyes looked moist! Surely there weren't tears in the eyes of the fiercest, toughest warrior he knew?

But before he could say anything, the huge double doors of the Great Hall burst open and crashed back against the stonework. A freezing blast of wind drove through the smoke and slightly fuggy warmth of the cavernous space. All the housecarles and werewolves leaped to their feet. Immediately, the guard poured from their positions around the walls and formed a shield wall in front of the Royal dais. The hunting hounds bayed and growled, their hackles raised and teeth bared.

"Who dares disturb the taking of the Royal meal?" Thirrin demanded, leaping on to the table and seizing the sword and shield that Oskan held up to her. "Make yourself known or die by the swords and teeth of my warriors!"

A tense silence fell, then into the hall strode a massive werewolf with a grizzled pelt and a gold collar about his neck.

"It's me, Grishmak Blood-drinker, King of the Wolf-folk, and ally of the House of Lindenshield. Put up your swords – I come with news!"

Immediately, the werewolves in the hall howled a greeting to their king, and the housecarle guard beat spear on shield in salute. Thirrin relaxed, and handing her weapons back to Oskan she ordered the guard to stand down.

"You are welcome, King Grishmak," she said formally. "Join us at the High Table and tell us your news. Not invasion, I hope?" she added, her voice suddenly tense.

"No, no invasion. At least not yet," Grishmak called as he strode down the length of the hall followed by a group of ten huge and hairy warriors. He climbed the steps to the dais, and thumped his massive weight down into the chair that a chamberlain had hurriedly placed next to Thirrin's. "But now we have confirmation that the Polypontian Empire is definitely preparing to invade in the spring, and that our old 'friend' Scipio Bellorum will be leading the way."

Thirrin nodded quietly. "So, it's come at last," she said. Looking down the table, she called, "Maggie, how soon can we put the evacuation plans into action?"

"Immediately. Everything's in place and ready," the old scholar called.

"Good," said Thirrin distractedly. Then, turning back to Grishmak, she said, "Why did you arrive unannounced, and why didn't the werewolf relay warn of your approach?"

"I ordered a silence. I didn't want to spread panic, or even speculation, amongst the people."

"Very wise," Thirrin admitted, and quickly returned to the matter of defending her realm. "Oskan, how soon can you gather the witches and other healers? We'll need them when the war begins."

"A matter of days. We've been ready for months," he answered calmly.

"Right. Captain Osgood," she then called to the Commander of the Palace Guard. "Send word for all generals present in the area to meet in the Operations Room in one hour. And tell the werewolf relay to order the presence of all provincial governors and Commanders, with special urgency and priority placed on the Hypolitan."

Captain Osgood saluted and hurried off. In the small oasis of silence that followed, Thirrin spoke to King Grishmak. "I'll need the Ukpik werewolves to take messages to Their Vampiric Majesties and to Tharaman-Thar. When can they leave?"

"They're already on their way," Grishmak answered.

Thirrin nodded, then asked, "You said you had confirmation of the Empire's plans to invade. What exactly do you know?"

"We captured a Polypontian officer just over the border, and judging by all his lace and ruffles he was pretty important. Anyway, I took personal charge of the interrogation and he soon told us all he knew. Oh yes . . ." Grishmak added as he fished about his thick pelt in search of something. "He was carrying these papers. I thought Maggiore might be able to interpret them."

A small leather case was passed down the table to the Royal Adviser, and they watched in silence as he read through them.

"Yes, invasion plans," he confirmed. "I'll need time to extract all the details. But you do realise that the Polypontians will change everything as soon as they know their officer is missing?"

"Yes, of course. But it'll give us some idea of numbers and weaponry," Thirrin said. "How long do you need to translate it completely?"

"I should have everything of worth by mid-morning tomorrow."

"Get on with it, then," Thirrin snapped. And as Maggie hurried from the hall, she returned her attention to the King of the Wolf-folk.

"Will the body of the officer be found?" she asked

Grishmak grinned enormously, his massive teeth glittering in the torchlight. "Never in a century of searching. They won't find his horse either."

Thirrin shuddered slightly and chose not to ask how the King had got rid of the evidence.

A commotion at the doors announced the first of the Generals to arrive, and Thirrin quickly dismissed all of the non-military personnel, including Charlemagne, from the High Table.

As he crossed the hall on the way to his room, Charlemagne stopped to look back at the heads huddled together as they discussed the imminent crisis. Already, werewolf and human messengers were scurrying away on errands about the city and beyond, and more soldiers were pouring in through the doors. He couldn't help noticing that Cressida and both his brothers were still in their seats, giving their opinions and asking questions. Medea was nowhere to be seen, but he'd hardly been aware of her at the table anyway.

He felt smaller and less important than the few mice that had survived the Primplepuss clan and scraped a living from the crumbs amongst the floor-rushes. Even his father's prophecy was forgotten as he slowly limped away back to his room.

The snows of the Icemark and the Northern World had flowed south beyond the borders into the Polypontian Empire, locking the world in their iron grip. Little moved in the vicious cold, and nothing could live here for long without shelter. Even so, a carriage risked the icy wastes, travelling fast; all brittle glitter under a frigid moon.

Ornately carved and gilded, the carriage looked like one of the beautiful pleasure boats that sailed the rivers of the Polypontian Empire. Six black horses, plumed and caparisoned in red, drew the vehicle through the snows of the foothills on the Empire's side of the Dancing Maidens mountain range, the driver and groom deeply muffled in furs.

Small charcoal braziers warmed the plush velvet interior of the carriage, where its three passengers sat in silence, occasionally passing round a small silver flask of warming spirits.

General Scipio Bellorum scrubbed away the rime of ice that had frosted the window, and gazed out at the frozen landscape. It would be several weeks yet before the thaw started and he could begin the invasion of the Icemark. But no matter, the army was still mustering, and several regiments would need time to recover from their long forced marches across many miles of the Imperial lands.

"Are the artillery batteries making good progress?" Bellorum asked his eldest son.

"Delayed at present in the mud of Isteria, I'm afraid," Octavius replied in a slightly bored tone. "The engineeers are laying new roads as we speak."

"Not through the southern marshes?"

"The very same."

"How very ambitious. What is the rate of progress?"

"Fair. Last reports had them halfway across. I expect them to be done within a month."

Scipio nodded. "Ten lashes of the whip for every day beyond that for the entire Engine-eering Corps, and two men hanged for every week."

Octavius nodded gently. "Duly noted, Sir."

"And your infantry regiments, Sulla. Any complaints?"

The General's youngest son leaned back into the plush velvet seat and stretched his elegantly booted feet towards the brazier. "Do you know, I actually received a *delegation* from the Iberian Light Mountain Foot Regiment last week, 'respectfully requesting' increased rations due to the harsh conditions."

Scipio was interested to know how Sulla had handled the situation. "Really? And what did you do?"

"Doubled the rations, of course. One cannot risk discontent in the ranks, especially when the men are being asked to march in such appalling conditions." He smiled, remembering. "I then had the Regimental Quartermaster flogged for not carrying out his duties of supplying and reacting to need correctly. Oh yes, and I also had the entire 'delegation' placed before a firing squad of their own comrades-in-arms, for impudence and insubordination . . . by the way, Octavius, I must commend you for your new training methods for the musketeers. They skilfully dispatched the little ring of mutinous scoundrels, despite low light levels and a howling blizzard."

"I'm glad to hear it. The gods know it took long enough for them to accept it, but once I'd made them use some of the more reluctant soldiers as target practice they soon buckled down. Still, I admire their stubbornness – twenty of their comrades were dead before they gave in."

"I'm not sure I like the sound of that. Such stubborn insubordination can infect an entire army," said Sulla with quiet intensity. "I hope you dealt with it."

"Oh, there's no need to worry. I sent all the ring-leaders to help with experiments in the munitions factories. They're all dead now, and our Imperial scientists at last know what ratio of gunpowder to body mass is required for total disintegration."

Scipio nodded in satisfaction; both his sons were avid and brilliant students of his own personal Art of War. Throughout the world, the Bellorum dynasty had become a byword for ruthless efficiency, and he somehow felt the coming invasion would only confirm it. The Icemark would soon experience the happy combination of his sons' elegant manners and vicious ruthlessness. Oh, how the barbarian Queen and her band of allies would suffer, especially as the Imperial scientists had made such advances in developing new weaponry. Bellorum could hardly wait to see the enemy's reaction to some of his new killing machines.

CHAPTER 4

As Tharaman-Thar and his army of Snow Leopards emerged from the forest, he called a halt and looked out across the plain towards the city of Frostmarris. The huge defensive earth banks that had been built during the last war against the Polypontian Empire still circled its walls, and in the brilliant sunshine they glittered and gleamed like carved quartz under their covering of snow.

"There, my dear, is Frostmarris, capital of the Icemark," he said in almost conversational tones to his Tharina beside him.

She purred and nuzzled his cheek affectionately. She was well aware of the huge importance the city held in Tharaman's life, and she also knew that the more casual his tone, the more deeply he felt.

"It looks strong," Krisafitsa-Tharina replied, her eyes expertly gauging the height and defensive capability of the walls.

"Oh yes, indeed it is!" her mate said, almost as if it was his own city. "But the Empire's war machine is massive, and by all accounts it's even stronger now than it was in the last war.

So much could be lost, so much . . ."

"Well, we're here now and the allies are gathering, so Bellorum will get a very bloody nose when he arrives," she answered in a brisk attempt to keep Tharaman's spirits up.

He looked at her and laughed, his enormous voice sending a flight of ravens calling and crying into the air. "Yes, he will get a bloody nose, won't he? A very bloody nose indeed!" And he threw back his head and roared into the frozen air.

Immediately, his entire army answered, and the massive wave of their collective roar rolled over the plain and up to the walls of the far-off city. A distant answering call from the werewolf guards wavered back over the snow-covered fields, and the Thar purred happily.

"Well, they know we're here. I hope the kitchens have been busy – I could eat a whole one of those cow thingies these people keep."

"I'm sure Thirrin's more than ready for your appetite," Krisafitsa said. "In fact, I'm quite peckish myself. Let's get going – there's sure to be all sorts of greetings and formalities to get through before we're allowed near the food."

A buzz of anticipation filled the streets and alleyways as the entire population of Frostmarris lined the route the Snow Leopards would take. It had become common knowledge that the leopards' presence had been requested because the Polypontians were going to invade again. Fear held the people in a powerful, slowly tightening grip.

Before General Scipio Bellorum had invaded the Icemark twenty years ago, he had never lost a battle, let alone a war. And he hadn't lost another battle since. A powerful and wily enemy, he was as ruthless as a fox in a henhouse and was certain to have learned some very valuable lessons from his last attempt to defeat the Queen and her allies. Not only was he clever, tough and totally vicious, but he had now trained his two sons who, rumours claimed, made their father look like some gentle old granddad.

Sulla and Octavius Bellorum were already a byword for ferocity and sheer lack of restraint. Both were guilty of killing on a terrible scale, wiping out entire populations merely to demonstrate the power of the Polypontian Empire. In fact, both Bellorum's sons had been campaigning independently of their father for the past five years, so it was ominous that the old General had enlisted their help in his proposed war against the Icemark. The only member of the Bellorum family not mustered for the war was the General's wife, the mother of his ruthless sons. She'd escaped into death many years before, preferring the Great Unknown to a continued certainty with her menfolk.

A fanfare of bugles brayed on the frozen air, interrupting the collective worries of the people of Frostmarris, and the gates of the citadel opened.

Thirrin rode out on a magnificent charger, its bridle polished and blazing in the bright sunlight and the crimson leather of its trappings gleaming in stark contrast to the horse's pure black coat. Beside her rode Oskan on his old mule Jenny, her long ears drooping with age. Even so, Oskan had insisted that Jenny wear her crimson and yellow ear-warmers, which made her look as though she had a roll of brightly coloured tapestry balanced on top of her head. But despite looking completely ridiculous, the old mule was obviously in high spirits. She brayed loud and long as she trotted along beside Thirrin's charger.

Thirrin had long ago accepted that one of the few limits to

her power was her complete inability to make her stubborn husband ride the sort of horse she thought more fitting for her Consort. In an effort to compensate for this, Thirrin assumed full *monarch mode*, staring proudly ahead as the people watched her ride by wearing her best parade armour. The helmet and shield were polished to a glittering brilliance that dazzled all who gazed on her. Beneath the rim of steel encircling her brow, the brilliant green of her eyes gleamed with excitement. Tharaman had arrived, and with him was his Tharina, Krisafitsa! Let the Bellorums launch their war; the Icemark and her allies would beat them down!

The people watched the Queen and her escort in silence. There was too much fear in the air to allow for cheering; the Icemark feared the vicious old General. He would have studied his enemy well, and had presumably found them lacking in some way if he thought he could defeat them this time. Even so, they were comforted to see the controlled power displayed by the columns of housecarles and werewolves who marched along behind Thirrin. The Empire wouldn't find this war any easier than the last.

With almost perfect timing the Royal party arrived in the square that led to the main gate just as the Snow Leopard army was beginning to climb the causeway up to the city. The marching troops stamped to a halt and a silence descended. In the cold air every tiny sound was magnified: the frost on the roofs and walls crackled continually like a cold fire, and the creak of leather boots and breeches rose like the murmuring of trees swaying in a gentle breeze.

The massive outer gates were opened and slammed back against the walls of the long entrance tunnel. Thirrin struggled to keep her face a mask of Royal composure as her heart beat in excitement. The softly muffled tread of thousands of padded paws whispered and murmured into the air as the first ranks of the Snow Leopard army advanced through the entrance tunnel.

At a signal from their Captain, who was peering through a small spyhole, the gate guards drew back the enormous bolts, and the inner gates swung ponderously open. And there, framed in the gateway, stood Tharaman, One Hundredth Thar of the Snow Leopards, Lord of the Icesheets and Scourge of the Ice Trolls, and with him his Tharina, Krisafitsa, Lady of the White Fire and his partner in rule and power.

For a moment, all was silent. The giant leopard then rose up on his hind legs and roared. His mighty voice reverberated through the frozen air and into the city, filling the ears of all those who waited to the uttermost brim.

Thirrin and Oskan rode slowly to the centre of the square and waited quietly for Tharaman and Krisafitsa to come to them. With all their natural grace and power, the Royal Snow Leopards seemed to glide forward. As they came to a halt, Oskan and Thirrin dismounted, and the people waited for the formal speeches of welcome to begin. But they never came. Their Queen cast aside her Royal dignity and rushed forward to hug the giant leopard. His booming purr filled the square with a rumble like distant thunder.

Wild cheering broke out. Tharaman-Thar and Krisafitsa-Tharina, the Icemark's greatest allies, had arrived, and the people could begin to hope again.

Charlemagne thought the Royal apartments were impossibly crowded. King Grishmak sat with his large feet resting on the hearth before the blazing fire, adding a slightly cheesy scent to the already stuffy atmosphere, while Tharaman and Krisafitsa had each managed to cram in their huge bulk on opposite sides of the fireplace. The human beings sat in a squashed semi-circle of chairs with Thirrin and Oskan at the centre. Maggiore sat on the extreme left with Primplepuss on his knee, and Charlemagne on the right. Cressida, as Crown Princess, sat next to her mother, while the twins, sitting next to Oskan, towered over him, laughing and poking each other happily. Medea on the other hand, sitting in a chair only a few feet behind her father's, managed to convey the impression of a massive physical chasm between herself and the rest of the family.

Sharley seemed to be dozing in the warm fug, but he was still listening to the conversation going on around him. "That was just what I needed," Tharaman purred contentedly. "Though I must admit I rather surprised myself by eating *two* entire cows. The journey must have taken more out of me than I thought."

"Even I could only manage one and a half," said Grishmak with admiration. "But then, I've done nothing more physically strenuous than walk from meeting to committee and back again for the last week. Still, I think we're as ready as we'll ever be to face the Bellorum clan."

"Oh, no business tonight, please!" begged Krisafitsa. "You can fill in the details tomorrow. But tonight, let's just enjoy each other's company and relax. We all know there'll be precious little time for such things in the coming months."

A general murmur of agreement greeted this comment, and for a while the only sounds were the crackle of the fire and the odd rumblings and squeaks of Tharaman's digestive system as it processed his gargantuan dinner.

Krisafitsa looked at her human allies and purred gently. Thirrin's family was growing fast, and Cressida was so like her mother that they could almost be sisters. The twins were typical of young males of any species – they were rapidly growing into a strength they had yet to fully understand and control. Even so, they were already of warrior height and would make a valuable contribution to the coming war.

Medea, on the other hand, was an unknown quantity. The Tharina gazed at the dark-haired young woman whose closed face and black, oddly unfocused eyes gave nothing away. She was staring into her lap and only looked up if her father moved or spoke, otherwise she remained utterly still as if no one other than those with the Gift were of any interest to her. Krisafitsa realised she'd never actually heard Medea speak. Polite conversation between ordinary people was something the Princess obviously had little time for

The Tharina's gaze then settled on Charlemagne, or Sharley as his family called him. He rarely spoke in company either, but his silence seemed to be more a lack of self-confidence than indifference to the people around him. His leg was obviously a problem for him, and he was small for a human boy of his age. Even so, something about him suggested there were unknown depths to his character. Krisafitsa could understand why Thirrin felt so protective of him.

"Charlemagne, what would you be?" Krisafitsa asked.

The boy looked at her, blushing in surprise that the Tharina had spoken to him, and angry with himself for not understanding the question. "'What would I . . .?' I don't know what you mean."

"If you could be anything you wanted, what would you be?" she explained.

"Oh, I see. That's easy. I'd be a warrior, like my mother and sister and brothers."

"And what would you be if you could be anything other than a warrior?"

"There's nothing else worth being."

"There are many lives to live in the world. Not everyone can be a soldier."

"No," Charlemagne agreed. "But you first asked me what I would be if I could be anything, and I would be a warrior."

A heavy silence told Krisafitsa that she'd found an old family wound, and she deftly changed direction. "And where would you live if you could choose anywhere in the world?"

"Here, in the Icemark," he answered immediately. But then he stopped and after a moment added. "I suppose. But I don't really know anywhere else. Not properly. Oh, I know I've learned about different places from Maggie. But knowing what type of food a country grows or what sort of minerals they mine only tells you about the . . . body of a place, not about its mind; not about how it feels and what it's *really* like."

"No, it doesn't," the Tharina agreed. "I'm sure there must be some mighty minds in the lands beyond our borders, Charlemagne. Perhaps one day you'll have a chance to find out."

"Sharley's going to explore the world anyway, according to Dad, aren't you Sharley?" said Eodred in a tone that suggested he thought the whole idea a bit daft.

"That's your brother's prophecy, Eddie. Leave *him* to decide whether he discusses it or not!" said Cressida sharply.

"Prophecy?" asked the Tharina with interest.

"Yes. He's going to a 'land of fire', whatever that means, and when he comes back he'll have a 'blade of fire' in his hand. All sounds a bit unlikely— ow! That hurt."

"It was meant to," said Cressida. "I've already told you to let Sharley decide whether he wants to talk about it or not. And don't you *ever* let me hear you doubting Dad's fore-tellings again!"

"I wasn't doubting anything! It just . . . well, it just all seems a little . . . odd. I mean, *Sharley!*"

"That's enough," said Thirrin with quiet force. "Eodred, if you're ever to become a Commander of any worth you need to understand that there are times when you should keep your opinions to yourself. And not least because they're likely to be wrong!"

"I don't mind what he says," said Charlemagne. "After all, it's true. It does seem unlikely."

"Prophecies often do," said Oskan quietly. "They tell us of the unlooked-for, the unexpected. That's their very nature. They come into our lives with news of shock and amazement and leave us to puzzle over what may seem unbelievable."

"And you had just such a . . . presentiment about Charlemagne?" Krisafitsa prompted gently.

"Yes, more or less as Eodred said. But there was more. He's destined to be listed amongst the very greatest in the land. How, I don't know, nor even when. But that's typical of the Sight. It only ever gives a tantalising glimpse of possibilities, never the full story. It would be so much easier if it would reveal things in their entirety! I can't imagine why it doesn't."

"Can you not?" said Maggiore Totus, and drained his mug of mulled wine. "I think it's true to say that if we were given a detailed view of our future we might well sit back and do nothing to actually bring it about. So, our future would be changed by our own inaction."

"Of course!" Oskan agreed excitedly. "That's it precisely. If we know too much, we could change our futures by our reaction to what we know. Thank the Goddess for the gift of wise men!"

"Thank the Goddess," echoed a quiet, yet powerful, female voice, and everyone in the room turned to look at Medea, whose deep eyes were resting on her father.

"Well, at least Dad's Sight didn't say Sharley's going to be a great warrior," said Cerdic. "That would have been too difficult to believe. *Ouch!* Why'd you do that?"

"Because identical twins should have identical injuries," said Cressida calmly.

In the amused and approving silence that followed, nobody noticed Charlemagne blushing deep crimson as he sank down as far as possible into his chair. His brothers' honesty cut him like a knife. The thought of him becoming a warrior was laughable, and yet the desire to do just that filled Sharley's every waking moment and, indeed, many of his dreams. Medea broke the silence by suddenly leaving the room without a word. Everyone stared after her, surprised by her lack of manners. Oskan shrugged his apologies to the guests, and quickly followed her.

He didn't try to reach Medea until they were in a quiet corridor deep within the labyrinth of the citadel. When she heard his footsteps she stopped and waited for him to catch up.

"You wanted me?" she asked quietly.

"What I want is an explanation for your rudeness, Medea," he said, his voice even and steady.

"The room was warm, and the conversation of no interest to me."

"Wouldn't it have been more polite to make an excuse and

ask permission to withdraw?"

"Apparently you think so."

"I do," he agreed, keeping a tight rein on his temper. "But it's equally apparent that you don't." Medea had always been a strange child, but he was usually able to reach her with patience.

Her odd, dark eyes held his gaze unflinchingly. "I have no time for social niceties."

"Even if a lack of those social niceties can offend important friends and allies?"

"Oh dear," she said, her tone quite flat yet bitingly sarcastic. "Have I caused a war?"

"Medea," Oskan said calmly. "Why must you be so rude?"

"I've already—"

"No, I want the real reason. Everyone in that room is your friend or your family."

"It is possible for family not to be friends," she pointed out softly.

"What do you mean? We *all* love you, Medea."

"That *may* be true, Father, but doesn't it occur to you that I may not love you *all* in return?"

Oskan stared at her, unable to answer. After moment or two Medea turned and walked away.

CHAPTER 5

There were still hours to go before dawn, and the air literally crackled with frost as Charlemagne crept across the stable yard as quietly as his weak leg would allow. There was no moon, and the stars blazed like molten silver spilt over the blue-black sky.

He reached the stable door without being seen, and lifted the latch. Once inside, he lit his lantern and held it up. Several long-faced, sleepy horses whickered at him gently.

"Shush!" hissed Charlemagne urgently. "Don't give me away!"

He limped along the row of stalls until he came to his mother's warhorse. Havoc stood well back in his stall, obviously unhappy about being disturbed, and Charlemagne swallowed nervously. The huge horse was as black as the shadow of a dark night, had hooves the size of a housecarle's shield, and eyes that glittered and rolled dangerously whenever he scented even the possibility of a fight.

Charlemagne hoped the warhorse recognised his scent and would respect him for the Queen's sake.

"Hello, Havvy," he said gently, his voice wavering, and

breaking into a high note just when he wanted to sound as adult as possible.

The horse rumbled deeply and snorted. Then, as Charlemagne climbed awkwardly on to the door and held out his hand to coax him over, he laid back his ears and let out a deafening squeal that echoed around the stables.

"Quiet, Havoc!" Charlemagne barked with an anger bordering on panic, and almost magically the horse's ears pricked up and he stood motionless. Acting before he could reason himself out of his plan, Charlemagne climbed down from the door and opened it.

The horse immediately began to dance lightly on his massive hooves. Charlemagne stopped dead as the sheer bulk of the animal loomed over him, but then the fighting blood of the Lindenshields coursed through his frame and he stepped forward. Better to die in a brave attempt to make the family accept your right to be a fully trained warrior, than to run away and fulfil only a fraction of your real potential.

"Havoc!" he said sharply, and reached up briskly to pat the strongly arching neck that rose above him. The horse's flesh quivered, and he snorted loudly, but he stamped to a standstill and allowed the boy to stroke him.

"We're going out for a canter, you and I. So you just wait quietly while I fetch your saddle and bridle."

He crossed to the tack room. First he fetched a blanket and, returning to the stall, he managed to drape it across the animal's plateau-like back. Then, back in the tack room, he seized the massive saddle in his strongest grip, and fell straight over backwards.

After a frantic struggle, he managed to climb out from under the tangle of buckles, stirrups and leather and stood

61

glaring at the saddle angrily. But he'd gone too far to give up now, so shrugging at the indignity he grabbed the thing firmly by the girth strap, and slowly and painfully dragged it to Havoc's stall.

The horse seemed a little surprised to see his equipment arrive in such an unorthodox manner, but after a few sharp words in a voice that had a familiar echo of Thirrin's powerful tone, he allowed the boy to put on his bridle. But now Charlemagne was stuck. He could barely lift the saddle, let alone raise it above his head and throw it over the stallion's broad back.

He held his breath, close to panic. But just as he was about to despair, he remembered one of the cavalry commands.

"Havoc . . . knees down!"

The stallion turned his massive head and regarded him solemnly.

It was one thing making the horse stand still, but it was something else entirely to make him act on specific voice commands. But Charlemagne knew he mustn't lose heart now or his plan would have failed before it had even begun.

He tried again. "Havoc. Knees down!"

The great horse blew down his nostrils contemplatively and, almost seeming to shrug, he lowered himself until he was prone in the sawdust and straw. Charlemagne heaved a sigh of relief. Then he began a struggle to get the saddle over Havoc's wide back. At last he managed it and, praying the tangle of leather and metal wouldn't slip off, he gave the order to stand.

Havoc sprang to his feet and Charlemagne hurried to fasten the girth strap. Finally, the horse was ready, and Charlemagne climbed on to the door of the stall and made an undignified scramble into the saddle. Taking up the reins, he urged the horse forward, and they surged out into the stable corridor with Charlemagne staring down from an incredible height. Eventually, he managed to lean over far enough to open the latch on the stable door, and they went out into the yard. The stallion's massive hooves rattled and rang on the cobbles, but amazingly nobody came to investigate the noise. Charlemagne settled himself in the saddle, and after five minutes' riding, the low postern gate in the outer circuit of the city walls came into view.

Only a solitary figure standing in the window of the highest tower in the citadel saw him go. The wind drew her long black hair out into the freezing night air, and her odd, unfocused eyes absorbed every particle and photon of starlight. As horse and boy dwindled away to tiny figures in the distance, she reached up and closed the shutters. She then returned to her high-backed chair at the centre of the floor. Her lips moved slightly as she chanted under her breath, and the icy whisper of her voice rose into the air, forming her name, "Medea, Medea . . ." over and over again.

Charlemagne was still getting used to the reality of riding a charger. But he was tingling with a sense of elation. He'd done it! They'd all said he couldn't possibly ride an ordinary pony, let alone a warhorse, and yet here he was out on the plain of Frostmarris on his mother's own personal charger. Havoc the fierce! Havoc the mighty! Havoc the barely controllable!

Charlemagne was beginning to suspect that although the stallion was undoubtedly a formidable charger, the rest of his reputation as a firebrand and demon in horse disguise was all a sham. Havoc was trotting along now as docile as the gentlest mare.

Charlemagne decided to see how fast he could really go.

He bent forward over the animal's neck and shook the reins.

Havoc leaped to the gallop, with Charlemagne clinging on desperately as the wind howled and roared in his ears and his spine jammed against the high back of the war-saddle. He was terrified, especially when the stallion took it into his head to leave the road, leap hedgerow and ditch and head for the forest.

Then, as suddenly as the closing of a door, Havoc slowed. Within seconds they were walking towards the eaves of the forest as though nothing had happened. Charlemagne's thumping heart gradually slowed to a reasonable pace and the sweat of his terror dried in the freezing wind. One of the veteran housecarles had once told him that even the greatest warrior experienced terror at some time in his life, but a truly brave man carried on despite his fear. After several steadying breaths, he sighed with relief. His plan was back on track and he began to look about for landmarks. Eventually, he spotted what he was looking for: a distinctively twisted oak tree in the distance.

He had chosen the tree for a reason: it had a crack in its side, large enough to allow a small youth such as himself to slip inside the wide and dry space where over the decades the wood of the ancient oak had slowly rotted away. As they drew level with the tree he reined Havoc to a halt, quickly dismounted and slipped through the crack. Inside, it was pitch dark and smelt, not surprisingly, of wood dust and rotting leaves. Charlemagne searched through the deep pile of crumbled wood. Uncovering a large sack, he opened it and pulled out a pair of hunting spears, a long dagger, a set of skinning knives, and three torches primed with pitch and bundled together with a tinderbox.

His plan was going better than he'd ever dared hope. All he had to do now was find a boar, kill it, and take the carcass back to Frostmarris in triumph. Deep in the barbaric past of the little kingdom of the Icemark, no youth would have been considered a man and no maid a woman until they'd killed either a boar or a Greyling bear. Charlemagne intended to use this old way to prove himself worthy of warrior training and status.

Outside in the cold air, Havoc whickered. Charlemagne hurried back to the horse, strapped the spear scabbard to his saddle and, when the horse obediently settled to his knees, remounted.

He'd never really expected to get so far with his plan, and now that his initial elation was wearing off, a nagging sense of doubt began to creep into his mind. He was untrained, untried and, he had to admit, unfit. What would happen if he really did find a boar and had to give chase?

After a few minutes of steady riding, Charlemagne reined to a halt as the eaves of the forest loomed darkly ominous before him. The massive brooding trunks seemed almost to be daring him to enter their domain. A cold wind breathed out at him, bringing with it a scent of decaying leaves and the blended smells of all the animal, insect and bird life that found a home under its spreading canopy.

Havoc whickered nervously, and Charlemagne almost turned back towards the warmth and safety of the city. But all his years of frustration and humiliation suddenly boiled up inside him, and he kicked the horse's flanks to urge him on. The stallion snorted and threw up his head in the dim light.

Charlemagne could see the whites of the animal's eyes as he bordered on panic.

"Havoc, forward!" he barked.

And the animal trotted on, blowing fiercely.

The blackness of the forest enfolded them like a stifling cloth, and Charlemagne hurriedly drew out one of the torches, lit it with his tinderbox, and held it high above his head. The darkness receded slightly, but clamoured at the edges of the small pool of light like an animal stalking its prey. He had no idea what time it was, but he hoped dawn wasn't far away. He longed for daylight now. Somehow it hadn't occurred to him that it would be impossible to hunt in the dark. How dim could he be? He'd been so determined to prove himself before anyone had even noticed he was missing, he'd reached the forest when it was too dark to do anything!

"Idiot! Pin-brain! Prat!" He slapped his forehead with his open palm. This was hardly the cool and collected head of a warrior and tactician. The only thing he could do now was to find a clearing, light a fire, and wait for daylight.

After stumbling through the dark, he didn't know for how long, a wide glade opened up. He rode to the centre of it and dismounted to gather fuel. Fortunately, the freezing conditions under the first layers of snow had dried the wood to such a brittle and fibrous state that it flared up as soon as he lit the kindling. Havoc drew close to the warmth, while Charlemagne sat on a fallen branch, staring moodily into the flames and willing the darkness away.

He must have fallen asleep because he suddenly found himself sprawled on his back, staring into a morning sky that was heavy with a blanket of grey cloud. He scrambled to his feet and looked about himself, open-mouthed.

The black and shadowed forest of the night was now a woodland of breathless silence. In the grey light, not even the wind stirred the crowding trees that flowed away from his searching eyes as far as he could see, fading slowly away to distant shadow. Tiny, misty crystals of ice filled the air, drifting on invisible currents, and everything, every part and particle of the forest, seemed to be watching him.

Charlemagne shivered and moved towards Havoc, immediately aware of his boots creaking on the snow. Once he'd got himself into the saddle the lethargy of the winter woodland seemed to fall away and he drew a spear from its scabbard. He struggled to raise the weapon to the correct position, but eventually managed it and rested the butt on his boot. Feeling more in charge now, he urged the horse on. Having never been allowed to hunt, he wasn't exactly sure what signs to look for, but just knowing he'd slept out alone in the wilderness without any harm coming to him had boosted his confidence. He felt ready for anything, and was sure he'd soon find his boar and be ready to ride home.

But Charlemagne didn't find a boar at all. Instead he found a Greyling bear recently emerged from hibernation, and hungry. It was perfectly camouflaged, digging for grubs and insects beneath a fallen tree. Havoc caught its scent and whinnied a warning.

The bear spun round. Seeing them, it rose up on its hind legs, towering almost five metres into the freezing air, and let forth a deep rumbling growl. Normally it would have made off through the trees, but it was still dopey from its long hibernation, and its sleep-slowed brain reacted instead with aggression.

Charlemagne gasped, and gripped Havoc's reins tight. His

thoughts raced. Should he fight or run? How could he possibly kill such a huge animal? He'd never hunted even a rabbit, let alone one of the most dangerous creatures in the forest. He'd surely die if he charged it. But if he didn't, then everything Cerdic and Eodred said about him would be true: that he wasn't a warrior and had as much chance of fighting in the coming war as a newborn baby.

He lowered his spear, jammed his spine against the high back of the saddle, and dug his heels into Havoc's flanks. The stallion leaped forward and raced fearlessly at the bear.

The animal roared, and lumbered forward to meet them. As its huge face filled Charlemagne's entire field of vision, he closed his eyes and drove the spear into the raging creature. The shock of impact almost knocked him to the ground. Horse, bear and boy all screamed. Havoc lurched and stumbled, but righted himself and automatically wheeled about to face the enemy. Roaring in pain, the bear raised a massive paw and knocked the spear from its shoulder.

Charlemagne drew his second spear and barely had time to level it before Havoc charged the Greyling again. This time he kept his eyes open. The roaring mouth seemed to fill his entire world, until the wrenching pain of impact ground his spine into the saddle back and his shoulder felt as if it had been torn from his body. The battle-trained stallion skipped nimbly aside, dodging the slashing great paws, but Charlemagne could do nothing but cling to the saddle as if he were just a spectator in a competition between horse and bear.

Havoc turned and readied himself to charge again, as the young Prince spied his fallen spear a few metres away in the snow. Without thinking he jumped from the saddle and ran to grab it.

On foot, unarmed, and hampered by a gammy leg, he was now at the animal's mercy. Charlemagne scrambled for his spear, seized it, and jammed the butt into the frozen ground at an angle, like a pikeman defending himself from a cavalry charge.

The bear attacked. Charlemagne gritted his teeth and gripped the spear shaft as though clinging to a ledge over a sheer drop. He was about to die, but he would die a Prince of the House of Lindenshield. But at that moment the bear crashed sideways and a ferocious snarling filled the frozen air. Charlemagne stared in astonishment at the viciously writhing tangle of limbs before him. Blood spurted into the sky, and a hairy figure sprang back from the bloody mass, raised its head to the sky and howled.

Sharley at once realised that it was a young werewolf scout, no doubt sent from the city to search for him. Faint answering howls echoed through the trees, but then the werewolf staggered and fell. He was badly hurt.

Charlemagne scrambled over to him and held his dagger protectively in his blood-soaked hands as the bear lumbered round to attack again.

Then, all of a sudden, a warhorse crashed into the clearing, and without pause its rider charged the bear and drove a spear deep into its chest. Expertly, the horse wheeled about, reared and struck out with its forelegs as its rider drove in a second spear. Stallion and rider fell back, and the huge forms of the Queen's bodyguard of Ukpik werewolves burst into the clearing, Havoc galloping with them. Howling and snarling, they struck the bear as a solid phalanx. At last, the creature fell in a tumble of thrashing limbs, teeth and claws. Within seconds it lay dead in the snow.

A terrible silence fell over the forest, and Charlemagne sank to his knees beside the young werewolf. Gently, he turned him over and his eyes flickered open.

"The bear?"

"Dead," said Charlemagne. "The Queen's bodyguard have finished it off."

The rider of the warhorse dismounted and, as she removed her helmet, the young Prince realised it was his mother striding towards him. He scrambled to his feet and was nearly knocked flat as she grasped him and hugged him tight. Almost at once, she released him and stepped back to make sure he was unhurt. In another instant the deep relief in her eyes was replaced by an incandescent rage that made her flame-red hair seem to rise on her scalp and storm about her head.

"How dare you? How dare you risk the lives of Wolf-folk and human by riding off like that? I could beat you to a pulp! I could tear you apart with my own hands! If you *ever, ever* do such a thing again I will *personally* beat you in the presence of the entire household and army of the Icemark, and I will disown you as my son! Do you understand?"

Shocked speechless in the face of such rage, Charlemagne could only nod dumbly.

"I cannot tell you how blisteringly angry I am. You have risked not only your own life but the lives of those who serve you, and they should be your *first* consideration! Did you even remember to ask permission from the Holly King and the Oak King to hunt the animals in their domain?"

He shook his head, shocked to see tears in her eyes, and quickly looked away. Then, remembering his fallen ally, he knelt down beside him again.

Thirrin quickly turned her attention to the young werewolf.

"Let me see," she said, stooping over him to assess the deep wounds in the youngster's chest and shoulder.

"Find Oskan Witchfather," she instructed one of her Ukpik bodyguard. "He's somewhere along the forest road. Send messages ahead, and say the Prince is safe."

The werewolf threw back her head and howled to warn of casualties, then loped off through the trees.

"Prince Charlemagne is a mighty warrior," the young werewolf suddenly said, taking them all by surprise, as they'd thought him unconscious. "He fought well."

"Rest now," said Thirrin, taking his paw in her hand. "The Witchfather will be here soon to treat your wounds."

"No, My Lady. I'm going to the Land of Perpetual Moon where I'll stand before the glory of the Goddess for ever."

Thirrin nodded sadly, recognising that his bravery deserved honesty. "Tell us your name, so that we may properly remember and honour you."

"Your Majesty, I am Sharp Fang Sky-howler of the Nashrack tribe."

"Then, Sharp Fang Sky-howler of the Nashrack tribe, I appoint you a soldier of my Royal Bodyguard, and your name will be proclaimed throughout the land as *bravest of the brave*," Thirrin said simply.

"Ma'am. I am more than content," the young werewolf said, his voice fading to a whisper. Blood then flowed from his mouth, and he lay still.

The Ukpik werewolves lifted their heads and howled to mark the passing of one of their own, their call rising into the air and fading into distance as it flowed to the very borders of the forest and even to the walls of Frostmarris.

Charlemagne quietly wept, mortified that his quest for

acceptance as a warrior had caused the death of a friend and ally. Nothing he did ever seemed to work out as he wanted, and he finally decided to accept whatever fate sent him. He would become the family burden he'd never wanted to be, and sit uselessly by the fire with the elderly, the very young and the sick, waiting for news from the battlefields. Charlemagne Athelstan Redrought Weak-in-the-Leg Lindenshield, the first and last of his unwanted line.

CHAPTER 6

Krisafitsa-Tharina trotted out across the plain of Frostmarris with her Royal mate. They'd just finished several long hours of battle training as the horse of the cavalry and the Snow Leopard troopers practised the manoeuvres of their unique style of warfare. It hadn't taken long to get back into the stride of charging, wheeling and regrouping, but to hone it all to a deadly precision would take time. Still, the passes into the Icemark remained blocked rock-solid with ice, and by the time Bellorum and his armies could get through they would be ready for them.

But it wasn't the preparations for war that occupied the Tharina, it was the problem of Charlemagne. Thirrin and Oskan couldn't afford to be distracted for one moment from the coming crisis, yet their youngest and most loved child seemed to absorb more of their time and attention than anything else. It couldn't go on, and Thirrin was enough of a tactician and soldier to know it. A decision would have to be made soon.

"What do you think will happen?" Krisafitsa asked Tharaman.

"They'll probably send him north to the province of the Hypolitan," he answered, as though they'd been discussing it all along. Obviously he was as preoccupied as everyone else with the problem.

"Poor Sharley," she said. "He does so want to fight."

"Well, it's just not possible. How could he hope to live for more than a few seconds on the front line? And with his death we'd then lose half of Thirrin. She'd be devastated. And you can bet Bellorum will know that. The killing of Charlemagne could lose us the war. He's the one chink in the Icemark's armour. I'm afraid he will have to go."

Krisafitsa remained silent, understanding Tharaman's reasoning perfectly. "Perhaps he could be trained. He managed to ride Thirrin's warhorse, and put up a good fight against the bear by all accounts."

"He's already admitted that the horse bolted and he couldn't control him. That would be crucial in battle. And being brave is no substitute for the strength needed to use weapons," Tharaman added gently but firmly. "Sharley can't even pick up a battle-axe, let alone swing one, and when he tried to prove he was strong enough to hold a fighting line by using his brother's shield, it fell on him and Eodred had to help him to his feet."

They trotted along in silence, enjoying the crisp cooling air after the rigorous training. Then Krisafitsa said, "Perhaps he could be physically . . . built up. He already gets good food, so proper training could do wonders."

"He'd need a year at least, and even then there's no guarantee he'd improve. There's just not enough time. And even if there was, no amount of training is ever going to make his leg better."

"No," Krisafitsa agreed in a small voice. "Poor Sharley."

Charlemagne sat quietly on his bed. A housecarle had just brought a message from his parents requesting him to join them in their private chambers. He wanted to savour a few last seconds of peace before he had to face whatever it was they had decided for him. It was now three days since the incident with the bear. Sharp Fang Sky-howler had been cremated with full military honours, and Charlemagne had found himself envying the young werewolf as his body was placed on the fuel-soaked pyre, with the people of Frostmarris looking on. If only he too had died fighting the bear, then at least his end would have been honourable, and the people would have mourned him as a true Prince of the House of Lindenshield.

But Charlemagne couldn't help thinking he was about to be punished for the crime of having a gammy leg. He was sure he'd be sent as far away as possible from the fighting, and felt he was being banished from his home and family. He already considered himself an exile.

After a few more moments of staring out of his window over the frozen garden of the citadel, he sighed and climbed wearily to his feet. Outside in the corridor, he was surprised to find that the housecarle who'd brought the summons was waiting for him, making him feel like a prisoner under escort. But all his resentment had to be put aside as he struggled to keep up with the soldier, who strode along the corridors of the palace at breakneck speed. Charlemagne was determined that his escort wouldn't have to slow down to allow him to catch up. Since the incident of the bear, even tiny embarrassments had become too much for his fragile self-esteem to cope with.

They finally clattered down a wide sweep of stairs and

strode out across the Great Hall. Immediately they were surrounded by a happy pack of wolfhounds, convinced they were going hunting. The housecarle hammered on the door of the private apartments, then saluted and stamped off. A Royal chamberlain opened the door and looked Charlemagne over critically. "Are they your best clothes?" he asked.

"Well, no, but I wasn't aware that I needed to dress up."

"I suppose they'll do," the chamberlain murmured almost to himself.

Charlemagne felt his temper rising.

"I'll just give them a brush down," the man added. And with that, he disappeared into a small cupboard and re-emerged with a clothes brush, which he whisked over Charlemagne's tunic. He stepped back, scrutinised him critically and finally nodded.

"Wait here while I announce you," he instructed.

This was too much for the Prince's fragile temper. "My parents already know who I am, thank you very much! And I certainly don't need *your* permission to see them! Stand aside and let me through!"

The chamberlain looked down at the bristling youth before him as though seeing him for the first time. Normally, the Prince was quiet and unassuming, but something had finally made him assert his Royal status. The chamberlain bowed low, and stepped back.

Charlemagne angrily dragged aside the heavy curtain that kept out the draughts, and strode into the room. But at that point his leg chose to let him down and he fell sprawling across the floor.

Sitting by the blazing fire, neither of his parents rose to

help him up from the rush-strewn tiles. They knew he'd resent it.

"Drag up a stool, Sharley," Oskan said. "And please try not to look as if you've just been drinking dog pee. We only want to talk things over with you."

Charlemagne placed a stool squarely in front of his parents, then sat down and stared at the floor.

"You know why we've called you to see us, don't you, Sharley?" Thirrin said quietly.

He nodded. "You're going to send me off somewhere, well away from the coming war."

"True," Thirrin answered with brutal honesty. "But first, there are things you need to know. The werewolf scouts have managed to get information about the Empire's . . . intentions, when they invade."

Charlemagne looked up, interested despite his overwhelming despair and anger. "What intentions?"

"Bellorum intends to 'cleanse' all regions of the Icemark he captures. Basically, this means the Polypontians will kill *all* survivors, whether they are military combatants or not. It can only mean death and mayhem for the civilian population of regions that fall to him."

"But you're talking as though you expect to lose land to him!" said Charlemagne angrily. "Aren't you going to try and stop him?"

"Yes we do, and yes we will," his mother answered calmly. "You seem to have forgotten that we've fought Bellorum before, Sharley. It's a simple and undeniable fact that we can't hold the South Riding against him. Two of the first laws of warfare are know your weaknesses and be prepared to cut your losses. We can only hope to hold him at Frostmarris, and defeat him in a long trial of strength."

"Like last time."

"Like last time," Oskan agreed. "But in this war we'll have all of our allies gathered and ready, apart from the Vampires, I suppose. But they'll honour the treaty, I'm sure."

Uncertainty flickered briefly across Thirrin's features before she went on. "So, we have to be as ready as possible. The army of the South Riding and all of the town's garrisons will slow the Empire down for as long as they can, and in the meantime we'll evacuate the civilian population."

"But where will you send them?" Charlemagne asked. Then, remembering his history lessons, he answered his own question. "To the province of the Hypolitan."

"No, not this time," his mother answered, studying her youngest child for a moment, then deciding to confide in him fully. "Look, Sharley, Scipio Bellorum has been planning his revenge against the Icemark since his defeat almost twenty years ago. The Polypontian Empire almost broke apart then, after he was forced to retreat, but now his army is honed and perfected through years of warfare and he's called his sons back from their own campaigns in the south of the Empire. We'll be pushed to the very edge . . . and . . . and perhaps even over it, into oblivion."

Charlemagne almost gasped aloud, but swallowed instead and turned his head away towards the fire, feeling the heat burning his face to a bright crimson. He'd never heard his mother talk like this before. It was the talk of the defeated! Oskan coughed and took Thirrin's hand. "Your mother and I actually differ on this. I don't think the situation is hopeless . . . just desperate. I think we can withstand Bellorum and his sons again, but it'll be close."

"Have you had a premonition about it?" Charlemagne asked.

"Not exactly. In fact, no, I haven't. It's more a personal *feeling* I have."

"I see. And have you spoken to the others about this, Mum – Cressida, the twins, Medea?"

"Nobody at all. And they mustn't know, Charlemagne! If I, the Queen, despair, then how can we expect the soldiers to fight on?"

"So why are you telling me?"

"Because I want you to understand exactly *why* I'm sending you away, and also why I'm sending you abroad, to the Southern Continent."

This time Charlemagne did gasp, and leaped to his feet, but his leg gave way again and he sat down heavily. "You're sending me into exile? I won't go! If the Icemark does fall, I want to be here with you all!"

"Listen to me!" Thirrin snapped loudly. "You're not going alone. I'm sending with you as many refugees from the fighting as I can. So, if the Icemark does fall, there'll still be a free people waiting for the chance to return. There'll still be a free people speaking our language, maintaining our traditions, learning our history. And they'll still be led by the House of Lindenshield!" She fell silent, and leaning forward she took his hand. "Don't you see what I'm saying, Sharley? If the Icemark falls you'll be King."

His mind whirled in a storm of conflicting emotions. He was being sent into exile, his family could all die, and if the worst happened he was expected to continue the line of Lindenshield! How could he do any of this when he couldn't even ride a horse properly or lift a housecarle's shield?

"I can't! I won't! How can I? I'm not ready, not trained! I fall over all the time! The people think me a clown, or a misery, or both! Why would they listen to me?"

"Because you're a Prince of the House of Lindenshield!" Thirrin said firmly. "And as for being ready, who could ever be? When the worst happens we either sink or swim."

"Then I'll sink!"

"No, you won't. I'm not sending you without help; Maggie's going with you."

"Maggie?"

"Yes. He knows he can do nothing to help directly in the coming war, so he's agreed to go with you to lead our people to safety. Though of course it'll be no exile for him – he'll be going home."

"In fact, it's thanks to Maggie that we'll be able to save people. He's spent the last few months negotiating with the Doge of the Southern Continent to accept our refugees," said Oskan. "Very few independent nations would dare to risk upsetting the Polypontian Empire. But the Southern Continent has a powerful navy, and also provides the Empire with many imports that otherwise it would find difficult to get."

"So it's all arranged. All done and dusted," Charlemagne murmured.

"Yes, it is," his mother answered. "We're about to fight in one of the greatest struggles this country has ever faced. We can't afford to have any of our soldiers distracted for even a moment by worrying about their families. The Icemark will become a fortress, with no room for non-combatants. Are you prepared to accept your duty as leader of the refugees in exile?"

"Do I have a choice?"

"Yes. You can disgrace your name and be exiled in shame, or you can accept your Weird and become Prince Regent to the Exiles." Thirrin's face was fierce and stern, but she looked at her youngest son with a surge of almost unbearable longing. Soon he would be gone, and she feared she would never see him again.

"Then I accept."

CHAPTER 7

With Charlemagne's talk over, Oskan had been left alone in his chambers. His mind turned to thoughts of his dark difficult daughter and a day not long before her fourteenth birthday, when he had gone to her tower for the last time as her tutor of magic.

"A day of days, Medea," he'd said as he'd entered the room at the top of the tower. "Where shall we go? What shall we explore? What will we create in this last tutorial together?"

Her eyes had moved slowly to rest on him; she'd been almost in a trance already. "You choose, and I'll do whatever you say . . . for this one last time."

He'd crossed the room to sit on a low chair beside one of the open windows. "What about matter manipulation? Create something for me from the dust and debris of this room."

Medea had sat in silence for a few moments, before saying, "I'm only the pupil. Let me see the work of the master first, so that I can model my work on your example."

"All right," he'd agreed, beginning to concentrate and call upon his Gift. "Let's make a life from the lifeless."

Medea had watched as he'd drawn dust particles, long

hidden in the nooks and crannies of her room, and gathered them before him. They writhed and rolled, and grew in mass as he lifted more and more debris from between the floorboards.

At last, a small ball of whirling matter had played before them, and he'd reached out with his mind to gently give it form. Medea had been trying to guess what would emerge. At last, a mouse had struggled into existence. Tiny shards of grit and stone became its bones, moisture drawn from the atmosphere became the glistening jelly of its eyes, and he'd sleeked fluff and lint from clothing and upholstery into fur.

It had been perfect!

As he finished his creation, its tiny chest began to lift, and light kindled in its eyes. Then, as the mouse sat up and looked around at the world it had entered, he'd quickly conjured a chunk of cheese. "For you, Mr Twitch-whiskers," he'd said, hoping to make his daughter smile.

Medea had seemed tremendously impressed and had looked at him with admiration.

Wanting to emulate him, she'd then concentrated her Powers and drawn dust and debris from about her room. But to her creation, Medea added something extra. Oskan had felt her drawing the very electricity and ions of the air, the negative and positive charges of the weather, and the threat of storms. And a creature, which he feared was at least in part a reflection of her own psyche, had begun to form.

Oskan had watched as his daughter moulded the beautiful bright scales and they trickled and snapped into place. Jewel-like in their perfection, they'd made patterns like rainbows along the creature's back. Then a tongue of lightning had flashed forth from its mouth and its jaws had opened to reveal fangs, each one a tiny ivory sabre glistening with a perfect crystal globe of venom.

Before he had drawn breath to congratulate her, the snake had struck out and seized the mouse he had created. It had twitched and squeaked for a moment of blind terror, but then its new life had been extinguished by the venom, and the snake had swallowed its prey.

Furiously, he had struck out and broken the creature into its constituent parts, leaving only a small pile of dust, which a sudden draught blew away. "Learn to control what you create, Medea!" he'd snapped, unnerved by the violence of his daughter's magical manipulation. "Otherwise you may fall victim to your own Power!"

But as Oskan had strode angrily away he could have sworn her heard her say:

"But I did control it, Father. I controlled it perfectly."

Oskan dismissed the thought. She was still his daughter and he was sure she would come to the Light.

But he recognised that Medea's heritage had given her unusually strong powers. In her, the blood of the Witch's Son ran deep. While Oskan's mother had never told him who his father was, the hints had been clear enough for him to guess, and although his father's people were undoubtedly intelligent and powerful, they could hardly be called human. They lived in a deep world of Spirit, and every one of them had to choose between the Light and the Dark. Oskan knew he must act as a guide to Medea in her choice. He could help her if she would open herself to him and learn from his experience, but she had become so difficult to reach. After many internal battles he had chosen to become helpmate to Queen Thirrin. Indeed, most witches and warlocks with their heritage chose the path of the Light.

Thankfully she wasn't a problem yet. He had time, and he had more immediate concerns. Anyway, the choice was ultimately hers and hers alone, just as it had been for him. His daughter would choose whether to use her Gift for good or ill eventually, and then her decision might be crucial, both for herself and the Icemark.

While Oskan was contemplating his daughter's Gift, Medea sat alone brooding in her high-backed chair facing the open window of her tower. Now that Charlemagne had been appointed Prince Regent to the Exiles he was everyone's darling and had an official status that was almost equal to Cressida's. Knowing that their mother was spending even more time with him than ever, if that were possible, filled Medea's young heart with a darkly jealous rage.

In the depths of her loathing Medea let her mind reach out into the night, untouched by the howling blizzard that raged and ripped at the physical world. Slowly, her thoughts flowed over the frozen world of the Icemark, exploring the unbroken blanket of snow as it travelled south. Eventually, Medea's consciousness found the Dancing Maidens, the low mountain range that formed the Icemark's southern border with the Polypontian Empire. She probed sticky tendrils of consciousness into its chasms and clefts, gorges and canyons, until at last she found the pass that led to the armies of Scipio Bellorum.

It was blocked by deep drifts of snow and immensely thick walls of ice that stretched across its width as if defensive walls had been built against the coming of spring. Slowly, her mind expanded, seeking the deep secret of climates that would tell her when the thaw would begin. The answer was not to her liking. There were at least two months of snowfall yet to come, and that would keep the Icemark sealed and safe from the threat of the waiting war. But Medea wanted the Icemark, and her whining little brother, to suffer *now*!

With the instinct of the naturally gifted, Medea called up the pressures and depressions that would mould the atmosphere and climate into a movement of warm winds drawn from the southern seas. Within days the ice would begin to melt. She smiled, safe in the knowledge that Bellorum had no idea that he had an ally deep in the bosom of the Lindenshield clan.

In the Polypontian camp, General Scipio Bellorum sat before the fire of his sumptuously appointed campaign hut. To either side of him, his sons, Octavius and Sulla, sipped mulled wine from golden goblets.

"So, the time has arrived, gentlemen. Spring has begun its opening salvo and ours shall soon follow," the General observed in a voice as cold as the ice that rimed the glass windows.

"Yes, Sir," said Octavius. "I've already ordered the artillery train into position below the pass."

"Good," said his father with quiet enthusiasm. "I trust the ammunition reflects our new tactics."

"As a mirror, Sir," his son assured him. "Seventy-five percent of our solid shot capacity has been replaced with anti-personnel chain and grapeshot, designed to inflict a high casualty rate on advancing soldiers. After all, with our new weaponry, the need for the artillery to breach city walls has almost been negated."

"Yes indeed," the General agreed, smiling into his mulled

wine. "How surprised our little Queenling will be when her cities begin to fall to *fires from above*."

"Perhaps the shock will be enough to drive them to submission," said Sulla.

His father glanced at him. "My dear boy, I really wouldn't count on it. The barbarians and monsters we're about to encounter know only how to fight. Surrender is a considered act, taken only by intelligent beings who have assessed the odds and found them less than favourable. But Queen Thirrin and her circus of monsters have a level of sophistication much the same as trapped animals, so you can be certain they will resist unto death."

"How very pleasing," said Octavius. "One would almost be disappointed to be denied a war at this late stage."

"Oh, you need have no fear of that," said his father. "The Icemark provides an army of almost gladiatorial entertainment value. Every single one of them is loyal to their cause to the point of fanaticism, and even when captured they willingly die rather than reveal any information."

Sulla laughed. "What a glorious challenge that presents to my inventiveness. I've several instruments at my disposal that are designed specifically for extracting useful information from reluctant captives. I'm almost eager for our first prisoner to be brought in."

"I think you'll find them tougher nuts to crack than you expect," the General said lightly. "Still, the act of trying will be exhilarating in its own right." He rose to his feet and raised his goblet.

"Gentlemen, to a happy war."

His sons leaped to their feet and responded loudly, "To a happy war."

Their laughter flowed out into the night and reached into the pass through the Dancing Maidens, where it echoed round the mountains with all the insane glee of an army of psychopaths.

Maggiore Totus stroked the gigantically fat Primplepuss occupying his lap, and for the second time in as many minutes a stiflingly rancid smell wafted up and engulfed the little scholar. Holding his breath, he hurriedly waved the book he'd been reading under his nose. He stopped briefly and sniffed experimentally, but then coughed and flapped the book even more frantically. Old age could be a terrible burden, but at least he hadn't yet succumbed to the horrors of uncontrollable and pungent wind.

He hoped the smell would clear before Charlemagne arrived. With this in mind, Maggie hurried across to the window and threw open the shutters. The howling blizzard outside erupted into the room like a wild white animal, shedding snow like scales and sending Maggie's papers and ashes from the fireplace whirling into the air. The room became a sound box for the wind, which bellowed and roared until Maggie managed to drag the shutters shut.

Muttering and tutting to himself, the old man pottered about his room collecting papers and straightening cushions. At least now he could be certain that the smell had gone. Surely not even 'Essence of Primplepuss' could survive a good blasting by an Icemark blizzard.

A knock at the door was immediately followed by Charlemagne. "What's that awful smell?" he asked, wrinkling his nose.

"Smell? What smell?" said Maggie innocently. "Come in

and sit down, or better still, help me tidy up these papers."

Sharley limped about the room, gathering documents and piling them neatly on Maggie's desk. The old scholar surreptitiously watched him as he worked, and was pleased to note that the Prince seemed calmer, or at least more resigned to his circumstances than he had for months.

Once the room was restored to some sort of order, they sat down. "You've spoken to your mother and father?" Maggie asked without preamble.

"Yes," Charlemagne answered flatly, giving nothing away.

"And your thoughts on the matter?"

Sharley shrugged. "It's a carrot-and-stick situation, isn't it? I'm in the way here, a distraction to the fighters, so I have to go. On the other hand, I'm to be Prince Regent to the Exiles. But I do wonder just how real my power to rule the people will be."

Maggie nodded, pleased to hear a voice of maturity rising above the boy's disappointed tones. "Very real, I believe. I'm to be your adviser, Sharley, and I don't serve mere puppets."

"Are you sure you won't be my puppeteer?" Sharley asked sharply, his narrowed eyes scrutinising the scholar with fierce intensity.

The old man laughed. "At last! At long last, Charlemagne Athelstan Redrought Strong-in-the-Arm Lindenshield speaks his mind with the voice of a true Prince! No, My Lord Charlemagne, I will not be your puppeteer. You are truly your mother's son, and I wouldn't dare try!"

The boy nodded grudgingly, apparently satisfied, and asked cautiously, "How much do you know of my mother's . . . attitude to the coming war?"

"She expects to lose, as usual. A more pessimistic monarch

I never hope to meet, and after all these years she still believes she can hide her thoughts from me." With an effort, Maggie lifted the giant Primplepuss on to his lap, and added, "Even so, she may have a point this time."

Sharley looked startled. Maggie's doubts echoed his mother's perfectly.

"I said she *may* have a point," said Maggie, seeing his reaction. "Bellorum's not going to risk defeat and humiliation a second time. Unless he's absolutely certain he's going to win, he wouldn't invade us. But no doubt he was equally confident all those years ago, and look what happened then."

"But you think he has more chance of success this time."

"Twenty years ago, we were an unknown quantity. This time he knows what to expect. Or so he thinks," said Maggie,smiling mysteriously into his beard.

"You have something in mind, don't you?" said Sharley, a glimmer of hope growing in his chest.

"I may have. But it will rely on so many untried factors, the greatest one being yourself."

"Me?"

"Yes, Charlemagne, you. How strong are you? How diplomatic? How determined? How *brave*?"

Sharley squirmed under his tutor's piercing gaze. "I don't know. Very . . . perhaps. I don't know!"

"Good. I dislike overconfidence."

"Just what are you planning? If I'm to answer your questions I need to know." Sharley's eyes locked on to Maggie's gently smiling face.

"I hardly know myself yet. It's still the merest germ of an idea, so My Lord will have to be patient while it develops and reaches maturity. Strategies and plans are like people in that way. They need to grow."

After a brief silence, Sharley nodded. "All right, I'll wait. But I'll want to know what you have in mind before we sail for the Southern Continent."

"My Lord may have to wait a little longer than that, I'm afraid. An old brain is very thorough, but unfortunately, slow. Still, I believe my cogitations may bear interesting fruit."

"Well, at least give me a clue. Are we talking of allies, or weapons, or both?"

"Exactly what sort of weapon do you think could help us against the Empire? Don't you think we would have made our own cannons by now if they could make a difference? Don't you think we could have regiments of musketeers all primed and ready to repel invaders? Well, of course we could! But the Empire's greatest technologies are less effective than our own longbows and ballistas. You know full well we can outshoot them in terms of range and rate of fire. So what would be the point? Harness me the lightning, and we may have a weapon that's greater than Tharaman's tooth and claw. Capture me the intense heat of the sun or the deepest cold of the arctic night, and we may have a means greater than your mother's cavalry to destroy the Polypontian armies. In the meantime, we must rely on our housecarles and werewolves, and even our Vampire allies."

"Then what else can we do?"

"Hope, my dearest Charlemagne, and trust to the determination of the ordinary soldier."

Charlemagne opened his mouth to protest, but immediately snapped it shut and slapped a hand over his nose, a look of disgust on his face. Primplepuss had struck again. Scrambling to his feet, he hurried for the door and wrenched it open before glancing back at Maggie. The old man was struggling to escape from beneath the enormous cat's weight. "We can discuss this later, Maggie," he said. "Perhaps tonight, on the battlements, where our thoughts might be clearer." And he hurried off, ignoring Maggie's pleas for help to get the cat off him.

"Sharley, wait! Give me a hand! This cat's so heavy – oh, my God! No! How can you smell like that and live? Sharley, help!"

An already distant voice floated back into his room. "Sorry, can't stop. I value my nostrils."

"Prince Charlemagne, for the love of all that's decent! My God, cat, if we could harness your arse we could repel any invasion! How do you do it?"

A small questioning meow was the only reply he received as he flapped a handkerchief under his nose and tried to breathe through his mouth without retching.

For years now, the Icemark had been preparing its people for a second Polypontian invasion, and now that the time had come, the actual evacuation had gone almost as smoothly as the theory. The land by the coast had been gathering a harvest of people all through the winter months. All non-combatants and the populace not essential to the war preparations had been resettled in large camps of small draughty huts built beside the harbour, which would be first to thaw at the coming of spring. The very young, the very old and those who would look after them, the sick, the disabled, and those without the temperament for war, had been waiting through the winter months for the time when they could set sail for the Southern Continent.

At long last the spring had come, and much, much earlier than was normal – a sure portent of danger. Already the harbour was clear of pack ice, although floes still populated the waters like miniature icebergs. The fleet would soon gather, and the first refugees would set off with their animals and all their possessions to set up new homes in the lands which the Doge of the Southern Continent had so generously offered them until it was safe to return to the Icemark.

The entire Royal Court had moved to Old Haven in the southwestern corner of the Icemark, to prepare for the day when the ships would sail. Maggie would be on the first ship in his role as envoy to the Southern Continent, and with him would sail Charlemagne. As Prince Regent to the Exiles, he would be acting as monarch in the absence of his mother Queen Thirrin. The people were already beginning to call him the Little King, which pleased Maggie a great deal. A new and affectionate name given by the people might help to boost Sharley's confidence and improve his outlook. Such developments were essential to the plans taking shape in Maggie's subtle brain.

For weeks the harbour had rung with the noise of hammering and sawing as shipwrights laboured to complete their work in time for the good sailing weather. The place was bright with new sails and paint, and seething with craftsmen and labourers hurrying to get the first of the fleets ready for the journey over the grey northern seas to the warmer waters and hotter lands of the Southern Continent.

At last, the ships were ready. The entire population of Old Haven had gathered at the harbour to watch as the refugees waited for the order to board. The sky was clear and the sun shone brilliantly, while a wind blew strongly seaward, bringing with it the faint scent of early wild flowers.

A fanfare was blown, its metallic rasp echoing back from the houses to cross the harbour and over the sea as if showing the way for the fleet. Then, as the beat of a marching drum sounded, a murmur arose, and all heads turned towards the main highway that wound down from the Old Haven town citadel. A column of housecarles and werewolves could be seen marching with a measured tread. A banner was held high at the head of each regiment, showing the fighting bear of the House of Lindenshield, the full moon of the Wolf-folk, or the galloping horse and charging Snow Leopard of the Icemark cavalry. Excitement tingled through the atmosphere, and erupted into cheering as Thirrin emerged riding her magnificent charger, while Tharaman-Thar and Krisafitsa-Tharina paced beside her. A deep braying of war horns heralded the arrival of a fighting fleet of Icemark dragon galleys. They were rowing in formation across the broad expanse of the harbour, their oars beating in unison like the wings of strange aquatic birds. Brilliantly painted shields studded every ship's hull, and their dragon-carved prows reared upwards out of the water to snarl a warning at anyone who dared to threaten the seas of the Icemark. These dragon galleys were to accompany the refugee ships as their fighting escort to guard them from marauding Corsairs and Zephyrs.

The twin columns of housecarle and werewolf infantry reached the harbour and drew up in silent ranks, waiting as the cavalry clattered over the cobbles to join them. The cheering increased as Thirrin and the Snow Leopard monarchs took up a position close to the quayside.

Just then, another fanfare brayed out from the walls of the citadel, and through its gates emerged a third group, led by a tall sombre-looking man riding an old mule. The animal's ears stuck out horizontally, and the huge dip in her long back meant that the man's feet almost touched the ground as she trotted along with a sprightly step. Her long camel-like face was split wide by a mouth that sent forth a rolling thunder of brays that echoed about the port.

Riding behind Oskan Witchfather were the Royal children: Crown Princess Cressida, fully armoured and astride a massive warhorse that snorted and sidled as though spoiling for a charge; the twins Cerdic and Eodred, also in full armour and riding chargers; and finally Prince Charlemagne, dressed entirely in black like his father and riding a quiet horse that paced along nodding its head with each step. Only Medea was missing, but if the people noticed her absence, none mentioned it. A few paces behind the family came Maggiore Totus, carried in a large sedan chair by a party of werewolves, looking about him at the land and the sky of the Icemark, and wondering if he would ever again see his adopted home.

Stomping along with them, his hands behind his back and his head thrust forward in a way that suggested impatience and a bad temper, was a scruffy little figure with wild hair and dusty clothes. Archimedo Archimedes was a renowned and brilliant military engine-eer from the Southern Continent. Cressida had hired him when he first arrived in Frostmarris, and since then he had become her most favoured adviser. She knew his usefulness in the coming war would be without equal, and she had already put him in charge of rebuilding and reinforcing the capital's defences.

The Royal party arrived at the quayside, and eventually the sound of cheering died down to a low murmur, which mingled with the wind sighing through the rigging of the ships.

Thirrin looked out over the crowds, her face set in its usual stern mask. Since arriving in Old Haven two weeks earlier, she'd spent as much time as she could with her youngest son, but now that time had come to an end and she must say goodbye. A knot of fear gripped her stomach. She would sooner be armed with no more than a wooden sword and ride Jenny into battle against an entire regiment of Bellorum's cavalry, than do what she must do now. How could a fighting monarch possibly hope to function properly when she was in so much pain? Her youngest child, gentle Charlemagne, was leaving, and she was afraid she'd never see him again. Oskan had assured her that she would, but he couldn't say when. And he would only add that at the darkest time Charlemagne would be an unexpected light. Mystics were such pains! They spoke in riddles even *they* didn't understand, when all she needed was some proof that Sharley would come home and that she would see him again.

Taking a deep breath, she urged Havoc forward and he paced out into a large square that was defined by the ranks of infantry on one side, the cavalry on another, and on the remaining two sides, the sea and the crowds. Charlemagne rode out to meet her, calmly holding her gaze. Thirrin felt the familiar longing to wrap the slight, vulnerable figure in her arms and protect him from the world. So intense was the pain in the pit of her stomach, she almost bowed forward over the high pommel of her saddle, but she made a show of adjusting her shield. None but Oskan and Krisafitsa saw and understood what had happened.

Charlemagne himself felt extraordinarily calm. He had expected to be terrified when it came to leaving his home and family, instead of which he felt merely empty. An invisible barrier seemed to shield him from his own emotions. As soon as he began to feel any sadness or panic, the barrier would drop, leaving him to observe events from an odd position of unfeeling detachment. He suspected his brothers and sisters felt the same emptiness. Cressida and the twins were far too excited at the prospect of fighting in the coming war to think of anything else; in fact, the Crown Princess was even now deep in conversation with Archimedo Archimedes as they discussed some point in the defences of Frostmarris. For days now anyone who had come within earshot of the pair heard nothing but strange arcane words and phrases, like *palisade*, *enfilade* and *killing ground*. Their excited exclusion – of anyone who wasn't a fighter, preparing to fight, or building defences to protect a city from invasion – made Sharley feel even more isolated from his family of warriors than he usually did.

And then there was Medea . . . well, Medea was a mystery in her own right. She wasn't a soldier either, but all similarity between her and Sharley ended right there. He'd last seen his sister the previous evening at the farewell banquet given in his honour in the citadel of Old Haven. She'd been surrounded by her own unique atmosphere – at once removed and broodingly present. But, feeling he ought to make some effort to say goodbye, Sharley had forced himself to take Medea's hand and hold it until some sort of human presence swam to the surface. The shock of her cold flesh had distracted him at first, but eventually he'd become aware of her staring at him.

"Medea, this is it," he'd said. "I'm leaving tomorrow, so I thought we should say goodbye properly now. We won't be able to at the harbour with all the people around us."

"I won't be there anyway," she'd answered, her voice deep and expressionless.

"Oh! Well, all the more reason for us to take our leave of each other now." But Medea's black eyes had stared at him unwaveringly and she'd remained silent.

"Erm . . . well, goodbye then." Naturally he'd waited for some sort of response, but her pale face had remained impassive, for all the world like a carving made in ice. Without a word, Medea had let go of his hand, and walked slowly from the banquet leaving small pockets of silence in her wake.

Charlemagne's thoughts jolted back to the present, to the beautiful, comforting sight of his mother mounted on Havoc. Oskan joined her, riding Jenny, and father and son smiled at each other. Charlemagne urged his horse closer to his parents, and he stroked one of Jenny's long ears. Oskan smiled at him again.

"Bye, Dad," he said quietly.

Oskan nodded. "Bye, Sharley. Don't forget us."

What a stupid thing to say! Of course he wouldn't forget them. The protective barrier wavered, but then slammed firmly back into place. Shielded within his unfeeling cocoon Charlemagne reined his horse back to the opposite side of the square, and sat waiting.

Thirrin straightened in her saddle, and her voice, pitched at battle level, echoed over the watching crowds:

"People of the Icemark, behold my son, Charlemagne Athelstan Redrought Strong-in-the-Arm Lindenshield, Prince Regent to the Exiles, and my beloved child. In this time of grave crisis I send him this day to be your leader in the Southern Continent until such time as our enemies are defeated and you can return to your homes . . ." She paused, and fought to control her voice. "Know you all, that in exile Prince Charlemagne is entrusted with the full power of the Lindenshield monarchy. His word is law. His thought is your action. His anger brings death. Look upon him now and tremble!"

On the quayside, Maggie couldn't resist a small ironic smile as he watched Sharley's slender figure astride his docile horse – hardly the fire and lightning of a great northern warrior. Still, he recalled, Sharley's mother had been no bigger when she'd first led her armies against the might of the Polypontian Empire.

"I call upon all here present to witness my act," Thirrin continued. "I now bestow upon your Regent the Great Ring of State. Know you all that sovereignty lies within the body and presence of the Monarch, but also with those who wear this symbol of our country's power. For the duration of the coming war my son Charlemagne will wear the Ring of State. From this day, the Icemark effectively has two rulers! The histories shall record that King Charlemagne reigned in loving duality with his mother Queen Thirrin for the duration of the war with the Polypontian Empire. All hail King Charlemagne!"

Maggie gasped as Thirrin urged Havoc forward, removed the Ring of State from her finger and placed it on Sharley's. This was unprecedented! This was unheard of! In all recorded history, as far as he was aware, no people had ever been ruled by two monarchs, unless they were fighting each other for the right to be the one and only ruler! Oh, happy day! Oh, joyous coincidence! How much easier this would make the plans he was busily making. Standing up in his sedan chair, he gustily added his own voice to the cheering.

But the time of parting had now come, and as the cheering

died away it was replaced by a deadly silence as the first of the exiles started to walk up the gangplanks and board the waiting ships. When each vessel had been loaded with its cargo of people it drew away from the quayside and was replaced by another, until it too was loaded and withdrew to wait in the calm waters of the harbour.

At last, the largest ship of the fleet moored at the quayside. Sharley dismounted and walked to the waiting gangplank. Maggie's sedan chair had already been carried aboard and he watched as the newly-made Monarch bowed to his parents and his brothers and sister, then walked the few steps up on to the waiting ship. No emotion was displayed by any of the Royal Family; only Oskan raised his hand, and Jenny, catching the mood, suddenly let out a long and doleful bray that seemed to carry the entire weight of the crowd's feelings.

The gangplank was drawn aboard and the vessel eased away from the quayside. Out in the wide waters of the harbour the rest of the first refugee fleet waited, and as their flagship took up its position at their head, they drew in behind and headed for the open sea. Only the rhythmic splashing of the dragon galleys' oars and the wailing of seagulls broke the silence.

Sharley watched the brilliant centre of the crowd, where the polished armour and colourful banners of the Royal Family and escort stood, and felt the emotion swell within him as they dwindled to a tiny speck like a star in cloudy sky. Then at last, as the first lurching swell of the sea hit his ship beyond the protecting walls of the harbour, the barrier that had shielded him was broken, and he quietly wept, his tears adding their tiny offering of salt to the vast, endless roll of the ocean.

CHAPTER 8

Oskan rode back to the citadel in silence. Saying goodbye to Sharley and the refugees had been emotionally draining, reason enough to make him want to ride quietly, but there was something more he needed to think about. Somewhere, a powerful Weather Witch was weaving her spells, and he couldn't quite work out where. Whoever she was, she was clever enough to cover her tracks so well that he had no hope of pinning her down, but the effect she was having was obvious. The sea and land around Old Haven was already free of winter's grip, and it had taken all of his strength to break her hold over the rest of the country.

Thankfully, controlling the weather of an entire region must have proved too much for her, and he'd managed to settle the climate back into its usual patterns. Added to that, he'd also ensured that the passes were still well and truly blocked by impenetrable snow and ice. Unlike the last war, Bellorum wouldn't be able to start his invasion during the winter, quite simply because Oskan had made the weather colder and used it as a wall to keep out the Imperial Army. The winter would continue its dominion for at least another month now, keeping the passes into the Polypontian Empire well and truly frozen solid.

But he'd allowed the harbour and surrounding regions of Old Haven to have an early spring, so that Sharley and the first refugees had got away early, well before any of the Corsairs, Zephyrs and other sea-going allies of the Empire would be watching for them. But that in itself presented another puzzle. Whoever this witch was, she obviously wasn't working *with* Bellorum because the early thaw hadn't sparked off any increased activity amongst the enemy. She must be a renegade of some sort with a personal grievance against the Icemark.

He had to track her down. The fact that she was female was obvious; the *tone* of the magic was undeniable, in much the same way that a speaking voice is recognisably male or female. But exactly where and who she was, was another matter entirely. The gateway to Old Haven's citadel loomed over him as he passed through without noticing. His agile mind was devising ways and means of finding the witch, and already he was planning Magical traps and relishing the mind games ahead. But, engrossed as he was by the coming struggle, deep in the recesses of his mind he was still thinking of Sharley and his journey. One day, he'd return, *a blade of fire in his hand.* But when would that be and exactly how would it happen? He could only wait and hope that the Sight would one day reveal more.

A tangle of seagulls kept pace with the fleet, the warp and weft of their flight patterns drawing Sharley's eye deep into their flock and lulling his mind away from the pain of that morning's departure. With an effort he drew his gaze back to the horizon, but eventually he had to admit there was no longer anything to see. Turning slowly, he looked out along the length of the ship.

Before being requisitioned for its work as a refugee ship, the *Horizon* had been a fast merchantman, one of the vessels used to bring perishable cargoes at speed from foreign ports and seas back to the Icemark. It was long and slender with four masts and raised areas of decking fore and aft. Sharley watched with interest as the crew scurried about scrubbing the planking with white stones, tidying away ropes and canvases and hurrying about on mysterious errands. It was all totally fascinating and completely different from anything else he'd ever experienced before and, as he watched the ship at work, his sadness began to lift.

After a few moments he made his way across the heaving deck to the hatchway that led down to the cabins. Grabbing the rail, he started to climb down the steps, his feet sometimes suspended in mid-air as the ship rolled hugely on the swell. Reaching the bottom safely, he entered a narrow corridor that seemed to run the entire length of the ship. It was lined by doors that opened on to the cabins of the rich refugees, whom he could hear retching and heaving as the sea did its best to empty their stomachs.

Charlemagne walked slowly along the passageway, peering at each door until he stopped outside the one next to his own. He listened, then knocked softly.

"Come in," a voice called strongly, and Sharley stepped inside. The cabin was surprisingly large, with a desk, two chairs, a comfortable-looking bed and a small table. "Ah, Sharley!" said Maggiore happily. "Or should I say *Your Majesty?*"

"Sharley'll do."

"How's the Ring of State?"

"Too big."

"You'll grow to fit it, in more ways than one," said Maggie mysteriously. "Anyway, sit down, sit down. Perhaps a little wine to settle your stomach?"

"My stomach's fine, thanks."

"Yes, I do believe it is. Obviously the Lindenshield clan remember their seafaring ancestry."

"And your stomach?"

"Ah, it's bred from a nation that once owned the largest maritime empire the Southern Ocean has ever seen. My blood is seawater and my digestion could hold down a banquet in a hurricane, with the fattest bull walrus jumping up and down on my midriff."

Sharley absorbed this image with difficulty, then his mind turned to what was really bothering him. "I thought it'd be a good idea to talk to you about the Southern Continent. What's it like, exactly?" What he actually meant was: how different was it from home, would the people like him, would he be overwhelmed with the massive responsibilities that faced him, and was he right to feel so terrified?

"Don't you remember any of your geography lessons?" Maggie teased, understanding perfectly what the young Prince meant. Then, deciding to put him out of his misery, he went on, "Sharley, I'd be lying if I said there's nothing to worry about. A war's about to start, and you're going to a foreign land that lives and thinks very differently to the ways you're used to. But you have every advantage at your disposal. You're young, you have a natural gift for languages, and most importantly you have Royal status." Maggie paused as he looked at the slight, vulnerable figure of the boy before him.

Sharley nodded, desperately trying to find comfort in his old tutor's words. But his fears continued to roll like a stormy sea through his mind. There were too many horrors to put into a single sentence, so he unconsciously condensed it all down into unimportant questions that pecked at the edges of the much bigger issue. "Will I meet the Doge? And will I be expected to . . . contribute in some way?"

"You'll certainly meet the Doge, yes," Maggie answered. "But he doesn't have a Court as such; he's not like a king in any sense of the word that the Icemark would recognise. He's an elected leader, chosen from several candidates put forward by the eight aristocratic families of the capital city."

"Which is?"

"*Venezzia*, of course," Maggie continued, frowning. "An ancient settlement built on a series of islands and connected by a network of canals and waterways, if you remember from our many lessons."

"Some of it. But what are the people *like*?" Sharley asked, his tone almost desperate as he tried to find some clue about what his personal circumstances would be.

"Sharley, you'll be fine," the old scholar said, answering his true question directly. "You won't fail, nobody will laugh. This is your greatest chance to get away from the smothering pity of your family that's held you back for years. Seize it now and you'll never look back!"

Charlemagne knew he was right, but somehow he couldn't quite believe that he'd really be allowed to think and act for himself. With an effort, he sat up straight and tried to look the part of Prince Regent and Monarch in Exile. "All right, Maggie.

Tell me more about the history of the Southern Continent."

Maggie looked at him closely. The Prince's mother had grown into her throne, and perhaps Sharley too would become the leader his people needed, if only everyone would trust him. "There's nothing left of the empire the Southern Continent once had," Maggie said quietly, "but they still have a strong trading fleet and a navy to protect it. It's their skill as merchants and seafarers that has kept them safe from the Polypontians. Scipio Bellorum and his Emperor have no navy to speak of; they're purely a land power and they need the Southern Continent and its trade links. Even they can't conquer every land that has some commodity or other they need, so they have to bargain for things they want to import. The Doge and his ships supply the Empire with tons of raw material every year. And while they're useful to the Polypontians, they're safe. Safe enough, in fact, to risk offering a haven to you and the refugees."

"That's what I don't quite understand," said Sharley, warming to the subject. "Why *do* they risk upsetting Bellorum and his armies? They can't really believe they're that safe."

Maggie chuckled quietly and walked over to his bed where he retrieved a very sleepy Primplepuss and settled down with her on his chair. It had been decided that the old cat should also go into exile, where she could live out her life peacefully in the gentle warmth of the Southern Continent.

"It's quite simple really," Maggie continued. "The Doge is playing a risky game in the hope that the wild card of Queen Thirrin Freer Strong-in-the-Arm Lindenshield, Wildcat of the North, will make his gamble pay off. When she defeated Bellorum last time, the Empire almost fell apart. There were rebellions and insurrections throughout its conquered lands and it took almost twenty years for Bellorum to bring them all back under control."

The old scholar poured a generous measure of wine for himself and a smaller one for Sharley. "The Southern Continent made an enormous profit selling arms and raw materials to all sides. They even had a chance of regaining some of their old empire as the struggle went on. For the Doge, the risk of upsetting Bellorum and having to grovel to him and the Emperor for a while is well worth the opportunity to make huge profits again. And, who knows, perhaps this time the Polypontian Empire will finally fall, and the vacuum could be nicely filled by a nation with a well-organised navy and a highly developed sense of business."

"A clever politician, then," Sharley said.

"Extraordinarily so," Maggie agreed. "In fact, I'd go so far as to say that Machiavelli III is probably the Southern Continent's greatest Doge in almost three hundred years."

Sharley nodded thoughtfully, then said, "How long will it take us to reach Venezzia?"

"With a good wind and even better luck, we could be sailing up the Grand Canal in about three weeks. But you'd be safer allowing for a month," Maggie answered.

"Well, if I'm going to be imprisoned in this wooden barrel for all that time, I'd better get to know it, and how it works," said Sharley, and climbed to his feet. "I'm going on deck to talk to the officers."

His departure left a sense of emptiness in the cabin. Maggie smiled to himself. It reminded him of Thirrin and her youthful energy when she'd first come to the throne. He was now almost convinced that, given a little more grooming, Charlemagne would not only be ready to fill his role as Regent to the Exiles but would also be able to carry out Maggie's plans for him to perfection.

Over the next five days the winds and sea slowly subsided to a state of virtual breathlessness. But with the sails on the three huge masts spread to their fullest capacity, they still gathered enough wind to move the ship slowly forward, gliding over an ocean that was as calm as an inland river. Even those with the weakest stomachs were able to leave their beds and buckets to stroll about the decks, looking pale, but happier than they had in several days.

Even Sharley seemed much more relaxed as he walked around on deck, but the same couldn't be said about the sailors of the fleet. They spent most of their time watching the horizon, sniffing what little wind there was and murmuring amongst themselves.

The fleet had already travelled a good distance south and the last ice floe had been left behind over two days ago, but still the crews weren't happy. The winds were unnaturally warm for such latitudes and they carried an unusual earthy scent, as though they'd originated over land, instead of over the sea as they should have done.

Maggie tried to apply his smattering of meteorological knowledge to the conditions, but soon gave up. None of the usual rules applied. Clouds and winds seemed to be moving independently of each other, and the sun beat down on the decks as though they'd already reached the coastal waters of the Southern Continent. It was almost as though some Magical Power had been brought to bear on the weather. But the Chief Royal Adviser dismissed the idea as utter nonsense. Living with witches and warlocks must have clouded his common sense.

Then one evening as Sharley and Maggie were eating supper, the Captain knocked on the door and walked in without being asked.

"Ah, Captain Lokri!" said the old scholar breezily. "You've come, I presume, to give us some doom-laden prediction about the weather."

Sharley looked at the old sailor and thought that he could have guessed his profession even if he'd met him up a mountain in pitch darkness. Everything about him screamed *sea captain*, from his grey beard, weather-beaten face and gold hoop earrings to his great big sea boots and broad leather belt. He even smelt of the sea: a not unpleasant mix of salt, tar, and the slightest whiff of fish.

"I've come to tell Your Worships that the weather's far from doing rightly what it should, that's a correct assumption, Your Worshipful Maggiorrirey. It's brewing up a storm. And what's more, it's brewing up a *tropical* storm, or my name's not Lokri Sigurdson, and that's a fact."

"Well, undoubtedly your name is as you say, so what measures must we take against this rising storm?"

"I sees it like this, Your Worshipfulnesses: we can either draw in our sheets and batten down hatches and passengers in the hope of riding it out, or since it's a good two days off yet, we can break out the oars and try and outrun it."

"And which do you recommend, Captain Lokri?" Sharley asked, determined to be noticed.

"Well now, Your Young Worshipfulness, there's an island, sou'-sou'-east of our present position, that's beyond any hope of reaching in the normal course of events. But with a following high sea to push us, and later some prodigious winds to come, we could just about get lee side of it and ride out the winds, be they ever so fearsome."

"So, we 'break out the oars and try to outrun it'?" asked Sharley, beginning to enjoy himself despite the grim weather warnings.

"That's about the size of it, Your Young Worshipfulness."

"Then, by all means give whatever orders are fitting and let's give race to this storm, be it ever so fearsome!" said Maggie, getting into the spirit of things nicely.

The Captain nodded, saluted and very nearly bowed. He then marched from the room, bellowing orders as he went and waking Primplepuss, who showed her disapproval by emitting a terrible smell that drove all thoughts of supper out of the minds of both Maggie and Sharley.

"Not all fearsome winds have yet to reach us," said Maggie, waving a handkerchief under his nose. "I suggest we go up on deck to allow this particular hurricane to blow itself out."

Later, Sharley stood in the prow of the ship. It was a clear, moonless night with stars reflected in the smooth dark water, like silver coins from a celestial treasury densely scattered over the blackness of the sky. It was perfectly calm, and though the sails still ruffled and creaked as they harvested the wind, and the oars splashed and groaned in a precise clock-like rhythm as they drove the fleet steadily onward, it was otherwise deathly quiet. As the ships flowed purposefully on it seemed to Sharley that they were sailing through the universe. In his imagination he was navigating the cosmos, a sailor whose ports were planets and whose seas were the wide empty spaces between the galaxies.

As he stood absorbed in the beauty of the night, a slow roll of the ocean told him that the first storm surge had hit the fleet. The smooth mirror of the sea buckled, and the reflected stars shattered into a million shards of light.

He shuddered. What was he doing here, so far from home? A strange sound reached his ears. A low, barely audible rumble muttered across the sky, and a distant flash of light illuminated a massive bank of clouds that seemed to be rolling over the surface of the sea. As far away as it was, the advancing wall of clouds was obviously enormous, towering into the sky like a vaporous mountain range, and accompanied by the remote whisper of a howling wind, the far echoes of the screaming rage that he knew was coming for them.

Sharley felt a cold touch of fear as the first breath reached the ship, carrying with it a scent of rain and ozone. The sails rattled thickly as the wind filled the canvases, and orders were shouted to furl them before the wind could smash the masts. Sailors swarmed up the rigging, and soon the spars and ladders were filled with men hanging like oddly animated fruit as they hauled and heaved at the heavy sails.

Sharley dragged his eyes away from the tiny figures to look out at the other ships of the fleet. Already they were rearing and rolling on the storm surge, their lights bucking crazily as they plummeted down a watery slope or rose up to climb a towering peak. Feeling even more helpless and hopeless than usual, he fought his way over the pitching deck and fell down the steps to the cabins. Dragging himself to his feet he stumbled along the corridor until he burst through the door of Maggie's cabin.

The Royal Adviser was calmly securing his books in a large chest that was bolted to the floor. "Ah, Charlemagne! I do believe the weather's becoming lively."

"Lively? It looks like the sea's boiling out there, and the storm's not even hit us yet."

Maggie gathered up every last inch of the enormous drooping Primplepuss and poured her into a large secure basket with a lid. "I'm afraid we may lose some of the fleet. At best, it'll be scattered to the four winds. But the storm will run its course, no matter what we do. I'm afraid the vagaries of the weather are quite beyond us."

"You sound almost happy about it!" Sharley squeaked.

"No, not happy, more resigned." Maggie waved Charlemagne towards a chair that stood with another, and a small table, against one of the walls. "Sit down," he said. "I'll make you safe."

The young Prince noticed that all the furniture was bolted securely to the decking. Obviously the ship was a veteran of many storms. Maggie fussed about him, fastening a strap around his waist, then sat down on the other chair and strapped himself in.

Long years of childhood had made Sharley automatically accept his tutor's orders, but he suddenly remembered his new status as Regent to the Exiles and he unfastened the buckle. "I can't just sit here and do nothing. There's a storm coming! I'll be needed!"

"To do what, exactly?" Maggie enquired gently as he settled the strap about his own waist. "Do you actually have any experience of foul weather at sea?"

"Well, no . . . but I shouldn't just skulk below decks while the sailors battle the storm. My mother would be with them, giving encouragement and . . . well, just *being* there. And surely that's right. Surely it would be better for the . . . for the senior figure of authority to be with them giving moral support."

"And precisely how is that going to help them save the ship, pray tell?" the old scholar asked pedantically. "The crew will have enough to worry about, without being distracted by the fact that the Prince Regent's on deck and likely to get washed overboard."

"I wouldn't be washed overboard. I'll tie myself to the mast."

"From where you'll no doubt call out stirring words of encouragement to the brave jack tars valiantly doing battle with the elements."

"Yes . . . no . . . it wouldn't be like that. Look, Maggie, I want to help!" he almost wailed.

The old man relented, and smiled. "I know, Sharley. But really the best thing you can do is to keep out of the crew's way. They've got enough to cope with without worrying about you as well." He looked at the young boy's earnestly frowning face, and understood perfectly that he needed to prove himself. Wisely, he added, "And there's one vitally important thing you're forgetting."

"What's that?" Sharley asked moodily.

"You are the Prince Regent, effectively the King of the population in exile. If you die in some pointless attempt to be useful, there'll be no one to lead them. It's your duty to survive, and to fulfil your appointed task as shepherd of the people."

Sharley calmed himself, and considered Maggiore's logic. Reluctantly, he nodded. "All right. But I'm going on deck as soon as the storm passes. I don't want you trying to keep me down here just because there's dangerous debris lying about the decks."

"Agreed," said Maggie, opening a box that was secured to the table. He took out two mugs and a bottle, poured out careful measures of wine and replaced the bottle in its compartment. "We might as well be prepared. I do believe the ride's going to be rough."

Almost on cue, a huge explosion of wind hit the ship and it rolled alarmingly. Sharley hung almost horizontally over the opposite wall of the cabin, and only mind-numbing terror stopped him screaming. He turned in rising panic to Maggie as the wall then climbed above them. Despite everything, he stared in fascination as the old scholar carefully kept his mug of wine upright.

"Oh really, Sharley! Now we'll have to share!" he said in annoyance.

Sharley took several seconds to realise Maggie was referring to the fact that he'd dropped his mug. "Sorry!" he screamed in a hideously high voice as the ship began to plummet towards the seabed. It then reared upwards as though heading for the stars Sharley had been contemplating only a few minutes earlier. The young Prince couldn't believe the amazing change in the weather. Where had the storm come from? And how could it be happening at such an unseasonable time of the year?

Up on deck Captain Sigurdson was wondering the same thing, but he didn't have time to devote much energy to such questions. He was fighting to save his ship, and it was proving to be one of the hardest battles he'd fought in more than thirty years at sea. His sailors had managed to furl the canvases in time, leaving only one small topsail to cup its hand against the raging power of the storm. But he was sure he'd seen at least two sailors fall into the sea. He'd lashed himself to the wheel and fought now to keep the ship on some sort of course. But any chance of navigating by the stars was lost to the deadly black clouds that spewed out a torrent of rain and lashed the air and sea alike with strike after strike of lightning. In front of him parties of crew members fought to keep waterproof canvases over the hatchways; if even one of the hatches gave way, the ship would be lost in a matter of minutes as gallons of water would cascade down from the deck and swamp the vessel. But the wind continually ripped the lashings away and the sailors were nearing exhaustion. More than five members of the deck-crew had already been washed overboard as mountainous waves crashed down on to the planking and shook the ship like a rat in a terrier's mouth.

Suddenly a huge explosion knocked the sailors flat, as searing, crackling bolts of lightning struck the ship, fore, aft and centre. The topsail erupted into a ball of fire, and was ripped away and thrown far, far into the raging night. The rain-soaked superstructure of the ship sent out great gouts and plumes of steam as the wood was rapidly and massively heated by the strike, but the cascading seas and lashing rain saved it from fire. On the deck, the dead rolled and slithered, until the seas washed over them and dragged them down into the waters. But the survivors climbed to their feet and fought on to keep the hatchways secure.

The storm raged for more than eight hours and Sigurdson still clung to the wheel, feeling his way across the heaving seas and heading more for a sense of place than any geographical point. Then at last, as a mighty burst of lightning lit up the ravaged world, a mass of rock gleamed starkly on the horizon and the Captain shouted aloud in triumph.

* * *

Down in the cabin Maggie rode out the foulest of foul weather
in a pleasant haze of alcohol, but Charlemagne ached to go up
on deck and do something. He couldn't deny the logic of what
Maggie had said earlier, but that didn't make his inaction any
easier to bear. All he could do was literally sit tight. The old
scholar had then started to sing sea shanties from the vast
store of his memory, howling almost as loudly as the wind in
a multitude of languages. Sharley had always enjoyed a good
tune and and didn't mind Maggie's howling too much. But
nothing could distract him from the horrifying power of the
storm, and he spent most of his time waiting for the ship to
break up and sink to the bottom of the sea. But as Maggie
drunkenly pointed out, anyone who wasn't afraid in this raging tempest would have to be a raving nutter – if, that is, they
weren't as "drunk as a badger's bladder", as the odd saying
went.

Maggiore Totus, Royal Adviser and tutor to the monarch's
offspring, belched loudly and grinned in delight at the way the
sound echoed from the walls. "Another small snifter is in
order, I think," he said and took a long swig from the bottle.

All about them the cabin was in the wildest motion; anything and everything that Maggie had not secured was now
tumbling about the compact space, slowly being reduced to
useless debris by its passage around the walls, floor and even
ceiling.

Oddly, despite the horrendous noise and the terrible pitching and bucking of the ship, Sharley began to feel tired. Terror
finally seemed to have exhausted him and he slipped away into
a gentle peace while Maggie held his fingers to his lips and
shushed dramatically. "Quiet, quiet, the Prince Regent is

sleeping, let all commoners hold their damn noise!" He hic-cupped, burped and then suddenly sank into an alcoholic stu-por, his snores echoing around the walls like a discordant lullaby.

Eventually, the stark rocks on the horizon began to resolve into a fully-fledged island. Captain Sigurdson even thought he could make out lights from villages and towns on the slopes of a central mountain that rose high into the storm, defiantly absorbing rain, wind and lightning. The sea and murderous winds were steadily driving the ship on towards the island and Sigurdson was ready to seize the opportunity of shelter as soon as it presented itself. But he was nearing total exhaustion, and all he could do now was pray that the ship would reach the sheltered side of the island before he collapsed.

They drew level with the island's coast, and even in the black of the storm it was possible to see the livid white surf crashing against the shore. A high-pitched, ear-bursting crack suddenly erupted above them, and lightning struck the mizzenmast. With a boom like a cannon shot, the entire mast burst apart, and ripped open the deck. The sea poured into the holds. Under the direction of the First Officer, sailors were scrambling around, fighting to secure a sail over the gaping hole. But it was a losing battle – the ship would soon be swamped. Sigurdson assessed the situation in a split second, and hauling mightily on the wheel he turned broadside to the storm as he risked all on a dash to shore. Better to beach the ship than sink in open sea.

Immediately, the wind seized the superstructure and it heeled over at a vicious angle, but then slowly, incredibly, the ship righted herself and cascaded down towards the shore.

Sigurdson noticed a gap in the raging white of the surf. It could mean only one thing: an inlet!

"Well, be it deep, or be it shallow, that's our berth, my lads!" the Captain roared into the wind.

The shore rushed to meet them and as they entered the shallows the waves grew even higher, crashing down on the decks and heaving the ship skywards as though it was a piece of cork. Now the roar of the surf was added to the howling and screeching of the wind. Sigurdson offered a prayer to the gods and goddesses of the oceans as he tried to steer the vessel towards the dark gap where safety lay. To port and starboard, raging white water erupted and boiled about them, the ship heaved and pitched, rolled and slewed in every direction, and for the first time in his long battle with the storm, the Captain lost his grip on the wheel as it spun crazily from his hands.

The vessel's prow climbed impossibly skywards, until it was standing vertical in the water, and they must surely crash over backwards. But slowly, slowly, like a falling tree, it dropped forward, gathering speed as it went and smashed down into the raging sea.

Sigurdson grabbed the wheel again and glared ahead through the flying spray. They were now pouring and surging down a mountainous wall of sea like a rock down a glacier. They hit the trough at the bottom, the ocean boiled up beneath them and they crashed back down again . . . into an impossible calm.

They'd made it! They'd reached the inlet, a small natural harbour surrounded by high walls of rock that kept the storm at bay. Sigurdson slumped against the wheel, his eyes closed for a moment or two before he looked out over his ship to assess the damage. The mizzenmast was gone, leaving a gaping hole in the main deck, the foremast had been snapped cleanly in half, and all of the yardarms had been torn from the mainmast. The gunnels had been smashed at several points and everything was buried under a tangle of ropes and fallen ladders. Added to this, the entire ship was listing heavily to starboard and he couldn't begin to guess at how many crew members and passengers had been killed or lost at sea.

"Not too bad then, considering," he murmured, and fell asleep where he stood.

Down in Maggie's cabin, the Chief Royal Adviser eventually registered the fact that the ship was now stationary and gently rolling on a relatively calm swell. He looked about him, checking for damage and injuries. Charlemagne still slept peacefully, and apart from the debris left by the few items Maggie hadn't secured, everything seemed fine.

He undid the strap that had kept him in his chair and slowly stood up. He staggered over to the bed and opened Primplepuss's basket. The old cat uncurled, raised a sleepy face and began to wash, meowing as she did so.

Maggie laughed quietly. "I doubt you even noticed the storm, Madame Pussycat. And now of course, you want feeding."

Primplepuss meowed in agreement and confirmed it by letting off a horrible fishy stench that made Maggie clamp the lid back on her basket and hurriedly tie it shut. There were times when he was almost happy they would be leaving her, with the rest of the refugees, in Venezzia!

Medea collapsed against the back of her chair and drew a long, shuddering breath. She was exhausted. It had taken every ounce of her skill as a Weather Witch to control the storm over such a vast distance, and she still didn't know if she'd succeeded in drowning her limping, whining runt of a brother. After a few minutes' rest, she tried applying her Eye and groped far out over the ocean again. But the fleet was on the very periphery of her power and the details were unclear. The fleet was scattered, and she guessed that at least two or three of the refugee ships had foundered, but she couldn't be sure which ones. Eventually, she gave up. If nothing else, her first attempt to murder her brother had been a very useful strengthening exercise. Sharley was either dead or beyond her range and rage, for now. But if he ever returned to the Icemark he would find a powerful and malevolent sorceress waiting for him. She was surprised, and darkly delighted, at her power and the pleasure it gave her.

Outside in the cold, star-sparkled night, Oskan stood staring up at the lit window in the high tower. Recent events had distracted him from his ever-growing concern for his youngest daughter. There were unresolved issues there that he really must address, but with the mounting worries of the coming war, time was against him. His increasingly Dark-minded daughter was weaving some magical web of intrigue and he could only hope her intent was more mischievous than dangerous. Before they made their choice Gifted children needed privacy, time to find their true selves, but Oskan had the feeling that Medea's self was something to fear. And worryingly, though he tried to make connections with her, her mind was becoming impenetrable, even to him. It was now obvious to anyone with even the tiniest spark of Magical Ability that

Medea was drawn to the Dark, the most evil and dangerous of all the seven circles of the Spirit Realm. Few who entered that circle in their search for power survived. There his daughter might suffer unending torture and a horrible death at the hands of the demons who lived in its frozen wastes. But Oskan also knew that if Medea survived those terrible torments she could become a danger to her family and her country. Mysterious and unfathomable, his daughter stood on the threshold of the biggest decision of her life, but she was scarcely aware of it.

CHAPTER 9

Eodred and Cerdic were spending an evening cleaning their arms and armour. They never allowed anyone else to do this, as a badly maintained piece of equipment or armour could quite literally cost them their lives. It took them hours to clean the swords and daggers, mail coats, helmets and shields and the countless number of belts, straps and buckles that held everything together. As they scrubbed away at the buckling of their sword belts, the repetitious nature of the task actually lulled them into a pleasant sense of peace. But at the back of Eodred's mind a troubling thought kept nagging. "I never thought I'd miss the snotling so much."

Cerdic looked up, startled. "What?"

"The snotling . . . *Sharley*. I never thought I'd miss him."

"Oh. No, me neither. He was all right, Sharley, in a way."

Eodred snorted. "You're talking about him as though he's dead or as if we'll never see him again. Dad said he'll be back, one day, with something or other in his hand."

"Oh yeah. That's right," Cerdic agreed, and worked on in silence for a while. "Odd, him getting the Ring of State. That means he could order us about if he was here."

"Yeah. He wouldn't though. Sharley's all right really. I miss the daft things he says. Could always make me laugh, could Sharley, even if I'd done something really stupid like fallen off my horse or allowed my shield wall to be broken in weapons practice."

"You know, he once rounded on Captain Blood-fang when I really lost it against his regiment of White Pelts," said Cerdic admiringly. "They'd completely routed my housecarles in the big practice ring and I'd all but lost the war game for that day. Old Blood-fang was calling me all the names under the Blessed Moon, when Sharley popped up from nowhere and called him an 'eater of vegetables' and a 'drinker of diluted blood'. I'll never forget it. The look on his hairy face was a picture. Then he complimented Sharley on his perfect wolf-speak accent and pulled back to re-form his regiment. Sharley then told me to strengthen my centre and use my wings to take him in the flank. I did exactly as he said, we broke the Wolf-folk's phalanx, and it was me calling old Blood-fang names then. Until Sharley told me to shut up, that is, and pointed out that Blood-fang was still four two up on me in the victory roster. Only fair really, I suppose."

"Yeah, only fair. No point in making bad blood with officers you've got to work with," said Eodred.

"That's right. Sharley never forgot things like that."

"You're doing it again!"

"What?"

"Talking as though we'll never see him again."

"Sorry."

They continued working in silence for a few minutes, then Cerdic said, "I can't see it happening though: us meeting Sharley again. I think we've seen the last of him, Eddie."

"You don't know that for sure. You haven't got the Sight like Dad, or Medea," said Eodred, a strangely wistful note in his voice. "Sharley's tougher than he looks, you know. He'll come home one day."

Cerdic worked on quietly, his young warrior's heart aching for the brother he felt sure he'd never see again. After a while he hung his coat of mail on its stand and left his sword unburnished. "I've had enough of this. I'll finish it off tomorrow."

Eodred watched his brother walk slowly from the armoury. He'd never left any task unfinished in his entire life, so it was deeply unnerving. Eodred considered finishing off the work for his twin himself, but after a few minutes he too put aside his polish and cloth and went off in search of company. Perhaps a few laughs with the lads in the guardroom would help him sleep and prepare him for whatever lay ahead.

Tharaman-Thar and Krisafitsa-Tharina lay in a comfortable tangle before the fire. They'd just eaten an enormous dinner, and a long digestive sleep would have been the perfect conclusion to their day. But both knew they were unlikely to get it. Thirrin was pacing up and down the room, and Oskan was doing his best to sit quietly while his wife silently raged her way from chair to door and back again. Only King Grishmak was truly asleep, his feet stretched out towards the fire and adding their own special aroma to the warm, crowded room.

"Well, can't you do something about it?" Thirrin finally burst out at Oskan. "You *are* a warlock!"

For a moment her Consort thought she was referring to Grishmak's redolent feet, but he quickly realised she was talking about the weather. "Yes, but my speciality isn't climate. I'm a healer and seer, and only occasionally a caller of lightning."

Thirrin didn't need reminding of the disastrous consequences of the last time Oskan had summoned lightning. She
could still recall the terrible stench of burnt flesh, and her own
grief and panic when she thought he'd been killed. "All right,
but this has nothing to do with storms. I only want you to
slow down the thaw in the South Riding until we're ready for
Bellorum and his mad sons!"

"Well, if the truth be known, we'll never be ready enough
for that family of military madmen. And besides, the thaw's
perfectly natural. It's spring at last and the snows are melting
at their due time, even though it is a little earlier than I
expected. I can't keep the mountain passes frozen any longer,"
Oskan added reasonably.

"We're as ready as we're ever going to be, anyway," said
Tharaman-Thar, abandoning all pretence of sleep and raising
his huge head. "You're simply being over-cautious, my dear,
as usual."

"He's right, Thirrin," said Krisafitsa. "Come and sit down
and let's enjoy the peace and quiet while we can."

"I just wish Maggie was here," said Thirrin, crossing to a
chair and finally sitting down. "I don't know why I let him
go, especially when we're in the middle of a crisis."

"Because he wanted to," said Oskan mildly. "What else
were you going to do? Chain him to his desk like some sort of
slave oracle, and seek his advice whenever you needed it?"

"I suppose you're right, really," said Thirrin. "I'm just
racked by doubts and contradictions. First I want the passes
to stay frozen and blocked by snow, then I just want the invasion to begin and to get on with the war. I want Maggie here
to give advice and at the same time I'm glad he's keeping
Sharley safe in the Southern Continent," she said, falling quiet

for a moment and gazing into the fire as the thought of her youngest son filled her with a hopeless sense of longing.

"You'll be fine once you've a row of Polypontian heads to separate from their necks," said Tharaman with bloodthirsty relish.

"I suppose so," Thirrin agreed. "And if the thaw continues at this rate, I'll have the opportunity to do just that in a very short time indeed."

Suddenly Oskan sat bolt upright. "Quiet!" he hissed, and crossed to the window where he opened the shutters on the cold, clear night. A thin wavering howl sounded mournfully across the night, and Oskan nodded.

* * *

Sharley woke up. It took him a few moments to work the stiff buckle loose before he could unstrap himself and get to his feet. Stretching enormously, he finally realised they were almost static, apart from a gentle rocking motion that barely disturbed the lamps hanging in their gimbals. Maggie was nowhere to be seen.

"We've made it! We're safe," he said aloud, and laughed. There'd been times when he'd really thought they were all going to drown. But now, peering through the porthole, he saw the harbour for the first time. They'd obviously found a safe haven, and he almost wept with relief. But instead he laughed again, and when he'd calmed down he saw that the sky was blue and still and the day had that odd, slightly dusty smell that meant it was going to be hot. He also noticed that the ship was listing badly, but the lack of shouting and urgency either meant that the *Horizon* had been abandoned, or that she was in no immediate danger of sinking.

Quickly, he crossed to the door and hurried along the corridor to the stairway at the end, down which sunlight cascaded like a waterfall of light. The noise of the crew working on the stricken vessel engulfed him. Sailors were sawing up fallen spars and cutting through impossible tangles of rigging. Others worked pumps or were cutting away all of the shattered rails and gunnels that had once gleamed so brightly with gold leaf and paint.

Sharley was horrified. The once beautiful ship was a barely recognisable heap of wreckage. And what of the rest of the refugee fleet? He hurried to the stern and stood looking out over the calm waters of the natural harbour where they were anchored. Nearby were two ships that were also badly damaged, but they were of an odd design he'd never seen before. It seemed that no one else from the Icemark had reached the harbour.

"Dhows." A voice beside him made him jump. "The ships you're looking at are called dhows," Maggie explained. "They came in just after us and were lucky to make it. In fact, six others of their type were sunk."

"And what of our fleet?" Sharley asked, surprising himself with the deep concern he felt for the other ships and their passengers.

"No sign of them so far. But the Captain's hopeful that some will have reached safety."

"Only some?"

Maggie looked at him in silence for a second. "Sharley, we've just come through one of the worst storms Captain Sigurdson can remember. It's not impossible that we're the only survivors of the entire fleet."

Sharley was stunned. He'd lost his people before he'd even

properly begun his responsibilities. "But what can we do, Maggie?"

"Do? We can *do* nothing at all. Only wait and hope that any survivors find us soon."

Sharley nodded dumbly, and he hardly noticed the old scholar put his arm around his shoulders. "Not even those who carry the Ring of State can be held responsible for the elements, My Lord Prince Regent. But there is one small nugget of hope. The crew tell me that the storm *faded*, as they put it, almost as soon as we reached safety. They'd never seen anything like it, apparently. It was almost as though the storm itself gave up the moment it realised it couldn't get us. Most odd. But this means that any ships still afloat at that time may yet make it to land. Your people could still be safe, and in the meantime, it's your duty to keep your strength up for when they need you. Come on, let's go and get something to eat."

After a good meal and a long drink of fresh cool water brought from shore, Sharley felt much better. Maggie was right, of course: there was nothing they could do but wait and hope that the rest of the refugee fleet would make it to safety. After all, the other strange ships in the harbour had managed to battle through the storm and most of the Icemark ships were larger than them.

"Maggie, what did you say those strange craft were called?"

"Dhows. They're ships of the Desert People, from a land far to the south."

"Why would desert people have ships?"

"Stupid boy, even the most arid and barren of regions can have coastlines," Maggie answered sharply. "Has my teaching made no impression on you at all?"

"Well, yes. It just never occurred to me that deserts would
have water anywhere near them, let alone a sea. I mean . . ."
He trailed off into an embarrassed silence.

"You know, the House of Lindenshield makes me despair
at times. I could have had a Chair in one of the foremost and
most ancient universities of the Southern Continent, and yet I
rejected the offer in favour of teaching the Royal offspring of
the Icemark. And what have I achieved? A Crown Princess
who dreams only of warfare, two 'shield-wall Princes' who can
barely write their names, let alone a full sentence, and a
younger son who believes the seas of the world will only con-
descend to lap the shores of fertile lands!" Maggie said nothing of Medea; it had been a major relief when Thirrin and
Oskan had finally decided that their youngest daughter no
longer needed to attend lessons. The memory of her pale,
vacant face and empty black eyes staring unwaveringly at him
could still bring the little scholar out in a cold sweat.

"All right, all right! I admit it, I'm stupid. But I'm willing
to learn. Tell me about these Desert People," Sharley said,
interrupting Maggiore's thoughts and bringing him back to
the moment.

"You're far from stupid, Prince Charlemagne," said
Maggie, relieved to put aside his memories of Medea. "But
you lack both application and a retentive memory."

"Well, I promise to try and remember whatever you say
from now on. Where precisely is the land of the Desert
People, and who *exactly* are they?"

The old scholar settled back in his chair and poured himself a beaker of fresh water – the idea of anything alcoholic
made him feel queasy. "Well, where shall I begin? With their

history, I suppose. Militarily speaking it's certainly very rich. The Desert People once had a cavalry that very nearly conquered all the known world. They were feared just as Scipio Bellorum and the Polypontian Empire is feared today – indeed, the sound of their charging hooves was the death knell of many armies and kingdoms, republics and empires. All the lands of the south fell to their unstoppable cavalry."

"But if they were so famous and feared, why have I never heard of them?" Sharley interrupted.

"Well, the fault can only be your own," Maggie snapped, annoyed that the flow of his lecture had been disrupted. "Especially as you carry a name that is forever linked with their first and most devastating defeat. If you'd bothered to keep your ears and your mind open, you'd have most certainly heard of King Charlemagne of Gallia."

"I've heard of Gallia, of course, and I know I was named after one of its kings, but I never knew why."

"Did it never occur to you to ask?"

"I've always supposed that if it was important, I'd have been told."

The old scholar looked at him sharply. "History *is* important, Prince Charlemagne. It tells us who we are and why we are, and sometimes a little historical fact can have a very large effect on our actions today."

Sharley was well aware of what Maggie was thinking, but he wasn't yet ready to admit that he'd allowed his ambitions for military training to overshadow almost every other aspect of his life. So he stayed stubbornly silent and waited for the old scholar to go on.

"The Desert People moved north and invaded Gallia over five hundred years ago, under their undefeated Sultan Abd al-

Rahman II. King Charlemagne was determined to defend his land, and in emulation of his enemy trained a cavalry of light and fiery horses, unlike anything that had ever been seen in the north before, or since. Consider your mother's cavalry, and that of Scipio Bellorum – the horses are huge and heavy, and use their weight as their greatest weapon."

Sharley nodded, remembering the trouble he'd had trying to control Havoc.

"When the day of battle dawned, Charlemagne sent his infantry to attack the the Desert People – a mistake that many had made against the Sultan, believing that no horse will charge a phalanx of foot-soldiers. But the cavalry of the Desert People were not daunted by the long spears of the pikemen, and they thundered down on the Gallian soldiers, forcing them back across the wide plain until Charlemagne had them exactly where he wanted them.

"The bugle call for the charge was sounded, and the Gallian cavalry swept out of their concealed positions and hit the Desert People in both flanks. Eventually, the Standard Bearer of the Sultan was struck down, and the Desert People lost heart. For the first time in their long and glorious history the signal for retreat was given and they fell back. Eventually they were surrounded by the victorious Gallians and prepared to die. But Charlemagne drew back his forces, and dismounting, he walked alone to stand before the horses of the Sultan. He then called on his fellow monarch to come forward and talk with him, and the two men stood eye to eye, each preparing to hate the other.

"But as they looked at their enemy they each saw not a fiend, but one who in different circumstances could have been a friend. It is said they even smiled and took each other's hand, and after a time, chairs were found, and food, and the two talked into the night, until at last Sultan Abd al-Rahman II and King Charlemagne agreed that the invading Desert People should withdraw without further harm and never threaten Gallia again."

"What! You mean Charlemagne let him go! After all he'd done to his people?" Sharley asked incredulously.

"So the legend would have us believe," Maggiore answered stiffly.

Sharley shook his head in disbelief, but somewhere deep within the recesses of his mind a small note of respect and even shared emotion sounded.

Suddenly, horns brayed deep and loud, echoing across the bay and bouncing back from the surrounding rocks. Sharley rushed to the porthole. The narrow entrance to the natural harbour was in full view and he saw two ragged and broken ships limping into sight. They were being towed by Icemark war galleys, their oars dipping and rising like the legs of disciplined centipedes.

"Maggie! Ships! Ships of the fleet have reached us!" And without waiting for a reply, Sharley limped hurriedly from the cabin.

CHAPTER 10

Three horsemen rode up to the towering wall of ice that stretched across the pass into the Icemark. It was melting fast, and water cascaded about the horses' hooves as the run-off sought a route from the rocky heights and down on to the fertile plains.

The men sat gazing at the ice, as they assessed how long it would be before they could finally begin their advance into the barbaric land north of the pass. Their horses stood in a loose arrowhead formation, and at the tip sat Scipio Bellorum, with his sons, Sulla and Octavius, behind him.

Scipio was over sixty years old, but years of campaigning had kept his body and mind as strong as that of a man less than half his age. He knew that much of the determination and drive that had kept him going over the years came purely from a need to exact revenge on the Icemark and its barbarian queen, for his defeat and the loss of his sword hand almost twenty years earlier. This time there would be no mistakes. His army was well honed by years of warfare, and even the least experienced of his soldiers had more than three years' campaigning under their belts. His staff officers were all veterans of the wars that had followed his defeat in the Icemark, and they were as ruthless and as cunning as him. He also had some new weaponry and ideas, gathered from the best that his enemies had used against him over the years. He intended to enjoy himself, but he had learned not to underestimate the opposition, as he'd done in the previous war against the Icemark. And this time the barbarian queen was ready for him, with all of her abominations of nature already gathered into her alliance.

He nodded to himself. Oh yes! She was good and her army was strong. They'd already defeated the hideous Ice Trolls that he'd sent against the Snow Leopards. And he'd learned that the alliance was reciprocal; humans would fight for Snow Leopards and werewolves, just as they would fight for humans. Only the Vampires were an unknown quantity, but he wouldn't allow himself to hope that they'd ignore the call in this coming war. He would proceed as though they were an active part of the alliance; at least then there'd be no surprises.

"Another week, I'd say," he stated, nodding at the ice barrier.

"Agreed," Bellorum's sons said in unison.

"Octavius, prepare your regiments as the vanguard of the invasion . . . Sulla, you'll be in support," Scipio said quietly. "Though I don't think there'll be much resistance. Reports say the South Riding has already been evacuated."

Only one of the ten Polypontian spies had survived the winter on the mountains as they crossed into, and then back out of, the Icemark. But he'd lived long enough to tell of empty settlements and skeleton garrisons. Obviously, the barbarian queen was employing a 'scorched earth' policy against them. No doubt this would take a literal turn when they entered the land: the garrisons would set fire to the cities and towns, and so deny the invading forces any shelter or supplies.

Scipio hardly cared about any of this. It would save his army a job. Had any of the inhabitants been left behind he would have killed them anyway and burnt the cities. This time the very identity of the Icemark was going to be expunged from the face of the earth. Already the new Polypontian population was waiting behind the army, ready to move in and work the fertile land, build new cities and exploit the natural wealth of the forests and the mineral deposits of the very rocks themselves. He would rename the country *Bellora* and it would become one of the most productive provinces in the Empire. These people were of good Polypontian peasant stock, biddable, strong, and willing to drain the resources of the wild northern land for the good of the Empire.

"Gunpowder will speed things up a little," said Octavius, with a nod at the wall of ice across the pass.

"Indeed it will," Bellorum agreed, emerging from his thoughts. "Sulla, your batteries are in the locality, are they not?"

"Yes, Father."

"Have your munitions officers survey the situation and let's see if we can hurry things along. We can't have the troops getting stale."

Both sons saluted and waited while their father and General turned his horse and trotted away. After allowing a respectful gap to open up, they followed, all three with hand on hip in the characteristically arrogant riding style of the Bellorum clan.

The werewolves' relayed report of Bellorum's inspection of the pass reached Frostmarris within an hour. Oskan stood at the window of the Royal private chambers and listened to the mournful howling, while Thirrin, the Thar and the Tharina waited for a translation.

King Grishmak had woken at the first sound of howling, and laughed aloud as soon as the message ended. "Well, well! The old monster's here at last, is he?"

"Not quite, Grishmak," said Oskan. Then, realising that the others were waiting impatiently for news, he explained, "Bellorum and his sons have been inspecting the ice wall in the pass through the Dancing Maidens. It sounds as though they're going to blast their way in."

"Can he do that?" asked Krisafitsa.

"Oh yes," said Oskan. "The ice is melting anyway. All he has to do is pile enough gunpowder at the base of the wall and he'll be through."

"How did he look?" asked Thirrin eagerly. "Is he old and decrepit?"

"It seems not. The relay said he was mounted on his usual tall horse and was wearing full armour," Oskan answered.

"That tallies with what I've heard from the Wolf-folk spies," said Grishmak. "He's still in full command of his armies and will even fight when the going gets tricky. Time's had little effect on our old friend, it seems."

Thirrin sat back in her chair and took a deep steadying breath. She wasn't entirely sure how she felt about the news. In one way, Bellorum as a shambling wreck destroyed by old age would have been very satisfying. But in another, it would have robbed her of the chance to confront him in combat with honour. If he was as strong as ever, then she still had the chance to finish the job she'd started almost twenty years ago when she'd chopped off his hand. She wanted him killed, and she wanted to be the one who did the killing, in fair combat.

"It seems to me your destiny's waiting for you, my dear," said Tharaman. And all eyes turned to Oskan, who merely shrugged.

"Who knows?" he said. "The eyes of the Sight are firmly closed."

High in her tower, Medea watched events with interest. She'd heard the Wolf-folk message about Bellorum and his visit to the ice barrier in the pass, and this had helped to fill in her sketchy view of events. She'd been able to see the General and his sons, but she'd had no idea what they were saying or planning. Now she knew that he was going to blast his way into the Icemark, she finally gave up the unequal struggle against her father to bring about an early thaw. The Polypontians could do without her help.

She lay back in her chair and closed her eyes. Slowly, her mind groped its way over the citadel, briefly sliding over her parents in the Royal quarters with Tharaman, Krisafitsa and Grishmak, and then on to her brothers singing pathetically obscene songs with the housecarles and werewolf guards in their barracks. Next, she found her sister Cressida already in bed in preparation for a long day's training in the lists. She then oozed out into the night to explore the possibilities of the city.

Medea's Gift of the Sight was different from her father's. She couldn't see the future, but unlike him she *could* see much of the world about her, though there were limitations and nothing was ever as clear as physical sight. Her mind returned to that tiny island far, far to the south on the very edge of her

Eye, trying to find out if Sharley had survived the storm of her greatest effort. Though she believed her father's prophecy about her younger brother's return to the Icemark, she still hadn't been able to resist the temptation to try to kill him. One day she would surely crush Sharley. He would eventually return to the Icemark as her father had predicted, and she would destroy him then – pay him back for the love and attention he'd stolen from her. Love that should rightfully have been hers.

There were now twelve ships of the Icemark in the harbour: seven of the larger refugee transports and five war galleys. Sharley and Maggiore Totus had spent most of one morning visiting each of the surviving Icemark ships on a tour of inspection that had made Maggie almost gleeful.

Maggie was so pleased the young Prince was at last seeing beyond his own problems and showing concern for others. Sharley had even insisted that the least damaged of the war galleys should mount a search for possible survivors from the missing ships, and he'd been inconsolable when they'd returned a day later with nothing to report. And then, as the repairs had got under way, he'd asked questions about everything, and even helped where he could. But it wasn't to last, and as the ships' carpenters carried out repairs to the vessels and it became clear that it was likely to be half a month or more before they'd be ready to continue their journey, Sharley soon got bored with the sound of hammers and saws. Now Prince Face-ache was back and looking for any reason to be miserable.

Maggie, desperate to keep him occupied, made a suggestion. "Well, Charlemagne, how about making a mini State visit to one of the dhows?"

Sharley looked across the water to where the strange ships lay anchored, his face a careful mask that hid his keen interest. "That might be all right," he conceded. "When do we go?"

After an hour or so, all the preparations had been made and requests to visit had been formally lodged. Maggie and Sharley climbed into the small boat that would row them across to the dhows. "Now, remember, Charlemagne, the Desert People come from a strictly ordered and formal society. Good manners are everything, as is your status within the social order. The fact that you're a Prince Regent and I'm a Royal Adviser has given us a very high standing, even if we are from a backward and barbaric land," said Maggie, slipping into his lecture mode.

"Backward and barbaric!"

"Yes. Compared to the civilisation of the desert, the Icemark is indeed barbarous and uncultured."

"I see," said Sharley. "I'm surprised they've decided to soil their ships with our presence."

Maggie decided to ignore the sarcasm and continued. "Never mind about that. Just remember that as a nation the Desert People are deeply impressed by the military strength of the Icemark, and that may help you to look them in the eye. After all, no other country has ever defeated a full-scale Polypontian invasion led by Scipio Bellorum – apart, that is, from themselves."

Sharley leaped up in surprise, almost upsetting the small boat that was ferrying them to the dhow. "They defeated— but I thought we were the only ones ever to have done that!"

"Sit down, you'll have us over! Yes, officially, yes, the Icemark is the only country to have defeated Bellorum. But many years ago when Bellorum was still a young officer, the army of the Sultan of the time killed the Imperial Commander of the Empire along with most of his Chiefs of Staff. This left Bellorum as the most senior officer and he had to lead the retreat back to the border. He showed, even then, a superb military ability, but he wasn't in overall command. The bitter war ended in stalemate. The brilliant cavalry of the Desert People was never fully defeated, and this fact, coupled with the harsh nature of the Desert Kingdom, meant that it simply wasn't worth the Empire's effort to carry on fighting.

"Even so, the Desert Kingdom has never recovered from the war. None of the destroyed cities and settlements have ever been rebuilt. Only the capital remains, deep in the heart of their land; that and one harbour town. But they continue to fight border skirmishes because the Empire kept up its policy of repression to ensure the Desert People will never rise to glory again. Or so they hope."

The boat finally arrived at the largest and richest of the dhows, interrupting the many questions Sharley wanted to ask. But soon he was distracted with new interests as he noticed the crew of the foreign vessel watching their approach. They were all dark of complexion and had black liquid eyes that returned his gaze with frank curiosity. Many of them wore swathes of cloth on their heads, and their straight, well-defined noses supported some of the deepest frowns Sharley had ever seen.

A ladder was let down over the side, and many willing hands reached to help when they noticed that Sharley's weak leg made it difficult for him to climb up. He soon stood on deck, smiling shyly at the men who gathered about him.

"It's your hair and eyes," Maggie explained as he struggled up to stand next to him. "Many of them have never seen such colouring."

"Oh," Sharley said and immediately blushed a deep crimson. In the sunlight his red hair had taken on a fiery quality and seemed to blaze about his head, and even his eyes seemed to have developed a deeper, more lustrous green colouring.

Seeing the young Prince's confusion, the old scholar stepped forward and salaamed deeply to a finely dressed man. Sharley assumed this was the Captain, and he was about to copy the greeting, which involved touching the heart, lips and forehead, but Maggie caught his eye and shook his head.

Speaking slowly and carefully in the tongue of the Desert People, the old scholar introduced them, taking particular care to mention all of Sharley's princely titles and especially his role as Regent to the people in exile. The Captain gave a start at Charlemagne's name, but recovered quickly to salaam deeply in return and then surprise them by replying in Maggie's language. "You are most welcome to my small vessel and to whatever hospitality I can offer you. I have never before entertained one of Royal blood aboard my ships, and the honour is entirely and undoubtedly mine."

"Ah, you speak the tongue of the Southern Continent beautifully," said Maggie with enthusiasm. "May I ask where you had occasion to learn it?"

"Indeed you may. I have been sailing the trading routes of the Middle Ocean for more than forty years, man and boy. And for the last twenty-five I have been master of my own fleet of merchantmen. I've found it is always expedient to speak the language of those with whom one trades; it reduces the risk of any *misunderstandings*."

"Ah, of course, of course. Then you probably speak many tongues."

"I am fluent in five languages, and have a working acquaintance with another four. But alas, I have no knowledge of the tongue of the great-hearted nation that defeated Scipio Bellorum and his accursed army," he answered, bowing deeply to Sharley once more.

"That doesn't matter, Captain," said Sharley. "Maggiore Totus has taught me his native tongue and we can communicate easily in that."

"I see the Prince of the Icemark is a linguist. May I ask how many tongues you speak?"

"Not many, I'm afraid. Apart from my own native tongue I speak only that of the Southern Continent, a little Polypontian and the language of the Wolf-folk."

"A strange name. Who are these Wolf-folk?"

"Oh, a backward and barbarous people with a language that matches their status," Maggie interrupted hurriedly. Then, sensing Sharley's outrage, he secretly shook his head.

The Captain sensed a mystery, but quickly collected himself, and said, "But where are my manners? I've yet to introduce myself properly. I am Captain Al-Khatib of the city of Algeras, that was destroyed, alas, in my youth by the accursed Polypontian Empire. Please accept my hospitality. Let us withdraw from the sun and take refreshment in my poor quarters."

He led the way across the deck to a doorway that opened on to a large cabin. The room occupied the stern section of the dhow and the back wall was a window that reached across the entire width of the ship. Many of the panes of glass had been smashed by the storm, but it was a warm day, so the light breeze that played through the gaps was pleasant and refreshing.

But Sharley hardly noticed the view over the harbour. Instead, his eyes were dazzled by the feast of colour and texture filling his senses. Everywhere were hangings and cushions, carpets and tapestries of every shade and hue, from gold and the richest red to silver and the deepest blue. An awning of orange silk was draped over a large divan that was populated by a tumble of silken cushions.

"Please sit and take some refreshment," the Captain said, and led them to the divan. When he was certain they were comfortable, he settled himself on a large cushion facing them and clapped his hands. Immediately, a young boy scuttled into the room and salaamed deeply, then after a brief word from his master he scurried about pouring drinks into silver goblets and bowing as he offered them to the guests on a silver tray.

Sharley was surprised to find himself drinking fruit juice instead of wine, and wondered if it was because of his age. But he soon noticed that Maggie had exactly the same as himself. The old scholar raised his goblet to him and said quietly, "The People of the Desert never drink alcohol; it's forbidden by their religion."

Sharley mouthed an "oh" of surprise, and drank deeply. It was delicious. Mainly orange – which he'd once had at a Yule celebration – he thought, and possibly grape, and there was something else he didn't recognise. But above all, it was won- derfully cool and made a fantastically chilly journey down his throat to his stomach.

"Pomegranate juice," Maggie explained, guessing that Sharley was trying to figure out the ingredients. "A fruit com- mon to the Southern Continent and to the Desert Kingdom. It's a rich ruby colour and delicately flavoured."

"The Prince, I hope, enjoys his sherbet?" the Captain

enquired.

"Delicious, Captain Al-Khatib," said Sharley politely. "A very pleasant change from ship's barrel-water."

"If it would please the Prince, he may take a cask with him when he returns to his own vessel."

"It would please the Prince enormously," said Sharley, and smiled brilliantly.

The Captain was obviously pleased by such enthusiasm and decided to risk asking a question that went beyond the normal bounds of polite conversation. "Would it perhaps be presumptuous of me to ask exactly why a Prince from the lionhearted nation of the Icemark is sailing south at the head of a fleet that seems to be transporting . . . erm . . . forgive me, *refugees?*"

Maggie drew breath to reply, but Sharley spoke first.

"Hospitality such as yours demands an honest answer, Captain. The Polypontian Empire is preparing to invade the Icemark again, and my mother, Queen Thirrin, thought it best for at least some of the population to be sent away to safety. And as my brothers and sister are all able-bodied and therefore needed to help in the coming fight, I was sent to lead the people into exile."

Al-Khatib almost choked on his sherbet. Such openness was unheard of amongst the ruling elite of any country! "But surely the Prince would be needed for the defence of his homeland?"

For some reason, Sharley was neither annoyed nor embarrassed by the Captain's direct question. Quite simply, he liked the man, and almost without prior consideration he said, "My weak leg doesn't allow me to ride warhorses or train in any way. Even carrying weapons is difficult because they're too heavy for me, so I was the obvious choice to lead the people into exile."

Al-Khatib's finely tuned ear, honed by decades of dealing with slippery merchants and port officials, heard the disappointment in Sharley's voice. "But a weakness of the legs should be of no consequence to a cavalryman; I could name at least three heroes of the Desert People who— who had weaknesses, such as your own, and led famous squadrons in our wars against the Empire! There was Mekhmet the Conqueror, who—" The Captain suddenly fell silent when he realised he was calling into question the decision of a ruling monarch.

"Please go on," said Sharley eagerly. "Who were these heroes?"

The guest was all-powerful in the culture of the Desert People, and doubly so if they were of Royal blood, so Al-Khatib bowed his head and continued. "Mekhmet the Conqueror; Suleiman the Great, who was our most revered Sultan – may the One grant him blessings and peace in Paradise – and General Zamerak who crushed the first Polypontian invasion of our desert lands. All of these men were . . . infirm, but are counted amongst the greatest of our cavalrymen. For them, bodily disability imposed no limitations on their military strength."

Charlemagne's eyes shone with excitement. Could it be true? Were these men really soldiers? Hope flared up within him and he almost choked on his sherbet as he took a deep and distracted gulp. But then his natural scepticism set in. Perhaps these heroes were merely figures of legend, with no more substance or reality than a fairy tale.

"But in the real world, Captain, disabled people aren't allowed to lead armies," he said quietly.

"In the world of the Desert People, they most certainly are.

I myself watched General Zamerak riding at the head of his army as it set off to deliver the deathblow to the invading Polypontians. And he was a man whose legs were so deformed he had to be carried in a litter and helped on to his horse. But once in the saddle he became a flame of the One, a scimitar in the hand of the Messenger – may the One grant him blessings and peace in paradise."

"But how, Captain?" asked Sharley, in the heat of his excitement forgetting Maggie's description of the Desert People's cavalry. "Warhorses are huge beasts, and maces, swords, axes, shields . . . they weigh an enormous amount."

Al-Khatib paused and took a sip from his sherbet as he pondered his reply for a moment. "In my life, I have seen many lands and more warfare than most, and I know that the countries in the north use size and weight to overbear the opposition. Their horses are gigantic and the weaponry used by the warriors is massive and heavy. But we Desert People fight with speed and agility. Our horses are slender and as dextrous as dancers; they outpace the wind and have the hearts of lions! The warriors who ride them are built likewise, and use weapons of finesse and subtlety like the scimitar, a sword with the cutting edge of a striking eagle's talon, with the speed of lightning and the weight of a breath of wind."

Charlemagne fell silent as he digested all this: stories of weapons almost as light as air, and famous warriors with greater disabilities than his own, that set his mind buzzing. Could it really be true? Surely yes; everything else Al-Khatib had said had the ring of truth. As he took a drink from his goblet of sherbet, the tiniest seed of an idea planted itself in his brain. And though it would be many weeks before it began to grow, it had a fertile imagination to nourish it.

Over the next few days Sharley became a regular visitor to the dhows, sometimes in Maggie's company and sometimes alone. But always he insisted that the Captain and his crew speak to him in their own language, and his agile brain eagerly absorbed the new vocabulary and grammar. Within a matter of days he was holding simple and stilted conversations with the highly flattered crew, who screwed up their faces in concentration as the foreign Prince attempted to communicate. Within an amazingly short period of time Charlemagne could make himself understood, in both the polite forms of Al-Khatib's vocabulary and the more earthy language of the crew.

But exactly why he threw himself into learning the tongue of the Desert People – though Maggie seemed inordinately pleased by it – remained unclear to Sharley. If he bothered to stop and think about it at all, he simply told himself that he was filling his time while the ships were being repaired. But deep in the unconscious recesses of his mind, the beginnings of a plan were starting to form.

CHAPTER 11

In the confined space of the pass the ear-shattering noise of the explosion was magnified ten times over. Huge chunks of ice cascaded into the air, thrust skywards in a bursting flower of flame and smoke. Slowly, the last echoes died away, leaving only the rattle and clatter of falling debris as the air emptied itself of the flotsam that had once been the wall of ice blocking the pass into the Icemark.

Silence gradually returned, disturbed only by the slow, deliberate clip-clop of hooves. Three horses approached the site of the explosion, each one ridden by a man with one hand on his hip and wearing highly polished armour. An enormous amount of gunpowder had been packed around the foot of the ice wall, as well as into tunnels that had been dug deep into the compacted snow. But even so, there could be no guarantee that the explosion had been successful.

The horsemen drew rein at the shattered remnants of the blockage. Great boulders of ice lay tumbled and heaped before them. But the ice wall had gone, and any infantryman worth his pay could easily scramble over the small hill of debris that remained. The cavalry, however, was a different matter.

"Organise the first three regiments into a working party and have them clear a way through. I expect to be marching in less than three hours," Scipio said quietly. His tone allowed for no argument, and his sons saluted and trotted away. Bellorum continued to gaze at the mound of ice before him, then dismounted and scrambled nimbly up to the top. The bitter, acrid scent of the gunpowder filled his nostrils, and the once pristine ice and snow lay blackened and crushed all about him.

Ahead lay the route into the Icemark. He was back, and this time he would take no chances.

He'd earlier sent another half-dozen spies ahead to report on troop movements, and the four who'd survived reported that the pass, and all land in its vicinity, were empty of human life. When Bellorum quietly pointed out that not all Icemark opposition would be human, the spies had hastily amended this to 'empty of life', and he'd nodded in satisfaction. Even so, the orders of the day were to advance in full armour and in defensive formations. After all, this was the land of Thirrin Freer Strong-in-the-Arm Lindenshield, Wildcat of the North, and nothing could ever be considered certain.

He continued to scrutinise the land ahead for another ten minutes or so, but all seemed as lifeless as his spies had reported. The sound of marching then caused him to turn, and he watched as the working parties arrived. He made his way back to his horse, mounted, and rode slowly to the cliff that made up one wall of the pass, where he watched as the men began to clear the debris. His silent presence spurred them on more than any number of whips in the hands of the most vicious overseers. This was General Scipio Bellorum, a man who'd once had a regiment's entire cadre of staff officers executed because it had been broken by an enemy charge.

After two hours the last of the ice had been heaved aside, and Bellorum gave the order for the advance regiments to march up. They approached with fife and drums beating out a rapid tattoo, announcing to the world that the Polypontian Empire was about to invade another land. As they passed the General each and every soldier turned his head, saluted, and marched on along the cleared route.

At the head of the vanguard marched Quintus Severus, a young and promising officer with over ten years of battle experience. He'd joined the Imperial Army as a private when he was only sixteen, and was the youngest of a large family from the slums of Romula, the Empire's capital. He'd been decorated three times with the Laurel Crown, the highest order of merit and bravery that the Empire could bestow, and he'd steadily climbed his way up through the ranks until he'd become a Deputy Commander of a Cohort, with over three hundred men under his command.

But on the eve of this invasion, the General himself had promoted him in a special ceremony to the rank of full Commander and granted him the signal honour of leading the vanguard into the Icemark. He was now the youngest Cohort Commander in the entire Imperial Army. He personally commanded over six hundred men and he was particularly proud to note that only five levels of rank stood between him and the General's own sons.

As he led his soldiers through the narrow pass into the Icemark he felt enormous pride. But he had taken the precaution of sending scouts ahead and had ordered that all weapons be in a state of readiness. Behind him the spears of the pike-men advanced like a disciplined and mobile forest, while the acrid smoke of the musketeers' matches – lengths of smouldering cord used to ignite the gunpowder – swirled about the advancing soldiers in a blue-grey fog.

He quietly gave an order to the Regimental Centurion, and immediately the command was relayed in a gravel-voiced bellow to the Company Centurions, who repeated it all along the marching line:

"Shield-bearers! Shield-bearers prepare!"

Immediately, the silken rasp of thousands of swords being drawn by the infantry echoed along the pass.

Quintus Severus looked about him. As usual, the army looked invincible. He smiled confidently; not even the legendary Snow Leopards would be able to stop them, although his thoughts remained silent on the subject of Queen Thirrin. Her name could strike fear in the hearts of the toughest soldiers. Even Bellorum's reputation was challenged by that of the barbarian queen.

The vanguard continued its march, the scouts maintaining visual contact and waving them on. After fifteen minutes or so the pass began to widen and the true entrance into the Icemark opened up before them. The drums and fife still shrilled out their martial music and Severus gave the order for the army to fan out. Immediately, pike and shield-bearer regiments began to manoeuvre to left and right, preparing to cover both flanks as the vanguard moved out on to the rocky plain before them.

But then a sudden blood-curdling howl erupted into the air and was answered by an entire chorus. The scouts had been wrong, the enemy *was* here! A murmur ran through the ranks of the Imperial troops. All of them had heard of the monsters who fought alongside the soldiers of the Icemark, and the hideous howling proved they were not the products of legend and imagination that the Polypontians had hoped.

Severus barked an order and pikes were driven into the ground, and the shield-bearers formed a defensive wall while the musketeers levelled their weapons.

None of the soldiers had fought werewolves before, and they gazed about them waiting for the creatures to appear. But then a sudden rain of arrows smashed into their ranks, and dozens fell. Orders were shouted and the vanguard tightened into a defensive half-circle, closing off the entrance of the pass and presenting a wall of shields to the outside world. Wave after wave of arrows rained from the sky and although the Imperial soldiers continued to fall, their discipline held and they waited grimly for the enemy to show themselves.

The arrows stopped and a silence fell.

Suddenly, werewolves erupted into view, cascading down the rocky slopes in a swarm of snarling, howling fury.

The muskets fired a volley bringing down a number of the monsters, but most got up and ran on till they fell upon the ranks of the shield-bearers, forcing them back with the ferocity of their attack.

The clash and roar of the fighting masked the steady beat of the advancing Icemark housecarles. They came on at a swinging trot, their shield wall holding solid so that they hit the Empire's defensive phalanx like a rock slide, and their axes rained down on the Polypontian soldiers in a deadly hail of razor-sharp metal.

As his line began to buckle, Severus desperately ordered reinforcements forward. Soldiers rushed to take the place of their fallen comrades and the line held. Drum and fife shrilled out a fighting rhythm, but it was drowned out by the howling of the werewolves and the insistent grinding beat of the housecarles' chant:

"OUT! Out! Out! OUT! Out! Out! OUT! Out! Out!"

More arrows began to fall, hitting the rear of the Empire's positions and bringing down rank after rank of soldiers. Severus looked about him, as close to panic as he'd ever been in his entire career.

"We must pull back, Sir!" the Regimental Centurion shouted above the din. "Take the lads back to that spur of rock and they won't be able to break us even if we're all dead," he said, nodding at an outcrop of granite that almost closed the pass a hundred metres or so inside the mouth of the entrance.

Severus nodded, gave the order, and the soldiers began to fall back in good order until they held the narrow point with an impenetrable hedge of pike and musket.

The housecarles reformed, then swung forward again with locked shields and smashed against the barrier, hacking and chopping at the enemy, holding their attention while the werewolves stealthily climbed the rock walls. For more than twenty minutes the Icemark soldiers pressed the enemy position, following the orders of their Commander as she directed them on, and redressed their line again and again as her soldiers fell. At last, their Wolf-folk allies were in position high up on the cliff walls, and with bloodthirsty howls the werewolf soldiers dropped down on to the Imperial troops beneath them.

Severus beheaded one huge monster with a single sweep of his sword and swung round to hack down another that was threatening to take the regimental standard. As they fought on more werewolves leaped down from the cliffs, and the housecarles drove forward into the Polypontian frontline. When

Severus realised he was about to lose his first engagement he decided to die rather than retreat any further.

"Centurion Catullus, order the men to fall back about the standard . . ." His voice faltered as he watched a huge werewolf grab the jaw of his Centurion from behind and almost casually rip his head off. For a moment, the corpse of the soldier stood upright as blood fountained skywards from its torn arteries, then it fell. Severus screamed. He'd fought against any number of barbarian armies and never once felt anything but a vague contempt for their puny efforts. But this was different. He was being asked to fight creatures that belonged in his nightmares, and nowhere else. And not only that, but they were winning!

The werewolf lapped at the blood of the fallen Centurion, then turned its attention on the enemy officer and grinned as it licked the blood from its teeth. Severus felt fear to a degree he'd never believed possible, and in blind terror he dropped his sword and ran. For a moment, the Imperial troops fought on, but the realisation that their Commander had left them gathered pace through their ranks and like a swiftly ebbing tide the entire vanguard broke and ran. If their Commander couldn't face it, neither could they.

The housecarles burst through the buckling line of pike and musket and joined their werewolf comrades chasing the fleeing enemy. For several long, confused and bloody minutes the rout continued as the Imperial soldiers ran from the teeth and axes that were hacking them down. But as pursuer and pursued rounded a long bend in the meandering path of the pass they all slid to a halt. Before them stood a line of six cannon, and with them, arrogant hands on hips, sat the three Bellorums on three tall horses.

The defeated Polypontian soldiers immediately turned to face the enemy, thinking them marginally less terrifying than the General and his sons. But it was too late. They'd shown cowardice in the field and they'd forfeited the right to live.

The General nodded, and the six cannon fired, spewing out a salvo of grapeshot that smashed through the air, filling the narrow defile with deadly shrapnel, and indiscriminately ripping apart werewolf and human soldiers of both sides.

Rank after rank of musketeers fired into the seething bloody mass. The cannon were reloaded and fired again. The ear-smashing boom of explosions slowly died away until all finally lay still in the broken phalanx of soldiers.

Scipio Bellorum gave a silent nod, and the order for ceasefire was given. His plan had worked beautifully. He'd drawn out the enemy and trapped them nicely, and as an added bonus he'd rid his army of Quintus Severus, a man whose bravery he'd always doubted – rightly, as it happened. The Empire needed loyal soldiers who took orders and were brave within the limits the General set them. There was no room for self-serving heroes.

Scipio Bellorum smiled as the real vanguard of the invading army marched through the pass and into the Icemark.

In Frostmarris, news of the invasion had already arrived, relayed by the werewolf messengers. It was just growing dark when reports of the massacre started to come in. Thirrin waited impatiently while Oskan and King Grishmak nodded grimly to each other, as the howling from the gatehouse sounded mournfully over the city.

"What is it? What's happened?" Thirrin asked.

"The defence force in the South Riding has been wiped out," Oskan explained.

Thirrin walked quietly back to the table, where a large map of the Icemark lay spread out. She picked out a coloured marker from the map, placed it in a carved wooden box and closed the lid. The army of the South Riding no longer existed.

Cressida slammed her fist down hard on the table. Like all of them, she knew that the small defence force had had little chance against the invaders. They were simply a token gesture made against overwhelming odds. But even so, thousands of human and werewolf lives had been lost, and such grim news coming at the very beginning of the campaign was far from welcome.

"I could lead a counterattack against Bellorum and drive him back through the pass!" she said with quiet venom. She knew full well that the strategy of the conflict had been decided for months and none of it included her leading a strike force against the invaders, but the need to do something, *anything*, made her almost boil with rage and frustration.

"No. Our plans are already made. The next stage of the war will begin at the Five Boroughs," said Thirrin, turning to the map. "The towns of Allenby, Collingham, Middlehampton and Crawsby will slow Bellorum's advance. He'll have to take them before he can safely advance on Frostmarris. And they'll die an expensive death. The Empire may well find it can't afford the cost."

"In the meantime, might I suggest a little lunch?" said Tharaman-Thar, immediately breaking the tension. "We must keep up our strength for the coming struggle."

"Good idea," said Grishmak enthusiastically.

Krisafitsa purred happily at her mate. "He's right, you

know, Thirrin – now's the time to maintain our strength and determination, ready for the delivery of the counter-blow."

Thirrin sighed. "Yes, I know. It's almost time for dinner anyway. Let's go and see if they're ready for us."

Almost instinctively they fell into the ranks of precedence, with Thirrin, Tharaman and Grishmak leading the way as ruling monarchs, and Oskan, Krisafitsa and Cressida following as Consorts and Crown Princess. The door from the Royal apartments opened on a rising wave of noise and they stepped out into the Great Hall, where soldiers of all species were arriving to fill the ranks of trestle tables.

"The Vampires have always been unpredictable," Oskan was saying calmly as he walked along. "But I'm sure they'll be with us when we need them."

"I wish I had your confidence," said Grishmak. "Personally, I'd sooner bet my pelt on a broken-winded nag than take a risk on them turning up for battle."

"The oath you made them swear before the last war will still hold them," Thirrin said with more conviction than she felt.

"Possibly," Grishmak admitted. "But an embassy should be sent to the Blood Palace to remind them of their obligations."

"Agreed," said Thirrin. "Does anyone have any objections to representatives from all of the allied species being sent?"

"None whatsoever, my dear," said Tharaman. "I think Taradan would be ideal for the job as Ambassador for the Snow Leopards – don't you agree, Krisafitsa, my love?"

"Absolutely," the Tharina replied. "He has just the right level of dignity and an acute intelligence. Nobody could even begin to guess that he's just a soft old pussycat at heart."

"Quite," Tharaman agreed.

"I've a few scholarly types in mind," said Grishmak. "But don't let's make it too easy for Their Vampiric Majesties. A bit of muscle might add weight to our argument. I'll send along Grinfang Sky-howler; he's well known for a few private tussles with their Royal Face-aches over the years. I'm sure he'll give them the right message."

"Not too heavy-handed, Grishmak," said Oskan, worried that werewolf haste might spoil their overtures.

"No, no, of course not. Skyhowler can be subtlety itself, if need be."

Thirrin nodded, keeping her misgivings about Wolf-folk diplomacy to herself. "Oskan will represent the human interest in the embassy," she said.

Her Consort nodded in agreement. "I'd like to suggest one other."

"Who?"

"Medea."

The talk at the table died away.

"You want to take *Medea* on a diplomatic mission?"

"Yes."

Thirrin sat back in her chair. "But why?"

"Because she has a fine brain and I want her to learn to use it," he answered irritably as all the faces round the table showed undisguised amazement. "She *is* a Lindenshield, you know! She has a right to make a contribution to the war, even if it doesn't involve wielding a battle-axe or decapitating as many Imperial soldiers as possible."

"Well . . . yes, undoubtedly," said Thirrin after a tense silence. "But are you sure she's . . . *ready* for such a responsibility?"

Oskan knew what she really meant was: could Medea be trusted to behave in a way that wouldn't endanger the entire mission? And the simple answer to that was: no, she couldn't. He above all others knew his youngest daughter was unpredictable, cold, and at times downright odd. But he desperately hoped that by showing her trust and by displaying confidence in her abilities, he could guide her towards rejecting the temptation of the Dark.

The silence at the table was becoming uncomfortable as all eyes watched Oskan closely. "Look!" he said finally. "An embassy to Their Vampiric Majesties is ideal training for a novice diplomat. Nobody will expect subtlety. For goodness' sake, Grishmak wants to send Skyhowler, a werewolf who's been conducting what amounts to a private vendetta against the Vampires! At least Medea's not likely to physically attack our hosts. Can you guarantee the same of your delegate, Grishmak?"

"Well, no . . . I suppose not."

"There you are, then! At worst, Medea will make the Vampire King and Queen feel . . . unsettled. And I for one intend to do much more than that," Oskan went on heatedly. "We need to trust her, Thirrin. We *must* trust her."

His wife sat in thought for a few moments. Medea was her most difficult child. It was almost impossible to get to know a girl who hid herself away in a tower and who, even when she did join the family, sat in a deep and brooding silence that seemed to threaten storms. But Oskan was right, they needed to trust her.

"I agree," she said at last. "Medea will join the embassy and begin to learn an adult's role in life."

A low murmur ran around the table, but no objection was

raised openly, and she sighed, almost as though the taking of such a decision had been a relief. Here they were, at war again, and the pressures on Thirrin were manifold. If she didn't get it right everything could collapse around their ears, and it would be her fault. She mustn't allow the enormity of it all to overwhelm her. Sometimes she felt like the untried fourteen-year-old who'd first stood against the Polypontian Empire over twenty years before, but now she had more than just a kingdom to protect – her children depended on her too. Doubts, despair, and horror of that time washed over her and she gripped the arms of her huge oaken throne in a state of near panic.

But gradually, Thirrin became aware of a warm hand resting on hers, and she turned to find Oskan smiling at her. He was grateful to her for agreeing to take the risk with Medea and he felt a need to give something back. "Whatever our fate, Thirrin Lindenshield, all the world and its history will say that you were the bravest of the brave."

"Truly?"

"Truly, my Warrior Queen," he said, and kissed her hand.

Thirrin looked about her quickly, but no one seemed to have noticed anything. She and Oskan had withdrawn into their own private world, and everyone around them was literally suspended in time. Grishmak's long, questing tongue was wrapped around a huge beef shinbone, frozen in the act of licking up a tasty droplet of gravy. Nearby, a chamberlain poured wine towards a waiting goblet, the rich red stream seemingly set solid, as if carved from blood-red glass.

Thirrin looked at Oskan; released from the presence of her allies her thoughts turned to Sharley. Unlike her strange daughter, Sharley had never been a mystery to her. She missed him dreadfully. The questions she'd been carrying with her were just begging to be asked. "Oskan, can you . . . *see* Sharley? Is he safe? Is he well?" Her voice rose with desperation.

"My Sight sees only into times and possibilities, not distances, I'm afraid," her Consort sighed. "Believe me, I've tried. To the eaves of the Great Forest is as far as I can get. I'm sorry."

Thirrin smiled sadly. "That's all right. I knew you couldn't see him really, otherwise you'd have said. But I had to ask."

"Of course you did. But take comfort in this, Thirrin: if anything ever . . . happens to Sharley I'll know immediately. I might not be able to see him, but if he enters the Spirit Realm I'll be informed."

"And he's not there now?" she asked, her eyes brimming with tears as she gazed intently into his.

"No, he's not. In fact, I don't think he'll be called for many years to come." He held his hand up in warning. "Now, that's not a prophecy – call it gut feeling if you will – but our little Sharley has one of the strongest holds on life I've ever seen. When he had polio and he stopped breathing before I could get to him, he lived without drawing air into his body for longer than any other being I've ever known." He paused. "Thirrin, I truly believe the Goddess has a destiny planned for our youngest child that will see him held in higher esteem than the very greatest in all the land. Higher even than you, my love. And remember, the prophecy says he'll return with a 'blade of fire' in his hand."

She leaned across and kissed him. "Thank you," she said simply.

"Now, I think it's time we were getting back, before someone misses us. Shall we?" Oskan asked, gesturing towards the others.

"Yes, let's," she answered, and all of a sudden the noise and bustle of the Great Hall crowded in on them as they slipped back into time.

"So that's settled, then," Grishmak was saying in his usual booming tone. "The embassy sets out first thing tomorrow under Oskan's command."

"It does?" said Thirrin in confusion, then, catching a wink from Oskan she added, "Yes, it does."

Cressida, in her usual place to the left of her mother at the high table, looked out over the hall. The talk was all of the war and the loss of the South Riding's defence force, but the overall atmosphere was one of anger rather than despair. Everywhere, soldiers could be seen, heads together, going through the details that had been heard by all when the were-wolf relay had come in. Cressida nodded to herself, satisfied that the army's morale was still high. The soldiers were still filing in for their dinner and she caught sight of the twins laughing and joking with a werewolf officer. All of the uncertainty and disruption of the past few days had finally got to her and she felt a need to chat with someone nearer her age than her parents. She stood to catch her brothers' attention, and beckoned them up to the places reserved for them near their parents. For a moment, they seemed rebellious, frowning and shaking their heads. They usually ate with their comrades down in the hall, but Cressida held their eyes meaningfully and eventually they gave up and made their way to the High Table.

"Good evening, Eodred. Good evening, Cerdic," she said

with sarcastic politeness when they arrived. "So nice to have your company, for once."

They pointedly ignored her and waved to their parents down the table. "Hi, Mum. Hi, Dad," they called as they sat down chatting with each other.

"Doesn't your sister deserve a greeting of some sort too?" Cressida snapped at them.

"Not really, no," Cerdic answered.

"Especially not if you're going to spend the entire meal pointing out our faults and reminding us we're nothing but oiks," Eodred added. "There are limits to the respect and politeness even a Crown Princess can expect, particularly if she's a moody cow."

Cressida shot them both a sharp glance. This was quite a speech by her brothers' standards, and deep down she was sorry that it was a dislike for her that had prompted it. "I'm . . . surprised you should both feel that way," she said, and with an effort ignored the spluttering that erupted as both boys took a swig of small beer from their beakers. "Perhaps everyone's been a little sharper than they should have been over the last few weeks. After all, we *are* at war with the Empire again."

"No. The only one that's been 'sharp' is you," said Cerdic. "Me and Eddie have talked about it and we've decided it's just the way you are."

"Yeah. So we've decided to avoid you whenever we can from now on. Tonight's the last time we'll eat anywhere near you, and if you try to force us we'll tell Mum and Dad. They think you're a bossy cow too."

"They do not!" she exploded.

"Yes, they do, or at least Dad does," said Eodred. "You've

always been the same. Sarcastic, bossy, moody—"

"Don't forget superior, cold, and generally nasty," Cerdic added. "One of my earliest memories is of you laying into us because you thought we were making too much noise. And what were we doing? Well, I'll tell you. We were *laughing*. Yes, that's right, laughing. Two little kids enjoying themselves. Terrible crime, eh? Nobody else was bothered, just Crown Princess Cressida, and don't let anyone dare forget the title or they'll get the sort of tongue-lashing we've put up with for as long as we can remember."

"Yeah," Eodred agreed. "I just hope Mum lives for ever. The thought of you as Queen gives me nightmares. When it does happen, I'm off into exile like Sharley."

"Good idea. Perhaps we could join him in . . . where is it? . . . Venezzia. I miss the little snotling. At least he didn't spend the whole time telling us how sodding noisy, stupid, impolite, and pathetic we are."

Cressida was shocked. She'd only criticised her brothers when she thought it was necessary to correct bad behaviour. And everybody knew they were noisy and rowdy, and had to be kept under a firm hand. She was only doing her duty as she saw it. And yet her brothers had resented her good intentions to such an extent they must have been fermenting this outburst for the Goddess knew how long! There'd never been even a hint of anger on their part before. She thought they'd always just accepted her scolding as part of her duty as the Crown Princess. How wrong she was.

She looked at them now, taking in their deep frowns and blazing eyes, and wondered how they'd kept their anger so well hidden. If she really was to be Queen of the Icemark, she'd have to learn to read people more accurately from now on.

But in the meantime, there was the dignity of the Crown Princess to be maintained. She was determined that neither of them would know how hurt and confused she was by their outburst, so with enormous and cold disdain she stood and walked away, ignoring the comments that floated after her.

CHAPTER 12

The *Horizon* slid through the water, the wind filling her newly repaired sails till she seemed almost to be flying at the head of the flotilla of refugee ships. Maggiore Totus stood in the prow, his eyes watering from the wind of the ship's speed and a smile playing around his lips. It had almost been worth being caught in the terrible storm, quite simply because it had saved him months of diplomatic work.

Now both he and Sharley had a standing invitation to visit Al-Khatib whenever it was convenient, *and* as one of the richest merchants of that hot and barren land, he had strong links with the Royal Palaces.

Once they'd arrived in Venezzia and paid their courtesy visit to the Doge, Maggie could begin to set the next part of his plans in progress. He smiled to himself; even a man of his advanced years loved the intrigue of secrecy. He'd told no one in the Icemark the real reason for his joining the refugees in exile, because he didn't want to raise any false hopes, but the fact was that the Icemark was completely isolated and had made every possible alliance with the peoples and powers in the region. So the time had come to look far beyond their borders, to a land that hated the Polypontian Empire and was still militarily strong enough to make a difference in the coming war. Provided, of course, it could be persuaded to do so.

He'd had no idea if contact with the Desert People would be possible, and even if he did manage to open diplomatic talks there was no guarantee that anything could be achieved. But of one thing he was certain: with a son of the House of Lindenshield involved, uncertainty was inevitable. And the more Charlemagne grew in confidence the more Maggie realised how like his mother the Prince was. He was certain his potential was enormous. "We'll see fireworks yet!" he said to the wind. "Fireworks that – who knows? – could set empires alight!"

For another week the *Horizon* led the fleet further into the warm waters of the south. The sea steadily lost the grey-green colouring of the cold north, and slowly the deep uncompromising blue of the Middle Ocean bloomed about them. The wind was still strong, filling the white sails to straining capacity so they seemed to blaze against the blue sky, and whipping the sea into white horses that raced the ships as they crashed on towards Venezzia.

Captain Lokri Sigurdson had recovered from the storm as well as his ship had, and stood now on the deck scanning the horizon ahead for signs of land. He calculated that they'd be in the lagoon of Venezzia before nightfall and he, for one, was looking forward to the end of a journey that had almost destroyed his vessel and had robbed him of eleven crew members. He'd take advantage of the Venezzian shipyards to finish the repairs, then he and what remained of his crew would have a well-deserved rest.

He watched now as Prince Charlemagne hauled himself up the ladder. The lad may have been a Royal but the Captain had to admit he'd certainly found his sea legs, even if one of them was gammy. He walked towards him now rolling and pitching like a gimbal, faithfully keeping himself upright no matter how the ship moved on the swell.

"Landfall soon, I'm told, Captain Sigurdson," he said brightly.

"That's true, Your Young Worshipfulness," he answered. "I'd say another two hours or so, judging by the scent of the wind."

Sharley sniffed deeply, but it smelled much the same to him as it had done since they'd begun their journey well over a month ago. "Great. It'll be nice to stand on dry land again." Then, fearing such a comment might be thought offensive by a sailor, he quickly added, "Not that the journey hasn't been . . . an extraordinary experience. It's just that it'll be great to have something lying still under my feet."

The Captain smiled. Personally, he found the idea of a static surface beneath his sea-boots slightly unnatural. "Well, I don't know that Venezzia's exactly what you'd call 'dry land'. It's the only sort of city a sailor can feel really at home in. It's half land and half sea – the streets are canals and the carriages are boats, of a sort. When I finally have to tie up at the dock of old age it's the only place where I'll be happy to wait for that greatest and most final of voyages."

Sharley nodded. "Yes, Maggiore's told me about the city's unique character. I can hardly believe it. Odd . . . if you'd told me only a year ago that I'd have left home and be sailing across the Middle Ocean to a city that stands on the sea, I'd have laughed. And yet here I am." He looked out over the swell in the direction of the land. "I wonder what I'll know this time next year," he finally said.

"Look!" Sigurdson shouted, breaking into Sharley's thoughts. He pointed to the sky.

Sharley squinted into the brilliant blazing blue but saw nothing. "What am I looking for?"

"There! And there!" the Captain said, excitedly stabbing a finger at the sky. "Swallows. At this time of year they're a-nesting in Venezzia and all over the Southern Continent, so they must be a-hunting to feed their young."

"*And?*" Sharley asked, the old irritability creeping back.

"And so, Your Young Worshipfulness, they won't have flown too far from their nests. Those swallows will be sleeping in Venezzia tonight, and so will we."

For several hours Sharley stood eagerly in the prow of the *Horizon* watching for land. Then, at long last, the lookout high in the mizzenmast let out a yell and pointed ahead. Sharley could see nothing on the hazy line where sky met sea, but then a faint shadow began to coalesce, as if from nowhere, and gradually a coastline appeared.

An hour later the coastline had resolved itself from a hazy suggestion of land to a solid view of dry hillsides and dark green groves of trees that Maggie told him were olives. Then suddenly the sea wind dropped. The sails rattled thickly, emptied for a moment of their driving power, as the wind started to blow from the land, bringing with it an almost stifling heat and the scents of dust and a spicy smell that Sharley would later learn was wild thyme and olive trees.

Sharley gazed long and hard until his eyes ached, and eventually he began to see the first domes and spires of a beautiful city evolving from the faintest shading of the mists to unmistakeable silhouettes. He let out a whoop of joy, and soon all the lookouts were shouting, "Venezzia! Venezzia ho!"

Sharley watched spellbound as the deep shadows of the city slowly gave way to the colours of fine marbles, gilded domes and bronze cupolas. Every wall seemed to have decorative niches containing fine bronze statues of men, women and animals, all sculpted with breathtaking realism. And everywhere were water craft of every description: small boats scurrying between the many quaysides; larger ships unloading cargoes and ferrying passengers to the city; gilded barges that shot along purposefully, thrusting through the waters as banks of oars rose and dipped in rhythm; and scruffy-looking rowing boats holding one or two men, who cast nets over the water. There was even a black, crepe-draped funeral barque, festooned with keening mourners.

Sharley drank it all in. This city of Venezzia was beautiful, and at the same time ragged, with crumbling houses alongside fine palaces. It was fragrant with flowers and green growing things, but it also stank of mud and mould and other filth thrown into the canals by its thousands of citizens. He breathed a great lungful of the oddly fresh and fetid air and realised he wouldn't happily choose to feel any other way. This was what it was like to feel alive, and he laughed for joy.

"I'm glad you feel happy when you look on my city," said Maggiore Totus, who'd walked up unnoticed while Sharley avidly absorbed it all.

"Who wouldn't, Maggie? It's beautiful, and dirty, and noisy and . . . and . . . completely *alive!*"

"Well, yes. All of those things and more, much more. Look, there are the Arsenal shipyards, where the Republic's fleets have been built and repaired for over five hundred years," Maggie said as they passed a huge pair of stout water-gates that stood open on a complex of docks, where long, predatory war galleys were in the process of construction or refurbishment. "Of course, the fleet is less than a quarter the size it was at the height of Venezzian power. Now there's no Empire to patrol, nor new horizons to conquer. But we still have our trading routes to protect and, who knows, perhaps in the future the Republic's galleys will once again strike out at its enemies."

Sharley glanced at the old scholar. There was something in his tone that suggested his words were more than just a guide's rambling monologue to an interested tourist. "Which enemies do you have in mind?" he asked casually.

"Oh, any individual or country that threatens the interests of Venezzia," Maggie answered airily.

Sharley didn't push for any further information; he'd learned long ago that Maggiore Totus only divulged his plans and ideas if and when he was ready. But even so, Sharley was beginning to think that his exile might not be quite as hope-less or worthless as he'd feared.

But his thoughts were interrupted as the already hugely wide canal broadened out even further into a basin of blue-green water that was teeming with ships and boats of every description. Sharley was thrilled by the noise and chaos as they prepared to dock at Venezzia's most important quayside, Sancta Markus.

Dominating the entire harbour was a massive bronze statue of a lion standing on top of a dizzyingly tall column. One of his mighty paws rested on an open book, which faced out-wards as if to let viewers read the gilded words that blazed in the sun. But it was the face of the beast that held Sharley's attention; he looked just like Tharaman-Thar, proud and dignified and ferocious.

Sharley suddenly felt horribly homesick. Tharaman would be back in Frostmarris now, perhaps drilling the cavalry with his mother Thirrin; or lying in a snoring heap in front of the fire with a dozen palace cats burrowed deep into his fur, sharing his warmth; or munching away at half a cow in the Great Hall before joining in with some of the more colourful housecarle songs.

Sharley's eyes filled with tears as he thought of his mother tucking him up at night as a child and his father bickering with her about any subject you cared to name, from the cost of the palace provisions to the colour of Jenny's ear-warmers. His brothers would be there too, giggling and boisterous and as big as houses; and Cressida, haughty and proud, but under it all as kind as one of the old palace drudges, always ready to stop and listen and offer advice. He even found himself remembering Medea with less than the usual level of dislike.

Maggie noticed the change in the young prince and quietly put his arm around his shoulders. "There are times when strangeness reminds us sharply of the familiar," he said, accurately guessing what the problem was.

"I'm just being daft, Maggie. Ignore me. I'll cheer up in a minute."

But Sharley was almost doubled up with the pain of his memories. He hadn't been such a little boy when his mother had last tucked him up at night. He drew a deep breath, fighting for control, but his thoughts wouldn't allow him any peace. Would he ever see his family again? Would he ever see Frostmarris again?

Would they even survive the war?

Abruptly, he scrambled away and ran to his cabin before he disgraced himself in front of all the crew and his people. He reached his quarters, slammed the door behind him and leaned heavily against it, trying not to cry.

The sudden thunderous rattle of the anchor being dropped made him swallow a sob and hiccup. Then he giggled at himself and felt better. He crossed to the porthole and saw that they were still a few hundred metres away from the quayside. He watched a barge cast off and head towards them, its oars rising and falling into the water like the beating wings of some fabulous bird. Compared with some of the other vessels, it was remarkably plain and unspectacular, but it moved with such a purpose it caught the eye, and Sharley guessed it carried important people on important business.

He quickly scrubbed his face, put on one of his better tunics and hurried from his cabin. If this was to be an official visit, he wanted to be there. By the time he'd got back up on deck, the barge was already drawing alongside and the crew were letting down a ladder. Sharley stood beside Maggie, who'd been joined by Captain Sigurdson. Nobody said a word as two men climbed on deck, immediately spotted the small welcoming committee, and walked elegantly towards them.

Sharley was amazed. He'd expected Maggie's countrymen to dress like him in sober blacks and muted browns. But these men blazed in gold brocades and brilliant silks so they looked like fabulous creatures of fire shimmering under the warm Venezzian sun.

They bowed deeply and began to speak in a rapid tumble of words that took all of Sharley's concentration to understand. "Greetings, Signor Totus, you arrive at last. We thought perhaps your plans had been altered, or you'd perished on the seas."

Maggie bowed in return. "Indeed, we very nearly did perish. Our fleet was caught in an unseasonal storm and five of our ships were lost. It took us almost twenty days to carry out repairs, but we have finally and gladly reached our destination, as now you see."

"But if that's the case, then the second refugee fleet will be less than a week behind you, and very little has been prepared," the younger of the two men said agitatedly.

"Signor Gabraldi need have no cause for alarm," said Maggie smoothly. "As soon as we have been escorted to our new home, then we shall begin the task of preparing the camp for those who follow."

An elegantly gloved hand was raised to lips and a polite cough interrupted. "May we extend our sympathies for the loss of your ships," said the older man, at the same time turning a frosty glare on Signor Gabraldi. "I hope that those who survived have recovered well and that they will enjoy their time in the Venetti." Maggie bowed in acknowledgement, and the man went on, "The Doge extends warm greetings to the Prince Regent Charlemagne and yourself. He asks that you attend him tomorrow morning, a quarter of the hour before noon."

Sharley, determined not to be left out of the proceedings, plucked up his courage and replied, "Please return our greetings and thanks to His Eminence the Doge, and tell him we shall be honoured to visit."

"Ah, the Prince speaks Venettian," the courtier said in genuine surprise. "And, might I add, very well indeed."

Reading the protocol perfectly, Sharley inclined his head

politely and added, "As part of his duties to the Royal Household, Maggiore Totus was my tutor, and he taught me the basics of your language."

"I think that I, Veraducci Vaspadi Permino, can safely say that I have never before heard Venettian spoken so well by a foreig— *visiting* dignitary. The Doge will be enchanted, especially by your charming accent."

Another flurry of bows followed this compliment.

"One *small* detail," Signor Permino went on. "It would be deemed the greatest of favours by His Eminence if you would lower the Icemark flag while you are in our waters. You see, the Polypontian Empire has spies everywhere and we'd prefer not to advertise your presence more than is strictly necessary."

Sharley found himself to be the only one bowing after this request, and he tried to look as though he'd been wafting flies away from his shoes as he stood up with a red face.

"Of course. We understand perfectly," said Maggie. "Erm, Captain?"

"Yes, Your Eminencesseses," said Sigurdson, bending in the middle and waving vigorously at the toecaps of his sea-boots. "I'll send one of the lads up and bring it down. WALLY ERICSON!" he suddenly bellowed over the heads of the envoys. "GET YOUR ARSE UP ALOFT AND BRING DOWN THE ICEMARK COLOURS!"

Both envoys looked pained at the volume, but Signor Permino recovered quickly. "Well, how very *robust*," he said, and smiled.

After a few more minutes of polite exchange, the Venezzian courtiers left to rejoin their barge, and the fleet weighed anchor to follow them to their berth. Sharley was disappointed to see that they wouldn't be staying in the city itself, as they were heading away from the complex of canals and elegant buildings and out over the lagoon.

After half an hour's sailing they reached a fully equipped quay in an area of reed beds and scrubland. "But where will we be staying, Maggie?" he asked.

"Well, in the ships for the first few days, then eventually in those," he said, pointing to mountainous piles of ready-made timber walls that stood on the quayside. "We simply have to put them together."

CHAPTER 13

There was no sign of the thaw this far north. The snow was frozen to a crisp outer shell over loose powder, and walking was an exhausting process of high-stepping and stamping through to the solid ground somewhere deep underneath. But Oskan and Medea were untroubled, riding comfortably in a sledge pulled by a team of Ukpik werewolves. The snow was no problem to creatures like Wolf-folk or Snow Leopards either, and Taradan, Tharaman's Second-in-Command, happily scuffed along through the icy covering as though he was on a jaunty stroll to work up an appetite before dinner. To him the temperature was wonderfully comfortable, and he gazed about like a happy schoolboy on an educational trip.

Beside him walked Grinfang Sky-howler, whom King Grishmak had insisted on appointing to add 'a little muscle' to proceedings, as he'd put it.

Ahead Oskan could clearly see the pass through the Wolfrock Mountains that bordered The-Land-of-the-Ghosts. The Ukpik werewolves raised their heads and howled when they saw it, and increased their pace so that the sledge bounced and rocked over the stony track and Oskan was forced to hold on grimly as they careered towards the border. He was determined not to fall out because the Vampire King and Queen would have spies watching their approach. They'd love to hear how the Witchfather had been spilled out of his own sledge like so much dirty washing.

Next to him, Medea sat in silence. She'd hardly spoken a word since the beginning of the journey, but as far as her father could tell she seemed perfectly relaxed and unconcerned. But the same couldn't have been said when Oskan had suggested she join him on the diplomatic mission to The-Land-of-the-Ghosts. He had climbed the spiral stairs of her tower with determination, and when he'd arrived in the topmost room, she had been waiting for him, her high-backed chair facing the doorway and her black eyes glaring as he stepped over the threshold into her domain.

"Ah, Medea. May I come in?"

"You're in already," she'd answered expressionlessly.

"So I am. Well, I suppose you're wondering why I'm here." She'd stared at him in silence until eventually he'd continued. "Your mother and I . . . well, your mother and I have decided that you're now old enough to take a more active part in the workings of the kingdom."

"Do you expect me to train as a warrior?"

"No, not at all. Your skills obviously lie elsewhere, so we've decided you should help me with a diplomatic mission to the Court of Their Vampiric Majesties."

"I see. And how will I help, exactly?" she'd asked, holding his eye with her own unnerving black gaze.

"Probably in no way whatsoever. But you might find it instructive to observe a diplomatic mission at work."

"Why?"

Oskan had been irritated by her studied, quiet insolence. "Because if you're not suited to raise a sword for the Icemark, and you're unwilling to learn the art and craft of healing, then politics and diplomacy remain your only options."

"What if I dislike all of those options?"

"Medea, if you were a private citizen you would have every right to pursue whatever career you wanted, but as a member of the Royal House of Lindenshield, you have no such choice," he'd said coldly. "Unless, that is, you want to relinquish your titles, your wealth, *and* your apartments within the citadel."

This had clearly enraged his daughter, but she'd restrained herself. "I'll need time to consider."

"*Medea!* When your country's at war, luxuries like time are strictly rationed. Make your decision now, or have it made for you!" His voice had cracked like a whip on the air. Patience and gentle persuasion had long since become victims of the crisis faced by the Icemark, and Oskan had no time to indulge a sulky adolescent who wanted to dabble with the temptations of the Dark. She had to be reined in and controlled before people got hurt, including herself.

Medea's eyes narrowed thoughtfully and their black depths seemed to sharpen. Finally she'd nodded. "Very well. I'll join your embassy to the Vampires."

"Good. Be ready to leave at dawn the day after tomorrow."

All of that had happened almost a week ago, and since then Medea had been polite, distant and mainly silent. But Oskan wasn't too worried. He'd sooner have her with him than leave her behind to simmer at home. Thirrin had enough on her mind without having to cope with Medea.

Just then, the sledge bumped over a rock, jolting Oskan back to the present and making him grab the rails in panic. The Ukpiks were strong and tireless, but they really needed to take more care.

Taradan and Grinfang surged ahead, having no sledge to hold them back, but their pace gradually slowed as they drew closer to the shadow-haunted mouth of the pass, and then stopped. The sledge finally caught up with them and drew to a halt while Oskan peeled his fingers, one by one, from the rail that edged his seat.

"It doesn't get any more cheerful over the years, does it?" said Grinfang, staring into the pass where ragged shreds of mist gathered and flowed, often against the icy wind that blew along the narrow cliff-lined track. "I wonder if there'll be a welcoming committee to meet us?"

Taradan laughed hugely, his voice echoing from the stony walls. "That's about as likely as an Ice Troll with table manners. When we passed through Their Vampiric Majesties' realm on the way south, we were attacked by a party of Zombies – never too bright, those things. And when we complained at the Blood Palace we were told they were renegades beyond the control of the King and Queen. Still, we got some small revenge when we left a pile of dismembered bodies in the audience chamber. They were still animated, of course, and flopped about like stranded fish leaving bloody smears everywhere."

"We'd better keep moving, then," said Oskan grumpily. "We don't want to get caught up in unnecessary skirmishes."

Grinfang led the way, howling out a statement in the language of the Wolf-folk as he went so that no one could be left in any doubt that they were an embassy from three of the five monarchs in the alliance against the Polypontian Empire.

But the response was rather less than welcoming: a huge roaring and snarling echoed along the pass from just ahead. At first, Oskan thought he was hearing a rockslide, but then five huge figures rolled like boulders down the almost sheer cliffs that lined the pass, climbed ponderously to their feet and blocked the way. The Ukpik werewolves stopped the sledge and stepped out of the traces, howling fiercely as they joined Taradan and Grinfang, who were already squaring up to the massive rock trolls.

There was a long standoff as the werewolves howled at the trolls, and the trolls replied with voices like erupting volcanoes.

"What's going on?" Oskan called from his sledge.

"We're trying to persuade them to let us through," said Grinfang. "But they don't know what an embassy is, and they're too stupid to see they're outnumbered."

Oskan wasn't entirely sure they were outnumbered. Even with seven werewolves, a giant Snow Leopard and two Gifted human beings facing them.

Medea watched the standoff with interest. She'd never been in physical danger before, and she was uncertain how to react. The sensation of adrenalin quickening her heartbeat and sharpening her sight was a completely new experience, and wasn't entirely unpleasant. Perhaps the non-magical world had some merit.

Oskan was just wondering what he should do to make the situation less fraught, when Grinfang's patience ran out, and with a vicious snarl he attacked. Taradan watched for a second, then he charged too, hitting the nearest troll at a run. The beast staggered back, but then threw off the Snow

Leopard. Taradan gathered himself and sprang back into the attack.

Now the Ukpik werewolves moved in as a solid phalanx. All was chaos and confusion as a seething mass of fur and hide rolled and wrestled before Oskan's eyes. Taradan's towering frame rose into the air, and with a mighty roar he smashed his paws down on the head of the troll he was fighting. With a loud *crack*, its skull split in two and it fell dead, crashing to the ground like a rockslide. Grinfang leaped on to his opponent and, clamping his teeth about its neck, ripped its throat out. Snarling savagely, he straddled the troll's body and howled in elation while the Ukpik phalanx, working with deadly efficiency, tore two more of the trolls limb from limb, and then gave chase to the only survivor.

Oskan struggled to his feet and, standing on the seat of his sledge, he bellowed, "Stop!" His voice seemed to be magnified by the narrow rock-lined pass. The werewolves and Taradan froze. "There will be blood enough for the most ferocious warrior in the coming war. Let the creature live."

Grinfang snarled contemptuously, and ran after the troll that was slowly dragging itself up the cliff face.

"You will STOP, Grinfang Sky-howler!" Oskan bellowed.

The werewolf turned to face Oskan, his snarling lips drawn back over massive teeth, but his mouth snapped shut as he looked at the Witchfather. The strange rags of mist that haunted the pass had gathered about him and now writhed and billowed as though moved by invisible currents, and the very air itself roiled and trembled as if a heat haze had managed to find its way north through the deadly cold of the Icemark winter.

"You will kill no more unless I sanction it! Do you understand, Skyhowler?" Oskan's voice had become unnaturally deep, and his eyes had rolled back into his head so that the blind whites held the werewolf in their deadly gaze. "Do you UNDERSTAND?"

Medea was fascinated. Her father rarely chose to display his Power in public, and she gazed in wonder and with new-found respect as she sensed the strength of his Gift beating from him in palpable waves.

The werewolf, driven to his knees by some unseen force, nodded. "Yes, Witchfather," he said through gritted teeth.

"Then there's no need for any more unpleasantness, is there?" said Oskan, his voice returning to normal and his eyes rolling back into their natural position. "Shall we get on?"

The Ukpik werewolves scrambled hurriedly back to the sledge and waited while Taradan and Grinfang moved the rock trolls' corpses aside.

"I do hope Their Vampiric Majesties were not responsible for that little display of aggression," Oskan said lightly. "Otherwise there might have to be some more un-pleasantness."

Taradan looked at the slight figure of the man in the sledge, and shuddered. Not for the first time he found himself grateful that the warlock was on their side in the war. The Snow Leopard shifted his gaze to Medea, who was watching her father as though she was seeing him for the first time. He hoped he was wrong, but he couldn't quite convince himself that she would use her Power so wisely.

An hour or so later, the envoys entered The-Land-of-the-Ghosts and were descending the steep route that led to the tree-line far below. It was almost midday, and at this time of year, night would fall before they reached the Blood Palace.

Oskan shivered as his sledge finally passed under the branches of the first trees of the forest. Already darkness seemed to have gathered under the evergreen trees, and it wasn't possible to see more than a few metres to either side of the track, before the shadows closed in and hid everything from sight.

"Odd place, this," said Taradan, drawing alongside the sledge. "I remember it when we passed this way coming south with the army. If you listen you can hear something talking quietly. You can never quite catch what it's saying, but it sounds pretty menacing. Like something muttering threats or perhaps some evil incantation. Not sure I like it much."

Oskan understood exactly what he meant. An odd murmuring undertone drifted through the trees, but if you tried to pin down where it was coming from, it shifted in a weird unsettling way, like some wind of misery uttering evil words and just waiting for an opportunity to make something hideous happen.

"It's not my favourite place either," Oskan answered. "I'd sooner be at home in front of the fire with a mug of my favourite beer."

"Ah, yes. Now you're talking. Perhaps from the South Riding barrels, in the third cellar along under the palace kitchens."

"You're very well acquainted with the kitchen undercrofts," said Oskan with an amused grin.

"Well, erm . . ." said Taradan, feeling all at once like a naughty cub. "I'll . . . erm . . . I'll just scout ahead for any problems."

Oskan watched the brilliant white pelt dwindling to a pale

glow as the Snow Leopard ran on ahead, and he laughed to himself. There was something wonderfully *human* about Taradan and all his people. What would the Icemark do without them?

Just then the distant grey shadow of the giant cat disappeared. "Commander Blood-lapper, increase the pace, please," Oskan called to the werewolf leader. "I'd like to catch up with Field-Marshall Taradan." Something was beginning to make his flesh crawl, and a warlock was always alert to all his senses.

Medea too was aware of her flesh crawling, and it excited her. She was listening hard to the murmurings of the forest, trying to decipher what they were saying, but try as she might she couldn't quite make them out. Nevertheless, she was enjoying the atmosphere of The-Land-of-the–Ghosts. It had a feeling of deep and abiding nastiness that she found quite charming. Perhaps being forced to join the embassy to Their Vampiric Majesties would prove to be to her advantage after all. She found herself looking forward to their arrival at the Blood Palace.

A high-pitched yowl erupted into the air – a Snow Leopard's alarm call. Immediately the sledge leaped forward as the Ukpik werewolves surged to top speed. Grinfang charged on ahead, howling as he went, and they thundered round the long bend where Taradan had disappeared.

Abruptly they scrabbled and slithered to a halt. Before them crouched the Snow Leopard in the attack position, facing a party of zombies that stood across the track.

"Wait, Taradan!" Oskan called. "What do they want? They don't look aggressive."

The great cat sat upright and waited, though a deep growl still rumbled in his chest.

"Hit them! Hit them hard now, before they can attack!" Grinfang snarled.

"No, wait," Oskan commanded, and climbed down from the sledge. The werewolf muttered mutinously. Medea watched and waited, but after the earlier display of warlock Power, the werewolf didn't dare go against the Witchfather.

Oskan walked forward and faced the zombies. "You are impeding the progress of a Royal Embassy sent by Queen Thirrin of the Icemark, Tharaman-Thar of the Icesheets and King Grishmak of the Wolf-folk to Their Vampiric Majesties of The-Land-of-the-Ghosts. State your business, or be swept aside by the Snow Leopard and werewolves!"

A silence fell, and Oskan gazed at the zombies in revolted fascination. There were more than twenty of them, in such an advanced state of decomposition that he could hear tiny damp thuds and tired slithers as pieces of flesh, and even hands and feet, fell to the ground.

Obviously this party had orders to stop the embassy, but beyond that their purpose remained unclear. Oskan was about to demand their business again when the largest of the zombies shuffled forward.

"Follow usss!" it lisped in a deep voice muffled by a tongue and lips that had almost rotted away.

"Why should we?" Oskan demanded. "How can we trust you?"

"Vampire King, Vampire Queen sent ussss."

"Well, well, we have a reception committee after all," Oskan said to Taradan and Grinfang.

"I don't trust them," said Grinfang.

"Neither do I," said Oskan. "But even if they're lying, at

least we won't have to fight them for a while if we do as they ask."

"We've no real choice anyway," said Taradan. "Apart from abandoning the embassy and trying to outrun them as we head home."

"Follow them it is, then," said Oskan. "I wonder how many other envoys have had such lovely escorts?"

The Ukpik werewolves took up the traces of the sledge again, and Oskan settled himself under the furs before calling to the zombies, "Lead on, then. We'll follow."

The undead creatures set off at a tremendous speed, loping and rolling along at such a rate the werewolves struggled to keep up. But for Oskan, the worst aspect of the journey was the smell of rotting flesh and the shreds of matter that flew off the zombies. Once or twice nameless lumps of meat landed on the sledge and he was forced to use a stick, grabbed from an overhead branch, to scrape them off.

"I'm sorry about this, Medea," he said as the sledge surged on. "But this is the true nature of any embassy: often beneath the elegant diplomatic speeches lies corruption and decay."

"There's no need to apologise," she replied giving him one of her rare smiles. "I'm enjoying myself immensely."

Instinctively knowing she was drawn to The Land-of-the-Ghosts, a spasm of fear rippled over Oskan's flesh, raising the hairs on his arms and making him shudder. It was time for further talks.

"It's beautiful, isn't it?"

Medea frowned in puzzlement. "What is?"

"The temptation of the Dark."

Her black eyes revealed nothing, but undeterred Oskan went on. "The excitement of going against what's expected of you; the glory of being . . . different, terrible, frightening! "

Medea stared ahead, her black hair rolling out behind her like dark smoke in the wind. She knew her father had magically drawn them aside from the physical world. The Ukpik werewolves were suspended in mid-stride, as was Taradan, whose huge powerful body remained delicately balanced on one grounded paw. She and her father had entered the place between the material and spiritual dimensions, and this alone warned her of the gravity of the situation.

"Have we really reached this point in my education already? I thought revealing the true nature of the Dark would come later, when the matter of my choice becomes critical," she said, her tone calculated to give just the right impression of unconcern.

Oskan could only admire her intelligence. He'd hardly begun the lead-up to that terrible revelation of true evil, but she'd guessed his intention and had disarmed him with easy contempt.

"Clever words don't dilute the truth, Medea. You're tempted by a Power that is corrupt and foul. Let me show you something." His mind began to weave an image of a wide snowy tundra under a dense field of stars. She immediately put up barriers against him, but his Gift was by far the stronger and she was forced to watch.

"This is the Seventh Plain of the magical realms, known as the Circle of Dark, Medea. Here dwell my father's people."

She gasped and stared at him. "Then you do know who he is!"

"Oh yes. And so do you."

She turned back to stare ahead again, her silence confirming what Oskan suspected. "You find him admirable and strong. But you're afraid of him too." Oskan smiled, his face transformed into a cat-like mask. "That's good, Medea. That's very good; fear enables us to control those ambitions that might otherwise destroy us. You have to accept that you're not strong enough for the Dark. Its evil would smother you; it would stop up your head and your senses with its cloying Power and you'd be lost, drained to nothing, empty and trodden under the heel of my father's strength."

The image he'd been weaving clarified into stark and startling brilliance. "Look, Medea. What do you see?"

Reluctantly, she let her mind wander over the wide vision he'd created. "I see frozen wastes, snow, ice. Nothing unusual for the northern world."

"But this isn't the northern realms of the physical world," he said quietly. "We see the Spirit Plains. We see the Dark."

"Surprisingly ordinary, isn't it?" she said lightly.

"Far from it, as you well know. Nothing is as it seems in the Dark. It can only reflect, and mock the reality of the spiritual and physical worlds. The stars in all their beautiful constellations are nothing but distilled hatred given form; the distant snow-covered mountains are built from the pain and horror that people have suffered down the long millennia—"

"And I suppose the snow is nothing but the powdered bones of little babies who died in innocence at the behest of Evil," she answered, her voice high-pitched, quivering and mocking.

Oskan found himself admiring the strength of her resistance. She was a sorceress with a potential that terrified him.

"No bones make up the snows of the Dark, Medea," he replied. "Look closer."

Under the pressure of his Magical strength she had no

choice. "I see flakes of ice," she answered defiantly. "I see crystals with a delicate lacy symmetry, and below that I see the void that exists between matter."

"But this is the Spirit World, Medea," Oskan replied with measured calm. "There *is* no matter. Look again. Look again at the crystals of ice."

With an exasperated sigh she applied her Gift and studied the snow again. At first, she could see nothing out of the ordinary, but then she discerned an odd structure in the ice crystals. She gasped. The snow was spirit! Each and every crystal of ice was a soul captured and held by some incredible Power so that the spark of life itself had condensed and frozen into tiny glittering shards!

"Now look around you," Oskan instructed.

Medea looked far into the immense, endless sweep of frozen waste that was the Dark, as far as her Magical Eye could see. She trembled uncontrollably, and her body slumped forward in the sledge.

Oskan looked at her and nodded. "The snows of the Dark are made up of the souls of those who were tempted by its Power. Does it tempt you still, Medea?"

She moaned and closed her eyes, then seemed to slip away into unconsciousness. Her father heaved a sigh of relief dragged from the very deepest depth of his being. At last, he'd touched her mind! He'd reached out and drawn her back from the edge of the most terrible abyss! For a moment he slumped back in his seat and allowed the cold winds of The-Land-of-the-Ghosts to wash and coil over him. Then, wearily, he sat up and with a nod of his head, he and his daughter re-entered the physical world.

* * *

They were back in the sledge. Medea felt the shift as they left the in-between state, but she kept her eyes shut; she had to think. Carefully, silently, she built barriers that hid her thoughts even from Oskan, the most powerful of warlocks. He might have been able to force her mind to look at the scenes he had created, but he couldn't force her to engage with them emotionally. Her real thoughts and intentions were hidden, even from her father. There was no witch, warlock or wizard who was better at that than her.

Only when every vestige of thought and emotion was hidden behind barriers of Magical Adamant did she allow herself to exalt. She had never even begun to guess at the extraordinary Power of the Dark! How incredible; how amazing; how wonderfully superb!

One day she would triumph, she would make her grandfather proud – but first, it might be worth getting to know some of the lesser evils. The wickedness of Their Vampiric Majesties seemed to stem from the Dark. So, perhaps they had some safe means of accessing it. She smiled to herself; this diplomatic mission was definitely proving to be useful.

After more than two hours without a rest, Oskan caught his first glimpse of the sickly green light that outlined the battlements and turrets of the Blood Place, the seat of the Vampire King and Queen. They thundered on through the icy night, and as they drew closer details added themselves to the dark mass of the building. At first the black eyes of hundreds of windows watched their approach. But then, unnervingly, a fitful green light began to grow in the topmost casements and spread to more and more of the windows, until at last the entire palace seemed aflame with the sickly fluorescent glow that oozed down the walls like mucus and flowed out on to the terrace that surrounded the building.

"Not a comforting sight," said Taradan, drawing alongside the sledge. "It looks like it's been carved out of the corpse of some giant animal."

"Yes," Oskan agreed. "And its occupants are like the maggots and mould that are slowly eating it away."

"How can you say that?" said Taradan in mock horror. "You're speaking of our allies!"

"Indeed I am. And it's our task to remind them that that's exactly what they are."

"Oh, what fun," said Taradan morosely.

"Precisely," Oskan answered. "So the sooner we get it over and done with, the better."

Medea shivered with excitement. She'd heard so much about Their Vampiric Majesties, and now she was actually going to meet them. There was something wonderfully sinister, and even romantic, about their rule that had continued unaltered and unchallenged for more than a thousand years. And if they did have some safe means of access to the supreme Power that was the Dark, then perhaps through them she'd find her true spiritual birthplace.

They'd almost reached the palace. The zombies led the party on to the terraces that surrounded the building, and finally stopped. The werewolves sagged in the traces of the sledge, gasping for breath, their hairy forms almost hidden by a haze of steam that condensed on the freezing air and settled on their muzzles.

"We're heeeeere!" the head zombie boomed, its brain too rotten to grasp that it was stating the obvious.

"So we are," Oskan said brightly. "Just run along in and

announce us, will you?"

The undead creature seemed confused by that, and turned to the palace, then back to Oskan, its cold face working as it tried to decide what to do.

"Oh, never mind, we'll announce ourselves." Oskan turned to the Ukpik werewolves, who had already recovered enough to be gazing around at the hideous beauty of the palace ice-gardens, where marble skulls and frozen fountains in the forms of spectres loomed out of the darkness. "You may as well all come along. You'll freeze out here, and who knows, perhaps it'll actually be warmer inside."

He led the way over the terrace to the towering double doors of the palace. Taradan and Grinfang joined him, and they all stared up at the iron-studded woodwork that stayed firmly closed.

"I'll announce us," said Grinfang, and he hammered on the doors with his massive fists. They could hear the boom echoing hollowly through the palace, but nothing happened. The werewolf hammered again, harder this time. The doors shook in their frame, but still there was no acknowledgement of their presence.

"Oh, enough of this!" Taradan said, and rearing up to his full height, he smashed his weight against the doors, which burst open, slamming back against the inside walls and falling off their hinges.

"Crude but effective," said Oskan as he and Medea walked through the now gaping doorway and into the darkness beyond. After a moment's hesitation the others followed, edging cautiously into the gloom.

Medea was entranced. Emerging from dense shadows was an elegant Great Hall with cold marble floors and cavernous fireplaces, dripping with icy chandeliers. The décor was exquisite, with fine alabaster statues standing gracefully in ornate niches, and beautiful furniture positioned for the most arresting effect.

For Oskan, the whole effect was one of unwanted nostalgia. He hadn't seen the Blood Palace since the first war against Scipio Bellorum, when he and Thirrin, young and inexperienced, had travelled together to The-Land-of-the-Ghosts. He strode forward, calling out the names of his party and their mission, but the hall remained dark and empty. "You," he said to the nearest werewolf. "Light that fire, please." And he pointed to a cave of a fireplace that was stuffed with logs. "The rest of you, light any torches and candles you find. Let's see what we're doing here."

The Wolf-folk were fairly new to the technology of tinderboxes, but they'd taken to them readily, and the fire was soon lit. And as their hairy forms ran about the hall, distant points of light began to flare up, like new suns in the void of space. The place soon looked as close to cheerful as possible considering its sepulchral marbles and high-shadowed ceilings.

At the far end of the hall was a raised dais on which stood two empty black thrones. Obviously, Their Vampiric Majesties had not yet deigned to appear, but showing neither awe nor fear, Oskan strode up to them and sat down on the nearest. He patted the seat of the other one invitingly, but Grinfang backed away.

"I'll have a go," said Taradan. "I've often wondered what it felt like to sit on a chair." After several attempts the Snow Leopard succeeded in perching his rump on the seat, with his back legs stuck out at a crazy angle and his front legs resting on the second step of the dais. "Personally, I think the floor's more comfortable, but each species to its own, I suppose."

Medea ascended the dais without waiting to be invited. She felt perfectly relaxed – almost, but not quite, at home. Everything about the place appealed to her, and felt right. She looked about, searching in vain for signs of the inhabitants of the cavernous hall .

The Wolf-folk gathered about the thrones and waited in an uncomfortable silence. After a few minutes, Oskan stirred himself and stood up.

"Fetch the torches from the walls," he said quietly. "And position yourself close to anything flammable."

The werewolves scuttled off to do his bidding, and when they were scattered about the massively wide hall, standing next to hanging tapestries, upholstered furniture, or long velvet curtains, he drew breath and called, "If you don't put in an appearance this minute, I'll burn down your palace and destroy any Vampires not quick enough to make their escape."

Slowly, the seconds ticked by, then Oskan nodded to the nearest werewolf, who stood next to a deeply upholstered divan. Immediately, she thrust her torch into the seat and stood back as the flames took hold.

Suddenly, the air was full of hissing and screeching. Vampires with bat-like wings soared through the space below the high ceiling, while some descended on the divan and smothered it in heavy cloths.

"Are you entirely without scruples or sanity?" the Vampire King fumed, as he stepped with enraged precision along the polished floor. His usually languid voice was icy with barely suppressed anger as he glared at Oskan, who still sat in his throne. "Would you expect such behaviour from me, were I to visit Frostmarris?"

"Would you expect to find an empty palace and a host ill-mannered enough to leave guests to their own devices in a cold and dark Great Hall?" Oskan replied.

"I think our social misdemeanours, if indeed they were such, pale into insignificance compared with attempted arson!"

The Vampire Queen joined her Consort. "Hardly the act of a friend and ally, I would say. Nor that of someone who has come to beg for our help in their new war with the Polypontian Empire."

Oskan held their angry glares unwaveringly. The King was still as effetely elegant and his Consort as loathsomely beautiful as they'd been over twenty years before. Of course, Oskan knew perfectly well that Vampires were immortal, but to actually witness their unchanging state was a startling experience.

Medea gazed at the Vampires hungrily. She found their elegance and intelligence deeply attractive. They exuded an atmosphere of evil that infected the very air around them.

With an effort, Oskan dragged his attention back to the situation at hand. He drew breath to speak, but then held it, and let the silence stretch into discomfort before he finally spoke, "*Beg* for your help in the war, you say? The Icemark has no need to beg Their Vampiric Majesties for anything. I have merely come with my daughter and two other representatives of the species within the alliance to remind you of your obligations according to the terms of the treaty you signed before the last war with the Empire."

"A scrap of paper that has no validity in your present crisis," said the Vampire King. "We fulfilled our commitment and are free of any further obligation!"

The hideously pale courtiers surrounding the monarchs

hissed in approval, but when Oskan turned his gaze on them, they immediately fell silent.

"If you care to study your copy of the treaty, you will find that it calls for mutual assistance in the face of all and any violence. No time limitation was added, and so the agreement is still valid."

The Vampire Queen laughed, trying to seem completely at ease even though she was standing at the foot of her own dais, looking up at Oskan and the giant Snow Leopard that occupied her throne. "The treaty was signed to deal with the crisis of the time and in the *spirit* of the time. So although there are no limits written within the *letter* of its clauses, it doesn't apply to the present war with the Empire."

Again the courtiers hissed their approval of this legal nicety, and both Their Vampiric Majesties smiled regally at their subjects.

Taradan yawned cavernously, showing his enormous teeth and red throat. "I always get so bored when people start quibbling over the small print." He then sat up and fastened his bright amber eyes on the Vampire Queen. "So just accept it, fang-face, you're still part of the alliance whether you like it or not."

Grinfang sniggered nastily from where he now sat on the top step of the dais. "Yeah. Don't forget we still have all these torches, and we werewolves can be really clumsy sometimes. Things might catch fire, and the so-called *undead* might get fried and find themselves just plain *dead.*"

"Threats of violence and atrocity hardly carry the weight of legality, my dear wolf-person," said the Vampire King.

"Oh, you are so right, my dear," the Queen said admiringly, stroking her Consort's hair. "Threats of violence completely undermine an opponent's moral position – as I'm sure you will agree, Oskan Witchfather. Besides, what can you do to make us join your little struggle with Bellorum? Send an army and begin a war? I don't think so. You barely have enough soldiers to keep the Polypontians at bay, even with the support of your allies. And if you have to fight a war on two fronts, against two enemies, I don't think you'll survive more than a month, do you?"

Oskan rose from his seat and stared down at Their Vampiric Majesties. The atmosphere around him shifted subtly and a faint shimmer glowed about him.

Medea watched him. Could the Vampire King and Queen actually defy her father's powers?

"I have not come here to play legal games with a people who are bound by all known laws to an agreement of mutual assistance in the time of war," said Oskan darkly, his voice slowly deepening and his eyes rolling back in his head. "The Vampire King and Queen and all of their subjects are bound by a dreadful oath to the treaty they signed twenty years ago, and if they refuse to fulfil their obligations, I, Oskan Witchfather, Consort of Thirrin Freer Strong-in-the-Arm Lindenshield, Wildcat of the North and Queen of the Icemark, will invoke the sanctions laid down in that treaty."

All the Vampires hissed and screeched in rage and fear. The awesome figure before them seemed to have grown. The air around Oskan shimmered as if it were surrounded by a heat haze.

"Of course, if they truly believe they are not still bound by the original treaty then they will have no fear of the sanctions." Oskan drew a rattling breath *"May all the goddesses and gods of the earth and sky, all the spirits of blood and death, all*

198

the watchers and keepers of oaths, see this act and hold our written names as binding. And may any and all who break this trust fall from the face of the Mother Earth and live an unending life skinned under the endless gaze of the blazing sun, mortal and immortal, werewolf, Vampire and human being! By garlic, wood, and cleansing fire. So mote it be!"

A great screeching and hissing arose from the Vampires. Many of them transformed themselves into their bat forms and flapped frantically around the hall's high ceilings, while others simply collapsed to the floor where they sprawled looking about, fearfully waiting for the terrible penalty to be paid.

The Vampire King's voice cut through the hideous din, and silence fell. "Enough, enough. There is no need to invoke any sanctions or clauses. We accept that we are still bound by the original treaty and will fulfil our obligations as you interpret them."

Gradually, Oskan's eyes rolled back to their natural position and the shimmering haze dissipated. "Well, that's better," he said lightly. "Now, what about a little wine to cement our rediscovered spirit of co-operation?"

Medea could have wept with disappointment. Their Vampiric Majesties were without depth or substance. They were weak, useless allies, and she would be left all alone, an island of shadow in the sea of the Icemark. All she wanted now was to return to the safety of her tower. And with every darkening fibre of her being she wished she had never agreed to come.

Cressida was sitting quietly in the private apartments behind the throne, the wolfhounds lying in a snoring heap around her. She was angry and hurt. The twins had turned against her without any warning, and worst of all, for someone who would one day lead the nation, she hadn't seen it coming. She'd managed to make enemies within her own family, and if she could cause such deep resentment amongst those who were supposed to love her, then what might she do with those who had no blood ties to her at all?

She was just thinking about how to make peace with her brothers, when her mother walked into the room. "A little quiet for you, isn't it?" said Thirrin, searching through the papers on her worktable. "Now, where are those listings for the infantry?" she said to herself, and looked up. "Are you all right?"

"Hmm? Oh, yes! Yes. Just a little tired," Cressida answered and underlined her all-rightness by smiling brightly.

Her mother found the papers she was looking for, then putting them back on the table, she drew up a chair and sat down. "So. What's wrong?"

"Nothing! Nothing at all. Except . . . except the twins don't like me."

"Ah," said Thirrin. "And this surprises you?"

"No, not any more. They've told me exactly why they find me the least likeable person in the entire Icemark, item by item."

"And they are?"

Cressida took a deep breath. "I'm bossy, rude, cold, aloof, superior, proud, generally unpleasant and humourless."

"I see."

"We had words at dinner last week. And I've thought about what they said and come to the conclusion that perhaps, just perhaps, they may have one or two points."

"So?" Thirrin prompted.

"So, I decided to change my attitude towards them. And today, when I met them in the lists I was friendly, I cracked jokes, and I never once told them to shut up or stop being so loud. I didn't have to; they never said a word. They just finished what they were doing and left in complete silence."

"And now you're angry and intend laying into them next time you see them, I suppose," said Thirrin, leaning back in her chair and watching her daughter.

"No. There'd be no point. They'd still hate me. I suppose I have to accept that it's going to take longer than I thought for them to . . . well, *forgive* me."

"So, you accept you were harsh with them?"

Cressida ruffled one of the dogs' ears in silence, and reluctantly admitted it. "Yes. But whatever I said or did was always for their own good. They just don't see it that way."

Thirrin drew a deep breath, and let it out slowly while she thought. "You'll be Queen one day, and the final decisions will be yours to make on everything from what to have for dinner to enormous weighty matters of State. But you'll also have advisers to help you, as well as ministers, Commanders of the army, barons and baronesses, and most importantly of all, a Consort who, if he's worth his salt, will tell you exactly what he thinks whether you like it or not."

"Like Dad, you mean?"

"Oh yes, exactly like your dad," Thirrin agreed with a smirk. "But for the moment, you have none of these things. You have only your parents, and you never ask us for advice if you can help it. Cressida, you have to accept that no matter what you think, no matter what conclusions you reach, all of it is *only* your opinion. You may think the twins are noisy, boisterous and rowdy, and so they are, but they're soldiers. I don't really expect them to be otherwise.

"I suppose what I'm saying is that you have every right to your opinions, and you also have every right to voice them," Thirrin continued. "But equally, everyone else has every right to disagree with you. And if you simply ignore what other people think, eventually they'll resent you. And if you continue to ignore them, they'll begin to hate you, and from hatred springs rebellion."

A silence fell between them, broken only by the crackle of the fire.

Thirrin stood and gathered her papers. "It's best that you learn this lesson now with your family, rather than later when you're Queen."

"But why didn't I know this already? Surely a future ruler should have an instinct for such things!" Cressida almost wailed.

"Instinct? Only bullies and tyrants think they have an instinct for dealing with people. Scipio Bellorum probably thinks he has an instinct for it. But he doesn't; he merely has a talent for terrifying entire populations. Everyone else accepts they have to learn these things. You're only just seventeen, Cressida. You can't expect to become a fully fledged monarch overnight."

"You did. You'd been ruling for three years by the time you were my age. *And* you'd defeated the Polypontian Empire, got married, and given birth to me!"

Thirrin raised her arms and let them fall in a hopeless gesture. "But I had to. My father was dead and Bellorum had invaded. I either learned quickly or died. At least you've had the luxury of a childhood and youth. Don't wish for the sort of maturity that comes with war and death. The price isn't worth it. Though the way things are going, too many people in this benighted little country will have to grow up very quickly indeed."

The Crown Princess stared into the fire, knowing that her mother was right. It would just take a little while longer to get used to it. "I'd better go to bed," she said finally. "I'll be reviewing the fyrd sections under my command tomorrow."

CHAPTER 14

It had taken just over a week to set up the first buildings. The ships' carpenters, and the builders and other artisans from amongst the refugees, had soon been organised by an enthusiastic Maggiore Totus into specialised work parties with their own gangs of labourers. And once the second fleet had arrived from the Icemark the small shanty settlement quickly began to develop into a proper town.

Sigurdson and his ships left not long after that, and Charlemagne felt his last link with home was being severed as he watched them head out over the lagoon. Still, the second fleet had brought letters from Frostmarris and he was soon locked away in his cabin reading sheets and sheets of paper from his parents, a longish and completely business-like letter from Cressida giving lots of advice, and even a note each from the twins. These both consisted of one small phrase:

Dear Sharley,
GET LOST!
Lots of Love,
US!

He could almost hear the twins giggling as they wrote them, and he found himself giggling too as he pinned the notes to the wall above his bed. Not surprisingly, there was nothing from Medea. Sharley tried to imagine what a letter from his strange sister would look like, and decided it would probably be written on black vellum with grey ink made from the ground ash of incinerated bones. He shuddered, then settled down to read his mum and dad's letter again.

His dad had done the actual writing; his mum was too impatient to write. She would have been pacing the floor and shouting out phrases and information to be included, until even his dad's slow-burning temper would reach breaking point and they'd have one of their shouting matches. After that his dad would write in sulky silence, until his mum could stand it no longer and would start offering advice again.

Sharley laid down the paper as it suddenly occurred to him how like children his parents were. This was quite a revelation, and he quickly scanned his memory for further instances of their childishness. After a while he gave up; there were just too many! Perhaps most adults were like that. Kids spent their lives expecting to act differently when they grew up, but perhaps they were wasting their time. Nothing changed but the body; the mind stayed much the same.

Somehow he found this a comfort. He'd expected to reach some stage in life when his childish self would be left behind, but now, if he was right, he didn't have to worry; he'd go on being himself no matter how old he got.

He tried to imagine what someone as old as the Doge of Venezzia would have been like when he was young. Charlemagne had met him two days before. He was tall, frighteningly thin, and had the face of an old hawk watching all about him with sharp, flinty eyes. He realised that he couldn't do it; the Doge's mind had probably always been old and calculating and manipulative, even when he'd been a toddler!

Sharley and Maggie's meeting with Venezzia's ruler had been odd, to say the least. The day had begun when the two courtiers, Signors Gabraldi and Permino, who'd first welcomed them to Venezzia, arrived at the quayside in a small State galley. Sharley and Maggie had been seated on plush divans in the centre of the vessel, and they'd set off to the palace. They'd crossed the wide lagoon to the city of Venezzia, in an amazingly short time and then dived into a dark labyrinth of narrow back waterways, where the oars of the galley almost scraped the banks on either side as they dipped and rose into and out of the murky waters.

The houses that lined these canals were dirty and crumbling, with shuttered windows or with dubious looking characters peering out. Most of these ducked out of sight as they approached, but at one large crumbling cliff of a building, several men appeared and started to shout something that Sharley could barely understand, but which seemed to be a demand for payment before they'd let the galley through.

Signor Permino waved a contemptuous hand, and immediately a hail of crossbow bolts were spat at the building from somewhere below decks, and two of the men fell screeching into the water. The galley glided on, and at another wave of Senor Permino's hand more crossbow bolts zipped through the windows, but this time they left trails of sparks, and soon the building was in flames.

Sharley was horrified. He'd never seen anyone killed before, despite his family's status as warriors. And the easy contempt with which Signor Permino had had the men slaughtered left him feeling both sick and angry. Killing an enemy in legitimate combat was one thing, but this appalled him. Then, with quiet indifference, Permino spoke to one of his young officials, "Remind me to have this nest of filth cleaned out before the end of the month."

Sharley knew his mother would tell him to harden his attitude: this was a different world to the one he knew and he could do nothing. He looked about him at his surroundings and tried to distract himself.

Exactly why they were taking such a roundabout route to the Doge's palace wasn't clear. In a desperate attempt to shake off the memory of the burning house he tried to ask Maggie what was going on, but the old man only smiled grimly and placed a finger on his lips. "All questions will be answered. But, for the moment, please be patient."

Sharley shrugged. He could wait, as long as he was told soon.

The galley was now nosing out into a broader waterway that seemed to be lined with the rear entrances of enormous buildings. Small docks and broad flights of stairs led down to the canal, where boats and galleys of all descriptions were unloading passengers and goods in equal quantities. But, unusually, this waterway was a dead end; no other canals intersected with it and there was only one entrance. Also, soldiers were standing on every dock and what looked like tiny war-galleys patrolled up and down the waters, each one containing men with crossbows. This had to be the rear entrance to the Doge's Palace. They drew up to a wide, elegant sweep of steps.

"His Eminence the Doge begs the pardon of your Royal

Highness in asking you to enter his humble establishment through the trade and kitchen quarters, but he is sure that your supreme intelligence will have informed you of the need for care," said Signor Permino, sweeping off his wildly plumed hat as he bowed.

The gangway was lowered, and several soldiers rushed to line either side of it as Sharley and Maggie were helped out of the boat and then whisked up the stairs and through an archway into the kitchens. Everywhere was fire and chaos as meats were roasted on spits, cauldrons seethed and ovens belched out heat in a seemingly solid wall that Sharley and his party were obliged to force their way through. Chefs in white aprons and ridiculously tall white hats screeched at assistants, and over all the human clamour clattered an accompaniment of pots and pans as water was boiled, meats fried and pastries baked. It was even more chaotic than Yuletide in the Frostmarris scullery!

They eventually emerged into a series of winding corridors, and after a journey that lasted several confusing minutes, they came to a passageway that was lined with wood panelling and was empty of anyone else. After Signor Gabraldi had tiptoed in elaborate silence to the door at the farther end and ensured no one was about to enter, Signor Permino stepped over to a section of panelling. He pressed a carved flower, and the panel slid open.

A secret passageway! How in keeping with Venezzian society, thought Sharley, but rather than let them think him an excitable barbarian boy who was easily impressed, he simply smiled knowingly and ducked inside. He then had to wait in a cramped and dusty stairway as the two courtiers squeezed by to lead the way. In less than a minute their guides were knocking at another piece of panelling, and it opened to reveal a sumptuously decorated room with a throne standing beneath a red velvet awning.

It took Sharley a few moments to notice the tall man gazing out of a huge window overlooking the Grand Central Canal. He looked like part of a moving painting, as galleys and full-sized ships sailed up and down, while tiny supply boats whipped backwards and forwards over the greeny-blue waters.

Eventually the man turned and, after looking at them for a second, his face folded itself into a well-practised smile. "Ah, Prince Regent Charlemagne, I can at last look upon the features of the young man I have heard so much about."

Sharley felt his gammy leg threatening to buckle under him, but locking his knee with determination, he smiled and bowed his head. "Your Eminence Doge Machiavelli, I am honoured and gratified."

The Doge's smile, having done its job, had been packed away, but now an expressive eyebrow climbed his forehead. "I see the reports were by no means an exaggeration. You do speak Venezzian."

"As I explained to your emissaries, Maggiore Totus has been a more than able tutor," Sharley said, and was relieved when the cold, flinty eyes turned from him and came to rest on Maggie.

"Signor Totus. You are exactly as I imagined: a man whose intricacies are packaged in an unassuming exterior. I must admit your plan amuses me. Its audacity is quite breathtaking, but there are times when danger is the only antidote to decades of careful and tedious government. Shall we sit?"

He led the way to a small table set with three goblets. Signor Permino took up a position behind the Doge's chair, while Gabraldi melted into the shadows at the back of the room. "Please forgive the charade of secrecy," the elegantly tall man said while they made themselves comfortable. "We all know that the Empire's spies will have reported your presence as soon as you arrived in Venezzia. But if we don't make at least a pretence of secrecy, the enemy will think we're getting arrogant, and that could be dangerous." He poured three measures of wine, and asked, "How long will you need to establish contact?"

"That has already been achieved by happy accident," said Maggie.

"Indeed?" the Doge said quietly, but didn't ask for details. "Then when will you begin your journey?"

"As soon as a ship is made available, Your Eminence."

"The day after tomorrow. It will be crewed by Hellenic mercenaries, and none of them will know that they are in the pay of the Venezzian Republic." Suddenly the flinty eyes held Maggie in a penetrating gaze. "It will remain that way."

"Of course."

"You will send no messages or reports of your progress while you are away. The Empire's spy network is far too efficient to risk contact of any sort. And if you're intercepted by the Imperial Forces, then the Venezzian Republic knows nothing about your mission." Machiavelli paused briefly to let Maggie absorb his words, then he added: "Do you understand?"

"Perfectly, Your Eminence."

Sharley felt as if he'd become invisible and had stumbled in on a private conversation. How dare they ignore him? He'd entered a world where people could be killed with an indolent wave of the hand, and where intrigue and secrecy seemed second nature. And now they were talking over him as though he had no right to understand their conversation! He was Prince Regent, and if plans were being finalised – let alone made – then he had a right to know what they were. In tones that his grandfather King Redrought would have been proud of, he said: "Excuse me, have I died or something? I just wondered because everyone seems to be ignoring me here!"

Maggie patted his arm. "I'll explain later," he whispered.

"Why can't you explain now? How could you have brought me to a meeting with the Doge without telling me what's going on?" he asked, his tone confused and hurt. "Are you trying to make me look like some stupid young nobody whom you control?" His eyes flashed around the room. "I see two rulers and three servants here, and one of the servants is called Maggiore Totus. Perhaps he's forgotten that!"

Machiavelli sat back in his seat, his eyes narrowed as he re-evaluated the boy before him.

"There has been no time to fill you in on details, Your Majesty," Maggie hissed. "I intended to explain everything to you after we had left the palace."

"No time in all the weeks of our sea journey? It's pretty clear you've been in touch with Venezzia for months, yet you've never thought of saying anything to me about it."

"The negotiations have been . . . delicate and complex. Everything may have fallen through, and I didn't want to raise false hopes. What can I say? . . . I thought it better that no one knew until I had something definite to tell. If I'd explained my plans and they'd come to nothing, the disappointment might have had a devastating effect on the morale of the Icemark."

"What plans? You *still* haven't explained," said Sharley

angrily. Then, before Maggie could answer, he asked, "Does my mother even know?"

"Well, erm . . . no," the old scholar said with a nervous glance at the Doge. "She already had enough to worry about. I didn't think it right to burden her with more."

"Didn't think it right?" Sharley was stupefied with anger. "She's the Queen! How dare you make plans without telling her, whatever they are!"

Maggie suddenly felt old beyond even his considerable years. There were times when diplomacy and international intrigue were too heavy a burden. And now even gentle Sharley was turning against him. Obviously he'd miscalculated, and if he didn't think quickly, then everything could fall apart.

The only solution seemed to be complete honesty. He sat up, took a deep breath and said, "Your Majesty, Prince Charlemagne. When the threat from the Polypontus was renewed I realised that Scipio Bellorum would never have contemplated another invasion unless he was absolutely certain he would succeed. He would have calculated all the odds, allowed for the abilities and the effect of all of the allies, and reached the conclusion, not only that he *could* win, but that he definitely *would* win. And so, I decided that the only thing to do was to upset his calculations by adding a factor that would make his conclusions null and void. Namely, something unexpected: new allies!"

He took a sip from his goblet and quickly glanced at his audience. Sharley was listening carefully despite his anger, and Machiavelli was watching proceedings with his calculating eye. Maggie took another deep breath and continued.

"Of course, your mother had made alliances with all possible peoples in the region. Short of signing a treaty with the birds of the air, there was no one else to turn to. So, I knew we would have to look farther afield, and it was then that I contacted the Doge.

"It soon became clear that Venezzia wasn't in a position to help openly and directly, but His Eminence suggested an . . . *alternative* solution. He proposed that I make contact with the Desert People."

"Captain Al-Khatib's people! Those of the brilliant light cavalry!" said Sharley, excited and absorbed despite his anger.

"Precisely. If we could get them to join our struggle against the Empire then we could still defeat Bellorum, no matter what he has planned!"

"But why should they help us?" Sharley asked, suddenly deflating after his initial enthusiasm.

"Because the Desert People hate Bellorum and his Empire; because the fame of the Icemark's victory has reached even them; and because they are desperate to strike at their enemy in a way that will finally rid them of the continuing threat to their borders and freedom," said Maggie.

"So have they agreed to join the alliance?"

"Erm . . . no. Not yet. Captain Al-Khatib was my first contact with them. The diplomatic work and negotiations have yet to begin. And that is where you, Your Majesty, come in, providing of course that you agree."

"What do you mean?" Sharley asked nervously.

"We must undertake an embassy to the Desert People. We must visit their Court and place our plans directly before the Sultan."

"You mean I'm to be a Royal Ambassador, just like my mother was to the Vampire King and Queen and to the Snow Leopards?"

"Precisely."

Sharley swallowed nervously. He wasn't sure he could do it. He was a gawky boy with about as much diplomatic skill as a clown at a funeral. After all, he'd just verbally attacked Maggie in front of the Doge, instead of waiting till after the meeting as he knew he should have done. He was just too hot-tempered and hasty. He was almost certain to do or say something ridiculous at just the wrong moment and spoil all of Maggie's efforts.

"Do you think I can do it?" he asked nervously.

"My Lord Charlemagne, when I look at you I see your mother when she was your age. You have exactly the same combination of pride and lack of confidence; you have exactly the same fiery temper and, forgive me, vulnerability; and I'm convinced you have exactly the same potential to achieve greatness beyond anything you'd ever imagine yourself capable of."

Sharley blushed so furiously his hair and his face were almost the same colour. But he was totally unable to speak. Embarrassment, confusion and fear combined to strike him dumb, and he buried his nose in his goblet of wine.

The Doge had been watching with an interest that rose above that of a mere bystander. He was about to commit his small country to helping an enemy of the mighty Polypontian Empire, and if he miscalculated then the wrath of Scipio Bellorum could well be turned against them – once, that is, he'd defeated the barbarous Icemark. However, if they succeeded against all the odds, then the political applecart would most certainly be upset, and perhaps Venezzia could rise to fill the vacuum left by the Empire. It was a risk, but he liked taking risks and there was much that could be gained. The Doge absently tapped his fingernail against the silver of his wine goblet as he reached his decision.

"It would appear that the Prince's anger has been quelled, for the time being," said Machiavelli. "But rather than risk his ire once again, might I enquire if the plan to begin your journey to the land of the Desert People the day after tomorrow is still acceptable?"

Maggie looked at Sharley, his eyebrows raised. Realising that everyone was looking at him, the boy choked on his wine. After spluttering and burping for a few moments, he managed to draw enough breath to croak, "Yes."

"*Bene!* Then, Your Majesty, and Signor Totus, we have an agreement. In two days' time you will have left our territorial waters and you will be travellers on a private journey to the Desert Kingdom. I wish you success, for all our sakes," the Doge said with quiet precision. He then sat back in his chair and closed his eyes.

Aware that they'd been dismissed, Charlemagne stood up as Signor Permino emerged from the shadows to lead them back out of the palace with rather unseemly haste.

As the boat drew away from the quayside, Sharley couldn't help feeling that something had begun that he couldn't now stop even if he'd wanted to. Excitement thrilled through his frame, swiftly followed by a rush of fear that almost made him gasp aloud.

Chapter 15

The deep, flawless blue of the sea was equalled only by that of the sky, and the all-pervading heat struck the back of Sharley's head like a hammer even through the hat and cotton scarf he wore for protection. Directly ahead he could clearly see a port where dozens of dhows were either being unloaded or standing a little way out waiting for their turn to dock.

Beyond the quayside was a bustling town. Sharley could see high towers with finely pointed tops, like the lances of a distant troop of cavalry, soaring out of a shimmering heat haze, and Maggie explained to him that these were minarets, from which the muezzin would call the town's people to prayer. In the distance, the town climbed a steep hill towards a high defensive wall that was pierced by a single gate and, above that, the hill continued its climb through a land of browny-orange rocks and red dust to a crest high against the blue sky. Sharley couldn't wait for his ship to dock so that he could begin to explore this exciting new world that lay before him.

Maggie had finalised arrangements with Captain

Al-Khatib, and now he, Sharley, was about to embark on his first mission as a Royal Ambassador, even though it was officially completely unofficial. The Desert People, the Empire's arch-enemy, had no wish to draw attention to this visit from a Prince of the Icemark. Bellorum needed few excuses to attack a country. This, added to the fact that he could mess everything up, had so horrified Sharley that he'd been unable to sleep for most of the journey.

Suddenly, orders were shouted and the anchor was hauled up. It was their turn to dock! Sharley ran to the prow of the ship as it slowly nosed its way forward. The closer they got to the quayside, the more the distant specks of the dock-workers began to resolve themselves into recognisable people. He stared at the chaos and bustle below him. Wooden cranes hauled barrels and crates from the holds of ships that lined the dockside, while teams of workers loaded the goods on to waiting carts which then headed off to join the shouting throng of drivers who were all trying to get through the port gates at the same time. The noise was incredible: men shouted, horses neighed, cranes and windlasses groaned and creaked.

Adding to the general atmosphere of mayhem were crowds of traders on the dockside, trying to sell their wares to the sailors on the ships. Everything from exotic foods to brightly coloured birds and strange creatures like tiny hairy people – which Maggie explained were called monkeys – was being offered for sale.

Sharley greedily absorbed it all, gasping at every new sight and demanding explanations. Then his eye was caught by a large and richly decorated carriage that was slowly fighting its way through the traffic. It was drawn by a team of six horses, each one bearing ostrich plumes on its bridle and a sky blue livery. But it was the driver who held his attention: every few metres he would stand up and flick his whip at the crowds, while screaming what Sharley guessed was abuse. Arguments raged around the driver, but even so the coach continued to make progress.

Eventually, the vehicle reached the dockside and drew up next to the gangplank of Sharley's vessel. Maggie smiled in relief. "I think our contact has arrived."

They both watched as the driver jumped down and opened the carriage door for a tall black gentleman in a bright red turban and white silk robes. Sharley had never seen anyone of such a rich mahogany colour before, and only just remembered to close his mouth as the man walked up the gangplank.

He stepped on to the deck and salaamed deeply. "Welcome to the Desert Kingdom, Your Majesty. I am Ibrahim Rahoul, Captain Al-Khatib's steward. He sends his greetings and felicitations and bids me escort you to his small home in the town, where he will receive you."

Maggie salaamed in return. "Greetings, Ibrahim Rahoul. We gladly accept Captain Al-Khatib's invitation."

As the carriage moved off, with the driver screaming himself hoarse, Sharley looked about him, gazing in wonder at the passing sights. Everywhere, goods spilled into the road from open-fronted shops, and crowds of shoppers milled about inspecting the produce and haggling. Sharley couldn't help noticing that the women kept their faces hidden behind silken scarves.

Soon they began to climb the hill away from the port, and headed towards the town walls. The houses became richer and richer as they trotted along, until eventually they were passing establishments that looked like miniature palaces.

At last the carriage slowed and finally stopped. Ibrahim Rahoul waited in dignified silence until the driver had climbed down from his seat and opened the door. As Sharley and Maggie emerged, they saw before them a huge house with a pair of enormous carved wooden doors set in walls that were blindingly white in the bright desert sunshine. They squinted at its brilliance, and slowly the massive double doors swung open, revealing a courtyard that was deeply shaded and green. Both Maggie and Sharley hurried towards the inviting cool of the courtyard without waiting to be asked.

Once they were inside, the doors closed and the sound of running water reached their ears. In the centre of the courtyard water cascaded from a beautiful marble fountain in a spectacular display, and pots of flowering plants stood under the tall trees that shaded everything from the glare of the sun.

A great shout went up, and Captain Al-Khatib himself appeared. He was dressed in a fire of brightly coloured silks and, after salaaming deeply to them, his face broke into a wide grin.

"Greetings and felicitations, Your Majesty, and to you, Maggiore Totus. Welcome to my humble home. May the One fill your lives with the greatest gifts of providence."

Sharley smiled. "May the One pour forth his benevolence on you and your family," he replied correctly, remembering the formality of his earlier meetings with the Captain.

"Ah, I see that you have remembered our language. My people and I are deeply honoured."

Sharley wondered if such extreme politeness could become a little overwhelming, but he smiled manfully and reminded himself that he was genuinely pleased to see the Captain again.

"Come, let us take a little sherbet in the cool of the

mirador." Al-Khatib led them from the courtyard and into a corridor, where a flight of steps led up to a room situated high up on the outside wall of the house. It had wide floors of polished wood, and fretted windows that drastically reduced the glare of the desert sun and at the same time seemed to cool the gentle breezes that playfully rippled the many silk hangings. From one set of windows there was a view of the town as it undulated down the steep hill towards the harbour, and from another, the desert glared and shimmered in many shades of red and gold as it swept away to the horizon under the oppressive heat of the sun.

"From here we can see both the benevolence and the power of the One," said Al-Khatib, waving his hand first at the town and his own fine house and then at the desert. "The most powerful politician and the mightiest warrior need only walk in the land beyond the walls of this town for one hour without coverings or water, to realise their true insignificance."

Sharley nodded, and Maggie murmured in agreement and said, "And yet, that is the very route we must take if we are to complete our mission and meet with His Majesty the Sultan."

"Indeed, yes. But you will be properly equipped and supplied so that you will be able to cross the desert in safety. I myself will be your guide, and we will have an escort of forty armed tribesmen and a caravan of more than twenty pack camels."

"Is the Sultan expecting us?" Sharley asked.

"Yes and no, Your Majesty," Al-Khatib replied with a small smile. "Unofficially he knows that a Prince of the mighty House of Lindenshield is within his Kingdom, and yet *officially* he knows nothing of this. You are simply a private individual travelling the world for pleasure."

"Do the Empire's spies reach as far as the desert, so that even here we have to pretend and hide?" Sharley asked in amazement.

"As far as the desert and sometimes even within our capital," said Al-Khatib.

"Do you know if any are within your lands now?" asked Maggie.

"Always. They try to report our every move. But it has to be admitted that just recently their activities have grown less," said the Captain with a knowing smile. "We believe that a certain Kingdom far to the north, mighty in arms and brave in heart, is keeping them busy."

"Then perhaps we can meet with the Sultan without Bellorum knowing," said Sharley hopefully.

"Perhaps. But if he doesn't know about your visit immediately, he will surely find out about it before you leave."

"Then there's no hope," said Sharley in despair.

Al-Khatib considered him in silence for a moment, then said, "I have no idea why you are making such a journey to meet the Sultan, but even so, perhaps I can make one or two informed guesses and say that the Empire is not the only Government that has spies. Our own people have told us that Bellorum is committing huge resources to his new war with the Icemark. So much so that if something as strange as an army of allies was to be gathered and prepared to strike at him from the south, then there would be little he could do to stop it. Only the sea and his naval allies the Island Buccaneers and the Zephyrs could try and prevent this force from reaching the Icemark. All of this, of course, assumes that such an army could ever be gathered."

"Of course," Maggie agreed. "But if such a thing should ever be proposed to the Sultan, would he, in your opinion, be likely to agree to such a venture?"

"Ah, now, that is the *golden question,* as we say in the Desert Kingdom. In truth, the Sultan is old and wearied by a lifetime of border wars with the Empire. In his youth he was a lion who would have leaped at such a chance to finally destroy the Polypontians, and the hated Bellorum. But now . . ." Al-Khatib shrugged. "Only the One knows the answer."

"So, even now we could be wasting our time, and the Icemark's as good as lost," said Sharley quietly.

"Nothing in diplomacy or warfare is ever certain," said Maggie. "But if we don't try, then there is no hope at all of achieving what we want."

"That is undoubtedly true," said Al-Khatib. "But there is another route to consider. The Sultan has a son, Crown Prince Mekhmet. To give him his full title, Crown Prince Mekhmet Nasrid, Sword of the Desert, Beloved of the One. Now, he has the fire that has long been extinguished in his father. An adventure such as you . . . *may* be proposing would appeal to his sense of honour. Might I therefore suggest that a word with him before approaching his father could be of value?"

"Your advice is invaluable, as ever," said Maggie politely.

Their host bowed his head in reply. "And now, the promised sherbet." He clapped his hands and a young boy hurried in, carrying a tray of goblets and a tall silver jug.

That evening they all went to bed early because Al-Khatib wanted to set out for the capital at dawn. Sharley's bedroom was large and stuffed with rich carpets and hangings. Not only that, but it even had a room attached with its own toilet and a place to bathe! Even Venezzia couldn't equal grandeur on this scale, and in celebration of such luxury Sharley used the bath even though he didn't think he was that dirty.

Sharley woke to a servant opening the shutters on a rose-coloured sky. The sun was rising over the desert, and the surprising cold of the night was already in retreat. The man then laid out some clothes on a chair and, smiling, bowed and left the room. Curious, Sharley crossed to the chair and inspected the garments. They were entirely black and consisted of the loose trousers and shirt like those worn by Al-Khatib's household staff, with the addition of a full-length tunic with long sleeves and a headdress. The weave of the cloth was surprisingly thick considering the heat, but having experienced something of the ferocity of the local weather in his short journey from the harbour, Sharley rightly guessed that the cloth was designed to protect the wearer from the worst effects of the sun.

Another servant then entered and placed a tray of dates, bread and sherbet on a low table. Obviously breakfast was going to be a hurried affair. Taking the hint, Sharley ate, quickly washed, and then dressed in the desert clothing. There was a huge mirror in the corner of the room, one of the largest he'd ever seen, and crossing to it he looked at his reflection. He was amazed by the transformation.

The boy from the barbarian north had disappeared, replaced by someone who looked almost like a young man. He stood as tall as his gammy leg would allow, and his reflection glared arrogantly back. He grinned at the effect and the old Sharley returned, but even the old Sharley looked different: less boyish, and more like someone who could hope to command authority.

He hurried from his room and down a long marble

staircase, then out into the courtyard. Maggie and Al-Khatib were deep in conversation, but they turned as he joined them. Obviously the transformation was more marked than he'd thought, because both men suddenly bowed as though they'd forgotten their manners in the presence of some high official. It was only as they were straightening up that Sharley remembered he *was* a high official, and as Prince Regent and Monarch to the Exiles he was one of the highest.

"My Lord is made for the dress of my people," said Al-Khatib. "Your physical form may have been born in the Icemark, but you have the soul of the desert!"

Maggie said nothing, but he looked thoughtful and secretly pleased. Sharley tried his best to look suitably impressive, but a delighted grin insisted on breaking out and he blushed the colour of sunsets.

They made their way out to the front of the house, where Sharley was startled to see what looked like an army preparing to march to war. There were enormous beasts called camels that were taller than horses but had faces not unlike Oskan's old mule, Jenny. These camels were supposedly riding animals as well as beasts of burden, but Sharley could hardly guess how it was possible to ride a creature that had something like a large hillock on its back. As he watched, the animals' keepers placed frames over the humps, and to these were attached more parcels and goods than it seemed possible for any animal to carry. Then the escort of forty desert warriors arrived. They, too, were riding camels, and sat on saddles that were moulded over the strange humps.

The warriors were a fierce-looking people with scowling faces, and they had long curved swords and daggers hanging from their brightly coloured belts. The noise of the camels roaring in rich, bubbling voices and the warriors and drivers all shouting and calling was indescribable. The smell of the beasts was also pretty overwhelming; it was an odd mixture that reminded Sharley of King Grishmak's cheesy feet steaming in front of the fire and a stable in need of cleaning out. He coughed once or twice, but nobody else seemed to notice it, so he kept his thoughts to himself.

Al-Khatib led Maggie and Sharley over to a group of camels. "These will be our mounts," he said, and nodded to the drivers, who barked short orders to the beasts. They sank slowly to their knees, just as Havoc, Thirrin's warhorse, had done for Sharley that night, so long ago, when he'd ridden to the Great Forest.

"I would advise My Lords to observe as I mount, and try to copy my actions." Al-Khatib placed a foot on the camel's shoulder and hopped into the saddle. At a touch from his riding crop, the animal surged to its feet, back legs first, throwing all its weight forward as Al-Khatib compensated for this by leaning far back in his saddle.

Eager to try, Sharley quickly scrambled into the saddle of his waiting camel. When it rose to its feet he flung himself backwards, and his perspective on the world took on a strange angle as the camel climbed to its full height. The beast was even taller than Havoc, and Sharley felt he was riding a mountain.

When Maggie scrambled into his saddle, things didn't go quite so well. The old scholar rolled to the ground with a thump when the camel stood up. Maggie's second attempt was better, although he only just managed to cling on as the camel rose to its feet. Then, as they made their way to the head of the caravan, poor Maggie bounced around like a pea on a drumskin as he clutched the reins and tried to stop his teeth clicking with every jolt. Sharley found it easier, copying Al-Khatib and swaying in rhythm to his animal's odd way of walking. It wasn't unlike the dip and sway of a small boat, so the months they'd spent at sea came in useful, though it wasn't so much "sea legs" that were needed, but a "desert arse", Sharley thought to himself.

By this time the caravan was almost ready to set off and the escort of desert warriors divided into two parts, half of their number leading the way and the other half acting as a rearguard.

Sharley concentrated on double-checking his equipment and camel. He didn't want to do anything stupid like falling off during the journey. He was having trouble enough trying to look the part of a confident and sophisticated Royal Personage, without anything like that happening!

The camels continued to roar and belch, while their riders screeched at them in return, and small boys scampered about on mysterious errands that required much shouting and waving of arms. Then, at last, Al-Khatib raised his hand and they lurched forward. Within a matter of minutes they had passed through the main gate of the town and were climbing to the brow of the hill outside, where the huge expanse of the desert opened up before them. Sharley stared in wonder. The rocks and boulders surrounding the town soon gave way to fine red sand that stretched away in gracefully undulating dunes to the far horizon.

The caravan paused while further checks were made on water and food supplies, then at last the camels roared and belched their way onwards, their huge plate-like feet thudding down on to the soft sands and carrying them deep into a hostile land of fire.

The sun had risen over the horizon and cast long early-morning shadows back towards the town, but already the temperature was beginning to rise. Many of the caravaneers began to wind lengths of cloth around their faces, leaving only their eyes exposed, as an addition to the protection given by their headdresses. On the advice of Al-Khatib, Sharley and Maggie did the same.

The first day passed under a crushing weight of heat. Sharley had never experienced anything like it. He felt as if every drop of moisture was being drawn from his body by the merciless sun that blazed unendingly in a sky that was no longer blue, but a bright uncompromising white. Every breath of air he took was hot, and he felt it travelling down his windpipe and into his lungs almost as though he'd breathed in boiling water. The land around shimmered and wavered in a heat haze that made it almost impossible to see more than a couple of metres ahead with any accuracy. He couldn't believe that anyone could travel more than a few kilometres in such conditions and live. But the other members of the caravan seemed relaxed and happy, chatting quietly amongst themselves and sometimes even laughing. Sharley couldn't believe it. He was closer to panic than he'd been since the storm at sea that had sunk so many of his fleet.

When night came they made camp, Al-Khatib directing operations as three large tents were pitched for himself and the Royal ambassadors, and a constellation of fires made from dried camel dung were lit. The white heat of the sky cooled to blue and gold, and finally to a rich deep red, before the black and silver of night finally claimed dominion.

Sharley was shocked by the sudden plunge in temperature as the sun dipped below the horizon and the heat of the day drained from the desert. He was glad to huddle close to one of the strong-smelling fires as a cold wind started to blow around them, and he even wrapped a blanket over his thick desert clothing.

The extremes of heat and cold seemed to confuse his body into a muddle of sensations. He ached horribly from the camel saddle and was almost convinced he'd be bow-legged for the rest of his life, but at the same time he shivered, as though with a fever, as his body shook in reaction to the heat it had been subjected to. He also had badly sunburned hands and feet, the only parts that weren't protected by his clothing, and on Al-Khatib's advice he rubbed a milk product he called "yoghurt" into the blisters, which helped to cool them.

Later that night, after supper had revived him slightly, he walked beyond the light of the fires and climbed to the top of a nearby dune. He wanted time to think about this new world he'd entered. He both liked and feared the harsh and unforgiving land, but was sure that if a traveller made only one mistake the desert would kill him. Yet it was beautiful, like a dangerous animal. Perhaps like Tharaman-Thar – beautiful, but at the same time ferocious.

And as for the people – well, the few he'd met were friendly, honourable and hospitable. Sharley had spoken with the sailors on Al-Khatib's ship, the servants who ran his household, and the men who worked on and defended his caravan. All of them had been the epitome of friendliness, but he felt they were also as fierce as the land they lived in. Even now, after such a brief time in the Desert Kingdom, he couldn't imagine a people who would make greater allies for the Icemark. And out of respect for them, their land and their religion he raised his hands in prayer and asked for help in his mission to gain their aid in the war against Bellorum and the Empire.

Sharley didn't know if he, a barbarian from the north, would be answered, but a strange sense of peace settled over him, and he lifted his head and gazed on the beauty of the night. Above him the moonless sky swept in a wide, graceful arc of stars, so densely scattered against the night that he could have been staring into the smithy of heaven as the starry sparks of creation flew from the hammer and anvil of the gods. As he walked back to the camp he stopped to watch as the moon rose over the horizon in full glory. Soon the desert was steeped in a subtle silver light that washed like water over the parched land and pooled at the feet of the great dunes like small lakes.

The next day they began their journey early again, in an attempt to travel as far as possible before the heat became overwhelming. But by nine o'clock temperatures were stifling, and once again Sharley felt as though he was being smothered in the dry furnace of the desert. He'd had to resort to wearing thick woolly socks on his feet and hands to protect them from the sun. He could only hope there'd be plenty of warning if any strangers approached, so at least he'd have some chance of preserving the Royal dignity of the House of Lindenshield. But he still felt dreadful. He was light-headed, and was now suffering from prickly heat, a horrible heat rash of red spots all over his body that itched as though he'd been sitting naked on an ants' nest. He thought he'd go mad as he scratched and raked at his skin, and felt thoroughly sorry for himself.

But Maggie was suffering even more. The few bits of the old scholar's skin that he could see had gone a deep red colour, and he seemed to be having difficulty breathing. Sharley did his best to manoeuvre his camel closer to Maggie's.

"It's a bit warm, isn't it?" he said with masterly understatement, hoping to make the old man laugh.

"No," he answered in short gasping breaths. "It's a lot hot!"

"I think we'll be stopping soon for a meal break. Perhaps you'll feel better then."

Maggie looked at him with a bloodshot eye. "Unless someone's been thoughtful enough to pack a mobile icehouse, I doubt very much that I'll feel any different. In fact, I fear I've been having hallucinations, a sure sign that the brain is overheating, which is hardly surprising."

Sharley looked at him. "What sort of hallucinations?" he asked worriedly.

"They're really quite interesting," the old scholar said, assuming his classroom voice, and taking several gasps for each word. "They take the appearance of young women, modestly dressed in flowing robes and with the most peaceful and calm expressions on their beautiful faces."

"Beautiful young women, eh?" Sharley said, and smiled.

"Young man, at my age, and in my present condition, I can assure you that their attractiveness, or lack thereof, is of little interest to me. Of far more significance is the fact that they appear to be transparent. In fact, as insubstantial as the ever-present heat haze that surrounds us."

"Then that's probably what they are," said Sharley, relieved to find a rational explanation.

"Undoubtedly. But the worrying factor is my brain's insistence in moulding a natural phenomenon into the appearance of young women."

Sharley nodded, trying to appear relaxed, but he was extremely worried. Even as he'd been speaking to him, the old scholar's face had become redder and his gasping worse. Sharley stayed with him for a few minutes making comforting comments, but then he urged his camel forward to catch up with Al-Khatib.

"My Lord need say nothing. I am aware of Maggiore's difficulties," the merchant said as the Prince drew level with him. "I'd hoped that he would be strong enough to cope with the desert conditions, but I'm afraid his great age has made it difficult for him to adapt," he said quietly.

"But he should get used to the heat soon, shouldn't he?" Sharley asked anxiously.

Al-Khatib shrugged. "Perhaps, but in truth it's unlikely. I hope that he will not get worse, but even if his condition doesn't deteriorate, he's already weak enough for it to be dangerous in the desert."

"What can we do?"

"I'm not entirely sure. We have few options, but those we do have I shall lay before you," Al-Khatib said with maddening precision and calm. "Firstly, we could turn back and try to reach the town before his condition deteriorates. Secondly, we could travel on and hope for the best. And lastly, we could leave him at the oasis we should reach by this evening. I have a small but comfortable house there and it is staffed by servants well used to treating maladies of the desert."

Sharley wondered if he should hit him. The choice was glaringly obvious! "Right. Then we settle him at the oasis and go on to the capital without him."

Al-Khatib bowed his head. "As My Lord wishes," he replied smoothly.

Sharley shifted in his saddle, then asked, "Is it . . . is it usual for somebody suffering from the effects of the heat to hallucinate?"

Al-Khatib turned to look directly at him. "Sometimes, though only in the more extreme and dangerous cases."

"I was afraid you'd say that."

"Then am I to infer that Maggiore Totus has experienced such disturbances?"

Sharley nodded miserably.

"May I ask what form these hallucinations take?"

"Young women, dressed in robes, beautiful young women, and he says they're transparent." Al-Khatib stayed silent, and Sharley was afraid it was worse than he thought. "Is that bad?"

"On the contrary, My Lord. Maggiore may have had the great good fortune to have received a visitation from the Blessed Women."

"Blessed Women? Who are they?"

Al-Khatib smiled. "Ah, they are the wealth of the desert and a benison on the land. Without them, no journey would be possible between the few cities and settlements the Desert Kingdom still possesses."

"Marvellous," said Sharley impatiently. "But that doesn't explain who or what they are."

"Forgive me," said Al-Khatib, bowing in the saddle. "I am forgetting the direct nature of the northern mind. Let me put your curiosity at rest. The Blessed Women are spirits bestowed upon the land by the One. It is their appointed role to protect travellers from danger during their journey through the hot lands."

"I see," said Sharley, perfectly willing to accept the existence of such beings. After all, he came from a land that counted werewolves and Vampires among its allies, not to mention giant talking leopards. "And do they do a good job?"

"But of course!" Al-Khatib replied, aghast that he should ask such a thing.

"Then, why do we need an armed escort?"

Once again the merchant bowed in his saddle. "Please forgive my stupidity, My Lord. It is all too easy to assume one shares common knowledge with a stranger. I was forgetting you would not know that the Blessed Women can only protect certain travellers from the dangers of the desert." Al-Khatib saw the puzzlement on Sharley's face and continued smoothly. "Indeed, many people are killed and driven mad by the desert despite the protective presence of the Blessed Women. But exactly why some people are protected by the spirits of good, while others die, must remain one of those mysteries of the One that are beyond our understanding. Some of our greatest theologians and thinkers have questioned such enigmas, but alas, they remain unsolved."

Sharley nodded and rode on in silence while he digested this. He was deeply relieved that Maggie wasn't going mad. After all, what hope would he have of achieving anything without the old scholar's superior brain to guide him? But now something else bothered him besides his deep concern for his beloved teacher. If Maggie didn't make a very quick recovery he, Sharley, would have to go to the Sultan's palace alone, without Maggie's guiding hand and calming influence. How could he possibly cope? He was bound to make a mess of things, and if he didn't forge an alliance with the Desert People, the Icemark would fall to Bellorum and his mad sons!

"Erm . . . will you . . . will you be there when I'm presented to the Sultan?" he asked Al-Khatib nervously.

"I have business to attend to in the palace, but if My Lord wishes, I can be your guide and help in your dealings with the Majlis."

Sharley nodded and smiled gratefully, a sense of relief flooding through him. Now at least there was still a hope that everything would turn out all right.

They stopped briefly for a meal, the warrior escort eating in the saddle with their curved swords drawn and resting on their knees. They were now deep in bandit territory where the likelihood of an attack was very real. Sharley sat with Maggie, then helped the caravaneers to set up an awning to provide shade for the old scholar. Once he was settled, Sharley gave him as much water as he could drink and insisted that he ate some bread, even though he wasn't interested in food at all. After a while Al-Khatib joined them, and the idea of Maggie staying at the oasis was broached.

"Out of the question! I'll be needed at the Majlis; Prince Charlemagne has no experience of such matters of diplomacy and negotiation," was Maggie's immediate and irritable answer, even though it took a laboured breath after each word to say it.

"That is undoubtedly true," Al-Khatib answered courteously. "But it is equally true to say that either you take refuge in my humble home in the comfort of the oasis, or you will die in a matter of days – a week at the very most. The Prince will have to conduct his meetings with the Sultan without your guiding hand, and it would be far better if your absence was due to your convalescence rather than to your death."

This bold statement shocked them into silence. Al-Khatib normally took three carefully polite sentences even to express an opinion about the heat of the desert. The seriousness of

Maggie's condition finally had to be accepted.

"That settles it – you're staying at the oasis. The Icemark can't survive without you," said Sharley firmly. "I want you with me when we go home, and I'd prefer it if you were sitting on a horse next to me, not ashes in a jar en route to your burial mound."

Maggie stared at Sharley. There were times when King Redrought, his plain-speaking grandfather, could be clearly heard in his rough youthful voice. "I really only need a day or two to recover. May I suggest a compromise? I can convalesce at the oasis, then we travel on to the Court of the Sultan *together*."

"No! It's going to be hard enough getting you back to the coast from the oasis in one piece, what with bandits and the heat to worry about. And who knows whether the Blessed Women will look after you, even if you *have* been lucky enough to have been visited by them already."

"Blessed Women! Who are they?"

"Maggie! For a scholar you can be pretty dense at times. You weren't having hallucinations earlier, you were visited by the good spirits of the desert."

"Firstly, I would say that as a scholar my expertise lies in the field of the rational, the scientific, and the generally quantifiable. That said, your news about these 'Blessed Women' is most welcome. If you're right, then I'm not going mad, I have been visited by spirits! What a relief! When one's livelihood depends upon one's intellectual clarity, the thought of insanity is quite disconcerting."

"Yeah, of course," said Sharley dismissively. "But, to get back to my earlier point, you are not coming any further with me. You're as frail and doddery as an old man's granddad, and

I'll need your brain working for me on the journey back to the Icemark. Just accept it, Maggie, you're ready for the knacker's yard and it's up to me to get you home before you pop your clogs!"

The old scholar looked at him in annoyed amazement, then he broke into wheezy laughter, as Sharley had known he would. "I hope you're a little more diplomatic than that when you meet the Sultan!"

"Tell it like it is, that's my motto!" Sharley answered with a wicked grin. Now he reminded Maggie of Oskan.

"You are the sum total of all your influences," the old scholar said fondly.

"Without question," Sharley agreed, a little surprised at the sudden change in Maggie's mood. "But there's also a large helping of me in here too."

"I have never doubted it."

Listening to these strange blunt-speaking people, Al-Khatib realised an agreement had been reached. Maggie would stay at the oasis. He was relieved, but the manner in which the Prince and his Royal Adviser had come to their decision left him feeling almost breathless! Barbarian honesty and plain speech was sometimes refreshing, but the supreme courtesy and formality of the Sultan's Court was beginning to look very attractive indeed.

CHAPTER 16

Scipio Bellorum rode at the head of his army, his false hand of gold resting arrogantly on his hip. It was engraved with battle scenes and studded with precious stones which flashed and sparkled in the sun. This glorious contraption was a result of his single combat with Queen Thirrin during his last invasion of the Icemark. Their long and vicious fight had ended when she hacked his swordhand off at the wrist, and Bellorum would have been killed if his entire cavalry hadn't intervened. But this time there'd be no theatrical duels between the two leaders: Bellorum intended to use precision and calculation to defeat the barbarian queen and her little country. To some extent the General regretted that he'd be denying the world the usual spectacle of a Polypontian war, but he'd been forced to acknowledge that Thirrin and her alliance of monsters were so formidable that they allowed no room for anything but total ruthlessness. The war would be a straight competition between the forces of science and those of abomination – between witchcraft and the modern world.

He was, however, allowing himself one small indulgence, which just might pay off handsomely and end the war before it had even properly begun. Here, right at the beginning of his campaign, he was laying a trap and baiting it with the citizens whose protection Queen Thirrin so misguidedly placed higher than even her own safety.

He'd allowed a refugee column to escape from the last town that had fallen in the South Riding, then he'd waited for it to walk right into his trap. Oh, how gullible are the desperate! thought Bellorum. They had no idea that their escape was essential to his plan to kill their Queen and crush their little country. He would draw her out of her stronghold by threatening these verminous refugees; she was bound to come riding out to the rescue. If he was right – and he was rarely wrong – Queen Thirrin would march straight into the steel jaws of his army and sacrifice herself in an attempt to save them. Such was the folly of compassion!

Behind him, the Polypontian army marched in stony silence. If commanded to do so, they would sing the martial songs of the Empire, but the General was in a pensive mood, so they stared rigidly ahead with only their boots tramping out the rhythm of conquest. Soon, Bellorum would exchange his golden hand for the steel construction he used for combat. Imperial engineers had designed it so that each finger could move separately and might be locked around the hilt of a sword or the haft of a mace. But even without weapon, the steel war-hand was deadly in itself. Bellorum had insisted that the cleverly jointed fingers should have elongated nails as sharp as razors, and in battle he'd been seen to slice open throats and puncture eyeballs with a casual flick of his wrist.

Strangely, his false hand actually itched, and when it was cold, as it always was in this frigid little land, it would ache just like the real one. Bellorum concluded that it was possessed by his living spirit and had, in effect, become a true part of himself. And as for the itching, he was sure a little bathing in fresh warm blood would soon solve that problem. Though, for that, he might have to wait until the barbarian queen arrived. If he himself took part in the fight against the column's rearguard they'd probably break and run, then there'd be no excuses left for not overtaking the refugees and slaughtering them. That would be the end of his plan. With no live bait he would have no trap, and he felt it was important that Octavius and Sulla both experienced action against Thirrin herself as early as possible in the campaign.

He turned in his saddle and beckoned to his sons, who'd been riding several paces behind him.

"My Lord?" they enquired as they drew level.

"You know your dispositions for the coming battle?"

"Of course, Sir," said Sulla. "I have command of the artillery. We'll use grapeshot. Not only is it effective against both cavalry and infantry, but broken and rusty metal is a fitting weapon to use against the barbarian alliance. Rubbish against filth, so to speak."

Bellorum nodded, satisfied. "And yourself, Octavius?"

"I'm commanding the cavalry on the right wing, though my main target will be the enemy centre and Thirrin Lindenshield herself. It'll be interesting to pit my troop against the cavalry of the Icesheets. A stuffed leopard's head will make an interesting banner, don't you think?"

His father smiled coldly. "I do indeed. And have you a particular leopard in mind for this honour?"

"Of course! None other than the so-called 'Thar' will do. He is a magnificent specimen, it has to be said, and his Tharina's skin will make a wonderful saddle blanket."

Bellorum gave a single bark of laughter. "It will at that! Let's see if we can furnish the entire cavalry with leopard-skin trappings."

Medea walked the moonlit corridors like a ghost, her face deathly white and her eyes as deeply shadowed as caves in a chalk cliff. Since she and Oskan had returned home this was her favourite time of the day, when the palace was asleep. Only the guards saw her pass, though the human soldiers avoided her with a shudder once they realised who she was. And the werewolves curled their muzzles as her faint but strangely unpleasant scent – like a fresh corpse, newly washed and perfumed – reached their sensitive nostrils. She particularly liked to visit the haunted parts of the palace, and told herself she had a special link with the phantoms that walked the night. But in truth, even the ghosts avoided her, and chose to watch her pass from the safety of their invisibility before manifesting in agitation once she'd finally gone.

But this night Medea walked for very human reasons: quite simply, she couldn't sleep. Scipio Bellorum was driving north, and even though her mother planned to defend the heartland of the Icemark, hoping that the Empire's armies would break themselves on the rock that was Frostmarris, Medea knew enough of the Imperial plans to know there was a faint chance she'd be drawn out of the capital. Details remained unclear – her Sight had only shown her a broad outline of the Imperial strategy – but she was almost convinced that they'd be effective, with a little help.

As she reached the Great Hall, all the dogs sleeping around the central hearth woke up and slunk off into the shadows. Medea rarely saw anything but the disappearing back of any animal, but tonight she didn't even notice the dogs. She was facing something of a dilemma: what should she do with the information she had on the Empire's plans? Of course, helping her family by telling her mother wasn't an option. She was strongly drawn to actively assist Bellorum and his sons – it would, she thought, be the most interesting course of action.

A distant tangle of voices stopped her dead and she listened as they approached. Laughter and the sounds of scuffling play-fights echoed across the hall. It was all too obviously her idiot twin brothers, Eodred and Cerdic. They'd probably been practising in the training arena with some of the housecarles and werewolves on late watch.

Medea could easily have slipped away, or simply stood in the shadows and watched them pass, but of all her family – apart from Sharley – she reserved her heaviest contempt for the twins. They were stupid, ignorant and loud. She had no intention whatsoever of giving ground before their unthinking male arrogance. She waited silently as they approached on a clamouring wave of giggles and cavernous burps.

The brothers burst into the hall, propelled, it seemed, by a particularly loud fart that made them dissolve into a welter of squeaks and snorts. Leaning weakly against each other they laughed until they could hardly breathe. Finally they regained some control, and wiping their eyes, they continued on their way to bed.

"Eh up, where are all the dogs?" Eodred asked, looking around the dimly lit hall.

"Here, doggies!" Cerdic called raucously into the quiet night. "Come and see your uncles Cerdie and Eddie! I can't believe this, Ed – they're usually huddled round the fire as close as they can get without burning their bums. Where could they have got to?"

"The pigsties perhaps, in search of some rather more intellectually stimulating company." Medea moved out of the shadows, her icy voice cutting the air like a frosted blade.

"Oh, hello, sis," said Cerdic, suppressing a shudder. "Didn't see you there."

"Well, that's not surprising, is it? She's about as hard to see as a shadow in the night's armpit," said Eodred, and both boys began to giggle again.

"Yeah, that's a good 'un. Yeah, no, what about this? She's about as hard to see as a mole on the world's bum!"

"Yeah, great! Or . . . or . . . she's about as hard—"

"I think we've exhausted that particular route of hilarity," Medea interrupted. "Don't you think it's time you both toddled off to bed before your mummy realises you're still awake?"

"And what about you?" Cerdic snapped, stung by her sarcasm. "Why aren't *you* in bed?"

"I keep different hours," she said quietly.

"Yeah, she's a bat," said Eodred. "She probably spends half the night flapping around that tower of hers." Both boys almost began laughing again, but the image seemed too near the truth and they fell silent.

"What I do in the hours of the night is beyond your limited ability to understand," she said icily. "Now step aside."

Eodred automatically moved away, glad to see the back of her. But Cerdic was annoyed by her attitude. Both of his sisters seemed to harbour a need to treat him with contempt, and he wasn't going to stand for it any more. "We may not be as bright as you, but at least people *like* us!"

"If you mean your bumpkin comrades of the shield wall, then I do believe I can survive without their approval."

"Well, yes, I do. But not only them. Mum and Dad don't like you either. None of the family do!"

Medea paused, shocked. It had somehow never occurred to her that her secret hatred for her brothers and sister would be returned. And could it really be true that her father disliked her? Deep, deep down in the fabric of her mind she felt a faint stab of pain.

"You liar!" she snapped at Cerdic, taking him by surprise. He'd scored a point. He'd actually managed to upset the icy cool of his strange sister.

"I'm not lying. Most nights we all sit around the fire telling jokes about you. About how weird you are, how animals avoid you, and how even the werewolves think you smell!"

Eodred frowned. Why was Cerdic saying such things? There were other ways of getting at Medea without telling lies about the family. "Erm, I don't think—"

"Tell her, Eddie. Tell her about how we all laugh!"

He was trapped now. He didn't want to go against Cerdic, and he certainly didn't want to be seen siding with Medea. "Erm . . . yeah. We all laugh about you a bit . . . yeah."

Medea seemed to blaze in the dark before them. A shaft of moonlight from the vents high in the roof mingled with the glow from the embers of the great central fire to cast an odd flickering miasma over her so that she looked like a will-o'-the-wisp, insubstantial and yet threatening.

"I don't believe you! No one would dare to laugh at me!"

"Why not? You're nothing special. Just a weirdo who mumbles in her room and thinks she can make things happen just by thinking about it."

Suddenly, the shadows seemed to clot and knot about her, forming a bank of darkness that beat and pulsated on the air. Medea whispered in a language the boys didn't recognise. They took a step back, realising, for once, that they'd gone too far and were about to suffer as a result. But then the shadows drifted away like wisps of smoke, and she smiled.

Eodred and Cerdic breathed a sigh of relief. They'd got away with it.

"Anyway, we can't stand here gassing with you all night. Some of us are actually doing something to help in this war and we need our sleep."

Medea said nothing as they carefully stepped around her and walked away. By the time they'd reached the far side of the hall they were teasing and laughing again, the clash with their sister already forgotten. But Medea would remember; in fact, the twins had helped her make up her mind. She, too, would allow herself some fun, and for that to happen she would have to *help* her mother make some unfortunate decisions.

The only problem was Oskan. If her father even suspected that a witch was manipulating minds, influencing her mother's allies for her own ends, he'd be after her, and she couldn't risk being caught. She'd have to tread very warily and feign indifference.

But, stronger than any caution, Medea was determined that Cerdic would suffer for what he'd said.

The time of choosing had arrived. A choice had been made, and in the end it had all been surprisingly easy, even trivial. Medea would follow the path that had fascinated her since childhood, and wander through the deep shadows of the Dark.

*   *   *

A few moments after Medea glided from the Great Hall, a werewolf soldier hurried across the echoing space, ignoring the barking wolfhounds and Great Danes that had now returned to the fireside. The werewolf arrived at the door to the Royal apartments and, after a hurried word with the guard, burst through.

Inside, Tharaman-Thar and Krisafitsa-Tharina leaped to their feet and roared, challenging all who disturbed their sleep in front of the huge fire. The werewolf cowered for a moment, then stood straight. "A message has come in from the relay, My Lord."

"Why didn't you say?" Tharaman boomed irritably. "I might have bitten your head off!"

"I don't think we actually gave him a chance to say anything, dear," said Krisafitsa, giving her mate's face a quick wash.

"Who is it? What is it?" A tousle-haired Thirrin had rushed in from her bedchamber, dressed in a white nightgown and incongruously carrying a sword and shield.

"Well, it's obviously Sergeant Throat-biter," said Oskan, wandering in after her, yawning and scratching. "What's the message?"

"The town of Bolby has fallen, My Lord, and a large refugee column is under threat from Bellorum himself. Werewolves and housecarles are fighting a rearguard action, but they'll soon be overwhelmed."

"How many in the column?" Thirrin asked.

"At a rough estimate, over a thousand."

"And how many in the rearguard?"

"After the last action, fifty Wolf-folk and two hundred humans."

"And they're holding Bellorum?" Thirrin asked incredulously.

"Yes, Ma'am. There've been two major engagements and each time the General withdrew."

"Could our venerable enemy be losing his touch?" said Tharaman.

Thirrin shot him a glance. "He'd better not be. I want to kill the man at the height of his powers, not as some senile old wreck."

"You need have no fear of that," said Oskan quietly. "The Sight shows a man as hard and as cunning as he ever was. Age has merely added experience and refined his ruthlessness."

"Then how can a scratch force of two hundred and fifty housecarles and werewolves keep him at bay?" Tharaman asked. "They should have been swept aside on first contact. Unless, of course, Bellorum's force is massively under strength?" He turned questioningly to the werewolf messenger.

"No, My Lord, the Imperial army is of normal size."

"Then it's a trap," said Krisafitsa decisively.

"A trap?" said Thirrin, a puzzled frown on her face.

"Yes. He's trying to draw you out. He knows exactly how strong Frostmarris is as a fortress. And, unlike last time, all of your allies are ready and waiting for him. If he can trick you into leaving your stronghold to fight him in the open, he has a chance to bring all of his power to bear without the need to overcome ditch and rampart."

"You could be right," said Thirrin.

"I'm certain she is," Tharaman boomed. "Let him rampage all over the South Riding – we'll just ignore him until he commits himself to the siege of Frostmarris."

"I'm not sure I can ignore him, Tharaman," Thirrin answered quietly. "My people are in danger. I can't allow more than a thousand refugees to die while I stand idly by."

"But can you knowingly ride into a trap and risk the loss of the Icemark for the sake of a thousand souls, when there are countless thousands more who will suffer because of your action?" Tharaman asked urgently.

"No! Of course she can't!" a voice boomed into the room, followed by King Grishmak who'd been asleep in a different part of the citadel. "It would be madness to ride out now! You sound like a woman possessed – what could possibly be achieved?"

"The saving of a thousand lives," Thirrin answered with quiet stubbornness. "And besides, a trap is only effective if the intended victim isn't aware of it, and I most certainly am! Bellorum's lost any chance of taking me by surprise. I'll ride out with both eyes wide open and my sword sharpened and ready for Polypontian blood!"

"Well said, Thirrin, I'm sure. But you don't even know what he intends to do," said Grishmak heatedly. "I'm sure he isn't just planning to meet you in a straight toe-to-toe slug-out. He knows better than that by now. He must have something else planned, and while we don't know what that is, he still has the advantage."

"I'll prepare for all possibilities," said Thirrin lamely.

"Ha! Then you'd better go ready for a war with your worst nightmares. Because that's the only way you could be prepared enough for him! Who knows what that man's planning? I can't even begin to guess, and neither, I'm sure, can you."

"I'm going, Grishmak, so you might as well get used to the idea!"

"What does Oskan have to say about it?" Krisafitsa's gentle voice asked.

They all turned to look at the warlock, who'd been quietly watching and listening. "Well, first of all, before you ask, the Sight has shown me nothing, so I can offer no practical advice at all. And secondly, let me pose a question: have any of you ever managed to change Thirrin's mind once she's decided to do something?" He listened quietly to the silence. "No, I thought not. The Queen of the Icemark will ride out to defend her people no matter how illogical, no matter how misguided, no matter how dangerous. And there's nothing that anyone or anything can do to stop her. As she says, 'you might as well get used to the idea.'"

Thirrin took his hand and squeezed it.

"I do hope that wasn't a gesture of thanks for my support, Thirrin Lindenshield, because I agree with the rest of them. I think marching off to confront Bellorum is a ridiculous act of misguided chivalry and crass stupidity. But I also know that you're going to do it anyway, so there's no point in trying to oppose you. Now, if you'll all excuse me, I'm going back to bed where I hope to enter the illogical world of dreams away from the barking insanity of my wife."

He walked away, leaving a silence behind him as they absorbed everything he'd said. Thirrin *would* go, with or without them, and if she fell in any battle that Bellorum had planned, then the entire cause was lost. They really had very little choice; marching with her was the only option, whether they agreed with it or not.

Eventually, the silence was filled by Tharaman's voice. "Well, now that we know where we all stand, we'd better start preparations to march."

"I suppose you're right," Grishmak agreed. "Madness has a certain charm to it, don't you think? It's so much simpler; nothing has to be considered, nothing assessed. You just make your decision and do it, no matter what. . ."

Overnight, officers of all species, apart from the Vampires, had been called in and a briefing given. The Hypolitan had at last arrived from their northern province and their Basilea, Iphigenia, her Consort Alexandros, and Thirrin's uncle Olememnon had been hurried into the meeting almost before their soldiers had been properly billeted in the city.

The fact that Olememnon was present at all showed just how many changes had occurred in Hypolitan society since Iphigenia had become Basilea. No man apart from the Consort would have been allowed at any important meeting in their home province, but this Basilea was far more flexible about such things, judging people on their merits rather than their gender. Thirrin greeted her uncle with delight: not only was she pleased to see him, but the Hypolitan army would be a valuable addition to the force she hoped to send south against Bellorum.

It was eventually agreed that half of the available soldiers and warriors would be led out under the joint command of Thirrin and Tharaman-Thar. King Grishmak would command the city and citadel of Frostmarris, while Crown Princess Cressida would act as Regent in her mother's absence.

Cressida was livid! Not only had these decisions been made in her absence – she'd simply been told that morning when she'd woken up – but both of her brothers would be going with the rescue force while she had to sit at home and gain *"valuable experience of administration".*

Cerdic and Eodred didn't try very hard to hide their gloating glee from Cressida. Despite her best efforts, things were still strained between her and the twins, and their thinly disguised joy at her disappointment didn't help matters. She even considered not attending the final meeting before the army set out, but knew her brothers would think they'd scored a point over her if she didn't. And not only that, but she'd miss her opportunity to voice her objections to a plan she believed to be ill-advised, to say the least. As she approached the conference chamber, still unsure of what to do, she squared her shoulders and strode through the door.

The room was loud with the talk and rumour of three species. Thirrin and Tharaman sat at the head of a large table, and Cressida took the empty seat next to them. She was genuinely worried about the operation. After analysing the message about the refugee column, she'd immediately spotted that Bellorum was laying a trap, and she had enough of her mother's spirit to bring up her fears before the meeting had properly started.

"Your Majesty," she began nervously. "Surely, it is obvious to all that the Empire wants to lure *you* and the army into an ambush, and yet it seems you are willing to fulfil your role as victim!"

This was rude even by Cressida's outspoken standards, and Thirrin gritted her teeth before answering with quiet care.

"Thank you, my daughter, for your valuable insight. Though perhaps you should be aware that your elders have already recognised that possibility and taken it into consideration."

Looking back later, Cressida was never really sure where

she found the courage to continue her defiance. Perhaps it was the disappointment of being left out of the first battle of the war between the Royal Army and a force under Bellorum's command. But whatever the reason, it caused quite a stir amongst the allied Commanders. Once the hubbub of shocked voices had died down she continued: "May I enquire if the *considerations* have allowed for the fact that Bellorum is a wily and cunning Commander who must know that we would spot the possibility of a trap in the situation? Obviously if this is the case he still expects us to walk into it, albeit with our eyes firmly open, and he still believes he can beat us."

Thirrin was furious, but managed to control her voice as she answered. "The Crown Princess need have no worries on that score. Though she may believe that her elders are on the threshold of senility, we nonetheless managed to reach exactly the same conclusion, and have decided to mount the rescue mission despite it."

"Then presumably a large reserve force will shadow the army as a fail-safe to whatever Bellorum is planning?"

"There will be a reserve force, yes."

"Of what size?"

"Of sufficient size."

Further down the table Cressida could see the twins smirking and nudging each other. She almost gave up her desperate effort to halt what she considered to be an act of tactical and inexplicable madness there and then, but then she realised that both Cerdic and Eodred were military fools who hadn't the intelligence to understand their danger. It was her duty to save them, and her mother, if she could.

"Ma'am, as acting Regent during your absence, I have the right to know details. How big will the reserve be?"

Thirrin narrowed her eyes as she observed her daughter. Despite her anger she admired her determination and had to admit she was a true scion of the House of Lindenshield. Cressida stood now, eyes blazing, red hair raging like a fire about her head, ready to face down even the Queen to receive her due rights. Eventually Thirrin nodded and said, "One thousand Wolf-folk and one thousand cavalry."

"One thousand leopard and horse cavalry, or horse only?"

"Horse only."

"Ma'am, it's not enough! It's not nearly enough! You will be riding to your deaths, and to the death of the Icemark!"

"Young Lady, you will *not* presume to question the decisions of your elders and, I might add, your betters when it comes to military planning. Both I and Tharaman-Thar believe we're acting correctly in this. Reducing the main force any further by increasing the reserve could endanger the entire operation. You will accept our plan as final!"

"And this is the decision of the entire Council of Allies?" Cressida asked, desperately clutching at straws.

Thirrin drew breath before answering and cast a warning glance about the room. "It was the view of the majority, and has now been accepted by the entire Council, yes."

Cressida saw a gleam of hope. "Then others agreed with my stance? This is madness, or *bewitchment*. Bellorum is waiting like a spider at the centre of his web, and you're happily marching into it!"

"This has all been discussed in the minutest detail. The planners are all agreed. Accept the decision!"

"Madam, I accept only that I cannot stop you. I want it noted that I object in the strongest possible terms and agree with not one article or point of your plan!"

"Duly noted," Thirrin answered quietly. "And duly marked."

A gentle cough broke into the crackling atmosphere. "Now that we've all thoroughly aired our differences, might I suggest that we continue with the rest of the agenda?" said Krisafitsa. "I'm sure that there are points on which we can all agree."

"I'm sure there are, Your Royal Highness," said Cressida. "Tomorrow is Thor's Day and not even a decision of the Council can alter such a certainty, so we must agree on that, I suppose."

Krisafitsa sighed. Sometimes humans would make no effort to heal rifts. She really found it very vexing.

The army was ready to march that same day. Speed was now of the essence, and Thirrin and Tharaman-Thar stood at the head of their force, impatient to be off. There was little ceremony. Oskan embraced Thirrin in the square before the main gate, he whispered something in her ear, and she embraced him again, but he only frowned in return and stumped off, hiding his fears under a veneer of anger. Grishmak howled loud and long, but nobody replied, and the entire force looked unhappy and uncomfortable. Cressida stood on the battlements of the barbican and watched as the gates were thrown wide and the army began to file out. It was mainly cavalry, but the human infantry sat on the backs of their Snow Leopard comrades, who, along with the horses, kept up a rapid trot while the foot soldiers clung grimly on in the interests of speed. They were soon winding along the road that headed out to the Great Forest. There they would join the main highway, and their progress would become even more rapid as Thirrin upped Havoc's pace to a canter.

Cressida had tried to say goodbye to Cerdic and Eodred properly, but they were too excited about going to war, and too pleased that they would be fighting Bellorum while Cressida had to stay at home. She'd had to more or less force them to hug her, and finally she'd left them to their preparations, feeling deeply sad and unwanted.

The main body of the army had disappeared from view before the small reserve force was assembled at the main gates. Cressida had waited to see them off too, and she watched as the werewolves and cavalry units took up their marching positions. Finally, the gates slammed open again and they set off, carefully grading their pace so they wouldn't catch up with the main army. By the time they'd marched over the horizon the afternoon was almost half over, but neither of the hosts would stop for the night. Cressida found herself wondering just how many of the soldiers really believed they'd still be alive by the same time tomorrow.

She sighed and, turning to leave the battlements, bumped into King Grishmak, who'd walked up quietly to join her. He had a strange, distant expression on his face as though he was thinking something through. At last he said, "Your mother was dead set on this battle and for some reason none of us could stand against her, not even Tharaman. None of us *really* wanted it, we just couldn't resist it. Odd, bloody odd." His face screwed into a puzzled frown as he remembered the debates. "But still, the die's cast, as they say. Now, if you want my advice, and I'm sure you don't, you'll keep yourself busy over the next few hours."

"And what exactly do you suggest?" Cressida asked listlessly, her usual boundless energy drained by her struggle to stop the march.

"War games!" Grishmak answered immediately. "Take every soldier and warrior we have left and put them through their paces down on the plain. Olememnon's in charge of the Hypolitan troops that have been left behind and Taradan's commanding the Snow Leopards. Put some fire back into their blood. No soldier likes to think they're expendable in any military operation, even if they're secretly relieved to be left behind. I'll join you myself and take command of the Wolf-folk!"

"War games?" said Cressida uncertainly. "Are you sure?"

"Never been more certain. I wouldn't mention anything to Oskan, though. Just go out on to the plain and start manoeuvres. An army at war games can sometimes march for miles. Who knows how far south we may go and what battle we may find? After all, we could find ourselves working as a reserve for some army or other – a reserve of a proper size, that could react to whatever any old warhorse of a General may have planned, and stop him in his tracks."

Cressida gazed at him, her jaw dropping, then she hugged him and laughed in pure, delighted relief. "You old stoat, I bet you've been planning this since the Queen first decided to march!"

"Could have been, I suppose. Those of us with our heads screwed on have to plan ahead, don't you think? Me and you together, girl, could out-think a whole sack of Bellorums. Now let's get this army marching!"

Once everything had been explained to Taradan and Olememnon they'd both jumped at the chance of marching in support of Thirrin and Tharaman's army. Officially, the order was for all soldiers to report for war games down on the plain of Frostmarris, but rumour of the truth spread through the rank and file faster than ink through blotting paper. A general silence was ordered with strict instructions that no werewolf should relay messages ahead.

This time Cressida looked forward with hope, even though they were taking a terrible risk. If they failed and Bellorum was victorious, then the capital was open to enemy attack. But if the main army was destroyed then the war would be as good as lost anyway.

Within an hour everything was prepared and ready. The Support Army, as they called themselves, travelled very light, bringing nothing but the armour they wore and their weapons. The housecarle and Hypolitan infantry followed the example of their comrades and rode on the Snow Leopards, and the werewolves could run for hours. Speed was everything now, and so was stealth.

They passed through the entrance tunnel of the main gate in silence, only the clop of hooves and the pad of paws echoing in the shadows as they emerged into the light of late afternoon and descended the winding walkway to the plain. The sun was sinking towards the western horizon in a blaze of crimson, throwing vastly elongated shadows back towards the city and burnishing the armour and weapons of the small army. Cressida turned in her saddle and looked back at her command. Everywhere spears and shields blazed, so that she seemed to be leading a host of fire spirits against the forces of the dark.

"We're doing the right thing, aren't we, Grishmak?" she said, suddenly seized by doubt. "We *are* right?"

"Ha! Never righter," the wolfman King boomed. "We're

the secret weapon that no one expects, not even your mother, and if even our Commander-in-Chief doesn't know we're on the way, Bellorum has no chance of guessing!"

Cressida nodded decisively, her confidence completely restored by the bluff power of the werewolf. "We'll hit him so hard he'll be knocked out of his skin!" she said, with such ferocity even Grishmak was impressed.

"That's it, young 'un. Tell it like it is!"

With the night came a new world for Cressida. Even after more than three years training with the cavalry and housecarles, and exploring the Great Forest, she'd never been beyond the walls of the city once the sun had set. It was the time of the Dark-of-the-Moon, when the Goddess was deeply wrapped in her Mystery – witches would call upon her at this time for help against evil, and Magic was most powerful. As Crown Princess, Cressida had always been more interested in the human activities of warfare and government, but now as she rode to her first real battle, her natural and understandable fears drew her to pray for help in the coming struggle. She looked at the wide sky, studded and littered with a cascade of stars as though some giant hand had scattered a handful of silver seeds over a black field, and tears rolled down her cheeks.

"If my eyes are to be closed forever on such beauty, I ask the Great Goddess to place my soul amongst the lanterns of the night so I may look on the home I have loved for ever."

"You'd be the brightest of the stars if that were to happen, and I for one would use you as my guide through the darkest of nights," said Grishmak's voice beside her.

She gasped aloud, taken by surprise. "You weren't

supposed to hear that. It's bad luck to pray in that way before a battle, I'm told."

"Who by? None of us forgets the gods before a fight, and those who say they do are either lying or stupid – probably both," the wolfman King said gruffly. "But you've no need to worry, my Princess – you've the blood of mighty warriors in your veins, and my knotted old guts tell me you'll not be spilling any of it in tomorrow's battle, though you'll certainly cause it to pour from the veins of many another."

As he spoke, a shooting star blazed a sudden scorching path across the sky, and Grishmak risked a short howl in greeting. "There, and on the right too! A star-dragon to greet you, My Lady – the luckiest of omens before your first fight! The Goddess is with you. Bellorum had better watch out!"

Cressida grinned in elation, the weight of her fears falling away. She was her mother's daughter, a warrior and leader of hosts. She was as ready as she'd ever be for her first battle.

Later that night, her uncle Olememnon asked Taradan, the Snow Leopard he was riding, to draw closer to Cressida's horse. "Hello, Your Highness," he greeted her in his deep, quietly powerful voice, with a teasing reference to her position as Regent. "It's all been a bit hectic today, hasn't it? No sooner do the Hypolitan arrive, than we're off on the road again with the promise of a punch-up at the end of it."

"Oh, I'm sorry, Uncle Ollie, you must be exhausted."

"No, not a bit of it. We took it easy on the way to Frostmarris, so we're as fresh as daisies, and in my case even prettier."

Cressida grinned. The veteran warrior was as creased and lined as an old leather armchair, and sometime during his many wars he'd picked up a broken nose that had set at a funny angle, making him look more like one of Grishmak's werewolves than her mother's much-loved uncle.

"Well, after hours of riding Taradan, you certainly don't smell like a daisy."

"He most certainly does not," Taradan agreed. "More like the Royal stables, actually."

Olememnon laughed. "Secret weapon of mine – no one can get near me when I smell like this. Better than any shield. And talking of which, what's the strategy for tomorrow?"

Cressida looked worried. "I've no idea, Uncle Ollie. We'll just have to remain flexible until we know what's happening."

"Fair enough, don't you think, Taradan?"

"Certainly. Let's just see how the land lies, so to speak, then hit them at their weakest point. Always the best way."

"What's that?" boomed Grishmak, as he made his way back to the head of the column after making an inspection.

"The tactics for tomorrow," Olememnon explained. "Hit them hard."

"Oh, absolutely. Hit them hard and keep hitting them hard until they bugger off!"

"Right," said Cressida brightly. "That's decided, then."

By the time the sun came up in a glory of crimson and gold, Thirrin and the main army were marching in battle formation. Werewolf scouts were ranging ahead and sending reports back every few minutes, but so far there were no signs of either the refugee column or the Imperial army.

But then, as the sun climbed to its mid-morning position, a scout came running to deliver a message. Bellorum had been spotted, and they were too close now to risk sending a vocal warning for fear of giving away the presence of the rescue force before they were ready.

The werewolf scout forced her way through the press of the Queen's Ukpik bodyguards and curtsied low. Thirrin had never got used to the sight of the huge creatures performing such graceful gestures, but she kept her face carefully neutral as she nodded her acknowledgement. "Warrior Flesh-tearer, give your report."

"Your Majesty, the refugee column is two miles ahead. They've just entered the Asgaard Cut and Bellorum is pressing them close."

"The rearguard?"

"All but destroyed. Twenty housecarles and ten werewolves are scrambling away as best they can, but in good order still."

"The Asgaard Cut. If I remember the maps correctly, isn't that the narrow valley the Great Road passes through before it reaches the Central Plain?" asked Tharaman-Thar, idly flexing his claws.

"That's right, two miles long and half a mile wide at the base. It's very steep-sided and the slopes are covered in trees and heavy scrub."

"A risky battlefield, then. Whoever commands the wooded slopes is almost guaranteed victory," said Krisafitsa quietly. "Anything could be hidden amongst the trees."

"Yes, but fortunately Bellorum is as new to the ground as we are," said Thirrin. "Now begins the race to take the better positions!" Standing in her stirrups she drew her sword and gave the order to advance, and the army leaped forward in a controlled gallop. It was imperative to reach the valley before Bellorum could survey the area in too much detail and seize the best ground.

Within minutes the entrance to the valley came into view, and Thirrin realised her force would have the advantage. They were at the top of a steep gradient with Bellorum at the bottom; the high ground was theirs!

On they swept like an unstoppable sea, galloping into the valley and on down the steeply sloping land. Far ahead at the southern entrance to the vale Thirrin could clearly see the refugee column coming towards them, and behind it was Bellorum's army! The allies now fanned out into a fighting front with the cavalry of horse and Snow Leopard in the centre and werewolves dividing themselves between the left and right flanks. Quickly, the infantry climbed down from the backs of their leopard comrades and formed up into their phalanxes, ready to sweep round on the left and right wings in a pincer movement with the werewolves.

Taking up a position close to his mother, Prince Eodred drew his sword and waited for orders. Scanning the infantry as they hurried by to their positions, he at last caught sight of his twin brother.

"Cerdic!" he called. "Cerdic, give them steel and fire!"

His brother grinned and raised his axe in greeting. "You too, steel and fire *and* a bit of horse and hoof!"

Thirrin, who'd been absorbed in assessing the oncoming army, suddenly remembered her sons as she heard their voices, and turned to watch them as they laughed and joked excitedly. She felt oddly detached from them, almost as if they were people she'd known long ago and in a different life. They were obviously feeling the same, because at that moment they seemed to remember her presence and turned to look at her. Both smiled shyly, even uncertainly. Thirrin nodded as a terrible fear for them suddenly threatened to overwhelm her with a rush that was almost violent in its power. She gasped aloud. Her boys could be killed!

A terrible screeching roar then crashed into the air, and she swung round to see Bellorum's army driving into the refugee column. Immediately, Thirrin stood in her stirrups. "The enemy is upon us! They kill our children, they burn our houses! Blood! Blast! And Fire! Blood! Blast! And Fire!"

With a roar, the warriors of all three species took up the war cry.

"Blood! Blast! And Fire! Blood! Blast! And Fire!"

And as one body they swept forward in a smashing charge.

The refugees scattered, throwing themselves clear of the two armies, and scrambled up the steep sides of the valley, leaving behind a broken litter of dead.

At the head of his force Bellorum smiled. He held up his steel war-hand and his troops stamped to a halt. The General watched Thirrin and the cream of her allies thundering down towards him. "Well, how very kind of you, my dear," he murmured. "You've really been most obliging." Slowly, he drew his sword and held it aloft, then chopped it viciously downwards.

All along the densely wooded sides of the valley hundreds of hidden cannon thundered, firing broken chains, rock and shattered metal of grapeshot that ripped into Thirrin's army. Hundreds fell in a welter of blood and torn bodies, the war cries drowned out by the screams of the hideously wounded.

Too late, Thirrin knew her mistake. Ambush! And they couldn't retreat; they'd come too far and would be wiped out by volley after volley of cannon fire. The only option was to charge onwards and hit Bellorum with all they had left. Her rage burst from her lungs in a wordless shout that rose over her soldiers like a banner, and back crashed the reply in a roar that echoed over the valley.

On they charged as a meticulously ordered sequence of cannon spewed shot into their passing ranks. But now the Commanders of the Icemark infantry on both flanks turned aside and advanced up the sides of the valley to attack the gun emplacements. Werewolf, housecarle and Hypolitan infantry rolled forward at a swinging trot as their disciplined ranks were ripped apart by the shattering volleys of grapeshot. But nearer and ever nearer they drew to the gun crews, who were working frantically to destroy the raging and howling warriors.

Bellorum watched and waited for his moment. He knew the guns would eventually be silenced, but they were expendable as long as he killed the barbarian Queen. His sons were in position, waiting for his signal.

Still the cannon roared, slicing into cavalry and infantry alike and bringing down hundreds of allied soldiers. Thirrin gritted her teeth and looked to right and left. Tharaman-Thar and Krisafitsa-Tharina were still with her, but many leopards had fallen, as had troopers of the human cavalry. Her body-guard of Ukpik werewolves were also still with her, their white pelts splattered with blood and gore, but they seemed undaunted, howling and raging as they fought on. Beside her, the Icemark's standard-bearer was slumped in his saddle, bleeding heavily from multiple wounds. But another trooper drew close and seized the standard of the cavalry so that the galloping horse and leopard continued to stream on in the wind of their speed.

Again, the cannon roared and more fell in bloody explosions of flailing limbs and screaming agony. But at last, the infantry reached the first emplacements and hacked and chopped, ripped and tore at the gun crews. Ranks of musketeers positioned to protect the cannon fired into the advancing infantry, but were quickly overwhelmed by the raging warriors.

Cerdic led his first command with a terrible raging pride. But deep down, under the frenzy of battle he was puzzled. There was nothing glorious in the horrible deaths all round him. Werewolves and housecarles he'd known since he was a little boy had been torn apart by rusty lumps of metal, the lucky ones dying quickly, the others screeching and yelping with terrible, unimaginable pain as their broken, mutilated bodies sank to the ground. Cerdic had even taken time to chop the head off one old comrade who was mortally wounded and screaming in agony. He'd also waited while a werewolf with a gaping stomach wound positioned the tip of his dagger exactly over her heart so that when he stabbed she'd certainly die.

He stood briefly on the barrel of a captured cannon waving his soldiers on, before he leaped down into the press and hacked at the Imperial troops who fought on defending the next rank of cannon that were still pouring grapeshot into the charging cavalry. Fighting furiously alongside his troops, he failed to notice an Imperial officer at his feet. The man, in the regalia of high office, levelled his pistol and fired at point-blank range into Cerdic's guts.

Cerdic was knocked off his feet.

Sulla Bellorum rose to stand over him, smiled and saluted. "Scion of the House of Lindenshield, I do believe," he said. The intelligence gathered by his Polypontian spies had been excellent. "Eodred, or is it Cerdic? But, whichever, you're most certainly dead." He stood, savouring the pure joy of inflicting pain and death. Then he smiled, saluted again, and withdrew to his hard-pressed artillery lines, where he mounted his horse and galloped away, leaving his soldiers to their fate.

Cerdic tried to rise to his feet and give chase, but an icy fire of pain burst in his belly and he doubled up, screaming. Blood spat and coughed from his mouth, and he bowed forward trying to breathe. Suddenly, a werewolf was kneeling beside him, supporting his head and holding a water bottle to his mouth. There must have been some drug in the water, because miraculously the pain began to dull and he managed to speak.

"I didn't see him, Moon-howler. He came from nowhere. How bad is it?"

The werewolf gently searched the wound. "Very bad, my friend. Gut wound, the worst."

"Any chance I'll live to see the morning?"

The creature's eyes turned away. "None, My Lord."

Cerdic started to cry as he realised he'd never again see any of those he loved. "Tell them I ended well. All the wounds in front, none in my back . . . didn't run away."

Moon-howler nodded, and then, kissing him, broke his neck.

Down in the valley Thirrin and her cavalry charged on. Their numbers had been reduced by almost half and still the cannon fired, though she was aware that they were beginning to fall silent in some areas. All around her were screams and death. She'd last seen the Hypolitan Basilea when her horse literally broke apart beneath her, and she could only pray that she was safe. The ranks had continued to close up as their numbers were reduced and she signalled that they should move apart, so presenting the cannon with a more scattered target.

Ahead she could see Bellorum's army quietly waiting, then she saw his arm chop down. She hoped and prayed that the cannon would fall silent, but nothing happened. How many would be left to hit the General and his army? Through the frenzy and the horror of the charge, she finally realised this was her last battle and the war was all but over. So be it, she thought. None could say the Alliance didn't know how to die!

Then with the suddenness of a door closing on a howling wind, the guns stopped firing. Faintly, she could hear ragged cheers from the wooded slopes, and realised that her infantry had finally captured the artillery batteries. She stood in her stirrups and looked about her. They were still a force, but only just. How could they fight on?

Tharaman-Thar raised his huge head and roared, and immediately his warriors answered. "Now we have them, my people! Now they will feel our claw and steel!" And he roared again. Thirrin raised her sword and gave the note for the battle paean, and all took it up, leopard and human and werewolf guard. Closing ranks, they thundered down on Bellorum's position. The General himself, seeing that his enemy had survived the cannon, gave the order to charge, and his army leaped forward while he quietly watched from the side with his staff officers.

With a shuddering clash the two forces met, the Icemark cavalry driving deep into the opposing ranks. Human, Snow Leopard and werewolf slashed and bit, clawed and stabbed at the soldiers before and around them, but they were heavily outnumbered and their charge slowly lost momentum. Now the Imperial army surrounded them, and the allies were in danger of being overwhelmed by the hugely superior numbers, but Thirrin rallied her cavalry and, turning about, they desperately fought their way clear until, at last, the enemy ranks began to thin and with a final heave the Icemark army was free, and they galloped back towards the head of the valley. But Bellorum didn't give chase. Thirrin couldn't believe it; perhaps they could escape after all. But then she looked ahead.

Rolling down the valley like a dark flood was a massive new force, and at its head rode Sulla Bellorum. The General's son had arrived in answer to his father's signal. The door of the cage was closed.

Thirrin reined to a halt and sat quietly watching as the Imperial trap was finally sprung. She slumped in her saddle. "Oh my brave, brave warriors, I have failed you. A madness was in my eyes and I led you into doom. Today we die, and with us dies the Icemark."

Krisafitsa-Tharina nuzzled her. "My dear Thirrin, you've ruled with skill and dignity, and you've never deserted your people. What more can a nation ask? The Great Creator has made its choice and we must play our part. So come, let's meet with our allotted end and feel no sorrow for what might have been; the die is cast and our time is here."

"But even now, don't presume to know what the Great Creator has planned," said Tharaman-Thar. "The day is not yet over, and neither is the battle."

Thirrin smiled at the unquenchable optimism of the Snow Leopard, and despite the desperate circumstances she hugged him, drawing new strength from the deep rumbling purr she felt inside his massive chest.

She then stood away and resumed her role as Queen. "The cavalry will dismount. Bugler, recall the infantry, all who can reach us. Here, we will stand in a shield wall and prepare for whatever end awaits us. Close ranks then, my people, and prepare to receive unwanted guests!"

The horses were tethered in the centre while the bugler sounded recall and the infantry began to stream down from the heights to join the last stand. The banner of the cavalry was raised alongside that of the Icemark and the Hypolitan, and a strange silence settled as the General himself advanced. With him rode Octavius, scanning the beleaguered enemy before him, a small smile playing around his lips.

The barbarian Queen's army was still of a formidable size, but even so, she was heavily outnumbered and her end was inevitable. Octavius gave the order for the cannon to be brought down from the valley sides and turned on the Icemark's pathetic shield wall. Now that Thirrin's infantry had rejoined their Queen the huge guns were once again under the Empire's control.

"Another small mistake, my dear," Scipio said quietly, as though his enemy could hear him. "If your soldiers had been trained in modern warfare, they could have turned the cannon against me, and I would have been the one standing at bay, preparing for a less than glorious death."

"Let me lead the next charge against her, Father," said Octavius, desperate to test his cavalry against her combined force of horse and Snow Leopard.

"I think not," Bellorum answered calmly. "The barbarian shield wall will be a difficult nut to crack. I expect it'll take a barrage from the artillery to finally bring them down."

"Do you doubt my ability as a cavalry, Commander?" Octavius demanded angrily.

"Not in the least; but as a general I do not doubt my enemy's ability either," his father said, and held his son's eye in an icy gaze. "I will not risk your life in a vainglorious gesture. You will obey my order and rejoin your men to watch the Icemark's final destruction at the behest of cannon and fire."

Scipio Bellorum had decided to stop the unnecessary waste of his soldiers' lives on the rabble freak show that was the Icemark army. The artillery would make an end of the abominations that were preparing to make their last stand. This would be the end of all resistance to the Imperial will.

Thirrin realised too late that Bellorum had sent troops to recover the cannon, and almost screamed aloud with frustration. Would nothing go right during this expedition? Truly it seemed bewitched! Thirrin could have wept with frustrated rage. There was nothing she or anyone could do to prevent the inevitable massacre.

Once again the strange waiting silence settled over the battlefield as Bellorum and his sons sat and gloated over their trapped foe and relished the coming bloodbath. But then a distant voice slowly unfolded itself on the still air, as clear as a chiming bell, and as fierce as a hunting hawk:

"The enemy is upon us! They kill our children, they burn our houses! Blood! Blast! And Fire! Blood! Blast! And Fire!"

The soldiers and warriors behind the shield wall held their breath, hardly daring to hope. But Thirrin grasped at Tharaman and strained to listen. "Cressida? It *is*! It's Cressida! Tharaman, it's Cressida!" But before anyone could react, a huge booming reply to the lonely voice crashed into the air.

"Blood! Blast! And Fire! Blood! Blast! And Fire!"

And an army swarmed over the brow of the hill. At its head rode Cressida, and beside her strode King Grishmak and Taradan.

"Our Queen is in danger and our army besieged. Drive forth the hated enemy! Rip their flesh and drink their blood! Long live the Icemark! Long live the Alliance!" And with a roar the army poured down the hill like an avalanche.

Bellorum raged as he saw his victory about to slip away, but he quickly regained his self-control and spat out orders that sent regiments of pikemen to the rear to dig their long spears into the ground. But it was too late. The force of the charge was unstoppable, and the pike regiments' barrier of steel broke under the momentum and was swept aside.

The rage and roar of battle filled Cressida's senses. All chance of her feeling fear had been ripped away in the first moment of the charge, and now, as she hacked and thrust at the enemy, the blood of her warrior heritage raged and sang through her veins.

Cressida's army of allies formed into a gigantic wedge, a fearsome spearhead with the Crown Princess and Grishmak as its glittering point, driving deep into the Imperial ranks, killing and smashing all before it.

Thirrin screamed aloud for joy, and as the Thar lowered his mighty form, she leaped on to his back, an example followed by all the human cavalry troopers as they scrambled astride their leopard comrades.

"Forward now, my people!" she shouted. "Forward the Alliance and destroy the hated invader!"

The coughing bark of the Snow Leopard challenge, the howl of the werewolves and the battle paean of the human soldiers rose in a raucous cacophony as they too drove into the ranks of the Imperial army. Bellorum and his sons fought with frenzy. The General's steel war-hand ran red with blood, as did the sword he wielded in his left hand, but he knew the tide was flowing strongly against him. Once again, the barbarian Queen of the Icemark looked like denying him the sweetness of her death! How many more times would she survive his carefully laid plans? "Not for much longer!" he screamed aloud in frustration. "I'll crush you, and your army of ragged mongrels! I'll rip the skin from your flesh and raise it as a banner before my regiments!"

But, after a few more despairing minutes, Bellorum was forced to admit defeat. He turned his horse and fled from the field, knowing his sons, too, would judge this the right moment to make their escape.

The Polypontian forces fought on with superb discipline, but as the rumour that the Commanders had left them spread through the army, they despaired and fled, their ranks breaking apart like dead leaves before a sweeping wind.

Now began the deadly pursuit, and the Alliance army cut thousands down as they ran, leaving the dead heaped in mounds over a distance of more than ten miles. But at last, the victorious soldiers were exhausted and turned wearily back to the valley.

There, the Queen and Crown Princess finally met. Thirrin climbed down from Tharaman-Thar's back and waited while Cressida dismounted. The two women looked at each other, then Thirrin stepped forward and hugged her daughter fiercely.

"I won't forget this, Cressida. Your action has saved the Icemark, the army, and my life!" She stepped back, tears of pride running down her face, and turned to the army of allies.

"Behold Cressida Striking Eagle, Crown Princess of the Icemark!"

All the soldiers cheered her fighting epithet, earned by this, her first action. At first, relief and elation filled Cressida to the brim, but slowly the horror of the fighting returned, and her memory's eye recalled the first Polypontian she'd killed, his throat spitted by her sword. A shivering, shocked reaction set in, and she stood gasping before the army until her mother, recognising the symptoms, folded her in a protective hug and guided her away from the prying eyes.

CHAPTER 17

After only a few days back in the desert, the oasis already seemed part of the dim and distant past. Sharley tried to conjure up images of Al-Khatib's beautiful home, and the natural pools of water lined with date palms and lush with exotic foliage and brilliant flowers, but all seemed a dream as the hot desert wind blew sand into his eyes and his camel broke wind like a storm in the mountains.

Maggie had shown signs of recovery from his terrible heat-stroke within an hour of being installed in the coolest, most tranquil room of the house, deep in the basement where jars of sherbet stood chilling in vats of water, and musicians played gently in concealed alcoves. Sharley and the caravan had rested for two days in the oasis before resuming their journey to the capital of the Desert Kingdom, leaving Maggie to build up his strength ready for the trip back to the coast when they returned.

They were following the ancient caravan route from the coastal port to the capital city of Haifolex, and when they were within two days' ride of the city, the towering importance of Sharley's mission began to weigh heavily on him. Without

Maggie to guide and advise him he was in a complete state of panic. It was all well and good having Al-Khatib as a sponsor, but Sharley *knew* Maggie. He was almost part of his family, like an old and slightly dotty uncle. And right now, Sharley would have given almost anything to hold the old scholar's hand again, as he had when he was a little boy. But Maggie was resting in the oasis house and Sharley would just have to manage without him.

He sank into a moody silence, mulling over his fears. But eventually, the rhythmic rocking of his camel lulled his mind and he looked out over the strange and beautiful land of the desert, seeking peace in the slow undulations of the dunes. The light was dramatically intense, searing his eyes to watery blinking as he looked at the white sky and the textured shimmering of the heat haze. But gradually, he became aware of an odd blue tinge to the air around him. He blinked, and rubbed his eyes in case they'd been affected by the heat, but when he opened them again the blue light was still there.

Quickly he glanced about to see if anyone else had noticed the change in the atmosphere, but no one seemed aware of any difference. Sharley could only assume that it was some fairly common phenomenon of the desert – like the dust-devils and sandstorms he'd heard about.

He'd almost convinced himself of this when he began to hear the faint sound of singing. It was strangely beautiful and wistful like a sad love song, but at the same time joyous and mischievous, like a children's playtime song.

The effect it had on Sharley was extraordinary. Tears ran down his cheeks as a terrible sense of homesickness crushed him under a merciless weight. But at the same time he was filled with a childlike happiness and couldn't help grinning and giggling. He thought he must be going mad, perhaps finally driven to insanity by heatstroke, but then all such thoughts fled from his mind as the surrounding heat haze slowly moulded and shaped itself into a semblance of transparent human forms.

He found himself gazing on a group of twenty or so beautiful young women, all modestly draped in flowing robes. He gasped aloud and stared about wildly, but still nobody else in the caravan seemed to have noticed anything amiss.

"Do not be afraid, Charlemagne Athelstan Redrought Strong-in-the-Arm Lindenshield, we mean neither yourself nor your cause any harm," said one of the beautiful women who moved a little ahead of the group, keeping perfect pace with his camel. "We have been sent to guard you and your mission from the dangers of the desert."

Sharley's mouth hung open, but he shut it with a snap when it suddenly occurred to him to ask, "Who are you? And if you have been sent, then who did the sending?"

"We are the Blessed Women, and it is our appointed task to protect you during your journeys within our lands."

Sharley's eyes widened. So these were the famous Blessed Women – the ones who had appeared to Maggie when he was ill. But they still hadn't told him who'd sent them, or why, so he asked again. The woman gave him a smile of such gentle peace, he seemed to fill with the knowledge that there was no need to know such things, and that if he cared to search his mind he would probably find he already knew the answer anyway.

"Be not concerned, Charlemagne. Only know that for as long as you dwell within the borders of the Desert Kingdom, no harm will come to you." The woman's gentle smile broadened, and she added, "Know also that at the time of your greatest need, the love you feel for another will call our power across the seas, even to the northernmost limits of the lands, and all will be made well."

Sharley was overwhelmed with such a sense of deep and pure emotion, he covered his face and wept.

But when he looked up again, the Blessed Women had disappeared, and the caravan was jogging along as though nothing had happened. He wiped his eyes and mulled over what had happened, but try as he might, his bewilderment refused to become scepticism, and eventually he shrugged and smiled to himself. He could only adopt the attitude of the Desert People themselves, and accept all that had happened as the "will of the One".

He began to look about himself again, and as he allowed the harsh reality of the desert to reassert itself, the strange visitation he'd experienced began to take on the quality of a dream.

As the day wore on he noticed that the sandy track they'd been following had slowly, almost imperceptibly, become flagstones, edged with what looked like marble. Perhaps the track had all been made of stones and they'd simply emerged here from beneath the desert dunes. But the fact that the paving was clear of sand now meant that someone, or more likely a group of someones, must actually sweep it regularly. An amazing thought, especially as they were still miles from the city.

That night when they made camp, Sharley questioned Al-Khatib about palace etiquette. He already knew that if any rules of social nicety were broken no allowances were made, even for foreigners. Al-Khatib's instruction calmed most of Sharley's fears, although he did think prostrating oneself before the Sultan was a little excessive. Even the Polypontian Emperor only asked you to bend one knee and declare your staggering inferiority when you came into his presence. But every Royal Court had its little ways, and at least Crown Prince Mekhmet sounded a little more human. To greet him, you were only expected to fall to your knees and bend your head. With the problems of polite behaviour and etiquette dealt with, all he had to worry about now was the very real possibility of his complete and utter failure as an ambassador!

The caravan was expected to arrive in the capital by noon the next day, provided they set out early enough. So everyone, including drovers, camel boys, merchants and warrior guards – apart from those on watch – bedded down for the night as soon as the evening meal was finished. Sharley lay in his tent looking out of the open flap at the stars arcing over the deeply black, moonless sky. Slowly, his eyelids closed on his worries . . . and the distant sound of singing voices wove a pattern of peace over the sleeping camp.

In the middle of the following day, some of the drovers suddenly sent up a cry. Al-Khatib drew his camel alongside Sharley's and pointed towards a city far away on the horizon. "We are almost there, Your Highness. Behold Haifolex, the 'jewel of the Desert'. We should be entering the Golden Gates in a few hours, and then your embassy can truly begin."

Sharley's stomach lurched and rolled enormously, and he was almost sick with nerves. He fought to control himself, thinking that depositing his breakfast in the sands would hardly be the best of omens for his mission.

As the day wore on, the distant cityscape became more substantial and solid, and Sharley became more and more miserable as he gazed at its towering walls. It was worse than going to see the tooth doctor, but for once he thought he might actually prefer the agony of that particular gentleman's surgery than having to face the Sultan in the Royal Palace of the Desert People!

Eventually, the main gate came into view, glinting and glittering in the sunlight as though it was made of metal. As they drew closer, Sharley realised that the gates and their surrounding frame were indeed sheathed in what looked like highly polished brass.

"Behold, the Golden Gates!" Al-Khatib boomed beside him, making him jump.

"Golden! You mean they're actually made of—"

"Yes, the finest cedar wood encased in pure gold."

Sharley's mouth gaped, until a particularly fat bluebottle flew into it and he gagged. "But that would have cost . . . would have cost—"

"A kingdom's income for an entire year."

"What an incredible waste of money," Sharley blurted out, before he could stop himself.

Al-Khatib looked at him sharply. "So thought and said many others, before the Sultan of the day removed their heads from their shoulders. But that was in less enlightened times. Nonetheless, I advise My Young Lord to keep such thoughts to himself while we enjoy the hospitality of the present ruler."

Sharley blushed deep crimson, and nodded in silence. He really must learn to think first, and speak a long time afterwards.

They were now close enough to the walls to see that they were made of finely dressed stone, rising to truly dizzying heights and topped with battlements that were faced with blue-glazed bricks. This beautiful extravagance was extended to the entire fabric of the gatehouse and its surrounds. The Desert Kingdom must have been fabulously wealthy at one time and could probably have afforded a large and brilliantly equipped army. Little wonder that Scipio Bellorum had decided to strike at its wealth rather than its military strength.

The Golden Gates stood wide open as a constant stream of traffic headed into the city. "We have been fated to arrive in Haifolex on market day when the bazaar is at its most busy," said Al-Khatib with a philosophical lift of his shoulders. "Which is fortunate for the mercantile aspect of our journey, but not for our diplomatic mission."

"Will it delay our audience with the Sultan?" asked Sharley.

"Perhaps," Al-Khatib replied. "But that may work to our advantage." He went on to explain. "In a society whose economy is under siege, those who can alleviate the problem will always be treated like kings; therefore the Sultan must entertain the merchants lavishly and flatter their abilities above their true worth. But Crown Prince Mekhmet is proud, and he will not join his father at these banquets. So it is, then, that he is available to those who know how to reach him."

"What's he like?" Sharley asked, deeply curious about the man whose name had been an invocation of power, brought out like an incantation by his guide throughout their journey.

"What's he like?" Al-Khatib repeated, in a tone that suggested this was the strangest of questions to ask about a member of the Royal Family. "He . . . he's the desert storm, he's the raging sun at midday . . . he's the great hope of our—"

"Yes, yes," Sharley interrupted impatiently. "But what's he *like*? How tall is he? What does he like doing in his free time? What are his interests? Is he funny?"

"*Funny?*" Al-Khatib roared in amazement.

"Yes, does he like a laugh? Is he good-tempered? Is he . . . *nice?*"

The older man looked as if he'd swallowed his tongue. "Well . . . I believe His Majesty enjoys riding, and he trains constantly with the Weapons Master—"

"Of course he does," said Sharley impatiently. "But you're not telling me anything about *him*. Look, let me make it easier. How tall is he?"

"I suppose a little taller than yourself. Just a little."

"Small, then," said Sharley, amazed that this man with a name of power wasn't a giant. "And is he good-tempered?"

"He has the perfect temperament for one of the Lords of Men: he is quick to anger, but even quicker to forgive. Yea, he is eager to teach us the error of our ways."

Sharley thought he sounded just like Cressida: pompous, arrogant and bossy. He could only hope that he also had his sister's saving graces: kindness, compassion and a genuine concern for other people and their needs. "And how old is he?"

"The same age as yourself."

"*What?*" Sharley almost fell off his camel. "The same age as me! I thought he was a man!"

"And so he is by the tenets of our society, but not yet a fully grown man."

"The same age as me?" Sharley repeated incredulously.

"Yes. Though, to be precise, exactly a week younger," said Al-Khatib, who clearly had unknown sources of information.

"A week younger!"

"My Lord is beginning to sound like one of the talking birds of Arifica; perhaps it would be wise for him to close his mouth before a swarm of flies decides to use it as a latrine."

"Yes, but he's only a boy . . . just like me!"

"I would say rather that both yourself and Crown Prince Mekhmet are young men, on the very threshold of manhood."

A commotion at the head of the caravan distracted Al-Khatib, and he rode off to sort out an argument that had broken out between a camel driver and the owner of a large cart.

Sharley had a lot to think about. He was amazed that Prince Mekhmet was only his own age, but thoughts on that would have to wait. It had become impossible to do anything other than concentrate on making sure his camel didn't trample anyone or crash into the dozens of carts being funnelled towards the city. He couldn't guess where all the traffic had come from, but the road was packed, and the closer they got to the gates, the more congested it became.

The caravan's armed guard now came into its own and cleared a path through the traffic. Camels and people were unceremoniously shoved aside by the fierce warriors, and Al-Khatib smiled and waved courteously as curses and screams of outrage arose from the crowds. Sharley tried to look as though he had nothing to do with the caravan, but no one was fooled and he was able to add some very colourful phrases to his growing vocabulary.

But he soon forgot to be embarrassed as he passed through the Golden Gates and the city opened up before him. It was like walking into an exotic forest. Everywhere there were trees and plants of every description, towering into the sky or growing in raised beds and huge pots. Fragrant gardens punctuated the rows of beautiful marble-built houses at regular intervals, the trees casting deep pools of shade over the streets and waving gently in a magically cool breeze.

If heaven could exist on earth it would surely look like this, Sharley thought to himself, but just then a group of ragged people shuffled into view, led by a man in a turban. Al-Khatib told Sharley the man was a sort of priest who had dedicated his life to looking after the beggars, who were all victims of a terrible wasting disease. Sharley noticed that the crowds gave the beggars a wide berth and even the caravan's warrior guards waited quietly until they'd passed.

"It is the will of the One," said Al-Khatib sadly. "We are as children before His mighty power and cannot even begin to understand His designs and plans."

Sharley nodded, but before he could say anything, a bugle call blasted into the air and the market-day crowds scuttled to the side of the road as a troop of horses thundered down towards them. Sharley was fascinated. These were the first examples of the almost legendary cavalry of the Desert Kingdom he'd seen since arriving in the country, and he wasn't disappointed. All the troopers were men. They wore close-fitting shirts of mail that shimmered in the sunlight, on their heads were steel helmets with a spike at the top, and they carried curved swords and round shields. But it was the horses that held his attention. They were small and light-boned, almost like deer, yet they all looked as fit and as fierce as miniature dragons. Sharley didn't doubt for a moment that they were superbly trained warhorses, despite being tiny compared to the animals of his mother's cavalry.

Al-Khatib bowed in his saddle as the cavalry drew rein and halted before them. "We are honoured indeed," he whispered. "The palace has sent an escort for us."

Sharley's stomach rolled uncomfortably again. He'd expected at least a few hours to prepare before he was called into the Sultan's presence. He was travel-stained and hot, and probably smelt worse than the camels, and yet he was about to be whisked away to the palace.

The Commander of the cavalry had the face of a vicious hawk, and his eyes glittered like the steel of his mail coat as he stared at them. "Where is the Prince of the northern lands who seeks audience with His Dreadful Mightiness the Sultan?"

Something told Sharley not to undersell himself before this fierce warrior, and with a flourish he removed his headdress and glared down at the cavalry from the height of his camel. "I am Prince Charlemagne Athelstan Redrought Strong-in-the-Arm Lindenshield, Regent to the Exiles, and offspring of the mighty Queen who defeated the Polypontian Empire and General Scipio Bellorum. Who asks my name and what is his business?"

The Commander's face stiffened at the sight of Sharley's flaming red hair and green eyes, but he quickly recovered and salaamed. "Greetings, Your Majesty. I am Commander Hussein. It is my duty to escort you to the palace, where my master awaits you."

Sharley nodded coldly, and said, "I will be accompanied by my friend Al-Khatib. His presence amuses me."

The Commander salaamed again. "It is well. Al-Khatib is known at the palace."

The caravan was left to make its own way to its quarters while the cavalry escort turned about, and Sharley and Al-Khatib drew in their camels behind them. The older man caught his eye and grinned. "So, I amuse you, do I?" he said quietly.

"I'm sorry about that," Sharley answered, blushing slightly. "I thought it best to appear . . . snotty."

Al-Khatib leaned across and patted his hand. "You did very well. Commander Hussein is hard to impress, but you soon put him in his place."

With the cavalry escort the journey to the palace passed quickly. The city seemed to flash by in a blur of faces, buildings, streets and wide graceful parks. But when they reached the bazaar even the cavalry was forced to slow to a brisk trot. Never had Sharley seen so many people crammed together in one place; he was amazed and a little unnerved. His own problems paled into insignificance in the face of this crush of humanity. Why should the Sultan agree to help *him* when his own people had so many needs to meet?

But then Al-Khatib pointed ahead at another huge defensive wall, where soldiers were slowly patrolling all along the parapet. They'd reached the perimeter of the palace complex. Sharley mentally squared his shoulders; if his problems were of no more significance than anyone else's, then neither were they any *less* important. He would present his case to the Sultan and place his trust with the gods. He could do no more than that. He immediately felt better, then almost instantly was swamped again by nerves. He didn't have butterflies so much as great muscular eagles flapping around in his stomach.

But there wasn't time to contemplate his fears. Within seconds, they were clattering through a long entrance tunnel, and reined to a halt in a courtyard where grooms came running to take their camels. Commander Hussein dismounted, but the rest of the escort turned about and galloped off.

"You will be so good as to wait here while I inform my master of your presence," he said, salaaming deeply. He then turned, and crossed the courtyard to disappear through a doorway.

"It is as I hoped," said Al-Khatib. "We are to be brought into the presence of the Crown Prince Mekhmet. We may not see the Sultan himself for some time."

"And that's good?" asked Sharley.

"Indeed, yes. The Crown Prince is the very *vitality* and energy of the land. If you make a favourable impression on him, then it's almost guaranteed that the Sultan will also give his support."

Sharley couldn't help thinking that *he'd* have about as much chance of influencing his mother's views on policy as he'd have beating a housecarle in a straight fight. But obviously things were different for Prince Mekhmet. Better to just bide his time and see what happened. Who knows, perhaps he wouldn't fall flat on his face or break nervous wind in a quiet moment. He might just get it right and make a valuable ally of the Prince – though privately he thought it unlikely he would change the habits of a lifetime.

He was just beginning to wallow in self-pity and pessimism when Commander Hussein returned with an immensely tall figure in what looked like a fire of brilliantly coloured silks. Both men salaamed deeply. Sharley nodded, and Al-Khatib returned the bow.

"May I introduce the Chief Eunuch of the Crown Prince's Household," said the Commander. "He will take charge of you now and escort you into the Presence."

Sharley nodded again with what he hoped was regal arrogance and followed the tall man, who drifted ahead in a cloud of colour and perfume. He led them directly across an antechamber to a huge set of doors that were studded with brass nails and had scrolled hinges. With exaggerated dignity he slapped the wood three times with his open palm.

Eventually, a small grille in one of the doors opened, and the Chief Eunuch announced the arrival of the 'special' visitors in a surprisingly high voice.

The doors swung ponderously open, groaning and rumbling on their massive hinges, and they were led inside. Immediately a hissing and bubbling started up amongst several groups of people waiting in the garden beyond. As Sharley passed them he gained the distinct impression that there was more than a little anger towards him amongst the groups of petitioners who'd probably been waiting several days to see the Prince.

Before Sharley lay a beautiful garden far greater and richer than any others he'd seen on his journey through the city. Orange and lemon trees were interspersed with palms, cascading fountains and quiet pools of water lilies, and brilliantly coloured birds and butterflies flew about the trees in small flocks. The Chief Eunuch bowed to him and politely indicated a path that crossed the lawn and headed towards a large pavilion at the centre of the garden. But Sharley would have continued to stand in open-mouthed awe had Al-Khatib not taken his arm and guided him forward.

"Come, the Crown Prince awaits us in his private apartments."

"He has his own apartments?" Sharley asked enviously, remembering his poky little room in one of the many towers of his mother's citadel.

"Indeed, and his own courtiers and retainers in the Court of the Lions. It was thought expedient by the palace authorities that Prince Mekhmet should learn of the workings and, shall we say . . . *intrigues,* of courtly life before he assumes the reins of power."

Sharley felt like the most awkward and stupid of country bumpkins as he gazed on the sophistication of the Desert Kingdom's palace society. He'd only ever associated with housecarles, the servants, Maggie and his family before he'd begun this journey into new worlds and strange experiences. But rather than falling into despair, a strange sense of resignation washed over him. He could never hope to be anything other than himself, and if that was found to be wanting by Prince Mekhmet and his courtiers, then there was nothing he could do about it.

Walking under the pavilion's gold-leafed ceiling was like entering a stone forest. A myriad columns and archways, striped with alternating blocks of light-coloured marble and dark granite, stretched away into the distance. His eye and mind confused by the mass of pillars and patterns, Sharley felt as if they were struggling through a labyrinth, but the Chief Eunuch led them through it until eventually they came to another set of towering doors. Once again, he slapped the wood with the flat of his palm, and once again a small grille was opened.

A terrified Sharley was about to meet Crown Prince Mekhmet at last, though he'd sooner have faced Scipio Bellorum and his entire cavalry, armed with a butter knife and wearing nothing but a pair of carpet slippers. After a few moments he took a deep breath, regained a little composure, and stepped forward into a wide and luxurious room.

At first, he was confused by the brightly coloured silken hangings, deep carpets and exquisitely upholstered divans, and thought the room was empty. But eventually he began to make out groups of richly dressed people – who, he assumed, must be courtiers – lounging about on the divans or standing about in small knots, talking and laughing. In one corner sat a small orchestra playing quietly, and in the centre of the room a fountain trickled its musical tinklings into the air.

The Chief Eunuch hurried to a point on the farthest wall where the only chair in the entire room stood on a raised dais. After a few moments a distant figure stood and clapped its hands. Silence fell, and then a powerful voice rose into the air.

"In the name of the One, give greetings to Charlemagne Athelstan Redrought Strong-in-the-Arm Lindenshield, Prince Regent to the Exiles and son of the warrior House that defeated the hated Polypontian Empire and Scipio Bellorum."

Sharley was amazed that all of his titles were known so well. Al-Khatib discreetly urged him forward and he realised that he was expected to cross the huge room to the throne. Gritting his teeth, and praying to whoever would listen that his leg wouldn't give way, he set off. By the time he reached the fountain he was sweating in panic but, as he'd forgotten to remove his hat, headdress and winding scarf, nobody noticed. Also, his slow, careful limp gave him a strange air of dignity that made even the most cynical courtier watch his progress with interest.

At last he stood before the throne and, heaving a quiet sigh of relief, he looked at the seated figure for the first time. His leg almost gave way then and there! He'd obviously been brought to the wrong place and he was standing before the Sultan. A man sat on the throne and returned his gaze from large liquid eyes that narrowed as he observed Sharley's small travel-stained figure. He had a neatly clipped beard that outlined his fine features perfectly, and on his head was a silken turban with a huge red jewel in the centre.

But then he stood up and Sharley saw that he was barely taller than he was, and when he spoke to a courtier standing nearby, his voice had the uncertain waver and growl of ado-lescence. This *was* Prince Mekhmet! But he had a beard! How could he be a week younger than him? Sharley was almost affronted. His own facial hair barely grew at all yet, and when it did, it sprouted in apologetic little wisps that he hurriedly shaved off before anyone could see them and start teasing him.

The silence began to grow uncomfortable.

Suddenly realising he was still wearing his headgear, Sharley swept off hat, headdress and scarf in a single move-ment, releasing his hair in a startling red halo that blazed about his head like a mane. The Prince and courtiers gasped aloud. They'd heard rumours of the barbarian's colouring, but they hadn't believed it. His skin was an amazing milky-white – where it hadn't been burned red by the sun – and his eyes were the colour of blazing emeralds.

Mekhmet bent forward in fascination to gaze on this Prince of the legendary north. He'd heard that the people there were almost savages, barely civilised at all, and that they even wore animal skins rather than clothes. Yet the boy standing before him seemed human enough. In fact, he looked scared, and he was beginning to blush, his amazing white skin changing to a magnificent red as though wine had been spilled on fine linen.

Mekhmet felt sorry for him, thousands of miles from home, in a foreign Court, carrying the burden of Royalty, and now subjected to the scrutiny of the sort of rich good-for-nothings that were all pigeonholed under the title of "courtier" for the want of anything better. He tried a smile of welcome, and was immediately rewarded with an answering grin that lit up the barbarian's face and made his amazing green eyes sparkle.

Well, that was a small success anyway. Encouraged, he decided to try and talk to him, hoping that Al-Khatib would join them quickly enough to translate. "Welcome to my Court, Prince Charlemagne."

"Thank you, Crown Prince Mekhmet. May the One smile upon your House for a thousand generations."

He spoke the language of the Desert People! Well, how amazing. Obviously intelligence wasn't lacking in the cold north. "I'm pleased to hear that we will be able to converse without the need of interpreters."

"No, indeed. I've been practising your tongue ever since I was invited aboard Al-Khatib's ship on my journey to your shores."

"But that can only have been a few weeks ago!"

"Yes, that's right. Maggie . . . that is, Maggiore Totus, my tutor, says I have a gift for languages."

"And he's right. You have a gift indeed."

Sharley smiled again as his confidence grew. "There's no great skill involved really. It's just a matter of listening, making the link between word and meaning, and then repeating."

Mekhmet was astonished. He'd never heard anyone deny the complexity of their talents before. Modesty was considered something of a weakness in the society of the palace – beyond the usual polite phrases of etiquette, of course, but no one believed *them*. Everyone knew that "Welcome to my humble home" meant "Look at my wonderful furnishings and décor. You could never afford it, and even if you could, you don't have the taste to carry it off."

Mekhmet decided to see this astonishing honesty as refreshingly barbaric. "Well, I'm sure I couldn't learn a language as fast as you obviously have," he went on, experimenting with the alien idea of modesty, and finding it oddly pleasant.

"Of course you could!" Sharley said firmly, ignoring the horrified murmurs from the courtiers that he'd dared to contradict the Crown Prince. "Say after me . . ." and he slowly enunciated an Icemark greeting often used by the housecarles.

"*Eh up . . . hairy arse . . . how's things?*" Mekhmet repeated slowly. "What does it mean?"

Sharley translated as best he could, and the dignity of the Crown Prince slipped slightly as he giggled. "*Hairy arse! And is that a polite greeting?*" he asked, incredulously.

"No," said Sharley. "It's what friends say when they meet."

"Oh!" said Mekhmet, trying to remember the last time he was greeted by anyone other than a servant, courtier, or immediate member of his family. "Oh," he said again in a small voice.

"Eh up, Mekhmet, hairy arse, how's things?" said Sharley, and stepping forward he held out his hand. "I'm known as Sharley to anyone who matters."

Mekhmet stared at the hand held out in front of him. Eventually realising what he was expected to do, he grasped it, and even gave up the attempt to maintain his usual unsmiling expression. The barbarian's grin was just too infectious, and he grinned back. "Eh up, Sharley, hairy arse, how's things?"

"They're great. For the first time in weeks, they're just great."

CHAPTER 18

Thirrin's moods swung between despairing grief and enormous pride. Cerdic had fallen leading his troops to silence the Imperial cannons, and the werewolf who'd brought news of his death said he'd fought like a hero of the sagas. But she couldn't get the sound of his absurd giggle out of her head, or the memories of him as a child with Eodred, playing tricks on the housecarles, or running screaming and laughing through the corridors of the palace with an irate soldier in pursuit. They'd once even set fire to a werewolf officer's pelt – fortunately no harm had been done apart from a few scorch marks and the terrible smell of burnt hair. Thirrin had always defended them, saying that their excesses were just 'warriors' exuberance'. But now there were no pranks or laughter – one of her beautiful boys was dead, and the other had retreated to his room and refused to come out. It had been almost a fortnight since the battle and Eodred had eaten next to nothing; Thirrin was beginning to fear he'd starve himself to death.

Cressida was doing her best, applying equal measures of bullying and sisterly love, and the fact that he was still alive at all was probably entirely due to her. In fact, it was only due to her, and her timely arrival on the battlefield, that *any* of them were still alive.

And above all of Thirrin's other griefs and fears was Sharley. There'd been no news from or about him for weeks now. The seas around the Icemark were blockaded by a mighty fleet of Zephyrs and Corsairs, allied to the Polypontians, and no messages or letters of any sort could get through. As a result, though Oskan tried to reassure her, she had no concrete way of knowing if she'd lost one son or two. At her lowest points she almost believed Sharley was dead, drowned under the waters of any number of seas or oceans, killed by hostile natives or suffering from some terrible disease. In the middle of one of the biggest armies the allies and soldiers of the Icemark had ever gathered, she felt completely and utterly alone.

Thirrin rose wearily to her feet and crossed to the window where the city opened up before her. As Queen she was expected to be strong and carry on no matter what. So far, she'd managed to do just that, pointing out to the people that theirs was the only army that had ever defeated Scipio Bellorum in the field, and in their last battle they'd repeated that feat. But they'd paid a high price for their victory, far higher than she dared reveal to the population. Not only had Prince Cerdic fallen, but so too had the Basilea of the Hypolitan and her Consort, and almost the entire sweep of experienced staff officers. The rank and file had been decimated too, with thousands killed from all three species: human, Snow Leopard and werewolf. In fact, the Snow Leopard numbers were so depleted Tharaman-Thar had said they could hardly be called an army any more. But at least that would be remedied when reinforcements arrived from the Hub of the World. Krisafitsa-Tharina had gone to the Icesheets to bring them south, while her mate did his best to salvage what he could from the survivors of the battle. But it was many days before the Thar's booming laugh was heard echoing along the corridors again, and it had taken a drinking competition with his old friend Olememnon of the Hypolitan to finally break his sombre mood.

Tears began to trickle down Thirrin's cheeks as her mind ran over the events of the last few days. It had been happening a lot recently, which was hardly surprising, but sometimes she wasn't even aware that she was crying until a tear dropped on to whatever report she was reading, or King Grishmak quietly handed her a hankie, gathered from somewhere in his thick pelt. She wiped at her face irritably. This wasn't good enough – she had a country to run and that allowed no room for private grief. There probably wasn't a single family in the entirety of the Icemark that didn't have some tragedy to grieve over as a direct result of this war, or the last one, and yet they functioned, they got on with life. As Queen she should be setting a good example, not drawing comfort from the strength of her subjects.

She took a deep breath and went to look for Oskan. She was secretly as worried about him as she was about Eodred. He'd said almost nothing about Cerdic since hearing the news of the battle, and had withdrawn into himself. He'd not only shut a physical door on the world – Oskan Witchfather had closed away his mind, and it would take an enormous effort to bring him back.

Thirrin strode through the corridors with a power and a purpose that made everyone stand aside and salute as she swept by. But Oskan wasn't to be found in the infirmary where the wounded survivors of the battle were recovering, or were slowly sinking into the Peace of the Goddess with the help of the healers who worked there. Thirrin asked some of the witches if they'd seen him, but none of them had, and she set off on her quest again, sending out messengers to all points of the citadel in search of her Consort.

But then it occurred to her that when Oskan needed time alone he often went to his cave in the Great Forest, or if there was no time to do that, he'd descend to the deepest part of the city's undercroft, where he'd been healed of his terrible burns in the last war with the Empire. She quickly retraced her steps to the infirmary and made her way down to the cellars. From there, she found the broken and crumbling spiral stairway that wound steeply down into the black of the natural caves that lay beneath the city.

On reaching the bottom of the steps the strong, acrid scent of the place filled her nostrils and she almost retched, but controlling herself she raised the torch above her head. The wet, glutinous mud of the cave floor sent up a myriad luminous reflections that dazzled her, but she could see Oskan sitting on a chair in the centre of the rough floor.

She splashed across to him, but then, startled, she took a step back. She'd expected him to be in a trance, and his white eyes and heavy broken breathing were familiar symptoms that didn't bother her at all. But sitting on the back of his chair was a fabulous eagle, its wings outstretched and its fierce head pointing directly at her. She raised her torch higher to see it better, and realised she could see right through it. The creature was obviously a protective spirit whose task it was to look after the warlock while he was vulnerable. But Thirrin had never seen such a creature before, and could only assume some other power had sent it to act as a guardian over her husband.

"Don't worry," she said in awe. "Oskan Witchfather is my Consort. I've come to watch over him too."

The eagle flapped its wings in a noisy display of strength, and proved its power to be effective even in the physical world as the blast of wind caused Thirrin's hair to stream about her head. But then the creature settled down and started to preen its feathers. Thirrin scrutinised Oskan's face, and with a sudden rush of affection she noticed the fine lines and wrinkles that were just beginning to mark the corners of his eyes. She was certain they hadn't been there when she'd marched off to battle – perhaps at last Time was beginning to write its story on his features. She watched as his face twitched and moved in his trance, the lines deepening and smoothing as the muscles contracted and relaxed.

"Where are you, Oskan?" she asked, leaning forward and gently taking his hand. "What battle are you fighting?"

The warlock was aware of her presence and was comforted by it, but this didn't distract him from his quest. Ever since the news of the battle had reached him, something had *shifted*, and he'd realised that the reasoning power of all the Icemark's High Command and their allies had been clouded and obscured by Magical means. Something or someone had wanted them to be destroyed. Thirrin would never have been stupid enough to fall into such an obvious trap if there hadn't been some sort of magical control influencing her. All the military leaders had years of combat experience, and yet they'd all willingly marched off to the slaughter. Not only that, but he, Oskan, had let them go! Whoever the witch was, he or she was powerful indeed, but not powerful enough to bamboozle them all. They'd made the mistake of not including Cressida in the bewitchment, and that had been enough to thwart their plans.

Oskan was seethingly, ragingly angry. His son had died as a direct result of this malign influence, and he was determined to avenge him. There was something else nagging at his mind too – something he almost didn't dare acknowledge. Could somebody closer to the family than he cared to admit be responsible? But who? Surely not Medea. Not his own daughter. His mind swerved away from the thought. No. It was impossible. Whoever it was, they'd covered their tracks well, but he would find them. He plunged deeper, through the mist of the Spirit Plane and into the Magical Realm . . .

As usual, the Spirit Plain had the atmosphere of a foggy day just before the sun bursts through and burns away the mists. Nothing was clear, and yet neither did anything cast any shadows.

Oskan knew this world well, and if the evil witch he sought was hiding herself here, she was in danger of terrible revenge from the warlock. His mind searched far and wide over the realm and settled on a tall ice-covered tower. Oskan's mind scoured the building, and he soon felt the unmistakable presence of another – a very powerful being whose true identity was cleverly hidden. Carefully concealing his own identity, he began the hunt.

He reached the foot of the tower's spiral staircase and began to climb. It was cold and dark, with only a mean trickle of light coming through the arrow slits that pierced the walls at regular intervals. But he was getting closer. He could almost hear the witch breathing. She was sitting in the room at the very top of the tower, gloating over the havoc she'd caused. She seemed particularly pleased by the death of Cerdic, and Oskan felt a rising wave of fury swelling through his spirit form. He crept up the stairway with extreme care.

All of a sudden, faint laughter echoed through the tower. He stopped. The voice was oddly familiar, but so evil and twisted that it had barely a trace of humanity. The laughing ended abruptly, and instantly a huge beating of wings sounded. Oskan raced up the remaining steps and reached the room – too late. From the room's wide window he could see a shadowy form flying swiftly away.

The warlock transformed himself into a peregrine falcon, the swiftest of all birds of prey, and gave chase. Below him, the world swept by in a blur of speed as he slowly gained on the shadowy form of a vulture that flew ahead. Suddenly, its ugly naked head turned to look at him and, opening its beak, it spat out a white-hot bolt of lightning. Oskan folded his wings and dived. The bolt flew by harmlessly.

Swooping skywards again, he returned fire. The vulture screeched, and tumbled from the sky in a desperate attempt to avoid the bolt. But the white-hot ball of energy caught its wing a glancing blow and the creature fell in a tangle of feathers until, with a clap of thunder, it disappeared.

Oskan hovered, then slowly spiralled down to the ground. The evil witch was unmistakeably female, but apart from that her masking was too strong to penetrate. There was nothing more he could do now. Once a witch had left the Spirit Plain she could emerge anywhere in the physical world. He resumed his human form and grimly re-entered his body.

Back in the cave he took a deep shuddering breath and slowly sat upright. His eyes rolled back to their normal position, and when he could focus them, he saw Thirrin watching him anxiously.

"Are you all right?" she asked quietly.

He nodded, and looked about him. Knowing exactly what he wanted, Thirrin took a flask from her battledress pocket and gave it to him. The raw spirit made him cough, but everything swung firmly back into its proper place and he smiled sadly. "That's better. I'm completely back now."

"Good. What did you find?"

"A witch, as I expected. Female. I wounded her but she got away."

"And she was definitely the one who befuddled us all?"

"Definitely."

Thirrin nodded. "Then she's responsible for killing Cerdic and all the others."

He took her hand. "Yes. And I shall avenge him."

Thirrin fell silent as grief overwhelmed her. "Oskan, what's going to fill the emptiness he's left?"

"Nothing. And nothing ever should. All we can do is remember what he was: a son, a brother, a soldier who died as a soldier."

"But he was more than that. He was laughter and fun, he was . . . kind when he thought fast enough. I can't quite believe I'll never see or hear him again. Oskan—?"

"No."

"But you could do it."

"Yes, I could. But I won't. He's moved on, and it would be wrong to ask him to come back even for the shortest of times. Be glad that you know he still exists and that at your appointed time, you'll be with him again."

Tears ran down her cheeks. "Will I?" she whispered, her tone so desperate that Oskan could hardly bear to hear it.

"Oh yes! Yes! You'll be with him in Valhalla drinking your

mead in Odin's hall and swapping tales of your battles. He's with Redrought now, laughing and giggling and waiting for you."

She fell silent for a moment, and when she raised her eyes to him she looked like a lost and frightened little girl. "But . . . but what about you?"

"Me?" Oskan asked, desperate to bring back the warrior Queen he knew and loved.

"Yes, you. You're not a warrior. You'll have no seat in Valhalla. Will I ever see you in the life beyond?"

He smiled. "Oh, don't worry about me. I'll be in the Summerlands and I'll visit every day. The Goddess and the Gods of Valhalla are good neighbours; there'll be no problems there."

She smiled sadly. "You make the afterlife sound like a suburb of Frostmarris."

"Do I? Well, let me tell you it most certainly is not. *This* world's a suburb of the *afterlife*, and we're all just waiting to get on with the real point of existence once we've finished dithering about in this unimportant little backwater we call life!"

Thirrin laughed, quietly at first, then with a full-throated glory that echoed around the cave. "Oh, Oskan, only you could cheer me up at this most horrible of times." She drew a deep breath, seeming to draw strength from the air around her. Then she stretched with a sense of relief as though waking up after a nightmare. "Well, come on. We'd better get on with 'dithering about in this unimportant little backwater'. Scipio Bellorum and his horrid sons are dithering about too and I don't want them doing it in the Icemark."

Oskan smiled, relieved that the warrior Queen was back.

"Yes dear, right away dear," he said in his best henpecked husband voice.

Tharaman-Thar waited beneath the northern eaves of the Great Forest with Olememnon and a small escort of Snow Leopards, Wolf-folk and human soldiers. The werewolf relay had said that Krisafitsa and the reinforcements would reach the woodlands later that night, and Tharaman-Thar was gazing eagerly ahead through the gathering dusk.

He turned to the werewolf officer beside him. "What exactly did the relay say, Captain Skull-cruncher?"

"That the Tharina and the reinforcements would be here two hours after moonrise, My Lord."

"Really? Well, what about trotting ahead a little, Ollie," he said to the Hypolitan officer beside him, "and meeting them on the road?"

"Sounds like a good idea to me."

The Thar purred, then raising his head he roared mightily and moved off with his escort.

The evening light slowly dwindled, draining colour from the sky and leaving the simple black and white beauty of the night. The escort of Snow Leopards, werewolves and human soldiers marched on and watched as the full moon rose majestically into the sky, its subtle yet powerful radiance slowly dimming the stars around it and casting a misty grey light over the land. Only the whispering tread of the Snow Leopards' giant paws, the pad of the werewolves, and the quiet clip-clop of the cavalry mounts could be heard. Even the wind had fallen silent, so when the Thar suddenly asked for quiet, the gentle murmur of the approaching army of the Tharina could clearly be heard on the still night air. A mutter of excitement arose from the escort and they hurried on.

Eventually, Tharaman called a halt, and raising his head he sniffed the air. "I scent thirty thousand warriors – truly the greatest host my people have ever sent into the field!"

Olememnon smiled. "Old Bellorum'll have his work cut out now! I don't care how big his army is. When he finally gets them all through the mountain pass, we'll carve holes through their ranks as wide as Imperial highways!"

At last they crested a hill, and there before them, stretching into the distance, was the column of the relieving army. Tharaman roared again, and back crashed the reply from the approaching force.

Escort and army then increased their pace to a steady trot, and within a few minutes they stood facing each other on the moonlit road. Silence fell as the Thar and Tharina stepped forward and met between the two groups. Their noses touched and they rubbed cheeks as a thunderous purring swelled and rolled into the night air. Krisafitsa gave her mate's face a thorough wash, as though he'd become particularly grubby in her absence.

"Welcome back, my love," said Tharaman. "I hope your journey was without incident."

Krisafitsa blinked slowly in cat greeting, then said, "Almost, dear heart. Their Vampiric Majesties saw fit to offer no hospitality, but as we didn't want any, no harm was done." She shuddered delicately. "I think if I'd been forced to stay in the Blood Palace, I'd have worn out my tongue trying to wash away the very scent of the place."

Tharaman purred understandingly. "But otherwise, can I take it that you passed through The-Land-of-the-Ghosts without problems?"

"Apart from a . . . what is the collective noun for rock trolls? A boulder, perhaps? Apart from a *boulder* of fifty or so rock trolls who were stupid enough to try and block the pass through the Wolfrocks, everything went smoothly. They were soon reduced to rubble, as it were, and we reached the Icemark safely."

The Thar growled fiercely. "The High Command will be interested to hear about that. It may be that Their Vampiric Majesties will need another ambassadorial visit to remind them of their obligations."

"Perhaps, but the Vampire King and Queen have always claimed the trolls are beyond their control."

"They're only as beyond control as the circumstances suit their Vampiric Majesties. I think Thirrin and Oskan will take a very dim view of this."

"The Pro-Thar Talaman and all the other cubs send their love and greetings, by the way," Krisafitsa said, purring softly as the mention of Thirrin and Oskan brought back the memory of Prince Cerdic's death.

"Ah, yes!" Tharaman replied, feeling a sudden upsurge of love for his cubs, especially his favourite. "And how is Kirimin?" he asked.

"Growing fast, but missing her papa," said Krisafitsa sadly. "And Talaman wanted to join with the reinforcements and march south to the war with us. He was so determined."

For a moment she daydreamed of her departure from the Hub of the World. Talaman had been so desperate:

"Please, Mama, everyone will think I'm a coward if I stay at home while so many others march off to fight. And you can't say I'm too young – there are dozens of warriors younger than me, and you're taking *them* with you."

"I know, my dear," she'd replied. "But you are Pro-Thar, and if anything should happen to your father and me, you will be needed to lead our people. Remember, the Ice Trolls may have been defeated, but they're not destroyed; one day they'll rise again and the Snow Leopards will need a strong Commander to direct the war. I'm afraid it's your duty to stay at home."

Talaman had bowed his head, understanding and accepting her argument, but the disappointment was almost more than he could bear.

"What's going to happen to you and Papa?" Kirimin had then asked, looking up from where she'd been gnawing her brother's paw. "You will be home before Nightfall, won't you? I couldn't bear it if Papa wasn't here to tell us tales about the ice-monsters and giant walruses when the blizzards are blowing."

Krisafitsa had licked her face lovingly. "Of course we'll be home before then, Kirimin. Nightfall's another five months away, and much can happen between now and then."

"Oh yes, I know," she'd said importantly, selecting another of her brother's paws to attack. "I can hardly remember the last Nightfall, it was so long ago, and five months is almost a lifetime."

"Indeed it is, my dearest one," Krisafitsa had agreed. "But before you know it, your Papa will be home bursting with new stories to tell you, and purring like an avalanche."

"Yes, he will," Kirimin had said with certainty. "And you can give me a good wash when you get back. No one else can clean the backs of my ears quite like you do."

Krisafitsa hung her head now, remembering the intense longing she'd felt to stay with her cubs and protect them from the world and all the evil it contained. But there was a war to be fought, and if they didn't put every effort into preventing Bellorum from winning it, it wouldn't be long before his hordes found their way to The Hub of the World. Little Kirimin's baby-soft fur would be too much of a temptation for the men of the Empire, with their guns and their knives and their liking for the skins of other creatures.

"The cubs sent love and greetings to Thirrin and Oskan too," said Krisafitsa, pulling herself together. "How are they coping?"

The Thar flattened his ears. "Cerdic's grave-mound has been raised and sealed, but the emotional wounds will take far, far longer to close."

"Yes, of course," the Tharina said glumly.

"But now, we still have a fair way to go before we reach Frostmarris," said Tharaman, attempting to lighten the mood. "Shall we journey to the Great Forest tonight and make camp there?"

"Yes, it's a beautiful night and none of us are tired."

Olememnon rode forward and Krisafitsa nuzzled him in greeting. "Hello, Ollie. If you're here, then I assume you and Tharaman made sure there was plenty of wine for the trip."

"And beer! There's some left, surprisingly, if you're thirsty."

"Perhaps I'll have a bowl later. In the meantime shall we continue our journey?"

Within an hour the army and its escort reached the Great Forest. Here they paused, and a fanfare was sounded as a herald stepped out of the ranks and asked the leave of the Holly King and the Oak King to travel across their realm. The answering silence was taken as permission and they continued on their way. Beneath the canopy of the trees the night condensed to an almost tangible darkness, like grainy black silk. But the eyes of the Snow Leopards and Wolf-folk soon adjusted and they stepped out with confidence, the humans trusting their companions' night vision and not bothering to light torches.

After a further two hours of marching they came to a wide clearing, and here they decided to settle down for what was left of the night. Only Tharaman-Thar and Krisafitsa-Tharina stayed awake, talking quietly, and purring in the pleasure of each other's company far into the night.

"Tharaman, could we live after the death of one of our children?" asked Krisafitsa, becoming suddenly serious and thinking of her cubs again. "I'm not sure how Thirrin and Oskan can carry on without Cerdic."

"They carry on because they have to, because their country needs them. In effect, they are the mother and father of the entire nation, not just of their own children," he answered quietly. "You and I would do the same, though may the One never call our cubs home while we still live."

Krisafitsa lowered her head on to her paws. "May you and I be long asleep in the Ice Mausoleum before any of our young ones are called by the One-Who-Made-All-Things. I offer now, at this very moment, every last second of my remaining life, rather than have that happen."

"And I too, my love, though let us remember our cubs are safe at the Hub of the World and we are needed by our allies and friends in this continuing war. We live as yet, and who knows, we may do so for many years, watching the night and day of our homeland's year and growing grey-pelted as our grandcubs play in the kindly snows. We could yet be grandpapa and grandmama to dynasties. What greater joy could there ever be? What higher good could we ever reach?"

Krisafitsa purred thunderously and gave her mate's face another wash. "You soppy old pussycat! You'd make a wonderful granddad – all bluster and bark on the surface and all gooey and soft underneath. Kirimin knows this already; she can twist her daddy around her tiny paw, so I don't doubt any grandcubs will do just the same."

Tharaman humphed and tried to look stern for a few moments, but then he said: "You might . . . just *might* be right about Kirimin, but I'm sure the rest of the cubs think I'm strict and fearsome."

The peace of the clearing was suddenly shattered as Krisafitsa's laughter rang out clear and joyful into the night air.

"Don't they, then?" asked Tharaman quietly.

The werewolf relay had reported that the Snow Leopard army would emerge from the Great Forest in half an hour or so, but Cressida had been waiting for almost twice that long already. Thirrin was determined that the Thar and Tharina would be accorded the respect they certainly deserved, and was taking no chances with slip-ups and late preparations. The entire Citadel Guard of housecarles was lined up on the plain of Frostmarris, as was the Royal Bodyguard of Ukpik werewolves and the surviving warriors of the Snow Leopard and human cavalry under the joint command of Taradan and Thirrin herself.

Cressida stood to one side with King Grishmak and Oskan. She was a little annoyed; obviously her first battle command, and saving the entire allied army, weren't considered important enough to grant her even a small command of her own.

Grishmak leaned against Cressida's horse comfortably and

picked at his fearsome teeth. He'd just had a very satisfying little snack to tide him over until the official welcoming banquet, and was feeling particularly contented. Nonetheless, he was aware of Cressida's mood, and scratched at his pelt as he wondered how to cheer her up. He knew Thirrin had a surprise planned for her, but he couldn't let that particular cat out of the bag and spoil everything. He glanced at Oskan, but the warlock seemed to be in some sort of semi-trance, so he could expect no help from there. Eventually, he belched cavernously, startling Cressida's horse, then stretched until the sinews in his strongly muscled arms and legs cracked.

"Weary work waiting for important types to turn up," he said. Cressida only grunted moodily in reply. He went on, "Especially when other important types insist that you turn up too early and wait for bloody hours before things get going."

Cressida grunted again, but then added, "You're an *important type* too."

"I suppose," Grishmak agreed. "But I don't expect anyone to wait around for me. Then again, Tharaman and Krisafitsa don't either."

"No. I think we can only blame my mother for this."

"Perhaps, but it's not really surprising. The Snow Leopards are pretty important to the war, and besides . . ." Grishmak paused as he considered how much he should say in front of the Crown Princess.

"And besides, she's probably half mad with the need to strike back at Bellorum," Cressida finished for him.

"Well, I wouldn't go that far. But the vicious old sod nearly did for us last time, and witchcraft or not, your mother's military pride has been well and truly dented. She wants revenge, and she's froth-at-the-mouth desperate to get it. Not that your mother's lost it, or anything," he added hurriedly. "It's just that a few months ago she'd have ridden north herself, way beyond the Great Forest, to meet Krisafitsa and her army en route, and she wouldn't have spent half the morning snarling at the housecarles as she did today. Loyalty like that deserves more respect. Still, *they're* loyal enough to know she means nothing by it. Give her another battle to fight and a glimpse of that old pirate Bellorum, and she'll be back to her old self."

Cressida nodded; her mother had been . . . *distorted* somehow by the terrible battle. They all had, but as Queen, Thirrin's reactions were bound to be more obvious and more closely watched. Even so, Cressida had no doubt that she'd recover; she just needed a little more time. If only she could get it.

A sudden howling from the werewolf relay announced the arrival of the Snow Leopards, and almost immediately Tharaman and Krisafitsa emerged from the trees along with Olememnon, Captain Skull-cruncher and the other humans and werewolves of the escort. Then into the brilliant light of the Icemark afternoon marched the Snow Leopard army: rank after rank of the giant cats in strictly disciplined order, all trotting forward in regimented step.

A murmur rose up from the warriors waiting to greet the reinforcements, but Thirrin remained silent and rigid on her horse as they approached. A fanfare brayed from the house-carle units, and the Ukpik werewolves howled a greeting. Thirrin gave a small nod and the cavalry eased into a slow walk. This was gradually raised to a trot, then to a canter, until finally Thirrin drew her sword, and horse and Snow Leopard thundered across the plain letting out the coughing bark of their challenge and singing the fierce cavalry paean. Tharaman and Krisafitsa rose up on their hind legs and roared and the cavalry slid to a halt in a flurry of flying stones and billowing dust.

Thirrin leaped from the saddle and strode forward to meet the Thar and Tharina who stood waiting, their thunderous purrs rumbling over the plain. "Welcome back, Krisafitsa," she called. "And welcome to your army. When can they begin training for cavalry tactics?"

"Immediately, if need be, my dear. But I thought a day or two of rest might be in order after their long march," said Krisafitsa, eyeing her old friend curiously.

Thirrin stopped and shook her head. "I'm being hasty again, aren't I? No, of course they can have a rest. Bellorum's quiet at the moment, licking his wounds and building up his forces, no doubt. Come on back to the city – a feast of welcome's waiting."

She turned to walk away when Krisafitsa's polite cough made her turn back. "And how are you, Thirrin? How are Eodred and Oskan?"

"Fine, fine. We're all fine," she answered airily, but then her composure slipped and she hugged the great cat, burying her face in her fur.

"Shall we go back to Frostmarris and have a good old-fashioned chat?" said Krisafitsa, nuzzling her friend's head. Thirrin nodded, then wiping her face, she said, "Yes, I'd like that, but I have to announce something first."

The Tharina nodded to her mate, and Tharaman roared the order to make the ranks stand to attention. After a few seconds the Snow Leopard army stood silently as Cressida, Grishmak and Oskan approached and greeted Tharaman and Krisafitsa. Then, remounting her horse, Thirrin trotted to a point equidistant between the Snow Leopard reinforcements and the welcoming troops.

"Warriors of the Alliance, all of you know of the Crown Princess's brilliance in the last battle against Scipio Bellorum and his sons. Not only did she and King Grishmak destroy their army, but she also undoubtedly saved the lives of thousands of your comrades, as well as myself, Tharaman-Thar and Krisafitsa-Tharina. In acknowledgement of this, the High Command is in full agreement that Cressida Striking Eagle should be named as Second-in-Command of the cavalry, where she will ride with myself and the Monarchs of the Icesheets. She will also command a personal squadron fighting under its own banner." Here she paused and nodded at a trooper, who rode out from the ranks, unfurling as he came a battle-flag on which the image of a striking eagle flew above the running leopard and galloping horse of the cavalry. "Welcome now your new Commander."

Slowly, a low murmur grew amongst the ranks of the cavalry as the human troopers gently tapped spear on shield, until the sound swelled in rattling power and rolled into the air. To this cacophony, the Snow Leopards added their coughing bark, and the huge crescendo of noise rolled across the entire Plain of Frostmarris, until gradually it died away to silence.

Thirrin then drew her sword, and standing in her stirrups she raised her voice to battle pitch. "The enemy will fall before us, like wheat before the scythe! Blood! Blast! And Fire! Blood! Blast! And Fire!"

The warriors immediately responded, booming out the war cry of the Icemark until it echoed back from the walls of the city. Cressida's face blazed with pride. She rode forward to thank her mother and acknowledge the cheering of the allied army. Then, her blood singing through her veins, she took up her position at the head of the newly formed squadron. Commanding even a unit of the cavalry of the Icesheets was better than having her own regiment. In fact it was almost as good as having an entire army!

But then, whispering through her moment of triumph, the image of Eodred appeared. This was something to tell him! This was something to bring him back to reality! She was even prepared to use jealousy to shock him out of his grief-stricken torpor. Better to have a brother who was green with envy and functioning in the world, than one who sat brooding in his room refusing to communicate with anyone.

Another fanfare rang out, and the escort and Snow Leopard army formed up to march into Frostmarris. Cressida rode proudly at the head of her squadron, planning exactly what she'd say to Eodred for maximum effect.

Medea watched from her tower room as the warriors approached across the plain. Ever since Oskan had almost caught her in the Magical World, she'd been lying low and had hardly used her Gift at all. In fact, she'd only used her psychic abilities once – to speed the healing of the arm that had been injured by Oskan when she'd made her escape back to the physical world. Now, even the charred skin and scarring were starting to fade. Obviously he hadn't seen through her disguise, because he hadn't confronted her, and now all she had to do was hide her injuries from him, which wasn't difficult under a long-sleeved dress. Even so, she wasn't ready to risk trying anything else yet. Her father was just too powerful a warlock; she couldn't face him again.

She leaned further out of her window, and caught sight of Oskan. It was almost as though her thoughts had conjured him up, and there he was walking slowly across the courtyard of the citadel.

She almost panicked. Her instincts told her he was heading for her tower, but then her icy calm reasserted itself. He knew nothing. All she had to do was play the role of the studious daughter and she'd be safe.

After what seemed an age of tense anticipation, the rattle of the latch on the lower door echoed up the spiral staircase, and she quickly sat at her desk and opened one of the books that were stacked high on its dusty surface. As Oskan's measured step climbed slowly to her room, she buried her face in her book.

For several long moments she pretended not to know he was standing in the doorway, then turning the page, she looked up. "Oh, Father. Come in."

Oskan crossed the room to a small chair that stood by the window and sat down. He had come because there was a dark secret deep, deep in his mind that he hardly dared acknowledge. Had Medea already made that most terrible of choices? But how could a father suspect his own child of being responsible for so many deaths? And, especially horrifyingly, the death of her own brother?

"Medea, how are you?" he began carefully. "None of the family have seen you for days."

"No . . . I've been observing the war and deciding how I can . . . help. The diplomatic mission to Their Vampiric Majesties was quite eye-opening. But I fear the time for diplomacy and politics is past. The armies are marching and . . . and people are dying."

Oskan held her blank gaze. Perhaps he was wrong. His mind reached out, desperate to find that she was innocent. But before he allowed himself to See, he withdrew, disgusted with himself and his suspicions. "There are many roles for a powerful Adept like yourself. But perhaps your skills will come into their own once the fighting's over."

"Yes, yes. Perhaps they will." For a moment she was surprised to feel a twinge of guilt and even regret. But she ignored them. Why should she be sorry for actions against a land and people she didn't recognise as her own? "I'd be more than ready to help rebuild whatever survives the war."

"If anything survives at all," Oskan said and watched to see her reaction. Anything! Any tiny show of emotion for the danger her family and country faced would convince him of her innocence.

"Oh, I'm sure we'll win," she said, too briskly.

"Are you? I'm glad."

She looked up, alerted by her father's flat tones. "Well, of course we'll win. Anything else is just unthinkable."

"Have you received a premonition, or any other indication?"

"No . . . no. I'm just certain, that's all." Her hand grasped the book in her lap until her knuckles showed white. *He knows! He knows!*

Oskan's eyes seemed to bore into her head, even though she knew he wasn't using his Gift to search her mind. But if he already knew she was guilty he wouldn't need to use psychic probing, would he? She almost broke then, and prepared to throw herself at his feet to ask forgiveness.

"You didn't come to Cerdic's funeral. Your mother was hurt," he said quietly.

Medea grasped at the slight change of subject and allowed herself some small hope. "No . . . I couldn't. I mean . . .

Cerdic dead! How could I believe such a— if I'd gone to the funeral I'd have to accept it, wouldn't I? I didn't see his body; I didn't see him buried . . . I can still hope it's all a mistake and he's still alive somewhere, perhaps injured in some way; a bang on the head that's affected his memory. Who knows? Allow me that. At least allow me that!" She trembled under the terrible pressure of her father's scrutiny and the tension caused her eyes to fill with tears. She blinked and they coursed slowly down her cheeks.

Oskan slumped in his chair. At last, emotion! He almost shouted aloud for joy. Medea felt sorrow for the loss of her brother! In desperation he seized the moment and thrust aside his suspicions.

After several minutes of savouring a deep sense of relief, he slowly climbed to his feet and crossed to where she sat. "Medea, you know as well as I that nothing is ultimately lost. Cerdic exists still, striding the moonlit fields of the Summerlands, drinking mead in Valhalla. Only his body was broken; his mind lives on."

He took her hand and kissed it, then with a sad smile walked slowly to the door. Medea watched him go and listened as he descended the staircase. She was exultant. She'd fooled him! She was safe! No one would suspect her now, not when the greatest living warlock said she was innocent.

A wide smile crept across her sallow face.

Scipio Bellorum was sitting in the Great Hall of the Guild of Weavers in Barrowby. "With the Icemark we must predict the unpredictable," he said, calmly pouring himself a goblet of wine. His ever-simmering rage was barely hidden behind a smile. Most of the town around him was in flames, but the artisans' quarter had been left intact as billets for the General and his officers.

"Impossible, you might rightly argue, so let us amend our phraseology and say: with the Icemark there's a need to *pre-empt* the unpredictable; a need to prepare for every possibility." He smiled thinly around the table at his sons and senior staff officers.

"But, Father, how could we possibly have prepared for the Crown Princess's completely unexpected relieving army? And it's ridiculous to think we can pre-empt the unpredictable in future. The only way to do that would be to have an entire army in reserve!" said Octavius Bellorum, holding his father's icy stare with confidence.

"If, as you suggest, that is the only way to prepare for all eventualities when fighting these barbarians, then that is exactly what we shall do," said the General with steely precision. "We have sufficient numbers to keep fifty per cent of our forces in a support role, ready to respond to any eventuality, and still be strong enough to crush the opposition. Commander Domitus, you and the Logistics Corps will formulate plans to this effect as of now. I want names of regiments that will fulfil this supporting role; I want numbers; I want strategies designed to place them in the most effective position at the onset of battle and I want tactics that will move them into fighting positions with power and precision as and when they are needed. Do you understand?"

"Yes, Sir," Domitus answered confidently.

"Then I suggest you withdraw and begin immediately. I'll expect a working report in two days' time. Is that clear?"

"Sir!" The Commander stood, saluted, and hurried from the room.

Commander Octavius inclined his head in acknowledgement of his father's ability to respond to any situation. There
was nothing new in keeping troops in reserve to react to the
enemy's tactics, but appointing an entire army as support
would need superb tactical control and discipline.

"I'm willing to command the reserve," Sulla said, in the
sort of voice a newly opened tomb might have. "The shock of
onset would be enhanced by fear." He almost smiled. "And
I'm good at fear."

The General nodded. Of his two sons, Sulla had inherited
the truest Bellorum attitude. Octavius was a superbly skilled
soldier, but Sulla actually enjoyed killing. Unlike many commanders, he wasn't content to sit aloof from the battle and
watch his tactics come to fruition; he had to be in the front
line taking lives and terrifying the enemy. He'd often fight
without a helmet, knowing that the sight of his raging face and
wild black hair was sometimes enough to make the enemy
break ranks and flee.

"Very well," said the General. "Your reputation would be
our most effective weapon. I appoint Commander Sulla as
Martial of the Shock Regiments."

Of all the tactics and weapons at his disposal, General
Bellorum was of the opinion that only one might be more
effective than his son's dark reputation. And, after months of
delay, that weapon was now almost ready for action. It would
be used first of all against the remaining four cities of the Five
Boroughs. Any problems and hitches could then be ironed out
before they marched on Frostmarris. His new killing machine
would sweep all before it. No shield wall, no werewolf phalanx, no human and Snow Leopard cavalry could stand against
it. All would die. All would die in fire.

317

CHAPTER 19

Sharley ached! His back ached, his arms ached, his sides and shoulders ached, even his hair seemed to ache! But worst of all were his legs, particularly the gammy one, which actually throbbed in rhythm with his heartbeat. He pulled back the covers on his bed and looked at it, just to check if it was actually pulsating. But, of course, it wasn't. He slumped back on his pillow, trying to find a comfortable position, and ran over the events of the last few days.

Most prominent was Crown Prince Mekhmet. It had been his idea that Sharley should train with the palace Dancing Master, of all people. It happened during their second meeting when Mekhmet had invited him to lunch in his quarters.

Just before the appointed time, Sharley had been ushered into the Prince's private apartments. Immediately, a small youth had appeared, wearing creased white trousers and a simple white shirt, and it had taken Sharley a few moments to realise that this was Prince Mekhmet, the very same person he'd met the day before with his courtiers. Gone were the bejewelled turban and the elaborately embroidered waistcoat, and the beard that Sharley had been so envious of looked much less impressive uncombed and with bits of fluff in it.

They had both suddenly been beset by a crippling shyness that robbed them of speech. But then they'd grinned at each other. "Hello," said Mekhmet at last, and having broken the silence he seemed to regain his confidence. "Come in, come in. Lunch is waiting."

He led the way across the courtyard, and into a smallish room furnished with low divans and compact mother-of-pearl inlaid tables. "I hope you don't mind, but I look after myself in here. I don't have any servants, courtiers or grovelling. It's refreshing somehow."

Sharley realised what an honour it was to be invited to Mekhmet's private bolt-hole, and he warmed to him again. "I'm lucky, I suppose; at home in the Icemark we don't have personal courtiers. The servants work for everyone, not just for me or anyone else in the family."

"Tell me more about the north," said Mekhmet, pouring two goblets of sherbet. "Is it true that there's snow even in those parts where there are no mountains?"

"Yes, in the—" Sharley realised that he didn't know the word for "winter". "In the time when the days shorten and the sun becomes less strong and the trees are bare."

The Crown Prince looked at him blankly. "Does that happen in your country? It sounds like the end of the world."

Sharley laughed. "Yes, it happens every year, and then the time called 'spring' follows, and the trees and plants begin to put out new leaves and the sun gets warmer, after which we have summer, when it gets hot. Well, *quite* hot. Not like here. I mean, no one would actually die if they stood in the sun all day without a hat, or anything like that."

Mekhmet tried to understand, but in a land of constant

raging temperatures, the idea of seasons was completely alien to him. "I've heard tell that your entire land is an oasis with water everywhere and plants growing across every bit of ground. Is that true?"

"Well, yes. On most bits of ground, anyway. In some places people have cleared away the undergrowth, and of course there are farms that grow crops."

"And when it isn't snowing, it rains?"

"A lot of the time, yes. But the sun shines too."

"Rivers!" Mekhmet said suddenly.

"Yes, what about them?"

"Have you seen one?" he asked, with an ironic grin on his face to show he wasn't fooled by silly legends.

"I've seen lots," Sharley answered. "I've got my own boat and I used to go fishing quite often with Hereward, one of the retired housecarles. Sometimes in the spring we'd stay out all day, and we'd find a clearing on the bank and cook our catch over an open fire. There's nothing like fresh trout eaten at the end of a good day's fishing with the moon coming up and a fresh breeze off the river . . ." Sharley's voice trailed away as a sudden sense of homesickness descended on him.

Mekhmet immediately knew something was wrong. "I don't understand half of what you've told me, Sharley, but it's obviously a happy memory for you and something you miss. I tell you what, one day I'll visit your home and you can show me these rivers and take me . . . *fishing*, was it? How can fish live outside the sea?"

Sharley smiled sadly. "I'd like that. I'd like that a lot. Fishing's about the only sport I'm good at, so I should be able to teach you easily enough. And if not, old Hereward will set you straight. He always carries a spare rod, and he'd be happy to have somebody new to listen to his war stories."

"He's a warrior, then?"

"He used to be, yes. A housecarle. They're infantry soldiers, the anchor of the Icemark army. My granddad, King
Redrought, used to say they are the anvil and the cavalry is
the hammer. They're solid, you see. They'll hold a shield wall
all day if need be, and wait for the enemy to batter themselves
to pieces on their spears and axes."

"I see. Good defensive troops, then?" said Mekhmet,
happy that the conversation was turning to a familiar subject.

"They're good in offence too," said Sharley. "A charging
phalanx of housecarles with locked shields is like being hit by
a rockslide . . . so I'm told."

Mekhmet caught the small note of regret in his new
friend's voice. "So you're told? Haven't you seen it for
yourself?"

"Seen it, yes. But never experienced it, not even in the
practice lists."

"Why not?"

Sharley shifted uncomfortably. Here it was again: that
moment when he had to explain that he wasn't thought strong
enough to train as a warrior. "My mother won't let me . . .
I'm not thought . . . my leg . . ." his voice trailed away miserably.

Mekhmet gave this some thought as he silently piled fruit
on the plates that had lain empty as they'd talked. This Prince
of the North had obviously come on an embassy to the
Sultan's Court to ask for help in their war against the
Polypontian Empire. And despite the thousands of miles sep-
arating the two lands, it was clear that both cultures had the
same values of military prowess and honour. And yet, here

was a Prince of the Royal Blood who'd not been allowed to train as a warrior – the very point and reason for his existence!

Mekhmet might have felt contempt for such a pathetic creature, but there was something about the boy he found deeply likeable. It was as though he'd known him for years even though this was only the second time they'd met, and Mekhmet would be prepared to swear upon the word of the One that he had the heart of a lion. So why did his *mother,* of all people, refuse to let him train?

"Charlemagne, you have the name of one of the greatest warriors of the north. Doesn't that alone inspire you? Don't you feel a need to honour your namesake by becoming the best soldier you can possibly be?"

Sharley slumped on his divan. He'd carried the contempt of family and strangers alike for years, but for some reason he couldn't bear the thought of losing his new friend's respect. "I've never been allowed to train. I've always wanted to, *always*, but no one would let me."

"Why not?"

"The weapons are too heavy, and the shields. I couldn't lift them. And the horses are too big for me to control."

Mekhmet was puzzled; he'd heard that the fighting methods of the north were big and clumsy, but surely this boy could have been built up in some way. "It is only your leg that's a problem, isn't it?"

Sharley nodded. "But everyone says I'm *delicate.* I hate being delicate. I want to be like everyone else. I want to ride a warhorse and charge in the cavalry. I want to stand in the shield wall and carry a pike. I'm sure I could do it; I just need the chance to prove myself. I'm no smaller than my sister and she's a great warrior!"

"Your sister *fights?*"

"Of course. She's the Crown Princess," said Sharley, surprised at the question.

Mekhmet wondered if the hot sun had addled his friend's northern brains. Women didn't fight. At least, not in civilised lands. The Lusu armies to the south of the desert were made up of men and women, but they were an exception. Sharley didn't seem the type to make things up, and otherwise seemed totally sane, so with a shrug he thought it better to avoid the subject and get back to the important issue.

Standing, he straightened his back and looked down at his friend, who seemed to have shrunk into his divan. "Charlemagne. I don't know why your family decided to deny you the right to be a warrior, but I, Crown Prince Mekhmet Nasrid, Sword of the Desert, Beloved of the One, offer you now the opportunity to train as a soldier of the Desert Kingdom. You will become a cavalryman, where your weak leg will be irrelevant and you will ride at my side in battle."

Sharley hardly dared breathe. If he even moved, something might happen to take away the blaze of excitement and happiness that was flooding through him. But at last he could stay still no longer. He looked up at his friend, who was still gazing at him with fiery eyes.

"Can I?" he asked in a small voice. "Can I really? Oh yes, please! When can we start?"

He leaped to his feet, and collapsed to the floor as his gammy leg chose just the worst moment to let him down.

"Right away. But first we'd better see about strengthening that leg as much as we can. And I know just the man to do it!"

So it was that Sharley had met the palace Dance Master for the first time. Mekhmet had hurried to the door and bellowed loud and long down the corridor until a boy scuttled up and was given a message. Within ten minutes a tall elegant man sailed into the room. His face was finely featured and he salaamed with deep grace before standing as though about to dive from the highest rock into the deepest sea.

He looked at Sharley, his eyes narrowed as he scanned the slight frame before him, then he salaamed, and smiled. "If My Lord would do me the honour of walking to the door and back?"

Sharley set out, his face burning and his limp seeming to get ten times worse with each step he took. Then when he turned to walk back he stumbled through sheer nerves. He wanted to learn to fight, not prove to this dancer that he could walk! First his hopes had been raised and now he was being humiliated by this little charade.

The dancer glided over the floor to watch Sharley more closely. Then, with an apologetic nod, he smiled and said, "If My Lord will allow me to examine him?"

Sharley felt he had little choice, and agreed. He was then subjected to an embarrassing ten minutes or so of intense prodding and probing as the Dance Master felt his leg from his buttock to his foot.

The man then drew himself up to his full height and smiled. "But there is power here! More power than has been allowed to develop. Give me a month and My Lord will have more strength in his leg than he ever believed possible. Give me a year and he'll barely have a limp at all."

Sharley immediately felt better. "When can we start work?"

"Only say the word, and my time is yours," the Dance Master answered.

"We'll need to draw up a programme," said Mekhmet. "I'll

consult with the Weapons Master, and once we've all agreed a timetable we'll begin. Prince Charlemagne must be ready for when we march to the north."

Sharley looked at his friend in amazement. Not only was he to be trained as a warrior, but he'd succeeded in his mission. Had the Crown Prince of the Desert People really just declared his intention ride to the aid of the Icemark? He felt he'd burst with excitement and pride. Maggiore Totus would be enormously pleased. And he, Sharley, had managed it all without any help!

All of that had happened over three days earlier, and since then Sharley had spent hours in the Dance Master's studio. His muscles positively screamed with strain and tiredness. Sharley had jumped, squatted, leaped, raised and lowered himself on his toes, kicked, sat down and stood up again, until he almost wept with the pain and exhaustion. And all of this torture was performed in a room lined with mirrors that stretched from floor to ceiling. If Sharley had ever wondered if he looked a fool or not, he could soon confirm it just by watching himself translating the Dance Master's elegant movements into the fumbling, bumbling clumsiness of his own. To his tutor's elegant swan, he was a shitty-arsed barnyard fowl! But he never once complained. He may not have seen a weapon, but this was only the prelude to his training as a warrior, and he was prepared to suffer any amount of humiliation and discomfort to achieve his goal. It had been agreed that the Dance Master would have at least a week to prepare him for weapons training, after which his dance lessons would continue in tandem with his coaching as a warrior.

In less than three days Sharley would at last walk into the

lists to be taught the intricacies of a soldier's craft. He stretched his aching muscles, and almost shuddered with delight as he covered himself with his silken sheets and settled down for the night. One good thing was that he didn't have trouble sleeping at all these days; once he'd thought through the experiences of the day he always nodded off within seconds. At least that way the next day came quicker, and so would the time to start training with the Weapons Master.

"My Lord should meet the scimitar. She sings and stings and strikes like lightning," said Aramat Ilaman Hussein, the Weapons Master. He drew a slender, curved sword from a leather scabbard and flashed it about his head in a dazzling display that made the air whoop and hiss with the speed of each thrust and cut.

Sharley gasped. The sword was beautiful, with a hilt that was encrusted with emeralds and a blade of such dazzling brilliance it was almost impossible to see the inscription, taken from the Holy Book, which had been engraved along its length.

"The Crown Prince himself selected this sword for you. I was to tell you that the emeralds on the hilt were chosen to match your eyes and that the inscription on the blade talks of the sanctity of friendship," said the Weapons Master.

"But why didn't he give it to me himself?" Sharley asked, puzzled.

"The Prince told me that you would ask this question. The answer is simple: it is a tradition amongst the Desert People that a man never directly hands a sword to a friend when giving it as a gift, lest they should call conflict into their lives together."

"I see," said Sharley, and an excited smile lit up his whole face. He gazed at the beautiful weapon in Hussein's hands but waited patiently to see what would happen next.

Aramat Ilaman Hussein finally sheathed the sword and stood watching the strange barbarian boy before him. Was he ready yet to actually train? Would he ever be ready? Usually Hussein worked with the sons of Sultans and aristocrats. They began with small wooden replicas and graduated slowly to blunted lightweight blades, before finally being allowed to use the real thing. The scimitar was the main weapon, of course. It was the sword of a gentleman, and not merely a means of killing the enemy. A scimitar was an *extension* of the Desert warrior who carried it. So should a barbarian youth wield such a weapon? Oh, he couldn't deny his enthusiasm – the boy was desperately eager to shine in all areas. But he was from the uncivilised north!

The boy was gazing at him now with his strange emerald-coloured eyes, waiting so trustingly for his word. Hussein sighed; perhaps it was providence that had sent him, and if so, who was he to question the designs and plans of the One? Slowly he raised the scimitar to hand it over, but as he did so, a strange weight fell on his back, and his legs gave way so that he was kneeling as he offered up the sword.

"Take this Blade of Fire and carry it home to the northern lands, and there let it rage and roar at the head of the Army-of-Friends who will be as steel in the hearts of the invader!"

Hussein nearly choked with surprise; the voice had not been his own. He hadn't even thought the words, let alone uttered them, and yet they'd leaped from his throat deep and powerful while his own vocal cords lay silent!

Charlemagne looked at him oddly, as if afraid, but then he strode forward and virtually snatched the scimitar. Quickly he unsheathed it, and shouting aloud some terrible cry in his barbarous tongue, he wielded the blade as though a veteran of many wars.

"The enemy is among us. They burn our cities and kill our people! Blood! Blast! And Fire! Blood! Blast! And Fire!"

Hussein watched, astounded, as the boy then perfectly executed every move from the training manual. He'd only seen the Weapons Master run through it once, barely minutes before, and yet here he was lunging and thrusting, parrying and blocking as though he'd practised for days.

Crown Prince Mekhmet looked out over the heads of his courtiers. He'd seen the door open and close at the rear of the audience chamber and he was hoping it was Sharley. Over the past week he'd had reports from the Weapons Master that read almost like Praise poems for his friend's abilities. He was determined to give it only another couple of days before joining him in the lists and testing his new skills himself. Obviously Sharley had the gifts of a natural warrior, and Mekhmet was enormously proud not only that he, Mekhmet, had caused them to be revealed, but also that his new friend should have these gifts at all. This was a new sensation. Before Sharley had arrived, he'd had ambitions and interest only in himself, and now he was just as eager for Sharley to do well.

The perfumed and be-silked courtiers began to draw aside, salaaming deeply to a small figure that strode confidently through them. It *was* Sharley! Mekhmet grinned.

"Eh up, hairy arse! How's things?"

"Great, fathead. Just great. How's things with you?"

"Good. What've you got to tell me?"

"Not a lot. Old Hussein's got me practising cut and thrust from the back of a wooden training horse, and he even gets some of his assistants to push it around so that I can have a go at slicing melons in two as we roll by. The wheels sound like thunder on the wooden training-floor. It's a wonder you didn't hear them."

Mekhmet grinned again. "What about letting you loose on a real horse?"

"No sign of that yet," Sharley answered, settling himself in a chair that a servant had hurriedly placed next to the throne. "I suppose he wonders if I can actually ride." He'd long ago decided never to mention the incident of taking his mother's charger, Havoc. Even so, ever since Hussein had presented him with the scimitar, speaking in a voice that obviously wasn't his own, Sharley had been content to let events unfold in their own way. He knew he'd be allowed to ride a horse when it was necessary for him to do so. Obviously there were powers at work beyond his understanding.

"You must have a mount. The sooner you get used to the ways of horses the better," said Mekhmet, who was secretly worried that this lack of experience could cause real problems. Many of the Desert People's cavalry troopers had been in the saddle since before they could walk.

Sharley nodded, but he wasn't really concerned. He'd been around horses all of his life and knew more about them than anyone in the Desert Kingdom realised. He might not have been allowed to ride them, but he'd helped the stable-hands since he was a little boy and was completely relaxed in the company of horses. Not only that, but he *had* managed to control Havoc for most of the time he'd been on him. Admittedly Havoc had bolted once, but he was known to be a horse with a strong will that not even the most experienced stable-hand could always control. Sharley was fairly confident that, given the right animal, he'd be just fine.

"Let's go to my apartments. I want to talk without too many listening ears," Mekhmet said.

Sharley looked about at the courtiers, almost embarrassed by the Crown Prince's distrust of the men with whom he spent most of his days. But no one seemed concerned. If he accidentally caught the eye of one of them, they merely smiled and salaamed politely.

The Majlis of the Sultan was a world that Sharley simply didn't understand. The most insulting attitudes and opinions could co-exist with friendship and loyalty, as long as they were decently dressed in the polite forms of society. In the Icemark a straight toe-to-toe fight would soon clear up any misunderstandings, but here the atmosphere was sometimes almost poisonous. The only other place Sharley knew of that was anything like it was the palace of the Doge in Venezzia.

He was jolted out of his thoughts as Mekhmet stood and touched his arm. "Come on, I've some sherbet cooling in my rooms. We'll talk there."

The entire Court rose and salaamed as the Princes left, and when the door closed behind them Sharley heaved a sigh of relief. "That's better; the air's fresher out here."

"No stench of plotting and distrust, you mean," Mekhmet said frankly. "I totally agree." With a shrug of his shoulders, he took off his embroidered waistcoat and his turban, grimacing like someone who'd just put down a heavy weight, then they set off along the corridor and across the lawn that led to Mekhmet's private apartments.

"The Weapons Master is more than pleased with you," he said. "In fact, he actually said he's amazed at how readily you've taken to the training regime."

"Did he?" said Sharley, enormously gratified. "I've been waiting for almost fifteen years to start living my life; I suppose I'm just making up for lost time."

"Yes, I expect so," said Mekhmet. "Everything's going nicely to plan, but there are two mountains to climb yet. First – the more difficult of the two – the Sultan has to be told about our expedition to the north, and second, you must have a horse."

"Yes," said Sharley quietly. "Will he be difficult to persuade?"

"Without doubt," said Mekhmet opening the door to the Court of the Lions and standing back to let his friend enter first. "He'll refuse to sanction even the idea of sending soldiers to help in your war against Bellorum, but that will merely be a show of diplomacy for the benefit of the Polypontian spies. Later we'll receive a message to attend him in his private quarters where we'll discuss logistics and details."

"But how can you be so certain that's how things will happen?"

Mekhmet led the way to his day room, where a jug of sherbet sat cooling in a bucket of ice. "Because I know the Sultan better than anyone. Even the Grand Vizier cannot guess his actions better than me. Everyone thinks he's just a fat old man waiting to die, but I know that in his heart my father is still the warrior he was in his youth. You simply have to know how to fan the embers of power so that they can burst into flames again." He poured two beakers of the icy drink and gave one to Sharley. "He doesn't know himself that he'll be lending his support to the expedition . . . yet."

"I see," said Sharley, feeling as loutish and unsophisticated as a peasant on his first visit to the big city. "Yes, I see."

CHAPTER 20

The Court of Sultan Haroun Nasrid the Magnificent was at least three times larger than that of the Crown Prince. Most of the courtiers had been with him for over twenty years, as they'd cleverly cultivated his favour when he was still only a young man during his father's reign. And now they were reaping the benefits of their gamble by living a luxurious life at the expense of the palace treasury. This they considered their proper due: after all, they created a Court that was populated with richly dressed and seemly men who provided a sophisticated, stable palace culture that reflected the society of the country around it.

But today held the promise of new events that would probably entertain the courtiers for weeks to come. Rumour had it that the foreign Prince Charlemagne from the barbarian north was to be given an audience with His Majesty, although his expected request for military aid would certainly be turned down. Refusals of the Royal Favour were always far more interesting than the granting of wishes and requests.

A flurry of movement near the main doors concentrated their minds, and they all salaamed deeply as the Sultan entered the Court of the Nightingales. The elderly monarch seemed a little more sprightly today, and he needed only one servant to help him climb the short flight of steps to his throne. The older courtiers, who knew the temperament of Haroun Nasrid the Magnificent as precisely as a drover understands the moods of his cattle, guessed that he was looking forward to an interesting change to the time-honoured order of his routine. Today, he was to meet Charlemagne Athelstan Redrought Strong-in-the-Arm Lindenshield, Prince of the country that had defeated the vicious Polypontian Empire. How could any-one with such a gloriously barbaric name fail to be anything other than entertaining, at the very least? Crown Prince Mekhmet had assured his father that the northern Prince was the most striking of individuals, not only in his physical appearance, but also in terms of personality and temperament. And this had been confirmed by the Sultan's spies.

The Prince's training in the Sultanate's method of warfare was going marvellously, he was informed. The barbarian Prince shone in almost every use of weapon and style of fight-ing, and overall seemed to be a most fitting bearer of the name Charlemagne. After all, was it not the ancient King of Gallia who had learned how to fight using the ways of the Desert People? And was it not also this very same king who had befriended the Sultan of the day, Abd al-Rahman II? Perhaps the One had decreed that the name should return and the bearer once again be an unlikely friend of the Desert People.

The Sultan nodded to the Chief Eunuch, who bowed and raised his hand to the door porters who stood far away across the wide room. The doors were opened, swinging outwards on to a courtyard where the petitioners usually stood, but which today was empty, save for two small figures staring proudly ahead. The Princes Mekhmet and Charlemagne had arrived for their audience.

As the doors to the audience chamber slowly opened, Sharley almost panicked, but then Mekhmet caught his eye and grinned. "Eh up, hairy arse," he whispered. "Let's go and show them how it's done!"

Sharley grinned back. The Crown Prince seemed to have a better grasp of the language of the housecarles' guardroom than even he had! Hardly a day went by when he didn't use some odd phrase or other he'd picked up from Sharley.

They both nodded and stepped out together, sweeping across the floor of the audience chamber. Sharley almost found himself swaggering! There was something about the clothing of the Desert People that gave a bearing and dignity to the wearer, and Mekhmet had assured him that the loose trousers, waistcoat and sash of his people suited him very well. With the addition of the long cloak he was wearing, the outfit made Sharley feel ten feet tall and invincible. Mekhmet's only regret was that his friend would insist on wearing black. There was a whole palette of colours Sharley could have worn, but he would only ever choose black. Still, he wore it well, and the colour set off his mane of red hair and his strange green eyes magnificently.

Sharley stared rigidly ahead at the throne as he advanced across the room. This was the first time he would see the Sultan, and though Mekhmet had hinted that his father was older than might be expected and was less than well, Sharley wasn't ready for the small fat figure they were approaching. Was *this* Haroun Nasrid the Magnificent, Lord of the Sands and Beloved of the One? He'd expected someone taller, more elegant and formidable. And even if he was old and ill, Sharley had expected a noble ruin of a once mighty form, not this almost circular little munchkin who was wearing a turban that seemed almost as big as he was!

Some of Sharley's nervousness evaporated. This may have been the most important meeting he'd had to date, on which the fate of the Icemark and literally millions of lives depended, but he really couldn't be afraid of a little man who made Maggiore Totus look fierce!

They stamped to a halt before the throne, and both Princes inclined their heads in keeping with protocol. The Sultan turned on them the fiercest eyes that Sharley had ever seen. Even the Greyling bear he'd fought so long ago in the Great Forest, when he'd tried to prove his worth as a warrior, had looked kinder! They were the deepest black, and somewhere far down in their depths a spark of ferocity burned, reminding Sharley of Tharaman-Thar. Fear reclaimed him and his mouth went dry.

"My Lord Sultan, Haroun Nasrid the Magnificent, Ruler of the Lands of Fire, and my most revered father, may I present to you Prince Charlemagne Athelstan Redrought Strong-in-the-Arm Lindenshield of the Icemark, Regent to his people in Exile, and beloved son of Queen Thirrin, vanquisher of General Scipio Bellorum and the armies of the Polypontian Empire."

The old Monarch faced Sharley full on, and the Prince felt his bad leg preparing to give way for the first time in days. He bowed his head in silence, and swallowed hard in a desperate attempt to moisten his dry mouth.

"I am pleased to meet a scion of the mighty House of Lindenshield. May the One for ever bless the lineage of the warrior clan who defeated Scipio Bellorum and made as dust his pride and ambition."

"And may the One forever smile upon the House of Nasrid who have been for generations as a scimitar in the flank of the Empire," Sharley replied with equal courtesy, hiding his terrible nerves behind the formality of his words.

"You speak our language well," said the Sultan with delighted surprise, even though his spies had already told him that the barbarian Prince was fluent. "You have the slightest trace of an accent that serves only to add charm to your words."

"Father, Prince Charlemagne has come as an ambassador to our lands and would make a request of us," said Mekhmet, coming to the point far more quickly than Sharley had expected.

"My son would finish our meeting before we have drawn breath, it would seem," the Sultan said. "Well, so be it; now that you have mentioned the purpose of Prince Charlemagne's visit perhaps he should reveal its details to us."

Now he had come to it! This was the point and purpose of weeks of travelling; this could be the fruition or downfall of all Maggie's plans, and most important of all, the survival or destruction of the Icemark depended on it. The terrible weight of the responsibility seemed to crush Sharley and he felt his back physically rounding as he tried to look up to the throne.

"My Lord . . . My Lord," he stuttered, and he almost despaired of ever pleading the case for military aid. But then a sense of his own destiny flared through his frame and his spine straightened. Had he but known it, both his mother and his sister had experienced just such a strengthening of resolve when their confidence was at its lowest ebb. This was the blood of the Lindenshield clan suddenly finding its courage under the threat of failure and defeat.

"My Lord Haroun Nasrid the Magnificent, Lord of the Sands and Beloved of the One. I am sent as ambassador from the Land of the Icemark to ask for your help in our continuing struggle with the Polypontian Empire. Our armies and allies are mighty indeed, but even so they are in danger of being overwhelmed by the uncountable numbers of the Imperial forces. Even the sharpest scimitar may be blunted against the immovable mountain, and even the mightiest sea can be swallowed by the unending deserts. So, too, are our forces in danger of finally succumbing to the limitless might of the Empire." He paused and looked out over the mass of courtiers, who'd all crowded nearer to hear him speak. Their heads were so closely packed together that they looked like an extraordinary mosaic, made up of a rainbow of brightly coloured turbans. "We have great need of help in the war that rages even now in the lands of my people, and I believe that the famous and formidable cavalry of the Desert People could help us to defeat the Empire and its plans once and for all. Help us in our struggle, and in so doing draw the Imperial war machine away from your own lands and so bring relief to your borders."

The Sultan gazed at the Prince before him. In the passion of his eloquent speech Charlemagne's amazing red hair had risen about his head like a halo of fire, and his green eyes sparked and blazed like those of a wild beast. Truly, here was a warrior of the House of Lindenshield. How odd that it took the training and fighting methods of the Desert People to hone it to this point of confidence. "Prince Charlemagne, the fighting might of your valiant land is known to all of those who struggle against the oppression of the Polypontian Empire, and what individual could resist your call to aid and arms? But those of us who carry the burden of rule must always consider the risks of answering such a call."

Mekhmet had warned Sharley that the Sultan would refuse his request in public, so he wasn't surprised at the direction his words were taking. Even so, he suddenly had an overwhelming need to convince all who heard him of his cause.

"Forgive me, My Lord, if I speak bluntly, but wouldn't it be better to finally confront the evil of the Empire and defeat it now, rather than allow this slow strangling war against your people to go on any longer?"

"We have maintained our independence in the face of Imperial aggression far longer than any other nation that has been subjected to the wrath of the Empire!" The Sultan spoke with a slow rising anger. Who was this youth to dictate policy to a man of his experience?

"And yet your cities are dying and your trade routes are drying up, and your people go hungry as you fight against the raids that go on year after year, decade after decade," said Sharley, quite unable to stop himself arguing. "You have the independence of a country that is doing exactly what the Imperial strategists want it to do: fighting within its own lands, damaging its own resources while it slowly grows weaker and weaker with each passing year."

The Sultan almost screamed in rage. "And what other option have we had, Little Lord Knowledgeable? When the Polypontians first attacked our lands there were no others to help us, and already we were weakened by the slow decline of our trade routes, lost to the Venezzians. And yet despite all of this we defeated two Imperial invasion forces and even blooded Scipio Bellorum's nose."

"Yes, but only when he was still a junior officer with little experience of war! If Bellorum truly wanted to add the Desert Kingdom to his domain he would have returned as a General long before now, and your exhausted land would have been forced to stand alone against the mightiest war machine the known world has ever seen."

The Sultan's heart pounded, and his hands and feet tingled with the sensation of rushing blood for the first time in years. How dare this little upstart argue with Haroun Nasrid the Magnificent!

"If the Desert People are so weak and unworthy, why do you seek an alliance with them for your barbarous little nation in the frigid and frosty north?"

"Quite simply because they are neither weak nor unworthy. They are, on the contrary, superb. Their army's name strikes dread in the heart of their enemies, and the thunder of their hooves is like the drum of doom to those who dare to oppose them! But here, within your borders, you are trapped. Come with me to the north and let your squadrons fly like the storming winds over the wide lands of the Icemark and drive Scipio Bellorum back to his lair never to come out ever again!" said Sharley with passion, astonishing himself with his audacity and eloquence. Now there were notes of approval tumbled in with the murmurings of outrage. "Your policies and tactics have been misguided. No, more than that, they have been wrong for decades and have allowed the Polypontians to inflict a long slow defeat on a people who should have been their greatest challenge!"

"*Wrong?* My policies have been WRONG?" raged the Sultan. It wasn't possible for a monarch of the House of Nasrid to be wrong. "At worst my policies may have been less successful than they might have been, but they were never *wrong!*"

Mekhmet was watching the argument in amazement. He had known his friend had depths he could only guess at, but this toe-to-toe verbal battle with his father left him speechless. He, too, was was outraged by what Sharley was saying, even though there'd been times when he'd thought the same things himself, and he was astounded that Sharley dared face up to the Sultan in this way. Mekhmet's loyalties were hopelessly divided, and all he could do was to watch in silence.

"My Lord," Sharley began again. "Now is the time to ally what strength you still have with a determined and experienced resistance against the might of the Polypontian Empire, and in so doing draw the load of oppression and warfare away from your lands. Let the killing grounds be in the Icemark far to the north, and allow your kingdom and people a respite from the constant clamour and damage of war."

The Sultan drew breath. He was angrier than he ever remembered being before, and yet, at the same time, he had to admit that he'd heard more opinions expressed in the space of the last few minutes than he had heard in more than twenty years of rule. Someone had *dared* to have a different view and to voice it with the sort of force and vigour that he himself would have done, and quite simply it incensed him. And yet . . . and yet he felt more alive and more *invigorated* than he had in years and years of Palace living.

"And if I send my squadrons of cavalry away to fight in the north, how will I protect my borders?" he asked in a quieter voice.

"If you send your squadrons to the north, the Imperial forces will need every unit, every regiment, every army it can possibly muster to hold at bay the greatest alliance of people the world will have ever seen!"

"So you say, a mere callow youth with little experience of life and no understanding of warfare," said the Sultan scornfully.

"No! So says Maggiore Totus, a venerable diplomat and politician of deep wisdom and long experience. I am merely his messenger come to deliver that which he would have said."

"Then where is this paragon of diplomatic virtue? Why has he left a child to speak in his place?"

Sharley ignored the intended insult. "He lies exhausted and ill at the desert house of Al-Khatib the merchant. It was he who begged me to go on and seek audience with the Sultan so that our mission might not fail."

Haroun Nasrid the Magnificent paused and took stock. "Al-Khatib is well known to me. He has many . . . uses and has helped in several important projects. What does he say of the plans of this Maggiore Totus?"

"My Lord, in truth we told him few details, but his mind is such that he guessed much of our mission and agreed with it wholeheartedly," Sharley answered, childishly crossing his fingers against the untruths and exaggerations he found himself forced to make.

"That rings true," the Sultan said. "He has a brain of 'lightning and oceans', as the old saying goes – both speed and great depth. If anyone could guess the secret within any mission it would be he! And you say that he agreed with your ideas?"

"Yes, My Lord."

"Then that . . ." The old monarch sat back in his throne, his eyes focused on the middle distance as he cogitated. "Then that puts everything in a different light. I must think on this for a moment or two." He suddenly looked up. "Where is the grace and hospitality of my Court? Bring seats and refreshments for my son and his friend, Prince Charlemagne!"

Under the rigid mask of his Princely face Mekhmet was in a state of shock. Never had he witnessed such a debate so heatedly argued in his father's Court. No one had ever dared disagree with the Sultan, and none in the entire history of the Desert People had had the temerity to tell the ruling Monarch that he was wrong and lived for more than a few seconds! He stole a glance at Sharley, who sat staring into a goblet of sherbet, the brilliant crimson of his face slowly fading to the colour of sunsets. Mekhmet was appalled to have witnessed such scenes, and yet he felt an enormous admiration for this strangest of barbarians who came from the lands of ice. How proud he was to call him *friend*! How horrified he was to be associated with him! He took a deep swallow of sherbet and spilled most of it down his embroidered waistcoat. What contradictions and calamities!

Sharley grinned when he saw Mekhmet pouring his drink down his front, and when a servant hurried forward with a cloth, he took it from him and started to mop up the spillage. Suddenly, Sharley started to shake and his face went crimson again as he tried to suppress the terrible giggles that were welling up inside him. The hideous and deeply terrible tension had to find an outlet somewhere, and in the alchemy of fear, youth and stress it translated itself into laughter. Mekhmet stared at him in amazement; not only was he dabbing at his damp waistcoat like a servant, but he seemed to be going mad!

He tried to grab the cloth from Sharley's hand, and a tug

of war developed that made his friend snort and squeak even more. "Stop it! You'll get us both in trouble," Mekhmet hissed urgently. But then he caught Sharley's bloodshot eye and the terrible infection of giggling was passed on. He started to shake and splutter himself, and the pair became desperately engrossed in cleaning up the spilt sherbet as they giggled in mortified fear and pain. "Give it to me. It's my drink!"

"I didn't think you wanted it. You threw it away quickly enough!"

They both looked at each other and spluttered with horrified glee. How could they stop themselves? It was hilarious and terrifying, and when they looked round at the outraged and puzzled faces of the courtiers they laughed even more.

"I think we're causing a scene," said Sharley between gasps, but Mekhmet could only nod as he continued to shake with nervous laughter.

The Sultan rose to his feet and glared over the audience chamber.

"Enough!" he bellowed, and both Princes stopped abruptly. Sharley somehow managed to swallow a giggle and then burp cavernously. What would happen now, he thought to himself? Would he be dragged away and slammed in the deepest, darkest dungeon for daring to laugh in the Royal Presence?

"Enough! I have reached a decision. The slow, strength-sapping war with the Polypontian Empire has been fought for too long. The time has come to seize the initiative and take the struggle to a region of *our* choosing.

"This barbarian youth has swept through my Court like a hurricane with neither care nor consideration for our sensibilities and customary politeness. He has rudely spoken his thoughts aloud and presented us with nothing but the barest of truths. And yet I was arrogant enough to consider rejecting the honesty of his words and expelling him from the land. Such is the folly of the Crowned Head!

"Prince Charlemagne has opened my eyes and offers a most important alternative. Namely, an alliance with the House of Lindenshield, and the opportunity to fight in a theatre of war many miles from our beloved land. Now we will no longer have to worry about goading the Empire into a full-scale invasion. Now *we* can take the initiative; now *we* can launch an attack on an aggressor who for too long has drained our land of its lifeblood. I now proclaim this audience at an end, but hear all present these words: the army of the Desert People must be prepared and ready to march within a month. And I say to my son, Crown Prince Mekhmet: look to your Guest Friends the Lusu People beyond the mountains in the south. Their regiments will swell our depleted ranks to a formidable size and the Polypontian Empire will tremble to look on our power!"

What had he done? What wasps' nest had he stirred up? Sharley felt almost dizzy with excitement and, it had to be said, fear. He sat now in the garden of the Court of the Lions, waiting for Mekhmet to join him, and his mind reeled with the contradicting emotions that rampaged through his head. He'd done it! He'd somehow persuaded the Desert People to join the alliance against Bellorum and his murderous sons! Maggie would be so proud of him. But what now? His lessons with both the Dancing Master and Weapons Master continued, but he was very aware of his limitations. He hadn't yet lifted any weapon in anger, and he knew full well that there was a world of difference between the training ground and the reality of the battlefield. And he hadn't even got a horse yet, and Mekhmet was already making plans for them both to go on an official visit to the Lusu People who lived far to the south. It was all happening too quickly!

He was on the point of panicking and running aimlessly about the garden of beautifully clipped hedges and trees when Mekhmet appeared. He looked suitably serious as he walked across the lawn to join him, but as he drew nearer he smiled. "I still can't believe what's happening. I thought you'd really messed things up when you started to tell my father that he'd been doing it all wrong for over a decade, but then he agreed with you! Unheard of! You really must be charmed, that's all I can say."

"Perhaps I am," Sharley said with a grin. "Something seemed to be talking through me, and saying all the right things, even though they sounded so outrageous."

"'Outrageous' is exactly the right word. I shouldn't think my father's been spoken to like that since before he came to the throne. I really don't know how you got away with it. But you did, and now we're preparing to march to war! Al-Khatib's been summoned to the palace and things are already in motion. He's good at arranging all those things an army needs: transport, food, billets. It's all in hand. And now we have to go to the Lusu and get them to join us."

"Yes . . . the Lusu. Odd name. Exactly who are they again?"

"My Guest Friends. I travelled to their lands over a year ago and met with their Queen, Ketshaka. I must have made a good impression because they named one of their *impis*, or regiments, after me." Mekhmet had been pacing about excitedly, but now he flung himself down on the grass next to

Sharley. "They have the most brilliant cavalry and they ride
. . . well, you'll see what they ride when we get there. Talking
of which, you need a horse. We've got a long way to go over
hard country, so you'll need the best." He lay back with his
hands behind his head and stared into the brilliantly blue sky.
"And I've found one for you," he added with a grin.

Sharley looked at him in astonishment. "Found me a—?
But I haven't enough money to buy a horse!"

Mekhmet frowned. "Who said anything about buying him?
He's a present from me." He leaped to his feet. "Come and
meet him." He rushed off across the garden, and Sharley hurried to catch up. After a few moments they came to a set of
double gates set in a wall that bordered Mekhmet's private
quarters. "Put these on," he said, casually handing Sharley a
pair of beautiful riding boots that just happened to be standing ready next to the gates.

"But . . . but who? What?"

"Yes, I'm sure," said Mekhmet infuriatingly. "Have you
got them on yet? Fine. Now go back and stand next to the
tree," he said, pointing.

A guard stood waiting on the wall. Mekhmet nodded to
him. "We're ready now. Send him in."

The gates were slowly opened by some invisible mecha-
nism to reveal an empty courtyard. A small dust devil skipped
and whirled over the flagstones, but otherwise everything was
still. Sharley began to wonder if his friend was playing a joke
on him, but then a distant sound of hooves echoed on the hot
afternoon air. Slowly, they came closer, neat and rhythmical as
a ticking clock, until their sound seemed to fill the courtyard
and Sharley's whole head. Then, walking elegantly through
one of the archways set in the back wall of the courtyard, a

beautiful horse appeared. He was completely black, but for a star on his forehead, and he moved with an odd mixture of fire and grace that made Sharley think of the wind blowing patterns through the long grass of the Icemark.

When he caught sight of the small figure standing by the tree, the horse stopped and snorted, nodding his head and dancing uncertainly on his neat hooves. Sharley instinctively put his hand out and called, "Come on then. Come and say hello."

The horse seemed reassured by his voice and walked forward, his beautiful head nodding in rhythm with his step, until he stood on the grass a few feet from Sharley's hand. "Come on. I won't eat you," he said, and the horse moved a little closer and whickered quietly. Sharley found himself holding his breath. Could this magnificent animal really be his? He held out his hand again, and after hesitating for a few moments, the horse stepped up to him and allowed his muzzle to be stroked.

In the brilliant desert sunshine his coat gleamed as though polished, and every muscle stood out in a relief of light and shadow along his flanks. Sharley was still amazed by how small the Desert People's horses were compared to the huge beasts of his mother's cavalry, but this one had even more of the sense of fire and pent-up power than most of his breed.

Mekhmet joined them. "He's called Suleiman, after one of our wisest and most benevolent sultans. He's very young – just reached his full strength and growth. And he's that rarest of things, a gentle stallion. I thought he matched your temperament perfectly."

"Suleiman," Sharley repeated, still hardly daring to believe that such a beautiful animal could be his. "Can I ride him?"

"Of course, he's yours. Do as you will."

The horse was already saddled in a beautiful war caparison of black leather trimmed with brilliant red. Sharley scrambled round to the stirrup but then hesitated. Would his leg be strong enough, or would he need to be helped into the saddle? Certainly Suleiman wasn't anywhere near as tall as Havoc, and he was sure his leg was stronger now than it had ever been, but a sudden fear of needing help to climb on to his very own horse engulfed him, and he stepped back. This would be the first real test of his new status as a warrior. If he failed this simple task, what hope could he have of ever leading an army to the north?

Suleiman turned to look at him and whickered gently, almost as though he understood his new master's fears and was encouraging him. That was all Sharley needed, and he strode forward, placed his foot in the stirrup, seized the pommel and sailed skywards into the saddle with no problems at all. Immediately, horse and Prince seemed to become one, as Suleiman blew and pawed at the ground impatiently, and Sharley took the reins.

"Where shall I take him?" he asked, looking around at the manicured garden and neatly trimmed lawns.

"That way! Take him through there!" Mekhmet shouted, pointing across the courtyard to where a set of double gates was slowly opening on to the desert. Sharley hadn't realised that the palace was set directly against the southern perimeter walls of the city, but now he could see out into the wilderness of hot sands and slowly undulating dunes.

The Prince of the North looked at the world lying before him, and leaning forward in the war-saddle he stroked the horse's proudly arching neck. "The day's waiting for us,

Suleiman. There, through the gateway, beyond the walls and this city of men! It's calling to.us!"

The horse let out a piercing squeal and leaped forward. Black horse and black rider thundered through the courtyard and shot out of the gates. The world was gathered under Suleiman's flying hooves and pushed contemptuously away as far distance became close, then passed in a dark flash of power.

Mekhmet ran to the gates and watched as horse and rider galloped through the burning sands of the desert. Their blackness against the emphatic brilliance of the landscape was as stark as a brushstroke on a blank canvas.

"The Shadow of the Storm," Mekhmet whispered, not realising he had named his friend's legend.

CHAPTER 21

Three horsemen sat on the hilltop, arrogant hands on arrogant hips, surveying the city before them. This was the third settlement of the Five Boroughs to be attacked. The first two had died hard, draining the invasion force of valuable men and resources before they finally fell, but this next operation would be different. Scipio Bellorum expected the city to be taken within a matter of hours. He also expected the casualty figures to be almost negligible – negligible, that was, for the Imperial forces. The garrison and the few citizens left within the city itself would be wiped out.

Sulla and Octavius Bellorum watched their father with a pleasant sense of excited anticipation. Today, a new weapon was to be deployed against the Icemark, another of the General's innovations designed to minimise costs to the Empire's exchequer and increase the rate of Imperial expansion. Unfortunately, the new equipment hadn't been quite ready until now, and the previous conventional tactics had proved costly. But now everything was set to go.

Scipio Bellorum raised his monoculum and scanned the southern horizon. "Ah! Nemesis has arrived," he said with quiet relish, and handed the instrument to Sulla, who soon spotted the series of dark shapes advancing across the sky. Octavius impatiently snatched the monoculum from his brother and greedily searched the horizon, and grunted in satisfaction.

"Bye-bye, townie!" he said in a grotesquely high-pitched falsetto, and laughed.

For the next few minutes the shapes steadily advanced until they began to translate themselves into solid forms. They were flying at several hundred feet, and the larger ones looked like sea-going ships. But strangest of all were the enormous balloons, made of hide and oiled canvas, that rose above them and were securely attached to the vessels by a series of stout ropes and nets. The Imperial scientists had managed to isolate a gas that was lighter than air and trap it in these massive canopies. And such was its power, entire fighting galleons could be lifted into the air.

This was Scipio Bellorum's new weapon, and he called it his Sky Navy. Every ship was fitted with sails that extended on long spars from its sides like horizontal masts, and by this means the navy swept across the sky like a flotilla of storm clouds. There was also an escort of hundreds of smaller craft, called wasp-fighters, mustered in squadrons. These were massive man-carrying kites, completely independent of the ground and controlled by a pilot who lay horizontally along the length of his craft in a sling. From here he could make his flying machine climb or dive, and bank to right and left at incredible speeds and with great agility. The fighters were heavily armed with muskets, pistols and a powerful crossbow, all attached to a bracket at the front. The new weapon had been thoroughly tested in a number of war-games, but this invasion of the Icemark would be its first real conflict.

There had then been weeks of delay as the unpredictable climate of the Icemark had plunged the land back into a brief period of winter again, and the ships had been unable to fly as ice formed on every surface, coating ropes and canopy, woodwork and even the metal barrels of the cannon. The higher the ships had climbed, the worse it had become, and eventually some of the galleons had become so encrusted and weighed down by ice that they'd become too heavy for the gas in the canopies to keep them aloft and they'd sunk to earth, completely defeated by the weather. But now the conditions had changed again, and everything was ready for the new weapons to be deployed.

As Bellorum and his sons watched, the navy swept overhead, the dozens of flying ships and hundreds of wasp-fighters oddly silent but for the distant groaning of wood and rope, and the thick rattling rumble of wind in canvas.

Down in the city, warning shouts and the clamour of alarm bells sounded. The enemy were attacking, and they were coming from the sky! Amazing as this was, it wasn't as shocking as it might have been to other soldiers who had stood against the might of the Empire. The housecarles and fyrd of the Icemark had a history of fighting an airborne enemy in the form of the armies of the Vampire King and Queen. Even so, it was unheard of amongst the warriors of mortal people, and the defenders of the city could only gaze in wonder as Bellorum's Sky Navy came on. All along the walls, housecarles, werewolves and soldiers of the fyrd could be seen scrambling to their battle positions. But against this new weapon there was little they could do.

The wasp-fighters suddenly peeled away from the larger galleons in squadron formations, and swooped down on the defenders waiting on the walls. The crackle of musket-fire erupted into the sky. But this stage of the attack didn't last long; in a matter of minutes, the fighters swept on over the city, where they climbed skywards again on the thermals that rose from the sun-warmed streets and buildings.

Now the huge galleons sailed over the walls, their hulls casting ominous shadows over the settlement. Then, with an awesome slowness, they broke formation and took up positions over almost every district of the city.

Scipio Bellorum followed every move with rapt attention through his monoculum, a cold grin like the rictus of a skull splitting his face. "Now!" he hissed. "Let them have it now!"

Large hatchways in the hull of each ship swung open, and barrels began to cascade in a tumbling avalanche, down on to the city. Within seconds the shattering 'crump' of explosions began to echo over the sky, followed a few minutes later by the delicate blooming of flames.

"Yes! Oh yes! Now we shall see how long these rat-hole cities can resist the Imperial will! Raise a shield wall against bombs, my little barbarians; send your werewolves to attack my sky-ships, if you can!"

Now the wasp-fighters swept back into action, dropping barrel after barrel of pitch and oil on to the city, fuelling the flames, then spiralling away on the huge waves of heat that blasted into the sky.

Bellorum was ecstatic; in less than half an hour the mainly wooden buildings within the stone shell of the city walls were fiercely ablaze. Thick black smoke poured skywards, and a strange song arose from the dying settlement as the crackle and roar of the flames mingled with the screams of the people still trapped inside.

The Sky Navy continued bombing, the huge galleons driving through the smoke and re-emerging like ships sailing through sea fog, while the wasp-fighters dived and swooped almost through the flames themselves, as they fed the conflagration with oil and pitch.

Scipio Bellorum now raised his hand, and units of infantry and cavalry that had been waiting out of sight marched forward to cover the gates and kill anyone who tried to escape. They were soon busy cutting down the fleeing civilians who hadn't already been evacuated. Even when the housecarles and werewolf guard had finally abandoned their blazing positions, they had put up only a feeble resistance, half choked as they were on the smoke, and many injured by the fires they'd fought long and hard with inadequate buckets of water.

The sky galleons at last turned ponderously from their target and sailed away as the wasp-fighters swept and tumbled about them. Their first mission was completed – the city was dead. Only its corpse continued to burn, like a body on a funeral pyre.

The General and his sons watched the spectacle of flame and death for another hour. Before they rode away laughing, they left orders with the Field Commanders to let the city burn itself out, then occupy what remained. With such spectacular results, Bellorum expected to be besieging Frostmarris in a matter of days rather than weeks.

Thirrin sat quietly holding Oskan's hand as she gazed into the fire in their private rooms. Eodred's continuing self-imposed withdrawal from life nagged and fretted on the edge of their minds, but now there were further worries to think about. The news was bad, very bad, and they both needed a few moments to digest it before they could even begin to react.

After several minutes of complete silence, Oskan drew a deep breath and kissed Thirrin on the cheek. "So, Bellorum's done it again – presented us with another impossible situation to which there seems to be no answer. Some things never change, do they?"

"Don't joke about it, Oskan!" she snapped. "This could be the end of us! How can we fight flying ships? How can we defend our cities and people from exploding barrels of gunpowder dropped from the skies?"

"I think you'll find the term is *bombs*. 'How can we defend our cities and people from *bombs*?'"

"Well, whatever they're called, it's impossible! Most of the time the ships flew too high for even the most powerful longbow, and we couldn't jack the ballistas up far enough to return fire effectively. And not even the best trained army can defend a raging fireball that was once a city. Don't you see what I'm saying, Oskan? We're beaten. We have no answer to this new weapon. We'll have to abandon the cities and fight from the forests, marshes and other wild places, like rebels in our own land!"

"Perhaps you're right, but don't send out orders to evacuate the cities just yet. There's still a chance we can get through even this."

"How? It's impossible. What defence could there possibly be?"

"The Vampires," Oskan answered simply. "Flying ships won't be out of their range."

Thirrin gazed at him in excitement as the truth of his

words sank in. "Of course!" she said in sudden and happy relief. But it was quickly cut short as she added, "But will they heed a summons to help? Don't forget, they're *still* trying to resist fulfilling their treaty obligations."

"Oh yes, they'll heed the summons," Oskan replied. "Either they come to help or I'll burn them alive – or rather, dead!"

Thirrin looked at her normally gentle husband, and shuddered. Even the suggestion that the Vampires might ignore their treaty obligations had caused his features to sharpen, so that she seemed to be looking on the face of some ferocious hunting hawk. She wasn't often reminded that Oskan was only half human, and that his father was from the oldest and most powerful People in the worlds of shadow and light. But when his heritage showed itself, she felt herself a stranger in the company of the very man she loved – something she felt a hundredfold in the presence of her youngest daughter, Medea.

"We'd better send a message straight away; even the werewolf relay will take several hours," Thirrin went on, thinking it better to ignore the matter-of-fact way her husband discussed burning their reluctant allies. Even the Vampires deserved more compassion than that . . . perhaps.

"We'd better get a favourable reply quickly, otherwise I might just decide to pay a less than pleasant visit to Their Vampiric Majesties."

"I'm sure we will," Thirrin said placatingly, not quite able to believe she was trying to shield the Vampires from the anger and vengeance of Oskan, of all people.

"I'll summon Sergeant Moon-howler," she said finally. "The sooner we send a message, the sooner we'll know what we're doing."

* * *

Cressida strode along the corridor to her brother's room, thumped on the door once, and burst in. As she'd expected, Eodred was lying curled up on his bed with his back to the door.

"It stinks in here," she said, and striding to the window she pushed the shutters open wide. Immediately, a blast of snow and ice exploded into the room, as the Icemark weather indulged in one of its little quirks and inflicted a late blizzard on the land. Although the spring flowers were now well in bloom and the Great Forest was decked in the brilliance of new green, the snows of the Icemark were no respecters of what people expected from the season.

Eodred looked up and blinked as the stale fug and debris of his room was blasted aside by the freezing wind.

"You've done more than enough lying around. It's time to get up and start living again," said Cressida, dragging the covers off the bed and throwing them on the floor. "You're coming down to the lists with me. Your weapons skills must be as rusty as an unpolished sword by now, and we're going to need everyone we can get in the next few months."

Eodred allowed himself to be hauled to his feet by his diminutive sister, then stood blinking down at her like a confused owl. "I . . . I'm not ready . . . I don't want—"

"Tough!" Cressida barked. "The time for kindness and kid gloves is over. Cerdic's dead, so get used to it. He's gone to Valhalla where he's probably giggling with Granddad right now. But remember this, Eodred, you have to earn your place in Odin's Mead Hall, so if you want to see your twin again you'd better start living the life of a warrior. They don't let milksops into Valhalla; you can't get in if you've starved yourself to death or pined away like some spineless Wally who's been thwarted in love. The Lindenshield clan are fighters and doers; we're righters of wrongs and defenders of lives. And if you can't live up to that tradition then you're no brother of mine!"

Cressida crossed to where Eodred's armour lay in a heap where he'd dropped it after the battle in which Cerdic had been killed. She grabbed the coat of mail and threw it at him. "Put that on," she shouted. "And this!" A rust-flecked helmet landed at his feet. "We'll worry about cleaning it after a few hours in the lists. Now move! I'm not letting you out of my sight, so you might as well get dressed now."

Eodred slowly slipped the mail shirt over his head and strapped on his sword belt. So far, he'd followed his bossy sister's orders almost automatically, but now his mind began to wake up, and with it came a spark of resistance.

"Why should I bother?" he moaned. "I don't care about fighting any more . . . I don't care about anything."

"Yes, well, that's been made pretty obvious over the last few weeks. But now you're going to care again," Cressida replied briskly.

Eodred unbuckled his sword belt and let it drop. "No, I'm not. Nothing's worth the effort any more."

Without warning his sister flew across the room, pinned him to the wall and slapped him hard round the face. "Cut the crap, Eodred!" she spat furiously. "You're a soldier in the army of the Icemark, and a Prince of the House of Lindenshield, and you *will* set an example to the rank and file who've also lost family and friends in this war! Either that or you will *become* an example, and I'll personally see to it that you're hanged for neglect of duty."

"You wouldn't . . . you couldn't! Mother wouldn't—"

". . . even know until it was too late!" Cressida interrupted. "She's too busy to keep an eye on everything, and as Crown Princess my powers are second only to hers. My personal squadron of cavalry would follow my orders to the letter, and by the time Mother found out you'd be swinging in the breeze!"

He gazed at his sister in horrified wonder. He'd always known she was determined and powerful, but this sort of ruthlessness was terrifying. Suddenly, the stress and grief of the war, the death of his twin, Cerdic, and the awful trauma of his first battle overwhelmed him and he broke down in a welter of sobs. Cressida watched him for a few seconds, then the hard mask of her fury melted and she gathered him into a hug.

"Come on, Eddie. Cerdic's dead and there's no point in living a half-life yourself. Mum needs you, we *all* need you. Now pick up your sword and let's go down to the lists and see what we can do about getting ready to avenge him. Just think how much better you'll feel once you've chopped off a few Polypontian heads!"

Slowly, Eodred's sobbing reduced to a few sniffs and hiccups. The world had gone mad. Nobody had warned him that war could be anything other than glorious. They'd never told of the blood and the stench of dying soldiers as they lost control of their bodily functions. They'd never mentioned the foul, groaning, hideously painful deaths that most warriors died, stabbed with sword, dagger or pike, shot with arrow or musket ball or burnt to a crisp and blown apart by cannon-fire. But perhaps that was because they couldn't bear to remember the truth of battle themselves. Perhaps veterans of real war knew better than to admit to the truth. After all, if everyone knew what it was really like, perhaps nobody would dare allow it to happen, and then what would they do? Some people had nothing to offer the world other than their fighting skills.

Besides, he was a soldier; that was what he'd been trained to do almost as soon as he could walk. There was no other role for him — what could he possibly do in a peaceful world? No, he decided, it was all too impossible. People had always fought and died in wars and probably always would. He couldn't change that situation; no one could. It was what he was meant to do.

Suddenly Eodred realised he'd made a decision. He would do as Cressida wanted. He'd take up his sword again and fight in the war. He knew he had no real choice. Eventually, he wiped his eyes and nodded. "All right. I'll start training again. I need to blow away a few cobwebs. Perhaps then I'll feel better."

"I'm sure you will. Captain Bone-splitter's in the training grounds, and so are my cavalry units and Commander Kalaman. Just wait till you get the feel of a sword and shield again; you'll feel much better!" Cressida said eagerly, a look of immense relief spreading over her face.

"Yes," Eodred answered, and smiled sadly.

His sister quickly seized his hand before he could change his mind, and hurried him out into the corridor where she virtually dragged him along to the training lists.

Medea was almost happy. The window of her room high in its tower was wide open to the storming sky, but she seemed completely oblivious to the cold. Physical discomfort rarely affected her, unless she was directly and severely injured, but even then her Gift could reduce the pain and shock. Her wounded arm had mended nicely thanks to the accelerated healing processes helped by Magic, and she was beginning to feel invincible.

She'd spent a memorable few hours watching the destruction of the city in the Five Boroughs. Science could be so clever. Who'd have thought that people could build flying ships? And, yet, true to form, they'd immediately used them for war and for the destruction of their fellow human beings. There were times when Medea found people quite refreshing. Of course nature, and particularly *supernature*, was far more powerful than science could ever be. Perhaps one day boring little people like Maggiore and Archimedo would understand that there was an entire limitless cosmos of plains beyond the constraints of the one material world they happened to occupy. Only then would science become a force that could challenge the greatest witch or warlock. But that, of course, would mean the mundane scientists would have become witches and warlocks themselves.

With a sigh she refocused her Eye to watch the dying city collapse to rubble in the raging flames. For unmagical mortals, Bellorum and his sons were really the most interesting creatures. They almost made a dull existence worthwhile.

CHAPTER 22

Their Vampiric Majesties sat in the cold and quiet Throne Room discussing the Icemark, and the answer they should give to their less than beloved ally's inconvenient demands for military assistance. A werewolf messenger, who had arrived earlier that day and was now growing rather impatient, was awaiting a reply somewhere in the palace grounds.

"It would seem, dear heart, that despite all of our hopes our allies believe the time has come to fight again," said the King, putting a voice to the abominable situation they found themselves in.

Her Vampiric Majesty sighed in tired irritation. "Yes; how unspeakably demeaning! That I, an individual of impeccably aristocratic credentials even before my elevation to the ranks of the Undying, should be expected to fight with and for mere barbarians, yet again! It really is too much, my ever-lasting love!"

"Yes, my dearest pumpkin," the King went on sarcastically. "Ripping the throats out of healthy warriors and gorging yourself on their thick, rich blood must be such an offence to your aristocratic sensibilities. I seem to remember

you screaming in disgust in the last battle against the Empire
. . . so clever the way you disguised your voice to sound excited and delighted, so as not to offend our less than noble
allies."

The Queen shot him a glance of near loathing, but then her
features softened. "Don't let's quarrel, Kingy, darling. We
work so much better together; my aristocratic instincts combined with your low cunning are an unbeatable combination,
and none can compare with your intelligence and wisdom.
Surely together we can word a reply to that renegade warlock
that will release us from this burdensome treaty."

They spent another hour in deep conversation, then summoned the werewolf to send their reply to the Icemark by
Wolf-folk relay. The huge creature stumped into the Royal
presence, its massive and uncouth physical power contrasting
sharply with the elegance of its surroundings. Their Vampiric
Majesties gazed imperiously down from the height of their
enormous gothic thrones and let the silence stretch out into
long uncomfortable minutes. To the immortal, time had little
power to either change or discommode.

"Well, wolf . . . *person*," the Queen said at last. "Are you
ready to receive our reply to Queen Thirrin and her Consort
the renega— the Warlock Oskan Witchfather?"

The huge creature inclined its head and waited silently.

"Then say this: 'Their Vampiric Majesties have neither the
time, nor the inclination, nor indeed the obligation to lead
any sort of army against enemies that are not their own. Therefore they most regretfully refuse, utterly and completely, to
answer the summons. And, as Sovereigns of an independent
land, they also refuse to recognise the right of anyone or anything to issue such summonses. This reply is open to neither

negotiation nor amendment." The Queen drew a deep and ecstatic breath, as though relieved and happy to have rid herself of a troublesome burden.

The werewolf raised a hugely expressive eyebrow, but said nothing. Then, bowing, he withdrew. A few moments later the melancholy notes of his howling sounded on the night.

"Come, my love," His Vampiric Majesty said quietly. "Let us take the air while we await the reply that will undoubtedly come sooner than we would like."

The Vampires looked at each other, understanding the position they were in perfectly. They really had no choice but to fulfil their treaty obligations; their reply had been nothing but a delaying tactic and an act of defiance in the face of a power they couldn't resist. Oskan Witchfather was implacable and remorseless. An enraged warlock of his phenomenal abilities would be unstoppable, and the rulers of The-Land-of-the-Ghosts were skilled enough as politicians and diplomats to know their limits.

Besides, it all mattered so very little. As a mortal, Oskan's control was limited by time itself. In fifty or sixty years at the very most, he would be dead and gone, and their Vampiric Majesties would once again be free to inflict havoc and terror on all the lands around. Patience was the greatest ally of the undead.

The Vampire King and Queen processed from the Throne Room and were joined by a simpering party of toothy courtiers as they made their way to the Royal gardens. Under a bright moon the displays of black and dead-white roses glowed in a glory of shadow and subtle light. Here and there fountains cascaded skywards, glittering like shards of crystal as they absorbed the radiance of the moon. All was elegance and beauty, and not one of the Undead was troubled by the freezing winds that blasted from the nearby mountains. Light laughter tinkled on the frozen air and courtiers sipped suspiciously red wine from cut crystal goblets.

The King was just in the middle of an amusing anecdote, when the distant wail of a werewolf insinuated itself into the night air. All fell silent and waited, until an acknowledgement was given from a nearby wood. They then turned and watched as a wolfman approached along the labyrinthine paths that wound around the symmetrical flower beds.

When he was a short distance from the party he stopped and bowed. The Queen slowly inclined her head, giving him permission to approach. "I assume you have brought a reply from our beloved allies," she said with deep irony.

"Indeed I have, Your Majesty," he said. And as they watched the creature began to shake, and his eyes turned in their sockets until only the whites could be seen. "To my fellow rulers and trusted allies I send this message that I know will be received in the spirit with which it was sent," the wolfman said, but the voice he used was not his own; it was light, human and immediately recognisable as that of Oskan Witchfather. The Vampires hissed in alarm. The warlock's Powers must have developed. He'd never displayed them in this way before; usually messages were simply reported, but here the werewolf was being used almost as though he were possessed by Oskan's spirit.

"Their Vampiric Majesties are very well aware of their obligations to our treaty of mutual assistance. And I need hardly remind them that if they attempt to break the said treaty then I will personally summon and inflict the penalties to which they will then be subject. Namely, I will flay their courtiers of their skins and expose their unblinking eyes to the raging sun; I will then destroy the Blood Palace and sow the ground with salt, after which I will hunt down the Vampire King and Queen, drive stakes through their unbeating hearts, and burn their inanimate bodies to a sifting of ash that will be blown away on the four winds. Such will be my wrath if their Vampiric Majesties should stand by their unwise decision to default."

"Careful, warlock!" the Vampire Queen hissed. "Your less than human side is beginning to show."

"Yes, I suppose it is," Oskan's voice casually conceded, changing from the formal timbre of his address. "But that in itself has its uses; I don't have to worry about things like a conscience or feeling remorse or pity. You see, even a seasoned warrior like Queen Thirrin might occasionally have a moment of weakness and hesitate before being as ruthless as a situation might demand. But I have no such problems; I'm happy to tell you quite openly that either you answer the call to arms or I'll destroy you."

"And what if we should choose to ally ourselves with Scipio Bellorum and his Empire? His attitudes and acts are those of an individual we could both admire and work with," said the Vampire King calmly.

The werewolf laughed Oskan's amusement. "Oh, please! When will you ever come to realise that Bellorum would never make an alliance with creatures he finds detestable, loathsome and, what's more, the very embodiment of all the irrationality and superstition he hates. But all of this you know. We've discussed every part and particle of this situation many times. So come, make your decision, and this time make it final and irrevocable. I'm fast losing patience with your long-in-the-tooth attempts to free yourself from a binding treaty!"

The King took his wife's hand and kissed it gently. "Well, my dear, it seems we have reached that point where we can no longer delay. What should we do?"

"Is there any real choice, my love?" she asked, stroking his hair and trying to ignore a rising sense of what she almost recognised as fear.

"None at all, it would seem."

"Then let us muster our soldiers and march off to this war that's neither of our making nor choosing."

The King nodded, and turning to the werewolf he said, "Put away your threats, Warlock. We will honour this dishonourable treaty and fight in your war. We will be with you in half a month."

"Make it ten days," Oskan said through the mouth of the werewolf, and suddenly the creature slumped to the ground as the warlock released his grip.

Scipio Bellorum allowed himself the smallest smile as he looked now from the gunnel of his Sky Navy's flagship, *The Fiery Jack*. He'd made sure spring had established its hold on the Icemark before he had allowed himself this first flight aboard one of the flying ships and now he was relishing the experience. Below him, the land looked like a beautifully drawn map. Every field, copse and river seemed to be a fraction of its real size, giving the illusion that the General could reach out, pick it up and drop it in his pocket. Which, in effect, was exactly what he intended to do.

There were, of course, disadvantages to the new method of fighting. At such altitudes the cold was intense, and the winds could drain life and warmth from an unprotected body within minutes. The Imperial scientists had designed special padded flying suits to protect the sky-sailors from most of the extremes, and their own natural toughness enabled them to work and fight in the new theatre of war with relative ease. But even so, there were still limitations to what the Sky Navy could do. Above certain heights the quality of the air began to deteriorate, and soon the strongest and most athletic fighters were left gasping for breath. But this wouldn't be a problem for the Icemark campaign. The Sky Navy's role would be one of low-level bombing at a height where the air was rich with oxygen and the screams of the injured and dying could still be clearly heard.

Ahead, the city of Learton was just broaching the horizon as the defensive walls and towers began to thrust up into the sky. This was the last of the Mid-Land cities to be attacked, and when it fell, the way to Frostmarris would be open. Bellorum was as happy as his oddly emotionless personality would allow. Beside him stood Octavius, who was as enthusiastic as his father about the new weapons. Sulla had chosen to lead the ground forces, which had been reduced to a minor supporting role in this stage of the war .

Spread across the sky, the entire fleet of sky-ship galleons swept forward in perfect formation, the crews scurrying to prepare the vessels for the attack on the city. On the deck of each ship, Bellorum could see the Captains issuing orders and scanning the flagship for directives, transmitted by semaphore. 'Hold steady' was the signal currently being given. Then, as the city began to loom larger on the horizon, the order to climb to greater heights was issued. Bellorum immediately felt the deck beneath his feet surge upwards as more gas was pumped into the huge canopy of the balloon above him. Now the wasp-fighters were launched, the dart-like craft spilling into the air as their pilots dived from specially constructed platforms that projected out beyond the gunnels of each of the galleons.

The faint sounds of the city's alarm bells and clarions drifted on the still air, and Bellorum smiled to himself. Learton was as good as dead already. He wondered why the defenders even bothered to try. But then a lookout gave a cry and all eyes turned to the city.

Issuing from the walls rose an odd smoke-like billowing that swirled up into the sky. Immediately, monocula were levelled.

Vampires! Vampires in their bat form, and with them thousands of giant Snowy Owls, the allies and vassals of Their Vampiric Majesties! The crews quickly drew cutlasses and ran small cannon into battle positions. Bellorum could have screamed in rage. So much for the belief that sunlight was as deadly as poison to these hideous abominations of nature!

Such was the General's loathing of these creatures, he'd neglected to study them as was his usual practice. Had he done so, he would have learned that they were of the sub-genus *Vampiris Arcticus*, and like their close cousins, *Vampiris Antarcticus*, they had a high tolerance to daylight due to the long hours of sunshine enjoyed by their native regions during the summer months. No creature, even if it was 'undead', could sleep for almost six months of the year without taking nourishment, and so this species had evolved an ability to resist the poisonous effect of sunlight, enabling them to hunt and feed at any time of the day or night.

They came on now in dense formation, the loathsome bat faces of the Vampires clearly visible through the monoculum

Bellorum trained on them. The wasp-fighters formed into fighting squadrons and swept down to meet this unexpected threat. The hideous screeches of the Vampires and owls began to echo through the air as they engaged. In the first few minutes dozens of the creatures fell from the sky, spiralling down in broken ruin to smash into the ground thousands of feet below. Bellorum roared in triumph.

The Imperial soldiers, though unprepared for a daylight battle with Vampires, had nonetheless come to the war equipped to take on the undead. They shot slender stakes of wood from their crossbows, and fired silver bullets from their muskets. But the Vampires and owls reformed and swept back into battle, dropping on to the flimsy canopies of the wasp-fighters and ripping them apart. The Snowy Owls tore and wrenched at pilot and fighter alike with razor talons, and soon as many fighters as Vampires and owls were falling to their death.

The crews of the galleons cheered and groaned as the dog-fight continued before them, the advantage swinging first one way and then the other. But eventually one of the largest bats broke away, leading at least half the force away from the battle and straight at the sky-ships. Immediately, alarm bells rang and musketeers lined the gunnels as the sky-sailors ran the cannon forward, ready to fire. Bellorum drew his sword and strode to the spot where he calculated the first engagement would occur.

The cannons opened fire, belching out grapeshot and bringing down seemingly hundreds of the Vampire army. But still they advanced, and the muskets began to fire in disciplined order, rank after rank. The crews, armed with pistol and cutlass, waited as the hideous enemy slowly made ground against the gunfire that was keeping them at bay.

Soon they were dropping to the decks, metamorphosing as they fell into hideously pale soldiers in black armour. Leading the terrified crew, Bellorum and his son strode forward to meet the threat. Soon the deck was swarming and heaving with fighting soldiers. All about them the Vampires fought with loathsome elegance, and when they killed they tore out the throats of their opponents and drank the gushing blood. The crews of the sky-ships were almost mad with horror. They'd never confronted such monsters before; it was almost as though their nightmares had come to life. Even so, the customary discipline of the Polypontian army held good and they stood shoulder to shoulder, hacking and thrusting with their razor-sharp cutlasses at the abominations before them.

Slowly, slowly, Bellorum and his force began to advance across the deck, pushing the Vampires overboard and forcing them to transform into bats once more. But then an odd gasping roar sounded on the air, and all eyes turned to watch as a sudden gust of wind cleared away the musket smoke. One of the galleons was on fire, or at least its rigging was, and they watched as the balloon began to burn. Wasp-fighters swarmed all around it, but soon they drew off as the canopy gaped open and the ship slowly rolled over and began a long tumbling fall to the ground. Small figures could clearly be seen plunging to their deaths, thrown wide of the ship as it plummeted to earth and smashed into the ground, sending up a great billow of dust and debris. A second later an ear-shattering crack split the air, followed by a massive explosion as the ship's entire complement of bombs blew up.

With triumphant shrieks the Vampires and owls renewed their attack, tearing out throats and splashing the decks with

gallons of blood. Again and again Bellorum drove the creatures from his ship. Again and again they returned to the
attack. His soldiers were beginning to tire, and here, thousands
of feet in the air, he had no reserves to call on. It was then
that the solution occurred to him. Of course! Quickly, he gave
the order to release the gas from the ship's canopy. He would
carry out a controlled return to earth and get help from the
ground troops. Slowly they descended, still maintaining discipline in the face of the insane attack of the Vampires and giant
owls.

Bellorum quickly glanced out at the rest of the fleet and
saw that they were following his lead. Now they would have
more than a fighting chance!

Then all went quiet. Bellorum turned to watch in astonishment as the fighting halted and the Vampire soldiers parted to let a tall, elegant man step forward. The Imperial troops
murmured suspiciously but held their positions, curious to see
what would happen.

"I do believe I have the honour of fighting General Scipio
Bellorum himself," the pale figure said in perfect Polypontian.
"May I introduce myself? I am the King of The-Land-of-the-
Ghosts, commonly known by my rather . . . shall we say
earthy allies, as His Vampiric Majesty." He leaned with bored
nonchalance on his viciously serrated sword, which dripped
thick globules of blood. "You can have no idea what a problem you have caused my people. It really is too ungallant of
you to continue in your attempts to defeat the Icemark. Didn't
you learn last time you attacked them that the House of
Lindenshield really is tiresomely stubborn? Now, why don't
you just be a good little General and go and fight somewhere
else? You know it makes sense. Then we can all go home and

get on with our hobbies and interests and things."

Bellorum glared at the figure before him with a mixture of loathing, contempt and outrage. Here was an embodiment of all that he hated about the Icemark and its region. Abominations of nature, superstition, witchcraft, and freaks that upset the balance of a rational universe. "I will never rest until I have rid the world of your pollution and the poison that you represent," he growled. "For every one of your kind destroyed, the balance and order of the world is a little more restored. May this war continue until all your unnatural species have been expunged from the land!"

His Vampiric Majesty drew a tiredly resigned breath. "You know, Oskan Witchfather warned us that you weren't really a fan of Vampires, ghosts and the like. Such a shame! For once, I feel that I have met an individual who almost approaches my own intellectual capacity, and yet his blind prejudice and boorish refusal to accept the astounding *variety* of the natural and supernatural worlds denies us the right to be friends. Oh well, on with the fighting, I suppose. Still, there are compensations: your soldiers do have such an exotic aroma, all sweet flesh and rare spices, and that, added to the delicious piquancy of their blood, makes this irksome war a rare feast for the vampiric palette!" And with the speed of a striking snake he leaped on the ranks of Imperial troops and ripped out the throats of three young men before anyone had time to react.

With a deafening roar the fighting resumed. Now the Vampire soldiers gained the upper hand over the exhausted Imperial troops, relentlessly pushing them back across the decks and over the sides of the ship. Screeching and raging, and moving with the elegance of loathly ballet dancers, the Vampires were unstoppable. But within five minutes the galleons were nearing the ground, and the support army led by Sulla Bellorum was advancing rapidly to their relief.

Warning shrieks rose up from the Vampires, and their king stepped forward once again. Raising his sword in an exquisite salute he smiled at Bellorum. "It was a pleasure to meet with a man of such inimitable refinement and taste. I can only lament that your chauvinism has blinded you to the fact that we share many virtues. So, until next time, General, when perhaps I'll have the opportunity to appreciate the more *sanguine* aspects of your person."

The Vampire King bowed, and leaped up into the air, where he transformed into a huge bat. His soldiers quickly followed and together they spiralled away, screaming and screeching in triumph.

Bellorum's Sky Navy had been successfully grounded. Four galleons had been destroyed as well as hundreds of the wasp-fighters. And not one bomb had yet been dropped on the city of Learton.

CHAPTER 23

Charlemagne and Mekhmet were riding south across the desert. With them were an escort of fifty cavalry and a baggage train of twenty camels, and as Sharley turned in his saddle to look back over the twin lines of the column he felt a swelling pride. To his inexperienced eyes the glittering cavalcade and stately pacing camels looked like an army. But best of all, actually riding away from the city and its intrigues had brought with it an invigorating sense of freedom. With every mile they put between themselves and the complicated politics and plottings of the Sultan's court, both Princes felt like a weight was being lifted from their shoulders. Soon they were chatting and giggling like a couple of schoolboys with no more worries than how much homework they had to hand in the next day.

Suleiman, completely adapted to the heat, trotted along in the blazing light as easily as if he had been strolling through an oasis, and beside him, Mekhmet's beautiful grey arched its neck proudly. Close behind them a cohort of cavalry that bore the name of the Crown Prince gleamed and glittered in the sun. These were the elite of the elite, the bodyguard of the heir to the throne. Riding the finest horses of the Desert Kingdom, they wore chain-mail hauberks that flowed over each trooper's body like the finest silk, and highly polished conical helmets not unlike the headgear of the northern house-carles, but topped by a vicious spike that rose six inches or so from the crown. In the fiercest heat of the day, these soldiers also wore loose surcoats of fine white linen over their armour, to prevent the steel of their panoplies from becoming too hot. And when the sun grew really fierce, they'd even remove their helmets and cover their heads with a deep hood.

Sharley still wore his now characteristic black robes, but Mekhmet had also presented him with a beautiful set of black armour, complete with a round cavalryman's shield. When Sharley had first tried on the helmet, his pale complexion had glowed beneath the black metal like snow under a night sky.From helmet to hauberk to shield, the armour had seemed as though forged from midnight and storms, starkly contrast-ing with the brilliance of the desert light. Sharley was now fully equipped as a warrior of the Desert Kingdom, but the young northern Prince was too shy to wear the armour while riding with the soldiers of the Royal Bodyguard until he'd proved himself in battle, so the armour was stowed safely away in the baggage train.

Mekhmet spent much of the journey describing the land to which they were travelling. "Trees and grass grow wild there," he explained as though the idea of vegetation growing beyond gardens and oases was truly amazing. "It can sometimes be quite dry, as it will be at this time of the year, but they tell tales of a 'rainy season' when they claim that even rivers flow. I've never seen it myself, but I've no reason to doubt them. The Lusu people are very honourable, and never lie."

Sharley nodded; obviously his own tales of the northern weather and rivers that flowed all year round must have stretched to the absolute limit Mekhmet's ability to believe. "What are the people like? Are they good soldiers?"

"The best. Like the Desert People, the Lusu have a brilliant cavalry. Many years ago one of my ancestors attacked their land, and a great war was fought in which neither side could claim victory. Eventually, the Queen of the day, Swazeeloo, agreed to pay tribute to the Sultan and acknowledge him as her overlord. But to this day, nothing has ever been paid. Sometimes smaller wars were fought to try and extract the payments, but they always ended in stalemate. Today we know better than to even try, and besides, we have other things to worry about."

Sharley nodded again. "How long will it take to reach the border?"

"At least a week, as long as we have no trouble with sand-storms."

For the next few hours the column walked on, conserving the energy of beast and rider alike by maintaining a slow but steady pace that gradually ate up the miles. Then at last the sun dipped below the horizon, the raging afterglow of its fire staining the sky a deep blood-red that cooled over the arc of the sky so that in the east, the dark of night and its field of stars were already claiming mastery of the heavens. Sharley still found the swift transition from daylight to full dark in the desert lands a thing of wonder. The dark arrived almost like the snuffing of a candle, and the biting cold that came with it always took him by surprise and had him rummaging through his baggage for warm clothing.

They continued on through the night for several hours,

using the easier conditions to increase their pace. But as the whisper-thin crescent of a new moon rose into the sky, horse and camel were reined to a halt, and the rich, bubbling roars of the baggage beasts echoed over the empty land, as a prelude to sinking to their knees.

With amazing speed, tents were pitched, animals tethered and fed, and fires were lit. Soon, the rich scents of cooking were added to the acrid smell of cooling sand and dust, and Sharley became impatient for his supper. Riding all day was hungry work, but as he and Mekhmet had no designated tasks in the well-practised art of pitching camp, all they could do was sit in the Royal tent and wait for food to be brought to them.

At last, a chamberlain appeared, leading a party of lesser servants who set up low tables and arranged the evening meal in a splendour of scents and colours.

"Ah, that's better," said Sharley to no one in particular as he helped himself.

"When we've finished eating I thought we'd look at a map of the route again," said Mekhmet. "The Royal Kraal of the Lusu people is only a couple of days' ride, so we needn't be too heavily burdened with food and fuel. We'll just have to pray we don't lose our way."

"What's a 'kraal'?" Sharley asked.

"A settlement. Anything from a village to a large town, really," Mekhmet replied. "But the Royal Kraal, Swahati, is huge. A city, I suppose, but it's built entirely of wood, reeds and mud-brick."

"You make it sound like a temporary camp."

"No. It's definitely not that. Swahati has stood for more than a thousand years, even though none of its buildings are more than fifty years old. In a way, the Royal Kraal, and all the Lusu settlements, are more like animals . . . they're more *alive* than the cities we know. They're constantly changing and being renewed. They even move."

"Move?" Sharley said incredulously.

"Yes, gradually, and over many years admittedly, but the city definitely moves. Swahati lies in a valley, and when you stand on the hills that overlook it, you can see where the boundary ditches and walls have moved to protect a new outcrop of buildings, or where they've been abandoned when an area falls into disuse."

"And the King lives there?"

"*Queen*," Mekhmet corrected. "The Lusu people are ruled by Ketshaka the Third."

When they'd finished their meal the boys sat over a map while Mekhmet pointed out the route they'd be taking over the coming days. "It's mainly desert – the Polypontians have destroyed most of the cities and towns – but there are several oases where we'll be able to rest."

"Fine," Sharley answered.

Finally, Mekhmet rolled up the map and led them into the inner chamber of their large tent, where divans had been set up and smothered in cushions and silks. Sharley couldn't help thinking their journey might be somewhat quicker if the camels didn't have to carry so much luxurious equipment. But then the noises of the camp preparing for sleep reminded him to appreciate the wonderfully civilised country he was in.

Maggiore Totus had been right, the Desert People had a sophisticated civilisation that was far more advanced than that of the north. But why hadn't they developed the science and technology that would have enabled them to fight off the

Empire? 'Necessity is the mother of invention', as Maggie often said, and such a clever people should surely have been able to make weapons to send Scipio Bellorum running back to his borders.

As Sharley began to settle in his bed he asked, "Mekhmet, why didn't your engineers and scientists use their expertise against the Polypontians? Can't they translate their skills to the field of war?"

The Prince smiled. "Oh yes, with great flair and inventiveness, which is why the Empire kidnapped all of our great thinkers and forced them to work for the Imperial war machine. Not only that, but they destroyed all our factories and centres of learning to make sure we couldn't cast any more cannon, or make any more muskets."

Sharley was stupefied. "You mean the Empire's firearms are an invention of the Desert People?"

"Absolutely," Mekhmet answered with pride. "But now we can't even make the simplest pistol. Every engineer, every technician, has been either taken or killed, and if anyone else shows even the slightest ability in these fields, they too disappear."

"But . . . but can't you seal the borders, keep your clever ones in secure compounds or hide them away?"

Mekhmet shrugged. "It's been tried, but there are just too many spies and Polypontian agents to hunt our people down."

Sharley felt overwhelmingly depressed and his eyes followed a huge moth that rattled and battered itself around one of the filigreed oil lamps that burned on the low ivory-inlaid tables. Sometimes even attempting to fight Scipio Bellorum and his murderous armies seemed like an act of total stupidity. It was almost like trying to put out a forest fire with a cup of water, or standing on the roof of your house and trying to blow away the storm clouds that were threatening to flatten your home. But then he thought of his mother and her network of allies, who'd stood against the Imperial forces and had defeated them. He remembered too that the longbow and compound bow could still outshoot the musket in both range and accuracy, and that both the trebuchet and ballista had won every duel with the Empire's cannons.

He smiled, and slapped Mekhmet's knee. "Never mind. We'll just have to make do with sword and shield. The Icemark and her allies didn't do too badly against the Imperial war machine last time, and I don't see why it should be any different now. All we need are enough allies, and that's already in hand."

Mekhmet returned his friend's smile. He admired such optimism, and if he didn't allow himself to think about all of the problems they still faced, he could almost be infected by it. Of course they had a chance, a fighting chance . . . it just didn't seem a particularly good one, that was all.

CHAPTER 24

Archimedo Archimedes, Chief Engine-eer, appointed by Cressida after the attack on Learton, surveyed the additions he'd made to the defences around Frostmarris. Each of the triple rings of earth embankment and palisade now had extra batteries of truly gigantic ballistas on platforms that could turn, dip and rise in exactly the same way that gimbal brackets on board a ship kept lamps and other delicate pieces of equipment steady during a storm. Each of the huge cross-bows – and they were four times larger than the biggest that had previously been used – could now be turned to shoot in any direction, and they could be raised to an almost vertical position to target objects flying overhead.

Archimedo Archimedes was a citizen of the Hypolitan province and had offered his expertise to the defenders of Frostmarris on the insistence of the newly elected Basilea. He was an engine-eer who would probably have been more at home working with the scientists and technicians of the Polypontian Empire but, in truth, there he would have been just another clever slave amongst many others. Here in the Icemark he had a high status that made him almost equal to the most powerful witch. Many of the citizens saw his feats of engine-eering as virtually magical anyway, and this almost satisfied his truly enormous ego.

He jumped down off the ballistas' firing platform and scuttled over to where a steel column rose into the sky. His small, grubby hand patted the column and he squinted up at the lantern and highly polished concave mirror at the top, which could be tilted in any direction. This was another one of his inventions: a search lamp that could cast a brilliant shaft of light high into the sky to illuminate any flying machines that might try to attack the city in the dark. Each of the firing platforms was supplied with two such search-lamps, and Archimedo Archimedes considered his success in convincing the formidable Queen Thirrin that they were necessary for the defence of the city to be one of his greatest achievements.

He stepped down into the deep ditch between the second and third of the defensive rings so that he could survey as many of the batteries of giant ballistas as possible. He was quite happy with the preparations as far as they went. Not only had he set up the defensive firing platforms, he'd also had deep shelters dug to protect the occupants of Frostmarris from the Sky Navy's raids and he'd laid out a series of underground aqueducts that supplied almost every street with a supply of water, to make firefighting easier.

"Archimedes, my dear fellow, how go your preparations?" Tharaman-Thar boomed as he and the Tharina appeared on the embankment above him.

"Slowly, and with a lack of appreciation at every turn," he answered sullenly.

"Well, I can assure you that both Krisafitsa and I fully appreciate everything you're doing for us. Don't we, sweeting?"

said the giant Snow Leopard, jumping lightly down into the ditch.

"Without a doubt, my love," his Consort replied, trying not to wrinkle her nose at the acrid smell that arose from the little man. He was probably one of the smelliest human beings she'd ever encountered; even King Grishmak's cheesy feet seemed fragrant in comparison. "Do you have much more to do?"

"Hah! 'Much more to do?' I haven't even begun the real work yet!" he snapped rudely. "None of you have even the slightest idea of what I'm trying to do here, do you? Or, for that matter, what new threat you're actually facing?"

"Ignorance may be our middle name, Mr Archimedes, but we have listened to the reports of the destructive power of the Sky Navy, and spoken to the few survivors from the cities already attacked, so I suppose we're as well informed as it's possible to be without actually experiencing an air raid ourselves."

"You've got no idea. None!"

"And your own experience of this new weapon – exactly how great is that?" Tharaman spoke quietly, a dangerous sign to those who knew him.

"I know enough, I can assure you. And if anyone in Frostmarris survives at all, it'll be entirely due to me."

"Our gratitude knows no bounds, Mr Archimedes," said Krisafitsa calmly.

"Aye, well. Even that probably isn't enough. Anyway, I've no time to stand jawing with the ruling elite. Some of us actually have to keep things working around here. I've jobs to do – important jobs!" And he stumped away along the ditch, barking out orders to people working on the embankments as he went.

"What a delightful little man," said Tharaman with quiet irony.

"Oh, he's probably just under a lot of strain," said Krisafitsa, in an attempt to be understanding.

"And nobody else is?"

"Well, yes. But some people do have awfully important things to do, and that must be a terrible pressure."

Tharaman looked at her. "There are times, my love, when it's possible to be too understanding! That little man is simply rude, and if he wasn't so important to us I might try and commission Oskan to turn him into one of those toad thingies that live under stones."

Krisafitsa purred in amusement. "Now, you know you don't mean that, Tharaman sweetest. You're just a little tetchy, that's all."

"That's true, I am tetchy. Is it really surprising, when you consider everything that's been happening?"

"No, of course not. Come on, let's go back into the city and see if we can find Olememnon. I think you and he could probably put the entire world to rights over a few bowls of wine, and I wouldn't mind a chat with the new Basilea if she's not too busy," Krisafitsa said brightly. "Have you noticed how she's always to be found with Olememnon?"

"Krisafitsa!" Tharaman rumbled.

"What?" she asked in innocent tones.

"Human people have their own ways of securing mates, and I'm sure the interference of a Snow Leopard would only complicate things."

"Interference? I don't know what you mean, Tharaman. I never interfere."

The two giant cats made their way back through the

defences towards the city gates. All about them, soldiers of all species were digging, building and carrying as Archimedo Archimedes' plans were put into action.

News had arrived only that morning that Learton had finally fallen. The Imperial Command had been forced to abandon their initial attack for two weeks while they carried out repairs to the Sky Navy. They had then mounted a combined land and air assault against the city that had stretched the defenders to the limit. It had taken a further ten days for the settlement to fall, and though the Vampire army had inflicted heavy losses on the fleets of flying ships and wasp-fighters again, the end was inevitable. The city that had once been the largest of the Five Boroughs was now a ruin.

Medea sat in her high tower contemplating the news. She'd known the city had fallen long before the werewolf relay reported it, and had watched as the survivors had been evacuated by the soldiers of Their Vampiric Majesties. But she was troubled. Bellorum and the Imperial armies were about to turn their attention on Frostmarris, the centre of the entire country, and if the capital fell, the war was as good as over. Her own safety and comfort could be compromised. By meddling in the war and helping the Empire, she could be endangering herself. But if she remained aloof and neither helped nor hindered either side, the very society she hated might continue to exist. In fact her decision could mean the difference between her survival and destruction. Her continued existence depended on her Magical skills. She pondered what particular weaponry she should add to her already formidable armoury, and arrived at an obvious conclusion. Mind control, and the spiritual *possession* of a host body, would give her enormous advantage. Her father was adept at this particular skill, and this made her even more determined to master it too. But how should she begin?

Her Eye searched the dark and dusty corners of her tower until she found what she was looking for. At first, the mouse resisted, but it soon succumbed and she folded her mind to fit the restrictions of its tiny form. For the rest of the day she practised moving the mouse to her will: sending it scuttling up and down stairs, making it roll into a ball and somersault across the floor, and finally sending it on a suicide mission to attack a palace cat.

She even waited to experience the terror of feeling the cat's fangs tearing into its flesh before she finally withdrew, smiling in satisfaction. It was really quite easy. Tomorrow, when she'd rested, she'd possess one of the hunting dogs, after which she'd try a horse, then slowly progress until she was ready to possess one of the more intelligent species.

She was so happy with her new skill that she almost forgot the war. Almost, but not quite. A true sorceress always kept her Eye on danger.

Frostmarris waited breathlessly for the next phase of the conflict to begin. Lookouts watched from the ramparts for the first signs of the Polypontian army, and werewolf scouts scoured the roads and byways for any evidence of the Imperial military. But for the time being, Scipio Bellorum and his sons seemed content to consolidate their hold over the southern regions of the country and allow the capital city to stew in a juice of its own fear. Besides, weather conditions seemed to be changing again, and at altitude the moisture in the air would condense on all parts of the galleons and wasp-fighters and

quickly freeze, weighing them down, and even causing ships
to crash in the more extreme conditions. The Sky Navy was
apparently happy to wait until the danger of icing was past;
after all, the weather would eventually improve, and for the
time being the ground crews could carry out repairs and refur-
bish the fleet ready for the next phase of the war.

The General may have learned that his new weapon was
not invincible, but even so, he'd managed to destroy Learton
in less than half the time that conventional siege techniques
would have taken. But the defenders of the Icemark took heart
from knowing that with the Vampires on their side, at least
the invaders couldn't destroy a city in less than a day as they
had done when they first used their Sky Navy.

As usual, Thirrin and her allies were adapting themselves
to everything Bellorum could throw at them. But the question
remained, could they adapt fast enough? This time, none of
the defenders were expecting any new allies to arrive in the
nick of time to save them. This time they had only themselves
to rely on, and some were beginning to wonder if it would be
enough.

As Tharaman and his Tharina reached the gates of the
heavily barred citadel, Tharaman searched for some good news
to comment on. "At least Eodred's back in the land of the
living."

"Yes. We have Cressida to thank for that, I think. She's
certainly a . . . forceful young woman when she needs to be,"
said Krisafitsa.

"So like her mother," said Tharaman. "She'll make a great
queen someday."

Slowly, the gates swung open and the Thar and Tharina
walked through, deep in conversation.

"Olememnon will be in the lists, I should think," said Krisafitsa. "Why don't you go and see if he's thirsty and would like to join us for a few bowls of wine?"

Tharaman gazed lovingly at his mate. "My dear, your every word is steeped in wisdom. I'll do just that and meet you in the Great Hall in a few minutes."

Krisafitsa purred affectionately as she watched him pad across the courtyard in the direction of the lists.

As she entered the Great Hall, the huge cat's enormous pupils dilated instantly to adjust to the dim light, and she spied King Grishmak approaching through another of the many doors. The young werewolf with him looked about as happy as a wet winter's afternoon, and the Tharina guessed he'd been receiving some forceful advice from the Wolf-folk King.

"Grishmak, are you busy? Tharaman and Olememnon should be here soon, and there's talk of a few relaxing drinks."

"Drinks, eh? Could do with a beer or two myself!" He rubbed his huge paws together happily and dragged a bench closer to the hearth. "Well, don't just stand there like a stuffed cow, find some sheepskins for the Tharina to recline on!" he snarled at the younger werewolf, who scuttled off grumpily. "One of my whelps," said Grishmak. "His mother's family have had enough of him and sent him to me. But as he's of an age to learn the art of the warrior I suppose he could be useful," said Grishmak, nodding towards his son.

"Such an awkward age," said Krisafitsa sympathetically as she watched the youngster grab a huge armful of sheepskins that lay stacked against the wall, then fall flat on his face as he tripped over the bundle. "It must be so trying for him."

"And for everyone else! My paws ache from cuffing him

round the ear, and he's still as daft as ever in spite of it."

Grishmak's son finally dropped the sheepskins in a pile before the Tharina, who thanked him kindly.

"Well, don't just leave them in a heap, spread them out!" Grishmak snarled impatiently, then sighing at the youngster's ineffectual efforts, he snapped, "Oh, leave them alone!" and waved to a passing human chamberlain who quickly arranged the pelts into a comfortable couch.

"How old are you, dear?" Krisafitsa asked quietly.

The werewolf whelp gave her a hunted look, obviously expecting to be lectured on how difficult life had been when she'd been his age. "I've seen one hundred and ninety-five moons," he answered sullenly. "Or fifteen years in human terms."

"I see," said the Tharina pensively. "Exactly the same age as Prince Eodred. Have you met him yet?"

He shook his head. "No, I've only been here two days, and Dad – I mean King Grishmak – has kept me busy most of the time."

"Hah, *busy?* You wouldn't know *busy* if it jumped up and bit you on the arse!" the King snapped.

"Perhaps a meeting could be arranged," Krisafitsa said to Grishmak. "It might be beneficial in all sorts of ways. Not only would both boys have a companion of a similar age, but your son would be spending time with a battle-proven warrior."

Grishmak's eyes suddenly shone. "I hadn't thought of that. Might help to cheer Prince Eodred up a bit too."

"Precisely," said the Tharina. "I'll have a word with Thirrin and see what she says. What's your name and tribe, my dear?"

The young werewolf drew himself up to his full height. "I'm known as Growlahowl, and as the King's son I'm of the Fengari Royal Tribe and bear the family name of Blood-drinker."

"Yes, of course. Do you know, I think you'll make an ideal companion for the Prince."

"And what happens if I don't want to be his companion? I hear he's a right misery guts, always moping about and going off to his room. I'd sooner spend my time with someone with a bit of life in them."

Grishmak growled threateningly. "Right now your arse is inviting my foot to give it a good kicking. Eodred's a fine lad, and if you end up half as good as him I'll be amazed!"

"There's good reason for his depression, Growlahowl," Krisafitsa explained. "His twin brother was killed in battle, but before that Prince Eodred was as boisterous and as fun-loving as any other teenage lad, and perhaps more so. Who knows, perhaps you can bring him out of his shell and make him laugh again."

"I'm nobody's nursemaid. Let someone else wipe his snotty nose. I'm a Prince of the House of Blood-drinker; we don't befriend invalids."

Krisafitsa sighed. Youngsters could be so trying.

"You'll be a good friend to the Prince or I'll want to know why!" Grishmak snarled. "Here's your chance to do something useful for once, and you're going to take it!"

To save his much-cuffed ears from a further battering, Growlahowl subsided into rebellious mutterings and stared moodily into the flames of the central hearth where they were sitting. The young werewolf had his own pain to bear and he'd asked no one to make concessions for him. He hadn't withdrawn from the world and sunk into some sort of soppy solitude. He got on with life.

Just then a booming laugh echoed through the Great Hall as Tharaman-Thar arrived with Olememnon, and all attention turned to the Snow Leopard as he padded across the wide space to join them.

"Well, well! Grishmak, are you joining us in a little refreshment?"

"I certainly am!"

"And who, may I ask, is this young wolf-person?" the Thar asked, turning his huge amber eyes on Growlahowl and purring benevolently.

"No one of any importance. He's just going back to his quarters now where he'll stay until I call him, if he knows what's good for him."

The werewolf Prince immediately sloped off, torn between relief and anger. How dare his father just dismiss him like that! He may not have wanted to spend his time with a bunch of old fogeys – they'd probably only get drunk and become even more annoying – but he should have been allowed to choose his own moment of departure, not be told to leave like some common lackey!

Never one to miss the opportunity for a good tantrum, he stormed blindly along one of the many corridors that led off the Great Hall, unsure of where he was, but totally certain he wasn't going back to his room as his dad had ordered.

He was soon totally lost, but rather than admit it he crashed blindly on, climbing stairs and bursting through doors as he wound deeper and deeper into the labyrinth of the palace.

As his temper gradually cooled he began to slow down. He

looked around, trying to get his bearings. As he entered another corridor a housecarle saluted, having recognised the silver collar of a werewolf Prince. Relieved, Growlahowl realised that if this passageway had a guard it must lead some-where important.

He was just about to go back and ask the soldier where he was, when a nearby door was thrown open and a tall human, dressed in armour and concentrating on buckling his sword belt, burst through it. He walked into Growlahowl, knocking him against the wall, and instantly apologised in wolf-speech. "Who are you?" he asked, catching sight of the werewolf's silver collar. "Should I know you?"

Growlahowl could have snarled in frustration. Everybody was asking him questions! If one more person, of any species, cast doubt on his actions or called him a fool, he wouldn't be answerable for what happened! But before he could do or say anything, something made him pause. The human before him was obviously young, as he had no beard. Only Oskan Witchfather and the Hypolitan men shaved. As far as Growlahowl could tell, the boy was probably about his own age. "I only arrived a few days ago, so no, you wouldn't know me," he said finally. "I'm the son of King Grishmak."

"Oh, I see," the boy said, still trying to buckle his sword belt. When he succeeded he looked up and grinned. "Didn't know Grishmak had any whelps. Want to come along to the training ground? We're pitching a shield wall and werewolves against Taradan's cavalry. We always lose, but this could be the day we finally hold them."

Growlahowl shrugged. "Well . . . yes, I suppose. Won't the Weapons Master mind a stranger just turning up?"

"No. Why should she? Captain Aethelflaed likes as many

as she can get in a war game. She thinks it makes it more authentic. What's your name?"

"Prince Growlahowl."

"Too long for the battlefield. Howler will do. Don't worry, you'll get used to it. In official circles I'm Prince Eodred Cerdic Thor-Hammer, Spiller of the Blood of the Polypontian Empire, but when going into action I'm known as Eddie."

Growlahowl took a step back. "*You're* Prince Eodred? I thought you were fading away and threatening to kill yourself!"

Eodred scowled ferociously, but then his face lightened and he grinned. "Now I *know* you're Grishmak's son. As blunt as a rusty sword. Still, at least your feet don't smell like his."

"What do you mean?" asked Growlahowl sharply, ready to defend the family honour.

"Don't tell me you haven't smelt them! Like old cheese with a fart problem," said Eodred, giggling at his own joke.

"Like old cheese . . ." said Growlahowl, then barked with laughter. A perfect description of his dad's pongy paws. "Yeah, that's right! Dad doesn't like soap near his feet. He says it softens the pads and makes marching over rough ground painful. Can't say it causes me any problems, though."

Both boys laughed again. "Come on, I'll introduce you to Captain Aethelflaed. By the way, she's called 'Ethel' in battle, but don't laugh at that – she's got a vicious fist and she'll use it, Prince or not."

They hurried along the maze of corridors, but Eodred obviously knew the way and hardly bothered to look up as he constantly checked his equipment, settling a belt here, adjusting a scabbard there or shrugging his shoulders more comfortably into the straps that attached the huge shield he carried on his back.

"Who's your mum, then?" Eodred asked suddenly.

"Princess White-pelt of the Ukpik tribe."

The human boy glanced at his companion respectfully. "Really? I thought your coat was a bit on the light side for an Icemark werewolf," he said. "You're tall for your age too. I suppose your mum must be a mighty warrior."

"She was," Growlahowl answered in a quiet voice. "She fell in battle against the Ice Trolls in their last big uprising."

Eodred stopped in his tracks and gazed at his companion. "Then you know what it feels like when someone in your family dies. My brother was killed in battle too. At least we can both be sure that they'll get their rewards and be with the gods in Valhalla."

"The Wolf-folk don't have Valhalla," said Growlahowl, trying to ignore the tightening in his throat. "We are servants of the Blessed Moon. She's above the pain and misery of mere mortals."

Eodred had long ago reached his own conclusions on this subject. He'd seen many of his werewolf friends die in his first battle, and couldn't accept that their Goddess wouldn't reward her people's faithfulness. The Wolf-folk may not have a tradition of an afterlife, but Eodred knew in his heart that they lived on after death. "The Blessed Moon is a Goddess who must love her people as much as any other. Your mother's not gone, she's not become just . . . nothing. No, she's become part of the Blessed Moon's Royal bodyguard as a great warrior should. She strides the sky now, full of strength and power just as she strode the earth before she was killed. Those we love don't die – only their bodies break down, or get broken. But the real bit of them lives on for ever."

Growlahowl looked at his new friend and thought that he

was probably the strangest person he'd ever met. Still, the tightness in his throat didn't feel quite as bad as it had – or, at least, it felt different. He liked the thought that his mother still existed somewhere. And if he had to imagine her as a bodyguard to the Blessed Moon to believe that, then so be it!

"Are we ever going to get to this training ground?" the young werewolf asked gruffly.

"We're almost there," Eodred answered and smiled, recognising a fellow warrior's inability to talk too much about feelings and love.

The human Prince was true to his word, and within a couple of minutes they'd arrived at the huge arena where the allied army of human beings, werewolves and Snow Leopards trained and played war games. Growlahowl was introduced as 'Howler', and so began a long afternoon of mock fighting presided over by the fearsome Weapons Master.

Later that evening as the Princes walked back to their quarters they happily compared cuts and bruises, and then made arrangements to go hunting in the forest together the following day. They parted cheerfully, neither of them realising this was the first day of a friendship that would span the years, and would grow up and grow old just as they did. Then as Eodred finally closed the door on his new friend's retreating back, he smiled. Suddenly the world had lightened, suddenly the sun was warm again, and he knew there were things worth fighting for.

The huge complex of underground caverns that lay beneath Frostmarris was filled with regimented lines of coffins. Some of them were closed, but others gaped open and their occupants sat up quietly chatting with their neighbours, or gathered in small groups discussing the next stage of the war. The Vampires expected the alarms to go at any minute, even though Bellorum and his Sky Navy hadn't yet attacked the capital. They were now all seasoned veterans of the war with the Empire, and they knew it was wise to expect the unexpected.

The battle for Learton had been ferocious, with both sides suffering heavy losses, and although the town had eventually been destroyed by the bombers, it had taken far longer than Scipio Bellorum had either planned or expected. The Vampires and their allies, the Snowy Owls, took enormous pride in knowing that the ferocity of their fighting had badly damaged the Imperial cause.

The Vampire King and Queen were being housed in the largest underground cavern of the city they had once ambitiously imagined adding to their Blood Kingdom. They had arranged for their thrones and a few other home comforts to be delivered to their new quarters, and had then taken up residence with such an air of intended long-term ownership that the human chamberlains forced to conduct business with the Vampire Court had become rather worried.

That very morning the Royal Vampires were expecting a visit from Thirrin to discuss tactics for the coming assault, and they were busy contriving just the right effects to make the Queen of the Icemark feel like a visiting dignitary in her own city. Their thrones had been raised on a dais that had been hastily cobbled together from spare coffins, but which were now draped in black velvet and gave the impression of having been *in situ* for centuries.

The King leaned back against the elegant upholstery as though the tedium of it all was almost beyond his ability to tolerate. "Perhaps we should offer wine – that'll put us squarely in the position as hosts, and Her Mortal Majesty as mere guest," he offered, in a languid voice that sounded as though it barely had the strength to pass his lips.

"What a good idea, light of my death," said the Queen. "Lugosi, fetch the best crystal we have and decant the finest vintage," she ordered. Her Master of Vampiric Ceremonies bowed with supreme decorum and then managed to both glide and hurry to do her bidding at one and the same time.

"I suppose the loathsome *Witchfather* will be in tow," said the King, his tones becoming almost heated as he spoke of Oskan. "No doubt we'll get the usual pep talk on how we're committed to the war and any attempts to renege on our so-called obligations will result in mayhem, and our destruction! Someone really should take that man aside and give him a few pointers on how to maintain morale amongst one's allies."

"Calm down, Kingy darling," said the Queen soothingly. "Think of your Royal dignity."

"I *am* thinking of my dignity, oh illuminator of the centuries. We're summoned and ordered about like the lowliest palace chamberlains, with no thought given to etiquette and the due respect our Personages deserve! When I think of their measly little lives, spent and gone in the blink of a Vampire's eye, I could almost laugh at their presumption, were it not for the gross impertinences we are forced to suffer!" He slumped back in his throne as though despairing. "Oh well, I suppose we can expect little else from a land of country bumpkins. One simply has to rise above it, and hope our example of proper behaviour will eventually influence the manners of our hosts and allies."

"Precisely, my undying love. See yourself as an ambassador

from the Court of the Impeccable to the lowly hovels of the aspiring barbarian. Which, might I add, is exactly what you are, my lord of the darkest shadows."

"Thank you, dear unbeating heart," said the King with quiet appreciation. "You always manage to raise my spirits. How could I exist without your steady support? The centuries would stretch to an eternity of interminable boredom and drudgery."

The Queen kissed him lightly on the cheek and smiled a glittering grin. "We have an aeon of evers before us, my love. Let us relish our immortality and bear the presumptions of these *little* people for as long as it takes their paltry lives to end."

They laughed quietly together, and only stopped when they became aware of Thirrin and Oskan standing before their thrones.

"Oh, I'm sorry," said His Vampiric Majesty. "We didn't see you there. Can we help at all?"

As a sentence designed to put a mere mortal firmly in their place it was almost perfect. But Thirrin was used to the tricks of the Vampires and, ignoring them, turned to beckon a group of chamberlains and housecarles, who quickly built a dais out of specially constructed boxes. They then placed two high thrones in the centre of the platform and laid a small set of steps before them. Thirrin inclined her head regally and, taking Oskan's hand, ascended to her throne. When Queen and Witchfather were seated comfortably, Their Vampiric Majesties realised that Thirrin's dais was higher than theirs. Someone had been spying on the Vampires' quarters, and Oskan's wolfish grin told its own story. He'd used his Eye to prepare himself for any tricks .

"Our small cave is a little crowded with regality," said the Vampire Queen acidly. "Monarchs almost outnumber subjects! Who, then, will be subservient?"

"Perhaps we should just accept we are all equally superior, if you'll forgive the oxymoron," said Oskan with quiet amusement.

"Oh, please! These games begin to tire me," said His Vampiric Majesty. "We have business to discuss – let us get on with it and have done."

"As you wish," said Thirrin with an air of efficiency. "I have important news, anyway. The werewolf scouts report that Bellorum and his sons are advancing towards Frostmarris. They should be here at any time, but we expect the Sky Navy to attack first."

The Vampire Queen took her Consort's hand and held it briefly to her lips. "Then, my love, we will be defending the skies over a city of mortals once again."

"So it would seem, my most precious of riches," the King answered, and smiled gently.

Thirrin was amazed to hear a note of genuine weariness in his tone, and scrutinised her reluctant allies. If she hadn't known better she might have believed that only a determination to save Frostmarris kept the Vampires fighting on. But she dismissed the thought as absurd. The Vampires loved none but themselves, and their loyalty was exacted only by threats and menaces. Even so, they had fought long and hard for Learton and had then covered the retreat of the housecarle and werewolf garrison. And when the pursuit by Polypontian cavalry became desperate, they'd finally swooped down on their allies and bodily carried them to safety. Could Oskan be wrong when he insisted that the Vampires hated them? Could there perhaps be the faintest spark of friendship somewhere in their dead hearts?

"Let us hope they attack soon," Her Vampiric Majesty snapped. "Our people grow hungry, and human blood is nourishing no matter what the source. Jugular of the Icemark or jugular of the Polypontus is all one and the same to the piercing fang."

Thirrin shuddered; her answer was given. "Any attack on my people or allies will meet with swift and terrible revenge, Your Majesty," she said with quiet venom. "You can rest assured that for every human death you inflict on my people, ten Vampires will be sent into the Dark."

"Well now, isn't this pleasant?" said Oskan. "Just a group of old friends passing time in idle chit-chat. How fortunate that we have so much in common."

"How fortunate for you that we have a binding treaty in common, as well as a mutual enemy intent on destroying us both," said His Vampiric Majesty.

"Quite," agreed Oskan. "And with that in mind, perhaps we should discuss tactics." He beckoned to a werewolf soldier who stepped forward with a low table that she positioned between the two sets of thrones, after which a housecarle unrolled a large map showing Frostmarris and the surrounding area.

"Shall we?" Thirrin said, stepping down from the dais.

Their Vampiric Majesties and Oskan joined her at the table, and together they pored over the plan. "As we know, the squadrons of Snowy Owls are billeted in the Great Forest. From there they'll be able to send out patrols to cover and hinder Bellorum's advance, as well as attacking the Sky Navy as and when it arrives. But I suggest your Vampires concentrate solely on protecting the skies directly above Frostmarris. Are we in agreement?"

"The Snowy Owls know of this plan?" His Vampiric Majesty asked.

"Yes. They understand the language of the Wolf-folk and have been in communication with myself and Oskan for a day or so now. They are in complete agreement."

"Would it perhaps have been rather more courteous if you had informed their Overlord, namely myself, that you were instructing his vassals in tactics for the coming battle?"

Thirrin glanced at the Vampire King and inclined her head. "It would," she answered simply. "Please accept my apologies."

His Vampiric Majesty raised an eyebrow in surprise. "It is of no consequence. War sometimes makes speed more necessary than etiquette."

Oskan watched this small exchange with interest. Normally, such a slight to his Royal dignity would have given the Vampire King an excuse to argue and wrangle for hours. So why, Oskan wondered, had he ignored such a golden opportunity to cause trouble this time? Thirrin might believe that the Vampires were warming in their attitude towards their human allies, but Oskan would have none of it. Their Vampiric Majesties did nothing that didn't have their own interests at heart, and the Witchfather determined to find out what it was.

"The tactics remain simple and basic, I suppose. When the Sky Navy appears, attack it; destroy what you can and hinder what you can't," said Thirrin, continuing with the briefing. "The land forces will then appear and take up a position on the high ground to the south of the plain, and the battle for

Frostmarris will have begun in earnest." She sighed wearily and sat on the edge of the dais. "It's just like the last time, I suppose. Only now Bellorum has his new Sky Navy to bomb us into submission, and we have no additional allies to call on. We can't fail to be the first ones to crack under the pressure."

Her Vampiric Majesty sat down next to her. "None of us will crack, Thirrin. You'll see. Bellorum and his legions will batter themselves to pieces on our ramparts, and when the remnants of his filthy army are forced to withdraw, we'll still be standing."

Oskan was astonished. He'd never heard the Vampires use anything other than their formal titles when addressing either himself or the Queen. What could it all mean? But before he had time to analyse anything, the sound of hurrying feet interrupted his thoughts.

A housecarle officer burst into the cave and bowed hurriedly. "Your Majesties. The werewolf relay has just reported Bellorum is fast approaching and the Sky Navy is flying ahead. They expect the first of the wasp-fighters to be over the city in less than an hour."

"Then the time has come, my love," said his Vampiric Majesty, taking his Queen's hand with a peculiarly gentle smile. Let us prepare for battle."

CHAPTER 25

The camels roared a rich concert of bubbling groans and growls across the silent dunes. The mules and one or two of the horses joined in, and Sharley stared nervously about the empty landscape. What had the animals sensed? He knew these creatures never wasted energy unnecessarily in the harsh desert conditions. This discordant chorus must be a warning of some sort.

Mekhmet was worried too, and reining to a halt he beckoned over the Commander of the Guard and the chief drover, hoping their greater experience would provide an explanation.

"Perhaps they scent water, My Lord," the Commander suggested. "Sometimes there are hidden springs beneath the sands."

The camel drover glanced at the soldier contemptuously. "No, no. This is not the song for water. My camels issue a warning of weather, My Lord."

"Weather?" said Sharley in amazement. "Then perhaps we'd better prepare for sunshine and heat tomorrow," he added ironically.

"Forgive me, but His Majesty, the Prince of the North, has

little knowledge of the desert's ways," the drover said courteously. "My camels have scented a shift in the strength of the winds, and soon we may expect a sandstorm."

Mekhmet and the Commander both looked alarmed. "When? Exactly how long do we have?" the Commander asked.

The drover raised his head and sniffed at the hot air. "An hour, perhaps. Enough time to prepare."

Mekhmet nodded. "Then do it. I want losses kept to the barest minimum."

"What's so bad about a storm? A bit of rain might cool things down for a while," said Sharley, puzzled.

"Rain? There's no rain in a sandstorm," Mekhmet answered. "There are only howling, burning winds, and hot sands whipped up to such a force that they can scour the flesh from the bones of anyone stupid enough to get caught out in it. We can only trust that the Blessed Women will help us."

"Really?" said Sharley. "But can't we outrun it and find shelter somewhere?"

"And where would you suggest?" asked Mekhmet, waving his hand at the wide unbroken landscape of undulating sand dunes.

Both boys fell silent, and watched as the chief drover and his men goaded and cajoled the camels into a wide circle almost nose to tail. The horses and mules were then tethered within the ring of huge hump-backed beasts, and were forced to lie down with their back legs hobbled so that they couldn't bolt in panic.

"Come on, Sharley, we'd better get ready," said Mekhmet, and hurried to a position downwind of two particularly large camels that were roaring and bubbling as the drovers draped tent hides on the ground and staked them down next to their beasts.

"Dismount, and lead Suleiman close to the camels. He won't like it, but he'll go with you," Mekhmet directed, and he waited while Sharley did as he was told before leading his own horse in. Then both horses were hobbled and given the command to lie down.

Without waiting for one of his many servants, Mekhmet started to unload the hide of one of the smaller tents. "Well, don't just stand there with your mouth open, give me a hand!" he shouted to Sharley.

The Crown Prince showed him how to peg down the leading edge of the tent and drape it over the nervously whickering horses, leaving a long trailing length downwind. "Come on," he said. "Follow me." Lifting the deflated tent, he found the entrance and crawled inside.

The horses continued to snort and whicker nervously, but the boys murmured to them and Sharley whispered Suleiman's name into his ear. Eventually, the horses quieted, but the heat inside the unerected tent was stifling ."Look, I'm still not sure what all the fuss is about," said Sharley. "I mean, I know it's going to get windy, and you lot seem to think that's dangerous, but how bad can it be?"

"Perhaps you have to experience a sandstorm to truly understand," said Mekhmet quietly. "We still have a few minutes yet; maybe you should go outside and see if you can make anything out."

"Fine!" said Sharley, beginning to get irritated. "I will. But what am I looking for?"

"You'll know when you see it," said his friend mysteriously. "But don't wander off. You could get lost."

Sharley fought his way out from under the heavy hide and stood up. Everything was quiet. All the soldiers, drovers and servants were hidden inside their unerected tents, which were huddled against the sheltered side of the camel circle like the flayed skins of so many dead giants. Only the huge lumps at the leading edges of the hides showed where the horses and mules lay, and here and there the lumps writhed wildly as the animals panicked.

After the relative dark of the tent, the brilliant sun dazzled Sharley, but as his eyes adjusted he stared out over the shimmering dunes that wavered and boiled in the heat haze. Then he saw it. On the horizon a tower of something that looked like thick black and ochre smoke rose into the air. It was stupendously high, reaching from the desert floor far into the sky. Sharley gasped, and the hairs on his arms and neck stood up.

Almost imperceptibly, a gentle gasp of wind stroked his face, and with it came an acrid scent of hot dust and a whisper of a distant howling and raging that made him gasp again. For the first time in weeks, his gammy leg gave way and he sat down hard on the sands.

"Can you see anything?" a muffled voice called from under the tent.

"Yes," he whispered. Then, clearing his throat, he repeated, "Yes. A wall of sand higher than the sky, wider than a city, and heading this way!"

"That'd be the sandstorm, then," said Mekhmet, stating the obvious. "You'd better come back in. *Now!*"

"I think you should take a look," Sharley answered. "It's truly enormous. Surely an ordinary storm can't be this big?"

A scrambling in the tent indicated that Mekhmet was hurrying to join him. He emerged red-faced and sweating from the hides. "You've no experience of sandstorms. It's probably not too bad."

Sharley pointed silently, and his friend fell to his knees. "May the One protect us," he whispered.

"I told you it was bad," Sharley said quietly.

"*Bad!* It's more than bad. It's massive!" Mekhmet croaked. "We'd better pray that the Blessed Women are with us. Without their protection we're dead!"

Sharley's heart gave a huge thump and then seemed to fall silent. He stared in horrified fascination as the thin dusty outriders of the storm started to steal over the camp. Slowly, the sun was dimmed and the light turned a tawny colour. The eerie non-dark made Sharley's flesh creep; it was like twilight in a tomb.

The shriek of the raging wind was slowly climbing higher and higher, filling his head with its fury. Sharley began to pray. He wasn't exactly sure who or what he was praying to, but remembering the beautiful mirage of the Blessed Women he made a desperate plea for help.

The day then seemed to draw breath, and a huge blast of hot, sand-laden air roared across the camp. Sharley was almost blinded, but coughing and wheezing he grabbed Mekhmet, and together they just managed to struggle back to their tent. The wind screeched and howled like an attack of the Vampire army. It was almost impossible to see anything as the light level dipped to near dark. The boys fell to their knees and crawled into the hot airless refuge.

They lay still under the fabric. Eventually, Mekhmet's hand found Sharley's, and he grasped it gladly as the full terror of the storm hit them.

All around the camp the wind screamed.

"We're lost! We're lost, there's nothing we can do!" Mekhmet yelled against the noise of the storm.

Was this it? Sharley thought. Was this where his mission ended? Dying like this was almost laughable: caught in a dust storm and smothered to death!

He huddled closer to Mekhmet, glad to have some human contact at the end. But then Sharley noticed a strange blue light that began to filter through the tent. Beautiful female voices began to fill his head. He could have cried out with joy; his prayers had been answered!

The gentle singing slowly swelled, filling the air with sweetness, and the roaring and raging of the winds abated slightly.

Now Mekhmet lifted a corner of the tent, and after a few moments scrambled to his feet, laughing.

"The Blessed Women! We're saved! Look!"

What looked like a bank of blue mist was slowly evolving across the dunes and gradually surrounding the camp. Soon, a barrier of light and song stood against the storm, and no matter how the winds raged, they were unable to break through the wall of ethereal blue.

Sharley crawled out from under the canvas and stood with Mekhmet, gazing at the light. Gradually they began to make out the forms of beautiful young women, who stood holding hands in a long unbroken line around the camp, their long robes flowing and waving gently as though undulating on a current of water.

Their song strengthened and rose in powerful harmonies that slowly drowned out the raging of the winds. All around the camp the sandstorm rampaged, but within the barrier of blue light an all-pervading sense of calm settled over everything and everyone.

After what seemed an age, the howling of the storm began to abate and the singing of the Blessed Women also began to change, slowly descending the scales and levels of volume until only a gentle melody whispered through the air, and the last of the wind died away.

The barrier of blue light started to flow and ripple as the Blessed Women, too, slowly moved away. And as Sharley and Mekhmet watched, one of the fabulous, transparent figures broke away from the others and drifted over the sands towards them. Sharley fell to his knees and looked up at the woman's outline, which glowed in the dimness like a gentle lamp. Sharley could see that she was smiling at him, and he was pierced by an acute sense of love and compassion that brought tears to his eyes. Here was the love of mothers and of fathers; here was the love of sisters and of brothers. But more than that, Sharley felt that this single Blessed Woman was one tiny spark of compassion from a source infinitely greater than he or anyone else could ever imagine.

The Blessed Woman began to speak. "Charlemagne of the North, Blessed of the One, I come to sanctify your travels. Know this, we are here for you always and hold you safe in the palm of our hand. Do not be frightened on our desert road."

She held out her hands to the two Princes in a gesture of blessing, salaamed deeply and silently withdrew.

The boys watched her go, and were suddenly overwhelmed by a sense of exhaustion that seemed to seep out of the very air around them. Completely unable to resist, they sank to the ground and fell asleep. The next thing Sharley knew, Mekhmet was shaking him.

"Well, you're a cool one, I must say. There are not many who could sleep through their first sandstorm. I'm sorry if the worst my desert can throw at you is so boring," the Crown Prince said with reluctant amusement.

Sharley instinctively knew that the Blessed Women were ensuring his friend had forgotten almost all of what had just happened, but that for some reason they were allowing him to remember it. He decided he could only accept their wisdom, so he said nothing and grinned apologetically.

The world was silent now. The strange veil of dirty light had been drawn from the sky as if it had never been there, and the sun's glare was as strong as ever. But the land had changed completely, or rather the landmarks had. All the dunes, all the sand-valleys and hills had been swept away and a new topography of sandbanks, hummocks and hills rippled away to the horizon. If Sharley had known where he was before the storm, he certainly had no idea now. He just hoped the others knew the way.

He needn't have worried. The chief drover took an instrument from his saddlebag and, lining it up with the sun, he took a reading. Sharley knew this would tell him their exact position, but *how* it did so he had no idea. He was quite content to let the 'clever ones' lead the way.

Within an hour the caravan was en route to Lusuland again, and apart from finding sand in the unlikeliest of places, there was nothing to suggest they'd just been through a howling desert storm, and seen the mysterious Blessed Women.

CHAPTER 26

Their Vampiric Majesties waited above the city with their squadrons, wheeling slowly on the thermals spiralling up from the stonework that was gently warming in the summer sunshine. In their bat forms they could see and hear with amazing clarity, and they eagerly drank in the opening moves of the battle for Frostmarris.

Below them on the city defences, the human, leopard and werewolf soldiers were taking up their positions, while the crews of the crossbow-like ballistas and rock-throwing trebuchets swarmed over their giant weapons as they prepared them for the coming struggle. In the far distance the barely discernible flash and glitter of Bellorum's advancing army could just be seen through the haze of the warm day, and the shrill of fife and rattle of drum whispered over the miles. But much, much closer was the Sky Navy, the shadows of its ships sweeping over the land as they advanced in battle formation. Their task was to weaken the city and, perhaps, if they were very lucky, to destroy it completely in the first attack.

The Vampire King and Queen now saw themselves as the champions of the great living and unliving multiplicity that was the universe. They were determined to destroy the hideous threat of the Empire, with its undiluted rationality and rigid, unthinking science, before it could do any more harm to the glorious sweep of their natural and supernatural worlds.

The hugely ponderous shapes of the bomber galleons sailed slowly on, while around them the dart-like wasp-fighters tumbled and soared as they patrolled the skies for enemies. The Polypontian pilots were taking no risks. As much as they desperately hoped that the Vampires had left the war for good, they were not going to lower their guard.

Nearby the warning howls of the werewolf lookouts sounded as the Sky Navy flew over the low hills that bordered the southern part of the plain of Frostmarris, and immediately wave upon wave of Snowy Owls rose from the massive living bulk of the Great Forest. In quick response, the wasp-fighters started to peel away from the bombers and flew to intercept the enemy squadrons.

The Vampires watched and waited for the bombers that were now sailing over the plain. As they came within range, the batteries of giant ballistas all tipped and pivoted to target the advancing galleons like the many heads of one gigantic creature. They spewed out a flight of steel bolts, each with a flaming head that streaked a smoke trail through the sky. Many found their targets, smashing into the wooden hulls of the bombers or tearing through the canopy of the gas-filled balloons. Immediately, the sky-sailors swarmed over the rigging to fight flames, or swung on ropes as they tried to douse the blazing woodwork.

With a roaring gasp the canopies of two of the galleons erupted into fireballs and they tumbled through the sky and crashed to earth with an ear-splitting rending of wood and steel.

A huge cheer erupted from the housecarles on the defences, and they screamed encouragement as the ballistas continued to spit out their steel bolts with devastating accuracy.

The admiral reacted quickly to the new threat, and the galleons began to climb away, but the ballistas followed their route, loosing bolt after bolt into the air ships as they climbed. Soon three more of the huge bombers were in flames. Dozens of the wasp-fighters swarmed back to rescue the sky-sailors, carrying them away to other ships, and then returning to take off more of the men who were desperately hanging over the gunnels of the blazing vessels. But for some there was no rescue. The fire raged through the wooden flying ships, and many threw themselves overboard, their clothing and hair in flames as they fell like miniature meteors to the ground.

Down on the defences the ground troops watched the aerial battle raging above them. They were restless and desperate to fight, but the werewolf relay said Bellorum and his mad sons were still several miles away. Cressida found it all enormously frustrating, not only because the Empire could dictate the rate and style of fighting, but because she had no way of personally striking back at the hated Sky Navy. Her mother seemed amazingly relaxed, moving along the line with Grishmak and laughing and joking with the soldiers. She could only envy her restraint. Cressida's very skin prickled with tension.

"They'll send in the land attack soon enough," Tharaman said quietly, understanding her frustrations perfectly. "And then we'll be far too busy to think of the air war."

"Oh, I know, but I just need to *do* something. It's more than I can bear, just standing here, watching!" As she spoke, several wasp-fighters fell tumbling and spinning to the ground, and the victorious shrieks of the Snowy Owls echoed over the sky.

"Patience, my dear, is a great virtue, and one that every military Commander should strive to cultivate. We must stand ready and unwavering for Bellorum's land attack."

"I *know* that!" Cressida snapped. "Don't worry, I'm not going to do anything stupid like break ranks, or charge up and down the plain to draw the wasp-fighters down low enough for me to get a shot at them!"

"Nothing was further from my thoughts," said Tharaman patiently. "I merely hoped to calm you with a few well-chosen words."

"Well, it's not working!" she answered crossly. She watched as the distant figure of her mother reached Eodred and Howler's regiment. Even from her position standing with Tharaman and Krisafitsa, she could hear her brother's laughter. For a moment she almost hated him for his cool head, but she took the thought back immediately. Wishing ill on anyone, apart from the enemy, before a battle was bad luck. But not only that, she was enormously glad that Eodred had found his military fire again. He was a warrior, with a warrior's values and virtues. Even if the worst should happen in the war, at least he was guaranteed a place in Valhalla.

"Perhaps we should have a small snack while we're waiting," Krisafitsa suggested, falling back on her faithful remedy of keeping everyone well fed.

Cressida managed to smile despite everything. "You make it sound like we're tired children getting tetchy."

"Well, we're certainly getting tetchy," the Tharina answered lightly. "And a little food can often distract from unpleasantness."

Cressida considered pointing out that a war with the Polypontian Empire could hardly be categorised as "unpleasantness", but thought better of it. Tharaman was already burying his face in a huge mound of meat, and she had to admit she felt much calmer as she munched an apple one of her troopers had given her.

In the opening minutes of the battle it had looked desperate for the Sky Navy. But the bombers climbed beyond the range of the ballistas, until they were able to look down on the powerful barrage of steel bolts arcing up to the limit of their range, before falling back to earth.

However, in the hideous carnage and scramble of the opening moves, none of the Polypontian lookouts had noticed the Vampires calmly spiralling on thermals way above Frostmarris, waiting for the right moment to strike. His Vampiric Majesty had been quietly formulating his strategy and tactics. Not only must his squadrons stop the Sky Navy, but they would need to strike hard and decisively against the pending land attack if the defence of the city was to be truly effective. Bellorum and his sons might still be several miles away, but the Imperial army marched at an astonishing pace and would soon be advancing across the plain of Frostmarris. When that happened, His Vampiric Majesty had a little plan developing that would, at the very least, nicely delay the General's strategy. A plan with a sweetly neat twist, that involved gunpowder and fire and using the enemy's own weapons against him.

But in the meantime the Vampires had an aerial battle to fight. The King called his squadron to him. After a few moments, shrieking hideously, the huge bats peeled away, formed into massive battle groups and swooped into the fray.

Many of the wasp-fighters were still engaged with the Snowy Owls out over the plain, but seeing the danger, several of the squadrons banked away from their engagement and started to climb the spiral stairway of thermals, rising to the defence of the bombers. The sky-sailors began to break out muskets and cutlasses as the cannon crews prepared their pieces by loading them with grapeshot.

Thousands of hideous Vampires flew in tight formations, yammering and screeching as they came, causing many of the sky-sailors to shudder in fear. Then, as they drew closer, the cannons roared a huge broadside from over fifty ships. Dozens of the giant bats fell, torn to pieces by the broken metal of grapeshot. Then countless more were ripped apart by the muskets and crossbows of the wasp-fighters. But most escaped, climbing the thermals to safety and immediately swooping back into the attack, smashing into the flimsy canopies of the fighters, tearing them apart and sending them tumbling and rolling to the plain below.

Dozens more wasp-fighters joined the battle, firing volleys from their muskets and sending out a hail of wooden darts. The air was rent with screeches, howls and musket-shot, and it was impossible for the sky-sailors in the galleons to tell which side was winning.

Orders were given for the Sky Navy to continue the advance on the city and to prepare the bombs. But before they'd sailed any further towards their target, new squadrons – this time led by the Vampire Queen – flew in to begin their murderous attack. The cannons roared again, but they were no match for the mass of deadly bats which drew closer and closer to the ships until they swarmed over the decks, transforming into their Vampire forms and drawing their viciously serrated black swords. Their armour gleamed like wet hide in the bright sunlight, and their deathly white faces were quickly smeared with blood as they ripped out the throats of the Polypontian sailors.

While his Queen attacked the decks, the Vampire King saw a new opportunity. He and his selected squadrons swooped up on to the canopies of the giant sky-ships, while the Snowy Owls dived into the fray, battling with the wasp-fighters and drawing them away from the exposed Vampires, allowing the King and his soldiers to work unmolested, tearing at the vulnerable balloons with sword, dagger and tooth.

But it wasn't to last. Imperial sky-sailors swarmed into view, expertly snaking their way up over the rigging with cutlasses clamped in their teeth and pistols in their hands, and a terrible fight for the control of the canopies began. The crew members fired wooden shot from their pistols and sent dozens of the Vampires crashing to ruin, but the King rallied his soldiers and they swept down on the sailors, tearing out their throats, or transforming into bats and plucking them from the balloons before sending them tumbling to the ground, hundreds of feet below.

A roaring crackle erupted as the King and his squadron succeeded in setting fire to one giant balloon. But the rest of the bombers sailed on with the unstoppable progress of ponderous storm clouds.

Moving closer and closer to the walls of Frostmarris, they opened their bomb flaps and made ready for the assult on the city walls.

From her room high in her tower Medea watched the struggle

with cold detachment as the aerial battle tumbled and raged high above the plain. If she applied her Sight she could see everything in pristine detail. She had to admire the Vampires. Here they were, fighting in a war not of their making, or choosing, yet they risked their undead existence in an attempt to destroy the Sky Navy. How completely unfathomable they were. She'd once applied her Eye to the minds of Their Vampiric Majesties and found almost nothing but an aching-ly long memory of years, and carefully stored-up resentments for which they continually plotted and schemed to gain revenge.

Not surprisingly, Oskan was right at the top of a long list of hatreds, but none of their plans to rid themselves of his control had ever had the remotest chance of succeeding. It was all rather pathetic really, especially as Medea could also See, amongst the detritus of their undead minds, the vestigial remains of their once-human emotions. And, worse, the longer they had contact with the living, the more these emotions were likely to grow in strength. They could be in danger of devel-oping human consciences again, and perhaps even a sense of loyalty and friendship.

Medea shuddered at the very thought, and turned her attention back to the battle. Three more of the galleons were in flames and His Vampiric Majesty had just landed on the rigging of a fourth. But here, the sky-sailors were already wait-ing for him, armed to the teeth with cutlasses and pistols.

Just then, a huge explosion rocked the very foundations of Medea's tower. The first of the bombs had been dropped nearby, and was soon followed by the sound of falling mason-ry and the ominous crackle of fire. Her window, already open, had been blasted back on its hinges and all the glass shattered.

For the first time she realised that this war between mundane humans could actually be a direct danger to her, and a blast of white-hot rage roared through her veins. How dare anyone damage her tower and endanger her life!

With an intensity of concentration that made her physically quake and tremble, she drew power into herself, and moulded the air currents and atmosphere into a howling rush of wind that blasted across the sky and smashed into the flying ships. She watched in satisfaction as the huge galleons keeled over alarmingly, and the Vampires, Snowy Owls and wasp-fighters were literally thrown across the sky.

But her tempest raged for no more than a minute, until she came to her senses. If she was not more careful her father would become suspicious again. Abruptly she cut the wind, and normality returned. All of the warships of the Sky Navy had been blown far back across the plain, four more of them had foundered, tumbling and spinning to earth, and more than fifty of the wasp-fighters had been ripped from the sky and dashed to pieces on the ground.

Already, the cost to the Polypontians of the Sky Navy's first raid on Frostmarris was enormous. They'd managed to drop only one load of bombs and yet altogether they'd lost eight galleons and over a hundred wasp-fighters. If such a loss rate was sustained, they would only be able to carry out another ten raids before the Sky Navy was wiped out.

Medea watched all of this with a sense of satisfaction. In the streets below her tower, the units of housecarles and were-wolves who'd been trained as firefighters were providing a show as they operated huge pumps under the direction of the engine-eer, Archimedo Archimedes, and played jets of water over the burning buildings. Some were breaking down doors and pulling out injured people, while others were ferrying the injured to the witches in the infirmary.

Medea sighed happily. This was as close as the physical world got to excitement!

But the sound of axes thudding into the door of her tower interrupted her enjoyment. As she listened it burst open, and she heard running feet climbing the spiral staircase. She turned to face the werewolf and the huge housecarle who burst into her room and skidded to a halt before her.

The werewolf was first to recover from his shock. "Your Majesty, you're safe?"

"Untouched, as you see," Medea answered coolly, ignoring the creature's involuntary wrinkling of its lips as the distaste of her presence registered on its senses.

"You must come with us, Your Majesty. The fire could spread," the housecarle said.

Medea looked at the tall woman until the soldier was forced to drop her gaze from black pupil-less eyes. "I can think of nothing in this entire mortal world that I 'must' do," Medea said quietly. "The fire wouldn't dare touch my tower."

Both the werewolf and the housecarle thought she was probably right, so they saluted and ran back down the stairs, relief at getting away from the hideous young woman, and her strange chamber, giving their feet wings.

"And fix my door!" Medea called after them. "Or you'll pay for it in ways you wouldn't like."

Thirrin watched as the scattered squadrons of Vampires and Snowy Owls reformed over the plain. The freak wind had blown them like leaves in an autumn gale, but as far as she could see, none had been lost. She sighed in relief. Without them the city would have been completely destroyed by now. Not only that, but they'd also inflicted terrible damage on the Sky Navy and were even now preparing to help against the coming ground offensive. Dark and evil they undeniably were, but the Vampires were also valuable allies.

She looked out towards the hills that flanked the southern part of the plain of Frostmarris, where Bellorum and his army would first appear. And if he followed the same pattern as his last invasion, that was also where he would set up camp.

She ran her eyes over the defences for the umpteenth time. With her stood Tharaman and Krisafitsa, the human troopers of the cavalry and the rest of the Snow Leopards. Not far away, Cressida was bullying her particular squadron into looking the smartest and alertest of them all, and Grishmak was sharing what sounded like a very dirty joke with Olememnon while picking his enormous teeth with a twig.

Why did everyone look so relaxed and at ease? She thought she'd scream if something didn't happen soon. Even Eodred looked happy. He'd come out of his depression at last, largely thanks to Growlahowl, or rather, Howler, who stood with him now. They were proving to be great warriors. The pair of them had come up with a novel idea during their weeks of training: they'd formed a mixed regiment of werewolves and housecarles. Normally, the Wolf-folk fought in their own groups, complementing the human units, but the boys had mixed human and werewolf troops, and they carried shields painted with the insignia of a red wolf's head. Even the Wolf-folk carried them, which was unheard of! They didn't need any weaponry – teeth and claws were more than adequate. Still, it did mean they could raise a truly formidable shield wall, bristling with spears, axes, and the sort of grins that would make anyone with even an ounce of common sense run a mile.

Thirrin smiled to herself. Eodred had even given up his horse to fight as a foot-soldier. He said it was because of the new tactics he and Howler had devised, but she knew it was in tribute to Cerdic, his lost twin, who'd been an infantryman. She was so happy that Cressida and Eodred seemed more settled. Only the unfathomable Medea remained unreadable and unreachable, while Sharley was too far away for his father's weak Eye to see.

The thought of her youngest son suddenly pierced all the careful defences she'd built against fear and sorrow, and tears ran down her cheeks. Quickly she wiped them away before anyone could notice; crying on the day of battle was a terrible omen. All she could do was hope that Sharley was safe and happy in his role as Regent to the Exiles. With no letters getting through, she had no way of knowing.

She shook herself like a wet dog. She daren't let herself be distracted by such thoughts and worries. The opening phase of the sky war seemed to be almost over, but the land attack was about to begin. Soon Bellorum and his sons would be advancing over the plain, and she was more than ready for them.

CHAPTER 27

It took four more days of riding to reach the edge of the fiery desert, and another four to pass through the mountains bordering Lusuland. Now the golden furnace was far behind them and in front was a land of green abundance. Wide plains and dark forests lay before them, stitched and embroidered with rivers of the rainy season, and here and there lakes placidly reflected the sun in a sheen of silver lustre that stained the very sky above them with a shimmering miasma of light.

Sharley looked up from the pommel of his saddle where he'd been tiredly running through the events of the last few days, and as his eyes took in the glorious sweep of Lusuland he gasped aloud. "It's beautiful!" he said, his voice reduced to an awed whisper.

"And dangerous," added Mekhmet. "This land is the home of strange and dangerous beasts, and it also bred the people who withstood the cavalry of the Sultans when they were at their most powerful. They are more than just warriors; they are learned and artistic. Their thinkers and scholars have influenced our culture more than many are prepared to accept, and their friendship, once made, is unshakeable. But despite their greatness, I don't think the mighty impis of the Lusu people have been fully tested yet."

"Then let's hope they'll come to the north with us and put themselves to the test against the armies of the Empire."

"Yes, let's hope," Mekhmet agreed.

As the temperature cooled, the tough little horses started to get skittish, and it was all Sharley could do to keep Suleiman under control as he danced and sidled on his neat hooves. The rainy season had made Lusuland lush, and on the wind Sharley could smell greenery and growing things. He had almost forgotten the perfume of rich fertile soil and foliage after being in the Desert Kingdom for so long, and he breathed deeply, filling his lungs with an exotic reminder of home.

But this was not home, and Sharley was soon made starkly aware that they were entering another strange and dangerous land. He constantly felt as though he was being watched, and once or twice he thought he heard an unnerving call, like evil laughter, but he dismissed the idea as ludicrous – obviously it was just a bird of some sort. The cry sounded again, nearer this time, and Suleiman whickered nervously.

"Strange how that call sounds like laughter," said Sharley.

"That's exactly what it is," Mekhmet answered. "It's the Laughing Ones you can hear."

Sharley shuddered. "The Laughing Ones? Who are they?"

"People . . . in a way," his friend answered mysteriously. "Don't worry, they shouldn't bother us in daylight, especially as we're armed."

The cry came again, sounding like something that took pleasure in pain and death.

"It sounds so evil."

"They *are* evil."

Before Sharley could ask more, the sound of a horn blasted into the air and was answered by a second from a different direction, slightly farther off. There was something in the quality of the note that was undeniably military. Mekhmet seemed unconcerned and simply trotted on, but some of the younger troopers in the guard were nervous and would have drawn their scimitars if the Commander hadn't barked out orders forbidding it. Within a matter of minutes Sharley spotted movement on the road ahead, as two cohorts of cavalry met and, without pausing, smoothly melded together and came on as one.

Mekhmet held up his hand for his own party to stop. Sharley gazed ahead. These were the first Lusu he'd met and he was eager to see what they were like. But in the event it wasn't the people that caught his eye, but their mounts. As they drew closer he suddenly realised they were riding black-and-white striped horses! He gasped aloud, then giggled, but stopped when he saw Mekhmet's ferocious glare.

He tried to ignore the strange spectacle of the horses, and concentrated instead on the people. They were a rich mahogany brown, like one or two he'd seen in the Desert Kingdom, but these men and women rode with a sense of pride that made every one of them seem like a king or queen. In their regal presence Sharley felt awkward, and for the first time in weeks he blushed. But this didn't stop him from scrutinising their weaponry and equipment as he almost subconsciously assessed their suitability as possible allies.

They wore no armour but carried kite-shaped shields made of hide, which were strengthened with a metal rim and central boss. Their weapons consisted of light throwing spears, a mace with a vicious-looking toothed metal head, and a long sword, the Lusu equivalent of a cavalry sabre. Their flowing robes were richly coloured, and on their heads they all wore plumes made from the feathers of what must have been truly enormous birds.

The cavalry stopped a few paces away, and their Commander and one of the other officers rode forward. "Who are you that enter the lands of the mighty Lusu people, armed and ready for war?"

"Truly, we enter your lands," Mekhmet replied formally. "But war is not our intention. These soldiers are merely the fitting escort for two Princes of venerable and famed Royal Houses."

The Commander's expression remained neutral. Sharley was struck by her beauty, even though like his mother she looked almost thirty years old.

"Name these Royal Houses, and we shall see if their fame merits such an escort," she continued, her voice cold and brusque.

"The name of one you know already: I am Crown Prince Mekhmet, Sword of the Desert, Beloved of the One, scion of the House of Nasrid. And this is Charlemagne Athelstan Redrought Strong-in-the-Arm Lindenshield. It was his mighty House that defeated the Polypontian Empire when General Scipio Bellorum invaded their land called the Icemark, far, far to the north."

The Commander urged her striped horse forward and peered closely at Sharley. "Let me see the face of this Prince whose House drove back the unstoppable army of the Empire."

Sharley slowly removed the cloth of his headdress, and then

with an unconscious flourish he threw it to the ground. All of the Lusu gasped aloud at the sight of his red hair and pale skin, and the Commander drew back several paces.

"What terrible disease have you brought to our lands? Leave now, and be glad that we do not kill you for fear of contaminating our soil with your sick blood!"

"Disease?" said Sharley, shocked. "I'm not diseased! Lots of people in my country look like me!"

"But your skin has no colour and your hair is like blood diluted by fire. Who could look so terrible and still live?"

In deep embarrassment, Sharley's skin blushed crimson and his hair actually rose so that it seemed to swirl about his head. But seeing the Lusu warriors cowering in horror before him, he suddenly saw the funny side of it. He hadn't known he looked so bad. Someone had once even described him as handsome, but here were people who thought he looked so horrible they were actually scared of him.

He struggled hard to maintain an expression of outraged dignity, but it was impossible. He snorted, then giggled, and finally let out a huge bark of laughter that echoed around the foothills of the mountain. Mekhmet didn't know whether to join in or to stop his friend. But, as usual, Sharley's infectious laughter got to him and he too burst into laughter.

It took a long time for the boys to regain control of themselves, but they eventually calmed down and wiped their eyes. The sight of the Lusu Commander's mixed expression of horror at Sharley's appearance, and offended dignity that anyone should dare to laugh at her, almost started them off again. With a supreme effort Mekhmet settled down and remembered that he was a Crown Prince, and this woman a mere Commander of cavalry.

"You should accept the knowledge that far to the north, all people have colourless skin, and some have hair like fire and eyes the colour of emeralds. I am told that some even have hair as fair as ripe wheat and eyes the colour of sapphires, and though I've not seen this for myself, I have no reason to doubt it."

The Commander heard the unmistakable note of authority in Mekhmet's voice, and bowed her head in reluctant acceptance. But she still wasn't convinced that their visit was entirely peaceful. "That the Prince from the north is not diseased, I will allow, and bow to your greater knowledge of such things, but you still haven't told me of the reason for your presence in our land."

"I am the Guest Friend of Queen Ketshaka III and would travel to her Royal Kraal, there to present myself and Prince Charlemagne to Her Mightiness and have discussion on matters too lofty for your concern."

"I am not aware of any friendship between the Desert Kingdom and Lusuland. I only know of unresolved disputes that periodically erupt into open warfare. Why would the Great She-Lion, Mother of the Nation, want to give audience to one of your House?"

Mekhmet's voice sank to an icy purr of suppressed fury that took Sharley completely by surprise. He'd never seen his friend look or sound so angry, and he watched in fascination as he glared at the woman. "That there have been differences in the past, I cannot contest. But obviously regular diplomatic contact is maintained between our peoples, as is proven by the fact that you speak to me now in the language of the Desert Kingdom. Why should you, a mere Commander of cavalry, speak our tongue so fluently, if you have no use for it? And further, must

I, a stranger in your land, remind you that it is your duty to escort all those who request an audience with Her Mightiness to the Royal Kraal in the city of Swahati? And must I also repeat that I am a Guest Friend of Queen Ketshaka, having travelled here at the time of my Coming of Age? Think of Her Majesty's wrath, when she hears that you bandied words with one who claims the sacred trust of hospitality – because be told, oh *Commander* of mice and ratlings, I will inform Her Mightiness of your impudence and demand retribution!"

For fully five minutes, Prince and cavalry Commander glared at each other in silence, until at last the Lusu woman nodded curtly. "It is well. I will escort you to Swahati and deliver you into the power of the Great She-Lion. She will decide your fate."

"It is well," said Mekhmet with quiet venom.

The Lusu cavalry led the way. A collective sigh of relief sounded from Mekhmet's own escort, and loosened scimitars were pushed more firmly back into scabbards. They may have been outnumbered more than three to one by the Lusu, but they had all sworn to defend their Prince to the death.

"Well, that was an interesting first encounter with a new people," said Sharley brightly. "Are they always like that?"

"Not normally, no. I would think the Commander is new to her post, and perhaps a little over-zealous in carrying out her duties."

"Right. No hard feelings, then."

"No?" Mekhmet asked ominously.

They rode on in silence while the beautiful countryside of Lusuland unfolded around them. The foothills soon gave way to a wide plain, submerged beneath a sea of tall grass that heaved and billowed like waves in the warm wind. Here and there, individual trees and small copses rose like islands out of the surrounding grassland, where an amazing variety of beasts could be seen grazing and moving in huge herds. Sharley didn't recognise any of the species at all, apart from some striped horses in the distance that he rightly assumed were the cavalry mounts in their wild state.

"Those animals are amazing," he said to Mekhmet, nodding at the Lusus' steeds.

"Yes, they are, aren't they? They're known as zebras, and they make superb warhorses, as we've found to our cost every time we've invaded."

"Are there no ordinary horses in these parts?" Sharley asked, still gazing around him at the amazing variety of animals. But without waiting for an answer he grabbed Mekhmet's arm. "What are *those*?" He almost squeaked in excitement as a herd of creatures with enormously long necks sailed by on equally long legs.

"We call them camelopards, but in the Lusu tongue they're known as giraffes."

"Incredible!" Sharley gasped, but before he could recover from the excitement of the giraffes, another sight almost made him fall from the saddle. A small copse of trees was literally brushed aside as a group of truly astounding animals emerged. They were huge – at least twice as tall as the biggest of his mother's horses – and were roughly grey in colour and had a tail at both ends! Their ears were the size of sails, and they had two horns like gigantic fangs growing either side of the front tail.

This time Sharley couldn't speak for excitement and incredulity. Mekhmet glanced at him and sighed impatiently. "Elephants," he explained in a loud voice, as though talking to an idiot. "They're called elephants. The Lusu say they're the biggest animals in the world, and I suspect they're right. There are rumours that in some lands far to the south they use them in warfare, a bit like oversized cavalry, I suppose."

He caught Sharley's excited eyes and shook his head emphatically. "Forget it! Nobody knows how to train them, let alone actually ride them to war. And besides, you'd never get them across the desert; they need to drink an ocean of water every day, not to mention the mountain of food they eat."

Sharley gazed at them with longing, but reluctantly let go of the image of himself at the head of a cavalry of elephants, sweeping Bellorum and his army aside as though they were ants.

At last Sharley's overloaded sense of wonder was allowed to rest when the huge red ball of the sun dipped below the horizon, and it became too dark to see.

Night had arrived as suddenly as it did in the Desert Kingdom, and with it had come the strange laughing cries that they'd heard that morning. All around, in the tall shadowy grass, something seemed horribly amused. Sharley stared out at the darkening savannah, but could see nothing, and had to concentrate on keeping Suleiman calm.

But no one else seemed bothered by the laughter, and soon the escort of Lusus reined to a halt and immediately set about making camp. Despite his worries, Sharley watched with interest as the troopers cut huge quantities of thorn bush and set it in a wide unbroken circle as a protective wall around them all. They tethered the zebras inside it, lit several fires and began to cook a meal. Mekhmet directed his men to tether their horses, too, and pitch the tents.

They ate listening to the nocturnal sounds of animals

calling and screeching over the wide plain. Something in the quality of the night air allowed the sounds to carry for miles, and several times Sharley leaped to his feet as a huge roar erupted seemingly just outside the protecting hedge of thorns. But worse even than that were the sinister calls of the Laughing Ones, which seemed to surround the camp. Sharley shuddered. The cry came again, and was answered by another that went into such paroxysms of maniacal screeching that Sharley got up from his seat and drew closer to the fire.

The Lusu troopers found this extremely funny, and would have sat in a circle watching him for the next round of entertainment if their Commander had allowed it. As it was, they kept stealing glances from their separate fires, just in case the weird looking northern Prince did something else that would have them in fits of laughter.

Sharley noticed this scrutiny, and, trying to set aside his worries about the Laughing Ones, he decided to exploit it. He walked over to the Lusus' fires and sat down amongst the troopers. The Commander regarded him with suspicion at first, but eventually shrugged and continued her discussion with her second-in-command. Some of the lower ranks of Lusu spoke the language of the Desert People, and soon Sharley was chatting and laughing with them. He also seized the opportunity to learn a few Lusu words. The troopers were amazed by him. Not only did he look so strange, but the few foreigners they'd met had always kept themselves well apart, and certainly wouldn't have spent time talking with the lower ranks.

Eventually, Sharley worked his way over to the pickets of zebras, where he stroked their muzzles and patted them until he'd satisfied himself that, apart from their rather flat backs –

which meant that the Lusu troopers tended to ride closer to the animal's shoulder than was usual for cavalry – and, of course, their fabulous stripes, they were just the same as any other horse.

The next day Sharley woke to brilliant sunshine and the sweet smell of warming grasslands. Mingled with this was the wonderful scent of griddlecakes and some unknown meat the Lusu were frying. He climbed out of his sleeping roll and joined the troopers of both nationalities, who were standing round the cooks, looking hungry. Mekhmet, as usual, kept himself aloof from such matters, and waited for his breakfast to be brought to him. But Sharley felt at ease with the troopers, and besides, he was hungry enough to eat a zebra. At least he'd get fed before the Crown Prince.

An hour later, everything was packed and ready, and both squadrons of cavalry lined up to begin the last stage of the journey to the city of Swahati. Only then did Sharley appear dressed in the full panoply of black arms and armour that Mekhmet had given him. There were times when you couldn't put too much emphasis on a little personal pride and dignity, and riding to meet the monarch of a new land was one of them.

The escort of Desert People murmured amongst themselves, and the name "Shadow of the Storm" passed to and fro amongst them. The Lusus seemed surprised by the reaction, but made no comment. Mekhmet merely smiled and waited for his friend to join him at the head of the escort's column.

They made good time, and as they'd set out extra early they expected to be in the capital before nightfall. But for some reason the Lusu Commander, Tigazi, seemed ill at ease and sent out several patrols, then took careful note of their reports when they returned. Sharley watched her closely. What possible need could there be to send outriders ahead? According to Mekhmet, the Lusu had been at peace for more than twenty years and banditry was almost unheard of. Besides, it would need a huge gang of bandits to take on their combined cavalry.

Eventually, after another hour of riding, the Commander left an officer in charge and galloped ahead herself. By this time Sharley was burning with curiosity, and determined to find out what the problem was. "I'll just give Suleiman a run. It'll do him good. He's a bit restless," he said to Mekhmet, and before his friend could protest he galloped after the Commander.

She'd obviously travelled a good way ahead; after five minutes or so of hard riding he still hadn't caught up with her. But then a strange cry reached his ears, a sort of broken braying, like a mule or donkey with hiccups. This was obviously the call of the zebras. He slowed to listen, but then a huge clamour of hideous laughter broke out, and lowering his lance he galloped ahead.

He burst through some low thorn scrub and into a sort of clearing, and there before him was Commander Tigazi, standing over her fallen zebra with sword in hand, and facing a pack of truly hideous creatures. They were huge, almost as big as a zebra, and their most striking feature was their faces. They had short, blunt snouts which seemed to be crammed with a hideous array of yellow teeth, but worse by far were their eyes. They were blank and black, without pupil or any spark of light, and Sharley was sharply reminded of his sister Medea.

The creatures didn't actually seem fully animal at all.

There was something almost human about the way they constantly called and signalled to each other as they deliberately circled the Commander and her fallen zebra. And when one of them turned its head in his direction, Sharley could see the face of a person, hideously twisted and deformed, staring out from the animal features.

Almost without thinking, Sharley called out a challenge, lowered his lance and charged. Suleiman screamed and leaped forward. The creatures turned to face them and rose up on their hind legs, screeching with laughter as he bore down on them. Sharley's spear hit one of them squarely in the chest and it fell to the ground, its claws gripping the shaft of the lance and giggling horribly. Now the others closed in, their blank eyes unwavering and empty.

It felt like fighting the Greyling bear all over again. Suleiman circled, snorting fiercely and watching as many of the creatures as he could. But now some truly enormous specimens were coming in and he was in danger of being overwhelmed.

"Over here, Charlemagne. Stand with me!" a voice called. He suddenly remembered Tigazi. She stood with her back to the thicket of thorn scrub – a good defensive position.

He galloped over, and soon realised there was no hope of them both riding away on Suleiman; the Laughing Ones would easily outpace an overburdened horse. He dismounted and drew his scimitar, but before either could say anything more the horrible beasts were upon them. The two stood shoulder to shoulder and slashed at the animals with their razor-sharp blades, while Suleiman reared and struck out with his hooves. The fight raged on in a welter of striking claws, deafening snarls, neighing and war cries.

Suddenly the first wave of the attack fell back and others took their place, rearing up on their hind legs and hopping along in a grotesque shuffling run. Sharley struck straight-armed and his blade sank into one of the creature's faces, driven deep by the animal's own strength and momentum. It pulled back with a shriek of agony and Sharley thought his arm would be wrenched from its socket, but then the scimitar came free and he whirled and struck at the neck of a second beast, and blood spurted. Suleiman turned and lashed out with his powerful hind legs, sending one of the creatures flying through the air and injuring many others. But more and more were crowding in on them. They'd soon be overwhelmed.

Sharley felt his strength ebbing away, and his weak leg throbbed painfully, but then a tingling sensation thrilled through his frame and the fighting blood of the Lindenshield clan began to roar through his veins. He drew breath and out crashed the war cry of the Icemark:

"The enemy are upon us! They kill our children and burn our homes! Blood! Blast! And Fire! Blood! Blast! And Fire!"

One of the creatures leaped at him, and he smashed his shield with its lethal foot-long spike into its chest. Then he threw himself into the attack again, standing with Tigazi who fought with lethal control and precision. But the odds were impossible; they were being outnumbered and it could only be a matter of minutes before they were killed.

Just then, the brassy braying of a war-trumpet sounded and the combined cavalry of Lusu and Desert People crashed into the clearing. Lances and swords flashed in a deadly display of fighting power, and after a ferocious and bloody few minutes, the hideous beasts were driven off.

For a few moments all was completely silent, and Sharley

drew a deep steadying breath.

"Well, that was busy, wasn't it?" he said brightly.

Commander Tigazi looked at him for a second, then laughed. "Yes, it was busy, very busy indeed!"

Sharley looked at the dead Laughing Ones that lay around them. This had been his first real battle experience! This had been the culmination of all of the years and months of long, long struggle to be allowed to take up what he saw as his true role as a warrior Prince. But now that the moment had come, he wasn't quite sure how he felt. He'd used his newly learned battle skills and had found himself able to confront the enemy and fight back against its power and aggression. But he'd taken lives – an obvious fact of warfare that somehow hadn't occurred to him. He was elated and horrified; he was happy and sad. But most of all he was totally confused.

The sound of an approaching horse interrupted his thoughts, and he set them aside with relief as he looked up. It was Mekhmet, trotting over with a face of thunder and relief. "Are you all right?"

"Fine. All of us, I think, apart from the Commander's zebra. Just a few bruises otherwise."

"Good. And now that I know you're safe, I can tell you exactly what I think. How bloody stupid can you get? Riding off like that without backup was just asking for trouble. I suppose *you* can be forgiven to a certain extent, Sharley – you don't know the land. But, Commander, you have no such excuse. If you were under my authority I'd recommend a severe reprimand at the very least! What were you thinking of?"

"The scouts I sent out earlier spotted a large party of Laughing Ones. I just wanted to make sure our way was clear. Unfortunately it wasn't."

"Obviously. And yet, knowing the danger, you thought it would be a good idea to ride out alone and look for them?"

"Just a minute," Sharley interrupted. "I'd like someone to explain exactly what these creatures are! I mean, are they animal, or human, or what?"

"Both," Tigazi answered. "They're part human and part hyena."

"And what, precisely, is a hyena?" asked Sharley, at last feeling himself to be on familiar territory. After all, the Wolf-folk were just such a hybrid of human and beast.

"They're a large hunting animal, of neither the dog nor the cat family, but ferocious and ruthless, as you've discovered," Tigazi explained.

"I see," said Sharley, thinking things through. "But they seemed more beast than human."

"I suppose so," said the Commander. "But they seem to take the worst parts of both. From humanity they've inherited a calculating sense of evil: they seem to actually enjoy being foul. And from the hyena they've taken a completely brutal and unfeeling trait: they lack all sense of pity or remorse."

"And even though you know this, you still rode out alone?" said Mekhmet angrily.

Sharley felt as if he and Tigazi were being treated like naughty children. And, as usual when faced with the disapproval of authority, he began to giggle softly and guiltily, but then stopped. The sound reminded him too sharply of the hideous Laughing Ones.

They resumed their journey, Tigazi taking a zebra from one of the other troopers, who then rode pillion with a comrade. They had no more problems with the Laughing Ones and Sharley began to relax. At least now he'd earned the right to wear his armour. He might not have fought any human warriors yet, but the huge creatures were easily the equivalent of three of the best-armed soldiers. His training with the Desert People had obviously paid off; between them, he and Commander Tigazi had kept at bay some of the fiercest and strongest beasts in the whole of Lusuland.

In less than half a day they were on the hills overlooking the city and Royal Kraal of Swahati. It was huge, sprawling over a wide valley with no apparent sense of plan or design. They could clearly see a wide enclosure in the centre of the city, in which stood what Sharley could only describe to himself as a "grass palace". In form, most of it was similar to the huts that made up the majority of the city, but it was huge, consisting of hundreds of individual buildings all connected to a tall central core that rose up several storeys.

"Behold Pirhama Palace. Seat of government and power, and home to Her Mightiness Queen Ketshaka III, Great She-Lion and Mother of the Nation. It is there that you will present your credentials and hear her mighty judgement," said Commander Tigazi.

Mekhmet nodded. "Good. Let us ride on."

Soon they were approaching the nearest gate of the city, and as an armed escort of foreign soldiers they were stopped by the guards. Tigazi gave the password and they were soon let through. The streets were packed with market-day crowds, but Sharley was riding bareheaded and most people reacted to him in exactly the same way as the Commander had first done. A great cry went up that a dead man was riding amongst them with hair of fire, and miraculously the streets cleared.

It took them less than half an hour to reach the palace complex, the cries of warning flowing ahead of them and emptying the streets as the people ran in mortal dread. The soldiers on guard duty had already heard the terrible rumours, and were visibly trembling as Mekhmet and Sharley's group approached the huge gates into the Royal Kraal.

Tigazi rode forward and addressed the soldiers. "These people are envoys from the Desert Kingdom, and from the Icemark, the kingdom far to the north that defeated Scipio Bellorum and his hordes when he invaded their land. They require access to Her Mightiness Queen Ketshaka, that they may have discussion on matters too lofty for your concern. Open the gates and allow us through."

The soldiers levelled their spears, and though their voices trembled they stood firm. "That we cannot do, Commander Tigazi. We are ordered to protect Her Mightiness from all threats and enemies. And, indeed, we will defy even Death Himself rather than allow the Great She-Lion to be harmed!"

"Very commendable, I'm sure. But there are no enemies here, only ambassadors on diplomatic business. Now step aside and open the gates!"

The soldiers stubbornly shook their heads and stood their ground. "With all due respect, Commander, no one will pass, and least of all *him*," they said, pointing their spears at Sharley. "First, he will have to take our miserable lives."

At first, Sharley had found his role as Death Himself quite amusing, but now it was getting in the way of his mission. Impatiently he searched his meagre vocabulary of Lusu words and painfully constructed a simple phrase in his mind. Muttering the words to himself, he urged Suleiman forward and blurted: "Let me in!"

His accent was appalling, and his startling green eyes, colourless skin and hair of fire almost caused the guards to run screaming in terror. But still they refused access, though one fell to his knees. "No, My Lord Death. Not even you will enter the Royal Kraal without permission of the Queen herself."

"Oh, this is ridiculous! He isn't Death. He's a living human being like you and me! His name is Prince Charlemagne Athelstan Redrought Strong-in-the-Arm Lindenshield, known as Shadow of the Storm," Tigazi said with annoyance, conveniently forgetting her own first reaction to Sharley's appearance. "Now let us through. You have performed your duties admirably and I will personally see to it that you are commended."

"You could easily be bewitched," said the soldier on his knees. "Death could be controlling you and making you use words that will allow him into the Royal Kraal."

"Well, I'm *not* bewitched, and neither is anyone controlling my words!" said Tigazi, struggling to control her temper. "But as an officer in the army of Lusuland, I have right of access to the Royal Presence. Therefore I will go now to the Mother of the Nation and tell of her guards' stupidity. Step aside!"

She strode through the gate and disappeared from view, and Mekhmet, Sharley and their escort had no choice but to wait. A thick, almost tangible silence fell, broken only by the buzzing of flies and the chattering of the guards' teeth. For once, Sharley hadn't the slightest desire to giggle; he was too impatient to move things on as fast as he could. For all he knew, Frostmarris could be under siege already and his family fighting for their lives.

Another fifteen minutes of near-perfect silence passed before a rumble began to insinuate itself into the quietness. Suleiman's ears pricked towards the sound, and he began to sidle and snort. Sharley looked up hopefully, but shivered as he felt the usual shyness and fear spasm through his stomach. Was this the Queen? Would he make a good impression? And, most importantly, could he persuade her to send soldiers to the war?

The noise grew to the recognisable sound of beating drums. Nearer and nearer they came, and intermingled with the rattle and rhythm were human voices: a great babble of words that swelled and grew until all the surrounding streets seemed to be awash with laughing and crying, singing and chanting. Music, too, filled the air: pipes fluted, stringed instruments sawed and strummed, cymbals clashed and gongs boomed, following, more or less, the rhythm of the drums. And all of this great cacophony rolled and weaved itself into a banner of such stupendous sound that their senses were almost overwhelmed. Sharley turned to Mekhmet in amazement, but the Crown Prince merely shrugged and smiled encouragingly. Then, abruptly, the music stopped and there was total silence once again.

Suddenly, the huge double gates before them groaned and rattled as they were seized from within and thrown open. And there, framed in the entrance, stood a truly amazing figure.

The woman stood well over six foot tall. She had a huge head, and a face that glared at the world around it with an expression that should have been carved from granite with giant rusty chisels.

"Who is it that stands at my gate demanding entrance? Death Himself, I am told. If so, let him come in and I will wrestle with him to see if I am ready to enter his dark kingdom!"

As though drawn by some invisible force, Sharley urged Suleiman forward and sat gazing in wonder at the giantess. The Queen turned to regard him, and her bushy eyebrows shot up.

"Hah, you are colourless indeed! Not even the paleness of the Desert People could have prepared me for your faded look. But Death you most certainly are *not*. A boy you seem to me, and one young enough to still miss his mother, though old enough not to admit it! Am I right, boy? Speak up!"

The Queen had spoken in the tongue of the Desert People, so Sharley was able to nod and croak, "Yes."

She threw back her enormous head and laughed loud and long. "Then be comforted! I am The Mother of the Nation, and I have love enough to give to all, including a colourless boy who is far from his home!"

The entire party including horses was taken into the palace and then into a cavernous audience chamber. Sharley looked about him in awe. Not even the Great Hall of Frostmarris was as huge as this massive space. It was constructed entirely of woven rush matting, thatch and mud brick anchored by a wooden frame that soared into the air. All of the walls were lined with gigantic and beautiful paintings and tapestries showing scenes of battle and wild landscapes populated with herds of animals, many of which Sharley recognised from his journey to the city. Other exquisitely painted scenes he guessed must show incidents from Lusu mythology, and he marvelled at their artistic brilliance.

In the centre of the chamber stood the Queen's throne, carved from black wood into the likeness of an elephant's head; the seat was fashioned from its raised trunk, and the arms from tusks that Sharley suspected were real, not just made from white wood.

Ketshaka leaped lightly up the steps of the dais and sat perfectly upright on her throne, frowning on the massive crowd of courtiers that continued to pour through the doors.

"Welcome! Welcome one and all to my Royal Kraal! And know you now, my people, that Prince Charlemagne is *not* Death Himself, and neither is he the victim of some terrible disease. I am reliably informed that the Greatest Spirit in Its Mysterious Wisdom has chosen to create Its children of the northern realms in the form that you see before you." The Queen glared round at her courtiers, who lowered their eyes and murmured amongst themselves. "Know you, also, that Prince Charlemagne is sufficiently burdened with his appearance and does not need to have his ugliness made apparent by any unguarded words or unseemly stares. He will be treated as though completely normal! Do my words cause confusion, or do they garner understanding amongst my people?"

Once again the murmur sounded amongst the courtiers and Ketshaka nodded, as though satisfied. She then turned to Sharley and Mekhmet and her face broke into a great beaming smile. Striding forward from her throne, she hugged Sharley, lifted him from Suleiman's back and swung him round before setting him on his feet before her. "Welcome Charlemagne Athelstan Redrought Strong-in-the-Arm Lindenshield, Shadow of the Storm. Welcome to my Royal Kraal. Welcome to the heart of Lusuland!"

"Thank you," Sharley answered quietly.

"And welcome, welcome to my Guest Friend Crown Prince Mekhmet Nasrid, Sword of the Desert, Beloved of the One. I see you have grown since your last visit, and now wear the beard of manhood. Nevertheless, no matter how mature a man becomes, a son remains a child to his mother, so get off that horse and give me a hug," and with that she seized Mekhmet in a rib-cracking embrace and covered his face with kisses. "Now to business." With the wave of a hand, an army of scribes and officials appeared from the shadows. "These scholars are the Royal archivists, and they will transcribe all of our discussions so that they may be preserved for posterity."

"Do they record every word?" Sharley asked, suddenly nervous that he might say something ridiculous or foolish and have to suffer the mortification of knowing it would last forever in the archives.

"Yes indeed, they are writing even as we speak, and from these master copies many others will be faithfully reproduced and sent to every library and place of learning throughout the land."

"I see," said Sharley, watching the quills busily scratching at the rolls of parchment. Once again, he felt like a barbarian lout in the presence of sophisticates.

Ketshaka smiled at him kindly. "My son, we are an ancient people who have walked these lands for many ages. Our society has been stable and strong, protected as it is by our mighty impis, so we have had the time and security in which to develop the gentler arts of learning and of art. True, we have fought many wars, but our civilisation has never been threatened with destruction, and from this certainty and continuity has sprung our great learning."

Her words reminded Sharley of exactly why he was there, and drawing breath, he prepared to begin the long processes of explanation and attempted persuasion. But before he could say a word the Queen went on: "We are happy to receive so important an envoy from the valiant kingdom of the Icemark. News of their mighty struggle and defeat of the Empire reached even as far from that glorious land as here. What mighty warriors they must be to have stopped the steel snake Scipio Bellorum in his tracks!" Her peal of laughter boomed high into the roof of the audience chamber, from where it echoed back with a shower of dust.

"But no matter how powerful a country's army, it fights better when allies stand with it in the time of war. And that, of course, is why you are here, Prince Charlemagne, my adopted son. You would ask if I will send my impis to fight in the cause of the Icemark, against the dreadful power of the Empire!"

Sharley was amazed. What had happened to the niceties of diplomacy, and the complex language of negotiation? All he could do was draw breath and squeak, "Yes, please." Hardly the most persuasive of speeches, but, arguably, succinct and to the point.

"Well, of course I will! And not only that, but I will lead them myself! How glorious will be Ketshaka III in her panoply! How mighty will be her sword arm that will fell the enemy as the scythe reaps the ripe corn! How prodigious will be her immense impis of cavalry that will wipe the Imperial army from the land, like the careless hand of a giant brushing dust from his tunic!"

Sharley gasped. He'd done it! Or, rather, he hadn't; the Queen had offered to fight in the war and he'd not had to say a word to persuade her! He was dumbfounded. "But why?" he managed to ask, before realising he sounded less than grateful.

Ketshaka turned her bloodshot eyes on him and laughed

again. "Because, my adopted son, the Lusu are a people of contradictions. We are fierce and warlike as well as artistic and scholarly, and for too long we have known peace. Our enemies have withdrawn and there has been no opportunity for 'the washing of the spears'. But now you have arrived, like a messenger from the gods of conflict, to offer us the gift of battle!"

"Erm . . . you do realise that first we'll have to cross a desert, then voyage across the sea and probably fight the Corsairs and Zephyrs before we even set foot in the Icemark?" said Sharley, wondering why he was pointing out all the difficulties and problems rather than just accepting the alliance with glee.

"The Lusu are a knowledgeable people, as I have said. We are well aware of the size of the Greatest Spirit's creation," Ketshaka answered. "We have not lived our lives with closed ears. We know that far to the north it can be as cold as the mountains. We now also know that the people are without colour and have eyes like gemstones. And we are eager to find what other wonders have been created by the Greatest Spirit beyond our own lands!"

Sharley felt the blood rise to his face in a great glory of a blush. An overwhelming wave of gratitude to this giant of a woman swept over him, and he ran forward and hugged her. Ketshaka laughed thunderously and, stooping, she swept him off his feet and swung him round again as though he was a child.

CHAPTER 28

Thirrin looked out over the plain. The bomber galleons had retreated, and only the wasp-fighters remained, circling above the hills to the south, where she expected Bellorum and his land army to appear at any moment. She scanned the skies until she found the Vampire squadrons above Frostmarris itself, regrouping in preparation for the next stage of the battle.

It won't be long now, she thought. Bellorum had planned this day for more than twenty years. He was thirsty for revenge and desperate to destroy the land that had defied him for so long.

A thin howling from the werewolf relay rose into the air, and the Ukpik Wolf-folk of her bodyguard responded deafeningly.

Grinelda Blood-tooth, the Captain of the Guard, curtsied. "Your Majesty, Bellorum has arrived."

"Where?" she demanded, scanning the hills to the south.

"There, I do believe," said Tharaman-Thar quietly.

They watched as a forest of pikes pierced the skyline and the Polypontian army flowed into view. The wind caught the sound of fife and drum, and the marching music echoed eerily over the plain.

"Well, now. Isn't that a sight to darken the heart of even the most inveterate optimist?" Tharaman went on.

"We've fought against overwhelming odds before, my dear," said Krisafitsa. "And we're still here to talk about it."

"Indeed we are, my love," her mate agreed. And, laughing, he added, "Obviously your heart is far from darkened, dearest Krisafitsa."

"No, I somehow feel the One has other plans for our demise, lord of my heart. And even if I'm wrong, the Winter Night of Perpetual Moonlight awaits, so what fear should we have for that?"

"None at all, my brave Tharina. Come, let us defend the homes of our allies, and thank the One for these greatest of friends."

Thirrin listened to the Snow Leopards talking and felt a huge swell of pride that they were prepared to sacrifice everything for the Icemark. Suddenly, her tiredness dissipated and she drew her sword. Laughing, she strode forward. Now was the time to rally her people; now was the time to straighten the spine and strengthen the spirit. Drawing a deep breath, she prepared to give the war cry of the Icemark, and her voice rose above the defenders as high and fierce as a hunting hawk.

"The enemy are among us! They burn our cities and kill our children! Blood! Blast! And Fire! Blood! Blast! And Fire!"

For a moment a silence fell on the allied army, but then out crashed their reply.

"Blood! Blast! And Fire! Blood! Blast! And Fire!" And all along the defences the boys and girls of the drum corps rattled out a stirring fighting rhythm that had the soldiers of all species swaying and stamping to the beat.

The huge roar of sound rolled across the plain and struck the Imperial army, so that all who heard it shivered. All, that is, but the three men who rode their horses with arrogant hand on arrogant hip. They merely smiled, their eyes glinting with ice.

"At last, gentlemen, the city of Frostmarris," said Scipio Bellorum to his sons. "Now we'll see our new tactics taking effect. Once we've defeated this nest of freaks, witches and barbarians, the entire Icemark will be ours."

Sulla nodded, gazing ahead at the curtain walls and the defensive ditches. "It looks strong," he said. "Its death will be costly."

"Undoubtedly," his father agreed. "The Sky Navy has already felt the bite of these abominations. But the Alliance is a cornered beast and its continuing resistance is mere stubbornness. Gentlemen, they are as good as dead already; all we have to do is convince them of it!

Octavius laughed quietly. "How surprised they'll be when they feel the full force of our 'Lightning War'; I dare say they're expecting only the merest feint at their lines until we've established our camp. How deliciously naïve." He laughed again, and added, "I claim the right to Lindenshield's skull. It'll look most striking hanging on the wall with my other trophies."

"It's yours, Octavius," his father said with a cold smile. "And unless I've badly miscalculated, you'll be able to collect it today." He scanned the defences as they advanced. "As you so rightly say, they'll be expecting us to stop and set up camp before we attack. But we're going to ride them down *now*, without pause, without ceremony; we're going to roll over them like an unstoppable ocean. And when the tide ebbs, we'll pick our way through the debris and detritus until we find the ragged remains of Thirrin Lindenshield and her sorry little clan." Then, drawing his sword, he led his sons to the side and watched as the massive Imperial army continued its advance without pause.

These were to be the final death throes of the small and barbarous land that had resisted the Imperial will for far too long.

The Polypontian army marched onwards towards Frostmarris, flowing relentlessly out over the plain. Pike, musket, sword-bearers, cavalry, drum and fife formed a huge steel battering ram. Behind them thundered the baggage and artillery trains, ready to drive the army on as it smashed through the defenders' lines. Above them, the wasp-fighters had reformed and swept forward, ready to rain down fire and death.

For more than ten minutes the enemy advanced across the plain before Thirrin realised what was happening.

"Tharaman! They're attacking now!"

"Well, yes, my dear," he answered in puzzlement. "I can see."

"No, you don't understand! They're attacking *now*! The entire army. Bellorum's throwing everything against us. He's not even stopping to set up camp! Look – it's like an avalanche. They'll just smash through everything, even the walls of Frostmarris. We could fall now, this very day. We've got to stop them!"

The huge Snow Leopard looked out at the advancing army and suddenly understood. He towered up into the air and roared hugely.

"Cavalry to arms! Cavalry to arms and advance on the foe!"

All along the defences, troopers rushed to the horse lines while their Snow Leopard comrades formed ranks and prepared to attack. Amongst the Hypolitan, the stern-faced young women of the elite regiment of mounted archers also ran for their horses, and within minutes the Icemark response was riding out on to the plain.

Thirrin, Tharaman and Krisafitsa led the Cavalry of the Icesheets, their now familiar formation of alternating horses and Snow Leopards fanning out into battle lines, while the women of the Hypolitan thundered ahead, bows drawn and ready.

Cressida looked along the line of her own personal squadron, and with a nod to the ensign, the colours were unfurled. The proud striking eagle flew above them as they rode out, and she stared ahead at the hated enemy who were even now rolling down to meet them. She drew her sabre just as her mother drew hers, and stood in her stirrups. The pace was raised to a canter and the Snow Leopards let out the coughing bark of their challenge.

But then, from nowhere, wasp-fighters swept down from the skies and the roar of musket shots crashed into the air. Several horses and leopards fell, and the fighters soared away to begin a second strafing run, reloading their muskets as they went.

But this time the mounted archers were ready for them. They turned and charged, and as the aerial assault began the Hypolitan bows sang as one voice. Three hundred arrows ripped into the flying fighters, bringing down at least a hundred of them in a tangle of canvas and wood. Then, as the others swept overhead, the Hypolitan shot a second flight and brought down hundreds more, while the rest flew to the safety of the sky above the advancing Polypontian army.

A great cheer rang out from the Cavalry of the Icesheets, but there was no time for celebration. Once more Thirrin stood in her stirrups, and her voice rose powerfully over the sound of their beating hooves. The pace quickened to a full gallop and they crashed as an avalanche of steel, tooth and claw into the Polypontian army.

Cressida settled firmly into her war-saddle, her nose-guard scraping rhythmically against the rim of her shield, and led her cavalry squadron towards the front ranks. Her horse held its position in the galloping line as the enemy loomed, growing larger by the second, until they seemed to fill her entire field of vision. Then, with a huge raging roar and clamour, they struck! Steel, pike, sword and musket-shot rang out all about her as she hacked at the enemy soldiers. But as they drove deeper and deeper into the Imperial army, their progress became slower and slower. Soon Cressida was at a standstill, her horse courageously striking out with his hooves, while the Snow Leopards leaped at the enemy, beating at them with their huge claws.

Over the hideous cacophony the high brassy note of a cavalry bugle blared out the call to regroup. Cressida turned about, fighting her way clear. Calling out her name, she galloped out of the melee, back to where her squadron could reform.

As soon as they were all back in formation, her mother gave the call for the cavalry to attack again. Once more they slammed into the Polypontian ranks, the shock of onset reverberating over the field. But still the enemy advanced, heedless of its terrible losses.

"It's no good, Tharaman, we can't stop them," Thirrin screamed over the rage and roar of battle. "We're lost. We can't stop them."

The Thar sent out a mighty roar. "We're not lost yet! Charge again! Charge again!"

Up on the city defences Grishmak watched the struggle with a growing rage. "We can't just stand here. The defences won't hold them anyway unless we slow them down!" And he let out a high, blood-curdling howl that was answered by all of the Wolf-folk. "Forward, my people! Stop them, stop them! Rip out their throats and drink their juices!"

Like the gates of a mighty dam opening, the entire allied army swarmed forward: Hypolitan and Icemark, Snow Leopard and werewolf. With a thunderous roar they smashed into the Imperial ranks. The enemy host shuddered with the force of the impact. Its pace slowed and for a moment its advance seemed to stall, but then the pressing ranks of the thousands upon thousands of soldiers slowly drove it forward, once again, towards the city of Frostmarris.

High above the plain the Vampires and Snowy Owls circled leisurely on a thermal, watching the battle with indolent interest. They had fought and defeated the Sky Navy and were now taking a well-earned rest. The huge roar of onset drifted up on the warm air as the allied army smashed into the Imperial advance, and they observed the Polypontians' momentary stall and their renewed push forward as though it was of no concern to them.

But then the largest of the bats peeled away and wheeled down towards the battle, sweeping low over the Polypontian host before climbing again. His Vampiric Majesty had confirmed all he needed to know to put his plan into action. The time was almost perfectly ripe; the Imperial army was fully committed and couldn't have withdrawn even if it had wanted to. The Vampires turned and headed off towards the city.

Down on the front line, Thirrin watched as the Vampire squadrons swept away towards Frostmarris, and almost despaired. But, setting her teeth, she fought on in desperation as her army was forced back towards the city .

She didn't see the squadrons then rise up from the walls again, each Vampire bat carrying a flaming torch in its clawed feet. As they swept over the struggling front line of the battle, the Snowy Owls dived into the fight. But instead of joining them, Their Vampiric Majesties flew on, over the ordered ranks of the Imperial soldiers who had yet to strike a single blow in the epic fight, on and on, until at last they came to the baggage and artillery trains to the rear – the driving momentum of the Polypontian army – and down on them they swooped, screeching as they dived.

As they reached the ground they stepped into their human-like forms and, snarling and raging with hatred, they overwhelmed the unprepared soldiers of the gun-teams, smashed their guns and broke open the limbers that carried the armies' gunpowder.

"Oh, I say, I do believe we've found the chink in your armour, General Bellorum," the Vampire King observed, a small smile playing around his lips.

And with a screech the Vampires leaped into flight once again and dropped the blazing torches into the gunpowder below.

* * *

Fighting deep within the ranks of the Imperial army, Eodred
and Howler had been filled with hope at the sight of the
Vampires flying overhead, but as they'd swept on past, the
Warriors of the Red Eye were forced to fight on alone.

"Something's happening, Eddie," Howler shouted to him.

The Icemark Prince laughed. "Something's happening?
What, you mean like a war?"

"No, no, not that. Something else – something bad, if we
get caught by it!"

"Can it be worse than this?" Eodred yelled, splitting the
skull of his opponent as he tried to spit him with his sword.

"Yes!" Howler answered. Then, screaming with urgency,
he shouted the order, *"Testudo!* Warriors of the Red Eye!
Testudo!" Immediately, the soldiers drew into a tight crouching knot, their shields locked rigid in a surrounding wall with
a tightly interlocked roof.

"What is it?" Eodred demanded, as he added his own
shield to the protecting roof and crouched low. "What's
wrong?"

"This!" said Howler simply.

A massive roar and an ear-splitting crack crashed across the
air as the entire complement of explosives for three Imperial
armies blew sky-high. The shock wave sent cannon, wagons,
horses, mules and human bodies flying through the air like
dandelion seeds on a breeze. Flames bloomed in deadly beauty to engulf almost a third of the Polypontian soldiers, and
beyond even that the debris of what had once been the baggage and artillery trains scythed in a deadly wave of shrapnel
through the Imperial ranks.

The mighty beast that had been the Polypontian army
writhed in agony, and at last shuddered to a halt. A shocked

silence descended on the battlefield. Thousands of the Imperial soldiers were unharmed by the explosion, but they were stunned by the devastation behind them. Regiment after regiment had been destroyed, and thousands more lay screaming in shattered and bloody heaps that were barely recognisable as human beings.

Krisafitsa-Tharina rose up on her hind legs and roared mightily. "They are broken! They are broken! Drive them from the land!" And with a bellow of rage and triumph, the allied army pushed forward, smashing into the bewildered ranks of Polypontian soldiers.

Deep amongst the debris of the shattered army a tight knot of shields opened like the delicate petals of a rare orchid. The Warriors of the Red Eye had survived. Their shields were charred and pitted with shrapnel, but thanks to their *testudo*, or tortoise formation, they stood unharmed.

"The enemy is broken!" Eodred called, echoing Krisafitsa. "Strike now! Strike now and drive them from the land!" And with a roar the mixed regiment charged the stunned survivors.

The discipline and strength of the Polypontian army finally gave way. With a despairing howl, they turned and fled from the terrible power of Queen Thirrin and her army of monsters.

Any lesser man might have despaired, but Scipio Bellorum observed the reversal of his fortune with chilling acceptance. Once again, the Icemark had stolen the victory out of his very hand. He raised his steel fist and brought it down gently on the pommel of his saddle. "Well, Octavius, it's fortunate that I took your advice and kept armies in reserve. How long before the first is with us?"

"They're still half a day's march away, Sir."

"Then we'd better make haste and find them, before we become victims of the rout!" And with that, Scipio, Octavius and Sulla turned their horses and galloped away.

In the infirmary, the witches worked with an air of harried determination that bordered perilously close to the frantic as more and more injured fighters were brought in. Oskan almost despaired of ever seeing the end of the continual relay of medics that ferried in the wounded, but after more than three hours, the flow slowed to a trickle and finally stopped. The wards were full of moaning, dying soldiers, and his resources were limited. Every healer had at least thirty wounded waiting for attention, and out in the side wards where the surgeons worked, scalpels and saws had become blunt with use.

All the witches were crimson with the blood of their patients. Oskan's hair stood in tufts where he'd run his bloodied hand through it. He felt like the worst sort of quack doctor, doing more harm than good to the patients he was supposedly saving. There seemed so little he could do, apart from stitch up the gaping holes made by spear, sword and musket ball, and most of the wounded soldiers were beyond even that simple measure.

He'd already been forced to give the order that poppy be given only to those who were likely to live, because the painkiller was in such short supply, which meant they had to leave the mortally wounded to die in agony. What sort of healer worth their salt as a compassionate human being could stand by and watch a thirteen-year-old drummer boy end his last hours on earth screaming in the absolute extremity of pain? Was he, Oskan the Warlock, really worthy of the title Healer, let alone Witchfather?

All of these thoughts and doubts ran through his head as he stitched wounds, set bones broken by musket shot, amputated impossibly damaged arms and legs, and did his best to soothe the mortally injured.

As usual the massive bodies of the Snow Leopards and werewolves put an even greater strain on the hospital's limited resources, as they always needed larger doses of painkillers, cleansers and other drugs and potions. But who could begrudge these most loyal of allies help and succour in their time of need? Oskan had even had to treat wounded Vampires and Snowy Owls, an area of the Healer's craft he'd never explored before, but was learning rapidly.

He worked on beyond the borders of exhaustion, trying to save as many lives as he could. But, at last, all that could be done for the injured fighters had been achieved, and the patients were made as comfortable as possible as night approached. Oskan was truly exhausted; it was almost more than he could do to remove his blood-soaked leather apron and the rest of his clothes before he sluiced himself down with bucket after bucket of clean water. He then dressed in a clean tunic and left the wounded in the care of his witches.

Crossing the courtyard en route to the palace, he couldn't help but notice how subdued the soldiers were. Several campfires burned across the cobbled space, but no one seemed in the mood to celebrate. The fighters were all totally exhausted. It had been a hard-won victory, and everyone knew only too well that if the Vampires hadn't hit on the idea of blowing up the enemy's gunpowder supplies, Scipio Bellorum would have been in control of Frostmarris that night.

Oskan entered the Great Hall and found it shadowy and silent. Only the central fire burned in its massive hearth, its flickering light making the distant walls and roof waver and tremble as though they were about to fall. The quiet icy hand of superstition ran its fingers down his back, but he straightened up and strode forward, calling for light and bringing life into the Great Hall.

It was only then that he realised there were people sitting huddled and silent around the central hearth. Thirrin, Tharaman, Krisafitsa and Grishmak, the very people who should have been inspiring their exhausted fighters with renewed hope and confidence, all sat in silent despondency, their faces slack with fatigue, their bodies hunched in despair. Only Their Vampiric Majesties were missing, but they were probably in their quarters deep in the caves beneath the citadel.

Slightly apart from the adults were the children of the High Command: Cressida, Eodred and Howler. Being young, they seemed less physically exhausted than their parents and elders, but they, too, were imbued with an air of loss and hopelessness. If the Queen and her allied generals had given up even though the Vampires had dealt such a dramatic blow for the Icemark, what hope could there possibly be?

Oskan took a deep breath. "What's this? What's this? The Commanders of the defending army slumped and silent? Get up and show some life! Get out and review your troops!" he bawled, his healer's presence driving away the torpor and filling the hall with energy.

"We've just fought a battle, Oskan. We're tired," said Thirrin in a frighteningly quiet voice.

"And I've just fought to save hundreds of lives, a battle that lasted approximately three times longer than your own little struggle. But do I seem tired?" he snapped, hoping that no one would look too closely at his drawn face and pale complexion. "Look alive! Frostmarris still stands! Bellorum has been defeated yet again! Tell me, has that man ever beaten an allied army that was commanded by any one of you?" Not waiting for an answer, he went on, "No, he hasn't! I sometimes marvel at his stupidity. Any other general would have worked that out for himself and have given up years ago! But if he wants to be defeated and humiliated yet again, well, so be it!"

"You know, Oskan has a point," said Tharaman, climbing wearily to his feet. "Bellorum *is* a fool. What chance has he got against all of us? The man must be about as bright as a half-eaten bacon sandwich. Come on, it's only a matter of time before he realises he hasn't got a hope in hell and toddles off back to Bellorum-land, or whatever it's called!"

The others looked at the huge cat, who was now stretching luxuriously and trying to wash his face without touching the deep sabre cut across his cheek. Everyone knew that Bellorum was the most successful General there'd ever been and that his tactical and strategic flair was unquestionably brilliant, but *they* had defeated him in the past, and had just defeated him again.

Cressida, Eodred and Howler smiled. A cool invigorating breeze seemed to have meandered through the dark stuffy chamber, bringing with it the scent of flowers and growing things.

"We certainly gave them a pasting today, didn't we?" said Howler. "By the time they broke, the rabble that survived couldn't really be described as an army!"

"No, that's right. They looked like the drenched survivors of a shipwreck!" Eodred agreed. "Though the only thing making them wet was their own blood!"

Cressida nodded. "It'll be a while before they're ready to strike at us again. Perhaps we'll have a few weeks of peace while they build up their numbers."

"Don't depend on it. Bellorum learned long ago to treat us with respect," said Thirrin decisively. "I'll be very surprised if reinforcements aren't already marching up the line. He won't want to give us any breathing space if he can help it."

"Am I the only one who feels a little peckish?" said Grishmak, deciding to change the subject. "I don't know about you, but a side of beef would go down very well."

"Good idea," said Eodred. "Me and Howler are going to the mess hall to eat with the regiment. They did brilliantly today. A few words of thanks and praise wouldn't go amiss."

"You're right," said Thirrin, smiling warmly at her son and his werewolf friend. "The Red Eye regiment were superb today. But no fighting unit's better than its commanders."

Eodred blushed with pleasure, but Howler looked at his feet before glancing shyly at his father. As a king of many years' experience, Grishmak knew very well when praise and thanks were due. He grinned at his son. "The best regiment of the day, in my opinion, and amongst the bravest commanders."

Howler shuffled his feet and coughed. "Yes, well . . . me and Eddie have things to do. You joining us, Cressida?"

"No, thanks. I'll have supper here, if that's all right."

"Yeah, fine. Come on, Eddie." And with that, the two Princes left the hall, clipping each other around the ears, trying to trip each other up and laughing as they went.

"You know, you're right, Grishmak. I *am* a little hungry," said Tharaman, as though nothing else had been said since the werewolf King's comment about food. "A side of beef and one of those sheep thingies would be most welcome. What do you think?"

"And some beer!" a voice called from the gloom, as Olememnon strode into the circle of firelight.

"And some beer," Tharaman agreed. "Perhaps a little drinking competition, eh, Ollie? Bellorum's even more battered than we are, so he won't be making any moves quite yet, and any hangovers will have plenty of time to clear up before the next phase of the fighting."

Krisafitsa sighed, and rising to her feet she placed herself firmly in front of Tharaman. "That cut cheek needs seeing to before you do anything else."

"I'll get my equipment," said Oskan. "It looks as if it needs a fair few stitches."

"Thank you, dear, but that won't be necessary," said Krisafitsa warmly. "A good wash will soon sort it out." And with that she began to give her mate's face a thorough clean.

Tharaman stood patiently while his face was licked, but he tipped a wink at Grishmak, who understood perfectly what he meant and shouted for a chamberlain to bring them all food and beer. "And bring some torches too!" he called after the servant as he scurried off. "It's like sitting in a coal mine in here."

Olememnon sat down with a huge sigh next to Cressida. "And how's my favourite grandniece?"

"Not too bad, Uncle Ollie, just a bit tired."

"Oh, a beer or two will soon clear that up," he answered breezily. "Why don't you join the rest of us and *partake of the brewer's craft*?" he went on with a sense of relish.

"Do you know, I think I will," said Cressida, visibly

relaxing. "Dad, come and sit down. I don't care what you want us to believe, I know you must be exhausted." She patted the space on the bench between herself and her mother. The Witchfather gratefully sank down and stretched his feet out towards the fire.

"The Basilea must be invited to join us," said Krisafitsa between licks. "It would only be good manners, after all."

"Yes, where is Olympia?" Thirrin asked. "Her mounted archers made short work of the wasp-fighters today."

"She'll be down in the horse lines, I expect," said Krisafitsa. "Ollie, why don't you go and fetch her? It'll take a while for the chamberlains to get supper ready, and we won't start without you."

Olememnon readily agreed, and Tharaman chuckled as he strode off across the Hall. "You really are incorrigible, Krisafitsa. I'm sure the Basilea is perfectly capable of making her own mating arrangements."

"Mating arrangements?" said Thirrin in surprise. "What do you mean?"

"My redoubtable Tharina thinks that Ollie and Olympia would make a good couple, and she's being less than subtle in trying to bring them together," Tharaman explained.

"Oh! Oh . . . yes. I see. I never thought of that," said Thirrin, immediately appreciating how suitable the arrangement would be. Olympia was a new Basilea, she was unmarried, and Ollie was a widower, with long experience of being Consort to a governor of the Hypolitan province.

"Well, you haven't had time to think of such things, my dear," said Krisafitsa. "But I thought bringing the two of them together would be, somehow, just right. It's almost twenty years now since Elemnestra died, and that's too long for anyone to spend alone."

"Indeed it is," Thirrin agreed, secretly squeezing Oskan's hand and causing him to wake up with a snort.

"Eh, what? What's happening?"

Thirrin looked at him and frowned. "You old fraud. What was it you said? 'I've just fought to save hundreds of lives . . . but do I look tired?'" Laughing, she leaned over and kissed him. "Still, at least you managed to wake *us* up."

He grinned sheepishly. "Well, I had to do something. You all looked half dead when I walked in."

"Yes, but that was before the food arrived!" said Grishmak, revealing his huge teeth in a welcoming grin as four chamberlains stumbled in carrying a hogshead of beer between them. "I suppose we'd better wait for Ollie, though. Where is he?"

"Here!" a voice bellowed. "I met Olympia on her way to join us." He stepped into the light with a tall stern-looking woman by his side. She inclined her head to the company and swept them all with her fierce blue eyes. At first sight she looked about as friendly as a she-eagle guarding her nest, but then she smiled and her face was transformed – she looked almost beautiful.

"Ah, Olympia, my dear," said Krisafitsa enthusiastically. "Now, if you and Ollie sit on the bench over here, I'm sure Grishmak can start handing out the food."

Tharaman purred deeply in amusement, but said nothing. His mate was perfectly right: twenty years was far too long for anyone to spend alone.

The two Princes stretched their feet luxuriously towards the fire. They'd stopped off in their room en route to their regiment's billets for a few moments' private reflection on the day.

There was nothing quite as comforting as toasting your toes after the horrors of battle. They were not surprised that everyone was saying their mixed regiment of housecarles and werewolves had performed particularly well. Their rock-solid shield wall and combined weaponry of axe, sword, tooth and claw was a formidable barrier for any enemy to overcome.

And now in the warmth of the chamber Howler could feel himself drifting towards sleep, and shook himself awake. "Come on, we'd better get over to the regiment's mead hall and show our faces as we keep saying; you know, morale boosting and all that."

Eodred climbed wearily to his feet and stretched, wincing as his aching muscles protested. "All right, then," he said through a cavernous yawn. "I need waking up anyway."

"Talking of which," said Howler, "we'll need to keep the unit on its toes, if we're not to lose our fighting edge."

"What do you mean?" Eodred asked as he struggled to pull his boots back on.

"Well, Bellorum got a bit of a pasting today thanks to us and the Vampires, and it's going to be quite a while before he's ready to attack again, so why don't we keep him busy while he tries to establish his camp, and lead a few raids against him?"

"Good idea, but are there any Imperial troops anywhere near Frostmarris at the moment?"

Howler nodded. "I heard a werewolf relay just before I got here. Your mother was right about Bellorum calling in reserves; the vanguard of a reinforcing army has started to arrive on the southern hills *already*. The old sod must have ordered it up the line before he marched on us today. Perhaps he *is* finally learning to treat us with more respect. He's certainly keeping quiet about the latest arrival. They didn't put in an appearance until after dark, all the soldiers are wearing black, and the wheels of the wagons and gun carriages are muffled."

Eodred laughed. "He has no idea, has he? Hasn't it occurred to him yet that the Wolf-folk can see in the dark?"

"Who knows? Perhaps," Howler replied, shrugging. "But it's going to take him a while to get up to full strength, and in the meantime we can have some fun harassing his preparations."

"Great. When do we start?"

"Well, I suppose we could ask for volunteers tonight. No written orders, though. We don't want any of the high-ups getting wind of it and stopping us."

"No danger of that. I can't remember the last time I held a pen," said Eodred with a quiet shudder. "Come on, let's go to the mead hall."

The Princes swung off through the door and clattered along the corridor, chatting loudly and laughing like two excited boys soon to go on their first hunting trip.

Meanwhile, on the southern hills that overlooked the plain of Frostmarris, the Blue Imperial Army of the Province of Isteria dug into its new position. Morale was not high. Everyone knew the first attack that morning had failed utterly and that three armies had been destroyed. What chance did they have if the barbarian Queen and her alliance of humans and monsters chose to advance on them now? General Bellorum might insist that the Icemark had taken heavy casualties too and were in no position to press home their advantage, but the General had said many things since the beginning of this war and none of them bore close scrutiny.

Still, for the time being, the Imperial troops were marginally more afraid of Bellorum and his sons than they were even of Vampires, witches, werewolves and ghosts, and so they continued digging in and preparing for the next phase of the attack. They were quite prepared to believe that a second army would join them by tomorrow, and that a further two were marching north at this very moment, but they were beginning to wonder if they'd make any difference. Even the greatest general could meet his match, and the Polypontian soldiers were beginning to wonder if Bellorum had met his.

Deep in the caves beneath the citadel, His Vampiric Majesty was still enormously pleased with his idea to blow up the artillery train. He knew full well that he'd saved the entire defending army, and probably the war as well. His fighting force had proved itself indispensable to the allied cause, especially now that Bellorum had the Sky Navy at his disposal. Without the Vampires and Snowy Owls, the struggle for the Icemark would already be over, and Bellorum would have added a new province to the Empire.

"What are you thinking about, my love?" Her Vampiric Majesty asked as she watched the small smile playing about her Consort's lips.

"Only that it is *too* deliciously ironic that we are now the Icemark's most useful ally. Even the mighty Snow Leopards can do nothing against the Imperial flying machines, thus proving that there are times when delicacy and elegance are of far greater worth than mere brute strength."

"Oh, how right you are, my sweet breath of carrion," said the Queen. "Without us, the hateful Bellorum and his insane sons would be sitting in Frostmarris tonight, a thought that I find oddly disturbing."

"Do you know, oh deepest shadow of my darkness, I know *exactly* what you mean," said the King, a small fretful frown creasing his brow. "There was a time when I would have found the idea of the Icemark's defeat a positive delight, and yet now I feel a mild sense of outrage at the very idea."

Neither of Their Vampiric Majesties heard the polite cough, or the meaningful clearing of the throat that followed a few seconds later, so engrossed were they in dissecting their newly found feelings for the Icemark. But then a huge booming voice shouted, "Oi, Fang-face! Thirrin wants a word!"

They both turned, with pained expressions on their pale features, to see that Thirrin and King Grishmak had entered the chamber.

"Really, Grishmak! Have you never sampled the delights of subtlety?"

"No, can't say as I have. Anyway, now we've got your attention, listen up."

Thirrin smiled her thanks to the Wolf-folk King, and said, "I only really came to thank you for your actions during the battle today. We'd have been lost without you."

"What exactly do you mean?" Her Vampiric Majesty asked suspiciously.

"What do I mean? Well, erm, nothing – just *thank you*. I dread to think what would have happened if you hadn't blown up the gunpowder." Thirrin shuddered. "I really can't imagine what we'd have done without you." She looked up and held their cold gazes unflinchingly. "We'd all have died, I suppose, so I thought it my duty to come and personally thank you on behalf of all of the allies."

She turned to leave, but then stopped. "No, that's not actually right. It's more than that. It's not only because I thought it was my *duty* to express our gratitude; I *wanted* to come and personally say how grateful I am for your help."

An astonished silence followed, until the Vampire King gracefully inclined his head. "My dear, I know what it must have cost you to come here and speak to us tonight. And I can only say that of all the members of the House of Lindenshield we have known down the long, long years of our death, *you* are the only one who truly deserves the title 'Queen of the Icemark'."

CHAPTER 29

Queen Ketshaka had set her country's affairs in order. A council of ministers had been appointed to rule the land in her absence, and the palace had seethed with dignitaries and messengers from all over Lusuland as preparations for her long absence were made. And then, when all was ready, she'd sent out orders for the mustering of the entire Lusu army of sixty thousand warriors.

Now, as they assembled on the savannah in front of Swahati, Sharley was almost breathless with excitement. Regiment after regiment of magnificent Lusu warriors, male and female, with plumed headdresses and striped mounts, stretched away into the distance. The mighty force was thirty impis strong – thirty thousand cavalry in Icemark terms!

Queen Ketshaka arrived to review the parade, sitting astride her own war-zebra, and armed to the teeth with assegai, cavalry sabre, mace and battleaxe. Her face was a fierce mask that seemed to be carved from the threat of storms, and about her brow was tied a huge uncut diamond that glittered almost as terribly as her eyes.

"We go now, my mighty impis, to fight in a land far to the

472

north where the cold of the mountains is found everywhere and every day; where the people look like Death Himself, and where the mighty Queen Lindenshield holds her Court. Honoured are we who are called to help in her war. The time has come for the 'washing of the spears', and those of us who must die will do so with bravery and honour!"

In the silence that followed, the army stared rigidly ahead, but then a single voice called out: "Mighty is the Great She-Lion! Mighty is the Mother of the Nation!"

And out crashed the single word of the Royal salute from sixty thousand throats:

"*Keshay!*"

Three times the salute was given, the single voice of the mighty host rolling round the savannah that surrounded the capital city. Then a slow whisper of sound began as sixty thousand assegai spears were beaten gently on sixty thousand shields. The sound grew to a rattling, crashing crescendo and gradually faded away to silence. Then out roared the Royal salute again.

"*Keshay!*"

What a fighting force! What an awesome responsibility, Sharley thought. What if, after all he'd been through, he couldn't actually get this huge army to the Icemark? And if he could, what if they arrived too late? There was such a long way to go, and so many barriers and difficulties in their way!

Just getting such a formidable host across the desert was going to be an enormous task.

After several days of preparation for the difficult journey to come, the allies were ready. Sharley, Mekhmet and Ketshaka led their soldiers out of Lusuland and deep into the desert, and the huge striped army moved as one over the burning sands.

Each of the Lusu mounts carried not only its rider and all of his or her equipment, but also an enormous bundle of fodder and two barrels of water! A supply train, made up of hundreds of ox carts, piled high with supplies, brought up the rear. On Mekhmet's advice they had decided to 'hop' from oasis to oasis; even though this was slower, it meant that they could refill their water barrels from the wells and water holes, and allow the zebras, horses and oxen to recover their strength.

Before night fell on the first searingly hot day, Mekhmet sent word ahead to the Sultan to warn of their approach, reassuring the army of the Desert Kingdom that they weren't about to be invaded by the Lusu, and ensuring they were met halfway by another supply train that would replenish their stocks. Then they began to bed down for the night.

All around him Sharley could hear the low buzz of the camp. It was so large it was like being in a mobile city, and there was a continuous hum and rumour of small, incidental noises. Nearby, the strange hiccupping bray of a zebra echoed across the night, and soon after he heard the mighty snores of Queen Ketshaka. When he had first heard the Queen's snoring, back in the Lusu palace, Sharley had thought in his half-sleep that he was being attacked by a swarm of giant hornets, but now he'd grown used to it, and when it stopped the breathless silence of the desert night was almost painful.

Sharley lay in the tent he shared with Mekhmet and stared into the darkness. It was impossible to sleep; so much had happened and there was so much to think about. Eventually he gave up, climbed out of bed and walked silently to the entrance of the tent. As he emerged a guard drew his scimitar, and a flash of steel glinted in the brilliant moonlight. Then, seeing who it was, the man saluted and stood to attention.

"It's a beautiful night, Omar," said Sharley as he gazed out over the tents and picket lines, campfires and guard posts.

"Truly, Lord, I have never seen the moon so bright. Surely it is a powerful omen that the One should send us a light to make even our hours of darkness as bright as day."

"Surely," he agreed. "And truly, the mighty Queen of the Lusu provides her own nightingale for the splendour of the night."

Ketshaka's snores resounded from her nearby tent, and the guard smiled. "Her Majesty is such a prodigious monarch that even her sleeping voice must shout across the land."

"Prodigious indeed. I'm so glad she's on our side."

Sharley walked a little way into the night and stared into the full glory of the desert sky. His leg was aching, but he soon forgot all about the dull throbbing as the beauty of the night overwhelmed him. Eventually he drew a deep, shuddering breath, and allowed his eyes to wander back to the camp.

This was what it was all about: bringing an army to help save the Icemark. He just hoped and prayed he could get them there, and in time. Sharley fell to his knees and touched his head to the sands three times, just as he'd seen Mekhmet and all the other Desert People do. Please, *please* let us get back to the Icemark in time to make a difference, he prayed.

He climbed to his feet, and remembering his northern beliefs he bowed deeply to the moon in honour of the Mother Goddess and asked for her help too.

Slowly he became aware of a distant, gentle singing and a

faint blue light in the skies to the south. He smiled. Obviously the Blessed Women were back and keeping a close eye on them as they crossed the desert. He was enormously grateful for the protection they seemed to give him. He bowed slowly in the direction of the blue glow and thanked them.

Shivering in the bitter cold of the desert night, he went back to his tent. He felt somehow calmer, as though the weight of responsibility he felt was now shared with the gods. After all, he reasoned, he was only a fourteen-year-old boy. There were limits to what anyone could expect him to do. He got back into bed and immediately fell asleep.

The next day the camp awoke to the cacophony of roaring camels, neighing horses, braying zebras and shouting people. Mekhmet prodded Sharley. "Come on! How can you sleep through all this noise?"

Sharley grunted, and peered at his friend through slitted eyes. He was still tired after lying awake for most of the night, but he soon caught the usual morning excitement of the camp and sat up. "Where's breakfast?"

"Adil hasn't brought it in yet."

"Any messages from your father?"

"Yes. There's been a huge purging of Polypontian spies. As far as anyone can tell, the kingdom's now clean. Which means General Bellorum will know something's going on – because all information will have dried up – but he won't know what."

"Let's hope we can keep it that way," said Sharley, getting dressed. "Who knows, perhaps we'll be able to take him completely by surprise and arrive in the Icemark before he even knows there's an army on its way."

"Perhaps," said Mekhmet. "But that's highly unlikely. Even if he has no spies left in the Desert Kingdom, you can bet they're still at work in Venezzia, and the sort of fleet that'll be needed for the transport of over thirty thousand cavalry is certainly going to draw attention."

"I suppose you're right, but let's live in hope until we know otherwise."

Mekhmet nodded in agreement. "Oh, there's one other thing. Your old friend Captain Al-Khatib has been promoted, he's now the Grand Vizier."

Sharley grinned. "Al-Khatib, Grand Vizier! But how? Why?"

"He was the obvious choice. He's worked for the Nasrid dynasty all his life. It was he and his network of counter-spies who kept the Polypontian espionage system under some control. And once my father had decided to declare war openly on the Empire, it was he who arrested all the traitors and cleansed the land of their poison."

Sharley nodded. It had always been obvious that Al-Khatib was more than just a merchant and sea captain. But even so, it was still a surprise to hear that after the Sultan and Mekhmet, Al-Khatib was now the most powerful man in the Desert Kingdom.

Just then, the boys' servant, Adil, arrived with their breakfast and they took their places at the low table to eat.

It was surprising how quickly the camp could be packed up and the army made ready to march, but the superb command system of the Lusu cavalry ensured that everything was under way within half an hour of the order to move out being given. Sharley looked back over the seemingly endless triple column of zebras and found himself praying again that they'd actually reach the Icemark and have a chance to strike at the hated Polypontian Empire.

"Ah, I see my son Charlemagne has the shadows of doubt clouding his sight," said Queen Ketshaka, who rode alongside the boys at the head of the column. "You must learn to trust in the will of the Great Spirits. I cannot believe that they would have decreed that you should reach Lusuland if you were not destined to have your new allies fight alongside you in the North."

"I hope you're right," Sharley answered in the Lusu tongue. "Even as we speak, my mother and her army could be fighting a losing war against the overwhelming numbers of the Empire."

The Queen turned her enormous head to look long and hard at Sharley. "A Prince must learn to have faith in the motives of the gods. The Wise Woman of my Kraal read the signs and omens before we marched and she said that in the realms of the spirits we are even now known as the Army of Death, led by Death Himself. Apparently it is our appointed task to 'change the established world order'."

"And you believe that?" Sharley asked.

Ketshaka laughed. "But of course. The Wise Woman is never wrong. However, the gods and spirits speak in riddles, so how do we know how our 'appointed task' will be accomplished? Perhaps it will be as we hope, and we will destroy the mighty host of the Polypontian Empire. Maybe we will also kill the hated Bellorum and wipe his foul dynasty from the face of the bountiful earth." She fell silent for a moment and her radiant smile faded. "But we must also accept that our destiny could be fulfilled when we are destroyed, and the world order may change with the death of Queen Ketshaka III, and the fall of the House of Nasrid, and of Lindenshield. Such may be the will of the Great Spirits."

Mekhmet caught his friend's eye, and shrugged. "Whatever happens is the will of the One."

Sharley found no comfort whatsoever in either of their beliefs and after a while he urged Suleiman ahead, taking consolation from the emptiness of the desert that stretched before him. Here at least were no fears, no hopes and no crippling sense of duty. The desert was a leveller of all ambitions and desires, and he rested his mind in its calm.

As he trotted ahead he noticed a growing smudge of distorted colour on the horizon. He reined Suleiman in and waited for Mekhmet and Queen Ketshaka to catch up.

"Something's approaching," he said when they were within earshot.

"I see it," said Mekhmet. "With a bit of luck it's the escort and supply train from my father. I'm looking forward to eating something other than antelope, aren't you?"

And then, as they gazed hopefully ahead, a forest of banners and lances began to emerge from the shimmering distortions of the heat haze.

CHAPTER 30

General Scipio Bellorum sat in his campaign tent, reviewing the war so far. He was hardly surprised that the Icemark was proving to be an extremely tough nut to crack, but he remained confident that eventually his relentless attack would break the resistance of the defenders and he could finally add this tiny, insignificant little country to the Imperial possessions – an ambition that had been with him for twenty years, and one that, with every fibre of his military being, he was determined to see fulfilled.

Some of his critics had dared to whisper that his determination to defeat Thirrin Lindenshield and her allies had become an obsession that was perilously close to lunacy. But such rumours of mental instability did little to tarnish the General's reputation. Some of his more extreme actions, in a long and illustrious career, could only have been carried out by someone who had an insane disregard for human life and suffering. For Bellorum, Imperial ambition outweighed all other considerations.

"There's talk of insanity in the family again," said Sulla, almost as though he'd been reading his father's mind. "Funny

480

how such ideas are forgotten as soon as we've won another victory for the Empire."

"I presume the source of such rumours is the Senate," said Scipio quietly. Sulla nodded in silence. "Then take this as a lesson, my dear boy: civil government has little nerve for costly military actions, and they'll attack the strategists and tacticians with gusto until victory is secured, after which they'll become your greatest ally and supporter."

Bellorum knew he was a grand master in the art of war, and he also knew full well that a lesser Commander would have cut losses and withdrawn by now. This was the essential difference between a military genius and a general who was merely superb. He would allow himself until the winter to finally subjugate the Icemark and wipe out all resistance. If he was not master of the land by then, he would simply rest his troops in the territories he'd already secured and employ a 'scorched earth' policy that would strip the land of all food supplies. He'd then blockade the ports, and sit back in comfort to watch the enemy starve to death. By the following spring, the Icemark would be his. Victory was almost guaranteed. True, there were rumours of unrest in the Imperial territories far to the south, and reports were coming in that the Desert Kingdom was at last waking from its decades-long torpor, and might well be preparing for war. But the Imperial armies of the south and east should be able to contain any threat. Here in the north, they would be little bothered by rumours of unrest in a kingdom that had long since ceased to be a problem to the Empire.

He strode over to the side of his huge campaigning tent, where he nodded curtly to a guard. The wall of canvas was immediately rolled up to give him a clear, unhindered view of the plain of Frostmarris and the hated capital itself. The abortive attempt to crush the city on the first day of his attack had proved enormously costly, but fortunately he was still humble enough to accept lessons from the younger Bellorums, and had followed Sulla's advice to keep an army in reserve. This had undoubtedly saved the day, and he was able to make a strategic withdrawal and gather his resources before advancing again.

"You may join me," he said quietly to his sons without turning, and they walked across the tent to stand respectfully beside him. "You are both fully aware of my plan to starve the defenders into submission if need be; however, I would prefer to inflict a final military defeat on Thirrin Lindenshield and her fighters. It must become common knowledge throughout the Empire that resistance, no matter how vigorous, is ultimately futile." He sipped at his wine before continuing. "The Icemark's resistance has unfortunately become almost legendary throughout the known world; I am therefore determined that the House of Bellorum will be known as the power that finally defeats it."

"We're both in full agreement with you, Father," said Octavius smoothly. "We simply await your orders and the task will be completed."

Scipio smiled almost warmly at the confidence in his son's voice. "Then let me explain the strategy I have devised." He led them back to the table in the centre of the campaign tent and pointed to a relief map of the city and its surrounding defences.

"The Sky Navy will shortly be ready for operations again. Its task will be to flatten the city and break the morale of the defenders. After that, the land army will pierce the defences and isolate the enemy in small pockets. It should be simplicity itself to eliminate any resistance once the defenders are detached from the rest of their comrades. And that, in essence, is it."

"As usual, masterful in its clarity and genius," said Octavius. "But might I respectfully ask if the Vampire squadrons have been taken into consideration? After all, their record in action against the Sky Navy is impressive."

For a moment Scipio's face became a landscape of anger, but with a supreme effort of will he regained control, and smiled. "You need have no fears on that score. I am devising a little *surprise* for the Vampire King that will eliminate both him *and* his squadrons. Soon the sky will become just one more territory to add to the Imperial possessions."

"Might one enquire as to the nature of this surprise?" Sulla asked.

"No," his father answered. "I am still finalising the details, and for the time being the plan will remain secret."

Both sons saluted, and Bellorum felt a surge of pride that he'd been blessed with such obedient and intelligent progeny whose energy and purpose so ably supported his own determination to crush the barbarian Queen. Bellorum was certain that the end of the Icemark was now in sight, and that victory would be his in a few short weeks, rather than months.

However, the defenders were still able to mount nuisance raids, and during the last week while the camp's defences were being built, the Imperial soldiers had been attacked every night, and casualties were surprisingly high. According to reports, the freakish werewolves and some very tough housecarles, led by a young warrior matching the description of the remaining Lindenshield twin, had carried out the raids. But this couldn't be confirmed, as no one had ever been captured. Even when individual raiders were injured, their comrades would take huge personal risks to carry them away to safety.

Bellorum was certain that such foolhardy acts of courage were a sure sign that the defenders were so desperate for numbers that they'd leave no soldier behind. It never occurred to him that a refusal to leave a fellow warrior for the Empire's interrogators to work on simply showed a strong sense of comradeship. How could human beings and such monstrous aberrations of nature feel anything for each other? No, Thirrin Lindenshield and her band of freaks were obviously on their last legs. All he had to do now was pick them off just as soon as he was ready.

Bellorum almost smiled as he raised his goblet of wine to the distant walls of Frostmarris before turning back into his tent. In less than a week they'd begin the assault, and he needed to finalise plans with his Staff Officers. Any who were less than word-perfect in their understanding of the tactics would find themselves at the wrong end of a flogging. And perhaps, just perhaps, he might allow himself a hanging or two; the jolly little jig performed by a man hanging by his neck from the end of a rope might just liven things up a bit.

Archimedo Archimedes stumped through the streets of Frostmarris checking on the progress of work. He was in his usual foul mood, though this time it might actually have been justified. Some months ago he'd been forced to accept that Frostmarris could not be kept safe by means of his engineeering genius alone, and if the precarious defensive line of Vampire squadrons should be broken, then no amount of giant ballistas, search lamps and supplies of water could stop the city burning.

So he'd inaugurated a new phase in the defences of the city, in which deep spiral stairways had been dug down to the underground complex of caves far below the streets. Before his plans had been carried out, there had been only one way into the caverns, and that was through the undercroft of the citadel. But now a series of steeply angled corkscrew stairs throughout the city gave access to their shelter, and Archimedo didn't like it. They were a testament to his failure to counter the attacks by the Sky Navy.

He came to the head of one of the stairways and stumped down it, noting as he went such details as head clearance, width of the tread and depth of the riser. It struck him that if any of the soldiers running down here to gain shelter from bombs should fall, they could cause a deadly avalanche of bodies. And in the worst-case scenario, the stairway could become blocked. The only solution would be to dig twin or even triple stairways next to each other and connect them with short corridors, so if one became blocked, people could escape to another.

But would there be time? The werewolf relay had already warned that the newly refurbished Sky Navy was almost ready to fly. He'd start his teams digging tomorrow. Even a few sets of double and triple stairways would be better than none.

He reached the bottom and looked about him. Torches burned brightly in sconces, and boldly painted arrows point-ed the way to the shelters. He was looking for his Chief-of-Works, a woman whose good sense and practical abilities perfectly complemented his flights of inventive genius. Long experience had taught him that if Ariadne said a new idea was unworkable, then it was.

Archimedo walked along the narrow corridor that had recently been cut through the rock, and emerged into a wide cavern where his Chief-of-Works was arguing with a group of Vampires.

"I don't care if this *has* been your barrack room for the past month; it's now a bomb shelter, so you'll just have to move your . . . your coffin things elsewhere!"

"Trouble, Ariadne?"

She turned as the engine-eer approached. "Ach, no. These ladies and gentlemen were just about to vacate the area – weren't you?" she added with steely determination as she glared at the Vampires.

"Well, I don't know. It's most irregular. The Queen herself allocated this cavern to us," said an effete creature that looked like a vicious classics master. "And I for one am determined to stay exactly where I am until I receive a direct order to the contrary from her."

"That's soon remedied," said Ariadne briskly. "She's only in the next cave but one, I'll go and get her to shift you."

"Not Her Vampiric Majesty!" the Vampire almost spat with contempt. "I mean Queen *Thirrin*."

"Ach, man, she's far too busy to worry about little squabbles over space. Move your arse now, or my fist might make contact with that snooty snitch of yours!"

"Aye, that's right!" said Archimedo. "And I'll be helping. We haven't time to worrit about every little cave!"

"Well really! I find this entire situation most peeving!" said the Vampire, spreading his arms as they transformed into bat wings, and hissing threateningly. His comrades immediately joined him, the rattle of their leathery pinions and the angry threats of the engine-eers filling the cave.

"What is going on?" a voice of undoubted authority barked, and everyone turned to watch as a compact redheaded figure strode into the cave.

"Ah, Crown Princess, this . . . this *woman* has told us we must leave . . ."

"Madam, these Vampires are refusing—"

"We're doing nothing of the sort! We're simply questioning your authority to—"

"Oh yes you were—!"

"If I wanted a conversation with a vulgar little man I'd—"

"Vulgar I may be, but my abilities have saved your undead—"

"Enough!" Cressida shouted above the din, and silence fell. "Now, perhaps someone could explain to me exactly why you're all arguing at such a pitch that you've disturbed the sleep of His Vampiric Majesty."

The Vampire looked suitably embarrassed, but quickly leaped in before anyone else could speak. "Crown Princess, these people have told us we must move from here, and as I was trying to explain, your mother herself allocated the cave to us as our barracks. Therefore, I reasoned that only the Queen had the authority to order us to be removed."

"I see," said Cressida wearily. Over the past few days there'd been several disputes between the Vampires and the digging teams, and by an odd coincidence she'd found herself on hand just as most of them had flared up. But being resourceful she'd used the small crises as an opportunity to hone her skills of diplomacy and find solutions without causing offence to either side. "Archimedo, I take it, then, that this area's to be allocated as a bomb shelter?"

"Aye, it is, and yon fang-faced—"

"Thank you!" Cressia interrupted forcefully, and turned to the Vampire. "And can your . . . belongings be moved easily?"

"Well, yes, I suppose so, but—"

"Fine! Do you know, the Queen was only saying the other day how gratifying it is that our allies have been so accommodating and understanding when it comes to the changes that are being made. She'll be so pleased to hear that you and your comrades are continuing in that spirit of cooperation. I'll certainly see to it that she learns of your willingness to help, Mr . . . ?"

"Christophoray Leela," the Vampire simpered after a second's delay, and he bowed deeply.

"Thank you, Christopharay. Now, I do believe there's a vacant cavern this way. It's closer to Their Vampiric Majesties and there's plenty of room for all of you. Would you like me to show you the way?"

"Oh, please don't put yourself to any trouble, Your Majesty. We can manage perfectly."

Cressida smiled and stepped aside as the Vampires seized their coffins and carried them away on their shoulders with unnerving ease.

"All yours, then, Archimedo," she said.

The engine-eer looked at her through narrowed eyes. "You're as tricksy as a fox with a farmyard to raid, aren't you?"

"I'm also as vicious as a wild boar with territory to protect, so don't risk it, Archimedes!" she suddenly snapped, forgetting diplomacy.

"Nothing could be further from my mind," he said, then with studied rudeness he turned his back on her and began to discuss technical difficulties with his Chief-of-Works.

Cressida considered kicking his legs from under him and loosening a few teeth with a well-aimed punch, but reluctantly abandoned the idea. There were times when diplomacy got in the way of personal satisfaction. Instead, she just turned on her heel and stalked off, walking briskly through the natural complex of caves and newly-dug corridors with complete confidence and ease. She'd made a point of securing a plan of the area from the engine-eers and had committed it to memory; you just never knew when such knowledge might prove not only useful, but absolutely vital.

Within five minutes she'd reached the foot of one of the new stairways, and quickly ran up. If her calculations were correct, she should be close to the city's main gate, and from there a few minutes' brisk walk would bring her to the outer defences.

She emerged into brilliant sunshine, and breathed deeply as a warm wind carried the scent of the nearby Great Forest into the city. The gate guards stamped to attention, and she nodded an acknowledgement as she hurried on through the entrance tunnel.

At this time of the day the Basilea should be reviewing her troops on their allotted section of the defences, and Cressida wanted a word about tactics. It was nothing vitally important, but in this quiet time after the ferocity of the opening battle, she liked to keep herself busy and interested. She'd even joined one or two of the raids carried out by Eodred and Howler's regiment. She wanted to keep her fighting skills honed to perfection, and thought she might join another one that night. She wasn't prepared to admit, even to herself, that one of the main reasons for going on the raids was to keep in close touch with her brother.

She and Eodred had reached a new understanding, mutual respect being the mainstay, but neither of them would even dare acknowledge the existence of affection. They were simply two warriors who appreciated each other's abilities. They may have had their difficulties in the past, but now they were mature enough to put aside their childish spats and rub along together well enough.

Cressida ran up to the summit of the first of the defensive rings, slipped through the palisade and ran down into the ditch between it and the second ring. There she found the Basilea deep in conversation with Olememnon. The pair sprang apart as she approached, and she was almost certain Olympia was blushing, if such a thing was possible for an eagle-faced fighter like the Basilea.

"Ah, Cressida!" said Olememnon loudly. "How nice to see you."

"Yes, it's been a long time since breakfast," she replied in puzzled irony.

The Basilea was still awkwardly bent in a curtseying position that must have been truly painful.

"Please, Olympia, stand up. You're making my hips ache just to look at you," said Cressida, who was beginning to feel embarrassed herself. She'd obviously interrupted something private, and didn't quite know how to withdraw without making it worse.

"I, erm . . . I wanted a chat about the Hypolitan position on the defences," she finally said, and the other two suddenly became enormously interested.

"Oh, yes!" said Ollie. "Funny you should say that, because that's exactly what we were talking about, wasn't it, Olym— I mean Madam?"

"Umm? Oh, yes . . . yes, we were, weren't we? How odd, how strange, what a weird coincidence . . . yes."

"Don't you think if you dismounted the Sacred Regiment, their compound bows would have a devastating effect on the enemy's advance?"

"Dismount the Sacred Regiment?"

"Only if they couldn't be used as mounted archers, of course," said Cressida, deciding to ignore whatever the situation was here, and battle on.

"Good idea, yes, compound bows . . . quite devastating, don't you think, dea— Madam?" said Ollie, reddening for some reason.

"Yes, Ollie. I do."

The sound of Olememnon's pet name coming from that warrior's rat-trap of a mouth suddenly made everything crystal clear to Cressida. Of *course*! Olympia and Ollie were having a . . . fling! At first, she was shocked. They were so old! The Basilea was at least forty, and Ollie was at least fifteen years older than that! How could they?

But then common sense reasserted itself. After all, Krisafitsa and her mother had been discussing this very thing only a few nights ago. Ollie had massive experience as a Basilea's Consort, and Olympia would be able to draw on his knowledge whenever she needed to. Although, if you thought about it, Ollie's expertise was available to the Basilea anyway; they didn't have to have an actual relationship and indulge in all that other stuff!

But then suddenly Cressida realised that they simply *wanted* the other stuff, despite their enormous age. To her surprise the thought made her feel warm inside; people still needed each other even when they were incredibly old. Having decided it was a good thing, she couldn't understand what all the fuss was about.

"Oh, for goodness' sake, you two. You don't have to get embarrassed in front of me. I know what's going on, and I approve. In fact, I think you should get married, and as soon as possible too. We could do with something cheerful to distract us from all the war and bloodshed around here."

The couple managed to blush in unison, and Cressida grinned. They were quite sweet really.

"Well, thank you for your advice and insight, Princess," Olympia finally managed to say. "That's something worth thinking about, isn't it, Commander Olememnon?"

"Eh? Oh! Yes, yes. Definitely. We'll start thinking about it right away."

"Good. Now that's out of the way, perhaps we can concentrate on military matters. What do you think?" Cressida asked sensibly.

"Absolutely," agreed Ollie, and his face assumed a suitably serious and martial expression.

But it was all rather spoiled when the Basilea suddenly snorted with laughter.

Medea observed and absorbed all the city's activity from her high tower. The war continued to take completely unexpected twists and turns that she found highly entertaining, and she applied her Eye with huge enjoyment. She'd expected the Sky Navy to end hostilities within a matter of days, but the Vampire's countering moves had almost rendered it impotent. Even so, she could see that Bellorum still expected it ultimately to be successful, and was at this very moment calling it up the line to attack.

His land tactics were surprising too. Any other commander would have secured the high ground to the south of the plain of Frostmarris, established a fortified encampment and only then thought about attacking the city, but instead he'd arrived and then immediately rolled down on the defenders in a seemingly unstoppable attack. Even she herself had almost panicked!

If the city had fallen, she'd have been trapped and possibly even captured by the Imperial army! She'd fully expected her mother and the allies to be overwhelmed, and she'd been as shocked and relieved as everyone else when the Vampires had blown up the Polypontian gunpowder stores.

But the fact that the Imperial forces could have taken Frostmarris on the first day of the struggle for the city had concentrated her mind. She'd been postponing making a decision about her own role in the war until it was totally necessary, and as she'd believed that they'd be under siege for several weeks, she hadn't thought that the time had yet come for a final choice.

She'd taken greater care since. The physical world was just as unpredictable as the Realms of Magic, and she'd learned to treat it with a proper respect at last. With this in mind, she'd established an escape route for herself through the Great Forest. The concentric rings of the defences ended just inside the trees, and if things became desperate, she'd slip through and disappear before the first Imperial soldier reached the citadel.

The image of Oskan rose unbidden in her mind. He was back working in the infirmary, tending the injured soldiers who'd been brought in after the first attack. Medea watched him, trying to understand why he bothered. A warlock of such immense Gift could have had enormous power in the Spirit

Realms. Medea was certain his abilities were such that he could have escaped the restrictions of a physical life and existed forever as a sorcerer, influencing all worlds and wielding almost limitless power. And yet he chose to live within the restrictions of the physical plane. Why?

As she watched, one of the patients in the infirmary started to cough, sending out great gouts of blood that splashed thickly on to the clean bedding. Irritated, Medea withdrew and plied her Eye elsewhere as she sought answers, leaving the feeble twitchings of humanity for other, more rarefied, planes.

Oskan rushed to help the witches fighting to save the man's life, and held him while they struggled to clear the clots of blood from his windpipe. But there was little any of them could do.

He helped carry the body to the mortuary, then stripped the bed of its soiled linen. There'd soon be more patients to take the dead man's place. Any day now the next assault would begin, and according to the werewolf relay the Sky Navy had been rebuilt. Only the Vampires could stop them, and it wouldn't be long before Bellorum sent in the ground troops too.

Oskan went to check over the supplies of herbs, drugs and medicines. He'd been fighting a sense of despair for several days now. They were well and truly on their own with no other allies to call on. The entire complement of defenders was already here, waiting to repulse the massive Imperial army whenever it chose to attack. But he kept his fears carefully masked from everyone, even Thirrin. There was nothing to be gained from pointing out that they had no tactical answer to the overwhelming power of the Empire. But anyone with even a smattering of military knowledge must have reached the same conclusion. What exactly could they do? Just sit stubbornly in Frostmarris absorbing everything that Bellorum and his mad sons could throw at them, and just hope they'd get tired and go away?

He sighed wearily, and sat down next to a bed occupied by a drummer girl who'd lost an eye. She'd been given a strong draught of poppy, so didn't move as he carefully changed the dressings.

Though he thought there was nothing that could be done against the might of the Empire, he had his own personal tactics worked out: when the Imperial army was ready to deliver its death blow he intended to be standing with Thirrin in the shield wall. And when it was absolutely certain that there was no hope, he'd call down lightning and kill them both. With a bit of luck he and the last Queen of the Icemark would be incinerated, so Bellorum wouldn't have a body to display and despoil. His last act of love would be to kill his wife. Thirrin the beautiful; Thirrin the downright bloody annoying; Thirrin the loving. How could the world still exist when she was gone?

He smiled sadly to himself, rolled up the remains of the bandage he'd used on the drummer girl, and then stooped to kiss her brow. How many other young people would be maimed and killed before the Empire had finished with them? The answer was starkly simple: too many, and perhaps all of them.

Just then, the mournful sound of howling spread itself over the night. Dozens of other voices joined in and Oskan frowned in concentration as he translated the message.

Sky-ships!

The attack had begun.

CHAPTER 31

The steady rhythm of Suleiman's pace lulled Sharley's mind until he was relaxed enough to think back over the extraordinary events of recent days. What madness and meetings there had been! What happenings, and what unexpected actions had been taken since Sharley and Mekhmet had set out for Lusuland! When they had arrived back in Haifolex, capital of the Desert Kingdom, they'd been greeted by crowds of rapturous people and overwhelming adulation. Ketshaka and her soldiers were cheered and fêted as though they were saviours, and this was reflected in their audience with the Sultan. They proclaimed an undying alliance between the two nations, and the huge Lusu Queen had engulfed the little Monarch of the Desert Kingdom in an avalance of an embrace. Despite being somewhat dazed, the Sultan had shocked them all by announcing that he had mobilised what remained of the Desert Kingdom's armies, which he would personally command to open a new fighting front on the southern borders of the Polypontian Empire. Meanwhile, Mekhmet and his personal cavalry regiment of ten thousand elite troopers would ride north to the Icemark, along with the thirty thousand Lusu warriors.

This had caused uproar. Mekhmet had never expected his father to fight in the conflict, but the fat little monarch told them he'd been training ever since his son had left on his embassy to the Lusu Queen Ketshaka, and felt more alive than he had done in years. And if he fell in battle he knew his son was a worthy successor for the throne.

It was all too much to digest, but there was more. The Venezzians, and their allies the Hellenes, had already started a naval war against the Empire, and had captured several important supply routes and ports. Doge Machiavelli had apparently decided that the mere absence of war hadn't been a real peace. He knew the Polypontians were bound to find out about his involvement with Sharley and the Icemark, so it was only a matter of time before the wrath of Bellorum would fall upon him. He had nothing to lose in declaring open war.

Suleiman threw up his head and neighed as a gust of hot wind sent a dust-devil skipping across his path. Expertly, Sharley drew in the reins and settled his mount as his mind continued to run over events. He felt almost dazed by the speed with which everything was now falling into place. For weeks things had plodded along stolidly, and now it was all happening in a wonderful rush. New fronts were opening up that would distract the Empire from its conflict in the north, and he, Sharley, had succeeded in gathering an army of new allies, which he was now leading to relieve the Icemark. He could only pray they'd get there in time.

Of course, they had yet to travel over miles of desert and cross the oceans, and no doubt things would again slow to a frustrating crawl, but they were on their way at last. The walls of Haifolex were already receding into the distance and Sharley felt very alone. Something of a feat, he had to admit, at the head of an army that was forty thousand strong – but nonetheless, he felt alone.

His weak leg was aching, and he absently rubbed it as he rode along, still thinking about all that had happened. Suleiman sensed his unease and whickered quietly, then snorted as Sharley stroked his neck. This simple act seemed to clarify his thoughts, and he squared his shoulders. There was nothing he could do about any of it now. The die was cast and all of their fates lay with the gods and goddesses. Even if he could go back to the beginning of his journey, he knew he'd have done nothing differently. The Icemark and his family needed him. He would even have ridden into the Polypontus to have it out with the Emperor himself if he thought it would have made any difference.

The rest of the journey to the seaport was uneventful, apart from one incident when they were a few days out from their destination. As usual, the army had been 'oasis hopping', and as they drew into the latest palm-fringed haven from the desert heat, Sharley recognised an elegant house built close to the water – it was Al-Khatib's house, where they'd left Maggiore Totus to recover from his heat exhaustion.

Overwhelmed with excitement, Sharley thought of all the tales he had to tell Maggie. In all the time he'd been in Haifolex, Lusuland and the desert, he guiltily realised, he'd hardly thought of the old scholar – but now he couldn't wait to see him. Urging Suleiman forward he trotted eagerly towards the house.

A regal figure emerged from the main gate of the courtyard, dressed in fine silks of sky blue and shimmering silver-grey. On his head he wore a wide turban adorned with a blue jewel that flashed and glittered in the sunlight. On each arm was an exquisitely adorned and beautiful young woman. Sharley stared; he'd seen so few women in the Desert Kingdom that it was like seeing a rare species displayed by a rich patron.

Gazing open-mouthed, Sharley was shocked back to his senses when the figure salaamed deeply and said, "Welcome, Prince Charlemagne Athelstan Redrought Strong-in-the-Arm Lindenshield, Regent to the Exiles, Shadow of the Storm. Would you care to step inside and take some refreshment?"

"Maggie?" said Sharley, staring at the figure before him. "Maggie! It *is* you!"

"Indeed it is," he agreed, bowing in the northern style and grinning. "I must say, I hardly recognised you dressed in that armour and riding such a beautiful horse."

"*You* didn't recognise *me*!" Sharley exploded. "*You* look like one of the Sultan's courtiers!"

"Ah, yes," said Maggie, looking down at his robes. "Well, native clothing is so much more comfortable for the extremes of the desert, and silk is wonderfully smooth and cool."

"And how exactly do your . . . companions help?"

"Jumelia and Haroozala, you mean? They're skilled nurses who have brought me back to health, and now help me to pass the time in perfect peace and comfort."

"'Perfect peace and comfort', eh?" said Sharley suspiciously.

Just then, they were joined by Mekhmet and Ketshaka. Maggie's eyes widened as he looked on the Lusu Queen, and he salaamed deeply.

"Hah, I see now you're not a freak of nature, Charlemagne!" she boomed. "There *are* other colourless people in the world. The Great Spirits will have their little jokes; sometimes my sides just ache with laughter. How will I cope when I see an entire nation of people as pale and faded as cloth left too long in the sun?"

"We can only hope you'll get used to it," said Sharley coolly.

"You know, I just can't see that happening," the Queen replied, and her gales of laughter boomed through the oasis.

Maggie led them into the house, where Sharley, Mekhmet and Ketshaka took sherbet in the cool of a courtyard that was shaded by trees. "Tell me, Maggie," said Sharley, taking a long draught of the deliciously cold drink and settling back into his cushions, "how did you know the name given to me by the Desert People? No one called me 'Shadow of the Storm' until I reached their capital."

"Simple, really," Maggie answered. "Al-Khatib has been good enough to send me regular reports during the weeks I've been forced to rest in this oasis. Little has escaped my attention, and I must admit that although the Sultan's attack on the southern borders and the Venetti's naval actions against the ports of the Empire are small escalations of the war, they'll certainly distract some of Bellorum's attention away from our own army and its northward march."

"True," Sharley agreed. "But speed and surprise are of the essence, so if you're coming with us, Maggie, you'll need to say goodbye to your companions and be ready to ride tomorrow morning."

When Maggie appeared the next morning, the army had already formed into its travelling columns and was about to march. He'd put aside his courtier's silks and turban, and once again wore the simple black robes of a scholar. From the main gate of the house, the two young women waved shyly, and

Maggie blew them kisses as he mounted a spare zebra loaned to him by the Lusu. But any sadness he felt was banished as he gazed in amazement at the beast he was riding.

"By the Holy Brothers of Latinum and all their unexpected children, a striped horse!" he exploded. Quickly he spat on his sleeve and rubbed it vigorously on the animal's coat, then he inspected the cloth for signs of any paint. "No. It seems real. A striped horse! Has the desert heat got to me already?"

Sharley grinned and pointed back to the column of Lusu cavalry behind them.

"Ye Goddesses and little fieldmice, more of them! An entire cavalry of striped horses. Hah! Bellorum will finally admit to himself he's gone mad! Great Creating Nature, what a world we do live in!"

And with that he galloped back down the line to inspect the zebras, and to try and communicate with their riders.

For the next two days Maggie was so engrossed in his study of the Lusu that he hardly seemed to notice the heat. Obviously the two young women had done a splendid job in nursing him back to health.

Having satisfied himself for the time being with the information he'd gathered about the new allies, Maggie interviewed Mekhmet and Sharley in depth, managing to take copious notes even while riding. He happily told them it was all being included in the second volume of his history on the Icemark's war with the Empire. "With a bit of luck, I'll then retire and buy a nice comfortable house in the South Riding."

"But what about the Southern Continent?" asked Sharley in amazement. "I thought you intended to retire there."

"Ah, yes, well . . . I've been forced to change my plans there," the old scholar replied.

"But why?"

"Because . . . well, because over the last few weeks I've found myself feeling homesick for the Icemark," he admitted. "One of the ancient sages – Archilocus, I believe I'm right in saying – states that a person has both a physical and a *spiritual* place of birth, the latter being by far the most important, and I've come to the conclusion that the Icemark is the birthplace of my spirit."

"What, with all that snow and ice and cold rain?" asked Sharley mischievously.

"Yes, every last bit of it. And also the greenery, the gentle rivers and woodlands. The loud, rumbustious housecarles and their rude songs, the werewolves and their filthy jokes, even the Vampires and their fey elegance. But most of all I realise now that I've come to love your mother and father and every one of their children. I'd even kiss Medea if I was there now!"

"Steady on, Maggie. I wouldn't go that far."

"Well no, maybe not. Perhaps I'd give her a friendly wave."

"Even that's pushing it a bit," said Sharley with a shudder, but he felt a warm glow for the old scholar, and leaning over from his saddle he hugged him and kissed the top of his bald head.

"What was that for?" he asked in surprise.

"For being who you are."

"Now, there's a fine philosophical point to be discussed in that comment. How can you know who I am? How exactly does one define the very *amness* of an individual, or indeed even oursel—?"

"Shut up, Maggie," said Sharley happily.

* * *

Two days later they were looking down on the port from the hills above. The entire harbour, and a huge sweep of the sea beyond, was filled with more ships and vessels of every size and design than Sharley had ever seen: the long, knife-like shapes of fighting galleys, massively broad horse-transporters, troop ships, fighting galleons and a teeming, tumbling tangle of supply ships, merchantmen and flat-bottomed barges.

A sea-cooled blast of wind washed over them, bringing with it the scent of salt and tar and the shouts of the sailors and stevedores who were working on the ships. The metallic blare of bugles and horns, the rattle of chains and the creaking groan of ropes and timber wove themselves into the rich tapestry of sounds rising up from the harbour.

"By the Goddess, there must be over four hundred vessels down there!" said Sharley in awe.

"More like five hundred," said Mekhmet. "And look at the insignia they're flying: everything from the Desert Kingdom and the Venetti to the Hellenes and privateers. And there are many others I've never even seen before. The entire Southern Continent seems to be under sail."

Ketshaka sat in uncharacteristic silence as she gazed down on the harbour. But then she said, "My eyes have never before seen such a wide body of water. Neither have they beheld such gigantic boats all congregated together like the flocks of migrating flamingos that fly from the storms of winter. You say this 'sea' is like a lake, but larger, and that the entirety of Lusuland itself could be swallowed up by its waters. But how can I contain the enormity of such an idea?" Her huge face gazed fiercely at the frantic activities below as supply boats scurried around the larger ships, and tiny, ant-like figures swarmed over the rigging and sails. "What human being, who

503

has never before seen such a mighty gathering of waters, could possibly comprehend such a vastness? Our minds can only understand new experiences by comparing them with what we already know. So, my beloved allies: tell me, make me understand, how much larger this sea is than a lake."

"Well, Madam," said Maggie, clearing his throat, "that rather depends on the comparative sizes of the sea and lake in question. But as an example, it takes over two days to sail across Lake Tintavani, the largest body of fresh water in the Southern Continent. However, the journey we're about to embark upon will take us several weeks."

Ketshaka bowed her head and gazed at the mane of her zebra for several seconds before she turned her stony features to regard the little scholar. "Old man, your words bring no comfort. It seems to me that even your undoubted wisdom could learn that there are times when knowledge is an unwelcome thing."

"But, Your Majesty, you asked me!" said Maggie, outraged at this Royal injustice. "Would you prefer I lied to you?"

"No. I would prefer you to unleash the danger of naked facts with care and over a suitable period of time. No one will tell my warriors how long we will be sailing on this water. Let them arrive at that knowledge with the passing of time and distance."

This was greeted with silent agreement, and after a few more minutes of gazing at the huge spectacle of the fleet, they turned their mounts and headed down into the port.

The plan was that the army should embark immediately and sail on the next favourable tide, but it would take many hours of manoeuvring ships to the quayside, loading them, and then moving them out to sea again, while other ships were brought in to be loaded with their passengers. Depending on how the horses and zebras reacted to the huge transport ships, it could be as long as three days before they were ready to set sail.

The army reached the quayside to be greeted by Venezzian and Desert Kingdom harbour masters who marshalled them into different holding areas while the ships were made ready. Progress was excruciatingly slow, and Sharley found himself riding around the quaysides getting in everyone's way and generally being unhelpful. He could have wept with impatience; every moment of delay brought the possibility of the Icemark's defeat closer.

Mekhmet was much more relaxed. He did have bouts of nerves, which manifested in sudden bursts of energy that had him rushing about demanding to see charts and maps, or having lengthy discussions with quartermasters about supplies. But otherwise he seemed quite content to wait in the sumptuous rooms they'd been assigned.

But by far the happiest was Maggiore, who spent his time tidying up his rough field notes or talking to any Lusu troopers who spoke the language of the Desert Kingdom. Sharley was almost envious of the little scholar; all he needed to keep him content was a supply of paper and ink, and someone to interview.

On the evening of the third day, a Venezzian official arrived and told them that the fleet was almost ready to sail. Only the last horse transport needed to be loaded with the mounts of Prince Mekhmet's and Queen Ketshaka's personal bodyguards. These were the elite of the elite amongst the cavalry, and once they were on board the fleet could begin its expedition on the next high tide.

Sharley felt sick. Here it was! The moment he'd been working towards for weeks. Not till the last ship had left the harbour would he believe he was actually on his way home with a relieving army!

They all hurried down to the quayside, the atmosphere alive with a strange tumble and contradiction of emotions: fear, excitement, elation, and good old-fashioned worry all buzzed through their heads. But in Sharley, fear had the upper hand. What would happen if they hit another storm? Could they defend themselves against pirates – and, worse, against the fleets of the Corsairs and Zephyrs, the Empire's sea-going allies? Would their food and water supplies last out? And what if they were becalmed?

So much could go wrong! Sharley's leg obviously thought so too, because it suddenly gave way and he fell sprawling on the flagstones of the harbour.

"Hah! A good omen," said Ketshaka, grabbing him by the collar and setting him on his feet.

"Is it? Why?" asked Sharley, climbing to his feet and hurrying on.

"If you fall on the way to a war, it means you won't fall in battle. The palace Wise Woman once told me this, and she's never wrong."

Sharley grinned gratefully, and then slithered to a halt as they reached the quayside. A huge horse-transporter was being slowly manoeuvred to dock gently against the timbers of the harbour. The ship was truly enormous – over sixty metres long, and about fifteen wide. Halfway up its cliff-like side, wide twin doors opened ponderously to reveal a dark, cavernous entrance, from which a long gangplank was lowered. Without waiting to be asked, Sharley and Mekhmet ran up the gangway and stood gazing into the interior of the ship.

Inside, it was deeply dark, despite the lanterns that hung at intervals from the tree-thick timbers along the length of the hold. But as their eyes adjusted to the gloom, they could make out incredibly narrow stalls lining each side of a central walkway. The boys looked at each other, and stepped inside. They found that each stall had a canvas sling inside that would cradle a horse's belly and keep it steady on its legs in the event of rough weather. The entire effect was one of a dungeon especially designed for horses.

"We're asking too much of them, Mekhmet," said Sharley in a horrified whisper.

"I know. But it has been done many times before. The crews will be experienced horsemen; they'll know how to keep the horses calm and well, and we can only pray for quiet weather and a swift passage," Mekhmet answered, with more confidence than he felt.

Continuing their exploration, they found a long ramp that led down to a lower deck, where the conditions were even worse. At least the animals on the upper deck had a chance of seeing daylight through the grids of the hatchways, but down here there was only lamplight.

"Suleiman will be on the upper deck, and under a hatch," said Sharley fiercely.

Already the cavalry was approaching, each horse or zebra led by its rider who murmured and whispered to his or her mount, so that there seemed to be a gentle, calming wind blowing around the harbour. The Princes stood aside as the animals were walked slowly up the ramp, some of them whickering nervously and one or two rearing as they approached the wide, open doorway into the dark. The vast majority of them passed inside, trusting their riders and allowing themselves to be led to the stalls. But some reared wildly, screaming and striking out with their battle-trained hooves as they panicked and fought to get away.

Sharley watched all of this in growing apprehension. What would happen if Suleiman refused to board the transporter? Obviously nothing would stop him, Sharley, from returning to the Icemark, and he could always be given another horse to ride when they reached dry land again. But Suleiman was his friend. He was an integral part of the new and swiftly established legend that was the "Shadow of the Storm". It would be horrendous to leave the Desert Kingdom without him – and, even worse, such a catastrophe would be seen as the most dreadful omen by the entire army. Suleiman *had* to go with him; there was no other way Prince Charlemagne could return to the Icemark.

The boys had now retreated to the quayside, and watched as the loading operation continued. After what seemed like hours, the last zebra was led inside and the huge doors in the side of the transporter swung ponderously shut. Amidst the shouts and cries of the stevedores, the ropes were released from the bollards and the massive ship began to ease itself away from the quayside.

"But what about Suleiman?" Sharley cried out in panic.

"Our horses will be coming with us on board our ship," Mekhmet explained.

"But how?" Sharley asked in bewilderment. "We're not sailing on a transporter."

But before the Crown Prince could answer, a familiar figure rolled across the quayside and bowed low before them.

"Greetings to you, your Highnesseses and Eminenceses. I

have the great and most enormous pleasure of transporting your good and Royal personages across the sea to the fair land of the Icemark, place of my birth and home of good Nancy, my wife, and mother of nine children, most of whom, I'm reliably informed, have been fathered by myself."

Sharley stared at the strange apparition, his fears and worries forgotten for a moment as he took in the vision of the wind-burned Captain, still in his enormous tarred sea-boots, ragged trousers and looped earrings. This was the man who'd brought him safely to the Southern Continent through the most terrifying storm ever.

"Captain Sigurdson! We're sailing with you?"

"Indeed you are, Your Young Royalness! And might I add that in the weeks since last I was honoured to set my rough old eyes on your good Eminent self, you've grown and filled out and now look as fearsome a warrior as I ever did see in all of my travels on the oceans and seas of this entire wide world."

Sharley blushed with pleasure. "Well, thank you, Captain Sigurdson. Erm . . . you look well yourself."

"And what, may I ask, if I may make so bold, has happened to your bad leg? When I left you at Venezzia, you hopped and hobbled like a boy with a limb made from wormy old wood. But now you just limp like a man with a bit of a cramp that's knotted his muscles after too long a sit!"

"I've been training," Sharley explained in a quiet voice. If Cressida had been there she'd have haughtily reprimanded the Captain for being "familiar", but he couldn't bring himself to do that. Captain Sigurdson was beyond the usual social conventions.

The old sea-dog then noticed Queen Ketshaka as she slowly

walked forward to join them. Falling to one knee the captain bowed his head, and even swept off his greasy old hat in a clumsy gesture of courtliness.

"May I offer my services to you, Your Enormousness?" He looked up slowly and appreciatively. "I may truly say that I have never before looked upon such a beautiful personage as Your Good Royal Self, Your Greatest of Majesties! I am your humblest servant to do with as you will!"

Ketshaka's granite face beamed. "You may stand before me, Captain!" she boomed graciously. "I accept your generous tribute right gladly. If our journey over the seas were to take a decade of lifetimes, it would seem short in your good company."

"Were I to sail from now until the Crack of Doom, it would seem but a second, enlightened by your Good and Abundant Royal Self!"

Maggie coughed quietly into the charged silence that followed. "If I might interrupt such courtly politeness, could I suggest we board the Captain's ship?"

"Ah yes!" Captain Sigurdson said, as though he'd only just remembered why he was there. "The good ship *Horizon* is waiting to receive Your Royal Highnesses just as soon as she's docked and you're all ready."

"Apparently we're taking our horses on board with us, Captain. Is that right?" asked Sharley, anxious to confirm exactly how Suleiman would be travelling.

"Aye, that's right, My Royal Hearty! We've built a stall or two on the main deck, and they even have flagstoned floors to stop the piss and poop spoiling them. All pegged in and neat they are, and with roofs and doors to keep out the gales."

"Gales? Are you expecting bad weather again?" said

Sharley, imagining the pure horror of a horse-transporter in a storm.

"Just a figure of speech, My Little Kingling! My old weather nose has never sniffed so promising a trip. We should have a sea like a glassy lake all the way home to the Icemark!"

"With your undoubted skills, Captain Sigurdson, I'm sure our journey will be as gently rocked as a snooze in a hammock," boomed Ketshaka, her face beaming.

"For your greater comfort, My Most Abundant of Ladies, I would wrestle the sea nymphs and fight a war with the Brewer of Storms his wind-ravaged self!"

Ketshaka would have tittered girlishly if that had been at all possible for someone of her stature. Instead, she chuckled in a voice that sounded like a landslide of boulders tumbling down a wooden hill.

The *Horizon* had now manoeuvred to the harbourside and was preparing to dock. A cascade of ropes flew through the air and were caught by stevedores, who then leaned into them heavily, drawing the ship to bump gently against the timbers of the quay.

"LOWER THE GANGPLANK, AND PREPARE THE ANIMAL STALLS!" Sigurdson bawled in a voice that made Sharley's ears ring.

As the crew scurried to follow his orders a strangely cool and refreshing movement of air began to flow over the harbour, and from the town came a great upsurge of voices raised in wonder. Sharley and his party turned to watch as a beautiful blue light moved down through the streets, accompanied by sweetly singing voices.

Holding his breath, Sharley watched as the light slowly descended through the town and crossed the quayside. Soon he could make out the transparent forms of the Blessed Women moving like flowing water towards him.

When they were just a few yards away they stopped, and a single figure stepped forward. Sharley immediately recognised her as the Blessed Woman who had spoken to him in the desert, and he fell to his knees. Smiling radiantly, she signalled that he should stand.

"Charlemagne Athelstan Redrought Strong-in-the-Arm Lindenshield, Shadow of the Storm, it has been our duty and our delight to protect you while you dwelt within the borders of the Desert Kingdom, but now you will leave our shores and cross the wide seas to your northern home. Be now told that you have the favour of the One; take comfort in knowing that all that comes to pass is the will of the One, and meant to be. Remember too that though we may not be by your side, in your greatest danger we will answer your needs even across the oceans of the world. The power of the One has no limit and recognises no distances or borders. Go now with our blessings, Prince of the North, and know that you will remain in our hearts for all eternity."

She salaamed deeply and Sharley fell to his knees again, completely unable to speak.

The Blessed Women then withdrew, flowing away from the harbourside and back through the town, singing as they went.

Sigurdson was the first to recover from the deep sense of peace and wonder that had settled on his Royal passengers and crew.

"LOOK LIVELY!" he bawled to the sailors. "PREPARE TO RECEIVE HONOURED GUESTS!"

Sharley and his party were then escorted aboard by the

Captain, where they were received by twin ranks of sailors and a blast on the bosun's whistle.

Still in a state of pleasurable shock, Sharley limped to the seaward hull of the ship and looked out over the harbour. He was always more aware of his gammy leg whenever anything stressful or exciting was about to happen, and as he looked out over the waters, he realised that he was about to embark upon a journey that would have equal measures of both. As far as the eye could see there were galleons and transporters, barges and merchantmen, supply vessels and galleys of almost every size and description. The fleet spilled beyond the harbour wall and stood out to sea, waiting at anchor for the order to sail. He'd already heard some sailors saying that they'd never been part of so big a fleet before, and others had said it was probably the biggest that had ever been gathered. An exaggeration, perhaps, but as he looked out over the forest of masts, peopled with scurrying sailors and festooned with fluttering flags, it all looked like a huge, wooden, floating city just waiting for him to give the order that would take them over the sea to the Icemark.

The responsibility was overwhelming and he almost panicked. Then he thought of the Blessed Women, and of his mother besieged in Frostmarris, and he forced himself to stand upright.

"Captain Sigurdson, give the order to cast off!"

CHAPTER 32

The Vampires were exhausted. Bellorum's rebuilt Sky Navy had been attacking every night for more than a week, and despite Their Vampiric Majesties' brilliant defence of the skies, some of the bombers had got through. But so far the damage to Frostmarris had been minimal. In one district a row of houses had been flattened, and in another, incendiary devices had destroyed several shops. Overall the defence strategy was working; Archimedo Archimedes' new water supplies and the firefighting housecarles and werewolves had kept damage to a minimum. But even so, everyone was expecting things to get worse – much worse.

The Vampires had identified dozens of new squadron insignia on the wasp-fighters, and the same was true for the bombers, which meant that Bellorum had already replaced his damaged ships with new fleets. Certainly the Sky Navy's attacking waves were hitting much harder again, but Their Vampiric Majesties were convinced the enemy hadn't revealed their true strength yet.

"Bellorum's holding back for some reason," the King told Thirrin when she visited the Vampires' caves. "We know he has the capability to launch a truly spectacular attack on the city. The Snowy Owl spies report a hugely enlarged Sky Navy base at Learton, with thousands of ground crew. But the wasp-fighters were too vigilant, so they couldn't get close enough to get an accurate number for the galleons."

"You could try a raid," said Thirrin. "Destroy them on the ground."

"We've considered it, and even sent out a squadron to check out defences. But only one made it back. The cost would be too high, and Frostmarris would be left defenceless."

Thirrin nodded in disappointment. "Then Bellorum still calls the tune."

"As ever," said the Vampire Queen. "Still, it didn't stop us winning last time."

"No, but I'd like to fight a battle with that particular gentleman just once, when I wasn't on the defensive, or outnumbered, or on the very brink of being beaten. Victory, if we get it at all, is always 'snatched from the jaws of defeat', as the saying goes."

The Vampire King refilled her wine glass. "My dear Thirrin, accept victory wherever and however you can get it. Especially when fighting the Empire. Every other country they've invaded has succumbed in a matter of weeks, sometimes even days. I don't think you realise just how far your legend has spread throughout the known world. You're a beacon of hope for every suppressed and enslaved nation and individual. You're an icon, my dear – enjoy it."

"Well, even if that is true, it doesn't help us here, does it? I'd sooner be unknown and living in peace, than famous and at war. Or even just unknown but with a few thousand more soldiers would do."

The King settled back into his throne and sipped at his wine. "I wouldn't be too certain that your fame isn't helping us here, you know."

"What do you mean?" she asked, grasping at any morsel of hope.

"Just rumours, dear heart, only whispers of rebellion in the Empire, and perhaps even action on the Imperial southern borders."

"Do you have details?" she asked eagerly.

"I'm afraid not. Bellorum's got us blockaded as tight as a drum by land, sea and air. It's impossible to verify anything. Still, the rumours are persistent. Species migrating north have heard tales, and they talk to the Snowy Owls. But our feathery allies do tend to be greedy and eat the messengers before they have time to say too much."

"The werewolves haven't said anything."

"Well, they wouldn't, sweeting," said the Vampire Queen. "The Wolf-folk don't eat anything smaller than a red deer, and the larger animals would never make it through Imperial lines with any news. Venison and the like is very popular on the tables of the Empire and they seem to have killed most of the deer already. No, these whispers come from the smaller beasts, the rats and mice, and more importantly, the birds."

Thirrin fell silent as she mulled over the information. "Perhaps Oskan could apply his Eye and find something out," she said quietly.

"I don't think the Witchfather's Gift of Far-Seeing reaches far enough to ascertain what *exactly* is happening in the southern parts of the Empire," said Her Vampiric Majesty, diplomatically suppressing a shudder at the very mention of Oskan's name.

"No, perhaps not. Though maybe . . . maybe Medea could help."

The Vampire King spluttered wine all over his delicately embroidered waistcoat, then spent a good five minutes having his back patted by his Queen while he coughed uncontrollably.

At last he sat back in his throne weakly and drew breath. "I *do* beg pardon for my unseemly choking fit. I really should learn to be less appreciative of these fine vintages; they really are very rich."

Thirrin eyed him narrowly, but didn't comment. "We were discussing the possibility of action on the southern border of the Empire, weren't we? That could mean Venezzia, I suppose, and isn't there a place called the Desert . . . something-or-other? No, it's no good, I'll just have to ask Medea to—"

"Madam! Thirrin. I . . . *we've* been putting off saying something for quite a while now for fear of giving offence," the Vampire King interrupted. "You see . . . well, it concerns . . . how can I put this . . . erm . . . it's about—"

"What my esteemed Consort is trying to say is that we don't think Medea can be trusted," Her Vampiric Majesty said defiantly. "Her spirit isn't quite human, and I'm afraid that the contaminant comes from your husband's line. As you know, his father was of an ancient species who view the concepts of right and wrong in a very different way from their distant human cousins."

Thirrin rose angrily and drew breath to speak, but then she paused, and slowly sat down again as she thought things through. It had to be admitted that Medea *was* odd. Even as a baby she'd hardly been normal. She had never cried and had never shown affection to anyone or anything. Not even a doll or a pet animal.

Things began to make sense to Thirrin – or rather, they were becoming as complicated as they should be where Medea was concerned. "What do you think she might do?" she asked at last.

"Thirrin, I really don't think she—"

"She could betray you – betray all of us," Her Vampiric Majesty interrupted again. "She has Powers that would be very useful to Bellorum, and she may well choose to offer them to him."

"I see," Thirrin said thoughtfully. As a mother, she had every right to be screamingly angry at these accusations, but as Commander of the Icemark's defence force, she had an obligation to take them seriously. "I assume you would advise me not to seek her help in any way, or allow her access to any plans."

"At the very least," the Vampire Queen answered. "Some might go as far as to suggest exile – and, considering her potential for chaos and disruption, perhaps even the death penalty wouldn't be too extreme."

A heavy, stifling silence fell on the cave, during which His Vampiric Majesty looked and felt very unhappy.

"I'll need time to think," said Thirrin quietly. And before she could say anything else, the unmistakable wail of the were-wolf air attack warning sounded. The King immediately sprang to his feet, more relieved than he'd ever been to prepare for battle.

"I'm sorry, dear heart," he said to Thirrin. "We really must fly."

* * *

They'd been at sea for more than a week, and Captain Sigurdson said it was one of the swiftest passages he'd ever made in such a huge fleet. The weather showed every sign of staying perfect: a brisk wind, a relatively smooth sea, and not a cloud in sight.

Sharley was as happy as it was possible to be, considering he was desperate to get home with his army. But at least he knew everything was going well.

The routine of travel had established itself and the massive fleet sailed uneventfully towards its destination. The weather remained kind, with clear skies and a brisk following wind that drove them ever northward. But then slowly, by barely noticeable degrees, the temperature began to fall as they grew closer to their destination, and the unsullied blue of the sky became hazy, until entire days were shrouded under a canopy of grey that seemed to unnerve the Desert People and the Lusu. Only Sharley's assurances that all was quite normal kept them relatively calm.

A day eventually dawned when low cloud hid part of the sprawling fleet from view, and everything was drenched in a fine mizzling rain. Mekhmet was frozen, and piled on almost every article of clothing he possessed. He may have experienced the sharply cold temperatures of the mountains, but never before had he encountered the bone-chilling damp of the north.

"Is it like this every day?" he asked Sharley miserably.

"No, of course not . . . not *every* day," his friend answered with a reassuring smile.

"Good, because I think I'd rust if I was wet all the time."

Sharley had to work hard not to grin when he looked at Mekhmet's woebegone face, but when Queen Ketshaka shuffled into view draped in so many animal skins that she looked like a mobile zoo, he hurried over to the rails where his gleeful chuckling was lost to the wind.

Lusu Queen and Crown Prince joined him and stared glumly ahead to the horizon. "How much longer before we reach the Icemark?" Ketshaka asked, her bedraggled ostrich plumes sagging under the weight of the weather so that they stuck out almost horizontally from her head.

"Captain Sigurdson reckons we'll arrive in less than a week."

"How much less?" asked Mekhmet, shivering.

"He wouldn't be more specific, I'm afraid. But one day soon we'll scan the horizon and there'll be—" He stopped in mid-sentence and stared through the grey mizzle over the grey sea to the grey horizon where he thought he could see . . . something.

"What? What is it?" asked Mekhmet, peering ahead himself.

"SAIL HO! SAIL HO!" Sharley suddenly bellowed.

"WHERE AWAY?" A voice answered from the crow's nest that swayed precariously on the highest point of the highest mast.

"FORWARD HORIZON!"

"SAILS HO!" the voice confirmed, and immediately the decks were swarming with sailors. A bugle sounded, and was faintly answered by the transporter closest to them. Soon the sounds of horns and calling voices relayed the news throughout the fleet, and the long blade-like fighting galleys almost leaped out of the water as they drove forward over the waves and took up a defensive position before the transporters.

"Friend or enemy, think ye, Your Royal Highnesses?" asked Captain Sigurdson as he joined them on the deck.

"The Icemark navy was expecting to be blockaded by the fighting fleet of the Corsairs and Zephyrs, according to the last news I heard," said Sharley anxiously.

"That's true enough," said Sigurdson, snapping open a monoculum and training it on the horizon. "And if that lot ain't Corsair galleys and Zephyr galleons, I'm a eunuch guard in the Sultan's harem – begging your pardon, Prince Mekhmet." With that, he strode off bellowing orders.

"CLEAR THE DECKS AND BREAK OUT THE CUT-LASSES! WE'RE FIGHTING OUR WAY HOME, MY HEARTIES!"

Cressida was striding with determination along the corridors of the citadel. She'd just come from the defences, where the Imperial army had made yet another attempt to break through the allied lines. They'd been pushed back, but as usual the losses on both sides were enormous. For Bellorum this didn't pose too much of a problem, as there seemed to be a never-ending line of reinforcements marching up the Great Road from the northern provinces of the Empire, but for the defenders of Frostmarris, the situation was reaching crisis point. They just didn't have enough soldiers to keep Bellorum out of the city for much longer.

Cressida burst through a door and out into the courtyard of the fortress. All around her lay wounded soldiers of all species. Some lay still and silent, blood seeping through the rough bandages their comrades had hastily tied, but others screamed in agony and terror as horrendous wounds gaped wide and glistening in the stark light of day. The courtyard was now being used as an overspill area for the infirmary, and everywhere witches could be seen fighting to save lives as they tied tourniquets, closed wounds, cut out musket balls and reset shattered limbs. But like the soldiers on the defences, there were just too few of them. Many of the wounded died before the healers could even reach them.

Cressida strode on, the horrors of the fighting and its results adding impetus to her determination as she reached the main gates of the citadel and went out into the streets. But a sudden breeze brought with it a welcome scent of greenery from the nearby Great Forest, and the Crown Princess slowed her pace and looked out across the roofs to the huge canopy of trees that edged the plain of Frostmarris. The dense woodland stood like a second city, huge towers and impenetrable walls set against the sky, though this metropolis was made of living trees instead of stone, and was peopled by animals, birds and the strange tree soldiers that sometimes appeared in times of great danger.

The Holly King and the Oak King hadn't appeared in the battle yet. But Cressida knew they hadn't helped until the final struggle in the last war either. The Monarchs of the forest were ancient and mysterious, and even her father found it difficult to fathom their minds. "They will fight when it is right for them to do so," was all he would say.

Obviously that time hadn't yet arrived, and perhaps it never would. Everyone in Frostmarris knew that Bellorum had taken to bombing the Great Forest with his Sky Navy. The mad Commander of the Imperial Forces was still thirsty for revenge against the Holly and Oak Kings, who had led their combined armies against the Imperial host in the last battle for Frostmarris.

Cressida scrutinised the trees now for signs of damage, but she could see nothing. At this time of the year the sap was green and the deep leaf litter on the forest floor was wet with rain, so there'd been no fires. But the bombs had still smashed apart many living trees and felled the mightiest of those that had grown for centuries. The only mercy for the forest was that Bellorum was far more determined to destroy Frostmarris; so far, as closely as Cressida could calculate, only one air raid was being sent against the trees for every ten against the city.

She dragged her eyes away from the forest and tried to ignore the hope that the Holly and Oak Kings would soon openly join the war. There was little point in relying on those you couldn't understand. Best to put your trust in your own fighting ability and the resources close at hand.

With this in mind Cressida set off through the streets again. She was heading for Medea's high tower set in the walls of the citadel. It was an odd building, not only because it had become her sister's undisputed home, but also because, despite being part of the citadel, you could only enter it from the street that ran around the curtain walls of the fortress, rather than from the courtyard or any other internal door.

She reached the entrance and paused. There were many odd things about Medea, but Cressida had just discovered a new one that very morning. It had never occurred to her, or to anyone else, to ask for the strange young woman's help in the war. Perhaps this was something to do with Medea's great Abilities – maybe she'd somehow managed to stop any of them wondering why she was doing nothing to help. But if that was the case, why on earth would she do that when her family and country needed her so badly? She may not have been a fighter, but surely her Magical talents could have been used against Bellorum. Of course, that depended on what form her Gift took, but even if she was only a Far-Seer, she could help to warn of attacks, and tell of Bellorum's plans even more effectively than the werewolf relay.

Why hadn't anyone thought of this before? It was only because Cressida had heard her mother muttering to herself about whether she should talk to Medea and ask for her help that anything had occurred to her! Well, now she was determined to put it right. The Queen may have some doubts about asking Medea, but she certainly didn't!

Thumping the door once with her mailed fist, she burst through it and stamped up the spiral staircase. Without hesitating Cressida strode into the room that occupied the entire width of the tower at its very apex.

Medea sat gazing out of one of the four open windows, each of which looked to a different point of the compass. "Wake up, woman, I've come to talk to you," Cressida boomed, sounding amazingly like her grandfather Redrought.

"I can assure you I'm not asleep," answered a voice that was not a whisper, but which hissed like one.

"Good, then listen to what I have to say. Your help is needed. We're desperate for any help we can get, so what can *you* do?"

Medea slowly turned her head to look at her sister. "Oh, I can do an enormous amount, I assure you of that."

"So why haven't you offered your services before? I mean, are you blind, deaf and stupid, or did it just pass you by that we're fighting a bloody war here?"

The strangely dead eyes seemed to bore into Cressida's mind, and for a moment she felt dizzy. But then she shook her head, glared, and said, "Excuse me, but didn't you hear me? Do you need me to repeat it, or shall I write it down in large letters and short words so you can understand?"

Medea was shocked. She couldn't see into her sister's thoughts! But she dismissed this possibility as absurd, and hissed.

Cressida took a step back and then gave a short, harsh laugh. "Are you part cat, or has hissing been integrated into the language without me realising it?"

Medea rose slowly from her chair, seeming to fill the chamber, even though she was much smaller than her warrior sister. The atmosphere slowly darkened as the shutters over the window drew closed, seemingly of themselves, and the shadows thickened like black, dirty cobwebs.

"Oh, for goodness' sake," said Cressida, drawing a mace from her weapons belt, striding to each of the windows in turn and smashing the shutters off their hinges. "I haven't got time for your theatricals. Are you going to answer me, or am I going to have to give you a bloody good hiding? It seems to me that if you'd had a few more well-timed clouts when you were younger, we wouldn't have had to put up with so many of your tantrums! So what's it to be, hmm?"

Medea sat down heavily. She could hardly breathe with the shock of it all. Cressida was immune to Magic! She'd heard of such things, of course, but dismissed it all as so much non-sense; and yet here she was confronted with the truth of it within her own family. She applied her Eye to her sister's mind and found walls of Adamant where no Magic of any sort could ever do damage. How had she, Medea, missed such an obvious thing? The answer came to her almost at once. Cressida's Gift had probably lain dormant until she'd reached adolescence, which sometimes happened, and she probably had no idea about it herself. This was the nature of Magic Immunity; it didn't need to reveal itself. Its strength lay in its secrecy, because if someone with the Gift wanted to do you harm and they knew of your Ability, they'd simply use an axe, or a sword, or anything else that could make a big hole in you.

"Medea!" a voice snapped. "This is your last chance. Either answer me or get a good slapping!"

"What? Help? *Me*? Oh, *please*," she said sarcastically. "Do I look the sort who would want to nanny some fool who's chosen to get themselves injured in some stupid battle?"

Cressida's reply was swift. Pulling off her mail glove she slapped Medea across the face. "Think again, *sister*. We're fighting a war, and at the moment we're losing. There's no room for passengers; either you contribute or—"

"Or what?" Medea spat, but the look on her sister's face was answer enough. She didn't have to read her mind. Medea felt real fear: here was someone she couldn't harm, but who could definitely harm her. "You wouldn't dare!"

"Oh yes, I would. I'm as ruthless and as strong as Mother, but with none of her compassion. You're a parasite, and I crush parasites. Please don't forget, dear sister, I've already killed more people than I could possibly remember. One more death would make very little difference to me. I'm afraid you'd just get lost amongst all the other corpses."

Medea realised that she wasn't the only grandchild of Oskan's father. The blood of that Ancient One ran in the veins of other family members too. "What do you want me to do?" she asked, playing for time.

"I don't know! What *can* you do?"

"Help the healers?"

Cressida deflated with disappointment. "Is that all? Is that really all your much-vaunted Magical Powers can do?"

Medea shrugged. Afraid she may have been, but she

certainly wasn't going to reveal all of her Abilities to her sister. In fact, she wasn't going to reveal *any* of them.

But then the Crown Princess looked up, her eyes alight with a determination that made Medea recoil. How many fighters' last view of the living world had been that fanatical gleam? she wondered.

"Why should I believe you?" Cressida spat. "How do I know you're not hiding some Magical Ability that could drive Bellorum and his army from the field in a matter of minutes?"

"You can't know," Medea answered with as much calm as she could muster, and surprised herself by feeling the slow return of her confidence. "But tell me: even if I could defeat the Imperial soldiers so easily, just how do you think you could force me to do so? Hasn't it occurred to you that if I was that powerful I would have reduced *you* to a pile of smoking ashes by now?"

If she was honest with herself, Cressida could have wept. But she didn't dare be honest. Once she started to weep, she'd probably never stop. She'd hoped for so much when she'd at last remembered that her sister could bring her Gift to their aid. She'd hoped for lightning and firebolts and withering diseases; she'd hoped for a great reading of minds that would reveal the enemy's plans before he could put them into action. But all she'd got was a mocking offer to assist the healers. "Fine. Well, the healers are wallowing in blood right now. Perhaps you'd better go and help them."

She turned away from her strange sister and strode about the room as she thought things through. The possibility of Medea's Powers had given her a greater surge of hope than she dared admit. Now she felt cold and empty. Perhaps it would be wiser to maintain an attitude of deeply sceptical optimism in the future. But right now she needed to restore her morale before she communicated any sense of despair to her soldiers.

She drew her sword and sent it whirling about her head in a display of fighting prowess that made Medea draw in her arms and legs. This was the power of Cressida; this was the reason and root of her very existence, and even the briefest display of her military abilities restored her mind, and filled her with a deep calm.

"Right, sis!" she said at last, sheathing her sword. "You'd better find yourself a leather apron and report for duty; there's a lot of bones waiting to be sawn!"

With that she turned and clattered down the stairs, wishing with every step that she was as ruthless as Medea now believed her to be. How long could they resist Bellorum's hordes before they were finally swept aside? It all seemed so hopeless. Her restored spirits sank again, and she almost sat down on the stone steps of the spiral staircase and gave herself up to despair. But remembering that her squadron of cavalry would be leaderless without her, she lifted her chin and walked on.

Bellorum's battle plan was simple but highly effective. During the daylight hours the Imperial land army would assail the defences, with heavy wasp-fighter support putting the entire allied force under enormous pressure. Then at night the Sky Navy would attack, the bomber galleons rolling in at high altitude, while the fighters swept in low, dodging the search lamps and dropping small pots of burning pitch wherever they could to start random fires throughout the streets of Frostmarris.

As a result, the Vampires were near breaking point. There were just too few of them to try splitting their numbers between day squadrons who could fend off the wasp-fighter support for the land attack, and night squadrons who could defend the city from the bombers and wasp-fighters at night. So they were forced to snatch only brief periods of rest between raids, and the strain was beginning to show. Such prolonged exposure to sunlight was also having an effect on their recovery rate. The inevitable wounds of combat, which would normally have closed within a matter of minutes thanks to their Vampiric constitutions, were now taking days to heal, and some were even becoming infected.

His Vampiric Majesty sat slumped in his throne. He was so exhausted he didn't even care who saw him in such an inelegant pose. It would probably only be their old chamberlain Legosi, anyway, and after more than three hundred years of service to the Vampire King and Queen, he could be trusted to keep such lapses of decorum to himself.

The thin wail of the werewolf air-raid warning wound itself into the cave. The King climbed wearily to his feet and looked at his Consort, who slept peacefully. He almost let her be, but realising she'd never forgive him if he did, he bent and kissed her gently on the cheek. "Oh, sweet breath of decay, I'm afraid they're here again."

Her Vampiric Majesty slowly opened her eyes and stretched, her beauty moving the King to step back and look at her as though he was seeing her for the first time. She was perfect, her skin as pale and translucent as moonlight on snow, her lips as red as fresh blood, her eyes as deep and as dark as death.

"I was dreaming," she said in sleepy surprise. "For the first time in two hundred years."

"Were you, my little corpse? About what?"

"After the war. We were at home in the Blood Palace, and we had . . . silly, I know, but we had children."

"Children, my love? But you know that is impossible. The dead cannot conceive."

"Well, of course I know that. But it was so vivid. We had a boy and a girl, Belasarius and Lucretia. How silly is that?"

"Ludicrous, my dearest," said the King sadly.

"Imagine that . . . a son and a daughter, made from our love."

"Imagine," came the soft reply.

At that point the chamberlain rushed into the cave and bowed. "The squadrons are assembled and ready, Your Majesties," he announced.

"Thank you, Legosi," said the Queen, and realising that her Consort was still deep in thought, she said, "The skies are controlled by the Empire, my love. Shall we see what we can do about that?"

"Indeed yes, my little pie of putrescence," he replied, and strode down from the throne.

CHAPTER 33

Down on the defences the land army were fighting ferociously again as the Imperial hordes swarmed before them. Tharaman-Thar and Krisafitsa-Tharina stood with Thirrin; they were tired and their muzzles and forelegs were red with blood. From the skies wasp-fighters harried the line, dropping pots of blazing pitch and regrouping to form fighting lines that swept down on the Icemark lines on their dreaded strafing runs.

The wasp-fighters often came within range of the defender's archers, and many had been brought down in a tangle of canvas and canopy. But the pilots had been quick to learn that they must avoid the ranks of bowmen and the ballistas; the competition was too unequal, and they'd already lost hundreds of flyers to their arrows. Instead, the pilots concentrated their efforts on other points along the Icemark's defences where they could inflict terrible damage, ripping ragged holes in shield walls and killing countless numbers of housecarles and werewolves, Hypolitan and Snow Leopard warriors.

Thirrin shouted encouragement along the lines as the fighting raged on. The allies had already been pushed back to the second ring of the defences, and this battle was barely an hour old. What chance had they of holding back the Imperial hordes if Bellorum sent in more of his men?

"Where are the Vampires, Tharaman? My people can't fight the land and the skies at the same time!"

The huge Snow Leopard reared up to his mightiest height and with a bellowing roar, he crashed forward like an avalanche of ice, scattering and smashing an Imperial pike phalanx that was threatening to breach their line.

"They'll be here, my dear. Never fret." His refined voice was a stark contrast to the vicious fighting that surrounded them. "And indeed, I do believe I can see them now," he added, as squadrons of Vampires and Snowy Owls began to rise from the walls of Frostmarris like billows of smoke.

With a ghastly shrieking, Vampire and owl bore down on the battle, smashing into the wasp-fighters over the plain of Frostmarris. But no matter how many Imperial flyers the Vampires sent whirling to the ground, the numbers didn't seem to diminish.

Wave after wave of wasp-fighter squadrons came on unabated. Their Vampiric Majesties realised that at last Bellorum was sending out the full strength of the Sky Navy. Screeching out a warning, the Vampires and Snowy Owls withdrew to reform and prepare for the major battle they'd been expecting for weeks.

Hundreds of ponderous galleons hove into view, massive and intimidating, their shadows sliding over the land like the outriders of storm clouds that would soon unleash a rain of death and fire.

The Vampire King silently watched the never-ending flow of enemy force. Then he rose high above his squadrons and, letting out a hideous screech, he folded his leathery wings and dived towards the Sky Navy. With him flew his ferocious Queen and his fighting Vampires and Snowy Owls. They fell upon the massive bomber galleons, tearing open the fabric of their balloons and releasing the gas within. Soon several of the huge ships began to list heavily, scattering a haze of sailors about them as they fell from the decks. One of the galleons began to tumble to the earth; with a gasping roar its canopy burst into a spreading bloom of flame. It hit the ground with a shattering explosion that killed hundreds in the rear ranks of the advancing Imperial land army.

Several others fell in quick succession, their complement of bombs erupting into the sky in a huge billow of destructive flame that flattened all around it. Even so, the Vampires had hardly made a dent in the vast numbers of the enemy fleet.

The King howled his frustrated rage as the Sky Navy sailed on towards its target. But then, at the very edge of his sight, he spied a galleon moving slowly into view. It was truly enormous, with double the usual size of balloon to keep it aloft. Its rigging swarmed with sailors and it was festooned with flags and bunting. It seemed to blaze with colour as it advanced. And, most interesting of all, it flew the personal insignia of Scipio Bellorum, a stylised red rose forested with deadly-sharp thorns.

This was the flagship of the entire fleet, and it was commanded by the General himself. With a screech of challenge and elation, the Vampire King rose into the air, and gathering his squadron, he swept into the attack.

Scipio Bellorum watched the aerial battles and the land war with a smile. In this chaos of killing and mayhem was an order of which he approved. From this seething contest would be born a new world, one in which the strongest would quite rightfully rule, and the weak, with equal justice, would be exploited.

He paced the deck of the Sky Navy's new flagship *The Emperor*, calmly observing as yet another of the bomber galleons slowly keeled over and fell with terrible grace to the earth. The explosion as the payload of bombs blew up on impact sent a brief vibration through the timbers of the flagship, but then it sailed serenely on.

There were actually very few crew members working on the decks; some were in the rigging, waiting for the expected Vampire attack, but the rest stood smartly to attention by the cannon that had been loaded and primed for action several hours ago. It was simply a matter of patience. Bellorum knew they would come.

A high-pitched screech echoed faintly over the sky, and the General smiled. "Prepare to repel boarders," he ordered quietly.

Soon the first musket shots sounded, and suddenly the ship was surrounded by the black leathery wings of the Vampires and the pristine white feathers of the Snowy Owls. The cannons fired a devastating broadside of grapeshot, clearing a swathe through the ranks of the Vampire King's squadron, then the Vampires were on the decks, stepping with loathsome elegance out of flight and into their forms as black-armoured soldiers.

Bellorum rapped out an order, and immediately Imperial shield-bearers appeared from all hatchways and doors, and charged. The General watched the struggle for a few seconds, and then, spying the unmistakeable form of the Vampire King, he drew his sword and strode into battle.

Wordlessly, he struck at the King, who smiled as though greeting an old friend, and their contest began. All around them the battle raged, but for the two men it seemed they fought in a perfectly empty arena. With a precise and breathtaking elegance they fought like two deadly ballerinas; the speed of cut and parry, thrust and riposte was a blur of polished light.

His Vampiric Majesty's blade struck, and sliced a small nick in Bellorum's cheek.

"First blood to you, My Lord," said the General, bowing.

The King smiled, revealing his glittering teeth. "Oh, I *do* trust that so much more will flow my way before this day's business is over, my dear Scipio. I may use your first name, I trust?"

"But of course," came the reply, accompanied by a lightning downward stroke at the King's head.

The Vampire easily parried the stroke, and they sailed away like well-rehearsed dancing partners over the decks of the ship, their blades little more than a blur of light between them. Such was the brilliant virtuosity of their swordplay that soon the battle around them slowed, and finally came to a halt as the soldiers of both sides stopped to watch. A circle formed about the fighters, and a cheer rose up as the competition continued. Both men displayed astonishing footwork and an elegance of fighting precision that drew gasps of admiration. But the crowd gave a groan as the Vampire King struck with a straight-armed thrust that found a way through the General's defence and gashed his left shoulder.

"Second blood to me, I do believe, my dear fellow. Perhaps you should retire and allow your sons to continue without you."

Bellorum smiled, and launched an attack of such ferocity that the Vampire King was driven back across the deck, and soon was bending dangerously backwards over the railings of the hull. He could easily have transformed into his bat shape and flown back to land behind his opponent, but his sense of honour ruled out any move that Bellorum could not use in their personal contest. Summoning every ounce of his strength the Vampire straightened and slowly drove the General back, until he was able to throw him off contemptuously.

On they fought, sometimes balancing precariously on the railings that lined the deck as they cut and thrust at each other. But then his Vampiric Majesty struck again, this time cutting a deep gash into the General's leg. Blood began to pour on to the deck, and the Imperial soldiers, aware that the struggle was going against their Commander, started attacking the Vampires again.

The clash of steel and the screams of the wounded and dying filled the air as Bellorum retreated before the brilliant swordsmanship of the King. Then, with a despairing gasp, he fell to the deck and his sword clattered away out of reach.

His Vampiric Majesty grinned in vicious triumph. He had done it! He had defeated the hated Bellorum! The war was as good as won! He raised his sword and prepared to deliver the final blow.

"One moment, if you please," the General said, politely raising his hand.

"But of course. A final request, perhaps?"

"In a manner of speaking," he replied, and nodded at his soldiers, who had stopped fighting as soon as he'd fallen. They immediately withdrew to the stern of the galleon. "There's one final bit of business I have to do before you are destroyed."

The King grinned at the futile bravado and bowed mockingly. "Please, be my guest."

Bellorum nodded his thanks. "Now would be a good time, Captain Horatius," he called, and suddenly every door, hatchway and stairwell was alive with musketeers as they poured on to the deck and formed triple ranks, one lying, the second kneeling and the third standing. "When you're ready, Captain," said Bellorum quietly.

A young officer saluted and turned to his men. "Present your pieces," he said, as the Vampire soldiers stood as though mesmerised. "Aim," he continued, and a deadly silence settled over the galleon. "FIRE!"

The triple ranks erupted in a crescendo of fire, smoke and the ear-splitting explosion of gunpowder as the muskets were discharged. The agonised screaming of the Vampire soldiers rose into the air as the wooden musket balls tore into their undead flesh. Hundreds fell, their bodies imploding with sickening tearing sounds as thousands of splinters, like tiny stakes of wood, cut their undead existence from the skin and bone of their bodies.

Only one black-armoured soldier still stood – His Vampiric Majesty. His face was blank and unmoving, and his eyes blazed with the concentrated hatred he felt for the Imperial troops that had destroyed his soldiers. But his undead body was trembling with the excruciating effort of stopping his flesh from tearing itself into thousands of shreds. He turned his head to look out over the skies where he could see the squadrons of his Queen, still tumbling and soaring in their dogfights with the wasp-fighters. To his own astonishment, tears began to course slowly down his cheeks as he realised she would be left to walk alone down the long years. The burden of the lonely centuries would bow her down with the weight of their emptiness, and he found it impossible to comprehend any form of existence or oblivion in which he wouldn't be with his Consort of so many ages.

"Oh, my love, I'm so sorry. I've failed you. I must leave you in the undead twilight and go without you to what lies beyond. Will you ever find it in your heart to forgive me?"

And as he spoke his chest swelled, expanding to accommodate his rediscovered compassion. He raised his hand to his lips and blew a kiss over the skies. "With you I found my heart once again. Remember me, my only one, my delight, my light in the Vampiric dark."

By this time Bellorum had struggled to his feet and limped across the deck to where the King stood. Casually he reached into his breastplate and withdrew a sharpened stake of wood, and smiling coldly he plunged it deep into the Vampire King's chest.

Slowly His Vampiric Majesty sifted away to grey dust, and as the Imperial soldiers watched, a small breeze gathered it up and blew it over the side of the ship, where for a moment it seemed to reform into the shape of a man, one hand outstretched to the distant squadrons of the Queen. But then it was torn apart and scattered over the sky. Only then did a cry of pain and sorrow echo over the ether, so loud and so heartrending that all who stood near covered their ears and bowed their heads.

Bellorum alone stood impassive, savouring the answering scream that rose into the air, raging, incredulous, and lost.

Medea seethed with hatred, anger and humiliation. Her sister had left her less than two hours ago and she'd spent all of that

STUART HILL

time devising plans to kill her. Direct use of Magic would be useless, but a Magically conjured wind could easily be made to blow loose rocks from the battlements to flatten her. Or so Medea thought, but the more she analysed Cressida's Gift the more complex it seemed to become. If Magic protected her from direct Magical assault, then could it also protect her from *indirect* attack? Medea had no way of testing this theory without actually trying to kill her, but she soon reached the conclusion that the only safe way to get rid of her sister was to use some direct method. Perhaps a dagger in the dark, or a rock smashed over her head.

But Cressida was a trained soldier, and the likelihood of Medea who'd never done anything more energetic than walk up and down the spiral staircase of her tower actually taking her sister by surprise and dispatching her, was about as great as that of a mouse taking on a fully armed housecarle and winning. The Crown Princess's sense of duty had obviously equipped her perfectly for her dangerous life. And there it was again, that horrible word "duty"! Why did her family have such a fondness for the idea, Medea wondered, when the most sensible and natural attitude to adopt was one of self-service and self-preservation?

Even the hated Charlemagne had gone into exile reluctantly, and only accepted that he had no choice when it was underlined that it was his duty to serve as Regent to the refugees! For all of her short life Medea had felt nothing but contempt for her family and its ludicrous concept of "Royal Service", feeling herself to be strong, individual and completely right in her stance of self-interest. Even as the war raged about the walls of Frostmarris itself, she was still convinced she was correct in her beliefs. She may have told

539

Cressida she'd help in the infirmary, but fortunately her sister was too busy with the fighting to know what Medea was doing.

She sat back in her chair and allowed her Eye to range out over the plain in search of Bellorum and his sons. At least the purity of their selfishness would distract her from the nagging thoughts and questions that nibbled away at her confidence. This war, she was beginning to realise, was a test for all manner of systems and beliefs, from the army and its training methods to the individual and his or her most cherished beliefs. Just who would be the victors? Medea was now no longer certain.

CHAPTER 34

The battle had been won. The enemy fleet of Corsair galleons and Zephyr fighting galleys had been enormous, but the allied ships had all worked together, despite the fact that more than six individual nations had contributed vessels to the sea-going force that had finally faced the enemy. Sharley felt a deep glow of pride for the sailors who'd conducted themselves with such bravery in the engagement, and he could only feel an unending gratitude to the Venezzian and Hellene captains who'd provided the backbone and fighting prowess of the fleet.

Sharley and Mekhmet had joined with the tough little Hellenic marines and had fought from ship to ship as their galleys rammed the slower vessels of the enemy. Sometimes they had to leap between ships that were literally aflame as the strange machines that shot out the terrifying 'Hellenic Fire' had ignited everything in their paths – including, it seemed, the surface of the water!

Some of the hand-to-hand fighting had been vicious as the Corsair sailors fought bravely to defend their ships, but every vessel Sharley, Mekhmet and the marines had boarded was captured.

And at last, towards the end of the battle, the Venezzian admiral had spied a weakness in the enemy line, and as one the allied fleet had surged across the crashing seas and broken the foe's formation. That had been the end for the Corsairs and Zephyrs, and after that the battle had become a large-scale 'mopping-up' campaign as individual ships were hunted down and captured.

The Commander of the contingent of Venezzian galleons, Coranelli Vespugi, had enjoyed himself immensely, and it was at his insistence that not one of the enemy fleet was allowed to escape. After all, he pointed out, their success as a relieving army depended on surprise, and any Corsair or Zephyr who got away would undoubtedly send news to Bellorum.

Not until the following morning did Sharley learn that during the night all of the enemy prisoners had been herded on to one ship and then systematically slaughtered by every archer, soldier and sailor of the fleet. And when everything had seemed lifeless, the galleys had turned Hellenic Fire against the vessel, and stood back and watched until it sank.

Sharley was enraged, his face a brilliant, glowing red and his eyes green sparks of fire as he confronted the Venezzian Commander and Hellenic Admiral. But Vespugi was unmoved. "It was necessary, my Lord Charlemagne. We have too few supplies to feed prisoners and they would be a burden to guard and prevent from escaping. Would you have your mother die because we allowed them to live and flee to warn of our approach? There is no place for sentimentality in war."

"They were people with lives and loves, with children and families. Had they lost the right to live just because they chose to fight us? Perhaps in their consciences it seemed right to make war on the Icemark."

The Venezzian shrugged. "Perhaps. And perhaps their deaths in this way should be seen as the price they had to pay for allowing their consciences to misguide them. How can we know?"

Sharley stormed away to stand at the rails, staring out over the sea. He didn't hear Ketshaka arrive to stand beside him.

"I too am appalled by this barbarous act, my son. For the Lusu people captives in war are sacred to the Great Spirits, and have their protection," she said after a moment's silence. "But Commander Vespugi is of a different tradition. I think he really believed they could not be allowed to live. He is convinced the survival of your mother and your country depended on it."

"And what price do I place on my country? How many others should die for the sake of its liberty – a thousand? Ten thousand? One hundred thousand? Even more? When do we become as uncaring of life as the Empire is? Are all lives expendable as long as my country lives?"

Ketshaka frowned. "But if you asked any of your soldiers they would say many thousands have died in this war already. Every battle leaves a debris of dead that stretches as far as the eye can see and the mind can guess. Why, they would ask, are these deaths different?"

"Because they were unarmed and had given up the fight. Because they had entrusted their lives to us and we betrayed that trust! Because they were not killed on the battlefield in an equal fight with an equal enemy, but murdered after the fighting was done, by their captors who alone carried weapons! That is why their deaths were different. And in allowing them to die in that way, I have dirtied the purity of my cause. Wouldn't any soldier say, Ketshaka, that we have become as bad as the Empire, that we have out-Bellorumed Bellorum?"

The Lusu Queen fell silent for several long minutes, her stony features staring out over the grey seas and sky. But then she drew a deep shuddering breath and said, "Charlemagne, my son, I know that the Lusu people would agree with your stance on this, and I believe that even some of your own soldiers would understand your anger and distress at these deaths, but many others would say that your thoughts and ways of thinking are not as theirs, and that this is the way of war. Commander Vespugi acted to help our cause as his conscience and philosophy allowed, and if in your philosophy that is deemed to be wrong, then there will never be a point where your beliefs will concur."

Ketshaka held Sharley's eye. "But know this, Prince of the North, and may the Great Spirits be my witnesses: if I could shoulder the burden of this wrong for you, I would. If I had the power I would ensure the world knew for certain that your pockets carry only air and innocence; your spirit is as light as charitable thought, and like the mother I undoubtedly am, for my children I would willingly accept the burden of blame and any wrath that may come."

She turned then and, stooping, kissed him before walking away to her cabin.

Maggie was having a wonderful time with so many eye-witnesses to give their versions of events for his history. He scurried about the decks talking to sailors and fighters, and even had himself rowed out to the Hellenic triremes and the Venezzian galleons as he gathered his information. He and Primplepuss then retreated to his cabin where he spent many long hours writing everything up into fair copy.

"Our names will live forever in the history of this war," he said excitedly to Sharley and Mekhmet one night as they had supper in the boys' quarters. "I must send the manuscript to the Holy Brothers in the Southern Continent just as soon as the sea lanes are open again."

"Do you think the ending will be to our liking?" asked Sharley quietly.

Maggie looked at him sharply. "We can but hope, My Lord. We can but hope. But now I think the time has come for you to put all memory of unlawful killing and slaughter behind you. You are a warrior with a war to fight. Attend to your conscience when you have the luxury to do so. Now is the time to wage battle!"

Sharley nodded silently and drew a deep breath. Straightening his shoulders he sat up, stretched and forced himself to smile. "Yes, yes. You're right as usual, Maggie. Now is the time to fight! Just as soon as someone has massaged my leg. It aches like hell after yesterday!"

The next day a grey smudge on a greyer horizon came into view.

"LAND HO!" called the lookout in the crow's nest, and everyone crowded on to the forecastle and stared eagerly ahead.

"WHERE AWAY?" Sharley called impatiently, his heart pounding so furiously he thought it would rip itself out of his chest.

"AHEAD TO STARBOARD!"

"There! Just there!" he said, pointing wildly. "It's the Icemark! It's the Icemark, Maggie! We're home! We've made it!" And seizing the elderly scholar in a bear hug he raised him off his feet. "I'm going to show Primplepuss!" Sharley said excitedly, and shot off to Maggie's cabin. He returned a few breathless minutes later, the huge old cat draped like a bag of blancmange over his arms. "Look, Primpy! Look! It's the Icemark. We're home!"

The cat looked in a bored manner towards the horizon and added her own unmistakeable comment with a terrible fishy aroma that assailed everyone's nostrils, even in the blustery open air. Everyone scrambled away coughing, apart from Sharley who stood with watering eyes, not daring to drop her in case she fell overboard.

"Nobody can deny your status as a warrior now," called Mekhmet from a safe distance. "You're displaying bravery above and beyond the call of duty!"

The fleet turned to sail further north, to where the ports and harbours were not under Bellorum's control. Now that the Corsairs and Zephyrs had been destroyed they could have captured a landing stage and unloaded their army in the south, but it was vital that they didn't reveal their presence. Surprise was going to be their greatest weapon and they had to maintain secrecy at all costs, so they sailed far out to sea, out of sight of any spies.

Sharley watched as the misty haze of the distant coastline sank below the horizon. He was desperate to reach land and set foot once again on the soil of the Icemark. Everywhere he looked, every scent, every sound, even every touch reminded him he was home, and he ached to hear his rough, slightly uncouth native tongue.

For some reason the memory of a small boy with a grubby face, having his cheeks scrubbed with a handkerchief moistened with his mother's spit, brought tears to his eyes. His

cheeks even tingled as though it had just happened. The
Queen, he remembered, had then tucked the hankie in the
sleeve of her best Court dress and straightened up with
supreme regality to greet some important ambassador.

He suspected mothers were the same the world over, and
he was now of an age when his had begun to embarrass him
to greater depths than he thought possible. But he'd have willingly let her call him by his soppy pet name and kiss him in
front of the entire army of the Icemark, if only he could see
her again. Every moment of delay seemed to him to bring the
moment of her defeat and probable death closer. He was desperate to land and lead his army in a thundering charge to
Frostmarris. But he knew he had to be patient. Everything had
to be prepared and executed with precision; everything had to
be perfect. It would take only the tiniest slip for Bellorum to
find out about their presence, and then all hope of rescue
would be lost.

According to Captain Sigurdson it would take only two
days of good sailing to reach a deepwater harbour where they
could dock and disembark. Then would begin the task of getting the horses and zebras back to condition and good health.
They'd spent weeks cooped up in narrow stalls, unable to
move more than a few feet, drinking bad water and eating
grain that was musty with age. They'd be unfit at the very
least, and a good proportion of them would be ill. Much the
same could be said of the human troopers. None of them had
eaten fresh food or drunk fresh water for the entire voyage,
and though they'd certainly had more than enough exercise
during the sea-battle, in the main there hadn't been enough
room to train or to maintain fitness levels.

Realistically they'd need at least a week after reaching dry land before they could set out for Frostmarris. They'd just have to hope that the act of marching south would improve their overall condition. Sharley was desperate to get started as soon as possible, but every hour, every minute seemed to contrive to delay him.

"It could take a fortnight after landing before we see the walls of the city!" said Sharley to Mekhmet as they ate their supper that night. "Not only will the horses have to recover from the journey, but then we'll have to march inland and through the Great Forest."

"Isn't there a quicker route?" Mekhmet asked.

"No. The best roads go that way, and also I want to make contact with the Holly King and the Oak King. Their army could make the difference between a successful strike against Bellorum and complete failure."

The Crown Prince drank his sherbet and wished he could take away the terrible pressures and fears his friend was obviously feeling. "I can't believe we could have made it this far only to fail. It'll all work out. Just you wait and see."

"I thought you only believed in the will of the One, and our total inability to know clearly what that might be," Sharley snapped.

Mekhmet shrugged. "I do. But one name of the One is 'The Friend'. Why would a true friend let us down now?"

Sharley ignored the unanswerable question and stood up to pace as far as their cabin would allow him. "When did Sigurdson say we'd reach port?"

"The day after tomorrow, early in the morning, as you know full well. Now sit down and eat your supper."

"I'm not hungry. I think I'll go up on deck and see what's happening."

"There's nothing happening but grey sea and grey skies. Try and relax."

"Later," said Sharley, diving out of the door and hurrying along the companionway to the stairs.

Mekhmet stared after him and sighed. The shy young boy with the amazing red hair and green eyes, who'd so badly needed his help only a few short months ago, seemed to have gone for ever. In his stead was a mighty warrior, an astute politician and a clever diplomat. But sometimes Mekhmet found himself missing the young boy with the infectious giggle and the brilliant smile. He might even have wished for his return, were it not for the fact that Sharley was so much happier. Or at least he would be, if he wasn't trying to save his country and family, transport an army across oceans and fight a war all at the same time.

When Sharley finally came back from staring over the cold northern seas, Mekhmet would try to help him relax properly over a game of chess or cards. Who knows, maybe he'd even smile again and giggle about some of the antics of Maggie's appalling farting cat. Mekhmet hoped so; he missed the boy Sharley had been before the war.

The next day Mekhmet was surprised to find he'd woken before Sharley, and he crept quietly around the cabin they shared as he prepared for the day ahead. But he needn't have bothered. A sudden thunderous roar of iron on wood shook the entire superstructure of the ship as the anchor was dropped.

Sharley leaped to his feet, grasping for the scimitar he wasn't wearing. "What? Who? Where?".

"Undoubtedly. But I'm not really sure. We're obviously stopping for some reason. Let's go and find out."

549

They both ran up on deck and found the crew milling about in that controlled chaos of sailors everywhere. The day was brilliantly sunny, the grey of the past week having finally given way to a beautiful summer's day. Out on the port side was the coast of the Icemark, and more importantly a huge harbour, its quaysides empty and silent, and with an air of watchful fear.

"Ah, there you are, My Royal Highnessesses," said Sigurdson, his voice sounding like steam escaping from a kettle. "We've made much better time than I calculated. Here we are in Michael's Bay. In truth, I thought we might make it pretty quick, but I didn't like to get your hopes up too much."

Sharley hugged him and planted a huge kiss on his hairy cheek. "Captain Sigurdson, you're a marvel of marvellousness."

"Well, thankee kindly, I'm sure," he said, looking flustered. "Now, if you'll just stand to the asides, so to speak, we can begin the process of unloading and disembarking."

So began an operation that would take almost three days to complete. The huge fleet could only approach the quayside four ships at a time, and the manoeuvring of the massively ponderous transporters, and the only slightly less cumbersome troop ships, took hours of careful work.

The town itself was almost deserted, as most of its population had gone into exile at the beginning of the war, and its small garrison of rather elderly housecarles had been preparing to fight to the death rather than surrender the harbour to what they thought was the Corsair fleet. When they were hailed in the language of the Icemark by the sailors and then by Maggie, they nearly collapsed with relief.

But their suspicions were aroused again when they saw the

warriors of the Desert People. Then when the Lusu appeared they raised their shield wall and refused to listen to any reason. It took the intervention of Sharley himself to pacify them, and even then they watched warily as the figure dressed in black armour limped slowly across the quayside towards them. As usual in times of stress, his gammy leg decided to exaggerate its condition, and he walked almost as badly as he did when he had first left the Icemark. It was only when he removed his helmet and barked at the old soldiers in the language of the parade ground that that they finally began to listen. Here was a true son of the Icemark, and not only that – as several of the old soldiers who'd once served in Frostmarris could clearly see – here was a scion of Queen Thirrin's Royal House.

"Housecarles of the Icemark, I am Prince Charlemagne Athelstan Redrought Strong-in-the-Arm Lindenshield, known as Shadow of the Storm, and youngest son of our ruler and Queen. I have returned from exile and have brought with me an army of new allies: the Desert People of history and legend, and the Lusu people of the fabled continent of Arifica." He stared unwaveringly at the shield wall that was still locked solid across the quayside. "Who of you will contest the landing of an army that can finally push the hated Bellorum far from our lands?"

A murmur ran through the ranks of the veteran housecarles, then at last a voice rang out, "None of us!"

Sharley smiled. "Good! Then stop arsing about and put down your weapons."

A huge cheer rose up and the old soldiers ran forward to greet him. As one they laid their shields and axes, spears and swords at his feet. "Lead us to war! Lead us to war!" they shouted, and suddenly all of the doors and windows of the houses that lined the harbour were thrown open and hundreds of people poured out cheering and waving.

Sharley was amazed. He thought he'd taken most of the civilian population into exile when he'd first left the Icemark. But all thoughts and questions were driven from his mind as he was swamped by the throng of ecstatic people. After months of fear and bad news from the front, here was hope once again; here was a chance to fight back against the Empire!

The veteran housecarles immediately remembered their duties, and taking up their weapons they formed a bodyguard about the Prince and forced the people back. Sharley had made it home, and for a few minutes at least, everyone was going to enjoy the sense of relief.

Medea was seized by a coughing spasm of shock and hatred. Charlemagne! Charlemagne was home! She ran to the windows of her tower, turning her Eye instinctively to the coast and to Michael's Bay, where Sharley's armoured foot had stepped from the gangplank of his ship and placed itself firmly on the quayside. She shook with unbridled rage, her white, icy skin beaded with a cold sweat that trickled delicate, lacy designs of hatred all over her body.

He had come back! Against all of her hopes and plans the hated snotling was back! So engrossed had she been in the struggle for Frostmarris that her Eye had failed her, and it wasn't until he'd physically set foot on the soil of the Icemark that she'd finally become aware of his presence.

Here he was, the reason and root of her inability to embrace the cause of the Icemark, her family, humanity, the mortal world . . . everything! She wasn't responsible for her actions. Sharley was.

Her Eye raged across the distance between her tower and the quayside of Michael's Bay, and there before her lay the fleet and the army of allies. She was incredulous, and bitterly, acidly furious. They could break the siege of Frostmarris! Immediately she began to withdraw. She must warn Bellorum!

But then she stopped: there on the quayside was Sharley himself. Dressed in strange armour and moving with barely a trace of a limp, he mounted a beautiful black horse and joined another boy. Together they rode up into the town, casually acknowledging the salutes of a weird collection of soldiers as they went.

Medea could have screamed until she threw up! Her hated little brother had achieved what he'd always wanted. He'd become a warrior, and a respected one at that, judging by the soppy expressions of adoration on the faces of the soldiers who saluted him. For fully ten minutes her mind howled and raged through the streets of Michael's Bay, bringing a storm of hail and freezing wind that ripped shutters off hinges and smashed open doors.

Suddenly she stopped. Her vehemence controlled by her acute intelligence, she was at last beginning to think. Quietly, she returned to watch Sharley and his exotic-looking friend. They were obviously close. She could exploit that. How crushed would Sharley be if anything was to happen to his special little friend? Oh, what glory would be a death that crushed her little brother with an unending grief. Or, better still, a betrayal from one loved and trusted. Perhaps now was the time to use her ability to possess the body and mind of a victim.

Medea laughed, her evil mirth translating itself over the

distance to an icy blast of wind that struck Mekhmet like a fist.

Mekhmet's horse Jaspat reared, pawing the air with his battle-trained hooves. Only the Desert Prince's brilliance as a horseman saved him from a bad fall. "Where did that come from?" he said as the wind blasted away into the sky.

"Same place as the squall that did all that damage in the town just now, I should think," Sharley answered. "Are you all right?"

"Fine. Let's get the horses stabled and safe inside before any more weather happens."

Medea's spirit form sailed above them, her brilliant mind already weaving its plans. She quickly assessed the allied army's numbers. Sharley's army was nowhere near big enough to threaten Bellorum, so it would be much more satisfying to let him reach Frostmarris and ultimately fail.

"NO! Better even than that," she screamed aloud, "let him reach the city and see it burning. And then . . ."

Her voice roared across the sky above Michael's Bay, but to the soldiers and citizens it sounded like the thunder of an approaching storm.

The Vampire Queen hung suspended on a thread of flight. The last echoes of her Consort's despairing cry still hung in the air, and her entire frame shook as the terrible meaning of it entered her mind. He was gone. He had left her to face all eternity alone. The man who had existed with her down the long, long centuries had been released into oblivion, leaving her to go on without his companionship, without his presence, and now – it had to be admitted at last – without his love.

All around her the Vampire squadrons screeched and

wailed in despair, but she remained silent, her mouth stretched around a scream that refused to sound. At last she closed her wings and fell, tumbling slowly to the earth like a black leaf from a giant tree. Her Vampires watched in silence as they ceased their own lamentations in honour of her greater loss.

Her faithful chamberlain, Legosi, dived after her, racing through the air to catch her and bear her up before she hit the ground. Others joined him, and together they climbed skywards with her unresisting body. Her mind had fled for a moment, leaving the void that was to be the rest of her existence, but now it returned and she opened her eyes to the renewed knowledge of the King's death.

"Leave me," she said in a toneless voice, and her courtiers flew a short distance away to watch her and wait.

She looked to where her Consort's existence had ceased, and she bowed her head. "How, *how* will I go on, my lost love? What point could there possibly be to this undying state without you to give it shape and meaning?"

She drew a deep breath and the scream came, erupting from her body with all the despair and pain of the centuries she'd known, and all those she'd yet to know. Such was the howl of despair, that the armies on the land below drew apart and gazed into the sky.

Thirrin shuddered, recognising the cry for what it was. "He's dead, Tharaman. The Vampire King is dead!" And, bowing her head, she surprised herself by weeping for the reluctant ally who had become her friend despite all that stood against the very idea of such a friendship.

The giant Snow Leopard drew breath and gave the coughing bark that honoured the valiant fallen, and all along the defences the cry was taken up by his warriors. The human soldiers joined in, beating spear, sword and axe on shield, and the werewolves keened their note of mourning.

But then something new insinuated itself into the sky – a thin, high-pitched note that climbed higher and higher, growing in strength until it seemed to fill the entire sky and land. It raged and bawled as a great bellowing note of fury roared over the plain of Frostmarris. The Vampire Queen gave vent to all the seething wrath of ages, and now her only desire was revenge.

She screeched again and again, and with her screeched her Vampires. The Queen now started to fly, slowly at first as she gathered her squadrons, but then with ever-increasing speed as they swooped down the slopes of flight and raged down on the Sky Navy's flagship where the King had been destroyed.

Bellorum saw them coming and quickly issued orders to reload the cannons with wooden grapeshot. The musketeers stood ready and the sky-sailors drew their cutlasses and waited. The Vampires rolled over the air like an ominously billowing storm cloud, then swept up and out of sight as they climbed above the trajectory of the cannon and dropped like black hail on to the giant canopy of the galleon.

The huge ship vibrated as the Vampires leaped on to its rigging. Gunshots were then heard as the crew defending the canopy fired. But soon their bodies sailed by on their journey downwards to the earth. Most were silent, their ruined throats sending out great gushing fountains of red, but some screeched in terror as they fell to their deaths.

As a great General, Bellorum knew when a tactical retreat was wisest, and after giving the order for the ship to descend he withdrew below decks to the cabins, where he removed all insignia of his rank and anything else that would identify him as a Polypontian officer.

Above his head he could hear muskets being fired by the ranks in quick succession, and the enraged shrieks of Vampires as they exacted revenge for the death of their King. He worked quickly, casting aside his lace and finery, constantly looking up to the ceiling as though he expected the Vampire Queen to burst through the planking at any minute. The wounds inflicted by the Vampire King were stiffening, but such was the adrenalin as he hurried to make his escape, he hardly felt the pain. Finally he collected a bulky pack from a chest, then crept out of his cabin and made his way through dark corridors and down stairways into the bowels of the huge ship. The route was completely deserted as the entire crew fought to save their ship from the wrath of the undead Queen.

Without warning, a Vampire burst out of the shadows before him. With a sweep of his sword he decapitated it, and walked contemptuously over its dissolving body. At last, he reached the huge holds where the barrel-bombs were kept. He found the required lever, and opened the hatchway. He listened to the battle raging on above his head, and knew that his flagship was lost. No matter. Everything would be more than compensated for, once the Icemark was defeated.

He looked down through the hatchway at the world spread out below him. He could clearly see the land army retreating from the defences of Frostmarris, as once again the contemptible little force of defenders managed to fend off the finest military machine in the known world. Revenge, when it inevitably came, would be superlatively sweet. As he strapped on the bulky pack he'd brought with him from the cabin, he amused himself with the happy thought of executing all of the officers in front of the rank and file once he had defeated them. Then, without a moment's hesitation, he stepped to the edge of the hatchway and leaped out.

As he fell he knew he would be just one more body falling from the embattled ship. No Vampire would follow; as far as they were aware he was as good as dead, if not actually dead already. When he judged the moment to be right, he pulled the cord that opened the pack, and the wide canopy of finely woven silk opened above him like a beautiful bloom.

He was jolted from his wild, careering fall, and floated serenely over the plain of Frostmarris. Fortunately the wind was blowing towards his camp on the hills to the south, and with a bit of luck he wouldn't have far to walk. This was the third jump he'd made with a para-descender, as the Imperial scientists called it. Soon it would be ready to be issued to every galleon in the fleet, but in the meantime he was more than happy to be a "guinea pig".

The Vampire Queen screamed in hating elation as the flag-ship burned. She watched as it suddenly lurched to one side and finally fell in a slow tumble as the flames burned through the rigging and the canopy exploded.

But now the pain of her loss returned, and with a screech of rage, she led her squadrons to attack the rest of the fleet. Hundreds of wasp-fighters were ripped from the sky, and dozens of the bomber galleons fell in flaming ruin to explode on the plain of Frostmarris, and yet still nothing could soothe the pain of loss, or fill the void left by the death of the King.

Eventually, Her Vampiric Majesty drew back her squadrons in pure exhaustion and, after gazing out at the empty space where her Consort's existence had ended, she turned and flew away to the north with her fighters, leaving behind the cause of the Icemark and the alliance, abandoning

Frostmarris to the mercy of the Empire and its flotilla of bombers.

Frostmarris burned. For three nights in a row and most of the daylight hours the bomber galleons had attacked, dropping thousands of tons of gunpowder on to the streets, destroying houses and barracks, gatehouses and citadels.

The Vampire squadrons had gone, retreating north in their grief to mourn the loss of their King, and though the giant ballistas of the air defences had brought down dozens of the colossal airships, and hundreds of the wasp-fighters, there were always more to replace them. Without Her Vampiric Majesty and her undead warriors and Snowy Owls, the skies were controlled by the Empire.

The firefighting housecarles and werewolves were led by Archimedo Archimedes in their valiant efforts to save the city from destruction. Rescue teams dug through the rubble of destroyed houses to reach those trapped inside, and poured gallons of water on to burning buildings using the pumps designed by the little engine-eer. But for every life they saved, five were lost, and for every fire they doused, ten more raged out of control.

The physical form of the city was broken and burned. Slowly, night by night, raid after raid, Frostmarris was dying. But deep beneath the streets, in the network of caverns where no bomb could reach, the spirit of the city lived on. Here the people took shelter and waited with a hope that was fading by the hour. Who could come to their rescue now? All of the allies were with them: the Snow Leopards, the werewolves and the Hypolitan. The Vampires had fled and there was no one left to come to their aid. But despite their fears, the spirit of resistance lived on. They told each other tales of the great heroes of legend, and of unexpected rescue from the most hopeless situations.

Thirrin and Oskan stood in the huge central cave that had been occupied by the Vampires. As the deep rumble and thunder of the bombing raid on the city echoed faintly through the caverns they looked out over a massive crowd of housecarles, Snow Leopards, werewolves and Hypolitan who waited expectantly. Before the dais where their Vampiric Majesties' abandoned thrones still stood was a tall imposing woman, dressed all in white and wearing a coronet of golden oak leaves. She was stern of face and silent, and stared straight ahead to the entrance of the cave as though waiting for some-one to enter.

After a few moments the Basilea of the Hypolitan appeared with Olememnon at her side. The crowd of warriors drew apart to form a natural aisle down which the couple processed arm in arm. Both wore circlets of flowers on their heads, and robes of light blue with long trains that were carried in the mouths of Tharaman-Thar and Krisafitsa-Tharina.

Thirrin smiled, and searched for Oskan's hand without taking her eyes off the couple as they approached the Priestess. She raised it to her lips and kissed it.

Oskan's face remained stony, but he squeezed his wife's hand in return. He was still amazed that this entire ceremony had been Cressida's idea. Obviously the Basilea and Olememnon were in agreement, but it had been the Crown Princess who'd first suggested it as a morale booster for the beleaguered defenders. Personally, Oskan thought the effort of organising the ceremony had been worth it just to see

Tharaman acting as pageboy. What more precious sight could there possibly be than the huge Thar of the Icesheets delicately holding Olememnon's train? Oh blessed, blessed relief! Something to laugh about, at last, in all of the horrors of the past few months!

The Basilea and Olememnon reached the dais where the Priestess waited, and bowed their heads to the representative of the Goddess.

"All those here present are called upon to witness the joining of these two people. Who will sponsor them in the eyes of the Goddess?"

"I will," said Cressida, stepping from amongst the gathered throng.

"Known to the Mother you undoubtedly are, but state your names and titles for those of mortal limits," the Priestess said, using the ancient formula of the service.

"I am Cressida Aethelflaed Elemnestra Strong-in-the-Arm Lindenshield, known as Striking Eagle," she said to an audience who all knew full well who she was.

The priestess nodded. "And who will guarantee the conduct of this male?" she said in reference to Olememnon.

"I will, you old hairy arse," Grishmak boomed happily, showing his huge teeth in a massive grin. Then, seeing the disapproving looks, he remembered himself and said, "I mean . . . I will, Ma'am: King Grishmak Blood-drinker, King of the Wolf-folk."

A quiet sniggering reached his sensitive ears, and he looked out over the crowd and spied his son Howler and Prince Eodred visibly shaking as they tried to control their laughter. Seeing his ferociously frowning face, they collapsed in a welter of spluttering and high-pitched squeaks.

The Priestess coughed meaningfully and silence descended. "Then let the woman and the man step forward under the eye of the Goddess and be joined in life and love."

Basilea Olympia took Olememnon's hand and led him to stand before the dais.

"The Goddess has decreed that companionship between people shall be blessed and solemnised by Her gracious presence. Know then that She is here and knows all your hearts, all your loves, all your fears, and all your hopes. Ask Her now in the quiet of your thoughts and, like the Mother She is, She will decide what shall be given for your greater good."

The huge cavern became charged with an atmosphere of desperate hope as all present prayed for deliverance from the wrath of Bellorum. Thirrin, too, asked for this, with a power and determination as befitted a warrior queen. But in the quiet moments between prayers for her country and people, her thoughts turned to Sharley, her youngest and most loved child. *"May he be safe, Goddess. May he be happy and live a long life after we have been wiped from the face of your earth,"* she prayed quietly. *"And may he always know that I loved him . . . my son, whose face I shall never see again, whose laughter I will never hear again. And may he know the love of a special one, as deep and as powerful as that I have known with Oskan, and may they walk down the years together in peace and contentment."*

"And now let us all bear witness to the union between this woman and this man," the Priestess called clearly into the cool air of the cave, drawing all of their minds back to the marriage ceremony.

"Olympia Artemision, Basilea of the Hypolitan, do you take this man, Olememnon, once of the surname Stagapoulos, and give to him your own name? Do you promise to control him and guide him and set to rights all of his male traits?"

"I do."

"Olememnon, soon to be Artemesion, do you accept this name and all restrictions upon your actions and conduct as decreed by Hypolitan law?"

"I do."

Tharaman-Thar spat Olememnon's long cloak out of his mouth. "Thank goodness for that! Can I have a drink now?"

Krisafitsa gently dropped the Basilea's train and turned to her mate. "You have about as much sense of style and occasion as a walrus with wind!"

Tharaman looked at her haughtily. "I am completely and fully aware that this is a highly important occasion, and one that befits . . . the biggest and best pie-eating competition ever! What do you think, Olly? The first one to be sick is the loser!"

Far above the caves, fires raged and roared through the streets of the city. On the walls a party of archers had had some success against the wasp-fighters, but now they were in danger of being cut off by the flames. They ran down the steps to street level, and coughing and choking on the smoke, they hurried to an intersection they recognised, and found the spiral stairs that descended to the caverns many feet below. The Commander of the small party waved his people ahead of him, and just before running down to safety himself he looked back over the blazing skyline. The night sky was red with reflected fires. Fallen roofs and broken walls stood stark and black against the searing yellows and oranges, blues and reds of the inferno that was destroying the city. Overhead, the black

shape of a galleon swept dangerously low, a scatter of gunpowder bombs tumbling from the open hatchway in its belly.

The Commander could clearly see a single tower rising
pristine and untouched by either bomb or flame, an undamaged island amidst the hellish chaos of the burning city. As
the barrels of gunpowder exploded all around, it remained
impervious, rising proud and defiant against the sky. A bomb
exploded nearby and the Commander fled below, still puzzling
over the undamaged tower.

Medea's Eye watched the man scuttle to safety, and she
smiled. She had no need of the bombing shelters; she was perfectly safe in her tower, protected as it was by her Gift. All
around its walls was a perfect microclimate that kept the
stonework at a comfortable temperature, and a constant mizzle of fine, drenching rain prevented anything flammable from
igniting. As for the bombs, well, air pressure was her forte. It
was the engine of weather, and as a Weather Witch it was
easy for her to counteract the percussion of explosions with an
equally explosive rise in air pressure. It had required a certain
amount of concentration, but over the past few nights she'd
become adept at reacting quickly and almost automatically to
dangers. So much so that her mind was now quite free to continue with her own thoughts and plans.

Sharley was riding towards Frostmarris. He would be here
in a matter of days, and she was determined to stop him. How
many years had she waited to destroy him? The final realisation would be so sweet. With a happy sigh, she watched the
city burn and savoured her brother's fast approaching death.

CHAPTER 35

The horses and zebras had been released into a series of paddocks and fields behind the harbour town. Some had barely been able to walk after their weeks of confinement, and much to Sharley and Mekhmet's horror, several had died in transit.

Thankfully, Suleiman, and Mekhmet's horse, Jaspat, had fared better than most, as they'd had stalls in the open air and had been walked about the deck whenever the weather allowed. But even so, both boys exercised their horses gently every day to slowly rebuild their strength and stamina. The human soldiers, too, needed fresh food and exercise before they'd be ready for the march inland, a delay that Sharley found almost unbearably frustrating.

But at least they were using the time to good effect. Maggie took charge of all intelligence-gathering, sending off the fittest townsfolk to investigate sources and find out what was going on. The little scholar had become a powerhouse of activity and efficiency; in fact, ever since setting foot on Icemark soil again, he seemed to grow younger by the day, zooming about the town like a youth of seventy and filling them all with his hope and energy.

For Mekhmet and all of the cavalry of the Desert Kingdom, everything was completely and utterly alien. Many of the soldiers found it impossible to believe there were no places of worship for the faithful. And the cold was a major problem; all the men had expected the chilling temperatures of the northern sea to give way to the proper warmth of the land once they'd docked, but here in this strange country it remained cold even when the sun shone. They'd acclimatise, given time, but until then most of the troopers rode about in their mountain gear.

It rained too, sometimes several times a day. Most of the troopers had never seen rain; they'd heard of it, and the vast majority of them had even believed in it, but now they'd had more than enough proof of its reality. Once there had even been a sprinkle of snow, even though the locals assured them it was summertime! Unfortunately, no one could predict how much time they would have to get used to the new conditions and prepare to march before Bellorum found out they were there. Maggie's spies had reported that there were no Polypontian soldiers north of the Great Forest, even though it would have been relatively easy to have transported soldiers around the barrier of the trees and land them in the north by using the Corsair fleet. Perhaps the great General hadn't wanted to split his force when he believed it wasn't actually necessary. After all, as far as he was aware, he had all of the allies trapped in Frostmarris and no one expected any relieving army to come to their rescue, not even the allies themselves. By concentrating his forces around the capital city, he could ensure its capture, after which it would be simplicity itself to destroy the northern towns with their small garrisons one at a time.

"It seems we still have the element of surprise on our side," said Maggie one night as the High Command of Sharley, Mekhmet and Ketshaka sat discussing tactics in the Guild Hall of the town. "But it's imperative that we strike soon, before our presence is discovered."

"I agree," said Ketshaka. "Most of the animals and soldiers are now fit enough to make a start. They'll build up strength and increase stamina as we go. After all, on the march they'll certainly be exercising every day, and with fresh food and water their recovery rate should be rapid."

"So all we have to do is agree a day to start," said Sharley. "Maggie, are all supply lines established?"

"Such as they are, yes. But it's high summer, we'll be able to forage as we go along. The peasants may have a hungry winter as a result, but the sacrifice will have to be made."

"All right. Then I suggest we begin the day after tomorrow. All agreed?"

The following day was taken up with briefing all officers and organising the line and order of march. When everything was finally ready, Sharley almost panicked again. If he and his army failed to relieve Frostmarris and push Bellorum back to the border, then everything would be finally and utterly lost. There'd be no second chance; everything depended on arriving unexpectedly and breaking the Imperial hold.

He'd ridden Suleiman to the top of a nearby hill that overlooked the town and the fields beyond where the army was mustering. As he looked at the ragged horses and zebras and the troopers who were getting them into some sort of marching order, he felt suddenly exhausted. How could they take on the finest army in the known world? They had only a thousand infantry of any worth, in the form of the Hellenic

marines, and the rest of the foot units were made up of rowers from the galleys, armed only with short cutlasses and a
belief in their own strength. They'd be smashed instantly by
the Imperial shield-bearers or pike phalanxes. The cavalry
needed a strong anchor of solid infantry to provide support
and backup.

The sound of approaching hoofbeats made Sharley pause in
his gloom, and he turned to watch as Mekhmet rode up.

"Now, how does it go? . . . 'Look at the ridiculous ragged
little force we're sending against Bellorum. What chance do
we have?'" said the Crown Prince, mimicking Sharley's northern accent perfectly. "'Oh woe, oh doom!'"

"It's not funny. We won't have a chance. Look at the
housecarles we've got – not one is under fifty, and most are
nearer seventy. How can we possibly expect them to fight
Bellorum's madmen?"

"But you're forgetting something important . . . they *want*
to fight them. One willing soldier, no matter how old, is worth
at least five who've been forced to fight."

"Maybe, and I might take comfort from that thought if I
didn't know that most Imperial soldiers actually enjoy what
they do. They're professionals; it's their job to invade, kill and
maim, and they're good at it."

Mekhmet took his friend's hand and squeezed it. "You're
underestimating your soldiers. We can do it. We may be a little tired right now, but give us a few days and we'll be fine.
And don't forget the Great Forest. You keep talking about the
Holly King and the Oak King – their forces will make us a
truly formidable host."

"If they'll join us. I don't even know if I can communicate
with them yet. I've only ever seen my dad summon them, and

he's a warlock. I have about as much Magical power as a table leg."

Mekhmet finally lost his temper. "LOOK! If you're going to find miserable answers to every solution then you might as well give up. Let's load everything back on the ships and we can sail home now. 'Sorry we're back so early, but we thought we didn't have a chance so we gave up without trying.' That would look really good, wouldn't it?"

Sharley shrugged crossly. "I never said we'd give up; I'm just having a bit of a wallow."

"Well, stop it! We've got an army to lead, and most of the troopers haven't stopped being seasick yet, so we can all do without your miseries on top of everything else. All right?"

"All right," Sharley agreed sheepishly.

"Good. Now let's go back to town and get an early night. It might be the last chance we get to sleep in a bed for some time."

Sharley grinned. "Yes, *Dad*."

The army set out at sunrise. They made an impressive sight: twin columns of cavalry made up of Lusu and Desert Kingdom troopers, and a sizeable body of infantry led by the Hellenic marines and the town's housecarles. The rowers from the fleet followed behind them and made a good attempt to march in step and keep ranks.

The citizens of the harbour town certainly seemed impressed, and their cheering was quite out of proportion to their small numbers.

Once beyond the town, the army made quite good time and Sharley began to relax a bit. He hoped to reach the Great Forest in two days, and following a further march through the trees, he then hoped to emerge on to the plain of Frostmarris two days after that. As to whether he'd manage to increase the size of the army by making contact with the Holly and Oak Kings, that remained to be seen. He'd decided there was just too much to worry about and too much that could go wrong, and that the only way to cope was to refuse to think about any of it. It was enough of a task just to get through the first day.

The weather was perfect for marching, with a coolish wind and bright sunshine. Ketshaka and her Lusu warriors seemed to have adapted well to the strange land, and they all sang as they marched along. But the Desert People, apart from Mekhmet, seemed to be in a state of collective culture shock. How was it possible for a land to absorb so much rain without actually being washed away, and how could the sun shine with so little heat? And everywhere was so green! It was almost as though a palace garden had decided to march on the surrounding land and conquer it with its plants and trees. It didn't seem natural.

Sharley had been a little concerned about their unhappiness, but Mekhmet had assured him that they were simply indulging in every soldier's inalienable right to have a good moan. They'd soon settle down.

By nightfall the army had covered half the distance to the Great Forest. Camp was set up quickly, with picket guards set at regular intervals around the perimeter and an armed guard on the horse lines. Sharley was taking no chances; he might be on home territory, and in a region where the Empire had yet to advance, but he wasn't going to risk anything stopping him going to the rescue of Frostmarris.

They were camped on a wide, undulating area of grassland,

and as darkness fell the cooking fires reflected the night sky perfectly in fiery constellations. Ketshaka was with her Lusus and Maggie was busily writing up his notes. Sharley and Mekhmet sat alone at the entrance of their tent. The Prince of the Desert Kingdom knew that this was the most testing and difficult time for his friend, but there was nothing he could do to help him. Every soldier and warrior in the camp that night was risking everything to fight the Empire, but for Sharley there was the added pressure that his family and homeland were in danger of being destroyed. What comfort could anyone offer in the face of such fears?

"You'll like her, Mekhmet," Sharley said as he stared into the flames of the campfire.

"Who?"

"My mother. You'll like Dad too, but he's a bit more . . . remote."

"Oh," his friend answered non-committally. He'd spent a few minutes saying goodbye to his own mother just before they'd set off from the Desert Kingdom, mainly because Sharley had been so shocked that he'd been prepared to leave without seeing her at all. It was a painful memory. He'd been more affected by her tears and kisses than he thought he'd be, and much more than he'd wanted to be. He'd promised himself then that if he survived the war and became Sultan, he'd change some of the Desert Kingdom's laws on women.

"She's funny."

"Um, funny?" said Mekhmet, dragging his attention back to his friend.

"Yes, my mother. She used to make me laugh when I was little, and she always knew when I was in one of my moods and what to do to get me out of it."

"Yes. You've told me that before. It must have been . . . nice to have your mother with you when you were growing up."

Sharley suddenly moved closer to put his arm around Mekhmet's shoulders. "I'm sorry, friend. I was forgetting you didn't really see your mother when you were a kid."

"Well, no. But that doesn't matter. I didn't know any different. Still, you make it sound like I missed something special."

Sharley nodded silently. "Never mind. You can share mine when we get to Frostmarris. With five kids I'm sure she could squeeze another one in."

Mekhmet suspected that this was a great honour, but didn't quite know how to react to it. So he was relieved when Sharley stood up with a frown on his face and his head cocked to one side as though listening.

"Can you hear that?"

"Do you mean the jackal howling?"

"We don't have jackals in the Icemark."

"A wolf, then."

"No! That's not a—" and suddenly he let out a howl that rose into the air and echoed far and wide over the camp.

Mekhmet leaped to his feet, convinced Sharley had gone mad, or was possessed. Armed guards came running and pandemonium broke out all around.

"Be quiet! I can't hear the reply!"

"Reply? Reply to what?"

"The message from the Wolf-folk, of course! Now, all of you be quiet!" He looked so fierce and so convincing that silence fell, and a thin, distant wailing sounded on the air. After a few seconds of silent frowning, Sharley howled again with amazing power and realism, his voice rising into the air and echoing on the stillness.

"Right, call a general stand-to. I want everyone on parade and ready to listen to me in less than ten minutes. Understood?"

The guards ran off, accepting his orders at face value. If the Northern Prince had gone mad, they'd find out soon enough; in the meantime it was their job to obey.

Maggie appeared, breathless and excited. Mekhmet almost wept with relief. At least Maggie would know how to deal with what he hoped was Sharley's temporary madness.

"What did it say? What did it say?" the old scholar bellowed as he ran up, disappointing Mekhmet mightily. Now he had two madmen to deal with!

"She's part of a group who didn't manage to return to Frostmarris before it was besieged. They've been trying to get back for several weeks now, but the Polypontian lines are too strongly drawn, and the trails through the forest have been disrupted by . . . 'bombs'. I didn't quite understand that bit. Perhaps it'll become clearer later."

"Oh, this is wonderful. They'll be able to give us all the information we need. How many of them are there?"

"That's the best bit, Maggie. Including her own patrol and five others that were also marooned, as well as the northern and southern operatives of the werewolf relay and sundry survivors from the garrisons of fallen towns—"

"Yes? Yes?" Maggie asked breathlessly.

"There are five hundred Wolf-folk and three hundred housecarles!"

Mekhmet stepped back and watched in amazement as the old man pulled up his robes and danced around the campfire like a teenager. "We have a proper infantry now! We have a proper infantry now!"

"Yes, we have. But listen. We've got to get them safe conduct into the camp. I've told them to wait until I give the word. That's why I've called a general stand-to. I'm going to have to explain things to the army."

Ketshaka took the news of werewolves with ease. To a people who had experience of the Laughing Ones, the Wolf-folk seemed a very ordinary prospect. And as an experienced tactician, she was also well aware of their lack of infantry and of the new arrivals' importance in that regard.

"The Great Spirits are smiling on you, Charlemagne my son," she said as they rode to address the gathered ranks of the army. "Remember to give them due honour by using their Gift well."

"I intend to," he said with determination.

It was a matter of a few minutes to explain to the soldiers exactly who the Wolf-folk were and their circumstances, and without realising it, in doing so he also enhanced his own standing as a commander immeasurably. Not only could he gather and control an army of a multiplicity of peoples, but he also had the loyalty of beings who, if he was to be believed, were strange, powerful and intelligent to a high degree.

"To some of you the werewolves will appear strange and even terrible, but there is nothing to fear. The Wolf-folk are our most loyal allies. I will now call them and they will march into our camp. Remember that these people and their human comrades have been fighting a war for many months. They'll be tired, and wary of treachery. They know that I am here, but it wouldn't be impossible for me to be a captive and under the control of the Empire. Even though I've used certain words and codes in our communications that have reassured them to a certain extent, they'll still be suspicious. Make no movement or noise as they approach. Leave it all to me."

Sharley nodded in the following silence, and rode Suleiman a little apart from the ranks of his army. Then, drawing breath, he howled loud and long into the night sky. A low murmur ran through the assembled regiments, but they immediately fell silent as a reply sounded from surprisingly close by.

In less than two minutes the steady tread of marching feet began to sound across the night, and then the massed ranks of three hundred housecarles began to emerge from the textured shadows. As they drew nearer it became clear that their lines were made up of alternating human soldiers and huge, dark figures that marched in perfect step with them. Then, as they entered the pool of light thrown by two massive campfires and the torches that Mekhmet's and Ketshaka's troopers carried, the ferocious teeth, long claws and glittering eyes of the were-wolves became apparent.

A murmur like a gentle wind ran through the watching army, but died away to silence as the new arrivals stamped to a halt. Sharley was almost beside himself with excitement. At last, here were trained housecarles and some of the Icemark's most loyal friends and allies, the Wolf-folk! He could have screamed with relief, but he knew he had to show restraint. One wrong move, or even the tiniest suspicion of treachery, and it could all go horribly wrong.

Gently he urged Suleiman forward. The battle-trained warhorse whickered nervously, but trusting his rider he loyally followed commands. Sharley reined to a halt as a particularly large werewolf stepped out of the ranks to meet him.

Mekhmet's palms were sweating with tension. Sharley looked tiny before the huge creature that towered over him and Suleiman both. His friend could be crushed before his eyes, and there wouldn't be time to do anything about it! Silently he offered up a prayer to the One, and tried to remember to breathe.

Sharley wore no helmet or headdress, so that the red hair of the House of Lindenshield could be seen, and as the werewolf approached he smiled in greeting. Then he and the huge creature began to make strange growling and yelping noises that rose and fell with a rhythm almost like words.

It took Mekhmet several tense moments to realise that they were actually talking. He was almost breathless with fear for his friend, and when Sharley dismounted and stood before the massive creature, Mekhmet thought he'd be sick. But he couldn't afford the distraction of vomiting – he needed to see what was going on.

For several more minutes the strange yelping and growling continued as Sharley stood before the monster like a small red-headed torch in front of a bank of impenetrable darkness. Then amazingly the werewolf slowly fell to its knees before the slight figure of his friend, and Sharley suddenly rushed forward and hugged it! Mekhmet let out an explosive sigh of relief, and was aghast to see that there were tears on the creature's hairy face.

Sharley took the werewolf's paws, raised it to its feet, and turning to the army of allies he said, "Behold Captain Bonesplitter and her command of infantry, loyal allies and friends!"

The release of tension spilled into the night in a glorious torrent of cheering. Spears beat on shields, horses neighed and zebras hiccupped. The Empire would look upon their ranks and tremble!

"Gentlemen, the city is ripe for plucking," said Scipio Bellorum, addressing the Staff Officers who sat in respectful silence around the map table. "The Vampire King is dead, the Vampire Queen has retreated to her fetid eyries in the far north, and the skies are ours alone."

He was enjoying himself enormously. His two sons, Sulla and Octavius, smiled with him, like corroded mirrors reflecting their father's power.

"The obvious consequence has been the unopposed bombing of Frostmarris. Our little Queenling no longer has a castle in which to sit, and soon she will no longer have a country to rule. Now, are there any questions?"

"Yes, Sir," said a young Captain of Dragoons. "When do we go in and wipe them out?"

Bellorum's smile broadened. The officers of the most recently arrived reinforcements had none of the reservations and worries of the more experienced soldiers. That may have had its disadvantages at times, but it was so refreshing to hear the note of enthusiasm again from his men. For too long the army had been fighting a two-front war: one with the defenders and allies of the Icemark, and one with their own pessimism.

"We will 'go in and wipe them out', as you so eloquently put it, tomorrow night," he answered.

A murmur ran around the table as the veterans of the campaign muttered their worries. "But, Sir. The defences are still unbreached and the allies a formidable fighting force. We'll lose thousands if we try to storm them."

"And you are . . .?"

"Major Lucius Primus Orestus, Sir."

"I see that you're an officer of the Dacian Shield-Bearers, Major Orestus."

"Yes, Sir."

"Your regiment will lead the assault tomorrow night, targeting Queen Thirrin and Tharaman-Thar, and you will not retreat. Do I make myself clear?"

The officer paled slightly. "Yes, Sir."

"Haven't you forgotten something?" Bellorum asked, his voice silken ice.

"Sir?"

"It is customary at this juncture to tell me that your, admittedly suicidal, role in the battle will be an honour. Am I to presume from your reticence that you find your appointed task less than pleasing?"

"No, Sir. It is indeed an honour, Sir."

"Oh good, I'm *so* pleased, otherwise I might have been tempted to send you and your entire regiment into battle unarmed and naked."

"Then the Queen would refuse to harm them. Her sense of honour wouldn't allow it," a voice clearly murmured.

"Who said that?" Bellorum snapped, glaring round the table. "Sulla, Octavius, did you see?"

"No, Father," said Octavius smoothly. "But it would give me enormous pleasure to . . . *question* any suspects."

Bellorum quickly calculated the consequences and thought better of it. "No matter. When this war is won, due payments will be received by all my officers."

There was too much dissent in the camp, but searching it out would only cause more discontent. It was hardly surprising. An army camp was a microcosm of the government and land that it served, and at the present time the Empire was in turmoil. The Senate was pushing for Bellorum's withdrawal from the Icemark so that he could deal with the war that was raging in the south.

The Desert Kingdom had woken from its torpor with a vengeance, and five major cities and countless towns had already fallen to the Sultan and his hordes. And to make matters worse, he'd defeated an Imperial army in a set-piece battle less than two weeks previously. Venezzia and their allies the Hellenes had also seized ports and harbours and defeated two fleets in the Southern Ocean. It was all too painfully reminiscent of events that had followed Bellorum's last invasion of the Icemark. But this time the rebellions and invasions had begun before his plans had been defeated. There was obviously collusion at work.

Once the Icemark had fallen he'd strike south with a wrath that would become the stuff of legends! Governments would fall, the seas would be paved with Venezzian dead, deserts would be irrigated with the Sultan's blood. The Empire would be saved and its borders extended . . . but first, the Icemark must be defeated.

"Tomorrow night, then, gentlemen. We will attack by the light of the city in flames. You all know your positions and roles, and you all know what the Empire expects of you," said Bellorum, his voice quiet and cutting. "Oh, and one further thought. You should know that I invoke the curse of the Deus Imperator. Silly superstition, I know; there is no such thing as the God of the Empire, and furthermore, it is a ridiculous belief that a government of such impeccable credentials of Reason and Logic should reject out of hand. But, times are as they are, and the belief that any soldier who does not give his *all* for his homeland will die by the slowest of degrees in pain and complete degradation, his name and family to be reviled and hated throughout the far lands of all the Imperial possessions, may provide the more reluctant among us with an added incentive." He smiled around at his officers. "Oh, and believe me: superstition or not, it will work, because I personally will be the instrument of the curse. Look for me after the war is won; I will be standing at your shoulder in the darkened room; I will be waiting in the unfamiliar alleyway; mine will be the knock at the door in the dead of night . . ."

The officers stood, saluted, and filed from the map room in silence.

The bombing had continued, day and night, for more than a week. The giant ballistas of the air defences had brought down dozens of the galleons, but many more sailed on to drench the city in fire and explosions. Few buildings remained unscathed, and in several areas entire streets had been flattened, or blazed uncontrollably.

No one but the firefighters moved above ground in Frostmarris, and even down on the defences the soldiers were forced to hide away between land attacks in deeply dug shelters, as the galleons turned their attention to the concentric rings of earthworks that surrounded the capital. Sometimes they also bombed the forest, bringing down huge swathes of trees and briefly setting fire to the canopy before the flames mysteriously spluttered out. But the city remained the main target of the Sky Galleons and wasp-fighters; it hadn't stopped burning for days, and the wasp-fighters poured more and more pitch on to the flames with every pass they made. It was as though they wanted to reduce the very stones to ash.

On the defences, Thirrin and most of her High Command were all squeezed into one of the shelters dug under the outer ring of the earthworks. There was a lull in the bombing, but the werewolves hadn't yet given their signal for the "all clear", so they continued to wait in the twilight cast by a single oil lamp.

"Is there anything to eat?" asked Tharaman.

"Is there anything to drink?" asked Grishmak.

"My belly's rumbling louder than those bomb thingies. I don't think I've had a morsel or crumb since—"

"An hour ago," Krisafitsa interrupted, "when you ate half an ox for breakfast. It really is fortunate we have no problems with supplies, thanks to the access we have to the forest."

"Are you sure it was half an ox? I thought it was about a quarter of a sheep," Tharaman insisted.

"Half an ox. I know because it was a leftover from the 'small snack' you had for supper."

"There should be a barrel around here somewhere," said Grishmak distractedly. "Commander Gunhild usually has some small refreshments stashed away to keep her going through her watch."

"You nicked it yesterday, Grishmak," said Cressida. "Don't you remember, you said you were going to replace it?"

"Oh, bum," came the quiet reply.

"They could be about to launch another land attack. Anyone want to take a peek and check?" asked Thirrin. Silence followed. "Oh, all right, I'll go."

"There's no need," said Cressida. "The galleons are on their way back."

"How can you tell? You can't hear them, surely?" said Thirrin.

"Well, yes, actually. Can't you? There! Didn't you hear the creaking of ropes and canvas?"

"No. Your ears must be very—" A huge explosion nearby drowned out everything, and was swiftly followed by other booms and rumblings all along the defences.

"I suppose I could try earthworms," said Tharaman mournfully. "That last explosion brought down quite a bit of soil from the roof and they're all over my fur. I should imagine they'd be quite nutritious."

"Don't you dare even consider it!" Krisafitsa snapped. "Disgusting things!"

"Oh, I don't know. At least there's no bones, and if you think about it there's probably more meat, pound for pound, on an earthworm than there is on the fattest ox."

"Oh, *please!*" said Krisafitsa. "Forget it, Tharaman – you're not eating earthworms. In fact, come over here where I can give your coat a good clean. I'm not having them burrowing into your fur – heaven knows what damage they could do in the long term."

A fraught few minutes followed, during which toes were trod on, heads were bumped and chairs were knocked over while the huge King of the Snow Leopards tried to manoeuvre himself around in the tiny space. "Sorry," he said sincerely. "Bit of a tight spot here."

"Yes, indeed," said Thirrin quietly. "Tighter than any of us have been in before, I'm afraid."

A silence followed. Everyone knew that she was referring to the war and to their almost inevitable defeat.

"We're not beaten yet, old girl," said Tharaman at last.

"Where there's life there's hope, and all that, don't you know?"

"Well, there's *life* for some of us at the moment, certainly. But what about hope?"

"There's that too, my dear. Who knows what will happen. Tomorrow's another day."

"Tharaman, you're beginning to sound like a book of old sayings and clichés!"

"Perhaps, but it's true. We were pretty desperate in the last war, but Grishmak and the Vampires turned up in the nick of time. You just never know what's going to happen."

"I think we know this time, though," Thirrin insisted quietly. "There's no one to come to the rescue at the last minute. We're all here already, trapped in Frostmarris." She fell quiet, but there was something in her tone that made them all wait for her to go on.

"Actually – come to think of it – we're not *completely* trapped, are we? Krisafitsa mentioned it earlier."

"Mentioned what?" asked Cressida.

"The fact that we have access to the forest. The defensive rings are open-ended in the trees, where we presume we're defended by the soldiers of the Holly and Oak Kings. At any rate, no Imperial soldiers have ever managed to get in that way."

"And what has that got to do with anything?" asked Grishmak.

"Quite simple, really. Some of us could escape through the forest, go north to a port and sail to safety. Who knows, per-haps you could raise another army one day and come back. You could even go to Sharley and help him in exile . . ." her voice trailed away as she thought of her youngest child. The time was almost here when she'd close her eyes for ever and never see him again.

"None of us would go, and it's too late anyway," said Cressida with determination. "Anyone with half a tactical brain could see that Bellorum's ready for his endgame. If the big push doesn't come tonight, it'll be tomorrow morning, and no doubt the old monster's watching our defences so closely that no one could slip away without him knowing it."

"All very true," said Grishmak. "Which means we're just going to have to make a fight of it. And who knows, we just might bloody Bellorum's Imperial nose so badly, he'll die of a haemorrhage. I certainly intend to try."

"You and me both. What do you say, Thirrin?" asked Krisafitsa, hoping to distract the Queen from her thoughts of Sharley.

"I think I'm the most fortunate of women," she answered quietly. "Who else could claim to have friends who were willing both to fight for her and to die with her?"

"Yes, well, we're not dead yet," said Tharaman decisively. "Let's see what the next round of fighting brings us."

"That's easy to predict," said Cressida. "The walls of the city are breached in several places, the citadel is virtually rubble and what remains is burning. The only defences we have left are these earth banks and our fighting ability. And if the shield wall is broken at any point, we're lost. Bellorum knows this, we know it – in fact everyone from the smallest drummer boy to the mightiest warrior knows it. The next land attack will be the last. I suggest we make what peace we can with whomever and whatever we worship, and prepare ourselves for the end."

The room fell deathly silent as each of them digested this

devastating analysis of their position. The enormity of it was overpowering. The Icemark was about to fall. They'd fought a long and intelligent campaign, thwarting almost everything that Bellorum had thrown at them. In fact, if their armies and resources had been equal in size to those of the Empire, the Imperial war machine would have been defeated months ago, and with a bit of luck they'd have captured the hated General and executed him. But as usual, they were just outnumbered – devastatingly so, overwhelmingly so. And now that the Vampires had withdrawn they had no answer to the Sky Navy either.

The only comfort they could possibly derive from their appalling situation was to know that their struggle would become legend. If they but knew it, their names were already known throughout the Empire and, ironically, the Imperial Senate was close to overruling Bellorum and suing for peace. Everyone, from the Emperor himself to the Inner Cabinet of Governance, was in awe of the Icemark and its allies. What a friend such a powerful and determined enemy would make! But for the time being Bellorum's cronies still had control of the Senate, and the war would continue until all defenders of the Icemark were dead.

Time was running out for Thirrin and her friends, and they had to accept it. Eventually, Grishmak scratched his massive head as though trying to dislodge all of the horror and pessimism. Then he shrugged. "Anyone know any good jokes?" he asked.

But before anyone could reply, the mournful howling of the werewolves' "all clear" sounded. The bombers had gone, and now the land attack would begin.

CHAPTER 36

The Great Forest rose up before them like a solid wall, and even with his army and friends riding beside him, Sharley couldn't help feeling nervous – *very* nervous.

"Well, this is it," he said, trying to keep his voice steady. "The last leg of the journey. On the other side of the trees we'll come out on the plain of Frostmarris where Bellorum and his hordes are waiting."

"I think it would be polite at the very least to announce our presence to the Holly and Oak Kings before we enter their realm with such a large army," said Maggie. "And if we do succeed in making proper contact with them, we can formally seek their help by calling them to arms."

"Good idea," Sharley agreed. "But I'm not sure how to do it. I've watched Dad a few times, but I didn't ever expect to have to do it myself."

"Yes, I know what you mean, but I've also watched Oskan summoning the soldiers of the two Kings and there seems to be little that is actually formal or even truly magical about it. I suggest we use a bugler to blow a fanfare, then make it up as we go along."

"Do we actually have a bugler amongst us?" asked Sharley. "The cavalries of the Desert People and the Lusu seem to make do with drums and pipes."

"Well, try those, then. I don't suppose the soldiers of the Holly and Oak Kings had ever heard a bugle before your father summoned them anyway."

Sharley beckoned up a mounted drummer of the Desert People and a piper from the Lusu. "Do you think you can produce something between you that sounds like a summons?"

The troopers nodded, and after a brief consultation they rattled out a stirring rhythm and tune that echoed through the dark trees.

Silence followed, followed by yet more silence.

"I don't think it's going to work," said Mekhmet quietly.

"It always took this long with Oskan too," said Maggie. "Then there was always a huge blast of—"

Suddenly, the silent trees were waving and writhing in a roaring wind which then stopped abruptly, as if someone had opened a door on a storm and then slammed it shut.

"Like that, you mean?" asked Queen Ketshaka, picking leaves out of her headdress.

"Yes, but then we'd see either the Holly or Oak soldiers. Now, let me see, which King is ruling at this time of year? I think it's the—"

A line of soldiers stepped out of the undergrowth wearing armour that seemed to be made from large and highly polished holly leaves.

"Holly King," Maggie finished.

One or two of the horses whickered nervously, and a murmur ran through the ranks of the soldiers near enough to see the strange creatures that now stood to attention before them.

Their eyes were as red as berries, their skin was the grey-green of holly bark, and the weapons they carried seemed to be made of wood!

Ketshaka said something nasty in Lusu, and Mekhmet called on the One for protection. Only Sharley and Maggie seemed happy to see the weird warriors. In fact, Sharley was almost beside himself with excitement. He'd called the soldiers of the woodland and they'd arrived. Just like they had for his dad! Quickly he settled down and urged Suleiman forward, trying to remember the sort of language he'd heard used whenever contact had been made with the Monarchs of the Wild Wood.

"Greetings to you and to your Monarch, His Majesty the Holly King, Lord of the Wild Places. Take to him the friendly greetings of myself, Charlemagne Athelstan Redrought Strong-in-the-Arm Lindenshield, known as Shadow of the Storm, and also those of Crown Prince Mekhmet Nasrid of the Desert Kingdom, Beloved of the One and Sword of the Desert. Add to these the deep felicitations of Her Mightiness Queen Ketshaka III of Lusuland, the Great She-Lion and Mother of the Nation. We ask the permission of His Majesty to cross his realm with our army, which we have transported at huge effort and cost from overseas to bring relief and aid to my mother Queen Thirrin and to the besieged city of Frostmarris."

The Holly soldiers regarded them all with blazing red eyes, and before anything more could be said, one of their number stepped out of the ranks and dropped to one knee before Sharley. He stood again, and the entire complement of tree-warriors beat their spears on shields. For several long moments the two groups looked at each other in silence. The strange wind then blew up again, crashing and roaring through the trees and sending up great clouds of leaf litter. When all had gone quiet the soldiers had disappeared.

"Well done, My Lord," said Maggie warmly. "You conducted yourself splendidly."

"But I forgot to ask for their help in the fighting," he answered, angry with himself.

"Oh, I wouldn't worry too much about that. We can call them again just before we emerge on to the plain of Frostmarris."

The infirmary had been moved down into the cave system even before the Vampires had withdrawn from the war, so the witches and healers had had quite a while to do as best they could in the conditions. Even so, a damp, dirty cave that had once been home to a colony of bats was hardly the ideal place to treat the wounded and dying.

They'd raised most of the patients off the floor and away from the oozing mud by improvising beds out of storage boxes and barrels, but some of the less seriously wounded had to perch on chairs as though they were sitting around at a social gathering. If it hadn't been so appalling, Oskan might have found it funny, in a grim sort of way. It was the way they lolled about, sometimes settling to rest on each other's shoulders as they slipped in and out of consciousness, like drunks at a party. For the Snow Leopards and werewolves with their huge bodies, the best Oskan and the witches could do was to throw down clean straw and check regularly that the mud hadn't seeped through.

Oskan was making yet another tour of inspection in the lull between land attacks. He wasn't entirely sure why he did this.

He knew exactly how many supplies they had: clean bandages, virtually none; poppy and other drugs, virtually none; available 'bedding' for new patients, absolutely none; floor space for new patients, disappearing fast. Perhaps his inspections had become a sort of mantra, something that calmed his mind by its very repetition and hopelessness, as he tried to get through another day of the siege.

The Sky Navy was again bombing the outer defences and city, and nobody could risk trying to bring the wounded into the infirmary while that was happening. The relative calm allowed his thoughts to range further afield as he checked the wards, and they turned again to the mystery of the unfriendly Power within the walls of Frostmarris.

Of course, he'd been monitoring the activities of his 'opponent', as he saw her – at least he knew the source was female – and in the past few weeks her Abilities had grown and improved. He also knew she was young and not yet at her full strength, but he still couldn't pin down her identity.

Just who was she? He'd probed the minds of every one of the witches, but their minds only showed a concern for the wounded, and fear for their own safety. All perfectly normal for a city at war. Once in the depths of his frustration he'd even suspected Medea, his very own daughter, of all people! And now, because the only building left undamaged in the entire city was his daughter's tower, he felt his suspicions rising again. But when he'd secretly inspected her thoughts he'd found only confusion. Nothing unusual for an adolescent. And when she'd shown terrible pain over the loss of her brother all those weeks ago he felt as though he'd betrayed her. Medea was powerful, and he'd wondered if her Abilities could be used to protect the entire city, but surely even *she* would have offered to protect Frostmarris if it was at all possible.

He could feel his opponent *now*, looking out from the city walls, watching the Sky Navy and plotting . . . something. He caught his breath and concentrated his Power, sending a lancing probe through the ether. But it was too late. Walls of Adamant slammed down and he found nothing.

He came across a relatively dry spot on the cave floor and sat down. Like everyone else he was exhausted. He needed to be with Thirrin. Perhaps a little of her tireless energy would rub off on him and he could face yet another day under siege. He knew that of late even she was less energetic than she had been, but nonetheless just being with her would make him feel better. How long had he and his wife had together in the past few weeks? Impossible to say; but the time they'd had *alone* together he knew precisely: eight hours and forty minutes, and most of that had been spent sleeping.

Still, just sitting beside her during the bombing would be better than nothing. As long as the Sky Navy was at work even Thirrin was forced to stay still. He smiled weakly as he climbed to his feet and headed off for the defences. She'd be surprised to see him, and frown in that way she always did when he acted in a way she didn't expect. But then, as always, she'd pat the seat next to her and make room for him.

If he followed the new passageways Archimedo had dug, he'd only have to make a dash across a few metres above ground to the outer defences.

Oskan had almost reached the end of the new tunnels when without any warning his mind was suddenly crammed full with a sense of Sharley. He was riding a small and beautiful black horse, and next to him rode a dark young man of about the same age. They were deep in youthfully earnest conversation, then as Oskan watched, their mood seemed to change and they both laughed. The Witchfather heaved a sigh of relief. At least their youngest child was safe.

But then a deep and terrible sense of foreboding filled his mind. He gasped aloud and slumped against the wall of the tunnel, weak with a sense of his own helplessness. Sharley was in mortal danger. But there was nothing he could do. His son was too far away, and Oskan's Powers were already stretched to their very limit by the needs of Frostmarris and its failing defences.

Oskan succumbed to despair.

But then his sense of duty and the needs of others reasserted themselves. He could do nothing to help Sharley; he could only trust to the truth of the vision he'd had so many months ago that had said he would return safely to the Icemark.

Clinging to this hope, Oskan straightened up and decided to keep his fears to himself. Thirrin must know nothing. She was virtually at breaking point herself; any extra burden could push her over the edge.

Sharley laughed again. All morning, Mekhmet had been telling him about the happenings of the camp, but if it was meant to stop him from dwelling on their being less than a day's march away from the plain of Frostmarris, it failed utterly. He'd enjoyed the gossip and appreciated his friend's efforts, but nothing could divert his mind from what lay ahead.

Sharley knew his army was nowhere near big enough to have much effect against Bellorum and his mad sons, but if they succeeded in keeping their presence secret, they might just have a chance of driving him back from the walls of the city. And if they could do that, then the defenders could ride out, and together they might finally be able to crush the old tyrant. But it all depended on secrecy and surprise, and with this in mind they'd been marching at night and resting during the day. So far it had all gone well, and by nightfall they'd be able to see the walls of Frostmarris.

To Sharley none of it seemed real. How could he, a crippled son of a warrior House, really be leading an army to defend his family and country? And yet here he was; he looked about him as if to convince himself it was all true. It was then that he thought he saw an odd greenish glow to both his right and left, far off amongst the trees. He was just about tell Maggie when the captain of the werewolves appeared and walked beside him.

"Your Majesty. We have company," she reported in wolf speech.

"Company?" said Sharley. "What sort of company?"

"Ghosts, zombies and rock trolls."

He immediately reined to a halt and told the others what the werewolf had said. Both Mekhmet and Ketshaka were hugely alarmed, but Maggie was interested.

"What do they want, Captain Bone-splitter?" he asked.

"They want to join us. They say they were drawn to the war from The-Land-of-the-Ghosts when Their Vampiric Majesties flew south to join the alliance," the Captain explained in human speech. "And when they heard of the King's death they'd already walked to the eaves of the Great Forest, so they decided to carry on. But when they came within striking distance of the plain of Frostmarris they didn't know what to do next. Our arrival was a lucky coincidence."

"How many are there?" asked Sharley.

"A thousand zombies, three hundred rock trolls, and who

could even guess how many ghosts," replied Captain Bone-splitter. "They're barely visible and keep floating about, but . . ." She shuddered. "They're truly hideous."

Fear was their greatest weapon, simple fear. Invaluable on the battlefield, fear and panic could break an army. But the presence of the rock trolls was what excited Sharley most. A single troll was the equivalent of up to ten human soldiers, and Bone-splitter was saying that three hundred wanted to join them! The only problem was that they were completely unpredictable and uncontrollable, but if they were determined enough to march hundreds of miles to join the war, then presumably they'd be willing to take orders that would enable them to fight in it.

"Bring their leader to us, Bone-splitter," Sharley said eagerly.

Within minutes a truly horrific sight stood before them. The smell of rotting flesh was overpowering, and whenever the zombie moved, small rivulets of putrid flesh fell to the ground with damp splattering noises, which made the horses blow and sidle in disgust.

Mekhmet and Ketshaka were horrified.

"What possible use could a moving corpse be to us in battle?" the huge Lusu Queen asked, her stony features deepening into frowning ravines of disapproval.

"My Lady," said Maggie lightly, "there was a time when I would have been equally sceptical, but I witnessed them in action during the last war, and they are truly devastating. You see, they cannot be killed. They're already dead. No matter what is thrown at them, they keep going until they reach their target and quite simply rip it to pieces."

Ketshaka stared at the creature, her frown lightening

slightly. "But they seem so clumsy."

"And so they are," Maggie agreed. "But how many soldiers do you know who would stand their ground against the prospect of fighting the living dead?"

She nodded. "I see. Then I remove my objections."

Mekhmet also nodded in agreement. He didn't dare open his mouth in case he vomited. He'd never realised how weak his stomach was before he got involved with these barbarians and their revolting allies. He just wanted the thing to go away.

"Can you control the rock trolls?" Sharley asked, disappointing his friend, who'd hoped the zombie was about to be dismissed and sent back to its own ranks.

"No one caaan!" the creature answered in deep and horribly fetid tones.

"An honest answer," said Sharley, covering his nose with his hand. "Well, will they at least accept orders?"

The zombie shrugged, losing a pound of flesh, which oozed moistly into the earth. "If they are the same as their own wishessss!"

"Which are?"

"To fight the Empire and Bellorummmm."

"Then our orders and their wishes coincide. Will they agree to fight with us and not against us?"

"You are alliessss. Our enemy is your enemyyyy," the zombie answered, and added irritably, "They're not stupid, you knowwww!"

"Are they not? Good. You may join us. March at the rear of the column, and maintain strict silence."

"Most of us are dead, we don't talk easily. Assss for the rock trollsss, they couldn't be quiet if they triedddd." The thing shrugged again, and watched sadly as more of its flesh slithered to the ground. "But the war should be noisy enough to drown out our approachhhhh."

"One thing before you go," said Maggie. "You told Captain Bone-splitter earlier that the Vampire King has been destroyed. Is this possible?"

"Bellorum ended his exissstence. We have all wept and the Vampire Queen has withdrawn her squadronsssss, leaving the city open to the Sssky Navy. But we want revenge!"

"What is a *Sky Navy*?" Sharley asked, struck by the odd name.

"Flying shipsssss. They bomb Frostmarrissss and the city burnssss."

"Flying ships! How can that be? The Empire has no magic."

"Sciencccccce has made them."

"How?"

The zombie shrugged again. "Ask your werewolvesssss. We found out about it from their relayyyyy."

"Bone-splitter, is this true? Why didn't you tell us before? What are these flying ships? How do they fly?"

The Captain was mortified. "Forgive me, My Lord. We've lived with the reality of the Sky Navy for so long, it never occurred to us that you wouldn't have heard of them, even in Exile."

Sharley was furious, but quickly saw that it was an honest mistake and contained his temper. After all, what difference would knowing about the flying ships have made to his plans? None at all. "How do they fly?"

"We're not sure, but the Imperial scientists seem to have invented a gas that is lighter than air. They trap it in a huge sail they call a balloon, and it lifts the ships into the sky."

"Fascinating!" said Maggie. "Ingenious. They must have produced huge quantities of helium and harnessed it in canopies. Quite, quite extraordinary!"

"It's possible, then?" asked Sharley.

"Oh, yes. But it took a singular mind to put a gas to such use! Amazing, truly amazing!"

The drums rattled and beat out a tattoo all along the defences. This was it. This was the decisive battle. Thirrin stood with Grinelda Blood-tooth, the Captain of her bodyguard of Ukpik werewolves, watching a truly enormous enemy force marching over the plain towards them. Bellorum had surpassed himself; never before had she seen so many soldiers gathered together under one banner.

She called encouragement to her shield wall and felt the weight of doubt and fear fall from her shoulders. She could only fight and trust in the goddesses and gods. It was their decision now.

Beside her, Tharaman-Thar and Krisafitsa-Tharina narrowed their eyes as they too watched the unhurried advance of the Imperial army. "It's strange, but now it's come to it, I feel surprisingly calm," said Krisafitsa. "I thought I'd be more conscious of the *significance* of it all."

"Yes," Tharaman agreed. "One always imagined one's final battle would feel especially dramatic. But in reality, it's just another fight in a lifetime of fighting." He purred deeply. "Still, my love, at least now we may rest together in the long and endless night."

Krisafitsa rubbed her cheek against her mate's. "My only regret is that I won't be there to see the cubs grow up. Will Kirimin be safe, my love?"

Tharaman's huge eyes glowed to deeper levels of amber as he thought of their youngest cub. "She will live and grow and one day become the greatest Queen the Snow Leopards have ever known."

"*Queen*, dearest one? Do you not mean *Tharina*?"

"Kirimin will be a Queen, my love."

Krisafitsa looked at her mate, unable to guess whether he was prophesying at the close of his life or simply joking affectionately about their youngest cub's nature. She decided to accept the words at face value, and licked his face.

"A fair few of the beggars, aren't there?" said Grishmak, strolling up and staring out at the slow advance. "They'll take some holding."

"Nothing could hold them, Grishy," said Thirrin. "But we'll take lots with us."

The werewolf sighed tiredly. "I suppose you're right." Then he let out a great bark of laughter. "HAH! But we've had fun trying, haven't we! Eh, Cressida? Bellorum will remember all of our names and faces whether he likes it or not. Do you think he has pet names for us?"

The Crown Princess left her position in the line to join them, smiling as she walked up. "I doubt they'd be repeatable in polite company if he does. Can't say it bothers me, though."

Then, standing next to her mother, she quietly took her hand and squeezed it. "Thanks, Mum."

Thirrin turned to her. "What for, exactly?"

Cressida shrugged. "Oh, I don't know . . . for being who you are, I suppose."

"In that case, thank *you*, too, Cressida," she said gently, and kissed her. "Now, where's Eodred?"

"With Howler and his regiment in the centre."

"Of course." Thirrin smiled. "And I wonder what your father's doing."

"Why don't you ask him?" said Oskan as he struggled up the steep incline of the earthwork.

"What are *you* doing here?" Thirrin snapped. "It'll be mayhem and murder in a few minutes!"

"I know," he answered quietly. "But I thought I'd like to be with my wife."

She nodded, then turned to look back out over the plain as the ballistas and trebuchets launched their darts and rocks. The Imperial army was now in range, and shields rattled all along the defences as the line tightened. Tharaman reared high into the sky and roared loud and long. His warriors all replied, and their voices crashed out over the advancing soldiers.

From his position on the hills overlooking the plain, Scipio Bellorum watched the advance through his monoculum. At last it had arrived: the final overthrow of the House of Lindenshield. It had been a long journey of many years and even more battles. Thanks to that mongrel family of barbarians and scraylings he'd been forced to learn the pain of defeat and humiliation, but now all of that would finally be expunged. The stump of his wrist throbbed where Thirrin's sword had severed his hand so long ago. Well, revenge was the sweetest of dishes. He'd already decided that he would chop off *both* her hands, whether from a corpse or a living woman, and send them as trophies to the Senate.

He smiled coldly as he remembered the governing body of the Empire. It had been almost as difficult to manage them as it had been to fight this war. Only the steadfast loyalty of his allies in the Ruling Council had ensured that he'd been allowed to continue the campaign. Things had been especially difficult over the last few weeks with such bad news coming from the south of the Empire. The Sultan was still advancing steadily, and almost all of the southern ports had fallen to the Venezzians and the Hellenes. Still, now the war in the Icemark was almost over, he was already devising tactics for the campaigns against the Desert Kingdom and Doge Machievelli.

He silently handed his monoculum to Octavius, and watched as he surveyed their advancing troops. Bellorum was grateful to his son for the simple reminder he'd given him at the beginning of the campaign: when fighting an enemy as unpredictable as the people of the Icemark and their allies, always have plenty of reserves to call upon. This he had done ever since, and even as the largest army ever gathered under one banner advanced towards the pathetic remnants of the defender's force, another two hosts stood ready and waiting to the rear. He wouldn't be taken by surprise this time. No matter what happened, he'd have a backup army to call into the fighting.

But he was probably being overcautious. After all, the little Queenling and her allies were all trapped in and around the ruins of Frostmarris. Apart, that was, from the hideous Vampires, but they'd withdrawn from the war, mortified by the loss of their King, no doubt. Bellorum smiled at their weakness. Their cowardice had probably shortened the fighting by anything up to a year. His plan to kill His Vampiric Majesty had been a masterstroke. The skies over Frostmarris, and indeed the entire Icemark, were now his.

Bellorum turned, beckoned a Staff Officer and gave orders for the Sky Navy to bomb what remained of the city again. A conflagration always made such a nice backdrop to a battle. Fire made everything so much more joyously apocalyptic. The Sky Navy would distract the rest of the field, and he and Sulla would be bathed in red light when they made their dramatic appearance at the head of their cavalry and targeted Lindenshield and her pet leopards. Oh, how surprised they'd be to see him; and oh, how surprised they'd be to die on the point of his lance.

Medea watched everything from her tower. Her Eye observed Bellorum unblinkingly and, as usual, found much to admire.

She looked at the earthworks around the city and observed the long unbroken shield wall. The Imperial army would reach the defences in a matter of minutes! She watched Tharaman-Thar rear up like a monolith of marble and roar out the Snow Leopard challenge. The ballistas and trebuchets were sending steel darts and rocks crashing into the Polypontian ranks, and as the advancing army drew ever closer the Hypolitan archers shot flight after flight of arrows down into the press.

The long spears of the enemy's pike regiments were lowered into the engage position, and their glittering barrier of razor-sharp steel pushed forward towards the defences.

Medea was almost enjoying the show, but all at once her senses writhed in agony. Something terrible was close. No, it was a someone. Charlemagne! She gave a snarl of pure fury and elation as her Eye searched the plain and the Great Forest. He was there! He'd arrived at last! Now he was going to die! She prepared herself, and entered the Spirit Plane to meet her brother for the last time.

Sharley could hear a strange rumbling. At first he thought it was thunder, as there were some huge clouds gathering in the sky ahead, but the sound was far too constant. "What do you think that is, Maggie?" he asked eventually.

"Bombs, My Lord. The amazing Sky Navy must be attacking Frostmarris."

"Ah, of course," he said, his casual tone hiding the deep fear he felt for the defenders of the city.

Ketshaka smiled encouragingly. "Well, Charlemagne, if we're close enough to hear the attack, we should reach the edge of the forest soon."

"That's true!" said Mekhmet excitedly. "Perhaps we should call the Holly King and the Oak King again."

"Not yet," Sharley answered quietly. "We need to be nearer."

They marched on in silence. Ketshaka had ordered her Lusus to keep their chants and singing for the battlefield.

Night came early to the forest as the shadows coalesced under the densely leafed canopy of the trees, and soon they were advancing in total darkness. The werewolves led the army, their night vision ensuring they didn't lose their way, as no torches could be lit so close to the enemy lines.

They could all see the sky ahead glowing as the flames of the dying city stained the clouds orange. Every now and then a bright flash lit up the surrounding trees as a bomb exploded, or sometimes as lightning flashed from the thunderheads that were rolling over the plain.

After a while, Sharley realised he could see the ranks of the army behind. The trees were thinning, and the light of the burning city reached deep into the forest. It was all he could do not to give the order to charge, and rush crashing through the undergrowth. His family could be dead already, or fighting to their last breaths, even as he crept through the trees! But he kept himself reined in; there was still quite a way to go.

Soon they started to come across huge clearings in the forest that were littered with fallen trunks and smashed timber. Many of the trees were burned and still smoking, and all about was the acrid stench of gunpowder.

"Why would they bomb the forest?" he asked Maggie.

"Because the Holly and Oak Kings are your mother's allies," said the old scholar. "Perhaps Bellorum thinks it will discourage them from joining this battle."

"Do you think it will?"

"Patently not," the old scholar answered with a nod to left and right, where rank upon rank of Holly and Oak soldiers had materialised from the shadows. With them were huge phalanxes of fighting animals – stag and boar, bear and wolf – and beyond them, rushing through the undergrowth, were the weird Green Men and Women of the Wild Wood, tusks erupting from their mouths, their naked bodies green and mossy like the bark of ancient trees. And ahead of them all, riding proudly on antlered stags, were the Kings themselves. On their heads were circlets of leaves and in their hands were huge maces of polished wood. They looked as ancient as the forest itself, yet they seemed as strong and as imposing as the mightiest trees.

Sharley shivered with excitement and reached for Mekhmet's hand. "They came! They answered the call! We can do it, Mekhmet! We can do it!"

The Crown Prince gazed at the strange soldiers and back at the army of monsters and people they were all a part of. "Yes," he said at last. "We can do it. If we get there in time."

But just then, Mekhmet suddenly started to shake uncontrollably, as if he were suffering an attack of the fever. His eyes rolled, and his spine arched backwards till his head almost touched the root of Jaspat's tail.

"Mekhmet!" Sharley cried in terror. "What's wrong? Speak to me!"

"Leave him!" Maggie snapped out. "It looks like some sort of fit."

They watched helplessly as Mekhmet shuddered and vibrated, but the spasms seemed to pass and he slowly sat up. Sharley sighed in relief – then gasped in horror as he saw that his friend's eyes were rolled up into his head. Only the whites showed, glistening and eerie in the fire-red light.

A hideous gargling sound emerged from Mekhmet's throat, then he coughed and an awful rictus spread across his face. "Hello, Sharley!" he spat, a look of pure hatred and contempt twisting his features. "So, you've come home. You just couldn't stay away and do as you were told, could you? You just had to come back and interfere, like mummy's little soldier!"

Sharley gazed in shock at the transformation in his friend. What could be happening? Was it a fit, or was it—?

"Don't you know me, little snot?" Mekhmet's mouth spat. "It's me, Medea!"

"*Medea!*" he whispered in startled amazement. "But how—?"

"By Magic, you moron! How else? You really are stupid, aren't you? Oh well, no matter. You'll be dead soon, so at least there'll be one less airhead in the world!"

"What are you doing? Why have you possessed Mekhmet?"

"So I can talk to you, of course. I've come to tell you that Frostmarris is burning, though even *you* have probably managed to work that one out for yourself by now. Bellorum's about to win his war at last, and everyone you ever knew and

loved is about to be wiped out. So you're too late with you.
army of freaks and fools."

"You're wrong! And they're not dead yet – I can still hear
the bombs. Bellorum wouldn't bother to bomb a fallen city!"

"I said 'about to fall', not 'fallen'! You're obviously deaf as
well as stupid. How on earth did I resist murdering you over
all those tedious years we shared in the nursery?"

Sharley stared in blank amazement at his friend's mouth
spitting out the vile words and vitriol. It was impossible to
equate Mekhmet's face with such hatred. He was also having
trouble adjusting to his sister's shocking revulsion and aggression towards him. Medea had always been strange and indif-
ferent to her family, but now Sharley finally realised she
actually wanted to kill him! He watched, mesmerised, as
Mekhmet's hand slowly drew his scimitar and raised it above
his head.

"Look out!" Maggie shouted as the razor-sharp sword
struck at Sharley with all the power and speed of lightning.

Suleiman leaped back just in time, his battle-trained
reflexes saving his master.

"Mekhmet, it's me, *Sharley*. My witch of a sister has possessed you. Resist her! Throw her out!"

"He can't hear you!" Medea sneered with venomous contempt. "Don't you think I've prepared for this moment? I'm
an expert at possession now, better even than Father. Your
little friend is mine to do with as I wish. And unless you want
to kill *him*, you won't be able to stop me."

Again the scimitar struck! Sharley ducked at the last
moment, and it missed him by a hair's breadth.

"Mekhmet! Listen to me – it's Sharley. She's trying to use
you to kill me. But you can fight her! Come towards my

voice!" He leaned from his saddle and slipped inside the striking circle of the sword. He had bare seconds of safety, and moving quickly he cupped his friend's face in his hands. "Please, Mekhmet, come back to me! You made me the warrior I am; you gave my life meaning. Please come back to me!"

With a convulsive effort Mekhmet threw him off and raised his sword, hideous laughter rattling from his throat. "It seems he chooses not to remember you, snotling. Such a shame when friendship is held so cheaply, don't you think?" Sidling his horse closer, the Desert Prince advanced menacingly. "You're just going to have to kill him, Charlemagne, my dear brother – if you can."

Sharley bowed his head. "I will raise neither sword nor shield against the one who gave me the gift of companionship when I was lonely; who gave me the right to fight when all others denied it to me; who gave me my pride when I thought myself beneath contempt." Slowly, he opened his arms and waited.

Mekhmet lifted his scimitar, and a scream rose up from the ranks of the horrified army. But as his arm reached the zenith of his strike it stopped, and his face contorted. "Sharley! Help me – she's too strong!"

"Mekhmet, look at me! She can't defeat us! We're invincible if we truly believe it! Look at me!"

With a shuddering effort his friend's eyes rolled back to their natural position. "Sharley," he whispered. "Her hatred is huge. Forgive me!" His eyes turned up in his head again and Jaspat surged forward. "Hah, no chance, snotling! He's mine, and you're about to die!"

Sharley closed his eyes, and slowly – on the edge of hearing, on the edge of thought – he became aware of gentle singing. With the stealth of shadows it stole into his mind and filled him with a strength that flowed through every fibre of his being – a spiritual strength drawn from the boys' friendship and returned to him with increased power.

"The Blessed Women!" Sharley whispered.

With a surge of new-found strength, he leaped forward and grasped his friend around the middle, inside the striking range of the scimitar. He tightened his grip, almost as though he was giving his friend a hug, and his lips brushed his ear. "Mekhmet, could you truly find it in your heart to kill me?" he whispered.

The Desert Prince shuddered and convulsed, his entire body contorting in a desperate muscular spasm that almost threw him from the saddle.

"NO!" he screamed at last, and his eyes focused on his friend. "No! Never! Not if the power of all the witchcraft in all the world was used against me! Not if I must lay down my life to stop it! My friend . . . my greatest friend!"

The gentle singing of the Blessed Women now swelled through the forest so that all could hear it, and despite the horror they faced, everyone felt a sense of peace flow through them.

But then, slowly, irresistibly, Mekhmet's eyes rolled back in his head again.

"Not strong enough, are you? Not even with the filthy power of these contemptible female spirits," Medea spat sneeringly. "Where did you find them – in some desert hovel? I smell sand and jackals on them. I smell heat and scorpions. Their strength is nothing compared to mine! Their puny efforts will not save you!"

But Sharley heard a faint note of doubt in his sister's tones, and desperately seized on it.

"Mekhmet! She's worried. She can't hold you! Fight her!"

With terrible deliberation, the Desert Prince's head was drawn back and then struck forward, smashing Sharley on the cheekbone. He reeled, but grabbed his friend's sword hand.

"I won't let you suffer the grief of killing me if that's what must be. I'll kill myself first!" Drawing his dagger, he held it over his own heart and prepared to thrust.

The waves of singing voices now rose to a pitch that caused the trunks of the surrounding trees to vibrate as the Blessed Women drew on the power of Sharley's offered sacrifice. And, slowly, a blue light evolved into the shadows, banishing the darkness with the beauty of summer skies.

Mekhmet convulsed and his eyes rolled back to normal. "No!" he screamed, and seized the dagger Sharley held over his heart. "Not one second less of your God-given life! Your time isn't now! We have to grow old and grey. We have to be fat old men in sunlit courtyards remembering our youth!"

Slowly, he sat straight in his saddle and dropped his scimitar. "In the name of the One, the Friend and Lord of all creation, be gone, hideous witch! Leave me, and may your foul designs know no power!" His body began to shake and with a terrible cry he fell.

Sharley caught him, and a dreadful shriek rose up around them, filling the surrounding forest with a raging hatred that reverberated from tree to tree. Sharley climbed from the saddle, helped by the werewolf Commander who had rushed forward. Gently, he laid Mekhmet's limp form on the ground, and grabbing his hands he rubbed them vigorously. "Don't you dare leave me now! We've defeated her! She's gone! Don't leave me now!"

"Who's leaving anyone?" Mekhmet asked, opening his eyes and grinning. "Sandstorms and scorpions, I thought we'd had it then!"

Sharley laughed for joy, then as he helped his friend to his feet they embraced. The singing rose to a crescendo, then slowly started to fade, along with the blue light. Sharley turned to gaze into the trees and salaamed deeply. "You said you would help me even at 'the northernmost limits of the world', and you have been true to your word. You have our boundless thanks." And both boys salaamed in unison as the light and singing dwindled to silence.

The army gave a collective sigh of relief and a troubled murmuring ran through the ranks. Maggie urged his horse forward. "Perhaps something should be announced," he said, pointedly nodding at the ranks. "Damage limitation, morale and all that," he added in a whisper.

Sharley understood immediately, and remounting Suleiman he faced the warriors of his host. "Soldiers of the alliance, we have defeated the second most powerful witch in the entire land of the Icemark, and the most powerful of all is our staunch ally, my father! What greater omen of good fortune could we have? All of you have just witnessed the good spirits of the Desert Kingdom who crossed even the grey seas of the north to help us in our time of need. What allies we have! Not even the Dark Arts can beat us, so what chance has a mere army of mortals against our swords, against our determination, against our power?"

A charged silence greeted this, but then a lone cheering voice rose up as Ketshaka stood in her stirrups and brandished her spear. "None can stand against us! The Shadow of the Storm has defeated even Magic in his war against his enemies.

Truly we are makers of history! Truly we are destroyers of empires!"

This time the entire army joined in with the cheering, and they prepared to march on. But now Sharley was almost overwhelmed with fear as he remembered what Medea had said about Frostmarris and his family. The city was burning, and everyone he ever knew and loved was about to be wiped out! Were they still alive? Were they already dead, trampled and bloodied beneath the feet of the Imperial army, or had they been taken captive to be humiliated and tortured by Bellorum and his mad sons? He must strike immediately and drive the Empire from the land! Standing in his stirrups he drew his scimitar.

"Ride now for Frostmarris! Ride now for the blood of the foe! The enemy awaits us! They are ready to bleed! They are ready to die!"

And as one the army of people and monsters, legends and nightmares surged forward, a wordless roar of hatred rising before them like a bow wave.

Medea smashed back into her body with crushing force, and lay, shuddering and vibrating, before being violently sick. She lay in the corner of her tower room heaving and vomiting as the physical shock to her system convulsed her stomach in great waves of nausea.

"Sharley!" she snarled. "I'll peel the skin from your body, strip by strip, and watch the bluebottles and maggots feed on your flesh!" She vomited again, bringing up bile in bitter gouts that tore at her guts. "It took an alliance to beat me: you, your fancy little friend, and spirits from a foul land! But I'll win in the end. I'll blast you and roast you, even as you ride at the head of your army of freaks!

CHAPTER 37

Olememnon watched as the pike phalanx punched through the fyrd regiment to the left of the Hypolitan position. "And so it ends," he said quietly, his voice lost in the terrible raging din of the battle as he pointed out the breach to his wife Olympia, the Basilea. She quickly gave the order to form a circular shield wall, and the men and women of their command moved with smooth precision to face outwards, their shields locked and spears bristling like an impenetrable hedge.

"Ollie," she said simply, and kissed him. "There won't be time later. Pity we had such a short time of it."

"Yes," he agreed. "But what we had was good."

"Wasn't it?" she said, and laughed, the glorious sound flowing out on to the air to mix incongruously with the sounds of fighting and death. A regiment of Polypontian shield-bearers advanced against them, breaking against the defiant wall of the Hypolitan and falling back, only to reform and charge again.

Further down the line Eodred and Howler watched as the enemy flowed through the breach to surround their position. "I'd sooner be with the Hypolitan," said Howler, nodding towards the Hypolitan's more easily defended position on a higher point of the earthworks.

"I'd sooner be in the mess hall with a pint of beer myself," said Eodred.

"Well, as that's a little difficult at the moment, perhaps we'd better move."

"Fine," Eodred agreed, and drawing breath, he bellowed out the order to charge. The mixed regiment of housecarles and werewolves formed a wedge of locked shields and smashed into the press of Imperial troops that stood between themselves and the Hypolitan. Axes, swords, tooth and claw carved a path through the enemy army, and as they approached the Hypolitan shield wall it opened to receive them.

Soon, two islands of resistance stood in a sea of Polypontian soldiers. In one stood the Basilea and her warriors with Eodred and Howler's regiment. On the other were Thirrin, Grishmak and the Snow Leopards. The banner of the white fighting bear flowed bravely in the wind, and alongside it flew Cressida's standard of the striking eagle.

Tharaman-Thar and Krisafitsa-Tharina reared high in the shield wall, striking down the enemy as they stormed around their beleaguered position. Grishmak, too, howled and raved, his teeth red with blood and his arms drenched to the elbows. But still the enemy came on, singing their war hymns and dying under the swords of Thirrin and Cressida as they fought with a frenzy against the unstoppable sea of the Imperial troops.

But then the impossible happened. The enemy began to draw back. The defenders began to cheer, but then fell silent as they saw what was coming in to replace the land soldiers. High in the sky, line after line of wasp-fighters were sweeping in. There seemed to be no end to their numbers. The canopies of the flying machines, stained red by the fires of the burning city, loomed in livid relief against the black storm clouds and darkening night sky.

Thirrin sagged, and leaned heavily against her sword. "My friends, we must stand against an enemy we cannot fight." She turned to Oskan who stood, seemingly deep in thought, at the foot of the banner. "It is time to say our goodbyes."

He looked up, and watched as the wasp-fighters bore down on them, making their strafing run, pistols and muskets cocked, and small barrels of gunpowder primed.

"Say our goodbyes?" he said. "No, not *quite* yet."

From the eaves of the Great Forest, Sharley saw Frostmarris in flames, and tears ran down his cheeks. His home was burning. Where were his family? Where were his people? Angrily, he dashed the moisture from his eyes and glared over the plain. There! There they were. Two islands of resistance surrounded by Imperial troops, with even more marching into the attack!

Slowly he drew his scimitar, the arc of his arm seeming to pull a controlled hatred and rage deep, deep into his slight frame. He urged Suleiman forward beyond the eaves of the trees and, as his friends and allies watched, he stood in his stirrups and held the slender curve of the blade high above his head.

A great growl and roar of thunder seemed to announce his arrival on the field of battle, and throwing back his head he gave the war cry of the Lindenshields.

"The enemy is among us! They burn our houses and kill our children! BLOOD! BLAST! AND FIRE! BLOOD!

BLAST! AND FIRE!"

And the vast army flowed from the forest like an unstoppable flood.

Thirrin turned back to watch the flying machines. She could clearly hear the wind whistling and rattling through their canopies, and raising her sword she roared out defiance against them as they streamed down the slopes of flight towards her.

Then a screaming ripping screech rent the air, and the lead wasp-fighters were punched from the sky. A rising shriek of triumph and challenge echoed over the plain as the sky filled with giant Vampire bats and Snowy Owls.

Wasp-fighters fell like leaves in a storm, their gunpowder exploding as they buried themselves into the ground. A great roar of elation rose up from the ranks of the Icemark defenders.

"THE VAMPIRES! THE VAMPIRES! THE VAMPIRES ARE HERE!"

Thirrin watched as the Vampire Queen led her squadrons in triumph against the Sky Navy, the ferocious screeches of the undead warriors piercing the eardrums of all on the battlefield. They tore into the squadrons of wasp-fighters, and soon a tangle of dogfights wove and tumbled through the night air, illuminated by the flames of Frostmarris.

But while Thirrin had been distracted by the aerial fighting, the Imperial land soldiers had begun advancing again, their pikes and spears, swords and muskets glittering as they marched forward. Bellorum was not finished yet. Thirrin could see the General coldly giving his orders as one of the massive reserve armies began to roll on to the field of battle. These were the elite soldiers of the Black Army. None of these veteran soldiers had fewer than twenty years' battle experience, and they were fiercely, blindly loyal to the General and to the Empire, in that order. Theirs was the task of finally wiping out the hated House of Lindenshield, and they sang as they advanced, proud and honourable, fierce and ruthless.

Thirrin's brief elation at the return of the Vampires was already forgotten. They could fight no more. These were fresh reserves, strong and vital, and eager to kill. She turned to Oskan in despair, and gasped. His eyes were white, and his frame shook as he drew power from the sky.

"NO! Oskan, NO!" she screamed as she realised what was happening. He was calling down the lightning, and the last time he had done that it had nearly killed him.

Medea saw. She felt the energy of the ionised air gathering and roiling in the sky above the distant figure of her father. She knew the lightning would fall, crackling and roaring through the air, and smash into his body. She knew it would sear and burn and boil as it travelled through his frame, before bursting out of him as he directed it against the enemy.

In a split second she saw that this could be her moment of triumph. She stood, and screamed. Sharley and his band of freaks were drawing near. Now was the time to strike. Raising her arms above her head she opened her eyes wide, and their pupil-less blackness burned and raged. Calling forth her full strength as a Weather Witch, she reached out her mind and snatched the lightning away from her father.

Exhausted, Oskan fell to the ground unconscious.

Crackling and roaring, the first bolt of Power was drawn through the sky and struck her with a mighty force. She smiled as she felt its raging strength fill her. But unlike her father, she could take yet more power from the skies. Her Gift as a Weather Witch was without equal. The storm she'd sent against Sharley and the refugee fleet was puny compared to the power she called forth now, her strength increased manifold by her hatred of the favoured brother, the cherished weakling. She called forth more and more of the limitless storm force from the sky. Bolts of lightning fell, hissing through the air as they came, driving her to her knees as they entered her body with smashing force. With supreme will she stood up, containing the searing heat of the storm's power and neutralising its ability to destroy her by drawing a blood-freezing cold from the upper atmosphere.

Oskan clawed his way back to consciousness. There was something to say! There was something to say! He cried aloud in horror and despair. He understood at last. Medea *was* the Dark Witch! *Medea* was responsible for the deaths of so many soldiers who'd fallen in the first major battle of this war. *Medea* was responsible for the death of her own brother Cerdic! And now she was going to kill Sharley!

"Thirrin!" he shouted, climbing out from between Krisafitsa's protective front paws. "Thirrin! He's here!"

She heard his voice, and cried out from the shield wall where she'd been fighting.

"Oskan, you're awake!"

"He's here, Thirrin!"

She shook her head as though to clear it. This was too much like the last battle for Frostmarris all those years ago.

"Who's here?"

A great growl and grumble of thunder drowned out his reply, but he pointed towards the Great Forest. The humid atmosphere seemed to magnify the trees and everything close

616

to them, and suddenly she saw a black-armoured figure ride
out on a neat black horse. The figure stood in its stirrups and
drew an oddly curved sword. She held her breath. Who could
it be? Then as she watched, the fires from the burning city lit
the blade of his sword, and words from the past leaped into
her mind.

"*He shall return, a blade of fire in his hand . . .*"

Her eyes filled with tears. *It can't be!*

The figure seemed to expand as it drew breath, and then,
incredibly, it gave the war cry of the Icemark.

"It is! Oskan, Tharaman, Cressida! It is!" she shouted
incredulously.

Medea roared, and released the power of the lightning.
Like a white-hot meteor, like a quicksilver spear it raged
across the sky, crackling and blazing towards Sharley and his
allies.

Oskan saw it coming. With the unthinking reflex of rage,
he struck out. A great burst of energy erupted into the sky,
deflecting the lightning from Sharley and directing it straight
back at Medea.

She screamed in terror as the power ricocheted and struck
back at her. It hit her squarely in the chest and hurled her
against the wall of her tower room. Electricity hissed and
snarled, crackled and snapped all around her. The room was
filled with a brilliant, searing light, the glaring white of boiling steel. The heat was like the heart of the sun, and everything around her burst into flames.

But still she didn't die.

Now she drew towards her the deadly cold of the Arctic's
bitterest winters. The power of blizzards and the icy,
death-dealing winds of the north's winter storms enveloped

her. Cold met heat, and the atmosphere exploded and shattered as two equal but opposing powers fought for supremacy, and burned themselves out in a roaring crackling conflagration.

Medea was hurt, but not mortally so. She'd had a split second to call for protection, and some of the lightning's power had been neutralised. She retreated towards the stairwell, walking through the flames that raged and roiled through her room. She'd escape to the Great Forest and gather her thoughts before deciding what to do.

But too late! He was there, filling the room with his anger. Medea gasped, and watched as her father walked slowly towards her. His face was immobile, but his dark eyes blazed with incandescent fury.

In desperation Medea struck out, sending energy to hit him squarely in the face. He barely flinched. She sent blizzard and maelstrom against him, but now nothing had any effect. She knew she couldn't stop him. His power had grown from his anger, and hers had been burned from her very core. She was terribly damaged.

Oskan's mind locked deep into his daughter's. "Medea, my beloved daughter. Why have you betrayed your people? Why have you betrayed your family? Why, my sweetness, did you kill your brother?"

She shuddered as his bitter pain and terrible anger filled her head. Never had she been so utterly terrified. She could see her father's mind with horrifying clarity, and suddenly understood how hard it was for him to hide his other, evil self, so powerful and cruel. Like her, Oskan Witchfather belonged to another species that was as old as time, unfeeling, and dreadful.

She sank slowly to her knees and marvelled that he had

resisted so much of his nature for so many years. She now knew that if he opened himself to the Dark he could be a greater sorcerer than she could ever have imagined; she now knew he had a far greater potential for evil than she had ever realised.

"I await your answer, my love," her father said with terrifying tenderness. "You have brought about the deaths of thousands by refusing to join with me. You happily ended the life of your brother, my son, and you have just tried to kill another. Why?"

There was a long frightened silence.

"Because . . . I was loved less than I should have been! Because my brothers and my sister are beneath my contempt, unmagical as they are." She felt a small spark of courage and defiance returning. She had nothing to lose by standing her ground. "And because I have chosen to follow the path of the Dark. I, at least, in this family of wooden warriors and cowardly makers of Magic, have the courage to accept my heritage!"

"How strange, my beloved daughter, that you see succumbing to the temptation of evil as an act of courage, rather than the weak-minded selfish stupidity that it is. Do you not think that resisting its call takes all of my strength every second, every hour, every day of my life? Don't you think I would relish having the towering strength of the Dark?" He opened his mind, and the Dark flooded in. He allowed his daughter to see the depth of his strength, expanding to fill her watching senses to the brim.

"And what, my dear daughter, should I do with my power?" His voice hissed like an angry cat. "With this I could blast Bellorum and his hideous sons from the plain of

Frostmarris for ever."

"Then why don't you, Father?" she asked, shocked.

"Because to use evil Magic, even for good ends, poisons whatever is achieved. Don't you understand, Medea? Bellorum would die and his army would be destroyed, undoubtedly. But the land would be destroyed in the process. What then, my beloved daughter? Should we rule a kingdom of ashes and death? Oh, my Gifted child, you disappoint me; you have forced me to learn that huge Magical potential, even in a human being who has been loved and nurtured with unflagging care, can be housed in the brain of a fool and a murderer."

"I need nothing more from you," she spat back angrily. "Least of all a lecture. Kill me and have done!"

"Very well, you shall die."

Medea was stunned. Even now she expected the gentle father she knew to regain control of his power and find some way to forgive her for what she had done. But a sneer of contempt played mercilessly around his mocking lips. She was helpless! The breath left her body in an explosive gasp and she fell flat on the floor.

"You shall die, my daughter. Or at least you shall be as though dead to your family, to your country and to the mortal world. You will go to the Dark as you've always wanted; but you will go unprepared and without terms. You will enter that realm without having studied it, without having readied yourself for it. You may live, if you're strong enough. More likely, you will be captured and tortured by your grandfather's people, and your soul will become one more grain of ice in the frozen tundra of their realm."

Oskan raised his arms, and a huge tear appeared in the wall

of Medea's tower. With one command he had opened the fabric of the world. Terrified, Medea looked behind her at the gaping hole and felt the deadly cold pouring into the room. A deep abiding sense of despair seeped into her mind. At last, Medea had realised the true nature of that which she most desired.

"No! Father, wait! I do understand. Now I see I'm wrong to want the power of the Dark. Don't banish me to that emptiness!" On her knees, she begged for forgiveness and mercy, pleading with her father, the only living thing she had ever loved.

But, standing above her, Oskan only smiled tenderly and shook his head. "Too late, my child. Too late."

And suddenly, her body was seized by some unseen force and she was dragged, screaming and kicking, through the wall of the tower and down into the Dark.

Where was he? Thirrin gazed out over the plain to the Great Forest, and gasped. Galloping out of the dark trees was another army. There were striped horses, rock trolls, zombies, werewolves, and thousands and thousands of the soldiers of the Holly and Oak Kings. And leading these new allies on a fine black horse was Sharley! Thirrin's eyes filled with tears. The sight was incredible!

With a roar, the army leaped into the charge and swept down on the flanks of the Imperial army.

"Fly! Fly like the wind, my friend!" Sharley whispered into Suleiman's ear. "Today will be a red day, a death day! Today the Empire will die!" And with a scream of challenge the small black horse charged forward.

They crashed into the Polypontian ranks, carving through

them like a hot coal through ice. Hardly slowing, Ketshaka's Lusu warriors sang the ferocity of their death chants as they drove forward over the falling soldiers. The great Queen smote all about her with a huge mace, laughing as she killed. Mekhmet rode beside her, proclaiming the mystery of his belief.

"There is no God but the One, and Mighty is his Messenger!"

All the soldiers of the Desert Kingdom took up the cry. Thousands fell before them, and the entire Imperial army writhed in agony as they carved through its cumbersome mass.

Sharley rode at the glittering, deadly killing point of a mighty spear that was his army. Never since the days of the Frankish King Charlemagne, his namesake, had the cavalry of the Desert People ridden their neat, powerful horses in the lands of the north. Never had the lightning precision of the scimitar flashed and flickered in such a vicious hail of killing. But now they had returned, and with them came the mighty Lusu, brave and joyful warriors who killed as they sang their battle-chants, and who rode steeds that were striped as night and day.

The Polypontian ranks watched their advance in horror, and with a roar of despair, many turned and fled.

But in the midst of the Imperial host, Octavius turned to face the threat. Rallying his elite regiment of cavalry he advanced at a trot, arrogant hand on arrogant hip. No one was going to deny the Empire this final victory over the barbarian rabble – he would personally see to that! He raised his sword, and nodding to the bugler, gave the order to charge.

With a deadly elegance the personal regiment of Octavius Bellorum flowed over the land, their hooves raising a mighty roar of power as they thundered on and smashed into the advancing enemy. Sharley and Mekhmet met the charge, and the roar of onset rang into the air. Sabre clashed with scimitar, and the screams of the dead and dying rose up to join with the smoke of the burning city.

But then some desperate instinct made Sharley turn his head. Mekhmet! Through the mass of struggling warriors, Sharley watched in horror as Mekhmet's horse, Jaspat, stumbled over a fallen enemy soldier. For a moment the Prince's bodyguard fought to get to him as he struggled to regain control of his horse, but before they could reach him, the fallen Imperial trooper thrust his sabre deep into Mekhmet's chest.

"NO!" Sharley screamed. Reining Suleiman round to ride to his friend's aid, he came face to face with the cold and arrogant countenance of an elegantly uniformed Polypontian officer.

"Would you run, coward, before I've had a chance to cut you down?" asked a coldly sneering voice.

Distracted and distraught, Sharley hardly heard him. Already the tide of battle was flowing towards where Mekhmet had fallen. He must reach him before he was trampled beneath the hooves of the cavalry.

"So good to see the Commander of the enemy horse is preparing to flee the field! No doubt his troopers will all go with him. As is the way with all cowards," the arrogant voice gloated.

Even in his grief and fear for Mekhmet, Sharley knew the enemy officer was right. Already the cavalry of the Desert Kingdom was faltering, now that their Prince had fallen. Weeping for his friend, he raised his scimitar and called his battle-name aloud to rally the troopers.

"What chance has an army that needs to be taught the fundamentals of command by their enemy?" taunted the sneering voice.

"You begin to bother me!" Sharley snapped, his fighting spirit rising again. Suleiman caught his mood, and with a scream leaped towards the enemy horse.

With a whirl of blade on blade Sharley and Octavius fought. Trading blow for blow they circled and cut, parried and slashed, until with a contemptuous gesture the officer lowered his sabre and spat. "You're spawn of the Lindenshield clan. I see your red hair and green eyes even disguised under your armour."

"I wear no disguise. I am Charlemagne Athelstan Redrought Strong-in-the-Arm Lindenshield, Shadow of the Storm, and I will have your blood in reparation for the harm you have done my land!"

Octavius laughed. "Your land is mine, little Princeling!"

"Oh, I think not, whelp of the Empire. Your *life* is *mine!*"

"If you believe that is so, Lindenshield, you should know with whom you fight," he answered with searing contempt. "I am Commander Octavius Domitian Lycurgus Bellorum, son of the mighty General who has defeated your pathetic little land."

Sharley's eyes widened fractionally. "Then all the greater will be my pleasure when you die." And they leaped back into the fight.

Time seemed to slow for Sharley as he circled his enemy. Nothing else existed beyond the small theatre of their contest. Sound itself was reduced to the clatter and clang of scimitar on sabre. And yet, during that entire clash of culture and wills, of fighting styles and personal loathing, not once did the look of supreme contempt leave Octavius' face. It was that which drove Sharley on, until with a lightning flash of his scimitar he chopped at his enemy's neck, and the head leaped from its shoulders and rolled away. Even then, he noticed with interest, the sneer still curled his enemy's lip.

A gasp rose up from the Imperial cavalry. Octavius was dead! As simply as that, the great and vicious son of the mighty Bellorum clan had been killed! For a moment they stared, unable to believe the true horror of the deed. They looked at one another, uncertain what to do. The impossible had happened – the Commander was dead!

Then, as one, they turned their horses and fled.

On the far side of the plain, Scipio Bellorum and his second son were leading their cavalry in a huge sweep around the twin shield walls of the defenders. They knew nothing of Sharley's arrival, and wouldn't have cared less if they had. They were fixed determinedly on one target and one alone: the hated Queen of the Icemark. If she fell, the war would be over and the Empire would at last be victorious!

The General smiled coldly as the galloping hooves of his cavalry ate up the ground; closer and closer they drew to the locked shields of the housecarles and to the seemingly impenetrable barrier of the Snow Leopards and werewolves. He was close enough now to see the white pelts of the Queen's Ukpik bodyguard gleaming in the light of the burning city. Well, this time they would die! This time they would all die! He set the steel fingers of his war-hand into a claw of razors and slashed the air.

Behind the barrier, Cressida was watching the events on the field, open-mouthed with amazement. Sharley had returned, and with an army! She was so elated, she was almost in a daze. But then, all of a sudden, she sensed something was wrong. Her military instinct warned her to look to the flanks. And there, in the distance, she saw a huge phalanx of enemy cavalry. In a split second she'd taken in the direction of the horses, and the long glittering lances, and that the phalanx was being led by Bellorum himself. Now she knew exactly where they were heading.

There was hardly time to think, but she knew they must be stopped before they reached the shield wall. She couldn't take too many soldiers, or the integrity and strength of the formation would be weakened. Then a solution occurred, and she rushed to Grinelda Blood-tooth.

"The Queen is targeted by Bellorum!" she said, pointing to the cavalry. "Bring the bodyguard and tell no one!"

The huge Commander of the Ukpiks nodded, and within seconds Cressida was running at the head of a snarling ravening wedge of werewolves towards the ever-closing cavalry.

But the General saw them coming, and thundering to meet the Icemark Princess he sneered in contempt. Nothing could thwart him now!

With a deafening roar the two forces met. Horses fell screaming, werewolves howled, housecarle and trooper bellowed their war cries, and the charge was stopped dead.

Cressida's sword flashed and darted like a striking snake, felling every Imperial trooper who came against her. "Bellorum! Bellorum!" she screamed above the din of battle. "Show yourself! Fight me now and lose more than your hand!"

Sulla heard her cry and forced his horse forward, his long cavalry sabre slicing throat and skewering chest as he surged towards her. With a final heave he was through, and Cressida stood before him.

"Here, Lindenshield!" he yelled.

The Crown Princess swung round and glared at him. "I called for the jackal, not its pitiful whelp!"

Without retort Sulla's horse leaped forward. Cressida stepped aside, and with an almost contemptuous flick of her wrist she drove her sword deep into Sulla's stomach as he stormed past. He fell screaming, and with a following sweep of her blade she smashed open his helmet and head. "So die you all!"

Scipio Bellorum screamed in frustration as his cavalry faltered and fell before the raging attack. He'd lost sight of Sulla in the chaos, and glared about desperately as he fought to regain control and initiative.

"Fall back!" he roared. "Fall back and regroup!"

A bugler took up the order and the brassy, cracked notes blared out.

The cavalry withdrew and gathered about the figure of their General, who stood in his stirrups, sword aloft. They turned, redressed their ranks and stared at the force of werewolves raging before them. They'd closed into a tight fighting unit and were moving forward at a crouching run, predatory and hideous. Cressida laughed as they advanced, and the Wolf-folk snarled and roared, revealing their huge teeth and bright red tongues.

All of a sudden, the cavalry troopers' fear of the terrible inhuman enemy became greater than that they felt for Bellorum. A murmuring and muttering swelled through the Imperial ranks, and the horses neighed in panic.

Bellorum stood in his stirrups.

"Stand! Stand, all of you, or die on the hangman's gibbet!

Stand or die in disgrace!" he raged as he fought to regain control of his soldiers. "You've killed enough of them already. One more charge and they'll be crushed!"

But, like a wind blowing against a bank of mist, the cavalry turned and fled. The General watched them go, and with quiet deliberation he sheathed his sword. In his calculating brain there was no room for heroics. He spat at the advancing infantry phalanx, and galloped away.

Sharley glanced at the headless corpse of Octavius Bellorum, feeling neither elated nor repulsed. There was no time for that; the battle still had to be won. Turning in his saddle, he raised his hand and watched the motley infantry of monsters and zombies, humans and ghosts hasten to join him, and together they drove into the massed Imperial ranks. Thousands fell in the first few minutes as chaos and panic gripped the massive army.

But deep in his chest, Sharley carried a burning pain for his fallen friend.

At last, Thirrin felt a shift, the slightest change of atmosphere. The Imperial army was no longer . . . certain. Their ranks wavered; something was coming! Something was approaching.

Like a many-headed animal the host swayed, and at last turned to face its worst fears.

With a roar the ranks broke apart, and a neat black horse leaped through. It reared and screamed fiercely, its rider holding aloft a shining scimitar.

Thirrin stared.

The figure seized the rim of his helmet and swept it off, releasing his hair to blaze in a red halo about his head.

STUART HILL

"They are broken! The enemy is broken! Come out, drive them from the land! Mother, come out and join me!"

Thirrin fell to her knees. "Sharley! It *is* you!"

Tharaman roared, and scrambling to her feet Thirrin leaped on to his back. "The enemy is among us! They burn our houses and kill our children! BLOOD! BLAST! AND FIRE! BLOOD! BLAST! AND FIRE!"

Now the cavalry of the Icesheets roared their response, and charged, human trooper astride leopard comrade, driving the enemy before them.

With a despairing wail the Polypontian army broke and fled. Horsemen of the Desert Kingdom had magically appeared to ride them down; monsters and ghosts tore into them. Vampires and giant Snowy Owls swooped down on them, tearing out their throats and drinking their blood. Werewolves tore them limb from limb, and worst of all, a giant woman with black skin led a cavalry of striped horses to kill them.

They ran and died, still amazed that such an alliance had been brought against them. The rout was complete, and soon their huge numbers had choked the escape routes and they turned at bay to die in their thousands before the ferocity of the Icemark.

CHAPTER 38

Scipio Bellorum stood in chains at the centre of the battle-field. He'd almost escaped. But as his horse had thundered down the road to the south and to safety, a party of Vampires had swept out of the sky and plucked him from the saddle.

He now stood before Thirrin and Her Vampiric Majesty, apparently at arrogant ease though surrounded by a guard of werewolves, housecarles and Vampires. The rest of the allied High Command were mopping up under Cressida's direction, and Oskan was desperately fighting to save lives with few resources and little energy.

"How shall we kill him, Your Majesty?" the Vampire Queen asked, licking her fangs.

Thirrin took a long time to reply, but eventually she said, "I'm not sure." She'd waited so long for this moment that it seemed somehow *unreal.*

Her Vampiric Majesty looked at her, fierce hatred for the defeated General lighting her eyes. "Then give him to me! I can assure you I'll find many entertaining ways to dispatch him!"

"You wouldn't dare," Bellorum said in an arrogant drawl.

"The Empire would invade with another full force within a month if they knew you'd murdered me."

"Could you actually be murdered, Bellorum? Such a crime requires humanity on the part of the victim, and I truly believe you possess none," said Thirrin with quiet venom.

The Vampire Queen laughed. "Anyway, *General*," she snarled, "you're fooling no one. We've found your papers, and Maggiore Totus has already translated them. The Empire's on fire; there's war in the south and the Imperial armies are losing. They couldn't start a war of revenge even if they dared! You're already dead, my dear Bellorum – though if I have anything to do with it, it's going to take you a very long time to realise it!"

"One thing," Thirrin said. "Did your ambition match the scale of the sacrifice? Did what you wanted to achieve really merit all this death and destruction?"

He smiled coldly. "Oh, yes. You've never actually understood, have you, that as far as I and the Empire are concerned, your lives are of no value. The defeat of this insignificant little land and the killing of its entire population was of no real importance to anyone. The cost would have been negligible."

An angry murmur rose up from the soldiers who guarded him, but Thirrin raised her hand for silence. "But, Scipio, this 'insignificant little land' and its allies have defeated you twice. If you consider us to be of no value, what then is *your* worth if you can't overthrow us?"

"A quibble of words with no bearing on the war," he answered dismissively. "You and your lands are worthless, that is the beginning and end of the matter. Therefore all of the Redroughts, Cerdics, Vampire Kings, and countless others who died in the fighting are equally worthless."

This time a great shout of anger rose up from the guards, and Thirrin went white with rage. "Do you really believe that you are immune to death, Bellorum?"

"Immune to *death*?" The General looked puzzled. "Oh, you won't kill me, Lindenshield. You wouldn't dare."

Thirrin was momentarily shocked into silence. Did he really believe he wouldn't be executed?

"I am the greatest General the world has ever known, and there is not a living person who would dare spill my blood."

"But *I'm* dead, Bellorum," said the Vampire Queen. "And I can assure you that I not only dare to spill your blood, I'll be very happy to drink it too!"

Thirrin raised her hand for silence. "I was going to keep you until such time as a show trial for all the people of the Icemark could be arranged. But I no longer have the patience for that."

Bellorum's expression gradually changed from defiance to panic, and then to terror as he at last realised he was about to die.

"I demand a fair trial!" he bellowed, his eyes huge with fear, as he finally understood that he too was mortal after all.

Thirrin laughed. "Oh, I don't think so, General. When have *you* ever offered anyone a fair trial?"

With the greatest of care, Thirrin drew her sword and looked Bellorum full in the face. For the second time in her life, she stared into the eyes of her hated enemy. Then, with a triumphant roar, she cried out: "The enemy is among us! They'll burn our houses and kill our children no more! Blood! Blast! And Fire!" and she brought down the blade, whistling and flashing in a vicious arc, and sliced cleanly through Bellorum's neck. His head fell from his shoulders and bounced away, its eyes starting from their sockets as though enraged, before finally coming to rest, face down, in a puddle of mud.

Thirrin watched as the corpse swayed for a second or two, before its knees buckled and it finally sprawled on the ground at her feet. After a moment she placed her foot squarely between Bellorum's shoulder blades and walked over his body to the mud-splattered head. She turned it over with her foot. The monster's sightless eyes gazed up at her.

At long last, the architect of two terrible wars was dead. The sense of relief was immeasurable. Thirrin walked slowly away. Looking back over her shoulder, she caught the Vampire Queen's eye. "He's all yours," she said. "Do as you wish."

In an instant, the sound of General Bellorum's body being torn to shreds filled Thirrin's ears, but she was hardly aware of it. She was already too busy planning the rebuilding of Frostmarris.

Mekhmet lay barely conscious on a blood-soaked mattress in the infirmary, the pain of the sabre wound raging like fire through his chest. Every now and then he would cough up more blood, flooding his already soaked tunic with more of the precious liquid. He was dying, and he knew it. But he had fought bravely and had earned his place in Paradise. He wasn't afraid. In fact, to die seemed to him easier than making the effort to live.

Only the pressure of Sharley's hand in his kept him from closing his eyes and giving up. He liked having his friend with him at the end. He was glad Sharley had achieved everything he wanted; he could die happy, knowing that. But Sharley wouldn't let him go. Mekhmet wanted to plead with him to let him leave, but he couldn't speak. When at last his hand was released, he lay back with a sigh.

Sharley was rigid with fear and limp with grief at one and the same time. Mekhmet was dying! When he'd found him on the field, he and two troopers had carried him to the infirmary, but there was no sign of Oskan. Some of the witches had run to find him. All Sharley could do was hold Mekhmet's hand and pray, *"Please don't let him die! Please don't let him die!"* again and again to every goddess and god he could think of.

Oskan arrived at last to find his youngest son sitting next to a badly wounded soldier of the Desert Kingdom. Gently he stroked Sharley's hair, and he leaped to his feet.

"Dad! Dad! It's Mekhmet – he's dying! Please don't let him die. Please don't let him die! I don't know what I'd . . . how I'd . . . please . . ."

Oskan quickly examined the wound. Punctured lung, dangerously near the heart, and massive blood loss. He sighed. What could he do? He drew breath to tell Sharley it was hopeless, but seeing his face he turned and beckoned to a young witch. "Fetch Old Meg," he said simply.

"Can you save him, Dad?" Sharley asked, his voice barely a whisper.

"I'll fight for him, Sharley. I can say no more than that."

A sudden rustle and bustle announced the arrival of Old Meg. "You asked for me, Witchfather?"

"Your skill is needed. Keep the boy with us."

"Only if the Goddess decrees."

Oskan smiled sadly. "There's only one way to find out, isn't there?"

The old witch nodded, and sitting beside Mekhmet she

took his head in her hands. "Hello, my lovely," she said gently. "What have you been doing with yourself, then? You *are* in a bit of a mess. Never mind. The Witchfather will soon put you right. Now you just stay with us. I'm sure the Goddess has got more plans for you yet."

"He only believes in one God," said Sharley quietly.

"Does he, now?" said Old Meg. "Well, never mind. The Goddess believes in him, and she won't mind. Mothers are wonderfully forgiveful like that." She turned to Oskan and nodded. "You can get on with it. He's going nowhere."

Sharley watched his dad wash his hands and wearily open his bag of instruments. "Please don't let him die!" Sharley prayed to all his new-found goddesses and gods. "Please don't let him die!"

As he prayed, the sound of quiet singing began to fill the room. A blue light softly infiltrated the shadows and fitful lamplight, surrounding Oskan and Old Meg and giving them strength in their efforts to cradle Mekhmet's soul and keep it from slipping away.

"Thank you," whispered Sharley. "Thank you." And taking his friend's hand, he willed him to survive.

Olememnon and Olympia sat wearily on a pair of old boxes in one of the quieter side caverns, still not quite able to take it all in. It was over. Bellorum and his mad sons were defeated. Both Octavius and Sulla were dead: one killed by Sharley, of all people – who would have believed *that* only a few hours ago? – and the other dispatched by Cressida. It really was astounding. But no matter how stupendous the events, they just couldn't keep awake, and were soon slumped against each other, snoring gently with their fingers interlaced and their swords leaning together against the cave wall.

Eodred and Howler found them a few minutes later, and stood nudging one another as they decided what to do. Eventually, they scraped some mud from the cave floor, and squeaking and spluttering, drew huge muddy moustaches on them both. Then, finding a nice fresh pile of horse dung from a nearby stable, they gently prised open the deeply sleeping couple's hands and popped in a nice smelly mound to rest between their palms. Satisfied they'd done a reasonable job in difficult circumstances, the boys went off to find some beer.

CHAPTER 39

The war had long been over. A huge mass grave had been dug on the plain of Frostmarris and the enemy dead had been tumbled into it, rank upon rank of defeated soldiers whose bodies would nourish the soil and help in part to make amends for the damage they'd done by ensuring long, long years of good harvests.

The city of Frostmarris was rising again, stone by stone, and wounds had slowly become scars to be carried as reminders of the most desperate of times. The Vampires had long since flown north, much honoured and thanked by all the survivors of the Icemark, and their lonely Queen now sat on her throne in silence.

Such momentous times, such conclusions. The Lusu had eventually embarked for the dangerous journey back to the Desert Kingdom and beyond, and Mekhmet's own people had gone with them. The exiles of the Icemark had also made their way home, arriving in the harbours to tumultuous, joyous greetings as once again the people and the soul of the land walked free under its skies.

Banquets and celebrations lit the country from end to end.

Thirrin, Tharaman, Krisafitsa and Grishmak had made a Royal Progress the length and breadth of the Icemark, along with Oskan and Cressida. Maggiore Totus had settled down to write his history of the war, accompanied only by a large bottle of sherry and a smelly old cat. And everywhere was action and activity, rebuilding and renovation, as the scars of the invasion were cleared away.

Only Charlemagne Athelstan Redrought Strong-in-the-Arm Lindenshield seemed quiet and pensive. As he carefully limped down a bank towards the gently flowing river, a cold wind blew, rippling the surface of the water and blurring the reflection of the half-moon that had been lying peacefully in its depths. The eastern sky was beginning to lighten, and soon the early morning frost would melt to a crystal splendour of dew.

As Sharley climbed into a boat moored at the edge of the water, old Hereward seated him in the middle of the craft. Sharley had once tried to explain fishing and rivers to Mekhmet, long ago when he'd first arrived in the capital of the Desert Kingdom, and when Mekhmet had found it impossible to understand, Sharley had promised to teach him how to fish when he returned to the Icemark.

He smiled at the memory, and then started to laugh gently as he saw Mekhmet edge carefully down the bank after him, then grasp the housecarle's hand and step with exaggerated care into the unsteady boat.

"Thank you, Hairywart, you old fathead," he said in his thick accent, and he grinned at Sharley. "See? I did it!"

"You did indeed," Sharley agreed.

"So, where are these fish?"

"Oh, we'll be a while yet afore we get to the trout pool,

Your Highness," said Hereward. "Just you sit back and enjoy the view while I get the oars out."

This was the first time Oskan and Thirrin had agreed to let Mekhmet out of the city since he'd been wounded three months earlier. And everyone had strict instructions to be back in Frostmarris in time for supper. Tharaman and Krisafitsa were on a State visit to commemorate the rebuilding of Frostmarris, and everyone would be there. There was still lots to do, but Archimedo Archimedes had insisted they have a banquet to celebrate what had been done so far, because it was, in his opinion, superb. Still, Sharley didn't mind too much – the Royal Snow Leopard cubs would be there, and Kirimin had a sense of humour that made Eodred's and Howler's look tame!

Of course, Maggie would still be annoying everybody by demanding the tiniest minutiae of details from them all so that he could make his history of the war as accurate as possible, but at least Thirrin and Oskan had forbidden him to bring Primplepuss to the feast. The smell of rancid fishy farts really wasn't very good for the appetite. Sharley laughed; he must have the best family and friends in all the known world. They were all eccentric, argumentative and bossy – especially Cressida – but now he could hold his head up in their presence. He, too, was counted as a mighty warrior, and that was wonderful – more wonderful than he would ever have dreamed possible only a year ago.

But best of all, Mekhmet was recovering well at last, and all he needed now was good food and gentle exercise. Sharley couldn't have been happier. Feeling a pressure on his knee he looked up at his friend.

"Eh up, hairy arse! How's things?" Mekhmet said, using

the first phrase of the Icemark language he'd ever learned.

Sharley's smile widened into a grin. "Just great, fathead," he said. "Just great. We're going to catch the biggest trout in the entire river. And then we're going to sit on the bank and eat it for breakfast, aren't we, Hereward?"

"We are at that, Your Highness," the old housecarle agreed.

"What do they taste like?" Mekhmet asked.

Sharley frowned as he thought about it. How do you describe a taste? "Well . . . well, think of one of Primplepuss's fishy farts . . . a bit like that, I suppose," he said at last. "But much, much nicer!" he added hurriedly.

But it was too late. Mekhmet had gone a funny green colour, and hanging over the side of the boat he was loudly sick. His digestive system hadn't fully recovered from his wounds, and the slightest thing could upset it.

"I don't think I like the sound of trout," he said in a small voice when he'd regained some control of his stomach.

"No," said Sharley sadly. "Never mind. We've got some apples."